Possessions

Lake Superior

Lower Canada

St. Lawrence River

Montreal

2nd. Terr.

Lake Michigan

Lake Huron

Lake Michigan Territory

Upper Canada

Lake Ontario

Lake Erie

New York

Vermont

New Hampshire

(Mass.)

Mass.

Conn.

Rhode Isla

Illinois

Territory

Pennsylvania

New Jersey

Indiana Terr.

Ohio

Washington D.C.

Delaware

Maryland

Virginia

Missouri

Kentucky

Territory

Tennessee

North Carolina

South Carolina

Mississippi Territory

Georgia

Atlantic Ocean

Louisiana

U.S. Florida

New Orleans

Spanish Florida

Gulf of Mexico

★ 1812 ★

⋆ 1812 ⋆

DAVID NEVIN

A TOM DOHERTY ASSOCIATES BOOK
NEW YORK

1812

This book is printed on acid-free paper.

A Forge Book
Published by Tom Doherty Associates, Inc.
175 Fifth Avenue
New York, NY 10010

Forge® is a registered trademark of
Tom Doherty Associates, Inc.

Design by Lynn Newmark

Maps by Ellisa Mitchell

Library of Congress Cataloging-in-Publication Data

Nevin, David
    1812 / David Nevin.
        p.   cm.
    "A Tom Doherty Associates book."
    ISBN 0-312-85510-9
    1. United States—History—War of 1812—Fiction.   I. Title.
PS3564.E853A615   1996
813'.54—dc20   95-52731
                                                     CIP

First Edition: July 1996

Printed in the United States of America

0   9   8   7   6   5   4   3   2   1

ONE

WHEN LOVE COMMANDS

★ ★ ★ ★

THE 1790s

1

★ ★ ★ ★ "You're sweet on young Jackson, ain't you?" Ma said.

"Oh, Ma," Rachel said. "He's . . . nice, that's all."

Of course she was sweet on him. Andrew Jackson was tall, rail-skinny but strong in that Scotch-Irish border way, long-limbed, and fierce. He had red hair that blazed like his temper, eyes that snapped and sparked and went from sky-blue to purple when he was angry, a laugh you could hear a half mile off, and a way about him like a pistol on cock—he was *vivid*, that's what he was, made you feel good just to be with him, made life itself seem exciting and full of mysterious meaning.

He lived with little Johnny Overton and the other young lawyers in the guest cabin Pa had built next to the blockhouse. After Pa was shot down in the woods they needed boarders, what with roving war parties—Creeks and Cherokees—still common. But it was white men killed Pa, she was sure of that; John Donelson was too old a hand in Indian ways to let savages ambush him. Now each boarder was another rifle, if it came to that. And Andrew . . . oh, my. The thing was, he made them laugh. It was like a weight off Ma's soul to throw back her head and laugh out loud, and as for Rachel, why she'd get to telling stories to match his and they'd go back and forth whooping and yelling and she'd laugh till her eyes ran. And that drove Lewis Robards into a frenzy.

"Anyway, Ma," she said, "I'm a married woman."

They were outside, Ma tending the fire under the black iron wash kettle on its tripod while Rachel stirred the clothes. It was a brilliant day. Sunlight bathed the bare branches of the pecans Pa had been so proud of, flashed on the rolling Cumberland down at the far end of the property, softened the winter air here in the lee of the peeled log blockhouse. Ma's flower beds were banked for spring, her little square of grass neat as a patchwork quilt, fruit trees in pregnant rows. It was a kindly place, demanding but good to those who tended it. She added soap they'd boiled in the fall and stirred with both hands on the oak paddle.

"More's the pity you're a married woman," Ma said. "Reckon Robards'll come back?"

"Oh, God. I hope not."

There was something wrong with Lewis Robards's head. She'd known it the moment they wed and not one moment before. Sick jealousy. Let her talk to anyone, tell a story, laugh, tap her foot to the fiddle, any old thing he took as her being unfaithful. Or getting ready to be. If she smiled while reading a book, he asked of whom she dreamed.

"I couldn't make him believe me, Ma. *He* was unfaithful, so he figured
. . . oh, I don't know. His head is just screwed on wrong."

"Andrew showing him that knife wasn't no help neither."

Rachel sighed. That was Lewis's fault, too. Lewis had talked his crazy
jealousy in front of the wrong man. Andrew showed him a skinning knife
a foot long and told him he'd cut his ears out of his head if he heard it again.
What was Andrew supposed to do—just ignore nasty slander? Anyway, he
was a coiled spring. She couldn't imagine him walking away from trouble.

Ma took the paddle. "I reckon you're well off he's gone."

"I guess . . . a married woman without a husband."

"Divorce, maybe? He sure deserted you."

"Oh, Ma! Go all the way back to Carolina and get the legislature to
pass a special bill to give me a divorce? How can I manage that?"

"Tennessee's gonna be a state. With our own legislature."

"What then? You know how folks are about divorce. No one gets one
without proving somebody sinned—adultery, just to say it flat out. Why,
you've about got to be a *whore*!"

"Rachel! You're not too big to get your mouth washed out."

Rachel laughed. "Sorry. But just the same, I'll never take Lewis back,
so how will I live, a lone woman?"

"Well, dear, you have brothers."

And she would be a maiden auntie, minding someone else's babies.
"Yes . . ." She sighed.

Ma gave her a knowing glance. "It's lonely, without a man?"

"I sure don't miss Lewis! But . . . I guess it is. At night, you know."

"I know," her mother said dryly.

"You miss Daddy, don't you?"

Ma nodded, biting her lip. Rachel said, "You never told me . . . well,
what it was like. You know?"

"Oh, Rachel, how could I?"

"It downright amazed me, at first, anyway. I remember thinking how
wonderful it was, night after night. But then he started going out to the
slave cabins and coming back in the morning, and after that . . ." Across
the river a man pushed a skiff into the water. She could see his fishing pole.
"And that crazy jealousy started. *Him*, jealous of *me*! I should've taken a
stick to him."

"Acting out his own guilt, I reckon," Ma said.

"And thank God he's gone. But just the same, the nights . . ." She
shrugged. "Well, it's lonely, that's all." She studied her mother. "Was it
that way for you, with Daddy?"

Ma sighed. "Yes . . . your father, he was . . ."

"Special?"

Her mother blushed and then they were giggling like girls.

"I don't know that it's proper talk," Ma said, "but I reckon it's the way life is."

"And it's denied me . . . when life is just beginning."

They heard hoofbeats, loud even before they could see the horse, and her mother shifted toward the door and the rifle standing just inside.

"I think it's Andrew, Mother," Rachel said, and then he rounded the bend at a lope, sun glinting on that shock of bright hair, his long, lean body rocking to the bay's rhythm, and her heart swelled with pleasure.

★ ★ ★ ★

He saw the women as he rounded the turn, the sun flashing auburn lights in Rachel's dark hair. She was in that deep blue gown he liked with white lace at the throat, a black shawl across her shoulders, the strength in her face and carriage evident even at a distance. She stood poised, both hands raised, like a bird with wings lifted to take to the air and soar. Rachel Donelson—he hated the last name that scoundrel Robards had fastened on her—the prettiest, liveliest, laughingest girl, the best horsewoman, the fastest dancer, the dandiest girl in the Cumberland Valley or the whole damned world!

And now this. And yet, it might yet play to advantage. He wasn't a lawyer for nothing. He reined up.

"Miz Donelson. Rachel." To her, he said, "Walk with me while I water Maxine?"

They led the bay mare toward the barn. "Didn't want to say it before your ma," he said, "but it's all over Nashville. Robards says he's coming back for you. Says he'll take you by force . . ."

"Oh, God," she whispered.

"I'll kill the son of a bitch, he touches you," he said. He heard his voice, cold as a stone in snow. It was exactly how he felt, but he knew it was too strong. She took a step back from him. "Andrew," she said.

"It's all right," he said gently. "It's all right." He touched her arm. He knew his capacity for anger frightened her sometimes. Frightened *him* sometimes, but by God, it was real.

"What'll I do?" she said. In the barn he pulled off the saddle, let the mare drink, and turned her into a stall. The barn was quiet, the light dim. Harness leather hung from pegs, saddles were slung over a bar. He heard the mare crunching oats. In another stall a horse stamped and threw up its head. Its halter clinked. There was a delicious privacy in the dark barn. They could talk.

"I got a plan," he said. He'd thought it out, made up his mind in a moment, made the arrangements. "I want you to go to Natchez. We have friends there. He'll never go clear to the Mississippi country to find you, but if he does he can be dealt with."

"But so far?" she said. "And how?" She was looking up at him with an expression of trust that made his heart swell.

"Colonel Robertson is taking his family down by flatboat." They'd float the Cumberland in the open boat, then the Ohio, then the Mississippi down to Natchez. Two months in the wilderness. "I asked if he'd take you, he said what I figured he would—he'd need an extra rifle. He'll take you if I come along. And I sure wouldn't let you go alone."

"Oh, Andrew." She swayed toward him. His hands found her waist. "What will people say?"

"That's the point. Folks around here, folks we care about, won't say anything. The Robertsons will vouch we weren't improper. But from a distance, maybe it'll look different."

"You mean to Lewis?" she said in a small voice.

"Maybe he'll go get him a divorce. And then you and me, we can marry. That's what I want."

It was the first time he'd spoken. "So do I," she said, as if she'd been holding her breath.

He could feel his own heart beating. "You mean it?" he said. "You'll marry me, once you're free?"

"Yes, yes, you know I will. But I'm not free."

"This might do it."

"Give Lewis grounds?"

"*Apparent* grounds. Everybody who matters, they'll know better."

She wore a new, open look, fetters dropped, a bird ready to soar.

"Maybe it'll work," she said softly. "Maybe it will." She began to laugh and he caught the edge of hysteria and tightened his hands on her waist.

"D'you realize what it means?" she said. "We'll sleep by a campfire for two months and never touch."

And then she was crying, tears streaming down her warm, smooth cheeks. Her arms went around him, held him hard.

"Let's go up in the loft," she whispered. "Now."

"Your ma will figure—"

"I don't care. I want you now." Her lips were parted. He could feel her breath on his face. She pulled away from him and darted up the ladder. "Come!"

The deep blue gown draped from her fine hips swayed as she climbed and the movement touched off a blast of desire that shook him. When he reached the loft she was on her knees in the hay, arms outstretched. "Oh, darling," she said. "Darling, darling, darling!"

★ ★ ★ ★

"I'm going," Andrew Jackson said. "Nothing more to say."

Little Johnny Overton, who knew he looked like a dried-up prune and didn't mind at all, peered at his tall friend. They were standing in the square in the shade of a sweet gum. The log courthouse seemed to shimmer in the July heat. The air was heavy as a winter blanket, and Overton wondered if the heat itself hadn't touched off his friend's restless tension. But no, Jackson was just wild. All that red hair. The man did as he pleased and stood ready for the consequences.

Like when he took Rachel Robards to Natchez. Good God, did *that* set the town to talking! Still, he wore out good horses coming back on the Natchez Trace with testamentary letters from both the Robertsons, and the Robertsons were pillars in this community. If they said nothing happened, nothing happened. So the talk died down. Jackson had slipped through that one, but he shaved things mighty close. And now this!

"It's just a report," Overton said. "No better'n a rumor."

"Yes it is," Jackson said."Sounds official, anyway—Virginia legislature gave Robards his divorce."

"On what grounds, do you reckon?"

"Who knows?" He smiled. "Robards has a brother-in-law in the legislature in Richmond. That smooths things along."

"Yes, but in six months? You know how hard divorce is. Come on, now—you're a lawyer, you wouldn't settle a dogfight without seeing the paper. Wait for confirmation."

"No, I'm going to Natchez in the morning and I'm marrying Rachel the minute I get there. She's free, Johnny. Hell, the family would never have tolerated me taking her down if it wasn't clear we'd marry soon as we could. Her brothers'll be looking for me, I don't go marry her now."

"Just see the paper. So you *know*."

"But how? Ride a thousand miles to Richmond? There's no mail, you know that. Suppose I ask a traveler to carry a letter there. Maybe he drops dead. Maybe a war party gets him. Suppose there's an answer. Someone agrees to carry it back. Maybe he changes his destination, maybe someone else takes the letter, maybe not. Maybe he dunks his bags fording a stream and the ink runs. Come on, Johnny—I'm not going to stake the very happiness of my life on a letter in somebody's saddlebag."

"But suppose it's false. You marry her and you're committing adultery. Adultery! It would follow you to your grave. They'd pillory you. And her."

"Pillory her, they'll be looking down a pistol barrel."

"There aren't enough pistols to kill gossip."

Jackson stared at him. "Well, Johnny," he said. His voice was soft but something in his expression made Overton shiver. "I'll tell you. Back in Eighty-one when the war had been on awhile, a British major came up in the Carolina hills with a troop of redcoats and they ransacked our house. Tore it all up. And the major, he says to me, 'Boy, clean my boots!'

"I'd just turned fourteen but I'd been riding with the troops and I was a soldier. I drew myself up and I said, real politelike, you know, I said, 'Sir, I'm a prisoner of war and I aim to be treated as such.' He was a pale-eyed bastard and he didn't say a word, he drew his saber in one quick motion and I saw it swinging down, saw it glitter in the firelight, and then it like to cut my head in half and over the next month I was pretty near dead."

He rubbed the scar in his scalp. "But, Johnny, the thing is, I never cleaned his boots. You see what I mean? There's times in life you got to decide. You got to stand up, act, you got to do what you think's best. I never regretted speaking up—he could have cut my damned head off, I wouldn't have regretted it."

He smiled, suddenly at ease, and Overton knew his friend had crossed some interior barrier. "You got to do what your heart tells you. My life don't mean a damned thing without her. She's like me, too—she'll grab on for the whole ride." He shrugged. "If we're wrong, we'll deal with it then. Whatever it takes." He put out his hand. "Wish me luck, old friend."

"Good luck. God bless you, Andrew." He watched the tall, lean figure swing resolutely away. That spirit would be the making of him if it wasn't the death of him.

2

PHILADELPHIA
May, 1794

★ ★ ★ ★ Aaron Burr was trying to seduce her, and Dolley was deeply amused. He was a handsome devil in his late thirties with a definite way about him, and she'd grown fond of him. But she had no thought of sleeping with him. Not that it wouldn't be . . . but no. It would cheapen her in her own eyes, and that would be intolerable.

"You're being very forward, Colonel Burr," she murmured. "Right here in my mother's drawing room." A clatter came from the kitchen, where her mother was supervising the evening meal she would serve. The windows were open, curtains swaying in cool air, and she heard a carriage pass, hooves on cobblestone.

"A tribute to your mother's hospitality, dear girl. She makes it my home, too. That I feel so free is a supreme indication of her warmth as a hostess."

He raised his second sherry in a mock toast. She was on the striped sofa, squarely in the middle to discourage him; he sat in a blue Queen Anne chair her father had liked that was carefully placed to hide a hole burned in the carpet. Burr was a bit of a dandy in buff breeches, blue coat with brass buttons, and an embroidered waistcoat. His legs were crossed, showing off fine silk hose. A well-blacked shoe jiggled nervously. He was a congressman from New York, a leader in the new Democratic movement; Philadelphia was still the capital, though they now were building a dreadfully raw new place down on the Potomac somewhere, and Congress sat nearby in the old State House. Congressmen rarely set up households in the capital. A few brought families, but they also turned to boardinghouses. Several, like Burr, lived here in the fine house Pa had bought before he lost everything.

Poor Ma, reduced from landed gentry to boardinghouse keeper. They were old Virginia stock but then Pa became a Quaker, freed his slaves, sold the plantation, moved to the City of Brotherly Love, and failed in business. When he couldn't pay his debts the brotherly lovers expelled him from church. He took to his bed and stayed there till he died; Ma took in boarders. Pewter long since had replaced silver. Dolley's enthusiasm for religion was low.

Mr. Burr had a volume fresh from McGregor the bookseller—that new London poet, she'd already forgotten his name—and was reading fervently, his mellifluous voice soaring. Dolley laughed out loud. He looked up, not at all offended.

"Thinkest thee to sway me with such lovely words?" she asked. Actually, she didn't much like poetry; its convoluted phrasing struck her as unpleasantly mannered.

"I certainly hope so," he said. "Many a maiden has yielded to the poet's grace."

"But I'm hardly a maiden, my dear colonel. I'm a widow—only six months a widow, may I remind you, sir?" Poor John Todd had lasted almost to the end of last year's horror—yellow fever that killed one out of ten in Philadelphia, more than five thousand dead, men, women, and children going under and scarcely anyone left to bury them. John had sent her and little Payne, not yet two, to safety at Gray's Ferry but had himself stayed to volunteer after Congress fled and state government failed and city government collapsed; he'd come through unscathed until the epidemic clearly was waning, and then he was stricken and came to die in her arms. The violence of the terrible black vomit, the voiding bowels spewing black stinking water, lived in her memory. It was the cruelest of deaths, and then she was down and near death herself, her new baby died, and but for dear little Payne life might as well have ended.

But the spring came, her health returned and with it life's juices, and here she was, a beautiful woman of twenty-five with a two-year-old son and no husband. There was no conceit in her perception of her own beauty. Men's eyes had been on her since she was fourteen. Just the other day her dearest friend, Eliza, giggling in a most un-Quakerish way, had whispered, "Oh, Dolley, thee must hide thy face—there are so many staring!"

"I haven't forgotten, madam," Burr was saying. "You had a fine husband, a monument of self-sacrifice." He raised his empty glass. "May I?" He made a slight face when he sipped it. The decanter was cut glass but it no longer held the best sherry. "And I've tried to be of assistance to you since that sad day. You'll admit I've had some success?"

"Indeed, my dear colonel. You've been superb. Else I couldn't have named you guardian of little Payne, should I die."

"And I'm honored, madam. But in my defense, you have rather returned to society. You're hardly in widow's weeds."

She felt the heat in her cheeks. Her gown of plum-colored satin was cut low enough in front to allow a glimpse of superb milky breasts through the froth of lace. Hardly widow's weeds.

"Why," she said, "I do believe you're proposing something improper."

"Madam! I'm proposing love. Joy. Nirvana."

Love. She wanted that, all right, but not as Burr meant. Love and marriage. She'd had the marriage but she wasn't sure about the love. Oh, John Todd had loved her—adored her. But somehow he'd never really stirred her, and she wanted to be stirred. She wanted to burn with love that would sweep her into a blazing marriage. Would she ever find it? She was a widow with a child and relatively few resources; her mother was going to live with Dolley's little sister, who'd made a most fortunate marriage. It was not a comfortable situation.

"Nirvana," she said, letting a touch of scorn sound. He wasn't fazed. "And you're married."

"Ah, well, a small detail in the face of nirvana."

She sighed, then gave him a soulful look. "Ah, Colonel Burr," she whispered, "do you know what I'd really like?"

Instantly he was on the sofa beside her. "Anything you want, darling girl," he said, his voice suddenly hoarse. "My God, you're beautiful. You stir me to my very core." He caught her hand; his was damp. "Anything at all."

She withdrew her hand. "I'd like to slap your face for trying to take advantage of a widow."

His head snapped back. Then, with a burst of laughter, he fell against the back of the sofa.

"Oh, you darling girl," he said, "I did seek to seduce you, I admit it, but you seduced me. No other word for it. Set me up like a tenpin and bowled me over!" Still laughing, he took his chair. "I'm to understand, then, that my suit has no chance?"

"None whatsoever. But you're still my best friend."

"Well, well, less than I wanted, probably more than I deserve." He beamed at her, not at all disturbed. "Then, one friend to another, I have a request for you on behalf of a third friend. Do you know Mr. Madison? James Madison?"

"I know who he is, of course." The gnomish little congressman from Virginia who'd practically written the Constitution and then defended it so brilliantly; Tom Jefferson's closest friend, George Washington's confidant and adviser, a formidable power in the newly emerging Democratic-Republican Party that had the Federalists so disturbed, onetime friend of Alexander Hamilton with whom he'd written the Federalist Papers before their great falling out—she snubbed her tongue just in time, remembering that Burr hated Hamilton. Everyone knew Madison, but his reserve was legendary and she doubted that anyone really knew him.

"I've seen Mr. Madison at dinners," she said cautiously. "He seemed, ah . . . quiet, you might say."

"Not so quiet that he hasn't asked to be presented to you." Burr smiled. "This very evening, in fact."

Madison? He was substantially older, somewhat shorter, and, yes, quiet if not dour, but she remembered wondering if his manner didn't reflect shyness more than ill humor. And he wanted to meet her? The implication of serious intentions was unmistakable. She felt a surge of excitement and, from Burr's amused expression, knew she had failed to hide it.

"You see my dilemma," he said. "That's why I advanced my case. I didn't really expect to prevail, but I wanted to find out before presenting Jimmy Madison. From your expression, I assume your response to him is in the affirmative."

She could only smile, sure she was scarlet at such transparency. Burr was a sophisticated man whose ease made her aware of her own youth and inexperience.

"Yes, Colonel," she said. "You may present Mr. Madison."

"He's quiet, as you say. But he's able, clever, very wise. Indeed, he's brilliant—more so, I'd say, than is Tom Jefferson, though with much less dash. Much more so than our venerable President whom I, at least, consider a dull fellow."

When she raised her eyebrows, he winked and said, "A great man, perhaps, George Washington, but dull."

"Really!"

"Do I shock you?"

"Not much, actually."

"I thought not. But Jimmy Madison is never dull. He's often tongue-tied in company, he's shy, he avoids debate, and I believe he's hopeless around women—I give you fair warning. He was in love once and I think he was very badly hurt. She was just a slip of a girl, sixteen or so, and he was thirty-two. Kitty Floyd. John Floyd's daughter—do you remember John? Congressman from New York? Before your time, perhaps; this was a decade ago, I suppose.

"Anyway, Jimmy was much taken with her and then she fell in love with somebody else and that was the end of that. These things happen, of course, but Jimmy took it terribly hard. So far as I know, he didn't go near a woman for years." He paused, studying her with that little smile. "But you see, darling girl, it's a measure of his strength that when he does show interest, it's in the most beautiful woman in Philadelphia."

She gave a little seated curtsy. "Thank you, Aaron. I'll look forward to meeting Mr. Madison."

"Then I'll go tell him the good news."

Burr clattered down the enclosed stairs to the street. And Dolley scrawled a quick message to Eliza, who'd told her to hide her face: "Thou must come to me. Aaron Burr says that the great little Madison has asked to be brought to me this evening."

★　★　★　★

James Madison followed the serving girl up the steps from the front door of the boardinghouse on Walnut Street. His heart lurched with a sudden sense of risk: it was two months since Aaron Burr had presented him, and now, having emerged abruptly from a near-monastic life, he was besotted. Her face filled his mind, her swift smile, the intimacy of her voice when they were alone, their easy laughter. But on this afternoon he had committed everything, and as his steps on the staircase slowed, he realized he was terrified.

She was stunning, and somehow that alarmed him more—black hair falling in soft waves to frame her pale brow, eyes a deep offsetting blue, cheeks pink, and lips wonderfully red. Yet what made her most striking was an inner quality of intelligence, assurance, strength. She wore a new gown the color of roses, a lacy throw draped over strong shoulders, and as she seated herself, patting the sofa cushion beside her, he glanced down at her gorgeous bosom and felt such an urge to press his face there that he colored, sure his desire was evident.

It had been eleven dry years since he'd been in love, since Kitty Floyd had crushed him so thoroughly that he'd shied from further risk. Her family had been living in his boardinghouse and he'd made friends with her, though he was twice her age. Friendship in turn overcame the cursed shyness that tended to separate him from women. Actually he liked women, though they often took his inability to make small talk as rudeness. But he wasn't always shy—with close friends he could be bright, gay, even talkative. And so, relaxing, he'd fallen in love.

Kitty played the harpsichord with modest skill; a young man who studied medicine somewhere hung on the instrument and sang while the men talked politics. She'd gone home with a marriage date set and a month later sent him a letter saying she was marrying the student. That's all. He knew his pain was disproportionate to the real loss, but it had hurt so much he'd kept his heart to himself ever since.

Until Dolley Todd became a widow and he found himself dreaming of her. The two months since he'd spoken to Burr had been all joy. Philadelphia society invited them together everywhere. Her very presence comforted him, her laughter warmed every room, and she told him his sober black coat and breeches perfectly set off her own high sense of style. He stayed near her, so soothed that he found himself managing small talk quite well. She had a gift for people, but he did too when he could release it, as witness his friendship with Jefferson. Now Dolley was opening him.

She poured him a second cup of tea from a pewter pot. Usually he liked this time best, here in her drawing room, boarders coming and going, her mother puttering in the kitchen while he and Dolley talked the hours away. She was highly intelligent, not profound or intellectual but shrewd and sensitive in her judgments of people. She enjoyed his ironic wit and matched his thrusts until they laughed like old friends. What a lovely wife she would be!

Yet the very thought set off a tremor.

The President's Lady had summoned him. He was very fond of Martha Washington.

"Have you asked that pretty young woman to marry you yet?"

He'd shaken his head, tongue-tied.

"So I thought," Mrs. Washington said. "I asked her if the two of you were to marry, and she said she really didn't know. So I told her General Washington and I would much approve such a match. Now, Jimmy, the rest is up to you."

It was June. The first heat wave had come and gone, the congressional session was over, he'd be going to Virginia soon. He felt he was on a flood tide with Dolley; if he didn't act, an ebb would follow. His brave note had committed him: might he call this afternoon? He had something to say.

Doubt crowded on doubt. His hand shook, his cup rattled in the saucer. She would never have told Martha Washington the plain truth that he was too old. His eyes fixed on the fingers encircling her cup—young fingers, supple wrist, face smooth, throat uncreased. Wasn't this a twice-told tale? There was even a young medical student, or his equivalent, William Winter, a handsome attorney about her age and hopelessly in love with her. Everyone knew it. Winter's eyes followed her in a room like a dog watching his master. Why shouldn't she, like Kitty, prefer a vital young fellow?

He was running down. Their talk stumbled. Her expression was puzzled, watchful. But what if he proposed and she made it a joke? Or was embarrassed? Or offended? She was only eight months a widow—would anyone but a boor even broach the subject? Glancing down, he saw the silver buckle on his shoe coming loose. His hose had a yellowish cast. He had come to propose marriage wearing old hose! He looked up, appalled, and just then she touched his arm.

"You said you had something to say. What is it, Jimmy?"

"Well," he said, "yes. I did. I . . . ." His palms were damp. Just in time he stopped himself from wiping them on his breeches. Then, feeling a fool but suddenly angry, he cried, "Well, talk is difficult if it has meaning!" Her eyes widened. He calmed himself, hurried on. "So cheap and yet so dear, you see. A million blathering words every day, instantly forgotten. But who can forget, 'Don't fire till you see the whites of their eyes'?" What did *that* mean? He was being idiotic.

She smiled. "A warlike metaphor."

"Well, love and war are closely allied." He felt himself blushing. He hadn't meant to say that, but it was in his mind that assaulting the ramparts of a woman's heart took the careful planning of a military campaign—and now, too late, it struck him that he had laid no such plans nor had even the slightest idea how to woo her away from her young attorney. Again she smiled, but in his flustered state he couldn't read her expression.

"Are we talking of love, Jimmy?" she whispered.

"Well, well . . ." Oh, God, why couldn't he just say, *Yes, madam, we are, because I love you and want to marry you.* All she could do was say no. Or laugh. Or be angry. Tell him he'd spoiled everything, ruined all his chances. Assassinated every hope he had in the world. That's all. "Well," he said, "metaphorically speaking."

"Ah." She settled back on the sofa. "Metaphorically."

"No! Or . . . not exactly."

"What, exactly?" Her voice was gentle and encouraging and suddenly he found himself wishing he weren't so much more a man of thought than of action, cursed by the intellectual's gift and flaw, the ability to understand and even accept both sides of any question. Just in time he managed to stop the observation that he could see clearly why she would prefer a young romantic draped over her harpsichord.

He wanted her to understand how much he would like to have the decisive energy needed to seize the high ground and thunder to his objective. He admired forceful men who took a position and then saw nothing else despite all odds and arguments. And yet, the very certainty of such men also irritated him—he knew there was no certainty in life and believed that to assume it was the mark of a weak intellect. He would never be a general.

She smiled. "Do you want to be a general?"

"God forbid. But I'd like to be President." He shrugged. "Not that it will ever happen."

"Perhaps it will."

"I wouldn't be good at it. It calls for a special kind of leader."

"But they say you're a leader in the Congress. And were in the making of the Constitution. Everyone agrees on that."

"Oh, yes, Dolley. I don't mean to denigrate myself. I'm listened to in the Congress, and yes, some of the key ideas in the Constitution are mine. I think anyone who was there would grant me that. And the writing I did afterward—persuading people who could influence each state's ratification— that went a long way toward getting the thing passed."

"And that's not leadership?"

"Well, yes, but in a very limited way, don't you see?"

"Aaron Burr said you have the strongest mind in government today. He drew quite a picture, I must say—he seemed to think this capacity to see both sides is a great strength."

"Well, yes, in the legislative arena, I suppose it lets me see how my opponents are likely to respond."

"And hence how to overcome them?"

He chuckled. "You do put it in the kindest light."

"General Washington listens to you. I suspect he doesn't listen to Aaron, and that's why Aaron says he's dull."

"Oh, Aaron—he can be so shallow! That's ridiculous. He has a small streak sometimes. Of course, he's a friend—"

"He did us a great favor," she said. She smiled in a way that surely gave her words special meaning, but he hesitated and then chose the safest course.

"Aaron has never understood the President's strength isn't intellect at all," he said. "It's wisdom. Wisdom and action. He has the capacity to listen, assimilate, weigh, balance, and finally decide wisely, and then, in action, he's indomitable. He can rally his forces, hold them together against all odds as he crashes through every opposition to triumph by the very power of his spirit. That's what makes a great man great."

She looked at him with a quizzical expression in which he saw something oddly motherly. At last she said softly, "We want to be what we're not. It's the human condition."

"I suppose so." He chuckled, feeling easier now. "But I'd like myself better if I could cast aside all doubts and seize the high ground." If, in short, he could crash straight to a woman's heart. That was the missing thought he couldn't express.

But perhaps she divined it, for she said, "Are you uncertain about everything, Jimmy?"

He smiled. "No. Of some things, I'm entirely certain." But he still couldn't say it.

"You are a lovely man, you know."

"I am?"

"I think so. I like your mind. I like listening to you. I like it that everyone in the room pays attention when you're serious. You're gentle. My baby boy sits on your lap and looks happy. I like it when you're relaxed and funny." She shrugged. "I wish you were relaxed today."

"Today, I'm—" Then, quite unable to help himself, he took the plunge. "I'm forty-three years old. And you're . . ."

"Twenty-five. Not exactly a girl."

"Your youth cries out, dear Dolley. Look at you. So smooth, so bright, so *young*!"

"Yes," she said, glancing at herself in a beveled mirror on the wall, "I *do* do well, don't I?" She smiled. "You realize there's artifice involved?"

"There is?"

"A touch of rouge, a little powder, applications of cream and whey." She laughed. "A good beginning deserves a little help, don't you think?"

He chuckled. "I'd never have guessed."

"You're not supposed to."

"But you *are* young. And I *am* forty-three."

"I'm a mother," she said evenly. "I'm a widow. My husband died in my arms. I'm not a girl, Jimmy."

"No, I didn't mean—God knows, you're fully mature, fully accepted everywhere. Everyone loves you, that's the fact. And I . . . I didn't know there could be such pleasure in a woman's company."

"You like me, then?"

What better chance? Shout it out, man: *I love you*! But he said, "Mr. Winter is in love with you, I believe."

"Yes. Poor Willy."

"He seems to adore you. That must be . . . exciting."

"Not really. My husband adored me, and please don't take that for vanity. Adoration as a steady diet makes thin gruel. I want a life with a man I can talk to, admire, be thrilled by. Someone who's interesting, who makes me laugh, who stands for something. I have style enough for two, don't you think? But I have a certain power, too."

He nodded, smiling. That she did—it was the real core of her appeal.

Her voice was very low. "Well, I want a man who matches me and I haven't met many. And then such a man must . . ."

"Love you."

"Yes. He must love me."

It was quiet in the room. He felt at ease in a way he couldn't remember since childhood.

"I love you, Dolley."

"Do you really?" She was poised, waiting.

"Oh, yes." It all seemed easy now. "From the beginning. That's why I've been so nervous today. I wanted—but was afraid—to ask you to marry me."

"Ah," she said. "Yes, dear Jimmy, I'll marry you."

He stared at her. She swayed toward him and he kissed her. There was no mistaking the charged response in her lips—she *wanted* him. Slowly he bent forward to lay his cheek against her lovely breasts. Her arms closed around him and his around her and the sensation was so thrilling he almost missed her whisper.

"I think you'd make a very good President, Jimmy."

"No . . . do you?"

"Yes. You're stronger than you know. Much stronger."

TWO

THE PLUNGING
HEART

★ ★ ★ ★

1812

3

★ ★ ★ ★ It was after eleven in the morning and Rufe Dumster's relief was late. He'd been on duty since dawn at the mansion's door, shifting his weight from one foot to the other in his tight boots and plain black suit, his cudgel in easy reach behind a pillar. It was a cool, pleasant day, sunlight spangling new green leaves, forsythia spears and dogwood blossoms come and gone. Dumster's feet hurt, he was hungry, he wanted a drink, he was by God *aggrieved*, and he wouldn't mind using his cudgel on Sime Puckett when Sime showed up. *If* Sime showed up. Sime needed a boot in the ass, and Rufe Dumster was just the man to deliver it.

A tall, skinny figure—not Sime—turned into the circular drive from Pennsylvania Avenue and came striding toward the door. Dumster spat. People thought they could just walk in and see the President of the United States any old time they chose. And often the President saw them, weakling that he was. If Dumster were President, they'd *kneel* when they entered the room. Not that he'd take the job and be pestered all the time.

Long and narrow and yet powerful, walking with a ramrod up his backside, a thatch of stiff gray hair rearing high on his head, a hickory stick in his hand, forty-five years old or so, the fellow wore buff trousers and a blue coat with brass buttons. He didn't *look* Washington, and Dumster wasn't surprised when he drew himself up and said sharply, "Andrew Jackson of Tennessee to see President Madison. *General* Andrew Jackson."

"President Madison ain't receiving today, mister."

"Call his secretary. He'll see me."

"Now, didn't I just tell you he ain't seeing nobody today? Come back tomorrow—maybe you'll have better luck."

The visitor's eyes opened wide, his face went pale, his lips parted as if he were having trouble breathing, his hand drew back, he took a quick step forward—and Dumster flinched. He couldn't even remember the last time he'd been afraid, but this was fear, all right. It reached to his core, a mindless sense that something terrible could happen. The fellow's shrill voice burst from his throat like a horn.

"Ring for his secretary, God damn you, and be quick about it!"

Dumster took a step back. "All right, all right."

He gave the velvet bell cord two savage yanks and turned to stand with his arms crossed, gazing out on Pennsylvania Avenue. Old bastard. Who did he think he was? But he didn't look at the Tennessean again. He didn't want to see those eyes locked on his.

★ ★ ★ ★

Climbing the staircase behind a young secretary in a blue kerseymere coat who'd given his name as Edward Coles, Jackson had an odd little feeling of trepidation, very unusual. But he *was* in what folks were calling the White House, here to present his troops and urge the President of the United States to action, and its grandeur, physical and symbolic, gave him momentary pause.

Only momentary, though. He squared his shoulders. He was a soldier on duty and it was time to move. The nation was poised on the brink of war and the President already had hesitated too long, which fit what Jackson took for a universal view: James Madison was no leader. Rachel's worried eyes and gentle voice came to mind. "Now, Andrew, please, don't you go up there and lay into him. Remember who he is." Of course he'd be respectful; the office demanded it even if the occupant didn't.

Plain and simple, he didn't like Madison. It went back to Aaron Burr's traitorous scheme to slice the American West into a new empire for himself. Or, at least, that was the charge made against Burr. No one really knew, there'd been no proof and no conviction, but Madison and Jefferson were convinced.

Jefferson was President then, Madison Secretary of State, and they'd suspected Jackson of involvement because he'd been friendly to Burr. God, they did hate Burr—it was a vendetta, and the suggestion that Jackson was involved still infuriated him. He'd fought off any real accusations, of course, and while he wasn't likely to forget base treatment, he'd set it aside.

Now all that paled before the fact that war was coming. War was long overdue, in fact—it was past time to stand up and show Great Britain that the new American nation had teeth and the courage to use them. The whole country was wondering what would happen. At first the outlook had seemed promising—six months ago, after years of shamelessly accepting British abuse, Madison had put the country on a war footing, ordered the army expanded, taken control of merchant ships at sea. And since? Nothing.

Maybe maneuvers were afoot, but it felt more like dithering than diplomacy, and Jackson wanted action. His Tennessee militiamen were on high alert, ears cocked for the call, rifles and blanket rolls ready. They needed answers and so did he: how long could he keep them poised on the balls of their feet?

Coles opened a door. "General Jackson, Mr. President."

Jackson walked in and bowed. "Good morning, Mr. President."

It was a corner room, oddly narrow, walnut wainscoting, and light blue wallpaper with an eagle design. The windows were open. Voile curtains rolled in a light breeze. Madison rose at his desk, long goose quill in hand. Jackson was always surprised at how small the man was, slender and neat in his black breeches and coat, white hose, buckled shoes. Jackson wore modern pantaloons for their ease.

"General Jackson." The President bowed perfunctorily. He had a cool patrician look, gray hair coming to a sharp peak on his forehead and flowing over his ears, long straight nose, long upper lip, strong chin, an expression of authority surprising in a man whom Jackson considered weak.

"I didn't expect visitors," he said.

A reprimand? Jackson stiffened. "Yes, I was ready to take my stick to that jackanapes at your door."

Madison's eyebrows rose, but he waved toward a chair and said, "You're up from Tennessee? Nashville, is it?"

He knew perfectly well it was Nashville. The conceit irked Jackson but he stifled a sharp reply.

"Sir, I've come to report my troops ready for action and in need of orders. I have two thousand militia available on a week's notice, well trained, well armed. Turn 'em loose and they'll take Canada like a bass takes a fly. And right behind them, couple of months to mobilize, I can give you four thousand more. Orders—that's all they need."

"Very well."

"Very well?" He stared at the President. "Does that mean I'm to call 'em up? Order supplies, wagons, livestock?"

"Of course not. We're not at war. Not yet. And many questions remain."

"Haven't the provocations been ample?" Jackson said as mildly as he could manage. "Seems to me we've knuckled under for years—scared kid to a schoolyard bully." Ever since Britain went to war with Napoleon, it had been forcing American trade, American ships, American seamen themselves, to support that war.

"That quite overstates, sir," Madison said.

"God Almighty, they won't let our ships even trade abroad without we pay 'em a fee—they slap a license on what in fact is every sovereign nation's free right, to trade with anyone it chooses. Now, sir, that's correct, ain't it?"

"Yes, but—"

"And our sailormen—what abuse! Stop our ships and steal our men. They need a dose of Tennessee long rifles, you ask me."

"You do have a knack for reducing the complex to a mere metaphor," Madison said. "Metaphors are cheap and easy, General. War isn't."

"I say metaphors tell the truth in a form any man can recognize. What the devil kind of people can the British be, they abuse their own sailors so bad the poor devils desert in droves? Those Royal Navy ships must be living hells. And they stop our ships on the high seas and seize our men to crew their hell ships and we don't lift a finger. That's no metaphor."

"They're looking for their own deserters."

"Yes, and along with their deserters they take any likely looking sailor. Ten thousand Americans abducted to rot below British decks, facing knout and lash."

Madison colored. "Don't lecture me, sir."

"I'm not lecturing, Mr. President, don't mean to at all. But that's the way we see it in Tennessee. Why we say it's time for action. Since the *Leopard*—"

"The *Leopard*! Oh, how tedious."

"Tedious? That isn't the view of it in the West, I promise you." Five long years ago, H.M.S. *Leopard* had opened fire on an American naval vessel, U.S.S. *Chesapeake*, forcing it to submit to a search for British deserters. Their navy attacking our navy. Not pouncing on some merchant brig but attacking a capital ship of a sovereign nation, killing our men, forcing them to strike the Stars and Stripes! "I guess that was an act of war!"

"Yes, it was an act of war," Madison said, "and it was answered. Doesn't have to be answered in like terms. War itself, it carries great dangers." He waved a slender hand. "I don't mean the usual dangers; I mean dangers specific to the American nation in its present state."

"Well, begging your pardon, Mr. President, our answer didn't seem to have much effect." He restrained himself from branding it for what it was, a damned fiasco—the administration called it a trade war but it really was a self-embargo. To punish them, we refused to sell them our goods! Maybe it hurt them but it sure as hell hurt us more—and any fool on a street corner knew it was inherently weak. He shrugged and added what seemed self-evident. "I expect men who've been in real war for years see trade restrictions as powder puff fighting."

"Powder puff? General, are you trying to provoke?"

"No, sir. Not at all. I'm telling you our feelings—the feelings of men who're ready to fight at your command. And let me assure you, sir, you raised a chord of joy when you put the country on a war footing a few months ago. My men danced in the streets. Because Americans are sick of knuckling under . . ."

He saw Madison stiffen at that. "Well, sir," he said, "'pears to me we impoverished ourselves in hopes of pushing them—and they didn't budge. They tell me grass grew in the streets of coastal towns, ships rotted at anchor. I don't know about that, but I can tell you what happened in the West. What little trade we had vanished. Fur trade died, and try to get Indians to understand why all at once their only trade item ain't wanted. Western wheat that used to go to British soldiers on the Continent? Now it's plowed under. So I ask you, Mr. President, how many questions can there be? Turning the other cheek already has made us a laughingstock."

There was lots more to be said, but he saw he'd said enough. Madison's face went a deep red shaded toward purple and his eyes—well, a lesser man than Jackson might have quailed.

"You betray your ignorance," Madison said. "Turning the other cheek, as you put it, saved the Republic from much worse consequences."

Jackson smiled stiffly. "Well, hell's fire, Mr. President, I'm a good Democrat, I've made that argument a hundred times. And for a while there, yes, it was tense as a dog on point. But that's long past."

"A mere dozen years past. When Jefferson took office, the whole thing hung in the balance."

"Well, sure," Jackson said, "when we whupped the Federalists and sent old John Adams home to Massachusetts, it was touchy would the people stick with us. I had a hand in that, you know."

How simple it all had been in his youth! In the days when there were no political parties, but just the men who ran the government, including old Madison. But you can't keep parties from forming in a free society. Liberal and conservative. Wide open to the people or constrained to a ruling class whose own prosperity will trickle down to common folk. He could remember when a ruling class just seemed natural, Washington himself and John Adams and Alexander Hamilton.

And then along came the Democratic-Republicans—Jefferson's boys and Madison's in their homespun shirts—to open it all up to the people. A revolt, if you wanted to call it that, and didn't you know it was welcome out on the frontier where every man was equal anyway? As if it were yesterday, he could see the bonfires and the roaring celebrations in Tennessee when Jefferson defeated Adams in 1800, glory be, and ushered in a new age. You bet he'd had a hand in it!

The President's lips were tight. That "laughingstock" phrase had stung him, all right, but when he finally spoke his voice had returned to its low, carefully modulated tone.

"You do see, I suppose, that free men governing themselves, ideal as it is, they're subject to the sudden passions that an elitist government would control with central authority—that's one use for a strong military and coercive taxes, you know, people held in economic bondage to the wealthy."

But this was old stuff. Did the little man think they were that ignorant in Tennessee? Spent their time rooting with the hogs instead of keeping up with the world? Jackson bit his lip as the President went on in that infuriating, patient voice. "Don't forget, when we came along, there hadn't been a successful republic of any size since the classical days of Greece."

The Tennessean could barely restrain himself as the lecture continued. "So the Federalists had a legitimate fear of failure—and even our people, they had to be shown the government we envisioned could succeed. And France followed us on the republican road and lost it all to the Napoleonic dictatorship, and he gobbled up the brave little European republics that had imitated us so that we're the only one left—and you tell me we shouldn't notice this is a perilous world for democracy?"

"No, sir," Jackson said, "I'm not telling you that. But I think we're so worried about the Federalists undermining our republic that we can't see the British are already doing it." Federalists were strongest in the Northeast, weakest in the South and the West. Their view, which folks in Tennessee denounced as self-serving, saw human nature as base and in need of control by power centralized in the form of aristocracy or monarchy.

Jackson raised both hands. "You don't have to preach agin Federalists to me. I've said for years what they really want is a hereditary aristocracy."

The President wasn't done patronizing him. "You overlook the fact that the very measures needed to resist Britain play into Federalist hands." Explaining as if to a child. "Start with a big army with all its potential to oppress the citizenry. Then heavy taxes to pay for it and inevitable boosting of the public debt—you can't build an army and navy without borrowing— and that runs up the national debt, and what do we have? The wealthy class holding the debt and everybody else impoverished. That's just another name for aristocracy."

Yes, yes, of course, if they acted like Federalists they might as well *be* Federalists and forget the dream of free government run by free men exercising democratic vote. But couldn't Madison see that the situation had reversed itself?

"I'm a loyal Democrat, Mr. President, but that dog won't hunt today, 'cause a government that can't defend its trade and protect its citizens won't keep the people's respect. Sooner or later they'll throw it out and get one that can. And that'll mean Federalist."

He saw Madison's face tighten. To hell with him. They'd never be friends, and the truth was the truth. There was just one question, really: would the man fight or wouldn't he? A lot of Americans thought he was all bluff. But if you duck a fight you're branded forever, and Jackson figured nations weren't much different. Anyway, how long could the Tennessee militia remain suspended without orders?

"Federalist power exceeds their minority status," Madison said. "They're strong in New England and getting stronger everywhere, sad to say. And separatism is growing, too—talk of breaking up the country."

"Huh! Separatism is another name for treason and ought to be treated accordingly."

"That's much too easy, General. There are real differences, North and South and West, slave against nonslave, farmer against manufacturer, coastal shipper against wheat in the West, cotton in the South. We're a patchwork nation born of compromise. The Declaration, the Constitution, all compromises, especially on the deadly slavery question. Do you know there's been a sounding in the North to try to split off New England and New York into a separate nation that might ally with Canada?"

"I'd hang the bastard proposed that!" he snapped. He saw Madison's eyes widen and thought of Rachel. Easy, easy.

Madison frowned. "Must be comforting to perceive everything as so easily settled."

"Most things are simple. This is, too, and——"

"No, sir, it's not! If you were sitting in my chair, you'd know that. And as for the war, whatever the past, the fact that the British are carefully giving us no new provocation makes the decision all the harder."

Jackson almost snorted. Why in hell should Britain oblige him with provocations when it already had everything its own way?

"That's the nature of politics," he said. "Problems and opportunities." He looked straight into Madison's eyes. "And decisions."

Madison flushed. "If you want to talk politics, General, I guess I'm enough of a politician to remember you supported my opponent in Ought-eight when I succeeded President Jefferson."

So. He was as small in spirit as in stature, remembering a personal slight when they stood on the brink of war.

"I supported James Monroe because I didn't like your vendetta against Burr," Jackson said quietly. "And now Monroe's your Secretary of State, so I suppose all's forgiven."

"Touché, General." Madison smiled, a sudden warm glint of eye as if he might have a sense of humor after all. Then, businesslike, "What's the sentiment in the West these days?"

"Solid for war. Anyone in Tennessee, or Kentucky either, will tell you it's years overdue. They're fed up. And on top of that, there's a major Indian war brewing."

"But the West always worries about Indians."

"This is new. British arms coming in a flood from Canada, and this fellow Tecumseh—you know he's been down in Alabama country agitating the Creek Indians?"

"No . . . all the way from the Great Lakes?"

"Down the Mississippi and back in a canoe. That's no small matter. He's serious—and that's how the war faction of the Creeks takes him. He's an Indian chief of a different stripe, you know. More like a French field marshal."

Madison nodded. "I hear plenty about him from Ohio and yes, he's remarkable. This alliance he's created—his own Shawnee, Potawatomi, Kickapoo, Mohawk, Winnebago, Ottawa—well, if there had been more such Indian leaders, white settlement in North America might have been very different."

"Could still be different if he succeeds in creating a single Indian buffer state to stop all white advance."

"Do you think he could?"

"Well, I was in plenty of Indian scraps in the old days," Jackson said. "Folks lived in forts then. My home today is an old log blockhouse, still has the gunports. And the thing about Indians, until now they couldn't get together. Fought each other more than they fought us. That's what Tecumseh is changing."

"People in Ohio take this buffer idea very seriously. They say it could seal up the West if it worked."

"Exactly. We'd never let it happen, blood would run in rivers, but now you're talking Indian war on a whole new scale."

Madison made a quick note. "They say he can muster ten thousand warriors in the North. In the South?"

"Good five thousand. Maybe seven. And, Mr. President, we war with the British, we'll be warring with the Indians, too."

"Just what they say in the Northwest. They say what you do, too—the embargo stopped the fur trade and the Indians took it personally, so to speak. How can they understand the intricacies of international diplomacy?"

"Which proves the British are the real threat." Jackson stifled the impulse to say that everyone had trouble understanding Madison's diplomacy. "Indians can't function without someone supplying them. They're a stone-age people. They fight with our guns and powder, skin with our blades, cook in our pots, decorate themselves with beads made in Belgium. Utterly dependent. The British are just using them, up north and in Alabama, too. Right now they're flooding them with arms through Florida, with Spanish connivance, obviously."

"Ah, Florida," Madison said. "It should have been part of the Louisiana Purchase. Texas, too."

Jackson smiled. "Sir, that's gospel in Tennessee."

With a sudden enthusiasm quite unlike his careworn manner, Madison sketched the new state of Louisiana with its bootlike shape and tapped his pencil on the toe. "We've moved east from the Mississippi here to the Pearl River; I think it obvious we must go on to the Perdido and make sure of Mobile Bay."

Jackson chuckled. "Authorize me to do that, you'll hear Tennessee's cheers all the way to Washington."

"Yes, well . . . first things first." Madison sighed. His worried look returned. "So," he said, "your people are talking war with Britain over this Indian threat?"

"No, no. Whip the British, that would put a crimp in Tecumseh, all right, but the West wants war because it knows that accepting abuse shames us nationally."

Madison's mouth tightened. "These easy generalizations . . ."

"That's not a generalization at all." He saw Madison stiffen at his tone and softened his voice. "You want to understand the men and women in the West. They're different from your easterners. Western man's a national man, a Union man, orients to the whole more'n any state. Back East, you have Virginians or New Yorkers, but Tennesseans are Americans first. Most all come from elsewhere, and who are they? Enterprising, tough-minded people, men and women alike, willing to live hard and take risks. People with the courage to fight for a better life. Your westerner, he's the key to the American future."

"Because he's 'national,' as you put it?"

"Because he has a continental vision. We'll be a continental nation one day, mark my words—we'll move west over everything Lewis and Clark unfolded, right to the shores of the Pacific, and your westerner is the man who'll do it. That's why we're Democrats—it's the party that sees the future. But the Federalists want to huddle in their tight little fiefdoms by the sea, build an aristocracy to keep it that way, and forget the West. I think we scare 'em."

"I grant you, Tennessee folk are good Democrats."

"Yes, sir. So they don't take kindly to their rights being abused. I meant no offense, you know, when I said a government that can't defend its people will be repudiated, but it's plain truth. Back in Tennessee, they're worried. Doubting. They say the British have abused us long enough—you hear it everywhere, they say we need a second revolution to remind the bastards who won the first one!"

The President pressed slender fingers to the bridge of his nose. "Tennessee's that certain, is it? I tend to distrust certainty. It doesn't serve complex times well."

Great God, was everything at risk? The man still dithering? Jackson leapt to his feet. "What are you saying? Can the issues be more clear-cut? You've brought us this far, you've put the country on a war footing, such as it is—surely you're not saying you're turning back?"

"I'm saying it's complicated. There are strong arguments against, too. So don't put words in my mouth. When I decide, you'll know my decision along with the rest of the world."

Jackson stared at him. He felt an immense contempt. A leaf blown by the wind—God help the country!

"We can win, Mr. President," he said hoarsely. He leaned forward, put both hands on the presidential desk. "March right into Canada and they'll beg for negotiations."

"Of course we can win," Madison said. "Canada is as vulnerable as a newborn babe. The question is, at what cost to ourselves? There's the danger."

"Danger?" Jackson shouted. "Danger's in doing nothing. That's what can sink us." He leaned closer, jabbed a stiff index finger in Madison's face. "We're at crisis. Don't you see—you must act. For God's sake, don't weaken now!"

Madison stood up so abruptly that his chair rattled against the wall. His face was crimson, his eyes glittered.

"Don't you put your finger in my face, damn you," he said in a low, intense voice, his lips flattened against his teeth. "You go too far!"

Jackson stepped back, caution bells ringing. He *had* gone too far. So be it. He would never admit it, never apologize. He could hear Rachel sighing—he very often did go too far, some thunderous impulse he'd never really understood driving him. But he'd never backed away from a fight and wouldn't now.

"I meant no offense, Mr. President," he said with icy formality. "I'm a soldier reporting to his commander. My judgment is that war is essential and that each day's delay exacts a penalty."

"But my judgment is the one that counts."

"Yes, but it's my duty to express my opinion."

The little man carefully straightened his chair and sat down. He leaned on the arm and rested his forehead on his fingers. He sighed.

"You do speak your mind, don't you?"

"Yes, sir. I don't regard that as a fault."

"I don't think I'm going to debate that," Madison said slowly. He sighed again and added, "Mrs. Madison is holding an open house tomorrow afternoon. Perhaps you'd enjoy attending."

Jackson would never have invited a man who'd poked a finger in his face. Poke at him, you'd be lucky to keep your finger. Even as he bowed and said he'd be pleased to attend, he decided that gracious as the President's invitation might be, it smacked of weakness.

★ ★ ★ ★

Late that night Dolley sat at the Hepplewhite dressing table in their bedroom. Madison was in his favorite wing chair, legs stretched out on a blue needlepoint stool, fingers tented under his chin, watching her. He'd been tense since Jackson's visit, with precious little accomplished in the afternoon as anger flared, ebbed, flared again. He wasn't over it yet, even here in his sanctuary, in slippers and the blue silk gown she'd given him, beyond the reach of visitors, secretary, waiters, and all the others who cared for him but so rarely left him alone. Usually the room soothed him with its fine Chippendale lowboys and highboys, its wallpaper of maple and roses, the moonlit view of the open pastures that stretched to the Potomac. His fingers under his chin pressed together so hard they trembled.

She was wiping her cheeks with a new unguent she said had extraordinary properties, Madame So-and-so's Fairy Elixirating Cream, or some such folde-rol, scrubbing away her rouge. All she had on was a lacy shift and a ruffled petticoat, and her fine milky shoulders were bare. He had an impulse to press his lips to that soft point where the strong pillar of neck joined shoulder, slide his hands under her arms to hold her wonderful breasts, but he didn't move.

"You know I love you, Jimmy," she said softly. "Sharing my secrets. No one would guess I use rouge." Actually, everyone probably guessed—she was unvaryingly a radiant pink—but the little vanity charmed him.

She was forty-three now, her figure more magnificent for a certain solidity it had acquired over the years, her face still riveting every eye in any room.

"I knew you loved me that day in Philadelphia when you revealed the artifice," he said, though, in fact, the extent of the gift in that comment had only occurred to him much later. He felt a stirring at the memory of those days and the stunning revelation she'd been when they married. He hadn't imagined such rapture existed on earth, nor would he have thought then that at sixty-one she could still stir him so. The mere recollection of passion was sifting through his being, mingling with the nervous tension of the day, quickening his pulse. Rapture . . . He flexed his fingers and she caught the movement in the mirror.

"You're nervous tonight."

"Oh, that damned fellow Jackson—he thinks it's all so easy! Just jump into war. Frontier barbarians, you know, in their leather shirts." What a petty comment. He knew he should be ashamed.

An ironic glance. "He wore a leather shirt?"

He laughed. "All right, all right. No, good broadcloth. Pantaloons— the latest fashion."

"You should pay some attention to fashion, Jimmy."

"Certainly not! Pantaloons? Breeches and hose will do very well, thank you. Jackson, now, you'll see him tomorrow, I invited him to your soiree."

Her eyebrows lifted. "And he accepted?"

He nodded.

"Then he's not such a brute?"

"Oh, he won't upset the party. But you know, he *is* wild. Famous for violent actions. Married another man's wife, after all—that's precipitous, I'd say."

"Don't be silly. He couldn't do that."

"Did."

"Bigamy?"

"More like adultery."

"Come, come. There's more than *that*."

"Something about a garbled report that her husband had divorced her. When it turned out he'd only started proceedings, they went through hell."

"Poor woman. I can imagine her bruises."

"Seems she's spent the rest of her life making up for it. She's a paragon of kindness, by all accounts."

She turned, her legs crossed under her petticoat. She was barefoot and he could see her smooth, slender ankle.

"And who's to condemn yielding to love?" she said. "You and I, Jimmy, we might've . . ."

"What? Before we married?"

"If you'd asked me."

"Why, I wouldn't've dared."

"And I, all the while, hoped you would."

"Why didn't you say so?"

"Ask you to make love to me?" She smiled. "Anyway, it worked out well enough, wouldn't you say?"

Again that quickening. "Very well indeed," he said. On the whole, though, it was just as well they had waited.

"And as for the Jacksons," she said, "apparently the community doesn't hold it against them."

"No wonder. He'd kill anyone who did."

"Jimmy! Aren't you ashamed?"

He grinned. "I am. But he *is* violent. Shootings, canings, horse-whippings—he's known for it. And duels. He's deadly, they say—young fellow named Dickinson, Jackson shot him down like a dog. He'd questioned Mrs. Jackson's virtue."

"Well," she said, "I know about gossip."

"Yes, darling Dolley," he said more gently. "And if a man defends his wife, I won't criticize him for that."

She flashed him a smile and turned back to her mirror. The Quakers had expelled her for marrying outside the faith, as they had her father for his bankruptcy, and she knew whispers were bullets. He sometimes wondered if her flamboyant dress—the vivid silks and satins, the bird-of-paradise feathers, the turbans that women in Paris were copying now—while certainly expressive of her taste and talent, wasn't also her answer to the plain folk. He loved every element of her dashing presence that warmed any room she entered. She had made herself the nation's preeminent hostess when she ran the President's table for poor Tom, the lonely widower, and now she ruled Washington like a democratic queen. She had a way of surveying her drawing room that assured total command of all she saw. He wouldn't be President today without her, he was sure of that.

For now he could see he'd been sinking into bookish torpor when he found her, turning in on himself and retreating from life. She had restored him. Yes, he still froze in a crowd, heard his voice go cold and dull when he wanted it warm and spontaneous, but what would he have been without her? And she had taught him rapture. She was brushing out her hair now, the five hundred strokes she gave it every night, her shoulders flexing, the motion emphasizing the flare of her hips. The tension of the day was refocusing itself in real desire. He wanted his hands and lips on her and wondered if she guessed. She often did.

He *was* a bit ashamed, bantering about what obviously had been a domestic tragedy. It was just that Jackson irritated him so with his certainty, his oversimplifications, the blind unwillingness to see the complexities and pitfalls, just take the future by storm and ask later of consequences. And yet, very possibly Jackson was right. There are men who are right by instinct, some intuitive concatenation of impulses that brings them swiftly, unerringly to conclusions that prove out as if by magic. Such men have the capacity to be great, to shake their times and change a nation's destiny. Not Jackson, of course, that was hardly likely, but still . . .

That smooth certainty, though—never doubting himself, waving off twelve years of diplomacy, twelve years of struggle.

Madison sighed. "Well, he's right in one sense. I mean, we saved republicanism, saved what I believe is the hope of the world, but we didn't move the British a whit. I thought we would and so did Tom. Still, you can see Britain's reasons, too . . ."

How easy it would be to take a stand as Jackson did and see nothing else. But the attitudes and pressures on the other side, the hopes and fears of his opponents, came too readily to mind. Having a window on an opponent's mind could be an asset, but it was a curse, too, hobbling him at the moment of action.

Britain, now, was fighting for its life against Napoleon. He accepted that. The Federalists claimed Madison was in the French dictator's thrall— if not his pay—but in fact he realized that the Emperor had subverted the French republic even as he'd conquered the European republics that sprang up in the wake of the French Revolution. Britain felt it stood alone in defending the free world and took as its due any assistance it might demand. He knew the British felt in their bones that Americans should be glad to have their trade crippled and their seamen stolen in the noble cause of helping contain the tyrant.

"You can understand it," he said. "As they see it, instead of helping, we're fattening on trade denied them by war. It infuriates them." He was deeper in his chair now, chin resting on doubled fists. She finished her hair and left it loose, giving her an open, uninhibited look as she put a cushion against the dresser for a backrest and sat facing him, her feet on the needle-point stool. After a while her foot touched his. He sighed, needing to talk. She encouraged him but sometimes he wondered if this endless talk at night was a form of abuse. Or perhaps she was a saint. Of course, she *was* interested—she conversed wittily and wisely with guests, and he'd long found her insights valuable. So he talked and she listened without saying much, and he felt guilty but went on talking.

"Well, Napoleon is no friend of republicanism—eating up the flower of the movement on the Continent. No friend of ours, either, but it's the British who molest us. Bullies—hard to believe we were once British ourselves."

"Isn't that why we no longer are?"

"Exactly. There's lots of talk about needing a second revolution to remind 'em who won the first. Jackson raised it."

She nodded. "I think it's a real feeling."

"Oh, it's real enough. Maybe it's what we need. God knows they assault our trade. They're jealous, too—fear we'll gain trade they're losing in the war and they'll never get it back. Maybe that's the real reason."

But he didn't need Jackson to tell him no sovereign nation could live with such abuse and retain its national pride. Since the Erskine imbroglio he'd known they would have to fight—the question was when. It still galled him—charming young David Erskine, new British ambassador, probably foolishly, perhaps malevolently, had offered concessions that settled all the differences between the two countries. Bells of thanksgiving pealed as the threat of war vanished. And then the British cabinet repudiated it all in a single stroke. The pure *contempt* of it ground salt in the wound—they didn't apologize, didn't even try to soften the blow. He felt the old fury rising.

"Can't you just see them sitting around that polished table guffawing at the image of the little American President leaping at their bait like a lapdog offered a morsel?"

She kicked his foot. "Don't talk that way!"

She was right, and yet the memory burned his soul, the slap in the face, big man looking down on the small man, tall Jackson looming over his desk this afternoon, *threatening* him. Like a British frigate running out its guns on a merchant brig. Damn it all! The man *had* upset him.

When to fight? The British were careful to give no new provocation, having things now exactly as they wanted. He'd seen Jackson's expression of contempt on that point—good God, did the man imagine he alone saw such things? And the French abused our trade, too. They tried to use us to punish Britain. Now there was a break; France had turned conciliatory— apparently, at least—so as to isolate Britain as America's only overt enemy. Was it real? He doubted it. A man was a fool to trust overly in the international world. But at least it was an excuse to move against the real enemy. If he really wanted to move.

"When? Tomorrow? Next week? Month? Year?" He sighed. Her bare foot nestled against his ankle, warm and comfortable. She didn't answer, understanding him. He was thinking it out.

What would he say to the purists in his own party who insisted that a strong military and the taxes to pay for it would lead to public debt that in turn was just a tool for the wealthy to control the common man—in short, the same old oppression they'd fought a revolution to escape. Why now? they would cry. They'd say he was giving in to the War Hawks, as they'd dubbed powerful newcomers in the House who demanded immediate action: Henry Clay of Kentucky, Felix Grundy of Tennessee, John Calhoun of South Carolina, and the others.

"Yet the last election was a revolution of sorts," she said. More than half the sitting Congress had been turned out, replaced by men who promised to vote for war. Nor was it just the West—except in New England, war sentiment ran strong in all sections. "I suppose you could interpret that as demand."

"A democratic revolution, really. Stunning. Remember Darndell in tears? Couldn't believe he'd been voted out."

"You always say, 'No stronger voice than the electorate's.' "

He sighed. "But such a confused voice."

He could tick them off. The philosophic core of his own party fearing for American freedom. The Federalists—in New England and New York and along the coast, representing the seamen and export merchants facing British mistreatment, the very people you'd think would want action—equally strong against. They'd been dying out but now they were like a tree clothed in new green. And for war, the strongest voice of all, Jackson's westerners and all the others who were near losing faith in a government that couldn't redress national wrongs.

"Remember the tug-of-war at the Orange County fair?" she said. "Twenty on each end of a long rope, back and forth? Suppose you cut the rope. Both sides would fall down."

"You're saying I should chop the electorate in half?"

She chuckled. "Wouldn't that be grand? Draw and quarter the opposition? *That* would teach 'em! But don't you think deciding will be like chopping the rope? Both sides fall down and by the time they get up there's a whole new situation."

He smiled, watching her, and slowly nodded.

"Perhaps . . . perhaps. But these are forces that can shred the national fabric, too. And it's so fragile . . . that's what the Jacksons of the world overlook—or refuse to understand."

And then the Indians, another element in this volatile mix. Yet he knew western sentiment didn't turn on Indians. Ohio agreed with Tennessee on that. Indians were a problem, but what mattered in the West was national pride.

He told her Jackson's views on westerners as a national people, ready to create a continental nation.

"That's exciting," she said.

"It is. No question. And why shouldn't we cover the continent? There's magnificent potential in Americans as a people. Free people, ruling themselves, forging their own destiny—it's glorious."

"But unrealistic, you think?"

"No, not really. Won't happen in our lifetime, I imagine, but the impulse to move west is powerful and it thrills millions of people who've chosen the frontier. Why not? A great idea, and it makes you impatient with this endless tussle with Britain—as if we need to settle it and get on with real business."

"Perhaps that's what Jackson's saying."

"I suppose it is. But he's so *arrogant*, so certain, so assertive. Telling me . . ."

"Why does he upset you so, darling?"

He smiled. "God, you do know me, sweetheart. I guess because he's so sure and I'm not. He's just a commander but talks like a leader; I'm the leader and I don't sound like one. Or look like one . . ."

"He's tall and you're not?"

He shrugged. "I try not to let that matter."

"It's never mattered to *me*," she said softly. "No one's stronger than you. No one's . . . better." She gave the word a curious inflection and glancing quickly at her, catching the fleeting smile, the kindling of eye, he read her message in the quickening of his own blood.

"I love you," he whispered. It was late. A setting moon filled the window with brilliance. He'd have to decide soon, but not tonight. He had the votes, he knew that. Congress would give him a declaration of war the moment he asked.

But could he afford to alienate so many in his own party, to strengthen the opposition party? The military men told him Canada would fall like a ripe apple. The very triteness of the metaphor delivered with such certainty made him wary, but with no military skills of his own he had to rely on them. And what if they were wrong? He supposed Americans would pull together in the face of real war, but what if they didn't?

He threw up his hands. "God, what an imbroglio. Even Tom thinks we should fight, did I tell you that?"

She raised an eyebrow.

"Yes. Isn't that ironic? The whole point of our policy when he was in my seat and I was Secretary of State was to avoid war. And now here's old Tom blithely saying, let's do it—let's do on your watch what we avoided doing on mine." He laughed. "Tom's a genius, but he was always able to say any damned thing that popped into his head."

She smiled but didn't answer. They were silent a moment. Then he sighed, sat forward in his chair, took her bare foot in both hands, and kissed it. His hands ran up her calf as he looked at her. Instantly he was tumescent, all the tensions and pressure of the day, the encounter with Jackson, the memory of Erskine, the overwhelming decision he faced, crashing full force into his groin. He saw an answering flare in her eyes.

"I'll go change," she said. There was a catch in her voice. She went into the dressing room. He heard the lid on the chamber pot, heard the washstand door close. When she returned she was in the revealing gown she wore when she wanted him. She didn't speak, nor did he. One by one she pinched out the candle flames between thumb and forefinger, and when it was dark she stood in the moonlight. Her gown opened to show her wonderful body, and she held out her arms to him.

4

★ ★ ★ ★ Dolley Madison watched her guests crowding into the splendid oval room she'd created in the center of the mansion. The air of tension among them seemed almost solid. She saw it in faces, heard it in voices too loud, too jocular, felt it in everyone who greeted her. They were all suspended—impaled—on the burning question, would there be war?

The evening was taking on a distinct military flavor, too—uniforms everywhere, the navy's dark blue, army's lighter blue, gaudy facings and medals of long-past heroics, gold-fringed epaulets, high collars faced with gold. Stephen Decatur, the dashing commander of U.S.S. *United States,* wore the vivid sash that denoted honors won in the Bay of Tripoli. Henry Dearborn bowed over Dolley's hand, major general's uniform strained across his girth, saber standing out at a ludicrous angle. The war, if it came, would be in his hands.

There was no reception line. Guests came by twos and threes up the marble stairs to enter through her lovely yellow parlor that lay between the great oval room and the larger state dining room. It wasn't really formal, though the men not in uniform wore black hose and the women wore their best, backs bare, fronts as revealing as they dared or could support, depending on their assets. *That* was a problem Dolley had never faced.

Waiters in white coats moved with strained quick steps, balancing trays with glasses of Madeira and champagne, porcelain demitasse cups, cut-glass cups of hard whiskey punch. She glanced through two sets of double doors to the dining room where a giant Virginia ham sliced in place, undersize loaves baked this morning and sliced on carved breadboards, candied peaches and kumquats soaked in brandy in silver dishes, almonds and cashews and the pecans Jimmy liked, awaited guests. The cut-glass punch bowl was already more than half empty. French John, her steward, prowled the room in his elegant cutaway, snapping his fingers at errant waiters. She caught his eye and pointed to the punch bowl; his eyebrows rose and he hurried off.

She was feeling good—she always did after making love—and she glanced around for Jimmy. He was in his usual spot at the rear of the oval where she had placed the great Gilbert Stuart portrait of General Washington centered between two offset doors that now were locked. He stood slightly away from the portrait, no doubt to avoid comparison with the first President. Of course his sweet, outgoing manner had already vanished behind the dull gray armor he wore when more than a half dozen were present, but given the day's tension, she couldn't blame him. She saw Dearborn talking to him around mouthfuls from a heaped plate.

This was her room, and she felt it really was only complete when it was full of people. The windows—so tall that with the lower sash up the guests could step outside without bending their heads—were open to the cool evening air, scarlet curtains drawn aside. A dozen people were outside now; beyond them the distant Potomac was fading into the dusk.

Inside, tapers in girandoles and oil lights glinting in multifaceted chandeliers cast a warm glow that flattered women and added an intriguing sense of mystery. She caught a glimpse of her own solid figure in red in the mirrors and paused to adjust her matching turban with its feather. A lovely room—its walls papered in a rich cream color overbrushed with flat white, woodwork shadowed in blue and gray to suggest masonry, ceiling shaded by a Philadelphia artist renowned for the delicacy of his colors—she felt it was a physical manifestation of her own rich inner self.

Of course, she couldn't have done it without Ben Latrobe, the brilliant curator, but every decision had been hers. The house had been drab under the widower Jefferson, and though Dolley often had presided over his table, she could hardly put her own imprint on what was, after all, his house. But the moment Jimmy assumed office, she and Mr. Latrobe plunged in. He'd won some arguments—he'd persuaded her that a simple Grecian motif in wood was most appropriate to the American democracy, and he'd designed the chairs with eagle and shield scattered about the room with matching sofas and small tables. Most of her guests, of course, were standing.

Over all this splendor was the tension that made the very air crackle. They gathered as against a storm, eyeing the man with the terrible ultimate responsibility, divining what they could from the timbre of his voice, the set of his shoulders. It was fitting that this room at the nation's heart should be where its destiny came to focus. That was the aim of her Wednesday Drawing Rooms, as she styled her open houses. She had made them the center of Washington society, a neutral ground on which people of all persuasions could gather in civility assured by the authority of host and hostess.

"Ah, Madame Dolley!" It was Henry Clay, the tall, dashing Kentuckian who was Speaker of the House and leader of the War Hawks. Making an entrance, he spread his hands dramatically. "How fortunate the President whose missus can manage all this!"

She laughed and curtsied, summoned a waiter to whom Clay turned eagerly, accepted a stiff bow from that handsome but puzzlingly dour young congressman from South Carolina, John Calhoun, who had drafted a war bill, and moved on. There was Peter Porter, their old ally from New York, a state that produced few allies. He stood firmly with Clay in pushing for war. She kissed him, whispering, "Now, Peter, don't agitate Jimmy."

"Sweet lady!" he cried. "Would I?"

"You would," she said, and whirled away. She moved from group to group, brushing cheeks with women, patting hands, nodding gracefully to men who bowed, disarming them with bright little quips before moving on. French John appeared at her side with a flute of champagne.

She sipped it to wet her throat, handed it back with a grateful glance, and turned to see a catastrophe in the making. A congressman from the Ohio frontier—a burly fellow with gray chin whiskers and a loud voice—was telling a story. At the climax he stepped backward with a braying laugh and collided with poor little Boney, their newest waiter, who'd come up from Montpelier only the month before. Squeezed among guests, Boney was holding a tray overhead. It tilted dangerously and was about to shower the Congressman with toast points covered with hot cheese when Joseph slid between them to steady it on outstretched fingers.

What a prize Joseph was! Smallish, slender, quick, and very intelligent, he was born on Montpelier and had been with them in Washington since he was a child. Dolley was proud of him, for almost entirely on his own, he'd become a voracious reader. Many people feared educated servants, but she and Jimmy encouraged it. There was something inscrutable in Joseph's black face that let no one really near, but she liked him and knew she could count on him.

The Congressman turned, startled. Joseph bowed. "Beg your pardon, Mr. Congressman Toms."

"Well, quite all right." The gentleman harumphed. She saw he was flattered that his name was known. "Just be more careful next time."

What nerve! She was ready to tell him so, too, when Joseph flashed her a quick grin. She laughed, looked about, and quickly sobered. Two of their archenemies, coming themselves from the opposite ends of the political spectrum, were huddled together like a couple of conspirators aping Machiavelli in the Florentine court. Two senators: Samuel Smith of Maryland, once a friend and fellow battler in the Democratic wars who had turned on them, and Josiah Quincy of Massachusetts, who entertained his Federalist constituency with vituperous attacks on poor Jimmy.

They saw her and started apart. Well they might look guilty! They were fighting the idea of war for opposite ideological reasons, but it was the underhanded cruelty of their unprincipled diatribes that infuriated her. And now, plotting together—they did test neutral ground to its outer limits.

She stepped forward, gave them a fierce smile, and said, "Welcome to the President's House, gentlemen."

The crowd was denser. Dolley took several deep breaths. The political pressures of war were as tense as military questions, but the uniforms had Jimmy's ear tonight. Decatur—a passionate terrier of a man, bright Tripoli sash marking him from a distance—was declaiming. She saw Commodore Rogers frown, Captain Bainbridge nod agreement. Dearborn raised a fork to take exception and, with the floor seized, talked vigorously around great mouthfuls of food.

Poor Jimmy. Dearborn dismayed him with his pontifical certainty, his slightly fatuous assurance. She had known the man for years—he'd been Jefferson's Secretary of War till he became customs collector in Boston. Life must have proved easy there.

Yet who else could plan war? Henry Dearborn had assumed the role to be his, reluctant as he was to give up his comforts in Boston, and in truth, there wasn't anyone else. Certainly not the Secretary of War, bluff, hearty Dr. Eustis, who was amusing at dinner but hadn't the faintest concept of organization. Still, Jimmy was terribly vulnerable to these men. Lacking military experience of his own, he found them hard to judge. They talked with authority, but did they really know?

French John threaded his way to her. The noise level was deafening, and he leaned close to say they had nearly three hundred guests who were eating and drinking at twice the usual rate. Collective nerves, she supposed. He was hurrying out to area kitchens and wine cellars for more supplies and would leave Joseph in charge.

She nodded, took a quick little pinch of snuff from her silver box, and sneezed gracefully into her kerchief. It left an exhilarating, stinging clarity that was better than champagne. It also made her eyes water, and when they cleared a tall man in a fine black suit with hair like a stiff brush was bowing to her. She knew him instantly.

"Andrew Jackson of Tennessee, madam," he said in a high but pleasing voice that carried easily over the din. "May I express my pleasure in being here and in meeting you? Your fame is cast wide in Tennessee and were I to fail to salute you in their name, folks at home would skin me."

My! *This* was the leather-shirted barbarian? She liked him immediately but saw just as quickly why he disturbed Jimmy. He was a man to whom the exercise of power came naturally. She'd known many powerful people, starting with George Washington and Martha, and she had a sure feeling for the inner capacity power required.

On impulse, she said, "You're a soldier. You see so many here tonight— tell me, sir, do you think soldiers as a class know of what they speak so confidently?"

He hesitated, taking her seriously, considering with what she sensed was a formidable intelligence. Then he smiled.

"First, madam, I'm a military man who does know of what he speaks. I know my people, what they want, what they'll fight for. But most military men I've met"—his lips pulled down in an odd, sour grimace—"why, I think doubts are on the mark."

She thought so, too. Politely she asked after Mrs. Jackson, at whose name an almost boyish smile lit his face. "She's very well, thank you, and she'll be delighted to hear you inquired." He rattled on happily of his wife's asthma, her discovery that snuff eased it, her talent with growing things, the formal garden she planned. Dolley listened with pleasure until he excused himself. Here was a man in love with his wife, and love never lacks for friends.

A willowy young woman in a gown as yellow as spring forsythia maneuvered toward Dolley with hands outstretched.

"Sally, darling!" Dolley gave her a quick hug. Sally McQuirk was one of her favorites, the only child and hence the heir of Micajah McQuirk, publisher of the *Democratic-Republican*, the one newspaper in Washington they could count on to tell the truth as they saw it, as if any other truth mattered. Sally said little about the paper, but Dolley knew she was close to her father and undoubtedly kept her eyes and ears open.

"What does Micajah think of Henry Dearborn?" she asked.

Sally hesitated. "Well, that he was a great fighter in the Revolution, but that that was thirty-odd years ago."

"And the Secretary of War?"

This time Sally giggled. "They play poker together. Papa says Dr. Eustis will draw to an inside straight every time."

"Oh, Sally, how dismaying!"

As if on cue, she saw Eustis enter the room, late as usual. He shook hands all around, blew kisses to the women, caught someone's arm to whisper, and both exploded in laughter. With him was a striking young officer, a captain whom Dolley was sure she'd never seen. He stood a full head above the crowd and looked around with such a blend of interest and self-assurance that she was captivated. Not quite handsome, too young to be distinguished, he had an air of authority she found compelling and yet touching in one so youthful. Who in the world was he?

Chatting with Sally, she watched Eustis worm his way into the circle around Jimmy, laughing and slapping backs as he deftly moved people aside. He knew how to get along, Eustis did, but she feared that was all he knew. Then she saw that the young captain who'd been with him had been left standing on the edge of a group that ignored him. He looked disconsolate.

"Oh, Sally," she said, pointing him out, "he looks so excluded. Go talk to him, there's a dear."

Sally's eyes brightened. So she *had* noticed the young man.

"If I can find a way without being forward."

"Oh, you will, dear."

★ ★ ★ ★

Well, it wasn't that simple. She could hardly just walk up to a strange man and say, why, hello there, I'm Sally McQuirk. It wasn't done and Miss Dolley knew it. Was she being naive or mischievous?

Of course she'd noticed the tall young officer the moment he arrived, though she was sure she'd concealed her interest. In fact, she concealed most of her thoughts, which was why people were so unguarded around her, and why she was so valuable to Papa. And why Papa someday would put the paper in her hands and leave her the voice of Washington—even if she chose to keep herself concealed, as she was now, behind male editors.

The moment she saw the man—mid-twenties, he looked, scarcely older than she—she knew she had to meet him. Sally tended to rate men by their ability to excite her, and she had a feeling this one would. Excitement meant more than good looks or good manners—it had to come from some genuine inner force.

She'd met one such man tonight. Felix Grundy, the gaudy Tennessee congressman wearing a waistcoat embroidered with rosebuds, had presented a militia general named Jackson who'd startled her with the intensity of his manner. He'd kissed her hand, rather more than she'd expected from a frontier soldier, and chatted with a grace and wit that left her strangely stirred. Not attracted—she struck a careful distinction—but invigorated in a forceful way she could feel in her body.

And the young soldier gave her the same sense, at least from a distance. He was still on the fringe of the group around Mr. Madison, whom she saw had lapsed into the monochrome persona he adopted in public. At small gatherings he was quite different; she found him downright charming.

Secretary Eustis had pushed close to the President and was talking in a loud voice and gesticulating while the naval officers frowned and Dearborn smiled like a fat cat. The Secretary of the Navy was there, too, rocking gently, glass in hand, silent. He was drunk, of course, poor Paul Hamilton, it being late in the day. General Washington's portrait gazed down on these talkers with stern disapproval—

The young officer sat down. Immediately she strode toward him. He'd taken one of those Greek-motif chairs that Mr. Latrobe considered so significant and sat with legs crossed, surveying the crowd with that same serene expression of confident interest she'd noticed when he entered the room.

"Pardon me," she said. "You're new at Miss Dolley's parties, aren't you?"

He leapt to his feet. "My first experience, thank you."

"Yes. In fairness, I thought I should inform you—one doesn't sit down. Not at our age. Only the infirm."

"Really?" He had a droll expression—doubtless he knew that she'd made this up on the spur of the moment, but she didn't care. "You've saved me from a gross misstep."

"My pleasure," she said, and turned away.

"But may I not know my rescuer's name?"

"Well, I suppose so. Miss McQuirk. Sally McQuirk."

He bowed. "Winfield Scott of Dinwiddie County, Virginia."

Just then Miss Dolley swept up.

"Ah," she said, "I see you've met. I'm Mrs. Madison."

"Winfield Scott, lieutenant colonel, Second Artillery. Miss McQuirk has been so kind as to rescue me from a grave faux pas."

Sally caught the edge of irony and thought Dolley did, too, for the older woman flashed her an appraising glance, then said to the officer, "I'm surprised, though. I took you for a captain."

In fact, he was wearing the insignia of a captain with the red facings of the artillery. Sally made it a point to know military and naval uniforms— easy enough, and it never failed to please their wearers.

He smiled. "I've only been a lieutenant colonel for an hour, but I like the sound of it."

Sally decided she liked *him*. Dolley hurried off, but her presence had legitimatized the encounter and they could talk easily. Tall herself, Sally was drawn to tall men. He had a strong, solid look, sandy hair, eyes blue or gray or mixed, forehead broad and rather high, chin square and slightly dimpled. There was something about him that was . . . formidable.

"An hour?" she said.

"Perhaps an hour and a half. The stress of war, you know."

"You think there'll be war?"

"Of course."

"You mean you want war."

"No soldier wants war per se. But the time comes when war is the only course consistent with honor."

Perversely—the thought hadn't struck her before—she said, "But soldiers prosper in war. You've leapt two grades in an afternoon, if I understand correctly."

He shrugged. "They could have made me a general."

My. She liked him better than ever. Just as she'd expected, there was a fierceness in him that stirred her. And almost as if on cue, he said with an intensity quite unlike their light, bantering exchange, "And they will, too— I'll be a general before this is over."

"Good for you," Sally said. She liked naked ambition—she had plenty herself. She could wait, but she intended in time to run the newspaper with a strong hand. In fact, as Papa had grown less well, she had taken an ever stronger hand behind the scenes. When it was hers she would have a voice heard across the nation, even if few knew it. She would know it.

"Arriving this morning, I read a fine newspaper on the stage," he said. "Very wise commentary. The publisher was a Mr. McQuirk, I believe."

"My father."

"Ah. Is he here tonight?"

"He's not well."

"I'm sorry. I'd like to have shaken his hand. So you're here as . . . surrogate? Agent? Source of information, perhaps?"

Damn. He was quick. He'd seen more in ten minutes than most people ever saw. Or so she flattered herself.

"I say, Scott!" Dr. Eustis called.

"Sir!"

"Come over here." The Secretary windmilled his arm. "I was just telling the President your story."

"Yes, sir." Swiftly he turned to her. "You're not leaving immediately . . . I hope."

"Not immediately."

"Please don't."

★ ★ ★ ★

"Winfield Scott, Mr. President," Eustis said.

Scott bowed, feeling preternaturally alert. They were all watching him, several naval officers, a fat general with a couple of colonels, several men in civilian garb whom he didn't know.

The President smiled but looked very tired. "Where are you from, young man?"

"Dinwiddie County, Virginia, sir."

"Then I expect I know your family. The late William Scott?"

"My father, sir."

"A fine family. You were saying, Doctor?"

"Gentlemen," Eustis said, "this young man is destined to rise. He came to my attention a couple of years ago when he was court-martialed for calling his commanding officer a scoundrel." He turned to Scott. "General . . . ?"

"Wilkinson, sir."

"Yes. General Wilkinson. In New Orleans. The court sentenced him to a year without pay. Out of the army, you understand. Well, one day I get a letter from him, and what do you think it says? That he's sorry, he'll never speak ill of a commander again? Not at all. The letter demands a promotion! Says he's just learned his regiment's major died of something or other, and he's the senior captain and he wants that majority!"

There was a sharp burst of laughter. Scott gave them an equable smile, fully at ease because he long since had thought the incident through. Speaking the truth was no sin, so he had paid a protocol penalty for a protocol crime. Only if he had been too cowed to demand a promotion that was rightfully his would he have felt demeaned.

"I like that," said a lean naval captain wearing a sash from the War of Tripoli. "He should have joined the navy. Ram and board, by God! So, Mr. Secretary, you gave him the promotion?"

It was peculiar, standing here the mute center of attention among the most powerful men in the nation, but not uncomfortable. The President's smile was warm, as if he welcomed diversion, and Scott liked Dr. Eustis. Liking and respecting, of course, were quite different.

He had landed in Baltimore the day before, come in by overnight stage, put on his best uniform, and gone straight to the War Department, a little brick building adjoining the President's House. He had passed down a hall lined with cubicles and found a larger room. A half-dozen clerks were writing

furiously at scattered desks. One in shirtsleeves and a bright waistcoat came
bustling by.

"Can you direct me to the Secretary's office, please?" Scott asked.

"I'm the Secretary. What can I do for you?"

"The Secretary of War?" Oh, oh, how clumsy to barge in here and
. . . but good Lord, *this* was the War Department? A handful of clerks
and a Secretary? Scott had never given the matter much thought, but he'd
supposed the department was quite an establishment, Secretary layered by
deputies, a general staff dealing with the intricacies of the military,
strategy and tactics, intelligence, manpower, training, supply . . . my
God, maintaining a national army is no small matter even if it's a small
army. Hastily he came to attention, explained he'd just arrived from New
Orleans with permission to seek an assignment in the army gathering to
the north.

"William Eustis. Medical doctor, I'm proud to say." The Secretary wrung
Scott's hand as if a vote might be concealed there and led him into a
corner cubicle. He was bluff, hearty, relaxed, the wrinkles in his fleshy face
suggesting easy smiles. He wore gray breeches with sagging hose, and the
buckle on his right shoe, which he placed atop his knee as he turned to his
visitor, was tied in place with white string.

"Henderson!" he shouted through the open door. "That hundredweight
of powder? Did we hear anything more?"

A skinny man in his forties wearing a green eyeshade began a frantic
search through a foot-high stack of papers. "Oh, God," Eustis said, "never
mind."

"I saw something on it, sir," Henderson said. "Today. Or yesterday."

"What'd it say?"

"That . . . uh—they're looking. I think."

"Huh! Well, light a fire under 'em."

Newspapers were spread on the desk. Eustis punched one with a forefinger.

"Scott, ever hear of Forbath & Sons?"

"Why, no, sir . . ."

"Hatmakers in Philadelphia. But who knows if they're any good? Still,
that's a good price, a dollar." He pondered the matter. Then, "Henderson!
This Forbath outfit—order a hundred hats, all sizes. No, make that every
other size. Offer eighty-five cents apiece—see what they say."

"Yes, sir." Henderson scribbled and spiked the note.

"Now, Scott, you're looking for a berth? Captain of artillery . . . let's
see." He went to a file cabinet and picked over the contents of a drawer.
"No, nothing here on you. Well, never mind, I'm sure you're competent."
Then he slapped his forehead. "Wait a minute! I remember you." Scott's
pulse raced, but the Secretary chuckled and began thumbing a sheaf of notes
as they talked.

"Here we go," he said. "George Izard's regiment—Second Artillery, making up in Philadelphia. You know Izard?"

"No, sir."

"Good man. He'll have a future, I promise you. Anyway, there's an opening . . . let's see, a major, a—here it is, lieutenant colonel. Second in command. Will that do?"

"Yes, sir! Thank you, sir."

"Very well. Oh, God, look at the time! Henderson! Why the hell didn't you remind me?"

"Sir?" Henderson looked confused.

"Oh, never mind. I'm due at the President's." He pulled on a blue coat with huge brass buttons. "Come along, Scott. Open house. You'll enjoy it."

A gravel path led to the White House. On their way over, Scott asked enough to learn that the entire War Department consisted of the Secretary and twenty-odd clerks. That was it, the whole controlling military establishment of the United States. It had been an educating if unsettling afternoon for a professional soldier on the eve of war.

Now, at parade rest in an audience with his Commander in Chief he'd never expected to have, he listened to his story spun out. In answer to the lean naval captain, Eustis said, "No, Decatur, I didn't promote him then, but I made up for it today—jumped him to lieutenant colonel. Izard's outfit."

But he grew tired of playing the passive object. "In my defense, Mr. Secretary, I put my time to good use."

"By God, he did," Eustis said. "Spent the whole year in Virginia studying the great military masters. Who all, Scott?"

"Machiavelli, Frederick, Vauban, Guibert, Napoleon's writings especially on artillery, Jomini, Clausewitz—"

"That last fellow, he ain't even in English," Eustis said. "Boy had to learn German."

Scott smiled. "Read with a dictionary at my side, I assure you, sir. He's very new—military journals only."

Eustis said, "I reckon this young fellow is as skilled a student of military science as we have in the army today."

Scott thought that a fair statement. It had been a lovely year, ironic in that at the start he'd thought seriously of resigning and going back to the law, but after a year with the finest military minds in the world he knew he would be a soldier forever. The beautiful precision was thrilling, the logic, the intellectual penetration of what looked like brute collisons and actually were intricate—and ultimate—dances with an infinite number of factors. He'd plumbed a friend's library, then ordered volumes from abroad, waited months for their arrival, and luxuriated in the time to study. He believed he could be a combat leader, but he knew he always would be a student.

"Well done, Colonel," Madison said. "I believe in study—it's a virtue in its own right."

Scott saw the fat general frown: a mere captain, knowledgeable? This must be Dearborn. When Scott had asked Eustis if he was making war plans, too, the Secretary said, "Thank God, no. It's all in Henry Dearborn's hands." He chuckled and added, "He's so fat he can't get close enough to the map table to see the maps, but what the hell."

Dearborn's belt was strained, which made his saber stick out like a rooster's tail. "That's all very well," he said, "but it overlooks the original crime. Denouncing his commanding general. Disgraceful—"

"Oh, I don't know," a tall man said in an oddly shrill voice. "Fact is, General Wilkinson *is* a scoundrel."

Scott saw the President shoot a look of surprising venom at the stranger before he turned to Dearborn and said, "General Jackson of Tennessee. Man of decided opinions."

Dearborn gaped. "What do you mean, sir? James Wilkinson commands the Southern Department."

"As well I know," Jackson said. "And he's a traitor. Been in the pay of the Spanish for years. Whatever Burr had in mind in his western imbroglio, Wilkinson was in it up to his hocks. I know—I was there."

" 'Twas Wilkinson brought Burr to our attention," Madison said in a voice that carried a dangerous edge.

"And how did he know so well what was afoot—which never was proved, remember—unless he was in it? Both of 'em tried to involve me, but I dealt with that in short order."

Dearborn sounded strangled. "If Wilkinson were here—"

Jackson's voice shot up several notches. "He were here, I'd pull his nose right out of his face!"

"I d-d-don't like such talk of a regular officer. Not from a militiaman. In *my* days, we respected regulars."

"Let me tell you something, General! My militiamen will outmarch, outmaneuver, outfight any soldiers on earth. As I told the President, give us the word and we'll march right up the St. Lawrence, take Montreal, and settle the whole matter."

"Ridiculous!" Dearborn said. "That's the trouble with amateur strategists. For your information, General, war is serious business. Canada can be ours, it's a ripe apple, its people will welcome us. They'll throw flowers under our feet. But we must show them massive strength—get control of the lakes, advance in the west, cross the Niagara, drive north from Lake Champlain. Three fronts, sir, to demonstrate power the Canadian people will thrill to."

Scott listened dumbfounded. He'd never thought it would be easy, but he knew the strategy Dearborn described was wrong. A glance at the map told the Canada story. The Great Lakes fed the mighty St. Lawrence on its way to the sea. That river provided the single avenue that connected settled Canada with the West, and Montreal was its key. A single quick thrust would take Montreal with Quebec a mere hundred-odd miles on. It would mean hard fighting, but in the end, taking Montreal would finish Canada. It was so obvious Scott had never imagined any other possibility. But this was not ground on which newly minted lieutenant colonels could speak.

Jackson sniffed. "Seems to me taking Montreal would impress 'em pretty fair."

Dearborn glared at him. " 'Tis a fool's trick to insist on error when it's just been explained."

In a voice that made Scott's skin prickle, Jackson said, "You're not calling me a fool, I hope, General?"

His tone struck instant silence in this end of the great oval room. It was in terrible taste in the President's House, but it seemed to Scott that the exchange said something profound about the two men. Dearborn was commanding general of the entire army, and in Scott's estimation men wouldn't follow him to an outhouse. But this fellow Jackson, of whom Scott had never even heard, had that fire that troops will follow right into hell.

"All right, gentlemen," President Madison said. There was no mistaking his authority.

Dearborn said, "I'm not calling anyone anything. If you take disagreement on strategy as an offense, so be it."

"Thank you, sir," Jackson said, his voice high but light.

Decatur stepped into the gathering silence. "Does make some sense, Henry," he said to Dearborn. "Go straight in and hit 'em fast and hard. That's good naval doctrine."

Dearborn wheeled like an old bear at bay. "Now, Stephen, it ill behooves the navy to advise the army when your ships are skulking in harbor."

"Skulking, sir! Now, by God, that's offensive! Let me tell you, General, ship for ship, gun for gun, man for man, we'll whip the British on any sea. Our sailors are free men, not held by force. They're better trained. Our ships are stronger and just as well handled. But the Royal Navy has six hundred capital ships, each a floating arsenal. We have sixteen.

"Skulking! You should be ashamed of yourself. I've recommended to the President that should war come he unleash us immediately. We'll prey on their shipping and when we can lure 'em into a fair fight we'll give lessons they'll never forget. By God, Henry, you must be under strain. If I didn't know you were a good fellow, I'd slap your jaws."

"All right, all right." Dearborn seemed a little befuddled, as if he'd been slapped and was still blinking. At last he said, "Maybe I did speak out of turn."

A slender, rather handsome man said in the manner of one just awakening, "Hear, hear. Can't have the army impinging—impugning the navy."

"Thank you, Mr. Secretary," Decatur said.

Ah, Secretary of the Navy Hamilton. It took Scott a moment to realize that the man was very drunk. No wonder Mr. Madison hesitated, his navy led by a man awash in wine, army planning in the hands of a soldier who appeared to have a snail's energy and scarcely more wit. How much confidence could the President have?

The navy itself admitted that it would be powerless in war. The Royal Navy could blockade the coast and cut off all outside contact. Yes, Yankee ships could slip out to harry enemy shipping, make them keep more warships on station that they'd like, maybe even challenge one to one, but nothing would change.

That meant it would be up to the army. And everything would depend on taking Canada, because there was no place else we could reach the enemy. But after listening to the war plans, he felt deep uneasiness.

Eustis had been right in one thing—the new lieutenant colonel was as expert on military thinking as anyone in the army. More so. He'd compressed four hundred years of the best military minds in the world into that year of punishment, and he pored over every new report. He traveled with a small military reference library, which his troops found strange but wonderful—they boasted of their brainy commander to other units.

But you needed no special training to know that strategic planning turned on striking where you could be decisive. The St. Lawrence River and Montreal were the keys to unlocking Canada; why fight on the periphery?

What's more, Scott had serious doubts that Canada really was all that ripe for the plucking. Canadian ships called at New Orleans, and he had talked to their crewmen in the oyster bars and coffeehouses and taverns along the riverfront and never a one of them voiced interest in being an American.

In his opinion, the commanding general who thought war would be easy hadn't thought much about war. He felt a wave of sympathy for the grave little President.

The talk became general. He felt it inappropriate to remain longer among men so superior in rank and withdrew unnoticed. The crowd's noise had evened out to a steady roar. He took champagne and a cracker with ham from a passing waiter and scanned the room. Maybe if he sat down she would reappear in some magic alchemy . . . ah, there she was in that striking yellow, talking to a young man. What a beauty—tall and willowy, hair coiled on the base of her neck like rolled gold—my! Whereas Mrs. Madison, for all her reputation for beauty, had turned out to be a slightly dumpy lady of middle age, pretty and charming but not Scott's idea of a dazzling woman. Sally, though . . . he saw her glance his way and smile, and that was invitation enough.

"Lieutenant Colonel Winfield Scott," she said formally, "Mr. Ambassador Augustus Foster. Mr. Foster represents the merry isle of England on our shores."

Scott bowed, as did the Ambassador, who murmured pleasantries in a rich public school accent. Foster was a slender fellow scarcely older than Scott, handsome in striped pantaloons and black coat cut to superb fit, light brown hair that fell in graceful waves, blue eyes as suited to a warrior as a statesman. There was an obdurate strength in his face. He would be formidable competition in the arena of love, but something in Sally's stance made Scott think she wasn't drawn to the Englishman, and he relaxed.

"Sally was just telling me I spend too much time talking to Federalists," Foster said, "and I suppose I do, but they're so reasonable. They understand how the world is, and the Democratic-Republicans, with all respect, live in dreams."

Scott smiled. "Because they believe a free nation should not have to pay tribute to another nation to exercise its right of trade? That was the Dey of Algiers's position, too."

"Oh, my dear chap, please don't compare the King to the Dey of Algiers. Oh, my, my, my."

"And ten thousand of our sailors stolen?"

"An exaggerated figure, I'm sure. And those given the chance to serve the King are engaged in a noble cause. That's the real issue, you know. Napoleon Bonaparte is the enemy every free man should want to fight. A few sailors borrowed by accident, a small tax on trade, that's nothing against the need to combat a tyrant who intends to rule the world."

"To rule *your* world, Mr. Ambassador," Scott said with a smile. "If Napoleon comes here, we'll fight him here."

"A shortsighted view, Colonel, if I may say so. England is fighting for the freedom of the world. You should be helping."

Sally laughed. "Augustus, please! Oppressing us in the name of freedom is a contradiction, don't you think?"

Foster laughed, too, smooth and easy. "Yes, Miss Sally, perhaps, perhaps. But the Colonel here understands military weight, I'm sure. We have a quarter-million men under arms with years of rugged fighting experience. I don't believe your army has reached ten thousand—has it, sir?"

"But as you've pointed out, yours is engaged elsewhere."

"True, true, but that may change."

"Oh?"

"We think Napoleon is embarking on his greatest mistake. He has decided to invade Russia."

"Really?" Scott said. "A madman's move."

"Ah," Foster said, "then you understand the implications. The man *is* mad, you know. That's what power does, which is why we limited our own king at Runnymede so many centuries ago."

If true, that was bad news. It was Napoleon's own dictum that an army travels on its belly. A march to Moscow would stretch supply lines impossibly. Yet there would be no living off the land, for the Russian peasant would burn his grain before he'd leave it to the French. And if the Russian winter smashed the dictator as England couldn't, that would free the whole British army to attack America. Scott realized that until now he hadn't really focused on how much American war plans depended on Napoleon keeping Britain busy.

"We believe he'll reel out of Russia in tatters," Foster said, "and we'll be waiting for him."

"But, my dear sir, by then you may find us in Canada throttling your own supply lines."

"Ah, Canada," Foster said. He smiled at Sally. "This talk of war doesn't offend you, my dear? We could speak of poetry."

She shrugged. "Poetry seems a little less immediate."

"Well, Colonel, I'm afraid you won't find Canada as easy as General Dearborn thinks. Or hopes. We have five thousand well-trained troops there, led by energetic officers who won their spurs against Napoleon. And the Indian chief, Tecumseh, is with us since you killed his brother last year at—where was it?"

"Tippecanoe."

"That's it. These odd, odd names. But Americans tipped Tecumseh right out of the canoe, if you'll forgive the pun."

Suddenly the Englishman's smile had an ugly tint. Scott said, "I'm surprised to hear you extolling the use of savages against women and children in frontier cabins." To Sally, he added, "A bit naive of me, d'you think?"

"I'm surprised, too," she said. "At least that you'd admit it, Augustus."

"Nothing of the sort, my dear. Tecumseh's legions are under tight British command. No atrocities planned, I assure you. But five thousand warriors added to our forces is no small matter.

"And then, really old man, the idea that Canadians will throw flowers under your feet, just can't wait to be Americans, that's laughable. I was in Halifax four weeks ago and it's full of loyalists who abandoned their homes in New England rather than abandon their King. Why should they change now?"

Since the comment mirrored Scott's thinking, he kept quiet.

"Mr. Madison is a very intelligent man," Foster said. "I believe we can count on him not to make a foolish move. And war would be foolish indeed." He pulled a turnip watch from a waistcoat pocket. "Oh, my, I must pay my respects to the President lest we have still another international incident."

Scott and Sally McQuirk watched him push his way into the circle.

"Poor Mr. Madison," she said, "the weight of the world on his shoulders. Do you think it'll be war?"

"Yes," Scott said. "I see a fundamental strength in the man, I don't think he'll back down."

"And Mr. Foster's views? Do you think he's bluffing?"

"I wish I did." His voice dropped. "I really do. But . . . well, war is ever hazardous and never easy—Foster is right about that. What worries me is, I think General Dearborn's telling the President it will be easy. Quick and easy."

"You don't find Dearborn wise?"

"Do you?"

She giggled. "No."

Scott had never met a woman like Sally McQuirk. She had a quickness of mind and a feeling for issues to match his own, but was as winsome as the loveliest belle of the ball. And yet he hesitated. She possessed some inner power that he found confusing and perhaps—he wasn't sure—alarming. Then, their talk ending, she gave him a brilliant smile that washed away all uncertainty and extended her hand.

He bent to kiss it and, not letting go, said with urgency that surprised him, "I want to see you again. Tell me I may call."

Something in her eyes deepened at that. Her hand tightened on his, a firm pressure that he found immensely erotic. He was instantly erect and knew it was visible, but she was looking into his eyes.

"Tomorrow at three," she said in a whisper that was like a kiss. Thoroughly shaken, he watched her move swiftly across the room and disappear through the double doors.

★ ★ ★ ★

James Madison could feel decision stirring. It was always this way, taking form after hours or days of pondering, like a ship emerging from fog. Two exhausting hours had passed with too many positive assertions and too few reservations raised.

He guessed Canada would be easy, but he'd like to hear a little decent doubt. Was the straight strike at Montreal that made such sense to him really simplistic thinking, as Dearborn said? He'd seen doubt on young Scott's face but to have asked would have embarrassed the youngster and infuriated Dearborn.

Dearborn and Eustis in his dithering War Department were weak reeds, but who else was there? At least Britain hadn't been alerted by genuine war preparations in America. He knew the young ambassador thought the American threat was all talk.

Foster put weight on the reports that Napoleon might invade Russia, which struck Madison as bad news for Britain. He didn't understand the military implications, granted, but the dictator had won so far, and taking Russia would make him impregnable. If the U.S. seized Canada in the meantime . . .

He'd noticed Dolley's encounter with the arch-Federalist Josiah Quincy and old Sam Smith, the Baltimore purist who now accused him of being insufficiently democratic. An asp in the bosom—apostate friends are the worst enemies. Dolley took it as simple treachery, but he could see their side, too, their conviction that—he stopped himself. He spent too much time seeing both sides and not enough in banging heads!

Put it to a vote today and he thought Americans would tip sixty-forty for war. A rage had built up over abuses that called the nation itself into question—were we free, strong, independent, a nation to stand on equal footing with others? Or were we a vassal state?

A second revolution to prove the first: he understood it well. It was the simplistic symbol of a sentiment that was entirely genuine and hence not to be dismissed. He knew the idea was growing that a government unable to protect national interests and its citizenry was unworthy.

Then there were the Indians. Could Tecumseh really establish a barrier state to stop western advance? Maybe, with British arms and tutelage. And eventually America must deal with a hostile Spain anchored in Florida and always ready with British connivance to threaten New Orleans. Put an enemy stopper in the Mississippi and the West would die, keeping the United States the modest competitor the British obviously desired.

Quincy and Smith . . . he'd like to slap their heads together and open their minds to the reality that the pressures for war exceeded those against. Still, violent political differences would follow so long as the President hesitated.

But even the very angriest of his opponents were Americans first of all. Commit the nation to war and they would rally to the flag as their fathers had done, as Americans always would do. Hardheaded New Englanders might disagree on everything but they were patriots, too—God knows they'd proved that in the Revolution. Love of country was embedded in Madison's heart and, he believed, in the hearts of all Americans. Faced with the test, they too would stand to the colors.

And it would be over quickly. He couldn't really doubt that Canada would fall, maybe not within a month as Clay liked to say, but soon; and with Canada in hand and Britain newly ready to negotiate, political opposition would have no complaint left.

The weight was shifting in his mind, and all at once he found himself composing the war message. The phrases leapt to hand, arguments and explanations that shaped themselves in powerful blocks to express finally the pain that had lain against the American heart for a dozen hard years. He felt a profound relief: he had decided.

"Gentlemen," he said, cutting across some rumbling voice, "I bid you good evening."

He turned to rap on one of the off-center doors at the rear of the room. The guard, Dumster, opened it.

"Walk me to my office, Rufe," Madison said. "See that I'm not interrupted."

Lake Ontario

Fort Niagara

Fort George

U.S. Camp

Queenston

Lewiston

Fort Gray

Wool's path

- - - British Forces
.... U.S. Forces
R   Redoubt
▲   Final U.S. Retreat

R

Niagara River

North

Detail of Queenston and Lewiston   North →

Wool's path
up the bluffs   The REDAN
                     18-Pounder   Vrooman's
                                       Point

                     Queenston   (British
                                       Battery)
Fort Gray   Road to Fort George

            LANDING   to Fort George
            Scott's guns   Lewiston   U.S. Camp

13 October, 1812

0   ½   1
       Mile

Niagara Falls

Lundy's Lane

Chippewa

Navy Island

E. Mitchell 9

5

★ ★ ★ ★ Winfield Scott was at the foot of Chestnut Street, a tall, stalwart figure in dress uniform, white breeches and blue coat faced with red, polished black shako on his head, white-gloved hand resting on his saber. He was alone. The Delaware sucked at deepwater brigs moored at the wharves. Hawsers groaned in the quiet as the ships moved. He saw a lantern on one and the ship's bell rang, eight clear strokes, midnight.

It was around here somewhere—yes, dim light spilling from a partly opened door, a sign barely visible. *The Thirsty Gull.* Inside, the air was heavy with smoke and the odor of bad rum.

"Sarenmajor Boone!" he roared.

From the rear came the Sergeant Major's answering bellow. "Ten-HUT!" A dozen men snapped to their feet, one falling down in the process. Scott saw Howell, Rainey, Beauregard, Filencia. Riordan was picking himself up from the floor.

A fellow at the bar with no neck and a striped sailor's jersey stretched over massive chest and arms bawled, "Well, lookit the soljer boys!" Scott had a feeling old differences were being renewed. "See an officer, their shit turns to water. See a redcoat, I reckon they'll pee their breeches."

Sergeant Major Asa Boone was a tall, rangy man, slender as a rail with long arms that Scott had seen work fearful damage. He was about forty, came out of Kentucky, and claimed old Daniel as an uncle, but you could never tell for sure about the Sarenmajor.

"Clamp down that pig's asshole you call a mouth, you slab-sided turd," he said. "You're in the presence of your betters. Colonel Scott, he don't cotton to that kind of talk."

"Well, Colonel Snot, now, he kin just kiss my ass," the sailor said. He smashed a bottle against the bar and lunged at Boone with the jagged glass. Scott thrust out his boot. The sailor crashed over it and landed on his belly. Boone kicked the glass from his hand and put a boot on the back of his neck.

"See, boys?" he said, laughing. "Didn't I tell you? The colonel, he's got a knack for this sort of thing."

A dozen seamen at the bar pointedly turned their backs. The man on the floor howled. Boone twisted his boot. The howl became a whine. "M'neck's busting."

Boone let him sit up. The sailor groaned. "Don't get up no farther," Boone said. "I'll kick your head off it you do."

"Let's go," Scott said. He let his saber, a foot out of its scabbard, fall back into place. "Fall out on the street."

"Yes, sir. Move it, boys, you heard the Colonel."

As the men formed up outside, Boone said, "Would it please the Colonel to let us know what's afoot?"

Scott laughed and popped his hands together. "Waiting's over, Sarenmajor. We're going to war." There was a ragged cheer, then they went swinging up dark Chestnut Street to Boone's low cadence. Scott smiled. He could always count on Boone.

★ ★ ★ ★

They marched at dawn, a battalion made up of the only two companies yet fully formed in the Second Artillery. Scott headed his little troop with a profound sense of relief that Sarenmajor Boone and the others couldn't imagine. For through the long summer, based on the evidence of the response in Philadelphia and in the nation, he had begun to doubt there would even be any action. Was war only a dream?

Oh, it had started smartly enough. The doughty little President had laid out a ringing call, as Scott had been sure he would, and the Congress had followed dutifully with a formal declaration of war. Scott, by then established in the Second Artillery's makeshift compound in a town square, had expected hordes of volunteers to storm their gates.

So what happened? Nothing happened. No tide of volunteers emerged. Recruiting remained a singular matter, one-at-a-time conversions, men listening somberly and many walking away without answering. The process was making him a damned salesman!—having to sell men on the virtue of defending their country. He wanted to shake them until their rotten little pea brains opened to understand that to rally to the flag in time of war is honor to the free man. Did they think they were free by accident? By some virtue of their own special worth?

If this was the attitude in Philadelphia, what of the rest of the country? Philadelphia was the most sophisticated, elegant, intelligent, accomplished city in the nation—the largest, the commercial and cultural center that until recently had been the political center, where the savants of the Philosophical Society were in constant touch with their peers abroad—and it couldn't be bothered with war.

Racks of newspapers from other cities that told their stories in agonizing detail were to be found at the old City Tavern near the Pennsylvania State House where the Declaration of Independence was written and the Constitution was drafted across the long hot summer of 1787. Scott went there daily to drink cup after cup of strong coffee while he studied the views from Boston and Hartford and New York and Baltimore and Charleston and from the nation's rude capital on the Potomac, to assess the national attitude, which in practice proved to be national lassitude.

Some papers cried yea and some nay, but collectively they made it clear the war hadn't caught the public imagination. Except in New England. They hated it there. In a fury of resistance, papers denounced Madison and the Democrats, antiwar rallies filled the streets, and the once moribund Federalist Party sprang back to life.

A new problem arose. The Constitution visualized militia as a defensive force, yeomen dropping the plow and leaping to arms in defense of their homes. But the only place England could be touched was in Canada. If the war was in self-defense, then striking Canada was in self-defense. But New England governors hadn't released their militia, and reluctant warriors were claiming a constitutional right not to cross national borders.

Scott sighed over the narrow columns of type, glad he was a soldier ready to respond to the crisp realities of flying shot and shell instead of a politician trapped in a morass of vagaries, unfeeling constituencies, confusing signals. Yet men were marching to war even as the public yawned.

A western army of fifteen hundred was cutting a trail through wilderness toward the village of Detroit. It was under a general named William Hull, of whom Scott knew only that he'd been governor of Indiana Territory. After Hull ejected the British from the west end of Lake Erie, he would advance along the northern shore into Canada proper.

Scott studied the terrain with care, poring over the available maps at the Philosophical Society, which welcomed him at its meetings. He still liked a strike straight at Montreal, but no one was asking his advice. Perhaps a three-pronged advance was safer, but obviously it was more problematic and difficult. It divided a still small force and provided that many more places for things to go wrong.

A second army under Alexander Smyth, a regular army brigadier, was forming on the Niagara River, through which Lake Erie flowed to join Lake Ontario. It would capture the British side of the Niagara, meet Hull's advance, and thus control Lake Ontario, which fed the St. Lawrence past Montreal to the sea. And General Dearborn would assemble an army at Lake Champlain and punch straight up into Canada to seize Montreal.

Then a confusion arose. Word crossed the Atlantic that just before our declaration, Britain had removed the sanctions on American trade that were one of our two great grievances.

"Well, hell, Win," said Nate Towson, the easygoing, rather solemn captain commanding Company A, "that ends it." They were in the City Tavern for the papers. Scott liked Towson, a dark-haired, even-featured man in his middle twenties who came from a storekeeper's family in western Pennsylvania and whose steady, merchantlike watch-the-inventory outlook made him a perfect subordinate. But Towson felt none of Scott's rage over public affairs and was forever chiding his friend for agitating himself. He confined his own reading to mercantile reports.

"No," Scott said, "Madison's tough. He won't back down, not with them stealing our seamen. Anyway, you read the British position carefully, you see they've left themselves an out you could put a coach-and-four through. Reimpose their restrictions whenever they like. And Madison's a careful reader."

"Nah. Bet you a rum toddy."

Scott laughed despite himself. "Done, damn it! If we can't protect our citizens, why be a country? Quitting now would kill republicanism. People want a government that can act."

He was right, of course. Madison held the line.

Nate chuckled and rapped the bar. "A rum toddy for the seer!"

Men whom Scott enlisted seemed more interested in the enlistment bonus than in national honor, and that certainly was the prevailing view among Philadelphia merchants. Cash on the barrelhead, sonny! Yet the government was strapped. Congress dared not ask a recalcitrant people to pay taxes, so its only income was from duties and its trade policies had cut import-export to a trickle.

Colonel Izard, the regimental commander, boiled with angry frustration. He couldn't even get his cannon.

"Scott," he said one day, "go push those foundry devils."

The foundryman had mustaches that curled toward his ears and arms like hams. "Ain't seen any money yet," he said.

"You'll get it. Government's not going to default."

"Well, I'll tell you. I got plenty of business, I'm making stoves and wagon tires and what all, and folks're ready to pay. You want guns, you know how to get 'em."

"My God, man, your country's at war!"

The foundryman shook his head. "Wasn't none of my doing."

Scott leaned on his desk. "We don't get those guns soon, we'll take over your place." He didn't have to fake the menace he put in his voice. He was far beyond his authority but doubted this ignoramus knew it. "Make it a government arsenal."

"You couldn't get away with that!"

"I've got the papers right here." He slapped his breast pocket. "I'm just giving you a last chance."

"Well, God damn it, I got four guns set up now. I'll pour 'em and bore 'em but that's the end of it till I see the cash!"

When the four guns were delivered and two companies had full complements, Scott presented his arguments to Colonel Izard. If Philadelphia's very own Second Artillery won heroes' laurels on the Niagara frontier, the four guns from its famous foundry blazing American wrath, perhaps city, people, and foundry would be inspired to rally to the flag at least a little . . .

Within ten days the War Department agreed and they were off. "Stick with Colonel Scott," he overheard Sergeant Major Boone telling Riordan.

"He has a way of getting what he wants. I tell you, I marked him for a comer and he ain't never disappointed me yet."

They went mostly by water as far as Albany, the boys hanging from the railings to hoorah the girls they passed. It was September. The days were full of summer but the nights suggested fall. From Albany the road to Buffalo stretched three hundred miles due west, dusty when dry, soup when wet. They would make it in fifteen days of marching or he'd know the reason why. All along the road to war, he met that same strange apathy. He had to fight down the urge to shake sense into people physically.

So: Company A, Captain Nate Towson, and Company B., Captain Jim Barker, each with sixty men and two of those pretty little black iron cannon from the foundry trundling behind their caissons, canvas muzzle covers and touchhole plugs lovingly in place. Wagons carried tents, cookpots, water butts, hardtack, and pickled beef in casks, Scott's famous military library, and gun gear—rams, picks, swabs, buckets, iron stakes, rope, shot and shell, black powder in kegs. Scott walked, his mount on a lead line.

Sarenmajor Boone's foraging patrol returned laden with ducks, chickens, eggs and vegetables, and a side of ham. The provender would be split among the messes, each a dozen men, with troopers doing double duty as cooks and, if they were good, leading charmed lives in battle while the boys protected them.

Boone was wearing a huge black eye. "Ask him about his shiner, Colonel," Riordan said. Scott raised an eyebrow.

Boone shrugged. "How was I to know her husband was in the next room? Lazy bastard should've been in the fields. *She* now . . . she was right interested."

Scott chuckled. He'd hate to go to war without Sarenmajor Boone, whom he'd pulled from a rotting guardhouse at Terre aux Boues south of New Orleans where men were dying right and left while that scoundrel General Wilkinson sold their rations to support a mulatto whore. He'd saved Boone's life, and the Sarenmajor had returned the favor a couple of times along the Mississippi where a young man could hardly avoid trouble.

The incident set Scott thinking about Sally McQuirk. What an appealing woman! He had called the next day and found several people there, met her father, chatted engagingly, and listened carefully to her responses to others. She was as intelligent as he and knew much more about Washington's affairs, so he said little but made sure that little sparkled.

When he called the next day she was by herself but for a maiden aunt as chaperone. She gave him sherry and cake and they grew flushed and laughed a lot, and after auntie went to sleep she fed him bits of cake with her fingers and poured a good deal more sherry. He was leaving the next morning, and when he told her good-bye at her door she suddenly pulled him into an anteroom.

"I like you, Winfield Scott," she whispered.

"Oh, Sally." His hands slid around her waist and drew her close. She raised her face and when he bent to her lips her arms went around his neck. Her mouth opened and their tongues met and he knew she could feel his erection but she pressed against him.

At last she tore away. "Oh, God," she muttered. He could hear her breathing. "You're dangerous. I could like you too much. Better go."

"Sally."

"Win—I have plans for my life."

"But I can write? See you when I return?"

"Of course. Oh, of course."

So he marched along thinking of her, her sparkling mind, the feel of her waist in his hands, her mouth opening on his. *I have plans for my life.* He knew exactly what she meant. He had plans for his, too. His plans would keep him in the field, hers would keep her in Washington. They were dangerous, each for the other. But what a glorious woman!

★ ★ ★ ★

They reached Buffalo in driving rain and found a place to camp between a couple of militia units whose men, huddled miserably under stretched tarps, assured the regulars they'd either goddam fight goddam quick or they'd tell the General to goddam stick it up his ass and they'd goddam go home.

Scott's adjutant, Lieutenant Isaac Roach, whom he'd sent ahead by stagecoach to scout the situation, appeared within an hour. Scott liked young Ike. He was a slender South Carolinian, his eyes bright blue in a dark, ruddy face. But his mood today matched the heavy skies and the cold steady rain.

"Have you heard about General Hull in the West?" he asked.

"No." Hull was to take Detroit and march eastward along the north shore of Lake Erie, in Canada.

"He surrendered," Roach said.

"Surrendered? With fifteen hundred men he lost the battle? Surely the British didn't have more?"

"There wasn't any battle. He quit without a fight."

Quit? It defied belief. Dearborn's whole strategy had rested on Hull and his strong army. But as the few who'd escaped and come overland through wilderness made clear, Hull had never put his own mind in a fighting mode. He wasn't a soldier, he was a governor. He'd served well in the Revolution but not since. He was old now, sick, exhausted. And he had women and children with him, including his own daughter and grandchild.

Facing him at Fort Malden on the British side was Major General Isaac Brock, a Napoleonic veteran who commanded everything west of Montreal. He sounded like a fighting man, alert and tough, if brutal, but his force was half Hull's size, three hundred regulars and as many Indians. He captured Hull's dispatches, read fear between the lines, and sent a cold-blooded warning: his Indians, once loosed, couldn't be controlled. Hull's dependents faced an orgy of rape and murder. Too bad, but there it was. He urged Hull to surrender immediately.

"Hull's officers were ready to depose him but he moved too fast. Now there's talk of hanging him for cowardice."

"By God, they should!" Scott cried. The poor tortured bastard, losing his nerve in the wilderness. When would we ever learn? Politicians all wanted to be generals and none of them were any good. Soldiering was a specialized craft, as the studied Scott knew well; why was every damned fool with a recognizable name sure he'd make a good one?

"Just inexcusable," he said, not sure if he meant Hull or those who'd appointed him. He felt sick. The nation had jumped into war and had its nose bloodied in the first exchange; what would this do for national apathy? "Give Brock credit, but—"

"Brock's our problem now," Roach said. "He's here, across the river at Fort George on the north end."

All right. The enemy was here and it was time to hit him. Cross the Niagara, whip this clever general, and drive on toward Montreal to link with Dearborn's move. Maybe Hull's loss was more a blow to morale than to strategy—after all, Montreal was the goal.

"General Smyth's ready to attack, then?"

"No, sir. A militia general's in command. Major general. He ranks Smyth."

"Jesus, Ike, you're full of surprises today."

"Yes, sir. Sorry, sir. It's this way . . ."

New York's governor had called out twenty-six hundred militia and named Stephen Van Rensselaer major general commanding—though in fact the new general had not had a day's military experience and relied totally on his cousin, Lieutenant Colonel Solomon Van Rensselaer, who'd been in the regulars years before. Stephen Van Rensselaer, it appeared, was a very big man in the state of New York.

Roach said Van Rensselaer's troops were threatening to go home if they didn't fight immediately, so he was planning his attack now. He intended to cross twenty miles north at Queenston.

"Let me get this straight," Scott said. "After Hull's loss, this campaign on which everything doubly depends is in the hands of a man who's never been a soldier and who lets his troops push his decisions?" Then he brightened. "But I suppose it means General Smyth will be de facto commander?"

"I don't think so, Colonel. They don't talk to each other."

"What? Are you serious?"

"You've got to meet General Smyth to believe him, sir. He *is* a talker, though. You should see his proclamations. The men laugh at him—call him Van Bladder."

General Van Bladder . . . good God.

He presented himself the next day. The General was a heavy man, belly bulging over his belt, with hooded, sleepy eyes and a pendulous lower lip that made him look a little like a pouting child. Van Bladder . . .

Scott reported the Second Artillery ready for action. "Will the attack be soon, sir?"

"How the defecating hell should I know?" Smyth said. He had a slight lisp and seemed perpetually short of breath. "I don't waste any time on this defecating militia rabble. We're regulars, sir! We won't demean ourselves with these defecating fools."

"But, sir—we'll support the attack, surely?"

"Bah! It's tomfoolery, won't come to a thing. Then when I'm ready, we'll—here!" He snatched up a paper. "What do you think of this?" He struck a pose. " 'Soldiers! Be ready! The day is soon to come when you'll have your chance to be an American hero, ready to die, certain to triumph!' "

There was a good deal more. "Very moving, sir," Scott said.

"I see you're a man who knows troops, Scott."

"Sir, you know how the militia complain?"

"Defecating whiners, exactly! But I've given 'em three hundred men from the Thirteenth Infantry at Fort Niagara. That should hold 'em."

"Sir, what would you think of supplementing that with my little battalion? Give my men a bit of experience, you know."

Smyth was studying his paper. He seized his quill to change a word.

"Oh, if you like," he said, waving a hand.

★ ★ ★ ★

Joe Totten was the first person Scott saw when he pounded down the long slope from the Niagara Escarpment to the flat that faced the hamlet of Queenston across the river. Totten was staring balefully at steep bluffs on the other side.

"Joe!" he bellowed. Totten turned quickly in the slanting rain, a stocky man with sandy hair cut very short, pale blue eyes, heavy shoulders. He was a captain of Engineers, a master builder full of energy even the heat in New Orleans couldn't slow. Despite an abrupt manner and a quick-ranging, often impatient mind, he was sound and Scott trusted him totally.

Now he wrung Scott's hand, laughing. "Win! What a sight for sore eyes. That Kentucky sergeant still with you? Remember the night he pulled us out of old Boudreau's shrimp house where we sure as hell didn't have any business being? Saved our necks, as I recall it."

"Why, Joe, I couldn't go to war without Boone. My battalion is coming on—I rode ahead for a quick look."

"Well, there it is, and it's going to be a bitch," Totten said. He'd come from Fort Niagara with the three hundred regulars from the Thirteenth Infantry that a lieutenant colonel commanded. Dark clouds boiled overhead. Thunder rolled on top of nearby lightning. Militia troops, some with muskets turned down, some unarmed, milled aimlessly about. Two militia majors passed, arguing like fishwives about whose men were most anxious to fight. Houses were scattered here and there but fences were down, crops trampled, the ground torn by too many men, horses, wheels.

The Niagara was comparatively narrow here but still two hundred fifty yards wide, its current making a continuous roar. They were five miles below the huge falls, the volume here compressed. It wasn't really a river but a channel that drained the Great Lakes through to Lake Ontario on the way to the St. Lawrence and the sea. Scott saw a log floating downstream at startling speed. It dipped into an eddy and spun like a top. This was deep and dangerous water. Low warehouses of logs stood near a small cove banked with stone where the ferry landed. A dozen lapstrake rowboats about thirty feet long lay on the beach in plain view.

"So they know we're coming," Scott said.

Totten shrugged. "General Brock's holding at Fort George, waiting to see. I figure this is so damned open and amateurish he can't believe it's not a feint, but we launch at midnight."

"Night crossing," Scott said. "Risky with untried troops."

"Especially in that water."

Scott could see a narrow shelf of beach on the other side, but then the ground rose sharply at least seventy-five feet to a sort of plateau where Queenston stood. He borrowed Totten's glass and saw British sentries behind rude barricades at the crest.

"Two companies of the Forty-ninth Foot," Totten said. "Brock's old regiment. Flank companies, highly professional."

To the left rose an awesome bluff. Part of the same Niagara Escarpment down which Scott had just ridden, it was distinctly higher and steeper. The side of the bluff facing the river was clifflike. Well up the face of the slope was a battery—a redan, open at the rear, holding a single long gun.

"Looks like an eighteen-pounder."

"You haven't lost your eye, Win."

"If they're using grape, it'll be suicide on that slope."

Totten grunted. "There'll be no choice. We've got to have that gun or they'll pound us to jelly."

They were joined by a smallish man, trim in a captain's uniform, his features even, his manner precise. "I hear there's a trail fishermen use that goes up that cliff," he said.

"That sounds a little better," Totten said. "Win, this is Johnny Wool of the Thirteenth." They shook hands.

"Well," Scott said, "I'd better report to our commander."

Major General Stephen Van Rensselaer proved to be an angular, handsome man in middle age with a distinct air of authority. He was sixth- or seventh-generation Dutch, patroon of most of two counties, the largest landholder in New York—which doubtless accounted for that easy authority.

He was in a command tent with several officers. The flaps were pulled
down against the rain and two smoking lanterns gave dim light. Map rolls
were weighted open on a table. With a worried frown that appeared habitual,
he introduced his cousin, Lieutenant Colonel Solomon Van Rensselaer of
the New York militia. A younger man with a crisp manner extended a hand.
This was the fount of all the General's military wisdom.

"General," said Totten, who had accompanied Scott, "Captain Wool of
the Thirteenth has heard of a fisherman's path that might take us up that
bluff the back way."

"Forget it, Joe," Solomon Van Rensselaer said. "A fly would have trouble
on that. Impossible for infantrymen."

Scott glanced at Totten. It was a poor officer who couldn't scent opportunity. To the General, he said, "Sir, I'd like a copy of your attack plan so I
can coordinate. My guns are highly mobile. I'd like to stay closely in touch
with you—"

"Oh," Van Rensselaer said, "I won't be there. No indeed. This is Solomon's show. I'd just be in the way."

"Sir? You're not crossing?"

"That's what I just said. Solomon's in command. Stay close to him, he'll
give you your orders."

"General," Scott said cautiously, "that presents a problem. My rank is
lieutenant colonel, and as you know, rank in the regular army is senior to
the same rank in the militia. I can't serve under Lieutenant Colonel Van
Rensselaer."

"The lieutenant colonel commanding the Thirteenth Infantry troops
didn't object."

"He should have."

"Well, he did, but when I put my foot down he agreed to go." He saw
Scott shake his head and his temper seemed to snap.

"God damn it," he shouted, "nobody cooperates! We need more boats,
more guns, more men. But my troops drive me insane. Fight or we'll go
home. And they will, too, independent bastards. Some've already gone.
General Smyth sits down there sucking his thumb and now you want to
take over the command. No, God damn it! This is the militia—Solomon's
in command."

"General, I want to serve, but under the law I can't."

He was dealing himself out of the fight and he hurt all over but he
didn't hesitate. This went to the heart of what he was. Professionalism
mattered. Rules and procedures mattered to discipline, to quick obedience,
to the skills he'd inculcated in his men. And Sally McQuirk—his professional
determination to win in the army would keep him from her in the end.

"No, sir. I can't do it."

"God damn you," General Van Rensselaer said, "you regulars are all
alike. Prima donnas."

Scott said, "I'm going to overlook that, sir."

"Dismissed, Colonel. Place your guns to support the attack and stay out of my sight."

★ ★ ★ ★

The first real battle of the war—Hull, after all, had not fought a battle—and Scott was sitting it out. The irony! Persuaded Colonel Izard, marched five hundred miles, slipped General Smyth's net, hurried as a soldier should toward the sound of firing, or where firing soon would sound and now, on a mere tic of technicality, he was denied his chance to serve.

The disappointment made him ache. He was a warrior, and a warrior's medium is war. Yet as he positioned his guns on a rise to sweep both the enemy town and the heights on the left, he had no regrets. He'd been right. Without the integrity of command, an officer has no integrity at all.

At midnight he left Towson with the guns. The ferry landing was very dark. The rain had stopped and soldiers sat huddled with their backs to a cold north wind. The three hundred regulars were steady, but confusion ruled the militia. Officers walked around swinging lanterns and shouting orders. One blew a whistle incessantly. They shuffled and reshuffled their companies, the men snarling complaints as they moved. British sentries could hardly miss the noise, the lights. He saw Solomon Van Rensselaer wearing an uneasy frown and avoided him.

The boats were launched about 3 A.M. Boatmen fought the current. Boats collided, oars splintered, oarsmen shouted. A fight started and officers jumped to stop it. The men waded out and hoisted themselves aboard, the boats rocking dangerously, boatmen cursing, soldiers snarling. They pushed off. A militia boat sheared the oars from the boat carrying the Lieutenant Colonel commanding the regulars, and it disappeared downstream.

Lieutenant Roach joined him. The last boat disappeared in the dark. They stood listening: at last a musket report came faintly across the wind. Sentry's signal. The British had been waiting.

Sarenmajor Boone joined them. "I found us a jim-dandy boat, small and fast. Place for two oarsmen and a rider."

"Over you go, then, Ike," Scott said. After watching the militia departure, he had a hunch he might get in this yet. He was sending Roach to keep him abreast of what happened. Two troopers in the boat would shuttle his reports back.

"Yes, sir!" Roach cried. Scott felt a quiver of envy.

A rattle of small-arms fire drifted in on the wind as he hurried back to his guns. It intensified, became a steady roar. Then the three-pounders in Queenston, deeper but still a light barking. Presently the heavy eighteen-pounder in that redan up the slope on the heights opened, and shell bursts blossomed on the beach where the Americans were to land.

He sighted his guns on the distant flashes. Matches flared; the shiny iron pieces from the Philadelphia foundry thundered and lunged against restraining lines. And he had a curious sense that this was real. After all the fakery and posturing and talking and political folderol, all the assurances that Canada would be theirs in a month, every bit of it absolute horse manure, now men were dying across the river and that made everything real. It was a warrior's lesson he would not forget. Talk is cheap; the price on the battlefield is always dear.

He belonged on the other side—he was *needed* there, he knew it in his gut—and after a while as if drawn by a magnet he left the guns to Towson and went back down to pace the riverfront. Presently the little boat came slicing out of the gloom. Riordan shipped oars and leapt out with field notepaper in his hand. In Roach's neat script, in this report and the next and the next, the battle took vivid form in Scott's mind.

> Ten of the boats make the beach . . . the others disappear . . . men splash out and mill on the beach, troops separated from officers, everyone yelling . . . a sentry on the bluff fires that signal shot . . . they're beginning to form when British grenadiers open fire from the bluff that practically overhangs the beach . . . it's a turkey shoot . . . Van Rensselaer is hit six times and is barely alive . . . men are screaming and milling but there's no place to run . . . they fire back aimlessly . . .
>
> The militia officers are down . . . command devolves to Johnny Wool . . . he takes charge, gets his men in order, charges up the bluff, and routs the grenadiers . . . he's taken a bullet through both buttocks making every step an agony, but keeps his feet . . . we must have the heights but charging an eighteen-pounder loaded with grape is suicide . . .
>
> He gambles, leading his men up the beach around to the sheer side of the bluff . . . they find that fisherman's path—good for you, Johnny Wool!—and inch up in the dark . . . while Wool climbs, Major General Isaac Brock of the British Army gallops in from Fort George . . . probably alerted all his forces . . . the eighteen-pounder is the key and he goes there to direct its fire . . .
>
> Wool and his men appear above the redan and charge straight down to overrun the gun . . . Brock lives up to his reputation for cool professionalism as he delays his retreat long enough to spike the piece with a ramrod jammed in the touchhole and broken off . . . Brock rallies his men below and leads a charge to retake the eighteen-pounder . . . American musket fire blazes . . . Britain's best falters . . . Brock's out in front, tall, handsome in brilliant red uniform, flogging his men on when he takes a musket ball in his heart . . .

Daylight came. What did it all mean? The cold truth was that we held the heights with a useless gun while they held the village and certainly were advancing troops in force to avenge their charismatic leader. We had put a mere three hundred regulars and six hundred militia across while two thousand more militiamen stood here picking their noses. Half the boats were lost, new boats were scarce, boatmen were losing their nerve . . . the wages of military amateurism were becoming horribly evident.

And now the two thousand who hadn't crossed were at the water's edge gazing on the wages of war. What boats remained were returning the dead and wounded. Here was the price the talkers forgot. Bloody bandages covered heads and eyes. Scott saw an arm severed but for a flap of skin. Bodies were carried ashore; by one a leg had been laid with the foot at the wrong end. A captain screamed with every bounce of the makeshift litter. A sergeant cried, "Ma, Ma, where are you, Ma?"

A wild-eyed boy with a bandage over his chest sat up suddenly on his litter and howled, "It's murder over there, boys, they're killing right and left, plain murder's all it is!"

Half sick, half fascinated, Scott wanted to turn his eyes away and couldn't. Then he heard a low moaning from the watching troops. He grabbed a militia major's arm.

"For God's sake, move these men out of here before their nerve goes."

The officer gazed at him blankly. Then, in the tone of an educated man drawn to service he doesn't understand or like, he said, "What do you expect me to do?" and walked away.

A boat approached. More wounded. But this one carried Major General Stephen Van Rensselaer, back from an inspection trip.

"Sir," Scott said as the General stepped ashore, "we must move these men before they're demoralized—"

"Well," the General said, "they'll be going over right away." He looked tired but seemed steady enough, the animosity of the night before apparently forgotten. Scott suspected Van Rensselaer respected him more for having held his position. "Now, Solomon's wounded and Wool is down, too. I want you to go over and take command."

He gestured toward the other side. "We're winning. We have the heights and we'll clear 'em out of the town if we can unspike that gun. They'll advance, but they can't muster more'n a thousand and I have two thousand here. I'll get my boys over, you get things set there, then we'll push north and take it all!"

"Yes, sir," Scott said. He felt a wild mix of anger and elation. "Sarenmajor! We're going over."

★ ★ ★ ★

Take it all . . . the General thought he'd won the battle, but all he'd had
was an initial skirmish leaving them with a spiked gun on the heights and
the enemy holding the village. Riordan and Howell dug deep on the oars.
Scott hunched forward on the stern seat as if body motion alone could hurry
them.

He had to get up that hill and get control of things. The men he was
to command had been up all night, they'd fought for hours, they were short
on ammunition and food and only now was the test beginning. He bit his
lip, fighting down raging anger. The great opportunity thrown away, the
waste of it . . .

The British hadn't been ready. If the Americans had had boats in number
and had put their whole force across—if they'd taken the village while they
seized the heights, if they'd put cooks over with tureens of stew, slapped a
hot meal into the men at dawn, refilled their cartridge cases, and started
them north—they could've kicked the enemy right into Lake Ontario.

Now it would be touch and go, all depending on how soon the British
came up in force, how soon Van Rensselaer could move his militia. Lost
opportunities . . . this was the reality of it. He thought of all that blathering
talk in Washington, the posturing and the politicizing, undermining and
backbiting, none of it meaning a thing when real time came and you called
on youngsters green as grass to execute the nation's policy.

He didn't lament war. It was his profession. And this *was* a second
revolution, essential to national health, and we were going to win it, too.
But damn the military amateurs, the poseurs, the politicians who wanted
military titles, the talkers who ignore its price as they commit others to
spill their blood. Even the doughty little President making his hard decision,
in the end he was a talker, too, went to bed every night with that dumpy
wife of his . . . and up on Queenston Heights with the redcoats coming,
the boys would be checking their powder, their guts all hollowed out by
the thought of bayonets aglitter.

The boat ground on sand as Boone leapt out and Scott followed. Totten
and Roach met him and they ran up the beach, a sniper's balls kicking up
sand. It was Scott's first time under fire; he felt a tremor but forgot it in
his urgency.

Soon they were alongside the sharp bluff that rose to the heights. The
beach angled in, leaving a shoulder that blocked fire from the village. A
narrow path leading upward was scarcely visible. Small bushes stood like
sentinels on the slope.

Larger bushes lined the base of the bluff. Scott caught movement in
one. He started. Yes, militiamen, and a lot of them. An oily-looking corporal
met his eye and grinned.

"Just resting a minute, Cap'n," the scoundrel called. "You go ahead—
we'll be right on up." Scott heard a low laugh.

Skulking cowardly bastards! He wanted to drive them up the hill with the flat of his saber, but there wasn't time.

"Let's go," he said, and started up the narrow path, his mind on the men above. "How're the boys?" he asked.

"Tuckered and shaky," Totten said. "About six hundred, half ours, half militia. The latter are flighty as birds and ours—well, shoot, Win, they're just recruits. I've seen the British drill—real professionals. Sheaffe'll have a thousand or so—"

"Sheaffe?"

"Major General Roger Sheaffe. You heard Brock was killed? Sheaffe was his second—"

Scott's boot slipped. His heart lurched. Boone's hand caught him and he regained his footing and climbed on, panting.

From elevation, the river had a hard, choppy look. On the far bank the militia regiments were lined up, the figures small at this distance. Van Rensselaer was on a long wagon bed, sword in hand, obviously haranguing them, but they weren't cheering. Scott thought they looked slack and irresolute.

The moment he stepped onto the crest, he knew Totten was right. Shaky and tuckered, the men lay scattered under small trees, uniforms soiled and torn. Many were asleep. Some gnawed on hardtack and beef jerky as they heated coffee in tin cups. He saw bloody bandages torn from shirts. They looked him over with the disdain men who've been in combat feel for the newcomer.

"Say, Cap'n," a peppery boy with orange hair called, "you going to get the rest of them scared-ass bastards over here?"

An older man laughed. "That'll be the day. Pushing high morning and they ain't come yet."

"They'll be along," Scott said. "How you boys doing?"

"Fought good this morning," another said. "Took that gun and kept it. But I reckon we're kinda wore out now."

"Well, brighten up, boys. It's not over yet." They were flat, victory's euphoria replaced by melancholy uneasiness. Their ammunition was low, some with a dozen paper cartridges of powder and ball, some fewer. The entrenching tools Van Rensselaer said he'd sent weren't here. More ammunition should be coming but probably wasn't. Still, strategy was forming in Scott's mind. When—if—the militia crossed, they should charge up the immediate slope to the village while he swept downhill with these men. With the village cleared, they could turn to meet Sheaffe—

"Colonel," Boone said in a low voice. He gestured. In the distance Scott saw a long line of marching men in scarlet coats, mounted flankers flung out against surprise. It was sinuous, flexing, as implacable as flowing water. It was . . . awesome.

At a crossroad the column swung right, away from the river. Sheaffe intended to circle out of range of the American guns, strike the escarpment inland, and advance to the attack. He knew what he was doing. The turn was faultless, ranks wheeling right like a machine. He had at least a thousand regulars, followed by a ragged covey of Mohawk Indian troops.

Totten knew the British officer. "Brock was a leader, men would follow him anywhere. But always impetuous," he said. "Sheaffe's the opposite—cool, methodical, a deadly tactician."

Scott sent Roach to Van Rensselaer with an urgent message: enemy in sight—contact in two hours.

The ground they held was a grassy flat scattered with small trees. With the river at their backs, the slope where the spiked eighteen-pounder overlooked the village was to the right. Some two hundred yards to the left stood an oak forest, most of its orange-gold leaves fallen, trunks starkly black. Ahead, open ground sloped gently down some three hundred yards to more woods.

He watched Totten take an engineer's skillful advantage of the terrain as he laid out their perimeter. They ignored the slope to the right and concentrated on the ground ahead and to the left. Scott placed his men carefully, regulars in front, militia to the left.

"Dig, boys. Get some earthworks up. Little something to lie behind, lay your piece against, draw a bead." They dug with bayonets, axes, knives, sharpened sticks, complaining loudly. Some were slipping away; he had fewer than five hundred now.

In the distance he caught a flash of scarlet. They'd made the second turn and were approaching the escarpment.

Time was shorter now. He sent Boone to look: were the militia coming? Presently the Sergeant Major said, "You'd better see this, Colonel." The militia regiments hadn't moved. Van Rensselaer was walking among his troops, pausing here and there. He mounted the wagon, looking very weary. He seemed different now. His arms were raised, palms up like a preacher. He was begging! Begging the men who'd pushed him to the fight, forced his hand, fight or go home. And now, hearing the guns and seeing the wounded, all their fight was gone.

Scott ran his glass over the ranks. They were sitting down; they were turning their backs on the lonely figure still beseeching them. Turning their backs on their own commander!

So there would be no concerted rush on the village, no forming to counterstrike Sheaffe. Could he march out and launch his own attack? Against a skilled army twice his size and entirely fresh? His own men exhausted, ammunition low? It was hopeless. For the first time, he realized fully what his country faced in going to war with a major power.

He hurried down to the eighteen-pounder. If he could clear it and turn it—but the touchhole through which it was fired was hopelessly plugged.

Professionalism, that made the difference. Sheaffe's calm approach, Brock's clear mind even as the enemy came at a dead run on his uncovered rear. Even then he took time to jam a ramrod into the hole and whip it back and forth till it broke.

And Sheaffe, on the escarpment by now, advancing steadily. Another ten minutes, another five. If the militia wasn't coming, Scott's little band couldn't hold alone; but neither would he retreat until he was sure. He knew he could tie Sheaffe up three or four hours if he had to, ample time for the militia to cross if Van Rensselaer worked some miracle of inspiration. He would hold the heights until ordered otherwise.

Suddenly a scream tore the air, high as a woman's shriek and yet so full of menace and cruelty as to ice the blood. He'd never heard such a thing but knew instantly what it was—a Mohawk war cry. And in another instant there were a hundred such cries and here they came, boiling out of the woods on the left—

His militiamen bawled and sobbed and a half dozen scrambled up to flee. Scott leapt at them with drawn saber.

"Down, God damn you, down!" he roared. "I'll cut you to pieces, you move. Grab those muskets and look sharp." They lay trembling.

"Hold your fire, boys, hold it. I'll give you the word. We'll kill a bushel of 'em. You'll see. Hold it, now."

The Indians came at a dead run, two hundred or more, dark faces painted with vermillion and white streaks like death's heads, feathers and bracelets and buckskin vests worked with quills and beads, running and screaming with muskets in one hand, hatchets or knives in the other. They stopped and fired and ran on again. Scott heard a couple of loud cries on his side.

When they were twenty yards out he swung down his sword. "FIRE!" The muskets roared in thunderous concert. When blue smoke cleared, several Indians were down and the others stopped.

"Let's go, boys," Scott screamed. He leapt over the barrier, saber in hand. "Bayonet 'em! Gut 'em!" He ran straight at the Indians, who were trying to reload, his saber point held before him like a lance. He heard the men behind him but didn't look as he fixed his gaze on a tall Indian with a top hat and braids and a bear-claw necklace.

His eyes locked with the Indian's, and when he was only twenty feet away the man shrieked something and turned and ran back toward the oak forest.

"Let's get 'em, boys!" Scott shouted and ran furiously on, all the frustrations and pressures of the day exploding. He heard howling, and there at his side and slightly in front was Sarenmajor Boone, long Kentucky legs pumping, a musket with a glittering bayonet thrust ahead.

The Indians darted into the trees and disappeared. The soldiers hesitated at the treeline. Scott started in, but Boone caught his arm.

"Begging the Colonel's pardon," he said in a low voice, "advantage 'pears to have shifted to them. I mean, they can see us and we can't see them. A quick boggle might be in order here, begging the Colonel's pardon."

Good advice. He waved an arm and they ran for their lines, a spattering of musket fire from the woods following them. They were laughing and yelling, spirits restored, when they tumbled over the low barrier they'd built. Rapidly he checked his men. Three had been pinked, one hit squarely, a lanky kid from Albany with a belly wound; his face was gray and he was grunting.

Roach handed him a folded message. He opened it to a spidery hand that made it official: the New York militia wouldn't fight. It stood on its constitutional right to serve as defense, not as offense. You're on your own, Colonel Scott. Retreat if you can. Van Rensselaer said he would send boats to pick them up but Scott doubted he could deliver even on that weak promise.

"Old man looked like he'd aged twenty years," Roach said.

There was a sudden exhalation from his men; Scott looked quickly ahead and saw Sheaffe's scarlet force filing out of the woods. The Indians had disappeared. The troops formed four long lines. Sergeants straightened the lines until they might have been drawn by a ruler. Scott focused his glass on a brilliantly dressed officer at the center. Sheaffe. He looked young, lean, capable, a man who knew his own mind.

The General was in no hurry. Probably he knew no relief was coming. Ten minutes passed. Scott's men watched in silence.

They were down to three hundred. Half his force had fled. His men weren't soldiers, not yet, but they could be. Watching those steady scarlet lines, Scott swore his men would be ready next time; he'd train them till they dropped.

A nervous giggle ran down his line. "All right, there," Sarenmajor Boone called, "Steady on. They're shitting their breeches, too, just like you, and don't forget it. Steady, now."

A drumroll in the distance. Jesus, they had drummers. And then two bagpipes sounded, some wild piercing air that made a man feel that he couldn't die today, and if he did a bright heaven awaited him. Scott looked down his own lines. The boys crouched, pale and shaking. Those damned bagpipes . . .

A musket popped. "Hold fire, hold fire!" he shouted. "They're far out of range. Reload, boy, reload!"

And then they were coming, bagpipes skirling and drums rolling, two lines out front and two in reserve, iron men in scarlet coats coming to kill the farm boys on Scott's line. At seventy yards they opened fire like a smooth, beautiful machine.

The first line knelt, braced, and fired. The second stepped through the first and advanced. The first reloaded. The second knelt and fired. The first stepped through the second and advanced. The second reloaded while the first knelt and fired. The first reloaded while the second knelt and fired.

They were delivering a half-dozen volleys a minute. It was devastating, and American muskets had a weak, ineffectual sound.

Several of Scott's men were hit. One began to scream, over and over. American fire stopped entirely as the farm boys hugged the ground and tried to burrow in. Boone was on his feet. "Fire back, God damn it!" he shouted. "You're giving them free fire, you ugly sons of bitches!"

Scott whipped cowering men's butts and legs with his saber flat. They moaned and tried to dig in. "It's suicide to stop firing, you fools!"

He saw movement at the corner of his eye and whirled. The militia on the left were breaking, scuttling away with downcast eyes, making for the path down the cliff. Scott leapt onto a log. "Hold the line, you regulars, hold the line! Fire between the volleys. Aim your fire, aim, cut 'em down. They're bigger targets'n you are now. FIRE!"

Some British soldiers were down, scarlet spots on tawny earth, but the implacable line came on. When it was near, that damned bagpipe keening, there was a shouted order and bayonets dropped to level and the men in the scarlet coats came at them on the run. Looking at that line of steel held as even as a picket fence, Scott felt a real tremor and his young soldiers shrieked with fear. Wailing, they hurtled back toward the cliff with such force that everyone was carried with them.

It was over and he knew it. His saber flashed in their faces, stopping a few.

"Take the wounded, damn you! We don't leave our wounded!" Faces like chalk, they nonetheless rolled wounded men in makeshift blanket litters and stepped onto the narrow path. Scott managed to stop a dozen men for a rear guard. Momentarily spirited, they leveled their pieces as the British soldiers jumped the low barricade and hesitated.

"Down you go, boys," Scott said. They hurried down the path and he followed. Down and down he went, bowed under the crushing knowledge that they, like poor Hull, had failed. They had fought honorably, but it was another defeat in a war that had yet to produce a victory, a war we'd started in all confidence and now were losing. What would an already apathetic people say to that?

On the beach below, under harassing fire from the slope, his men disorganized and demoralized, Scott had no choice. He tied a white cravat to his saber tip, advanced to surrender, fought off a knife attack from the big Mohawk in the top hat, and was taken to General Sheaffe. The General was calm, his uniform unmarked.

"I have the honor to offer you my sword, sir," Scott said.

"You may keep your sword for now, sir," Sheaffe said.

After a moment Scott said, "My compliments, sir. Your men's precision amazed me. I've never seen anything like it."

The Englishman gave him a curious look. "Why, Colonel," he said, "training is the key to everything. Everything, sir. No man is born a soldier but any decent man can be made a soldier. Training, sir. There is no substitute."

"Thank you, General," Scott said. "I shall remember that."

6

On the Great Bend of the Cumberland
Fall, 1812

★ ★ ★ ★ Andrew Jackson turned in at his gate and came up the avenue of yellow poplars leading to his home, the buckskin mare at an easy trot. He was sunk in gloom, mouth turned down, heat in his eyes—it would be a poor time to cross Tennessee's general, by God. Not that anyone would dare. Get his head on a platter, someone tried that. His country in the greatest peril it'd known in his adult lifetime, and those fools in Washington . . .

Still, the sight of his well-kept acres always soothed him, the fences even and true, fields banked for winter, fat cattle and swollen haystacks, fruit trees neatly pruned, cotton fields cleared, ginned bales sent downriver to New Orleans and saltwater ships, and in a pasture near the house, thoroughbred yearlings for whom he had soaring expectations.

Rachel really ran the place. He loved his land and directed it with obsessive interest, but duty regularly called him away. It would be a shambles without her steady hand. They had an overseer, but overseers have to be overseen.

She was sitting under a shagbark hickory in her garden, afternoon sun spangling still-dark hair, and he waved with a surge of pleasure. Her answering wave was quick and joyous. His return—even from Nashville, an hour's ride away—was an event. She loved him the more for what they'd been through; he knew now that love dies or it deepens to a communion of souls.

She was in a blue gown not so different from the blue she'd worn that day he'd galloped in to find her stirring clothes with old Mrs. Donelson, the day that changed their lives and shaped all that followed. But as he swung from the saddle, it struck him too how infinitely wiser was her face, undaunted but now fully aware of life's capacity for cruelty.

The day was cool and brilliant, as in that earlier memory. End traces of summer softened the air. Sunlight glowed on the worn logs of the old blockhouse that was their home. Like Mrs. Donelson's place, this once had been a picketed compound, log-walled against attack. Its core was the main two-story blockhouse. A second blockhouse stood nearby, flanked by kitchen shed and various outbuildings, including generous guest cabins and a roomy barn.

Her garden held it together as a hub holds a wheel. Watering channels from a fine spring and walks of brick laid in sunburst design wound among boxwood, honeysuckle, lilac, lilies, peonies, verbena and pinks, spicebush, sweetshrub, all well mulched against winter. It was her special creation, and he thought it served for the children they couldn't have.

She was beautiful, his slender girl of long ago now round and heavy as he was thin and light, her face fat and full under glossy skin, warm brown eyes guileless and clear, a face that bespoke solace discovered. She was smoking her old corncob with the reed stem, and he bent to kiss her.

He took tea and lighted his own pipe. At once he saw in her expression the query she kept herself from uttering and his anger flared anew.

"Not a single word. Oh, Rachel, it's just outrageous!"

For months Washington had ignored his offer of himself and his troops. The war cried out for men, and he could muster two thousand in a fortnight, fighting men, hardy frontier farmers as ready to defend country as homestead. But the call hadn't come. Nor had any explanation.

Yet the war was a disaster—the army weak, recruiting slow, national enthusiasm fading, defeats on every side, Hull's pitiful disgrace and now another at Queenston. And Andrew Jackson was sitting it out. Forgotten. Humiliated!

"Those idiots!" he said. "Miserable old grannies—hand-wringing old women who wet their drawers at decision time!" He saw her stiffen at the mention of old women, but he was in full cry. "I tell you, Rachel, it's enough to make me puke!"

"Now, Andrew."

"Well, it is! And you know why they're doing it, don't you? It's no accident. Oh, no—it's because I once spoke for Burr. That's what it's all about. I supported Monroe against Madison in Ought-eight, don't forget, and this is that pettifogging little man's revenge."

"Oh, Andrew, really! He's the President of the United States. He has more to do than that—"

"Then why hasn't he called me? I'll tell you why—"

"Oh, darling, you're so quick to suspect, quick to anger."

"Oh, is that so? But wait—talk about quick, why are you so quick to criticize? Why do you take his part against me? You see what he's doing to me!"

"Andrew!" She sat up straight, suddenly as fierce as he. "Don't you dare take it out on me, do you hear? You should find it in your heart to grant others your own high motives. Let me tell you something, sir—this anger, you are riding a wild horse."

He quivered with rage, but she was strong as a lioness guarding her den and his heart opened to her.

"That anger saved us," he said. He was breathing hard.

"Yes, but more and more it's a wild horse that will throw you someday. And don't you be snapping at me, either."

His mood shifted suddenly and he grinned. "You're as tough as I am, you know that?" He wanted to kiss her. He loved that strong-grained fiber in her; they wouldn't have survived without it. But what a price she—both of them—had paid! It was etched in her face, it was in the lonely anguish she felt when he was gone, in her shaky longing for his return, even in the gentle self-effacing kindness she offered to everyone.

His pipe had gone out and he relit it. His hands shook but he was calm. She feared his anger, but he knew it was the key to survival. The beating they'd taken had been brutal, worse on her than on him, armored in anger as he'd always been. But there were no regrets—he would do it all over again and so would she. Looking back across the years, nothing could have kept him from spiriting her off to Natchez with Colonel Robertson's party to force Robards's hand, or his sprint to Natchez to marry her when he heard Robards had divorced her. He'd realized he willingly would kill to protect her; what were legal technicalities in the face of that?

Two years later, the thunderbolt. They learned there'd been no divorce, just a preliminary step. And so, their marriage having given Robards prima facie evidence of adultery, he demanded and won a real divorce. And a court had named them adulterers.

Tennessee talked of little else, and Jackson approached every encounter as stiff-legged as a bulldog under challenge. He stared at everyone, watching for the flickering eye, the hesitation, the following glance.

Before his eyes, his laughing, dancing, storytelling girl began to change. She turned to her Bible and to the church and thence to Jesus Himself, and maybe that saved her. Jackson faced the world with his hand on his pistol.

One rarely has to use a pistol that's always ready. Often a horsewhip or a hickory cane will do. And had done often enough over the years to make the point. Not for pride, either. He was proud of not being proud. But he was ready to protect the woman he had exposed to the crowd. Let who would traduce them take heed. General Sevier had learned that in the exchange of gunfire that followed his loose remark.

And Dickinson . . .

That whole business had hurt both of them in countless ways. Yes, but God damn it, the man had wanted to kill him, too, boasting, laughing. And he'd taken Dickinson's bullet in his own chest, people forgot that. His own blood was filling his boots when he raised his pistol . . .

His breath was short and he felt that rush of wild anger that was like an old sustaining friend.

She touched his arm. "Rebecca Donelson is ill," she said.

"Oh?" he said, knowing she had read his emotions again.

"Consumption, I'm afraid. Listless, exhausted, coughing. She has those two darling little girls and she can't really care for them. Could they live with us for a while, Andrew?"

He smiled. "Of course." He drew her hand to his lips. Maybe Jesus had saved her, but in her husband's view, it was her own gentle, generous kindness that had brought her through the storm. Denied children of their own, they had taken many to raise, and as she was to the children, so she was to the community at large. Everyone ill or distressed or afflicted turned to her as naturally as flowers turn to the sun.

But she had paid, too, and he could see it in her weight, the shortness of breath that snuff and pipe could ease but not cure, the way her heart churned so that sometimes she must sit quickly, the heel of her hand pressed to her chest. A court had branded them adulterers, and that had dominated their lives.

★　★　★　★

Dusk was falling outside the blockhouse but inside candles glowed warmly in girandoles. Her long table was set for twelve as always and it was clear she would need it tonight. You could never tell: inns were rare in this new country and it was the custom to pause unannounced at the great country homes if one had even a nodding acquaintance.

Tom Benton, her favorite of all the young officers for whom Jackson was practically a father, had arrived about four. He had a trial the next day in Lebanon. He was tall with a cap of tight auburn curls, a prominent nose, and forthright blue eyes that gazed on opponents with disconcerting steadiness—it was no surprise to her that Thomas Hart Benton had a way with juries. She knew Andrew liked him and suspected he saw the young man as he remembered himself at that age.

Tom had bumped into Governor Blount on the road, and the Governor had said he would probably be here, too. And he'd seen Ebenezer Clute, who also said he would stop over for the night.

Andrew had frowned at that. He said Eb Clute was a blowhard, a small fellow who passionately wanted to be seen as bigger than he was, a dreamer living on hopes. He headed a little two-company battalion near Franklin and had the gall to talk of going head-to-head with Jackson for election as major general. You'd think he would have better taste than to impose himself for dinner and lodging on a man he talked of challenging, but all kinds came to her table.

John and Eliza Allen were over from Gallatin with a guest, as John's letter a week ago had forewarned her. Rachel warmed instinctively to the guest when John presented him. His name was William Thornton and he was a slender, saturnine man in his early fifties with wisps of black hair combed across a nearly bare skull, his chin bluish from a heavy beard close-shaven, something quick and strong in his eyes.

"He's a Bostonian, hence his accent," John said, touching his small, neat mustache. She saw he liked his guest.

"Well," she said as Mr. Thornton bowed over her hand, "he'll hear plenty of accent in these parts."

"Yes, ma'am," the newcomer said, "but more melodious than at home, I must admit."

"William is a lawyer," John said, "and I see the tiger in the courtroom becomes the diplomat in the drawing room."

Mr. Thornton struck a pose. "Why, sir, a lawyer must be all things to all men. It's quite a chore."

She smiled and said, "Say what they may, land wouldn't be half so interesting without lawyers to dispute it."

"Exactly, madam!"

John had served as agent on a ten-thousand-acre tract farther west that now was in litigation. Thornton represented the bank that had underwritten a Boston combine's purchase and he'd been here a month making little headway in untangling deeds.

Governor Blount had arrived. His round, deceptively simple face cast in the genial smile she had learned bore little relation to his thoughts, he said, "Why, sir, an amplitude of lawyers is a mark of civilization. I'll warrant they're in good supply in Boston?"

Thornton threw up his hands. "Oh, more than enough, sir!"

The Blounts were one of the great names in Tennessee, and Willie was a good governor as well as an old friend. He treated their home as his own when he was nearby and had arrived quietly an hour ago.

"And how are you finding our Tennessee juries?" Tom Benton asked. Andrew tended to gather bright young men on the rise, but in Tom's case, she was drawn to more indefinable qualities that could be summed as power of heart. He passed all tests.

"Fully as skeptical as Boston juries," Mr. Thornton said.

"If juries were easy," she said, "I suppose justice would falter."

Andrew smiled. "Well said—that's the nub of the system."

Ebenezer Clute walked in. She didn't know him well but remembered his wife as a worn little woman to whom an indefinable sadness clung. He was around fifty, fleshy but strong, thinning sandy hair cut short, little eyes with a choleric look. He hadn't shaved and his breeches were soiled, but then he was traveling. She frowned as he plucked a glass of whiskey punch from the tray Hannah was offering and downed it before he could be presented. Even his boots were muddy; you'd think a man would clean his boots before dinner.

Her brass clock from France chimed, and she led them to the long table at one side of the room. Andrew placed Eliza Allen to his right, reducing her to bright laughter as he seated her. He always took the center of the table, to be part of all conversations. Rachel sat across from him, the Governor to her right, Mr. Thornton to her left, and then Tom. John Allen took Andrew's left and Mr. Clute sat next to Eliza. Eliza's expression made Rachel wonder if the man smelled.

"You'll give us the prayer, Mr. Jackson?" Rachel said. They always addressed each other formally in the company of others.

She was a connoisseur of prayer, and Andrew's was a good one. Dear Andrew. He refused to join a church, said his enemies would take it as false piety done for effect, but she heard faith in the very timbre of his voice! She gave quick thanks to the Lord for this unspoken testimony.

"I've been admiring your home," Mr. Thornton said as they served themselves. They were in the main blockhouse with its massive fireplace, the inner walls now finished, generous windows cut and framed in varnished oak where once had been gunports, rawhide-bottomed chairs, and two comfortable sofas. On the walls were paintings by friends, most of them scenes here on the farm. She didn't know how good they might be—from the awkwardness of a potbellied cow in one of them, she thought perhaps not very—but their familiarity pleased her eye.

"An old blockhouse, isn't it?" Thornton added. "Handsome place. I saw one like it last week at Buchanan's Station."

She smiled. "Did they tell you the story? That was the site of the last great Indian raid in these parts."

"But that was long ago," Mr. Thornton said.

"Not so long," she said more sharply than she had intended. "Twenty years. Seventeen-ninety-two, the year after we married . . ." Her eyes were on the guest, awaiting the telltale flicker of interest, but his expression didn't change.

"That recently?" he said.

"Well," Andrew said, "it tells you something about how Tennessee looks at things—why it don't see things quite the way the settled East does, don't think the way Boston thinks. We're direct 'cause we grew up in a time when direct action was essential to staying alive."

Eb Clute slapped the table, a startlingly loud noise. Silver jumped and so did guests.

"But don't let's act like it's over, 'cause it ain't!"

She saw Eliza Allen flinch.

"Down south from here," he said, "in Alabama country, the Creeks are raising unshirted hell. I got a claim down there that'll be big if we can perfect it, got a cousin watching it, and he's scared witless. They're raiding all along the rivers and swapping the plunder with the Spanish in Florida for more weapons. Folks are starting to get out. Giving up on some mighty fine land and running their families to Fort Mims."

"We have military down there?" Mr. Thornton asked.

"Naw. Trading post. Mims runs a forted fur station. One of these days they'll overrun it, too, kill everyone there. Since Tecumseh come down last year, the Creeks been going crazy."

"The northern chief," Mr. Thornton asked. "Down here?"

"Damn right!"

She'd had enough. "That'll do, Mr. Clute," she said. "Such language has no place at the dinner table."

She saw she'd angered him but she didn't care. Glancing at Andrew, she said, "Tell Mr. Thornton about Tecumseh's visit."

Andrew sketched the familiar story—the great chief's arduous journey down the Mississippi and back by canoe proving his seriousness, the militant Creeks celebrating his mad plans for an Indian buffer state to stop the western advance. That couldn't survive, but it could mean years of hardship and war. And the certain decimation of the Indians, stone-age people dependent on a foreign power for their weaponry.

This Clute person—she was still simmering—said, "Creeks have been a hundred times worse since he built a fire under 'em. Not that it takes that much to stir 'em up anyway."

"Tecumseh's people were involved in the Hull debacle, weren't they?" Mr. Thornton asked. "That's why he gave up?"

"They were at Queenston, too," Tom Benton said. "That's the real concern. We're at war and they're on the other side, Indians and Spanish both. What's to keep a British army from invading through Mobile, using the Creeks for rangers and guides? Maybe that's why they press settlers so hard—our settlers would give us warning if the British landed."

Mr. Clute's sunken little eyes flicked from Andrew to Governor Blount. "What we ought to do, we ought to saddle up and go down there and clean 'em out."

She saw Tom Benton shake his head in disgust.

"Well, Eb," the Governor said, "that's foolish talk. You know we're awaiting federal orders."

"Maybe we've waited too long." He hesitated, licked his lips. "Well, I don't get to chin with the Governor all that often, so I reckon I'd better speak up. You've got the power to order the boys out. To put it plain, why don't you?"

Governor Blount's genial manner disappeared. "I don't like rabble-rousing chatter, Eb. You know we're awaiting a federal call. No state can prosecute war on its own."

"I'm surprised Tennessee troops haven't been called," Mr. Thornton said.

"Haw!" Mr. Clute said. "*You're* surprised? You know what our trouble is? Our general ain't in very good odor in Washington. That's the problem."

Appalled silence fell over the table. The fool was challenging Andrew in their own home. She glanced at her husband; he was staring, face pale as paper save for glowing red on his cheeks, that wildness she'd come to fear blazing up—

"That's enough such talk," she said, then turned to the visitor. "Newcomers' views are always interesting. Do tell us how you find the West."

"Maddening," Mr. Thornton said. "I hope I don't offend."

At the end of the table the Clute person stood and made a clumsy bow.

"If I may be excused," he said, "I reckon I can make Nashville tonight. Thank you for your hospitality, madam." He glanced at Andrew. "I meant no offense, General, but—"

"Good evening, Mr. Clute," she said.

"Yes. Well . . ." He ducked his head and left quickly.

"Maddening, Mr. Thornton?"

"Oh, madam, you've been so hospitable. I'd hate to offend. Better I keep my views to myself."

"Nonsense!" Andrew said. "Honest views moderately stated are always welcome. That's the essence of republicanism."

"Thank you, sir. But I, like so many of my people in New England, am of the Federalist persuasion. And we fear the West—with good reason, I think. It represents danger to the nation."

"My, my," Andrew said, and there was a general murmur. She thought for a moment she might have to rescue the visitor, but he didn't seem disturbed and Andrew was smiling.

"Well, I hardly expect such a view to find favor here. But the West . . . it's loose, it's big, it's all over the place. Hard to tell where it starts, impossible to tell where it ends. Hasn't many people but they're always wanting, always pushing. It's a classic case of the tail wagging the dog, and that's because it's too spread out to keep proper control."

"Control?" Andrew said. "What do you mean? Free men voting their convictions as they please equals self-control, and that's the key to a democratic society."

"Yes, sir. That and focus, manageability, cohesion. We created democracy in the original thirteen colonies—and we were a stronger country when we only had thirteen states and folks knew where they stood and could look to their betters for guidance."

"There's your difference, Democratic-Republicans and Federalists," Andrew said. " 'Betters' don't mean much. Out here, leaders emerge on their abilities, not on birth. That's the future in America, too, you wait and see."

Thornton waved a hand. "Well, that's appropriate enough. But in a properly stable society those leaders in turn become those to whom the common folk look for guidance. But the bigger and more far-flung we become, the harder it will be to maintain stability. We've already gone too far, patching on states, Ohio and Kentucky and Tennessee—" With a charming smile he added, "Honestly, Mrs. Jackson, I don't mean to offend."

"You're forgiven, sir."

"Thank you, madam. But there's my point, General. This very year we've done it again, added Louisiana. It weakens us as a nation. Where's it to end?"

"On the shores of the Pacific, sir," Andrew said. "That's where it'll end and not until. The West don't weaken us as a nation. It strengthens us. Now, sir, you've spoken frankly, so let me do the same."

"Please do."

"What you're describing is the opposite of strength, a small seaboard nation, forever weak, forever the victim of the European powers, never to be taken seriously."

"Having Ohio and Louisiana makes them respect us?"

"Having the continent, sir. The day will come when the United States will be a power to match any in the world. We'll stretch from sea to sea; we'll fill a broad continent with settlers; we'll open trade from the Pacific shore to the Orient. We'll be a great nation—the world, not just Europe, will listen to us. Ah, sir, don't you see? The West is our salvation."

Mr. Thornton smiled. "In Boston, they call it a millstone."

She laughed. "Could Boston's view be, perhaps . . . narrow?"

"Perhaps, madam," the visitor said. She saw he was amused. "But what about New Orleans? Where does it fit in this vision?"

"Why," Andrew said, "it's the key to everything. The Mississippi drains the great rivers, Ohio from the east, Missouri from the west, Appalachians to the Stony Mountains that young Lewis and Captain Clark described so well. Control New Orleans and you control the Mississippi. Thank God Mr. Jefferson acquired it, 'cause it's the lifeblood of the West. Ask the Governor, here. I know he agrees."

She leaned back in her chair as the Governor turned his genial smile onto the visitor.

"Oh, yes, that's western gospel, but I leave all that to the General. Truth is, I have trouble enough with state policy without worrying about national."

Then Mr. Thornton surprised her. "This Tecumseh business," he said, "isn't his threat really to New Orleans?"

The Governor's eyes opened as if he were awakening. Andrew chuckled softly.

"You have a better grasp of it than I thought," he said. "Yes, there's the danger. If the British invade with Creek and Spanish help, their aim will be to cross Mississippi Territory to the river and then go downriver—attack from above."

"This Democratic-Republican war—forget our opposition to it in Boston, we can agree it's not going well in the North?"

"Which exacerbates the danger in the South, of course," Andrew said. "If we can't keep the British busy in Canada, won't they invade us? And isn't New Orleans their logical target? They share the Federalist ideal, you know—they'd love to keep us a seaboard nation huddled on a rocky coast, keep us in control. If they held New Orleans, the West as we know it would die. Ultimately it would become part of Canada."

"There!" Mr. Thornton had a look of lawyerly triumph. "You've just proved my point, sir. The West as millstone."

Andrew laughed. "Why, I've done nothing of the sort."

"But it's exactly as you've described. Two of three attempts on Canada have failed miserably and the third hasn't even started, with winter beginning. Canadians have shown no interest in joining us and they've fought like terriers. The dream of taking Canada is proving only a dream. Yet surely Britain will retaliate, and New Orleans is our most vulnerable spot. And it can't be held against determined attack."

"Can't be held?" Andrew cried. "Of course it can be held. It *will* be held. It's the fulcrum of the West, and we'll defend it to the death."

"Yet they'll come one day with their vast fleet, their well-trained army. They'll be at the gates, from north or from south. What then, General?"

"Then?" He drew himself up with the look of an eagle. "*I* shall be there, sir. I shall be there."

★   ★   ★   ★

Tom Benton hurried along the road to General Jackson's place on his big bay gelding. Eb Clute, he'd decided, was a damned fool, carving out territory bigger than he could handle. Pushing Jackson was dangerous business. Only ten minutes ahead of Clute and the others, he touched spurs to the bay's ribs.

Clute was a little man who wanted to be big but lacked the capacity, that's all. His dirty boots and loose tongue had offended Aunt Rachel the other night, but to Benton that just said he was no gentleman. You'd never duel with him, for example, challenge him or accept his challenge. You'd cane him if he needed it, but dueling with its code of honor was for gentlemen. That granted, Benton found Clute just another vulgarian. But Jackson wasn't very forgiving these days.

Benton had known the General a couple of years now and had found him consistently honest, honorable, big-spirited, possessed of a huge intuitive intelligence, and very likable to those whom he liked. But he could be strident, suspicious, quick to anger, to say nothing of his suffocating sense of his own unquestioned rectitude. Stunning personal force assured his magnitude but left him vulnerable to arrogance. This, Benton was afraid, would not be his best day.

He reined up as Jackson opened his front door. "General," he said, touching two fingers to the brim of his hat. "Bad news, sir. Tecumseh's come back."

"Again?"

Benton heard a note of outrage in Jackson's voice, as if he'd caught a burglar at his window. The General had the peculiar ability to assume the whole weight of his fellow citizens, his state, his nation. Tecumseh's return became a personal affront.

"A runner from Fort Mims came in this morning. Says the chief came down by canoe like before, with twenty warriors. Hell of a trip if he's just sightseeing. Everyone's in an uproar."

"One of these days—" Jackson said.

"There's talk of doing it today. Eb Clute is right behind me, with some of the captains. They want to go hang Tecumseh now and keep right on going into Florida."

"Without orders? What idiocy," Jackson said. "Others are with him?"

"Yes, sir."

Contempt flashed across Jackson's narrow face. "Good God, won't they ever learn? Burr taught us that lesson."

Aaron Burr, in Benton's private opinion, must have been a hell of a fellow in those days. He certainly drove Jefferson and Madison up a tree, and they'd never forgiven him. Ran for vice president on a ticket with Jefferson in 1800 and when he found he had the same number of electoral votes, a quirk of the Constitution let him claim the top spot. It took weeks to settle that one, after which they amended the Constitution. Burr served as a discredited vice president, killed Alexander Hamilton in a duel, and headed west for a new start.

Of course, that's what the West was for, new starts—that was Benton's experience, too—and Burr was welcomed. Naturally he attached himself to Jackson, and naturally the general agreed to help when Burr insinuated that seizing Florida had become national policy. Florida was a thorn in the western side.

General Wilkinson, commanding in New Orleans, was in it, too, which added to its official color. Westerners knew Wilkinson had sold himself to the Spanish; it was a joke that he and Burr would lead a long overdue American upsetting of Spanish hopes.

But hints arose of different plans—to use Wilkinson's American troops in New Orleans to peel off the West itself into a Mississippi Valley empire. Split the Union, in other words, Burr a new king. Always the patriot, Jackson was said to have gone wild. Burr was so mysterious you couldn't be sure of anything, but Jackson severed relations and fired off warning letters.

And then Wilkinson lost his nerve and to clean his own skirts denounced Burr—and suggested Jackson was part of the conspiracy! Of course the Tennessean's letters cleared him, but the administration so hated Burr that it happily took Wilkinson at face value. To this day he commanded our meager forces in New Orleans, and Jackson had been persona non grata ever since.

The story had stirred Benton's litigating impulse the moment he heard it. Stick a slander suit up Wilkinson's ass, see how he jumps. He had tempted Jackson for a moment, too, but reason finally prevailed. This was serious business.

"The point of Burr," Jackson said, "is that only a nation can challenge another nation. National actions have the color of law by definition—personal actions don't. Lead an expedition into Florida without official sanction and you're no better than a filibusterer, a pirate. No nation can support pirates."

He cracked a crop against his thigh. "Damn it all! If that pusillanimous man in Washington would give the order, we could take Florida in a trice. But on our own we'd be branded pirates and rightfully so." He sighed. "I'll straighten 'em out."

Clute was in the lead of the column of horsemen that cantered up the lane. "You hear the news?" he bawled.

"Down to the barn, gentlemen," the General said. "We won't disturb Mrs. Jackson with such talk."

He walked with that ramrod up his backside, his very posture threatening, and they followed, looking a little sheepish but for Clute, who strutted ahead of them. Clute wore green breeches and a black coat over a shirt with no collar, and his stocky, strong body had a prideful roll as he walked. His face was wide and fleshy and he was missing a couple of teeth. The men with him were influential, Bennett Wood of Gallatin, Jake Smilie of Lebanon, Ogle Love from down toward Franklin, Baz Harris from Castallian Springs, and a couple of others. Half the state's militia would follow their call.

At the barn, the General said, "So, Tecumseh's back, but I gather the Creeks haven't hit the warpath."

"That don't matter," Clute said. "It's the perfect excuse to clean them bastards out once and for all—and settle the Florida question, too."

"When Washington turns us loose, that's what we'll do. Smash the Creeks and take Florida. But not until then."

"General, I reckon you're out of touch." Clute's confidence was growing. "There's a clamor to git on down there and take care of it—these Indians and their God damned buffer state and the Spanish, too. Am I right, boys?"

"No doubt about that," Ogle Love said. He was a cadaverous man with a potbelly. "Boys in my company, they're hot to go."

"We all are," Jackson said. "But we can't do it on our own. Don't you remember Burr?"

"I'm sick of hearing about Burr," Clute said. "This here is different. We're at war, case that's escaped your attention."

"Burr was talking piracy. That's what you're talking, too."

Clute's voice rose to an angry squeal. "What matters about Burr, they hate him so bad in Washington they hate you too for being involved—"

"God damn you—"

"Everybody here knows you really weren't," Clute said hastily, "but up yonder they think you were." He looked at the others and Benton saw they were taking him seriously. "Except for that, they'd welcome us. Think they don't want troops, them getting their ass whipped all over the North?"

The bastard had become an orator. Benton thought a good kick in the crotch would settle his mind.

"Boys, I say we can't wait for Washington to get over its snit. We go take Florida, they'll smother us in kisses."

Jackson had regained control, but not by much. "They'll stretch your neck, that's what they'll do," he said.

Benton relaxed. For a minute there Jackson had alarmed him. Something burned in him, always ready to explode, now more than ever. Was Clute trying to provoke him, playing Dickinson's role? Dickinson hung over everything.

When Benton came to Nashville he heard more than he wanted to hear about Dickinson. Twice the man, drunk, had made ribald speculations about Aunt Rachel and the marriage. Twice he'd apologized. Then a horse race provoked the old animosity and blew into the duel.

Dickinson was said to be the best shot in Tennessee, fast *and* accurate, a rare combination. The duel became a betting matter, odds against Jackson because of the other's skills, and Dickinson bet heavily on himself; Benton found it hard to have much sympathy for a man who expected to kill and looked for a profit therein. Knowing Dickinson fired fast to upset an opponent's aim, Jackson deliberately gave him first shot. He stood there like an iron man and took a bullet in his chest. Let himself be shot, waited for it. Then, left arm clamped across the wound, he raised his pistol and took careful aim . . .

Well within the dueling code—but my God! What passions this man could raise!

And Clute, the damned fool, was pushing him.

"Look here, boys. You get right down to it, for all his talk, General Jackson ain't never led troops into battle. Ain't that right? Now he's got his chance, maybe he's feeling a chill in the boots, know what I mean?"

"Well, now," Jackson said. He spoke softly but the hair rose on Benton's neck. "I'll warn you. You've walked right up to the danger line."

"Is that so? Well, shit on that line! What I say, the time for action is here and you're not up to it!"

Jackson started for him but stopped himself. "Get off my property," he said. His voice was like paper tearing.

"Let's go, boys," Clute bawled. "You got your answer. He won't do nothing. But I'm gonna put out a call for volunteers to go down and clean that Indian bastard out and keep right on going, and I believe the boys will flock to the colors—"

Clute was turning to his horse when Jackson went for him with a cry of rage that was more like a horse's whinny than a man's voice. Benton had a confused impression—the sudden movement, the alarm in the other men's faces, something implacably wild in Jackson's, and then the General had Clute by the shoulder, spun him around, snatched him close, and slapped him again and again, Clute's head jerking with each blow.

And timed to the blows, Jackson shouting, "You miserable turd—you'll call out *my* army?—you'll beat your God damned drum in *my* camp?—you pissant son of a bitch—who in the hell do you think you are?"

When Jackson threw him down Clute rolled on the ground and a knife appeared in his hand. *None of that!*—but even as Benton jumped forward, Jackson kicked the knife away.

"You *drew* on me!" he cried with stunned outrage and snatched a coiled whip from a stable door. Clute struggled to his knees; the lash curled around him and threw him down. He screamed and scrambled up but Jackson followed, the lash snapping like pistol fire. Bloody welts stood on his cheeks. He fell to his knees, hands raised, pleading.

Enough, enough—Benton saw dismay, even horror in the others' faces, and was ready to intervene when the General turned and faced them, the lash slack at his feet. He was panting.

"Get him on his horse and away," he said. He sounded strangled. "You men know me. Pass the word—I'll *destroy* any son of a bitch tries to call out my army. And I'll be armed, let any man who dares draw on me think on that . . ."

When they were gone he cupped his hands in the rain barrel and doused his face. He didn't look at Benton and didn't speak.

★ ★ ★ ★

She was at her desk planning menus with old Hannah—about the only person on the farm fatter than the mistress, alas—when she heard Andrew returning from Nashville. The minute he entered the house she knew something had happened; he was drawn tight as a rawhide lashing. He put too much sugar in his tea and stirred so fiercely it slopped into the saucer. She waited.

"Orders from Washington," he said finally in a low, distressed voice. "I've called out the troops."

Something else was wrong, she knew it. But the enormity of the news— he would be *leaving*—crushed every other thought. That it was long expected made it no easier to bear.

"I'm . . . happy for you," she said.

He looked at her sharply.

She managed a little laugh and said, "I'll be all right. I'll be fine. You'll see."

But immediately the dread set in. When he was gone for a week, her very being seemed to empty out like water spilled in the dust, as if the implacable scandal that had consumed them for so many years had opened great rents in her soul that never healed. She knew well she wouldn't have made it without her husband's utter rejection of any implication of error. It was in the shadow of his absolute refusal to hang his head that she could hold hers high.

Yet she also knew she was strong, and given that strength, it was odd for her to be so dependent on his presence. She wondered about it but could find no tools for analyzing it, and so in the end she came back always to the basic fact—she just *was*. Full, solid, whole when he was there; drained, bereft, and finally desperate when he was away.

Oh, she kept going, ran the farm well enough, made her kindly rounds, but her weight soared, her breath grew short, and finally late some night when she couldn't sleep she'd seize quill and foolscap and write him passionate screeds of misery, hysterical wails of loneliness. And once the letter was on its way, guilt would impose a new layer of misery.

"I'll be fine," she said. "Don't even think of me."

He smiled. "I'll write. And you'll answer."

"Yes, but not crazily." But she knew she would be crazy . . .

He was still tense. New dread assailed her. Orders for where—the dark, freezing woods of Canada? He'd be gone for months, years—he might never return! Her heart thundered.

"Where . . . where are you going?"

"We're to attack Florida."

Thank you, dear Lord! She offered instant prayer. Florida wasn't far and he'd always predicted the small Spanish forces there could be brushed aside. It was what he'd wanted most and the best she could have hoped for, a sheer gift from heaven. Yet he still seemed disturbed.

"We report to New Orleans. To General Wilkinson. *He* will lead the attack."

Ah, Wilkinson.

"That blackguard," he said. "That scoundrel." He shook his head. "I know you say speak no ill—"

"General Wilkinson deserves what Job got," she said.

She remembered Aaron Burr's charm. He'd been their guest for a week, bright, witty, full of stories, ennobled at least in her mind by his deep affection for his daughter, Theodosia, to whom he wrote almost daily. And then he'd betrayed them, linked them to a plot against the nation—Andrew besmirched when no greater patriot than he ever lived! And Wilkinson had used Andrew to clean his own filthy skirts.

But now . . . Wilkinson in command, snapping orders as if Andrew were a corporal, wasn't an explosion inevitable?

For she was learning to fear most of all that violent force in him that had blown up into so many wild encounters. It was part of the strength that long had sheltered them, but now it was taking on life of its own. As his own magnitude expanded—he had *grown* so from that slim young man with whom she'd gone to Natchez—so had this violent other side of his nature.

But the community long since had granted him full respect. Senator, judge, general—surely he'd moved beyond the need to punish every affront.

For her, Dickinson had been the turning point. Couldn't it have been avoided? Not after it progressed, of course; she understood the dueling code, and the time came when you couldn't turn back and survive. And the fight was fair, no matter the talk. But for three awful months she wasn't sure Andrew would live, and Dickinson had left a young widow with young children.

"The other day when that Clute person was here," she said, "something happened, didn't it?"

He stiffened. "An encounter," he said at last. "He's no friend of ours."

"He looked as if he was having trouble sitting his horse when he rode away. Another man was holding him up."

That sudden ignition in his eyes. His nose, his whole face thinned, and he looked . . . dangerous.

"He thought he could call out my army—*my* army!"

"You whipped him, didn't you?"

"I disciplined him."

"Andrew—"

"Took the lash to him. Taught him a lesson. He won't try to call out my troops again."

"Was it necessary?"

"Of course—what in tarnation are you driving at?"

"The other men—how did they react?"

"They were startled, I suppose . . ."

"Didn't expect the General to explode?"

He studied her, looking suddenly uncomfortable. "I know—you think I go too far."

"Could that foolish man really have called out the army?" When he didn't answer, she said, "I'm afraid . . . when your greatest strength turns on you, it becomes your greatest enemy."

"Oh, Rachel, really!"

"We're often our own worst enemy," she said. "We're the only ones who can really undermine ourselves."

"You think I lose control?"

"Don't you?"

She saw anger flare. Then he grinned. "Think I'll give Wilkinson a caning, do you?" He chuckled. "Tell you what—I promise I won't abuse him unless he really asks for it."

Her heart sank. He hadn't heard her.

He stood, smiling, his dark mood shaken off, drew her to her feet and into his arms.

"I love you," he whispered.

She sighed and pressed against him, but the weight on her heart didn't ease.

7

WASHINGTON
Late Fall, 1812

★ ★ ★ ★ That odious, sly, slinking, self-satisfied *oaf*, with his slippery manner, his false smiles, his duplicitous, cheating, lying cries of patriotism— Dolley Madison quivered with rage as she threaded her way through the crowd in her oval drawing room with the brilliant red curtains. She nodded, smiled, waved to others, but she never stopped. The *nerve* of the man—that the arch-Federalist, Josiah Quincy of Massachusetts, could come to her Wednesday Drawing Room as if nothing had happened—as if this were a public building!

"This is our *home*," she said when she reached him, her low voice forceful as steam from a teakettle, "how dare you enter it!"

Quincy stared at her. He was tall, slender, handsome, his talk witty, his manner urbane. This smooth elegance angered her the more, for she considered him an evil man.

"I believe you call it an open house, madam?"

"Not open to our deadliest enemies."

"Oh, come, come, madam. I'm a Federalist, we're the opposition party. Our sainted President can hardly expect us to dance to his tunes. That's politics, madam—nothing personal."

"Oh, no, you don't! I respect opposition and so does my husband. But this isn't politics. It's, it's—treason!"

"Treason, madam?"

"Undermining your country in time of war."

"Because we oppose—"

"This rotten pamphlet." She had it in her hand and had to resist the urge to slap him with it. "Full of filthy lies." Five minutes after Congress reconvened, Quincy as House minority leader had forced a full-scale debate on the war. What kind of message did it send the enemy, coming on the heels of defeats and disasters in the field? She had been so sure—and so had Jimmy—that common patriotism would overcome political schism once Americans were actually under fire. Instead the Federalists were worse than ever. Harder, more implacable, infinitely more vitriolic. And now this pamphlet, a half-million copies spreading like a black tide over the country.

She shook it under his nose. "That thirty-six of the thirty-eight Federalists in the House would sign it stains your party with dishonor!"

"Madam, I—"

"And the things you say on the floor of the House, hiding behind congressional privilege—do you think we don't hear? The President of the United States a snake leaving a trail of slime across the carpets of the halls of state? And your cohorts applauded!"

"The record won't show such a statement."

"No—because shame overtook you and you had the record expunged. Do not deny it, sir."

He stared at her, pale as paper.

"Your presence is not desired, Mr. Quincy," she said, "not so long as this is our home."

"Which may not be for long." His grin was ugly. "Eviction papers may soon be served."

This reference to the election campaign that was breaking Jimmy's heart made her so angry she couldn't speak for a long moment. To think that a sitting President in the midst of war should be required to stand for reelection not against the opposition party but against an apostate *from his own party*. Yes! A fellow Democratic-Republican, DeWitt Clinton of New York, was running against Jimmy on a promise to end the war however he could— throw up his hands, collapse, surrender.

The fool was talking the Federalist line, and she'd seen immediately what would happen. Sure enough, Quincy's minions threw their weight behind the apostate Democrat—and Federalist votes added to the Democratic votes he would draw made Clinton a real threat. And this vile man dared taunt her in her own home—

"Get out," she whispered. "Or I'll have the guards eject you bodily. And don't come back."

Quincy bowed, wheeled, and strode from the room. Her eyes burned holes in his rigid back.

★ ★ ★ ★

Pete Peterson of Philadelphia, party chairman for Pennsylvania, appeared in Madison's office with buff trousers tucked in high boots. His coat was bottle-green.

"Now, Mr. President," he said, "I got the most dismal God damned news you'd want to hear. Out West in our mountain counties, out where they like to shit their drawers when they heard Hull surrendered, figured Tecumseh would be coming down on them next, out there Clinton's got people telling them he'll take over the war and fight it better!"

Peterson gazed around him as if in search of a spittoon. His voice was nasal and rasping. "Same time, you understand, his speakers in the East are telling how he'll get us out of the war. But out West, they say he'll reorganize the army, get some good generals, and chase Tecumseh and his murderers all the way to Canada. Out where folks want to fight, he's selling himself as the fighter."

Madison sighed. Everything about this election was outrageous. He had been renominated in the usual way, by the congressional caucus, and then the Democrats in the New York legislature nominated Clinton. Of course, the legislature could do whatever it wanted. Clinton was New York's mayor and popular as the builder of the Erie Canal. But to separate himself from Madison, a fellow Democrat, after all, Clinton had made himself a pawn of the Federalists . . .

This wouldn't have happened to old Tom. Mr. Jefferson would have demolished them. But an opinion seemed to be forming that Madison was a failure, somehow untrustworthy. He was a thinker, a constitutional scholar—he wondered if he'd always been out of place in this office.

The voting process itself was an agony. Each state voted separately, whenever it chose, election days stretching from September to near December. Of course, individuals didn't campaign. Office was the gift of the voters, and to solicit it directly would be unseemly and instantly self-defeating. One simply agreed to serve if called—and then state by state, it was up to the state party. Pete Peterson's job, in short.

"Now," Peterson said, his ill-fitting green coat reared behind his neck, "time for a good statement from you that tells folks what this scamp is doing."

"A statement? You're asking me to campaign?"

"No, no, just a good statement. You know, well crafted, plenty of dignity—you're above it all, see, but you just want folks to know this is one lying son of a—"

"Why, I'll do no such thing!" Madison said. "I won't grovel for office, sir. The people know who I am."

"Sure, they know who you are. I want them to know who Clinton is—a liar."

Struggling to control his desire to throw the fellow out of his office, Madison said, "That's your job, Mr. Peterson. I would demean this office by making angry statements, by seeming to petition. It's out of the question."

Peterson slumped back in his chair. A surprisingly malevolent look flashed and disappeared.

"And maybe it'll cost you the damned election," he said.

Madison stood up. The remark wasn't worthy of an answer.

★ ★ ★ ★

For Dolley, Mr. Clinton personified their winter of discontent. Whatever could possibly go wrong had gone wrong. Events beat against them as this early winter rain beat against her bedroom window. Sitting in the dark, watching bare branches whip in the wind, she shivered and drew her robe close.

She'd always assumed the phrase "bowed by troubles" to be figurative. But Jimmy *was* bowed. His shoulders had taken on a perpetual slump, his never very grand height reduced. There was something gnomish about him now that made her heart ache, for in truth he was a giant.

Oh, they'd cried for him to start the war, but that was then. Shouting for a second revolution to prove the first, but it turned out that abstract goals like free trade and sailors' rights weren't the same as redcoats at your door. The people were querulous and Congress apprehensive. The War Hawks hadn't been able to move Congress beyond the declaration of war itself, and she knew Congress did reflect the people.

There was apathy in the land, that was the real problem. Taxes to pay for the war? Not a chance. Congress authorized still more loans, but most all of the nation's cash money was in the hands of Federalist bankers. Apathy slowed enlistments to a trickle, but mention conscription and solons would faint dead away. A bare ten thousand men were under arms.

Even the great naval victories didn't change things. American heavy frigates smashed enemy frigates in single-ship actions that stunned the Royal Navy. U.S.S. *Constitution* sank H.M.S. *Guerrière*; U.S.S. *Wasp* sank H.M.S. *Frolic*; U.S.S. *United States*, Captain Stephen Decatur, crippled H.M.S. *Macedonian* at sea and brought her into New York harbor as prize. Bells rang and Americans cheered for an evening, but everyone knew Royal Navy numbers must prevail. Now British ships sailed in squadrons and our great frigates lay locked in harbor.

This would be a land war, and on land it was all defeats. Hull's disaster, and now Queenston. Ironic that that charming young officer—Sally McQuirk had been quite taken with him, she thought—should emerge the hero of a cruel defeat. Pompous old Dearborn's three-prong attack . . . two prongs down and the third, under Dearborn himself, about to stall in the snows of the Canadian woods. My Lord, it was cold here; what must it be like there? And they'd said Canada would fall like a ripe apple!

Wind gusts shook the windowpane. A lightning stroke turned night to day as a horseman passed at too fast a trot, hat pulled low against rain.

The Federalist press delighted in the defeats, and never mind the American casualties. And the Democrats retaliated, mobs tarring and feathering critics of the war. When they burned out the most vitriolic editor of all, Alex Hanson over in Baltimore, she'd felt a momentary thrill—surely no one deserved misfortune more—and then, dismayed, she learned the fighting left two dead and a dozen injured. A stunning description in Mr. McQuirk's paper from someone who'd been there left her shaken. The very fabric of the nation was being torn.

Hotheaded Democrats in Congress wanted to silence Federalists with a new sedition law. Imprison people for their speech. Jimmy rose to a fury she'd rarely seen in him. He'd veto such a bill before its ink dried! She'd been thrilled: free speech makes free people, a point on which she felt Federalists took full advantage.

Oh, she understood the rationale for supporting England against France, when England had given us heritage, language, faith, culture, common law. But the truth was that the excesses of the French Revolution had made Federalists fear the very idea of democracy. She shrugged. The French revolted against their own elite, and Federalists were elitists at heart. The revolution there had long since been crushed by the tyrant Napoleon who now wanted to control the world. The *opposite* of democracy—so for Federalists to stand in your drawing room and accuse you of letting your fascination for the original high ideals of the French Revolution make you a partisan of Napoleon today was enough to make you laugh if you could keep from crying.

She sighed, sick with weariness. The clock chimed softly. Three in the morning, and Jimmy still at his desk. A tumbler of milk and a loaf wrapped in cloth had awaited him here for hours. She was ready to go fetch him when the door opened.

Even in the dark she could see he was farther bowed. He sounded like a ghost, his voice a whisper.

"The returns are in from New England. A disaster. Mr. Clinton carried everything but little Vermont."

"We knew New England was against us," she said. "We'll win everything south of New England. You'll see."

He smiled, a pale, exhausted smile.

"Yes . . ."

He sat on a sofa and rested his face in his hands. She moved beside him, held him in her arms.

He sighed. "If I were a real leader . . ."

"You are! Clinton is a demagogue."

He didn't answer. Rain beat against the windows.

★ ★ ★ ★

"I want to go to New York, Papa," Sally McQuirk said.

For a moment there was that old penetrating flash in Micajah McQuirk's blue eyes, the stare of a man who hears more than has been said. They were at home, a brick house on the President's Square, catty-cornered from Captain Decatur's new place. Through a leaded glass window Sally glimpsed a carriage turning from Pennsylvania Avenue into the President's circular drive.

The moment passed. Papa, in robe and slippers, sat with legs spread and belly slumped. His sparse gray hair was awry, his ankles swollen, he often paused between phrases to draw breath. He'd never been the same since Mama died.

"But why, Sally?"

"New York is charming in the fall. Etta Margolies invited me." She'd already booked a through stage.

"And Etta's brother, as I recall, is a member of the New York legislature, and the legislature will be voting soon on presidential electors. That the real interest?"

She laughed. "You always see through me. Johnny Margolies will seat us in the gallery, we'll meet the leaders, hear what happens in caucus—and, Papa, you know how important it is."

The election outraged the Papa, whose paper spoke for the administration, but Sally loved the excitement. DeWitt Clinton, once the tasteless pretender challenging his own party's sitting President, might actually win. He'd already taken all of New England except Vermont, just as Papa had predicted, giving him fifty-three electoral votes to the President's eight. Then Madison slid ahead a little as the states slowly voted. He won Virginia, South Carolina, Georgia, Kentucky, Tennessee, and the new state of Louisiana.

A New Jersey coup delivered its seven to the New Yorker. He certainly would get five or six of Maryland's eleven and all of Delaware's four, giving him seventy votes or so to Madison's eighty. North Carolina and Ohio could go either way.

So New York's twenty-nine and Pennsylvania's twenty-five would decide. Pennsylvania chose its electors by popular vote, winner take all, but in New York, as in about half the states, the legislature chose electors.

"Do you still think the New York vote will break about evenly?" she asked.

"Oh, Clinton's loved and hated in equal measure at home," her father said, "but predicting the New York legislature is like lighting your pipe in a powder magazine, baby, you know that."

He sighed. "God, I wish your mother were here. She'd know about this writing business—whether it's proper, I mean."

"Papa, we've been over and over this. Margaret Smith wrote for her husband's paper. And for magazines and she's started a novel. And she's a Bayard of Philadelphia. And there are others, too . . ."

"Yes, but . . . well, ever since Baltimore—"

"That was a good story. You said so yourself!"

A very good story, thanks to her good luck in being in Nellie Farbinger's carriage when it blundered into the mob that attacked Mr. Hanson's newspaper. She could still hear the crowd's menacing roar, still feel the coach rock as fists pounded on its sides.

"Your luck," Papa said, "was in the quality of men who opened that carriage door." She would never forget the startled look the big blond fellow gave her.

"*Mein Gott,*" he had cried. "Ladies!" And then, to a friend, "C'mon, Bill, we save 'em."

"Baltimore is full of German immigrants," she said, "and I love them all." The man called Bill had swept Nellie into his arms, but Sally had said, "I can walk. Lead the way."

"Well," Papa said, "you're courageous, I'll give you that. Pushing your way to the roof, and all."

There was, of course, a little more to it than that, but Papa didn't need to know everything. A cadaverous fellow who smelled of whiskey had slipped both hands around her from behind to grab her breasts and whispered, "Come to see the sights, lassie? I've got a sight to show you." She stamped his instep with her heel and when he yelped her rescuer turned and showed the fellow a huge fist. Getting to the roof wasn't much—when the big German deposited her on the stoop of a row house she'd simply dragooned the householder into taking her up.

"But, Papa," she said, "it was the most awesome, frightening, thrilling, beautiful sight I ever saw."

Neither the politics nor that they were burning a newspaper had entered her head at the time. What was etched in memory were the leaping flames, the crimson smoke, the muttering roar of the mob, and her basic reaction: what a story!

The next morning she'd learned two men were dead and a dozen injured. She wrote all the way to Washington on the rapid stage.

Papa set the type himself, fingers flying, and an hour later they were on the street.

Stories would never carry her name, but all Washington was reading her words. Her words, unchanged. So was the rest of the country, for editors elsewhere copied regularly from local papers; that's how news was transmitted. What satisfaction!

"Well, it *was* a good story," Papa said. "You know, I won't be here forever."

A moment of alarm: he'd never spoken of death before.

"With your mama gone, I've always assumed the *Democratic-Republican* would have to be sold when I go. But lately I've been thinking . . . is it possible that you could run it?"

"Yes." She heard the quiver in her voice and from his expression knew he heard it, too. What a keen old bird!

"Oh, I can run it," she said, her voice now steady, "but, Papa, you must teach me everything you know. Everything."

"Yes . . ." He seemed to speak more to himself than to her. "That's the right thing. That's what we'll do." Then, smiling, "Go on to New York. The election may be decided right there."

★ ★ ★ ★

Menu list in hand, Dolley pushed open the pantry door to find French John in tears.

"Oh, madam . . ."

She dropped into a chair. "What is it, John?"

He touched a letter lying open on his desk. "My brother—Henri, the youngest—he is dying, in New York.

"The lady of his boardinghouse, she writes for him. The doctor says he'll be lucky to last a week." He wiped his eyes. "Oh, madam, he's the only one left, he and I, there are no more. You understand, the whole family loved the Revolution, we fought for it, and then the imperial villains seized power in France and we were the enemy! My parents died of broken hearts and two of my brothers went to the knife, and little Henri and I fled to America. And now I'm to lose him, too!"

"Oh, John, I'm so sorry." She had two dinners to give, to say nothing of her Wednesday Drawing Room. "You must go to New York at once, of course."

"Thank you." He seized her hand and kissed it. "You are my best friend in America."

She extracted her hand. "I'll borrow Pompey from Colonel Tayloe. He can handle things here, don't you think?"

"Oh, madam, no need for that. Joseph can manage."

"Joseph? I don't know. He's bright, but he's only a boy."

"He's twenty-five, madam."

"Really? But he's . . . no, I don't think so. I'll ask Colonel Tayloe, I know he'll agree to—"

"Madam," John said, more sharply than she really liked, "you are mistaken about Joseph. He's a very capable man. Very. And intelligent. I've grown quite fond of him."

"We're all fond of him, John. That's not the point."

"Oh, madam, perhaps you will detest me, perhaps you will banish me forever from your sight, but at this moment when my family is dying, when everyone but me has been sacrificed to the ideals of republicanism, I cannot remain silent. Joseph is an able man, a proud man. He should not be a slave."

When she didn't respond, he drew himself up and said with Gallic fierceness, "Madam, I must say it. Forgive me, but I must. Slavery is wrong. An evil abomination!"

Dolley sighed. "Go to New York, John, and see to your brother. As to slavery, of course you're right."

He blinked. "I am?"

"Every thinking Virginian understands that. Mr. Madison argues against slavery, so does Mr. Jefferson. My own father freed his slaves and sold his plantation. Ned Coles has only delayed selling the plantation he inherited and taking his people to the Northwest Territory to free them because we need him in the war. He denounces slavery every day."

She stood up. "Go on to New York, John. I pray that Henri will live. And, yes, Joseph will be fine."

She watched him go and sat thinking for a few minutes. Papa, having prayed over Quaker doctrine and decided he must not be a slaveholder, had gone to Philadelphia to enter business and died a bankrupt. Leaving Mama to tend a boardinghouse—and someone else to put other slaves on what had been his land. Ned, too—he could free his people but others would take their place on the land under a hand probably less kind than his. Slavery was the labor system in the South.

Yet she well knew it to be incompatible with a free nation. Jimmy knew it, Tom knew it. Would the evil institution end in her lifetime? She didn't know, and it wasn't an issue she would die for, as Papa had and Ned would. The change would come in time, but the process might well be bloody. Now, only twenty years after Mr. Whitney invented his gin, cotton had spread across the South—the Cotton South, they were calling it, the Cotton Empire—and that was fastening slavery ever more firmly in place.

And French John thought it should end with a finger snap!

★ ★ ★ ★

"Cook has a treat for us."

Madison heard the happy note in Dolley's voice that sweets usually produced. He squared his shoulders, shaking off gloom.

"Fresh Irish scones," she said. "Ned and I waited for you."

The scones were puffy and golden, studded with black raisins. Coffee steamed in blue china cups. Sun poured through a fretted half-circle window in the graceful family parlor, laying patterns on the blue carpet. Dolley's block-front desk was piled high with cloth swatches, notes, Mr. Latrobe's drawings. She sat on a yellow settee with claw-and-ball feet, attending the tray on a low table before her. Smiling at her pleased, greedy expression as she spread butter on a scone—she would be a round little old lady someday— he put his troubles out of mind.

Ned Coles hurried in. The secretary was a handsome young man whose luminous brown eyes radiated sweet-tempered assurance. He was Dolley's cousin; she had countless relatives who extended Madison's family ad infinitum.

"Have a scone," Dolley said, buttering her second one. "Let's be merry while we wait on voters, bless 'em or curse 'em."

"Curse 'em, I'd say." Ned held his cup in both hands.

"Not at all, my boy," Madison said. "Voters are a force of nature, like the weather. Neither good nor bad. If a leader doesn't bring them along, it's his fault, not theirs."

"Oh, ta ta, Jimmy." Dolley licked butter off her fingers. "They're supposed to have some sense of their own."

"Well," he said, "they're confused. The reason Congress won't do anything is that it reflects the people and they haven't decided. Look at the confusion in the New York legislature."

"We'll get our half of that vote, won't we?" Dolley asked. He heard the anxiety in her voice and felt foolish to have been pontificating, for in fact he was as anxious as she. This damnable election had become truly dangerous. Madison felt that for him to get only half of New York's vote—when the state's interests weren't with Clinton, native son or not—was a travesty. And of course, the New York vote would have great influence over Pennsylvania . . .

Her mouth tightened. "I wish you'd released those papers earlier," she said.

He sighed. Dolley was very basic and partisan; he knew it was because she loved him, but he couldn't stoop to political maneuver. It would demean him and the office and the country. Yes, the diplomatic papers established clearly that Britain had pushed them into war and that they had not favored France, and when Congress asked for them, he'd been delighted. But to inspire a congressional request—no, he couldn't do that.

She wasn't smiling when she said, "I think that attitude can cost us this election."

The door opened and the Secretary of State walked in. Monroe's long face was ashen.

"We've lost New York," he said. "Lost it all."

Dead silence in the sunny little parlor: Madison felt the words as a fist in the chest.

"All? We didn't get our half?"

"Not a vote. Not one." A letter in Monroe's hand shook. "These are the returns. Not one . . ."

"But we were sure of half!" Dolley cried.

"Outmaneuvered, outsmarted, cheated wholesale, who knows?"

"They sold us out," she whispered.

Madison sagged back in his wing chair. It didn't matter how it had come about. The worst was happening, the bottom dropping out of his world. He'd never taken Clinton seriously, never believed American voters could be so thoroughly gulled. But with New York gone, losing was not just possible but probable. Only Pennsylvania stood in the way of disaster.

And the polls there had closed, the slow, laborious count under way. He could only wait.

★ ★ ★ ★

"Wal, Madison," Jacob Stuckey said, "I hate to be the one telling you, but I reckon your ass is mud."

The Congressman from western Pennsylvania was a skinny fellow in a homespun wool suit. He sat before Madison's desk, one yellow shoe resting on an American Chippendale chair with a blue needlepoint cushion.

"Way I see it, you deserve to know, so I come right on over soon as I got back to town. Figured you'd want to hear how you done stepped in shit in the mountain counties. Folks out yonder, they're really scared of Indians, you know, and what Clinton's men were saying sounded good to them. Course, it's a damned lie, he'll do just the opposite, and I told 'em, but it didn't do no good. You're dead meat in Pennsylvania and I reckon that's going to put Clinton right where you're sitting, and that's just a God damned shame!"

He droned on. Madison waited, doing penance for a failed presidency. He didn't doubt Stuckey's assessment. It just meant that the truth had lagged the charlatan's lies.

No fault of westerners. Through the mountains of Pennsylvania, the wilds of western New York, the vast forests along the Ohio, Tecumseh's dream of a buffer state backed by the British army was their nightmare.

Yet the consequences of losing Pennsylvania were terrible, too. Not for him—he'd be happy to go home to Montpelier and watch the distant Blue Ridge—but for the country. Clinton as President would destroy the United States. Surrendering to Federalists, quitting the war, accepting whatever terms a vindictive Britain might impose, would shatter America.

The die would be cast, not toward a great continental nation proudly taking its place in the world but toward a small country along the coast living in the British shadow. Tecumseh would have his buffer state. The West, dependent on the Mississippi, would break away and in time become part of Canada . . .

The American dream . . . sacrified to a selfish politician's overweening ambition—and a failed Virginia gentleman's inability to communicate his passion and his hopes for the most glorious national experiment on the face of the earth!

★ ★ ★ ★

The door burst open. The Pennsylvania chairman—still wearing that bottle-green coat, now wrinkled and travel-stained—pushed his way into the room ahead of Ned.

"Mr. President, I come myself on the fastest stage to tell you we've carried Pennsylvania!"

Madison stared at him.

"I've got the canvass in my pocket, Philadelphia and surrounding counties—you've carried 'em, sir, by a substantial margin. I mean, substantial! Fat! You've won Pennsylvania and that'll give you the election."

"Wal, now," Stuckey said, "I don't know about that. I just been telling him he's a horse gone lame in the western counties. Truth is, his goose is cooked."

Peterson, who knew Stuckey well, grinned. "Well, sir, let me tell you the joys of representative democracy. Every vote stands equal. Now, how many people in your district?"

"A good ten thousand, probably."

"Area I'm canvassing has polled a little better' than a hundred thousand votes. Mr. Madison's running right at sixty-two point six, or about twenty-five thousand ahead. Against that, your western counties don't amount to a pile of—"

Dolley swept into the room.

"Ned told me," she said. Her eyes filled with tears. "Oh, Jimmy, it's the most wonderful news!"

"Why, that's right!" said Stuckey, who was counting on his fingers. "Them numbers outvotes the West to a fare-ye-well." He seized Madison's hand. "Wal, old feller, you done it! Makes me feel better'n a dog with a bone."

Much later, in their bedroom, Dolley came into his arms.

"Oh, my lovely husband, let's drink a lot of wine and talk and laugh and make love . . ." His hands on her waist drew her close.

"And we'll give a big ball at Tomlinson's Hotel."

He pulled back. "I don't know . . . the margin so narrow, the nation so divided, the dissatisfaction—"

"Darling Jimmy." Her arms tightened around his neck. "Don't you know that's just when you should celebrate?"

★ ★ ★ ★

Three weeks later, watching the merry throng, women in flowing gowns and jewels and peacock feathers, men in their finest—why, he himself wore his best black hose and the shoes with sterling buckles—he knew she was right. Victory was victory, narrow or not. Could he ask for more in troubled times?

A drumroll. The noise level fell. Four officers from the U.S.S. *United States* entered the hall, each holding a corner of the battle flag taken from H.M.S. *Macedonian.* They circled the room to the pounding drums, stopped before Dolley, and spread the British ensign at her feet.

The drums stopped. In breathless silence, Dolley nodded to the orchestra, which burst into "Yankee Doodle." Slowly she stepped onto the center of the Union Jack and, to the marching song of the Revolution, danced a little jig.

Applause, shouts, laughter, piercing whistles.

"What a pity," a Federalist congressman said, "that the ship of state won't sail so smoothly as the ship of war."

Madison leveled a finger at the Congressman. "It would, sir, if the *crew* would do their duty as well."

That felt good! The Congressman scuttled off, flushed with anger. The music started again, dancing began, the gay clamor soared. Yes, the country was alive and growing in strength, and so, by God, was its President. Both had a war to fight—so let's get on with it!

8

★ ★ ★ ★ Winfield Scott walked into the ballroom as if he owned it. His full dress uniform was freshly sponged, his boots newly blackened, shako tucked smartly under his left arm. He heard the band strike up "Yankee Doodle," then an explosion of cheers.

"Your invitation, sir?"

He looked down at a harried clerk. "I'm Lieutenant Colonel Scott. The Secretary of War expects me."

"The Secretary hasn't arrived, sir."

"That's the point. I'm here in advance." He stepped past the man. The President was here and Scott intended to see him. His business was too urgent to wait.

The room seemed vast, its twenty-foot ceiling supported by pillars carved to match the plaster frieze on the wall. Candles flashed warmly in girandoles and hundreds of sperm-oil lights flickered through countless brilliants on four massive chandeliers, giving a warm glow to paper rosettes and miniature flags and red, white, and blue paper streamers entwined in long chains looping from pillar to pillar.

Waiters with champagne and whiskey punch on trays moved through a huge crowd, at least three hundred, Scott guessed, men formal in broadcloth and breeches, black hose and buckled shoes, women bejeweled and begowned, only an occasional uniform. That he was impressed irked him; war itself, let alone an icy prison camp in the snows of Quebec, seemed cruelly remote from this vivid scene.

Then he saw the object of the cheers. Mrs. Madison was doing a clumsy dance on what looked like a British flag.

"H.M.S. *Macedonia*'s battle flag," someone said.

Something dark rose in him. Men had died taking that flag, others had died defending it. He well knew the British were worthy opponents. Battle trophies deserved to be—

"Win!"

He turned quickly. Sally McQuirk approached with hands outstretched and his mood shifted instantly. He stood transfixed—she was even more stunning than he remembered. Golden hair was coiled atop her head; her gown was golden velvet with an effusion of white lace at her bodice that drew attention even as it concealed.

He caught her hands and barely stopped himself from kissing her and creating a scandal.

"Sally."

"Oh, Win, I'm *so* glad to see you. We knew you were captured; there were reports you were dead—or sent to England. And here you are at the ball!"

Clinging shamelessly to her hands, he sketched the prison ship across the lake and down the St. Lawrence to Montreal and Quebec locked in winter. There they'd been exchanged for British prisoners of like rank and dispatched on a scurvy-ridden ship that fetched up through winter gales in Boston.

Her hands pressed his, hard. "No wonder you seem different. Older, stronger somehow. I like it. You've seen terrible things . . ."

"Grown up some, perhaps."

She nodded. "Yes, that's it. Come to tea tomorrow. You must tell me everything about it. Everything." Her voice dropped. "Dear God, it's good to see you. I was worried. I . . ."

She broke off, a vulnerability in her eyes he hadn't seen before. She'd almost said she loved him, he was sure of it. It was intoxicating, but alarm bells were ringing.

Then she jerked them back to the lighthearted present. "So you arrived, heard there was a ball, and invited yourself!"

"Actually, I heard the President would be here. I have urgent information I must find a way to give directly to him. Dr. Eustis is a fine fellow and all that, but as Secretary of War he leaves a good deal to be desired."

"Well, we can get you to the President easily enough. And as for the good doctor, he's been sent to pasture."

"No!"

"Yes. And high time. Everyone knew he had to go, but the President delayed and delayed. That's a problem of his, you know—he hates to challenge anyone, so he hesitates."

That was disquieting. The situation that had brought Scott here by day-and-night coach wouldn't wait. He spotted the little President in a corner, all but obscured by taller men.

"So who's the new Secretary of War?"

"Mr. Monroe for the moment. Then he puts on his Secretary of State hat and negotiates with the British. But negotiations are going nowhere, so I guess it hardly matters."

"Can he do both jobs?"

"Oh, he lacks no confidence in himself. But he won't let himself be saddled with the War Department. That would preclude a military command, and I think that's what he really wants."

"He's a soldier, too?"

"No, but he's confident. And a couple of victories in the field would assure him the presidency in 1816, that's the point."

Another amateur general. Good Lord. He remembered poor Van Rensselaer in stumbling confusion facing General Sheaffe's redcoats whose bayonets were as steady as fence pickets.

And Sally? She was gorgeous and intelligent and great fun, but her insights into official Washington—which he found downright uncanny—were somehow disturbing. They reminded him of how far her world was from his world of men marching to war.

At the moment she was explaining why she thought John Armstrong of New York held the inside track for the appointment. A Revolutionary War officer who'd been in hot water with General Washington, he'd most recently been ambassador to France.

"That pugnacious manner of his worked well," she said, "since Napoleon is just about as hostile as the British King."

"How will pugnacity fare here?"

"He's well hated, Win. One of those people whose pride in their own honesty compels them to point out the faults of others. There's talk the Senate won't confirm him."

"Then why pick him? New York's a problem?"

"The country's so split," Sally said with that disconcerting assurance. "New England charts its own course. And Clinton did win New York, if by a piece of legerdemain that was startling when you saw it up close."

Startling? *He* was startled. "You saw it up close?"

She hesitated, as if suddenly wary. "By chance, I happened to be in Albany, visiting friends."

By chance. Gazing at her, he said, "Traveling, I picked up an old paper that had reprinted your father's fine article on the subject. I don't suppose . . ."

"Oh, I told Papa a few of my impressions."

To his utter surprise, she blushed, quite unlike her usual poise. Could she actually be writing? Herself? Quickly he added, "Your father is a fine writer."

She smiled and beckoned to a young man whom she introduced as Ned Coles, the President's secretary. He had dark and soulful eyes that he turned worshipfully on Sally. She told him Scott needed to speak to the President.

"Ah, Queenston," Coles said. "Of course. Let me see."

They watched him whisper to Mr. Madison, who looked up with a quick smile and beckoned. Feeling immensely alert, Scott stepped into the charmed circle in which he recognized only a few faces. Henry Clay, the lean Kentuckian who was Speaker of the House, was finishing a story, long finger tapping his snuffbox for emphasis. Mr. Monroe murmured something that produced a chuckle from a slender man, dark and balding with very canny eyes, whom Scott recognized as Albert Gallatin, Treasury Secretary and a great favorite of the President's.

A woman in scarlet velvet danced into the group, pecked the President on the cheek, and seized Mr. Gallatin's hand to draw him onto the floor. All of it—the complacent men around the President, the aura of power, the glitter, the music, and the whirling figures—seemed only to sharpen

Scott's senses. For he was here on a special mission. He intended to force the hand of the President of the United States, whatever the cost to himself.

"Thank you, Mr. President," he said. "Sir, I—"

"Tell me about Queenston," Mr. Madison said. "I expect you can give me the straight of that dolorous day. What went wrong?"

Scott hesitated. "Sir, General Van Rensselaer was commanding. I was just—"

"Come, come, Colonel, I know what you did there. And what Van Rensselaer did. For your information, he has left the army at his own request and General Smyth—who probably deserves court-martial—is on extended leave from which he's not expected to return. He'll regret it if he does." He paused, his expression suddenly stern. "Now, young man, you're a student of military matters; I want your insight on this."

"Yes, sir!" Swiftly he sorted key points. A night crossing demands elaborate practice. Far too few boats were used, though others were available. Naval boatmen wouldn't have panicked under fire. The British eighteen-pounder downriver that savaged the boats should have been silenced. Proper barges could have crossed their artillery; instead troops faced British guns with small arms. Smyth's brigade remained idle. No attempt was made to shield untried militia from the agony of the wounded, the real key to their ultimate refusal to fight.

"Cowardly militia," Clay said, closing his snuffbox with a loud snap. "Kentucky militia wouldn't have faltered."

Scott wheeled on him. "Sir, New Yorkers are no different from anyone else. They were allowed to become demoralized. Leadership is the issue, and they had none."

He turned to Madison. "Mr. President, if I may say so, I watched General Sheaffe's lines march into our fire as if on a straight edge and the difference was driven home. Training is the key, sir. Drill and drill and drill, get 'em so used to the commands that even under fire the command is what makes them comfortable. Training gives them confidence, in themselves, each other, their sergeants and officers. Confidence, sir. We shot down more than one of those redcoats, but the line never faltered. New York militia, Kentucky militia I shouldn't doubt, regulars—training is what our army cries for."

"I like the sound of that," Madison said. "But at Queenston, then, everything from top to bottom went wrong?"

"No, sir! Begging your pardon, sir, but that's not true. The men who made the first crossing fought well. They took that gun on the slope over the town and they kept it. And on the heights that afternoon, my men fought hard and when they were overrun they retreated in good order. Mr. President, we lost, but by God, sir, we gave 'em a fight!"

The President's eyes flashed. "Well said, Colonel." He hit his palm with his fist, a curiously warlike gesture, and said, "Now, why did you want to see me?"

"Sir, I was taken prisoner at Queenston." The President nodded. "We were released on prisoner exchange, but just before that the British committed an atrocity. Twenty-three of our men have been sequestered and sent to Britain to be hung. Men who are no different from any other American soldier."

"Hung? Prisoners of war? What the devil is this?"

Explaining, Scott was swept back to the foul little brig, moored under the guns of Fortress Quebec, that was to return them. He had been below decks when Sarenmajor Boone burst in.

"Better come topside, sir!"

He had followed Boone in a rush up the narrow ladder to find his men mustered on the snowy deck, a group standing to one side looking utterly miserable.

"What's going on here?" he shouted.

A squad of redcoats with fixed bayonets were behind a slender British captain who leveled cold blue eyes on Scott.

"That's enough from you. You're a prisoner."

"I'm a prisoner *of war*. I'm these men's commander and you will deal with them through me. What is the meaning of this?"

"General Prevost's orders. These men are Irish nationals, citizens of Great Britain. Taking arms against their country is a capital offense. General Prevost has ordered them hung."

"Are you mad? They're American soldiers. They're not Britons." He saw Riordan in the white-faced cluster.

"Listen to their brogues," the Captain said. "Any fool can hear Ireland."

Snowflakes dancing on the damp breeze grew thicker, settled on the British officer's shoulders, and whitened the deck.

"We're an immigrant nation, Captain." Scott kept his tone even. "Some of these men may have been born in Ireland, but they've long since emigrated. They are all American citizens."

"Citizens!" The Captain snorted. "Of a mongrel nation, not that it matters. Sir, the rule is well known—once a Briton, always a Briton. And Britain knows how to deal with traitors."

"That is insane! Riordan—where were you born?"

"Ulster County, New York, Colonel. My paw come from Ireland—I talk like him."

"There!" Scott cried. "You shall not have these men, Captain. They're Americans all."

"You'll shut your God damned mouth!" the Briton shouted. "I'll put a bayonet up your arse, you muck with me." He pointed to a man standing beside Boone. "You! Step forward and speak up. Let's hear how you handle the mother tongue."

The soldier hesitated, fear etched on his face. Scott remembered him dimly, an older man, come from Scotland in the 1790s—and Scotland lived in his speech.

Scott's hand shot out. "Don't move, soldier! Don't answer." He turned to the others. "All of you men, not another word. Hold your tongues no matter what."

He leveled a finger at the British officer's face. "And you, sir—I warn you, this is piracy and murder. The United States government will punish this atrocity."

The officer approached the Scotsman—Calhoun, that was his name—and a trooper put a bayonet to his throat.

"Speak up," the officer said.

"Silence!" Scott shouted. "That's an order." Calhoun's legs shook but he didn't speak.

The moment stretched. Then, abruptly, the officer jerked his head at the sequestered men.

"Get 'em ashore!"

Helpless, Scott watched his own soldiers march toward a hangman's noose. Now, standing in a warm ballroom full of music and dancing figures under red, white, and blue streamers, he shivered.

"Sir," he said, "they intend to hang those men."

Madison didn't answer for a long moment. The band ended a piece and there was loud applause. A leaden feeling overtook Scott. Madison was the Commander in Chief. He had an obligation to his men that even transcended the presidency. But did he understand that, having had no military experience? Scott remembered Sally's comment: he hesitates.

But he'd known all along that it would come to this. He'd prepared himself, knew exactly what he must hurl in the President's face: *Sir, these are my men. But, sir, they are your men, too*! But before he could plunge, the President spoke.

"That's the most outrageous story I've ever heard. By God, I won't have it!" He turned to Monroe. "How many British prisoners have we?"

"A little more than a hundred, sir."

"I want you to get orders out in the morning. I want—Scott, how many did you say, twenty-three?"

"Twenty-three, sir."

"I want forty-six Britons sequestered immediately. Officers and men alike. No exchanges."

"Yes, sir," Monroe said. "But—"

"No buts, Mr. Monroe. Call in the British chargé immediately. Tell him that for any one of our men he hangs, I'll hang two of his—right up to the whole forty-six. Understand?"

"My God, Mr. President, the British won't like that."

"That's my expectation."

"Sir, this could upset any chance for negotiations."

"Well? I'm to let them hang my men in hopes of a treaty?"

"No, sir, but we should find a way to soften—"

"I don't want to soften. I'll hang two for one and that's that. They're damned barbarians and we'll treat 'em so. Just *do* it, Jim. Tell that chargé to get word to Whitehall fast."

And they said the man was weak! Couldn't decide. Hesitated. Scott felt like hugging him.

"Thank you, sir," he said.

"You did well to report this, Scott. I don't think your men will hang."

★　★　★　★

Sally was chatting with three older men. When Scott caught her eye she moved her head, beckoning almost imperceptibly, and started separating herself. He hurried toward her, his heart full of thanksgiving.

Ned Coles joined them. "If I may intrude, a message from the President. First, you're a full colonel now. I'm to notify the department in the morning."

"Thank you, Mr. Coles," Scott said. Colonel!

"And, informally, you're to make it a point to call on him when you're in Washington. He says he gets a clearer idea of military realities from you than from his generals. Come through me and I'll see to everything. Understood?"

"Yes, sir. It will be an honor."

As Coles hurried off, Scott caught Sally's hand and whirled her onto the floor. 'Round and 'round he swung her till she was breathless. He stopped suddenly, laughing like a boy, and cried, "Colonel! Colonel Scott. My, Sally, doesn't that have a fine ring?" He bowed deeply. "*Soldat extraordinaire!* At your service, mademoiselle."

★　★　★　★

Madison had never liked John Armstrong and he'd known him for years. He found the man arrogant, ambitious, self-centered, petulant, usually angry, and often petty. So why give him the War Department? Why make him the cabinet's leading figure, the man who must convert failure into success?

Because he didn't have anyone else. Because Armstrong had national and international experience, because he understood organization, which poor Eustis didn't, because he had at least a little military background, because the war was a disaster and Dearborn was an imbecile and somebody had to take hold and make it all hump and maybe Armstrong could. Maybe.

The two men on whom Madison depended most—Albert Gallatin toiling night and day at Treasury to pay for a war Congress refused to finance, and Monroe at State—hated Armstrong. They said he was treacherous, foul-tempered, self-serving, ambitious. Which was true enough. As ambassador, he'd been famous for his temper. But Madison considered Napoleon's having hated him as a mark in his favor.

Anyway, Gallatin understood finances better than politics and Monroe's real interest was to unhorse a potential rival for the presidency. Monroe should talk—in ambition he had no peer.

And yet . . . State, Treasury, and War at each other's throats across the cabinet table? Not a pleasant prospect.

For ten days Madison pondered the underlying question: do you need him *that* much?

The answer was yes. He needed Armstrong. He needed New York. Clinton carried it by legerdemain, perhaps, but he'd carried it. Its militia balked on the Niagara. The old patroon, Van Rensselaer, had gone home in silent dismay. Federalist agents from New England were hard at work trying to align New York with the North, and if it joined the bloc New England was forming, the nation could break in two.

And Armstrong was the only acceptable New Yorker not in the Clinton camp; indeed, the man hated Clinton, another mark in his favor. He was a good Democratic-Republican, bloodied in the wars with the Federalists. He had gained some military staff experience in the Revolution, and while in Europe he'd studied Napoleon's tactics. He had headed New York City's defenses last year as a newly appointed brigadier and was organized, efficient, energetic. What the devil more could one ask?

Madison sat at his desk tapping pen on blotter, watching Pennsylvania Avenue fade into darkness. He put on a heavy black coat and walked the ellipse, boots ringing on frozen ground. He mounted a bay gelding and with Rufe Dumster in silent train galloped along Rock Creek, startling deer come down to break the ice and drink.

This miserable agonizing over the decision . . . wouldn't a real leader just know?

Monroe's negotiations with the British to end the war were futile. British ships sealed the Atlantic coast from the Hudson to the Chesapeake in a blockade that pinched the American economy ever harder, ships rotting in New York, Philadelphia, Baltimore.

The nation was so divided. Trade with the enemy flowed regularly to Canada coastwise and over northern borders. Small boats sailed out to supply the very ships imposing the blockade. Licking the hand that whipped them! And as New England fattened on profits, it became ever more disaffected.

Recruiting still depended on the bonus. Where were loyalty, ardor, old-fashioned patriotism? The army had inched up toward fifteen thousand. Supply was slightly improved. There were new Quartermaster, Ordnance, and Engineering departments but still no general staff and no serious planning. Any new man would be on his own.

The South was moving, at least. Jackson's Tennesseans were going to join Wilkinson in New Orleans to take West Florida. He had a momentary qualm, remembering Jackson's feelings for Wilkinson, but put it aside. They'd learn to get along or he'd bounce them both! The important thing was to get Florida, at least as far as Pensacola. Protect New Orleans and snatch a province that had long been a boil on the nation's underside. Madison had always believed Florida was included in the Louisiana Purchase, but it remained in Spanish hands. Authority for the Florida expedition was before Congress now, approval assured. So the leaders said.

Dangerous news from Europe . . . Napoleon's invasion of Russia had failed totally. The French were in disastrous retreat, weapons and bodies littering a thousand miles of snow. For years American diplomacy had depended on France keeping Britain busy. If Napoleon failed, the full might of the British army would fall on the little United States.

Of course, one defeat, even of the magnitude of this Russian debacle, didn't end a war. But from young Scott he'd heard the most interesting things, the rhythms of big armies and the interlocking issues of supplies, arms, key units, and, most of all, morale. Scott had an idea Napoleon's days were numbered, and Madison had an idea he was right.

Scott's insistence that training would make any man a soldier, including militia, made sense to Madison. But there was a larger issue about militia, too. Could a force designed for defense be used in offensive war? Or was the reliance on militia that was basic to the Constitution actually a fallacy for an established nation? War, after all, was an extension of politics; what recourse against British wrongs did they have but to strike Canada?

Training, preparations, recruiting, militia—all these lay behind the disasters in the North. All those much heralded prongs were broken, Hull's disgrace, Queenston, and now Dearborn's third column turned back from Canada in waist-deep snow. He sighed. It had been a year of unrelieved military failure, the surprise so possible to achieve last summer all wasted, Canada anything but welcoming, British defenses superb . . . of course he needed someone to take it all in hand!

★ ★ ★ ★

When the subject of Madison's anguish strode into his office radiating self-assertion and dropped into a slender American Chippendale chair with an impact that made it creak, his heart sank. Armstrong was in his fifties, stout though not fat, gray hair worn too long, side whiskers too long, a nose too bulbous . . . something sly in his expression, the look of a man focused on his own interests and none too scrupulous in their pursuit. But Madison rebuked himself: dislike was coloring his estimate.

"Mr. President, I accept your offer," Armstrong said. His voice was shrill and forceful, a tone schooled in anger. "You'll see an end to the tomfoolery so common here."

Restraining his irritation—after all, there *had* been tomfoolery—Madison laid out the problems. Armstrong listened with an expression that gradually shifted from patronizing to impatient to bored. Finally he raised an interrupting palm.

"Mr. President, this really isn't germane. I can't do anything about the navy but I sure as hell expect to turn the rest of it around. Dearborn, now, it's a mistake to assign any weight to him—why, all his weight's right in his ass."

Madison frowned; gratuitous crudity offended him.

"But I'm formulating a plan that will bring immediate success. I don't see Napoleon as an issue—even if the British do dispose of him, it'll take a year and they'll find me in Quebec when they raise their heads. I'll lay out my plan, then go to the field myself to make damned sure of its execution."

Madison stared. Armstrong as field general?

"Go personally, you mean?"

"So I intend."

"I don't know . . . do you think it appropriate? I really need you here to get control of the entire department."

Armstrong raised his palm. "I'll have that in a month."

"No," Madison said. "I don't want you in the field. I need you here."

Armstrong paled and his lips drew into a taut line.

"As you wish, Mr. President."

Gradually his color returned as they talked, but his speech remained clipped and brittle. Madison wondered if among his faults was a tendency to hold grudges. When the man rose to go half an hour later, Madison sighed with relief. It was a bad beginning.

★   ★   ★   ★

"Colonel Winfield Scott, sir, Second Artillery."

He stood at attention in the Secretary's office. A month had passed since he'd reported the atrocity threatening his Irishmen. Madison had sequestered forty-six hapless Englishmen, men and officers alike, ready to hang two for one. The press in Halifax and Quebec had screamed, echoed by the Federalist press in Boston, but Britain hadn't hung any Americans.

The War Department didn't look much different, filling the little brick building cater-cornered from the President's House. The rows of clerks were still there, including the harried Henderson who had carried such a load for Eustis. Scott had seen more senior officers in the halls, wearing insignia of the new departments, but the air of frantic dithering remained.

The new Secretary—the Senate had confirmed him the day before by a margin of only eighteen to fifteen—made a show of examining papers, letting the Colonel wait. At last he looked up.

"Ah, Scott. Let's see." A pause. "Second Artillery? Izard's outfit? Yes. Well, Scott, Izard's going on to greater things. I'm making him a brigadier. You'll take the regiment. Get it on the road to the Niagara frontier."

"Very well, sir. Thank you, sir. Mr. Secretary, my experience at Queenston urges the value of training. I'd like to spend a month putting the men through rigorous—"

"No, no, get 'em moving. Train en route if you must. My view is that if they know which end the bullet comes from, they're all right. Properly led men will fight—show 'em the enemy and tell 'em to go. What else can they do?"

Scott didn't answer. Armstrong should have seen the skulkers in the bushes at the base of the cliff at Queenston. He should have seen the slump in Van Rensselaer's shoulders, visible even from the heights, when his men turned their backs . . .

"Now, Scott," Armstrong said, "I have something else for you, too. You'll be adjutant general—chief of staff, in effect—to General Dearborn."

"In Albany, sir?"

"Dearborn will be on the Niagara frontier by then. I want you to stick a corn shuck up his ass and set it afire. I want to see some action out of that lazy sluggard."

Scott hesitated. He intended to command the United States Army entire one of these days, and the road thereto didn't lead through desks. But Dearborn was a damned old woman who would come immediately to depend on anyone with vigor.

"Sir, I want an assurance that when action comes, I'll be leading my regiment."

Armstrong grinned. "Not a desk man, then?"

"No, sir. I'd like that written into my orders."

"Oh, you would, would you?"

"Yes, sir. I'm a fighting officer."

"Well, by God, you're about the only officer around who fights worth a damn. It'll be in your orders."

"Thank you, sir."

"Dearborn objects, see me. I'll be there."

"On the Niagara, sir?"

"Exactly. You can't run a war from Washington. That's crap. People don't understand, let 'em live and learn."

Scott kept his expression neutral. "Yes, sir."

"Fine. Can you leave today?"

"Ah." He was thinking very fast. He'd been invited for the weekend to Colonel Tayloe's Virginia estate, courtesy of Sally McQuirk. In the last month he'd seen her often, calling at her home, escorting her to parties, joining her at important dinners. It had been sweet agony, occasional kisses exploding into passionate embraces from which she jerked away, trembling but determined. And now, Colonel Tayloe's invitation in his pocket and the prospect of four glorious days with Sally burning his mind, orders came.

"Sir, I believe Colonel Tayloe's an important figure?"

"Of course. Owns half of Washington and runs the other half, so they say."

"Sir, I'm invited to his country home for the weekend."

"Are you indeed? I haven't been so favored."

"It was my thought that if it meets with the Secretary's approval, I might do some good for the army there."

Armstrong smiled. "A bit more to it than that, I'd guess, but by all means go. Pick up your orders when you return."

★ ★ ★ ★

It was eleven on Monday night. Scott would leave in the morning and take the afternoon stage to his command in Philadelphia. The four joyous days with Sally almost behind him, he was restless and unhappy.

Her room was next to his. He had tried the door the first night and each night since, feeling increasingly foolish. Locked tight. He knew she heard the knob turn, but she'd said nothing. He wouldn't try tonight. He ached for her, in his loins and in his heart, but he couldn't shake the notion that they were dangerous for each other. She was wise to resist, since he couldn't. Sally . . .

A sharp click. He turned quickly and his breath caught in his throat. She stood in the open doorway between their rooms, a fireplace blazing behind her. The light outlined her magnificent body—her gown was sheer and she wore nothing beneath it.

There was a tremor in her voice. "Some sherry?"

Her nipples stiffened before his eyes. He could see the shadowy center below. Her bed was neatly opened.

"Ah, God, Sally!"

He was near choking. He lifted her in his arms. Her mouth opened to his; he laid her gently on her bed and fell beside her.

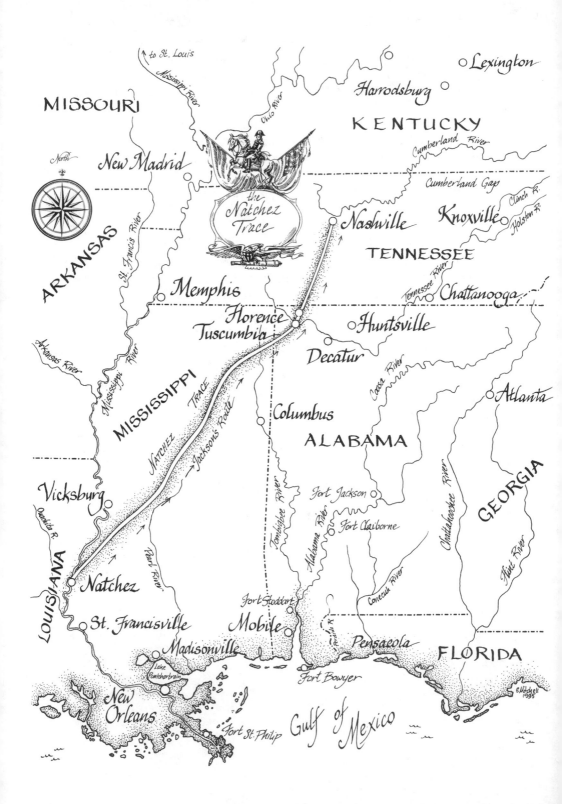

9

★ ★ ★ ★ Something was wrong. With each day that passed, Andrew Jackson's suspicion hardened. He and two thousand of Tennessee's best were pinned in wild, rollicking Natchez on the lower Mississippi, the only stopping place of note between St. Louis and New Orleans, held there for an interminable month by orders that made no sense when he'd received them and now seemed downright sinister. This was the reason his troops had been called to hurl the Spanish out of Florida? To rot here? No, sir! Something was going on.

Yet he wasn't quite sure how to proceed, and the uncertainty intensified his feeling that he'd been drawn into a trap. He shook his head. We'll see about that: catching Andrew Jackson short was no easy matter. Less so now, after two months of feeling out the nuances of field leadership. Every expectation of his ability had been proven; his metier was the capacity and the courage to command.

A soldier by instinct, he'd carried for years an inner conviction that he was capable of greatness. And if greatness came, it would be in the form of military grandeur, triumph on the battlefield. But destiny also depends on circumstance, and during his ten years as the elected major general of Tennessee militia, there'd been no war.

So the call to arms came as destiny's trumpet. It started uncertainly, for the Madison administration tried to squeeze him out. It asked for Tennessee troops without their general for the march on Florida from New Orleans, but Governor Blount refused to separate the men from their commander, and Jackson swallowed the affront. Harder to swallow—though he did it— were the orders to serve under General Wilkinson, an unmitigated scoundrel.

Everyone understood that for years Wilkinson had sold himself to the Spanish as secret agent while he commanded American troops in the West from headquarters in New Orleans. It also was common knowledge that he took fat profits for leaving smugglers unmolested. And there was that old score still unsettled from the Burr imbroglio, when the blackguard accused Jackson to hide his own complicity. But Jackson swallowed, wormwood on his tongue.

He mustered his troops, sent the cavalry regiment overland, six hundred hard miles on the Natchez Trace, and floated the two infantry regiments downriver on long flatboats. At Natchez, a hundred fifty overland miles north of New Orleans, Wilkinson's orders awaited: hold here until further notice. Jackson raised his tents and lean-tos along a creek where he and

Rachel once had talked and dreamed, where tulip trees and black willow scattered on open ground left room to drill.

Initially he was in good spirits, but letters from Wilkinson in New Orleans continued to hold him in place with no mention of plans. Florida as an objective seemed quite forgotten, and he began to smell betrayal in the air. His troops grew restless. Rain fell in torrents. Rations shrank. He was out of ammunition. His medical supplies ran out and his sick list soared beyond a hundred fifty—malaria, dysentery, Mississippi Valley ague . . .

And the French disease, for his boys still came to stare and stayed to play in the fleshpots of Natchez-under-the-hill, the saloons and whorehouses on the flats below the bluffs of Natchez proper that served the boatmen plying the long, lonely reaches of the Mississippi. He put it off-limits and posted guards, but the lure of women and whiskey, fiddle music and laughter and gunshots, was irresistible.

He often rode the creek, taking solace in warm memories of Rachel and the happy hours they had spent here weighing their future together in that wild time when he'd hurried down the Natchez Trace to marry her on news of Robards's divorce.

Looking back, all they'd dreamed had come to pass. There had been hell along the way, harder on her than on him, but no regrets. The trouble had strengthened them—well, yes, she said it made him too ready to fight, and maybe she was right. He shouldn't have whipped Eb Clute. She'd been upset and Clute had left the militia. Still, God damn it, his willingness to challenge every imputation of scandal had saved them, too, and she knew it. It gave him control of a situation that would have destroyed them if he'd let it dominate. Control . . . by force of personality, by force of action.

And now he was stranded on the banks of the Mississippi, thanks to a worthless scamp in New Orleans who treated the Tennessee army as a plaything. No question, that was the problem, and Jackson knew better than to let control shift from his hands. He'd built a life on that premise.

His fist smacked into his palm. Yes! It was time to force the issue. Go to New Orleans and face the man down.

His mind made up and equilibrium thus restored, he was headed for camp when he saw Tom Benton and Jack Coffee hurrying toward him. Coffee, who commanded the cavalry regiment, was an old friend who'd proved his constancy; always there, always ready. He was a big man with black hair and wrathful complexion, his voice a slow, deep rumble full of authority. Benton, of whom Aunt Rachel, as he called her, was so fond, was younger, quicker, a good lawyer who never forgot his profession. He wore his shako at a rakish tilt over those auburn curls and his men admired him.

He was waving a letter from the Secretary of War.

Sir,

 The causes for embodying & marching to New Orleans the Corps under your command having ceased to exist, you will on receipt of this Letter, consider it as dismissed from public service, & will take measures to have delivered over to Major General Wilkinson, all articles of public property which may have been put into its possession.

 You will accept for yourself & the Corps the thanks of the President of the United States.

 Very Respectfully I am Sir your most obt Humble Servant

John Armstrong

He felt oddly dizzy, as if the world quivered as he trotted into camp. What in hell was going on? Dismissed? In the middle of the wilderness, six hundred miles from home? It was idiotic. Was the new Secretary mad?

What were the Tennesseans to do? Food, ammunition, and medicine exhausted, Mississippi Valley miasma felling more every day, and he was to dismiss them? Give them the President's thanks and tell them to go to hell? It was criminal.

"I smell a dirty trick," Coffee rumbled.

As he swung off his horse he saw immediately that the men were disturbed. A small crowd had gathered and more were coming. Then he saw Pinkney Mims with an iron grip on a horse-faced captain who was squalling like a castrated calf.

"What the devil, Pink?" Sergeant Mims had biceps like hams and the Captain struggled helplessly. Jackson liked Mims; he served as orderly, guard, cook, and wrangler, and though weak on military protocol, he was a natural reflector of army feeling.

"Sir," Mims said, "I had to drag this sumbitch along, but I figured you'd want to know he's recruiting right in our camp."

"Recruiting?"

"Trying to get the boys to sign up with the regulars."

Jackson stared. "Who the devil are you, Captain?"

Mims released him and the fellow shrugged his uniform straight. He looked aggrieved.

"Matthew Derden, General Wilkinson's staff. I'm just giving your men an opportunity, General. What the hell, they're being discharged here. They might as well sign on with the regulars, that's the whole idea. What else'll they do?"

So! There *was* a plot, by God! They'd always wanted Tennessee troops without Jackson, and that was still their aim. Governor Blount had thwarted them, so they'd engineered this little scheme. Dump the Tennessee men here without supplies, and they must join Wilkinson's regulars or starve. And their general could go home a laughingstock.

Three young soldiers whom he recognized from his sick bay approached. One was flushed with fever and staggering; the others steadied him.

"Sir," the feverish lad said, "you ain't gonna leave us, are you?" His eyes glistened, his cheeks glowed red.

"Leave you?"

"We hear the gov'ment is going to cut us loose right here in Natchez. General, you got a lot of sick boys, some of us can't hardly move, ain't no way we can care for ourselves, we get left here in this godforsaken wilderness we'll just flat die—"

Derden, trying to implement this Madison-Wilkinson plot, had alerted the whole camp. The men crowded closer.

"All right, boys." Jackson raised his voice. "Nothing has changed. You're still under orders. You're not discharged—" He hesitated an instant and the decision formed, swift as a bird taking flight. "And you won't be discharged till I turn you loose on the square in Nashville. I'm taking you home, every last one of you. Now go spread the word: we're going home!"

He saw Benton turn, a lawyerly objection forming as the men began to cheer, but this was challenge as direct as a glove across the face, and he never refused a challenge. What did leadership mean if it collapsed at the first obstacle? This was testing time: he could take control and care for his men or he could go home with his tail between his legs.

Abandon his men? His army was an extension of his very being, and any son of a bitch who thought to tear it from him had plenty to learn!

★ ★ ★ ★

"Sir, this is a recipe for disaster," Benton said. "You are disobeying a direct order."

Coffee grunted. "Some orders want disobeying."

Good old Coffee. Jackson smiled, feeling at ease for the first time in weeks, the decision made, action in the offing.

"Discharge them," Benton said. "Then they're free agents. You can take them home just the same, but you won't have disobeyed orders."

Benton didn't understand the compact between leader and led.

"Well, Tom, to discharge them would be to abandon them. Sure, we could all walk home together, but they'd be a disorganized mob. Moving two thousand men through six hundred miles of wilderness—that's no easy matter, you know. If they're just a mob, they'll break up—the strong will forge ahead, the weak fall behind."

Control was the essence of leadership. The men owed him fealty; he owed them care, support, rescue. Discharge would break the contract by surrendering the control that was the glue holding the military relationship together. Discharge would be fatal to his army, because it would cease to be an army.

Benton wasn't really convinced. "General," he said, "we're at war and you'll be needed. I'm afraid this could destroy you."

Jackson shook his head. In fact, if he failed his men now, he would never have another command. He could go back to Tennessee and rot on his farm. No fighting man would serve under him. He would be finished.

★ ★ ★ ★

"Thank you for coming, gentlemen," Jackson said to the men who sat in a half circle around the table he leaned against. They were at Mickie's tavern, the splendid central meeting place of Natchez proper. The mahogany bar, the long mirrors, the heroic mural of Washington crossing the Delaware had come up from New Orleans by keelboat. Mickie's was very familiar to Jackson; he'd been a guest on many a business trip to Natchez. Noon was coming on and rich odors flowed from the kitchen. He knew all the men and had done business with most of them: Joe Bingham, whose store had everything from ladies' notions to hardware to strap leather; Handsom Gage with his ropewalk; Felix Embry the wainwright; William Wofford in feed and grain; the miller, Van Manning; and a few others.

"I'll need rope in hundred- and two-hundred-foot coils, three-quarters and three-eighths, axes, sledges, nails, saws, and, let's see . . . yes, wagons, about a dozen, and horses to draw them. Some packhorses. Medical supplies. Cornmeal, flour if it's on hand, coffee, sugar, salt, beans, rice, plenty of fatback—well, that's the idea. Colonel Benton has the full list."

"God Almighty, General," Joe Bingham said. He was a tall man but badly stooped, one eye milky and blind, the other shifty, though Jackson had known him for years and always found him straight. "That's one hell of a big order."

"Amen," Handsom Gage said. Jackson had never liked Gage, a perpetually hostile man with a big voice and hair so light it looked white.

"Well, I'm moving two thousand men over six hundred miles. We'll be a month."

"What's the matter with what you got?" Bingham asked.

Gage laughed, a grating sound. He stretched his legs and crossed them. "He ain't got nothing. Had to turn it all in. Captain Derden told me Jackson's boys'll be starving before long."

"Well, General," Bingham said, "that do bring up a point. Who'll pay for all this?"

"Who do you think, for God's sake? The War Department."

"Way we heard it," Gage said, "you ain't under War Department orders no more. Captain Derden says you'll be court-martialed and the gov'ment ain't going to pay shit."

Bingham rolled his shifty eye, looking embarrassed. "I wouldn't put it that way," he said, "but I guess it's about the fact. You got to see it from our side, General. This is big—the gov'ment don't pay, we're ruint."

"Very well," Jackson said. "Then I'll sign for them on my own account."

"General," Benton said with a look of alarm. Jackson raised a restraining hand. Yes, certainly, he would be ruined should the government refuse to honor his vouchers, but he didn't need Tom to tell him that. He shrugged. Duty's duty.

"Put your own personal signature on it?" Bingham asked.

"Exactly. You gentlemen know me. We've done business. You know the value of my word."

"Well, maybe it's good and maybe it ain't," Gage said. "Way I hear it, he's in a peck of trouble."

Big Jack Coffee stood up. He loomed over Gage. "You got something to say, mister?" His rumbling voice was menacing.

There was a long silence. Then Bingham said, "All right, General, I reckon we'll do it. But you know me, too. I want to tell you right here and now, we don't get paid, we'll file a joint action in Nashville. We'll come after you. Just so you understand."

Jackson smiled. "Why, Joe, that's what I'd expect."

★ ★ ★ ★

The first seventy miles from Natchez were relatively easy. The Trace—French for trail—ran parallel to the river through bottomland. Then it bore eastward, into the Chickasaw Nation and on to Choctaw country. They made thirty miles the first day, twenty-five the second, the cavalry marching a half day ahead, the two infantry regiments a mile-long snake winding through occasional settlements, pastures, cornfields. Then the trail turned into deep forest. It narrowed to a dozen feet, and trees full of new leaves joined overhead to make long green alleys.

White men had used this trail for seventy years, Indians for centuries, following animal paths. The Natchez Trace tied to the Great Lakes Trail from the north and the long route from the east that passed through the Cumberland Gap. Jackson could remember when it was just a path—when he and Rachel, newly married, came home on horseback in a large party for protection, there'd been plenty of places where horses had to go single file.

It was an avenue now. President Jefferson had ordered it widened to twelve feet for wagons, stumps cut to a height axles would clear. There were scattered Indian settlements, ferries at a couple of the biggest rivers, a few rude inns like the miserable hole where Meriwether Lewis had killed himself. Travelers—flatboatmen walking home; merchants carrying bags of gold from the sale of tobacco, hemp, flour, pork, iron taken downriver; caravans hauling the wines and silks that gave Nashville its cosmopolitan air—banded together in large parties. Between bandits and Indians, it was as good as a man's life to travel the Trace alone.

Jackson rode the line on his favorite mare, a bay with a white blaze. Some fifty of the sickest men rode draped on sacks and boxes of supplies as wagons jolted over deep ruts. The merchants had delivered—he shut from his mind the consequences should Washington default—and the boys had visibly relaxed when the wagons rolled into camp.

His decision to pay if the government wouldn't had flashed across the camp.

"Boys know what you done," Pink said. "They ain't gonna forget it."

And he could see that the leadership dynamic had changed. It had been commander to soldier, but the national government had cut them loose and they were on their own, a Tennessee family again. As they passed into the third day and into deep forest, there was an air about them he hadn't seen before—easy smiles, an occasional wave as he rode the line. Still, he was mounted; he looked down and they looked up.

That afternoon, two hours from camping, twenty miles behind them since dawn, he noticed a towheaded boy with a slouch hat jammed on long hair begin to stagger. Jackson reined up. The kid glanced at him, then his eyes rolled back and he fell.

Jackson swung down. The boy's cheeks burned. Malaria? Blue eyes opened. "Ah got the shits something awful."

A rangy youngster with a fierce blue-black beard—Forsyth, that was his name, a corporal—said, "That's Jasper Johnson. Doc's been giving him laudanum and belladonna, but it don't do no good."

"He should be in the wagons," Jackson said.

"He didn't want to ride when we was walking. Anyway, wagons're full, General."

Another decision that took only a second. "Couple of you get hold of him," Jackson said. "He'll take my horse. Boost him up."

"But what'll you do?" Forsyth asked.

"I'll walk."

A slow smile came over Forsyth's face. "Well, how about that?" he said. "Come on, boys, hoist ol' Jasper up."

Officers rode horses for quick mobility to the point of any trouble. But walking with his men, striding ahead on the hourly break—they marched fifty minutes, rested ten—and then working his way back, he had a whole new sense of them as individuals, heard a willingness to talk openly, and realized he was making a new connection.

That evening he summoned his officers. "From here on, gentlemen, we walk. Search out your sickest men and mount them on your horses. I don't want to see an officer riding tomorrow."

★ ★ ★ ★

He chopped out a hickory sapling to below the root ball, trimmed top and branch, and used the ax to shape the ball to a rough knob. Then he walked the line, smoothing the ball and peeling the length with his razor-edged clasp knife. By midmorning he had a serviceable staff. It became his constant companion, a walking man's tool. He was a foot soldier now.

★ ★ ★ ★

"She-it! Lookit the General shovel!"

It was dark. They were working by torchlight. The army had come to a stop in a chestnut stand only to find the cut leading out of a gorge they must cross broken down beyond use. The creek itself was shallow at the ford with a stony bottom, but it had carved a deep gorge with nearly sheer walls. The cavalry regiment's passage had left the far side unusable for wagons.

They broke out tools but had only a dozen shovels and a few mattocks, so Jackson assembled crews to work in half-hour shifts, then pass the tools to a new crew as they dug a deeper cut and stacked the overburden on cedar logs set in the outer edges. When one of the shifts was short a man, he took a shovel himself.

He'd forgotten the pain of shoveling. Five minutes and his back demanded relief; fifteen and he could feel blisters forming on his hands. He dug deeper, faster—lifting, tossing, fighting to keep his breathing if not even at least not gasping. The pain climbed from lower back to shoulders. It began as ache, turned to burning, sent threads and fingers of pain thrusting here and there, exploring possibilities for new agony. He stepped up his speed, keeping pace with the young lads beside him.

"Lookee, boys, ain't he something?" Silas Burger, a moon-faced boy from up around Gallatin, leaned on his shovel for a moment. "I didn't know you knew how to shovel, General."

"I live on a farm, Silas," Jackson said, willing his voice even with great effort. "Think I've never lifted dirt?" He tilted his head toward the other's stilled shovel. "But that don't mean I want to do it all by myself!"

There was a bray of laughter. "Get to work, Silas," someone yelled.

Jackson finished his shift at the same fierce pace, lips drawn against his teeth, and when he was done he stood quietly to one side, resisting the overwhelming impulse to sit down.

"Ol' General just keeps on going, don't he?" he heard Burger saying, and felt a burst of pride that was quite surprising.

★ ★ ★ ★

"Hunnert'n-one, hunnert'n-two, hunnert'n-three . . ."

It was late one night and Jackson was prowling the bivouac strung along the trail. He heard the voice chanting and turned in among the trees, curious.

Other voices picked up until it was a chorus. "Hunnert'n-thirteen, hunnert'n-fourteen . . ."

He came to a grove. Men lay around a blazing fire watching a wiry lad on the far side doing pull-ups on a pawpaw branch. Jackson could see his face clearly in the firelight each time he cleared the branch. A broad face that seemed to have no eyebrows—and then he realized the eyebrows were so light in color as to be near invisible, and knew why the face was familiar.

He'd seen it this afternoon. The soldier had been riding Tom Benton's big gelding, slumped over in pain, and here he was—

Jackson stepped into the firelight. The soldier saw him, dropped from the limb, staggered, put his hand to his forehead, cried, "I don't feel so good, boys."

The General was on him in a stride. ""You little shit!" He slapped him hard, knocked him down. "On your feet, God damn you!"

"What the hell?" a tall sergeant said.

Jackson whirled. "I'll tell you what. He's ridden all day while sick men walked."

"Ah, Rufe," the Sergeant said, "you always were an asshole. What're you gonna do with him, General?"

"Lay that hickory stick on him, General," someone yelled.

The court-martial convened fifteen minutes later, two officers, two sergeants, two privates. It heard testimony for ten minutes, took five more to convict, two more to set punishment: fifteen lashes. Jackson ordered the lout strung to a red oak.

He chose a husky soldier who said he didn't know the prisoner to swing the strap. On the first stroke the miscreant—Rufus Peeler was his name—began to cry, and on the second he started to scream. With each stroke he screamed louder. On the seventh his back began to bleed. Jackson watched with a stony face. The malingering bastard deserved everything he got.

★ ★ ★ ★

He trotted up the stopped line. A group had formed around a man lying in a riot of dandelions. Jackson's pretty mare with the white blaze stood to one side, patiently cropping around the bit. Yes, on the ground was the lad he'd given his horse.

"He just fell off, General. Done passed right out."

"We'll get him in a wagon," Jackson said. There was more wagon space as supplies were used.

They lifted the soldier in a blanket. His eyes fluttered open.

"Where am I?"

"You're going home, son." Jackson smoothed the boy's long hair off his hot forehead and put his slouch hat on his chest. "Be there before long. You rest easy, now."

★ ★ ★ ★

A blazing full moon in a cloudless sky. It was too good to pass up, and he ordered the march to continue till midnight. Brilliant stars dimmed as the moon controlled the night. It was dark under the leafy limbs that canopied the trail, but light glowed around leaf edges like holy fire and bathed them in benediction when branches parted.

"Hell's bells, General," said a soldier with a very young voice, "I am shore wore out. How far you reckon we're going today?"

"More than thirty, less than forty," Jackson said.

"Well, Goddam, m'legs feel like a couple of stumps."

The boy was so young, the voice so innocent and artless, that Jackson had to laugh out loud.

An older voice—Sergeant Kimbrum, Jackson thought—said, "You get the General's point, sonny boy? He's got a few gray hairs but you don't hear him crying."

"Well, shit, Sarge," the boy said, "I wasn't—"

"You was getting ready to. You take a lesson from the General. That way you'll grow up to be a man."

★ ★ ★ ★

"Heave, God damn it, heave!"

Jackson's arms and shoulders ached. They were at the Tombigbee; Pink Mims swam over with a three-eighth line and pulled across a small float to which a pulley and a three-quarter line were fixed. He rigged the pulley to a stout chestnut, swam back, and with the light line pulled the heavy line through. With a second pulley set well back on this side, the line attached to a log raft and men to heave, they had a serviceable ferry hauled by muscle power on the shore and were crossing wagons, supplies, the sick, and those unable to swim.

It was donkey work. Jackson took a place on an open spot on the rope but he hurt all over. He had walked four hundred miles; his boots were broken; each step sent pain to weary muscles and joints forty-six years old and a frame scarred by bullets.

He heaved, catching the rhythm, willing the pain to diffuse, his body to absorb it, his mind to forget it—

A rough hand caught his arm. Sergeant Mallet, a towering lumberman from the Duck River country, said, "Give me that rope, General. We need you for more than hauling line, now that's a fact. We'd be in the shitter if you wore out on us."

★ ★ ★ ★

They were getting close; the Tennessee River was up ahead, and fresh supplies awaited them at Colbert's Ferry. Though state-purchased, they brought his debt to the Natchez merchants to the front of his mind. His signature would destroy him if the government let him down. Could Madison be so small? Benton had said he would go to Washington to press their case personally with the Tennessee congressional delegation.

Still, nearing the end, Jackson was ebullient. He awakened long before dawn, Venus still brilliant, to prowl his camp stretched along the trail. He didn't post guards, since neither Indians nor bandits would attack so many. His enemies were shrinking rations, medicine chests exhausted, his sick list growing, space in the jolting wagons at a premium. Day after difficult day they marched, muscles aching, feet blistered, fording streams, wading swamps, drenched by downpours, and warmed by spring sun. They were bearded now, their butternut shirts and breeches torn, but they didn't stink, nor did he. They camped by creeks, drinking upstream, bathing and washing downstream.

And their spirits were high as they neared home; walking before dawn he heard laughter and smelled coffee and frying fatback, probably the last of both. Listening, smelling rude breakfasts on little fires, he was suffused with love for these men. It had to do with cutting loose from the government, assuming the obligation that kept food in their bellies, stepping down from the heights of the saddle and walking with them, sharing experience that bound leader to men and men to leader.

Individually they could be sons of bitches in need of the lash; collectively they were noblemen. They were American bedrock, their strength what assured the future and made the pirouettes of leaders possible. Presidents and generals were, after all, creations of the led who themselves were the gut center of the nation. They were the men who would drive westward, who would fill the incredible country that Lewis and Clark had blazed in the national mind a few years ago. They were the reason you could count on jurors and trust voters, the reason democracy must grow till narrow elitist Federalists disappeared. Democrats in yellow shoes . . .

"Don't let them gray hairs fool you," a voice said. He knew they were talking of him and he stopped, listening shamelessly, leaning on his hickory stick. Over the sound of fatback snapping in the pan he heard the voice add, "He's a tough old son of a bitch."

"It don't pay to fool with him." Another voice, high, almost squeaky. "Just ask Rufe Peeler. He ain't likely to forget the old man."

"But don't forgot what he done for us. Told the gov'ment to kiss his ass and pledged he'd pay the way. You can't beat that."

"Ol' Jackson's all right," the squeaky voice said. "Walked the whole distance, running up and down the line . . ."

"Tough as that damn hickory stick he carries."

★ ★ ★ ★

That evening, Pink Mims said, "You know what the boys are calling you? It's all over the camp." He hesitated, then blurted, " 'Ol' Hickory,' that's what."

"The hell you say." He didn't smile. "I'll lay a length of hickory up their backsides, they don't move along right smart."

10

★ ★ ★ ★ It was one of those brilliant days that bless Washington in winter, when spring is near, the air is soft, and forsythia buds can hardly wait. Madison was taking a rare afternoon away from his desk. He'd moved to the garden, where rosebushes were strawed against cold and bentwood furniture stood in a cluster. He sat in the sun, a red muffler around his throat, reading Frederick's *Tactical Elements,* to which young Scott had introduced him. Frederick the Great had changed the very notion of warfare in Europe, and Madison was stirred as work of true intellectual force always stirred him.

So the sound of a door opening was an intrusion, the more so when he saw Rufe Dumster lead Secretary of War Armstrong into the garden. He sighed, put a bookmark in Frederick, laid him by the now-cold teacup. The Secretary wore a black greatcoat too heavy for the day carelessly thrown open, and an expression that was an odd mix of satisfaction and uneasiness, and reminded the President of how little he liked the man.

It wasn't that Armstrong hadn't done well in the eight weeks since the Senate had confirmed him. By sheer force of will he'd snatched the department out of the chaos Eustis had left, he'd reorganized supply systems, he'd created a professional tone long lacking. That part was fine.

But he was boldly arrogant and kept the cabinet in turmoil. He immediately elevated Albert Gallatin's worst enemy, when Gallatin's Treasury Department was so essential, and he was openly contemptuous of Monroe at State, whom he viewed only as a rival for the presidency. Indeed, everything he did appeared shaped to that single end—succeeding Madison in the next election.

"Alfresco, eh?" he said. Madison took it as a sneer for a leader who would spend time sitting in the sun. The Secretary bowed, dropped heavily into a chair, waved aside Madison's offer of tea, and then quite casually presented devastating news. Madison sat rigidly, scarcely breathing, the story beating on his mind, drum taps on an acutely sensitive membrane.

An express was in from the west. General Harrison, advancing at the head of Ohio volunteers to reclaim Detroit after Hull threw it away, had received a plea for protection from American settlers at Frenchtown on the River Raisin a little below Detroit. He sent General Winchester, a planter-cum-general, with six hundred Kentucky volunteers to the rescue. A force of redcoats and Indians under General Proctor swept down from Detroit to meet Winchester on the River Raisin, feinted and darted and struck him from all sides, and when he was reeling, took his surrender.

Another defeat. Another disaster that would dismay the war's supporters and delight its opponents. Could we do nothing right? Were British soldiers so superior? And the instant answer followed: no, but their generals were. Raw Americans fresh from farms were meeting officers who'd honed their skills in the field against the best troops in the world.

But there was more. A hundred of Winchester's wounded were sheltered in Frenchtown houses. While the British looked the other way, their Indians went from house to house and murdered the wounded Americans with knives and tomahawks.

Hacked them to death in their beds—he could hear the screams of wounded youngsters too weak to lift their arms in defense, see the gouts of blood spattering rude log walls . . .

Suddenly all the rage he'd kept himself from voicing against Hull seemed to explode in his mind. He was silent, much too disciplined to cry out against the roaring in his ears but shaken to his core. A court-martial had sentenced Hull to death, and the miserable toad deserved it. Deserved every bit of it. A reservation flared in Madison's legal mind—Dearborn had sat on the court-martial when his own failure in the East had left Hull without support—but he thrust it away.

"My God!" he cried, but in a moment he realized the cry had been only in his mind and his heart, for Armstrong was still talking. Gradually, alerted by the Secretary's satisfied, almost pleased expression, what he was saying penetrated Madison's agony.

"Well, it do say a mouthful on the way the war's been run, don't it now? Bad, bad. Before my watch, of course—I'd never have countenanced it. Monroe's doing, I expect—you know what they say in New York? Too many Virginians spoil the broth. Haw!" He gave Madison a brazen look. "Present company excepted, of course. This Harrison—what's his name, Henry?"

"William Henry Harrison." He'd heard Armstrong was repeating the Virginia slur wherever it might advance him. "Harrison's been governor of Ohio Territory for years. He's the one who destroyed half of Tecumseh's force two years ago at Tippecanoe. I'd have supposed the name would be familiar to you."

"I've been serving abroad, you know. Paris is a bit remote from places like—what, Tippecanoe? I suppose it is a place?" He chuckled.

"You're damned casual about it!" Instantly Madison regretted his outburst. But he knew the River Raisin story would stir violent alarm in the West, where Indians were viewed with special horror. The murder of a hundred wounded prisoners summed up the American view of Indians: they might be honorable by their own measures but they cared nothing for our standards of honor and fair play. Yet these were, after all, the only standards Americans had to live by.

But the message Madison read was British cynicism. Britons understood honor and fair play precisely as Americans did, while considering themselves to be infinitely more civilized than their country cousins. But they willingly sent savages against women and children and winked while a hundred helpless men to whom they'd promised safety were slaughtered in their beds. It was unconscionable, by God!

Armstrong had not missed Madison's tone. "I don't suppose I'm indifferent to any man's suffering, Mr. President. But in the grand scheme, the success I'm planning will soon wipe away the stain." He leaned forward in his chair. "My plans are all set. Very simple, very direct. From our base at Sackett's Harbor on the New York shore of Lake Ontario, we sweep westward. We cross the St. Lawrence while the ice still holds and grab Kingston. Then we've got the head of the St. Lawrence plugged, we've cut their lines to the west, and we run right down the St. Lawrence and take Montreal!" He slammed his fist against the table.

"Then, by God, you can take your pick—we can have the rest of Canada if you want, gobble it all up, or you sure as hell can bring the British to the bargaining table. Talk about twisting the lion's tail—this'll damn near tear it off!"

Madison liked the sound of that; it was what he'd advocated all along. His generals had insisted in fighting on the periphery—everyone remembered Montgomery dying on the heights at Quebec in 1775—but he'd wanted to strike at the heart. And reading Frederick had confirmed all his instincts.

"Yes, sir," Armstrong said, glancing at the book, "we don't need any European theorists to instruct us. This is a smashing plan. I'll get right on it—stir up Dearborn and I'll be in Kingston by May, in Montreal by fall."

Madison assumed the personal pronoun was rhetorical, since he'd long made his position clear—cabinet members belonged in Washington and civilian leaders shouldn't try to be generals.

Success against Montreal would be more than welcome, for nothing else had gone well. It daily was more clear that the devastating defeat Napoleon had suffered in Russia had crippled him, which would free more redcoats to descend on America. Congress, its Democratic margin cut in the painful last election, was ever more craven—it cut the soldier's bonus and refused to lower the enlistment age to eighteen, though boys of sixteen enlisted in the Revolution. At least it did cancel the edicts of corrupt courts in New England that were aiding venal young men in a scheme to defraud the government with false enlistments—claim the bonus but arrange not to serve.

New England . . . what a thorn that lovely region with its deep harbors and pretty towns had become. Once it was at the very heart of American patriotism; now the governors of Massachusetts and Connecticut still refused to release their militia, and Vermont's governor had just called his men home from Plattsburgh on Lake Champlain when everyone knew the lake was a direct invasion route from the north. The British could run down Champlain to Lake George, jump to the Hudson and on to the sea, and split off New England and New York City with one stroke. Plattsburgh was the place to stop them.

"Whoa, whoa, whoa, Mr. President," Armstrong said, laughing and holding up both hands. "It's not all that dark. I know Napoleon, dealt with him all the time as ambassador. He's a fireball, that one. He'll raise a new army and take Wellington to the dances. Lake Champlain? Hell's fire, the British won't be thinking invasion when I'm in Montreal looking at Quebec. Enlistments? Frankly, I don't give a damn. I can take Canada with what I've got and then they can all go home anyway."

"All's rosy, then?" Madison said. "But a British fleet's in the Chesapeake. Admiral Co'burn has burned several towns."

"Mere pinpricks."

"What's to keep him from attacking Washington?"

"Oh, for God's sake, Washington has no strategic value. This Admiral Co'burn, he'd like nothing better than to see me divert my resources to deal with him instead of taking Canada." He raised his hands again in that peculiar rejecting gesture. "Don't worry about it. You've put the war in good hands. Just rest easy."

"Be so good as not to patronize me, sir," Madison said.

Armstrong colored. "No offense meant, Mr. President. I thought you were asking."

"Not for reassurances, Mr. Armstrong. On another matter, why did General Jackson march his force home so precipitously?"

Of course, the immediate need for Tennessee troops had vanished when Congress lost its nerve and backed away from seizing all the Spanish outposts in Florida. It authorized General Wilkinson to take Mobile, an easy matter, but nothing more.

This flowed from the only good news Madison had had in months. Russia had offered to mediate the differences between Britain and the United States. That was fine; everything at stake in this war could—and should—be settled at the table. Britain already had abandoned her coercive trade orders; let her drop her mean policy of kidnapping American sailors on the high seas and they could solve matters overnight.

Since Spain was an ally of Russia, Congress feared that angering it could undermine the Russian move. And the next thing Madison knew, Jackson was marching his men home overland.

"Precipitous to say the least, the damned scoundrel!" Armstrong said, voice rising. "Those men were in for a year's enlistment, and I wanted General Wilkinson to have them. Now Jackson's demanding we pay for the march. What cheek. Sent one of his officers—Benton, I think—to push the matter, but I'm damned if he shall have a cent."

"Jackson dislikes Wilkinson, I believe."

"Proof of his own sorry nature, I'd say. Wilkinson is a good man. Friend of mine—we served together years ago. I'm thinking of bringing him north.

Nothing's going to happen in New Orleans anyway, and we can use his talents agin Canada."

Madison frowned. Wilkinson had been useful when old Tom wanted to sink Burr, but it was hard to imagine him—corpulent, complacent, devious, self-serving—in a field command.

"Anyway, I ordered Jackson to release his troops and he refused."

"Really? I think I'd like to see that order."

"Not necessary at all, Mr. President. It's an internal department matter. I'll deal with it."

Madison put iron in his voice. "I'd like to see the order."

Armstrong stood up. His face flushed scarlet, his eyes seemed to bulge. "Very well, sir." It was close to a snarl.

The Secretary left, but Madison's mood had changed and he couldn't go back to his book. The department copy of the letter to Jackson didn't arrive for a week, and Madison didn't have time to read it for another week. When he did, he saw instantly why Jackson had reacted with such fury.

He sat at his desk a long time, drumming his fingers on his blotter. Jackson's march to Nashville had shown the instinct of a real leader. If he faced court-martial, if he was destroyed financially, so be it. He saw his duty and acted. Felix Grundy, the Tennessee senator, said that Jackson came home a hero. "Old Hickory," they were calling him, the whole state.

Well, by God, Jackson deserved it. A leader who could seize the moment. Madison shook his head. No one would ever dub *him* Old Hickory. It must be nice to be loved by one's people.

He sharpened a new quill and wrote two orders to Armstrong. The first set aside the death sentence the court-martial gave Hull. Send the old man home and forget him. Sometimes the frailty of mankind was overwhelming.

The second ordered the department to pay all Jackson's charges for the march.

The next day he received a cautious note from a War Department clerk. The President's orders would be obeyed immediately. Then they would be forwarded to the Secretary, who had gone to join the army on the Niagara.

★ ★ ★ ★

The new carriage was a beauty, crimson and black and gold, Philadelphia's best. Shiny whip springs anchored braces to new Conninge axles that could go a month or two without oiling. It was exactly what she'd wanted, though Dolley did have to admit that the cost had given poor Jimmy a turn. Glittering in the sun, full of the delicious odor of newness, it went drumming across the Long Bridge and into the open Virginia countryside, the road to the left winding toward Alexandria, the half-done hulk of Arlington House looming on its hill to the right.

"Oh, Ned," she said, "isn't it a beauty!" Ned Coles had called her down to see the new carriage and on impulse she'd dragooned him for a ride with

Sime Puckett on the box. Sime, unlike Rufe Dumster, didn't eavesdrop. It was a glorious day in April, leaves bursting on trees, forsythia blazing— she just had to be in the open with the landau top down.

"So tell me everything," she said. Her young cousin was just back from Annapolis. Jimmy had sent him down to see the workings of the new embargo that was supposed to stop the infernal trading with the enemy by stopping all traffic, and then at the last moment the Congress had backed down—as usual—and refused to impose it. Jimmy was furious. Most of what escaped American ports was with British connivance, trade for its benefit, and the little that was left was sub rosa, braving the blockade and dodging the custom's collector as well. The embargo—if Congress had had any courage—would at least have slowed it.

"Well," Ned said, "what I wanted you to know was that he mentioned you. By name. Admiral Co'burn did."

By name? It gave her a queer turn and she needed a moment to get ready. "But first," she said, "tell me your adventures."

He grinned, looking very young. "I was on the gunboat *Ticonderoga* and it was something!"

When Congress lost its nerve on the embargo, Jimmy told the navy to do all it could to stop the brazen little boats sailing out to supply the very ships manning the blockade. Some people prized British gold far above honor!

"So," Ned said, "our gunboat pushed off looking to catch a certain sloop that the skipper said planned to sail at dawn."

Dolley loved the sea. Until the blockade, of course, passenger brigs were the basic means of travel. Passage from Washington to Philadelphia or New York, for example, was an agony by stage, a vacation by ship. Ned described it well and she could see it all unfold in her mind's eye, the chill pearly dawn, fog wisps on the sea suddenly lifting to show the sloop a quarter mile on with sails only lightly filled, the long sweeps on the gunboat splashing rhythmically, and then the breeze freshens abruptly, the sloop's sails snap full, her sleek hull slices ahead.

The gunboat galley turns and crowds on its own sail, its long oars dig deeper, it strikes an angle course to cut off the sloop as she bears toward a thirty-two-gun British frigate hove to in the distance. A huge jib billows off the sloop's bowsprit and she lunges ahead, but *Ticonderoga* still gains, the men working the great oars faster and faster to the bosun's chant—

And then the frigate comes about, slowly, lazily, her gunports drop open with a clatter you can hear across the ruffled water and her starboard guns run out bearing right on the gunboat and poor Ned's heart almost stops. He gazes into the muzzles, big, black, round, deadly, his mouth falls open, he feels the most stunning shaft of fear—they're going to run into *that*?

The gunboat is a bare sixty feet in length with a single twelve-pounder on her bow that would be like a pistol shot to the frigate. Ned is dizzy but can't cry out, and then the bosun's chant dies and he hears the skipper roar, "Belay the sweeps, belay the sweeps, stand by to come about!"

"Poor Ned." Dolley patted his hand. "Thank God the Captain had the sense to stop."

"But it hurt, you know, seeing that impudent devil running out to supply the enemy and not a thing to be done."

She was ready now. "So," she said, "what did the nasty British admiral have to say?" Not that Ned had been near him, of course. Admiral Co'burn was raiding towns on the Chesapeake. He would appear at dawn, lead a party of Royal Marines ashore, and an hour later the town would be in flames. He had hit a couple of towns up the bay above Baltimore, and now there was a new report, a tower of smoke over Havre de Grace visible for ten miles.

"Apparently he's a truly malicious man," Ned said. "Tall, skinny, overbearing, bombastic, fancies himself a wit. He always refers to President Madison as 'Little Jemmy.'"

"And how does he refer to me?" she asked.

"Well, Miss Dolley, I hesitate—"

"Say it, Ned."

"As Little Jemmy's fat wench, begging your pardon."

"My. He *is* a British gentleman, isn't he?" Still, it was disturbing, this desire to personalize and ridicule those who were enemies yet not without dignity. But this war brought out the worst—Quincy's talk of snakes leaving trails of slime, the worst Federalist papers calling Jimmy an impotent little man and implying that his wife turned elsewhere for marital comfort . . .

Filthy rubbish!

"So what is his message?"

"I heard it from half a dozen men. He always says the same thing. 'Tell Little Jemmy's fat wench I'm coming to see her. Tell her I intend to make my bow in her Wednesday Drawing Room.'"

She shook her head. "What a disgusting man. You think he intends to attack Washington?"

"That's what I think."

"So do I," she said.

★ ★ ★ ★

The man from the bank consortium in Boston was named William Thornton. He came as Dolley was serving an afternoon snack, and he smiled with pleasure when she invited him to join them. She liked him. A swarthy fellow with a bluish jaw, he displayed a touch of vanity she understood perfectly—always make the most of what assets one has. Mr. Thornton combed wisps of black hair across a bare skull. His eyes were warm and direct.

Albert Gallatin accompanied him, slender, swarthy, bald as an egg, looking his usual worried self. Dolley was fond of Hannah Gallatin, and when the Treasury Secretary despaired and wanted to go home to his Pennsylvania farm, Dolley would remind Hannah what a crucial role Albert played.

She led them into her lovely oval drawing room where comfortable Chippendale armchairs were grouped around a low table on which Joseph placed her silver coffeepot on its alcohol stove with plates of biscuits and scones and delicate cakes and little beef sandwiches at which the visitor's eyes brightened. Late afternoon sun poured through the tall windows. Over one window she drew the red curtains that had so disturbed Mr. Latrobe— "Oh," he'd cried in mock horror, "those red, red, red curtains, won't they be the death of me!"—so they sat in shadow and the rest of the room glowed in incandescence.

"My," Mr. Thornton said, glancing about, "how magnificent. Surely it speaks to a nation whose greatness is in potential." She was immensely pleased.

"I was in this room once before," he said, "years ago. I don't remember it quite so . . . golden."

"Mr. Latrobe and I have worked hard."

"To good effect, my dear," Jimmy said. Then, to Thornton, "I understand you've come to speak for our friends in the Boston banks on the sixteen-million-dollar loan authorization."

"Yes, Mr. President. Except that"—he hesitated—"I'm not sure 'friends' is quite the right word."

Jimmy smiled. "I was a little afraid of that. So what is the response?"

She held her breath, noticed Albert's hands trembling. So much depended on the answer and she was pleased to see that Jimmy's calm, assured expression showed none of her worry. The point was that the Congress, quailing again, had finally agreed to a small taxation but had delayed it until next year— and 1814 was still eight months away, and who knew when collections actually could be made? Or whether people would pay? The normal revenue source, customs collections for export and import, had dried up when trade died under the British blockade.

So Congress authorized still another loan, this time for sixteen million. But the nation's available money in a country much given to barter had pooled in banks in New England, the center of the shipping trade. There was just enough capital in banks in Philadelphia and Baltimore and Charleston to keep the local economy fluid.

Mr. Thornton cleared his throat. He glanced at Albert, whom he seemed to know well.

"Well, sir," he said, "you understand, I'm just a lawyer. An errand boy, so to speak."

"How much, Mr. Thornton?" Jimmy asked. He was so calm!

"Seventy-five thousand dollars, sir."

"Out of sixteen million?" Jimmy said.

"William," Gallatin said, his voice shrill, "that is an insult!"

"I think it's intended so," Jimmy said.

Mr. Thornton didn't answer. Then he said, "In fairness, Mr. President, they think the war is evil. They believe they'd be abetting the devil's work—"

"Oh, come, come, Mr. Thornton," she said. "Surely no rational person believes the devil lives in this house."

He smiled. "I hope they don't personalize it so, but the feeling in New England has gone far beyond political disagreement—ministers are attacking the war from the pulpit."

"They're demonizing the war," Jimmy said. "Demonizing *us*."

She knew he was right. It reminded her of Admiral Co'burn's venomous personalizing—it clothed an abstract in flesh and blood, and that put fire in the heart.

"Actually, though," Jimmy added, "I think they see the way the war and the embargo clamp down on their profits as the greatest evil."

She saw something flash in Mr. Thornton's warm brown eyes. He bowed without answering. Then, after a long pause, he said, "Of course, not everyone in New England feels that way. Some are much more sympathetic."

Albert frowned. "But not the ones who count."

Dolley said, "Perhaps Mr. Thornton describes himself."

"I'm just a small cog, madam. However, I did take the liberty of stopping in New York to speak to Mr. Astor. He's a warm admirer of yours, Albert."

Gallatin smiled. "We're from the same part of the world."

"He mentioned that. Called you a countryman, though I believe he's German, and you're Swiss, are you not?"

"But long since an American," Albert said. "Long since."

She winced. Their enemies always attacked poor Albert as a foreigner. She had met John Jacob Astor, a stout, solid man whose German accent was still strong, his mouth a slash that radiated determination. Importing, exporting, strong in the new and difficult but highly rewarding China trade, already dominant in the fur trade . . .

She signaled to Joseph for more coffee.

"Mr. Astor said he would see David Parrish in Philadelphia and Stephen Girard," Mr. Thornton said, "and he thought together they could take a substantial portion of the loan. Factor some of it out to smaller men, of course."

"What nice news," Dolley said. She smiled. "I believe you're sympathetic to our problems."

"A traitor to my class, you mean."

"A patriot, I meant—who perceives reality, I might add."

He nodded. "I had a broadening experience—spent several weeks in Tennessee on land matters and got to know General Jackson rather well.

He gave me a view of the West—and hence of the nation—that certainly expanded my thinking."

"Really?" Dolley said. "Did you meet Mrs. Jackson?"

"Oh, yes, I was a guest in their home several times. She's a charming woman—intelligent, socially adept, gracious."

"Ah. Not a rustic, then."

"Not in the least. Broader accent, you understand, like Jackson himself. Some whars and thars creep into her speech. She likes her pipe, and the art on her walls isn't much, though I think she knows that. Mostly scenes on her own farm; she says they give her comfort."

"My," Dolley said. "What's their home like?"

"An old blockhouse. Very interesting. Some of the original loopholes are still intact. Makes you realize how new that country really is. Fighting Indians only twenty years ago."

"But you found Jackson thoughtful?" Jimmy asked.

"Highly impressive, sir. He's a man of vision. His sense of what the country can be, of its great continental sweep, a nation entire with coasts on the Atlantic and the Pacific, draining down its center in a single great channel guarded by New Orleans—well, it stirred me so that when I returned to Boston and heard such insular talk . . ." He smiled and shrugged.

The room, which had turned from gold to orange, softened to blue as the sun disappeared. Thornton stood to go, thanking Dolley for her hospitality. Then he added, "Well, New Englanders, they're my people and my fortune is tied to theirs. Too late to change that. But they're wrong on this and in time they'll see that. They want a seaboard nation they can dominate— the sweep of the West frightens them—but they'll lose. I think Jackson's right. Our destiny lies in the West."

"Oh, sir," she said, her hand in his, "and in the democratic spirit as well. Never forget that."

★ ★ ★ ★

Joseph, of course, had listened carefully. Seventy-five thousand dollars out of sixteen million sought? That alone told how this war was going. But he shrugged as he put dishes on his tray, brushed up crumbs, straightened chairs. It wasn't his war, it was the white man's war. When it was won, and he thought it would be, he'd still be a slave.

To be free was all in life he asked—and someday, somehow, he would have it. You couldn't read Hume and Locke, Montesquieu and Voltaire, Mr. Jefferson's Declaration or Mr. Madison's Federalist Papers, and not long for freedom. But freedom had burned in his heart when he was a child puzzling the alphabet, so it wasn't just reading, though he knew he was fortunate that the Madisons encouraged education. Few of his friends in the servant class of Washington could read, but all of them yearned for freedom.

Still, Joseph wasn't a fighting man. He was slight in stature and incapable of violence. Why, he wouldn't know where to begin. Nor would he run away and face the slave hunters, the floggers, the poor whites for whom abusing blacks was proof of superiority. The Madisons were haven against the real terrors of slavery. They didn't flog, they didn't sell. A man could marry and raise a family, and if he married off the plantation, Mr. Madison would buy his wife.

The Madisons were perfect owners, but that was the point. No man could own another's spirit, and it was intolerable that they could own his body. And sooner or later, Joseph would find a way to free himself, a way that didn't expose him to the slave hunters. He was as certain of this as that the sun would rise. It was the spark that fueled his life. Nothing else mattered—he must have no entanglements; when the day came he must be free to walk away.

He saw the darkening in his heart, the slow death of laughter, the price of the barriers he erected. But freedom was worth any price. Of course he envied the man who had a woman to love in the warmth of his own family. Could a man who denied himself family be whole? But then, family or no, could a slave be whole?

"Sst! Joseph!"

Heavy-laden with the tray, he was pushing the kitchen door open with his shoulder. He set down the tray and saw little Jennie beaming at him. Still skinny but filling out, she was like a little fairy, a dancing sprite, and she was in love with him. He knew it by instinct, not by experience. When he appeared her face lighted, and if he gave her one of his rare smiles, her delight was palpable.

She was as beautiful as a fairy, too, dark eyes clear, her skin a smooth chocolate that made him want to take her face in his hands, her neck strong and her carriage commanding, her budding breasts looking fuller every day. He'd been dreaming lately, he would lift her chemise, touch lips to rising nipples, and then start awake in a blaze of desire that left him shaken.

But Jennie was a snare. Give in to that hunger, that sense of her beauty, that joy he felt at the very sight of her, and he might as well throw away his dream. Yield himself forever to slavery's shackles. Was love worth that? He thought not, and he shook himself. Remember that. Remember what matters!

"What you want?"

Her smile dimmed slightly. "Cook, he say he need a ham, and I ain't got the smokehouse key."

"Very well. I'll get it." He turned away.

"Joseph?"

"Yes?"

"Oh, Joseph, don't you like me even a little bit? I do all I can to make you like me." She was trembling and he saw she'd summoned her courage. "I'd sew for you, I'd cook for you—"

"Don't talk foolish, girl."

She stepped close, her hand on his arm. "I'd love you, Joseph," she whispered. "Like a woman loves her man."

He could feel her breath on his face. Smell her faint scent, sweet and warm and lovely. He could feel himself slipping, slipping—

"Damn, girl! Stay offa me!"

She stepped back as if he'd slapped her. She stared at him, tears starting, then whirled and ran, hands over her face.

He'd never felt worse. But he was going to be free. Someday.

★ ★ ★ ★

Sally McQuirk found Miss Dolley in the family sitting room. It was late on a May afternoon, shadows on the ellipse lengthening, the sleepy buzz of foraging insects at the open windows. Sime Puckett, knowing her well, had sent her up alone; Ned Coles was still on the Hill in some probably fruitless maneuver with the recalcitrant Congress.

Poor Dolley! She looked exhausted, new lines in her face, gown slack over lost weight, graying hair pulled back in a careless bun from which strands escaped. The President was dangerously ill—for weeks there'd been talk he might not live, and Boston preachers were calling it divine retribution—and Miss Dolley had been his nurse through long days and longer nights. She sat at her kneehole desk with an oft-cut quill, her fingers ink-stained, correspondence stacked on her blotter. She rested her head on her hand.

"How is he?" Sally asked.

"Well . . . a little better, I guess. The fever's eased. If we just knew what's wrong! But you can't tell, the fever just comes—has all his life. Still, he's lived long in spite of it, and I think he will this time." Miss Dolley gestured wearily at the pile of letters. "People everywhere are writing, and must be answered. Go in and see him, Sally. The sight of you always cheers him."

She stole softly into his room. His eyes were shut, a book open on his chest. He looked . . . wasted. The thought made her realize she'd always seen him as square and strong. He seemed different though he looked the same, gray hair long on the sides and sparse on top yet with a widow's peak, new deep grooves from beside his nose to his straight mouth, lips so precisely shaped. Then she realized it was the eyes she missed, his dominant feature, light in color, steady, richly capable of compassion, fiercely intelligent. At which, he opened them, saw her, and smiled.

"Sally!" His voice was a whisper. "Dear child, how nice. Here, sit, sit. Had I dozed? Perhaps." He tapped the book. "I'm reading Jomini. Young

Scott says—you remember him, don't you? Anyway, he says Jomini is the key to understanding the military side of the French Revolution—and of Napoleon as genius. Genius . . ." His eyes closed.

She sat quietly. Oh, yes, she remembered young Scott. She thought of that night—and of the morning that followed. She'd known all along she would open her door and it had been all she'd imagined. Every delightful bit of it. He'd left before dawn, and she'd awakened two hours later in sheer horror—where did the night leave her? It wasn't the time for love. Maybe it would be, someday, but not now. She had a dream and there wasn't room in it for a man. Especially a soldier.

She didn't want to see him. She sent down a message—a headache, she would nap until noon. From behind her curtain she watched him make his departing bows and mount his horse. He looked at her window as the animal wheeled, but she didn't touch the curtain. A note awaited her. It was stiff and conventional, something ambiguous, perhaps slightly unpleasant between the lines that suggested he had reservations, too. She was at once relieved and deeply hurt, and those conflicting feelings had not changed.

A knock on the open door startled her. The President opened his eyes. Sime Puckett leaned into the room.

"Sir, there's a Mr. Webster from the Congress, says he has a message for the President from the House of Representatives. Says it's official, he must deliver it in person. I can't find Miss Dolley and Mr. Ned, he's not back, and I don't know what to do."

"Very well, Sime," the President said. "Bring him up."

Daniel Webster, a new congressman from New Hampshire and an arch-Federalist, had established himself rapidly. Everyone talked of him. Henry Clay had told her in that poetic way of his that the newcomer was a raven-haired fellow with an eye black as death's and as heavy as a lion's, and she'd looked forward to meeting him, if under circumstances more neutral than these.

But he scarcely noticed her as he strode into the room like a barrister taking command of a courtroom. He was thirty or so, not tall but powerful, thick-necked, a man of supreme assurance. She was struck immediately by his massive head, the leonine features, the protruding brow. Then he began talking and there was only the rolling thunder of his voice.

The resolutions . . . she'd never quite understood them, though Papa had explained. Something about those dangerous days before the war when Mr. Madison tried to play France off against Britain to the American advantage. Now the Federalists were saying it all had been a fraud—Napoleon had tricked the American leaders, meaning they were fools, or had connived with them, meaning they were venal and in the Emperor's pocket.

When Webster finished what amounted to an oration, he dropped his papers on the end of the President's bed.

"They shall be read," Mr. Madison said, "and the House shall have an answer." Then he moved his foot under the sheet and kicked the papers onto the floor.

Webster stiffened. "Well you may eject them from your sickbed, sir, for they are a prescription to bring you no great pleasure." He raised a finger. "Oh, sir! You have so much to answer for, fastening this damnable war on a suffering people who honored you with this great office, to which you've brought such shame! Bound yourself to the cause of an evil emperor, repudiated the brave British people from whom you sprung and who now fight alone for the freedom of the world. Ah, but now your vassaldom to the French is in deep arrears as that low Corsican staggers beaten from the snows of Russia . . ."

He went on for some time with this Federalist rhetoric, standard enough except for that magnificent voice and for the enormity of delivering it in an ailing President's bedroom, and Sally was thinking of jumping up and telling him so when the President sat up in bed, leveled a long, shaking forefinger at the young man, and shouted, "That will be enough, sir!" in a voice that was anything but a whisper.

"Do not come to me to criticize, sir, with your hands black with the tars of Federalism. Do not prate cheap Federalist doctrine blind as the snows of New England. Haven't you yet learned there's more to this country than your parochial little corner? Don't dare to criticize me, sir, when Federalists have done all they could to hobble their nation and cripple it in war."

She stared at him, amazed. He had come to life like the report of a pistol. He was staring, eyes burning, face flushed, with that intensity that she knew can come with fever when everything is clear and pours from the mind with utter force—

"It's your people who undermine their country, who encourage its enemies, who supply the very ships that blockade us—curs licking the boot that kicks them, sir!—your governors who refuse their duty, your militia who hide behind governors' skirts, your courts that connive with venal young men to defraud the government with false enlistments, your bankers who squat on their money like hens on their eggs, your ministers who cry from their pulpits of the devil's work when young Americans are dying for lack of support—oh, no, sir, do not dare preach to me, do not dare! Now begone, sir! This instant, sir!"

Webster's dark face had gone ashen. He stood a moment in silence, as if the President's voice still rang. His mouth worked, he raised a hand—

And Miss Dolley came into the room with the force of a Washington thunderstorm rolling thunder and lightning.

"What is the meaning of this? What are you doing?"

Webster made a half bow. "Daniel Webster, madam. I delivered official resolutions of the House—"

"What? Invade a sick man's room? Attack him in his own bed? Have you no shame, sir? Have you no decency?"

"Madam, I—"

"Get out, you miserable excuse for a human being! You utterly disgusting—get out or I'll take a broom to you!"

She was standing squarely in the doorway, one hand raised as if to strike him. Webster took a step toward her and stopped. She was blocking his escape and all at once Sally saw that he had taken on the mien of a whipped dog looking for a way to flee. Then the President's Lady stepped to one side; the Congressman scuttled out the door and was gone.

Sally wanted to cheer.

Miss Dolley's breathing slowed. "Oh, Jimmy," she said, "I heard what you told him—I've never been more proud of you."

11

ON THE NIAGARA FRONTIER
Spring, 1813

★ ★ ★ ★ On a morning in April when a brilliant sun hinted of warmth to come and dark branches were flecked with green, when the lake was clear but ice lingered in the coves, Winfield Scott walked from the waterfront of Sackett's Harbor, New York, past the navy yard and Fort Tompkins to the square stone house with wide porch serving the northern army as headquarters. A man sitting on the porch, feet on the railing, chair tilted far back, leaned forward to fire a jet of tobacco juice between the banisters.

Scott had brought the Second Artillery into Fort Niagara where that swift river poured into Lake Ontario, only to find that General Dearborn was at Sackett's Harbor, the American naval base one hundred fifty lake miles off at the eastern end of the lake. Secretary of War Armstrong was with him, as was Commodore Isaac Chauncey of the U.S. Navy, who had built an American fleet on the lake. Scott boarded a swift courier sloop.

He landed just after dawn wearing his best uniform, found Dearborn at Mrs. Boston's boardinghouse with his suspenders hanging around his knees as he shaved, took breakfast himself at Mrs. Boston's bounteous table, and walked to headquarters for the meeting the General said would start at nine. As for Dearborn, he reserved judgment; no man can stand serious scrutiny with his suspenders at his knees and shaving soap on his cheeks.

The fellow on the porch dropped his chair with a bang as he stood. He was forty or so, slender but wiry, with bright blue eyes. He brushed back a wisp of mustache with a forefinger and said in a curiously metallic voice, one used to command, "I reckon you must be Winfield Scott."

"At your service, sir."

"Jake Brown, brigadier general, New York militia. Had us a little scrap up to Ogdensburg on the St. Lawrence, them sons of bitches come across the ice in force and drove us back, and we don't like that one damn bit.

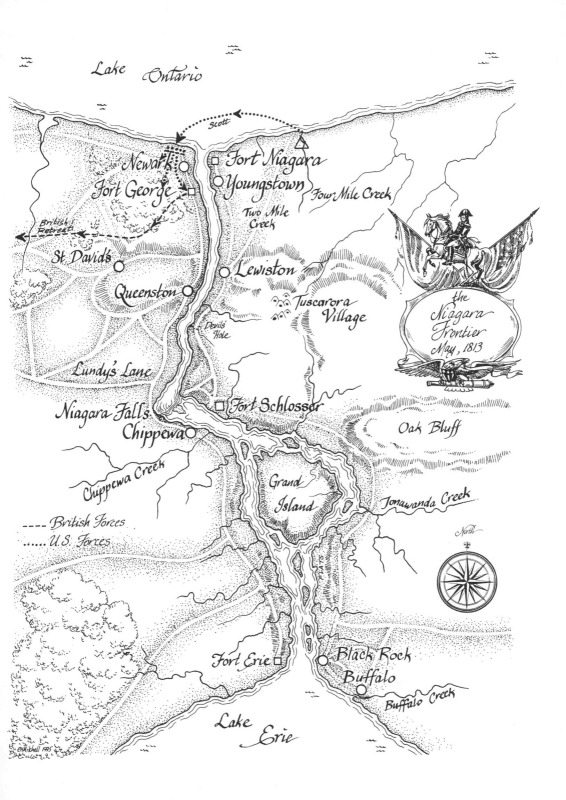

Lake Ontario

Scott

Newark
Fort George

Fort Niagara
Youngstown

Four Mile Creek

Two Mile Creek

British Retreat

St David's

Lewiston

Queenston

Devil's Hole

Tuscarora Village

Lundy's Lane

the
Niagara
Frontier
May, 1813

Niagara Falls
Chippewa

Fort Schlosser

Oak Bluff

Chippewa Creek

Grand Island

Tonawanda Creek

North

---- British Forces
...... U.S. Forces

Fort Erie

Black Rock
Buffalo

Buffalo Creek

Lake Erie

We were fixing on going back up and evening the score—righting the tally, know what I mean?—and the old woman says no."

"The old woman?"

"You met him yet? You're gonna love him. Just like being home with your mama." He cast his voice in falsetto. "Watch out, junior, lest your precious little butt gets shot off."

Scott laughed, liking him immediately.

"Now, Scott," Brown said, "I hear you like to fight."

"What we're here for, right?"

"If only everyone understood that. Well, I know about you from the Queenston story. The New York militia didn't shine there, but let me tell you, my troops fight like bastards or by God, they answer to me! Look— here's the old lady herself."

Dearborn lowered himself from a carriage. Even fatter than on that day when Scott saw him at the White House, he lurched when he stepped down. He wore a major general's uniform, no saber, and carried his shako. Wispy white hair left a round pink spot on top and his pale blue eyes had a rheumy, uneasy look.

"Well, Scott. Brown. Ah, yes, so to speak—well, let's go in."

Secretary Armstrong, black greatcoat thrown open, stout but fit, jumped down from the carriage and bounded up the stairs to pump Scott's hand and then Brown's. Behind him a tall, portly figure in naval uniform, cocked hat in his left hand, stepped down ponderously, florid face unsmiling, something remote and perhaps disdainful in his expression. Commodore Chauncey. He bowed perfunctorily when Scott and Brown were introduced.

Inside the front room, Chauncey marched directly to a window framed in oak and stood looking out, distancing himself, his very stance making clear that *he* reported to the Secretary of the Navy and was here as a mere courtesy to the Secretary of War, who had no say in naval matters. Armstrong went behind a table, pinned foolscap to the wall, and sketched as he talked. Chauncey watched but didn't leave the window. Dearborn's wooden armchair creaked when he moved. Scott took a seat by Brown in the back of the room.

Armstrong drew with quick, hard strokes. He was full of forceful enthusiasm and purpose, rising on his toes as he made points, rolling his shoulders like a fighter. The plan he laid out was superb, in Scott's estimation—the war might be over now if they'd followed such a plan at the start.

He intended to strike at British Canada's heart—starting with Kingston, where the waters of the the Great Lakes poured into the St. Lawrence River to run northward to the sea. Kingston with its major shipyard and naval base in American hands would cut Canada's lifeline to the West and open the way downriver to seize Montreal and then Quebec, and finish the war.

Armstrong looked hugely pleased with himself. He touched pointer to map with fierce little taps. Once they had Kingston and Canada could see the handwriting on the wall, they could tidy up the rear—take the village of York on Lake Ontario's north shore, then seize the Niagara peninsula itself, starting with Fort George across the river from Fort Niagara.

He turned confidently, planted both fists on the table, and smiled at his audience. Chauncey didn't speak.

Dearborn, sitting with legs spread, nodded several times as if making up his mind.

"Strong plan, Mr. Secretary." He puffed when he talked. "Yes, sir. Risky, but effective. And risk, after all, is the nature of war. Nothing is easy. Risk much and gain much obviously is your view, and I think it's daring of you. Yes, sir, daring."

Armstrong's smile disappeared. Dearborn went on in this vein for quite a while.

"Well, sir," he said at last, "no one ever said war was easy. High stakes. Disaster if you're wrong, glory if you're right." He drew himself up. "But be assured, sir, we'll execute your plan to the best of our abilities. And we'll see—the country will see—what happens."

Scott thought the slight emphasis Dearborn put on *your* wasn't lost on the Secretary.

"As for the navy," Chauncey said from the distance of his window, "be assured I'll help when I can. I am not under your authority, Mr. Secretary, but I know my superiors would want me to cooperate within the boundaries of the safety of my command."

General Brown glanced at Scott and rolled his eyes.

Chauncey raised a pontifical finger. "With great exertion, sir, untold hours of labor, and expenditure of treasure, we've built a strong fleet. At the moment we're stronger than the British fleet, but Sir James Yeo is hard at work and is not to be underestimated. At any moment the balance of power on the lake can change. Even now, a sloop of war is under construction at York. It will make my position perilous."

He eyed them with his head thrown back, imperious as a figurehead on one of his ships.

"Can we count on you to land troops and cover Kingston from the sea?" Armstrong said.

"By all means, sir. Provided, that is, that Sir James doesn't press overhard. Of course, my first duty is to my ships."

"Well, God damn it all," Armstrong said, "one point of taking Kingston is for its naval base."

"But that's of little use if my fleet is lost. You understand, I'm sure, I must be guided by caution."

"You men don't sound very confident," Armstrong said.

Neither man spoke. Then Dearborn said, "I shall obey your orders, sir." Again that faint emphasis on *your*.

"Suppose I left this to you gentlemen. What would you do?"

"I'd wrap it up slowly," Dearborn said. "First I'd take York, so it couldn't attack our rear when we move ultimately against Kingston. Then I'd cross the Niagara, take Fort George, and clear the peninsula. With that done, there'd be nothing to stop our taking Kingston and moving on to Montreal."

Scott sighed. This was idiocy. York was small and inconsequential. The Niagara was more important but still was peripheral. And by the time they succeeded at York and the Niagara, the British would have Kingston so fortified that taking it would be chancy indeed. But grabbing Kingston now while the St. Lawrence was still frozen and troops coming to the rescue from Montreal would have to march overland—that made perfect sense.

"Kingston last would be your choice?" Armstrong's voice was small.

"Yes, sir," Dearborn said, "but I'm a cautious man. Your plan is daring. Win all or lose all." Then, as an afterthought, he added, "I understand the British have seven thousand men in Kingston now."

Brown laid two fingers on Scott's sleeve. Two thousand in Kingston. Brown operated on the St. Lawrence; certainly he knew.

"Seven thousand? That's all we have, isn't it?" Armstrong hesitated. "Commodore?"

"Kingston last, I'd say," Chauncey said. "I'll happily attack York and add that sloop of war to my fleet. Kingston first . . ." He shrugged. "Well, I wouldn't want to be responsible."

Armstrong looked from one to the other. He shuffled papers on the table. "Well," he said at last, voice smaller still, "I don't like to go against professional opinion. I mean, I more or less have to be bound by what my professional officers tell me. Ultimately, they . . . well, they must be responsible."

Neither Dearborn nor Chauncey spoke.

"Very well, gentlemen. Do as you think best."

Outside, Brown said, "The damned old woman."

"Which one?" Scott said.

"All three. You know, one of these days these old hens'll lay an egg right on the President's desk, and as the preacher says, the scales will fall from his eyes. And you and I will be here. Stay in touch, Scott, we have work to do."

★ ★ ★ ★

A month later Scott was at Fort Niagara near where the river met Lake Ontario, laying plans to cross and drive a small but highly professional British army from the peninsula. He remembered Van Rensselaer's wretched planning and botched crossing with its cost in lives, national defeat, and wrecked careers. No more of that!

Major General Dearborn had welcomed his new chief of staff like an old man whose ambition in life has shrunk to staying warm by the fire, and within a week had given him the army. Or, at least, its planning. The more attack problems Scott solved, the more the General leaned on him. It was heady work, practice for when he wore stars of his own, which at this rate wouldn't be long.

But a wily opponent waited across the river to unhorse his ambitions. Brigadier General John Vincent had polished his skills against the French in Holland, and his force, though small, was formidable. He probably had fewer than a thousand soldiers, but they were good and he knew how to handle them. Knowledgeable men along the river talked most of the Glengarry Fencibles, a small band of Scotsmen in kilts who'd emigrated to Canada after service in the Royal Army and now were re-formed in a special combat unit—men who were well trained and fighting for their homes, a dangerous combination. He also had five hundred Mohawk warriors.

Scott had an army of five thousand supported by heavy artillery and Chauncey's guns. They were inferior in training man for man but sheer numbers should prevail if they were well led—and he would see to that.

The Niagara had moved to center stage after an expedition seized the village of York. Taking the peninsula wouldn't unlock Montreal but at least it would reverse the sorry failure of American arms and give the country something to cheer.

Which victory might—or, he feared, might not—assuage the dull ache that accompanied his every thought of Sally McQuirk's lissome figure, her golden hair piled atop her head, her vivid knowing eyes. Trouble was, it all had careered out of control. Their night together lived in bright memory—but so did the warning bells the next morning. Sally was not a woman to be taken lightly, nor had she led him to her bed casually. And my, what a woman!—intelligent, wise, clever, quick, so utterly knowledgeable in her milieu, to say nothing of beautiful.

But her milieu was not his, nor his hers, and they could spell disaster for each other. Did she mirror such thoughts? He took her decision not to come down before he left as a message. Still, he was heart-stricken when he looked up to give her a last salute and her curtain didn't stir. And neither time nor distance had healed the distress in which he'd ridden away that morning.

Work was antidote to pain. He plunged into the attack, assessing troops and commanders, studying the ground from the masthead of Chauncey's flagship, sketching careful plans.

When he presented them, Dearborn's pink pate glowed with pleasure and relief. Daily the old man grew more unsteady on his feet. His guts ached, he told Scott, he probably had dysentery, his head hurt, his heart raced—dear God, but he would like to be home in Boston. Sleep in his own bed, settle his stomach with food as the missus made it, see his friends, smoke a cigar, not *worry* all the time . . .

Still, seeing the attack take shape seemed to lift Dearborn's spirits. They would start with two days of artillery fire from the American side of the

river and from Chauncey's ships to destroy Fort George and force General
Vincent into the open. Scott sketched a quick map showing the Ontario
shore broken by the Niagara's entrance. Two miles on was a sandy shelf of
beach perfect for an amphibious landing.

"We'll hit in three timed waves forty minutes apart, committing four
thousand men with a thousand in reserve. I'll lead the first wave with my
Second Artillery fighting as infantry, Forsyth's Riflemen, the Fifteenth's two
flank companies and a flying battery, one three-pound gun.

"General Boyd's brigade will take the second wave. It will swing right
to turn Vincent's left flank and crowd him into a pocket against the river."
If Vincent let himself be so caught he was less expert than Scott expected,
but it was worth trying.

He thought Park Boyd could handle the second wave. The Brigadier
was a blowhard, but he'd heard hostile lead in the air, having been twenty
years a mercenary soldier hiring out his own army to various princes in
India intent on killing each other. A big, fleshy man of nearly fifty with a
booming voice and an aggressive manner whose watery blue eyes often had
an oddly vacant look, he was forever spitting and announcing, "Well, shitfire,
if 'twas like the old days, me with a dozen elephants mounting field pieces
in their howdahs and eighteen hundred hearties with turbans 'round their
skulls riding the plains of Hyderabad for the old Nizam, God rest his soul,
I'd put you in Quebec in a week."

John Winder's brigade would land on the third wave and follow the
strike at Vincent's left. Winder made Scott uneasy. He was a small man
with a potbelly and a silly little mustache, forty or so, a wealthy Baltimore
lawyer whose mind ran to lawyerly rules and limits rather than military
opportunity.

Dearborn would observe from Chauncey's flagship while Major General
Morgan Lewis, his second, would be in immediate command at Fort Niagara.
Scott trusted Lewis even less than Winder. An amiable lawyer from New
York who'd known Madison at Princeton forty years before and had married
into the all-powerful New York Livingstons, he weighed every idea on an
imaginary scale. Portly, face as gray as his hair, he was bent with dyspepsia
and covered frequent belches with a delicate hand.

Dearborn's glow slowly faded. "But won't it be dangerous?"

"No, sir. We'll overcome General Vincent on numbers alone."

"I mean at the start. From the beach you say you'll face a steep bluff,
a hard climb. That's dangerous. They'll be shooting down, it'll be a natural
parapet . . ."

"We may lose some men there, but—"

"That's just it. I don't want you in it. I can't afford to lose you."

"Sir," Scott said, "that's a critical moment. You want someone there
who grasps the whole—"

"Others can grasp it. I need you at my side."

"My regiment's in the lead. My place is with it."

"You're at army level now, not regimental. No, that's definite. I want you here."

Scott stared in consternation. Damn! He'd been reveling in power but he should have forseen this. The old fool had grown addicted to having a vigorous mind decide things for him.

"Sir, with all respect, my orders clearly say that I'm to take the field. The Secretary of War agreed."

"I don't care what the Secretary says—I want you here!"

Scott stood slowly to his full height. He leaned over Dearborn and stared. The silence began to stretch.

"Well, what?" Dearborn said.

Scott didn't speak. He made his expression dark and thunderous. His stare bored into the General's eyes.

Dearborn's hands began to tremble.

There wasn't a sound in the room.

"Lord, I wish I were home in Boston." The General sighed and flattened his hands to still them. "All right, all right, carry on. But the moment the victory is secure, I need you here."

★ ★ ★ ★

Fog in swirling tendrils that muffled all sound bled slowly from dark to gray to pearl. The stern of the schooner towing their flatboat and the others in a chain behind them became a vague dark spot in luminescent morning. Scott could hear the schooner's sweeps dipping rhythmically into the water.

Then, muted and distant, felt more than heard, came the heavy thump of American cannon on the Niagara opening fire for the third morning. The guns should have demolished Fort George by now, but he knew Vincent's army would be out in the open, and waiting. The fog was unexpected cover, a mixed blessing because it slowed them while it hid them, but with or without notice of their coming, Vincent's army would be ready.

A half-dozen chains of flatboats were passing through the gloom, the mouth of the Niagara hidden to the left, following the beach line toward Chauncey's marker buoys. Just as he was wondering if the buoys could be found in this murk, the wind picked up, the fog swirled away, and there they were spread across a glittering expanse of water for all the world to see.

"Jesus!" Poppy Poppenheim was staring at the slope they must climb and the British soldiers waiting like so many statues at its crest. "We're going in first? Mother of God!"

"C'mon, Poppy," Sarenmajor Boone said, "you join the best damned regiment in the U.S. Army, you think you'll go last?"

Scott winked at Ike Roach, his onetime aide now commanding the three-pounder battery going in on the lead. Poppy was sixteen; he'd lied when he enlisted and Poppy Sr. had lied for him, and he'd been a bright and willing soldier, but now he was learning what soldiering really means.

"Say, Poppy," Boone said, "see that big son of a bitch on the hill up yonder? He's waiting for you."

"Ah, shit, Sarge." The boy sounded near tears.

"That'll do, Sarenmajor," Scott said. "You scared, Poppy?"

The boy nodded, shame-faced.

Scott clapped him on the shoulder. "Everyone thinks pretty hard when he goes into battle, but you'll be too busy for fear. Follow the Sarenmajor—you'll be fine."

A hail from the schooner: "Ahoy, the boats! Stand by to cast off. We're abeam the lead marker. And good luck!"

Lines splashed into water, oarsmen dipped deep, the ungainly flatboats turned toward a pallid surf washing the beach. Scott leveled his glass to study the stalwart men atop the slope. They were in kilts. Glengarry Fencibles. Vincent's best.

A shocking roar came from behind them as the ships opened fire. Shells burst atop the slope and the soldiers there fell prone but didn't leave. The flatboat ground in sand and Scott stepped off its bow and splashed ashore, saber in hand. As he rallied his men across the sandy beach, flat sunrays broke the east and flashed on his saber. He windmilled an arm—come on, come on!

He ran in the lead, boots heavy in soft sand. The slope was steeper than he'd thought, sandy footing with sawgrass in ragged clumps, and when they were halfway up, spread across the slope like a line of ants, musket fire rattled from above. He heard a cry, saw a man down on his left, and plunged ahead.

Five hundred men were climbing that slope, and more from the first wave were on the beach. The Glengarry Scots waiting above numbered scarcely a hundred, and some already were down. Surely they would start their retreat soon. They had no choice.

Shell fire dosed the ground between beach and fort. A volley fell short of the crest, so close it sprayed Scott with sand and made his ears ring. He glanced at the ships—get your range, God damn it!—and then he was up and climbing, windmilling them on. His men were aiming, firing, then kneeling to reload, break the paper cartridge, pour powder down the good old 1795 musket's barrel, save a smidgeon for the pan, ram paper and ball down, replace your ramrod, aim, and fire with that soft popping of black powder and the puff of blue smoke—

The Scots were taking terrible punishment, big gaps in their line. Suddenly they leapt up and fired a rattling volley, presage to retreat.

"C'mon, boys," Scott yelled, "they'll break now!"

And then the kilt-clad warriors lowered their bayonets and charged!

Down they came in a wild run, blades level and steady, and Scott saw a big devil with sergeant's chevrons bearing straight at him. The kilted soldier was tall, heavy, he had orange hair and an orange handlebar mustache and his face was red as brick, and for a horrible frozen moment Scott watched that awful face, that glittering blade plunging toward his chest, and then as if wrenching himself from a dream, his own saber flashed down, slid against the swift blade, steel screaming on steel, guard locking against the bayonet as he thrust it aside too late, too late—he felt it sting into his side, and hang in his uniform, and for an instant he saw the dismay in the other's face as he tried to extricate his blade, and then Boone's bayonet swung in a great upward arc that caught the Scot in the ribs and sliced up through heart and lungs, and the hurtling body crashed into Scott, a blinding spray of blood exploding from the mouth, and the impact sent him tumbling down the slope.

He lay sprawled, head down, face in the sand, and then he sat up, wiped blood and sand from his face, felt his side curiously—no, by God, it was a scrape, stung like hell but the bastard missed! He was whole!

He leapt up. Boone started down toward him and Scott imperiously waved him forward and ran back up the hill. There were men down all along the slope, plenty of them in kilts. The Scots still on their feet had pulled back, started their careful retreat.

He saw a blue-clad soldier flat on the sand, face hidden in his hands, shuddering. It was Poppy. He knelt beside the boy.

"You hit, Poppy?"

"No, sir. I'm—I'm scared."

Scott caught his collar, snatched him up. "Get up, God damn you. You're going to fight!" Then, more gently, "Listen to me, son. You fail yourself—never mind us—you fail your duty and you'll be bent from this moment on for the rest of your life. Now get up."

The boy whispered something, face scarlet. Scott bent close, heard him say, "I done shit my pants."

"Run back to the lake and wash yourself. Then catch up with me within ten minutes or I'll have your ass, do you understand?"

Boone knelt beside them, doubled a heavy fist in the boy's face.

"Ten minutes—or you'll wish you was dead."

From the top of the slope Scott could see Fort George two miles off, some of its upper structure shot away, one end a jumble of timbers like a child's game of pick-up-sticks. Directly before him the ground sloped toward a steep ravine that would be the next line of resistance. What was left of the Glengarries retreated toward an intermediate line, which also began to give way toward the ravine. Shells screamed overhead and burst among the British, but their steady, controlled movement didn't change. Scott saw an officer on a wheeling, dancing horse directing his men: General Vincent, he was sure.

Ike Roach's gunners were dragging the little three-pounder up-slope on long lines while horses and caisson were led up separately. Ike grinned at him, teeth flashing white against his dark face, caught in the thunderous joy of attack.

"Bear off to the right," Scott said. "They'll take shelter in that ravine. I want you to get in there and lay a flanking fire of grape along its length."

The first wave was in hot pursuit as the second wave came ashore. Boyd was on horseback, aligning his men for the march to the right to turn Vincent's left flank and herd him toward the river. But nothing Scott had seen so far made him expect the Briton to allow himself to be trapped.

Far ahead he could make out Boone in the lead, and he set out at a hard run to catch up. The last of the British were ducking into the ravine. A blast of musketry followed. Scott saw Ike leading the horses into the ravine at a fast trot, the little gun bouncing behind the caisson, and as he reached Boone where his troops had paused, he heard the gun's distinctive high-pitched bark. Vincent's horse scrambled up the far side of the ravine. The British soldiers came after him, retreating again.

"Colonel! Colonel, I'm here!" He turned to see Poppy Poppenheim grinning at him. The boy's clothes were wet, but he had musket in hand and looked as if he'd been set free.

A riderless dapple gray careened by, eyes rolling.

"Hyah!" Boone roared and caught the reins. Scott bounded into the saddle and jumped the horse into the ravine. The stirrups were far too short but the horse was energetic and clever, adjusting quickly to a new rider. It took the rough ground of the ravine like a trooper and clawed up the other side as they poured out in hot pursuit of the retreating British.

He wheeled the horse, pulled the men into a rough order, and launched them toward the hamlet of Newark. A dirt road straggled down its length with log cabins helter-skelter and what could be a courthouse on a square in the center. A patriarch with a long white beard and a white shirt under heavy black coat was standing by the road. He held up a hand when he saw Scott.

"Sir, I'm the mayor here. Come out to ask you not to trouble our little town. All the soldiers have gone, only women and children left, and a few aged, like your humble servant."

Scott saw Ike Roach on the caisson approaching at a gallop, gunners clinging to the piece, others following.

"Mr. Mayor, I'll take your word. But if one shot is fired I'll blow that house apart with cannon fire and if women and children are inside you'll have yourself to blame."

The old man swallowed. "Soldiers are all gone. It's the truth."

Scott waved his men on. They fanned out as they walked, muskets bearing left and right. The village was silent, shutters pulled, no human in sight. A big dog with a basso profundo voice addressed them furiously from beside a house; at the far end guinea hens set up a great clamor as they passed into the open.

The enemy line was only a hundred yards away. Scott deployed rapidly, fanning his men left and right as the British resumed their careful retreat, ready to sting the unwary. There were perhaps five hundred redcoats before him now as Vincent's withdrawal scooped up more of his troops. The British were losing men but so was Scott, and the battle wasn't over.

They came to the fort and encountered no fire. Its gates stood ajar, shattered logs were knocked into kindling piles, flames licked at one end, a gun barrel on a bastion was cocked up at the sky. Scott scanned the distance with his glass, saw Boyd's men advancing rapidly off to the right, and turned to the fort. The redcoats were pulling away, but he must be sure he wasn't leaving an armed stronghold behind him.

As he trotted through the ruined gates at the head of a small detail he saw immediately that the fort was deserted. Then a vast explosion thundered against his eardrums.

Magazine exploding, he knew instantly, but the noise was so shattering, so shocking, the rush of air so forceful that he felt as if his whole body were being turned inside out. He had an image of fire and of black particles, wood and stone, darkening the sky; a violent blow struck him from above, ferocious pain darted through his shoulder, a rough hand threw him flat with his face in the dirt.

The dapple gray was down, too, but it scrambled up, snorting and swinging its head, and he saw it wasn't hurt. His head cleared, he felt his shoulder cautiously. By God, he was as fit as the horse! He leapt up, screamed at the shattering bolt of pain that struck his shoulder, fell—and the pain vanished. What the hell . . .

Boone knelt beside him, expert fingers probing his shoulders.

"Broke collarbone. You're out of it, Colonel."

"The hell with that! I don't even hurt."

"You will if you stand up."

"Help me sit up, then. Must be a stable in the fort. Find me a horse bandage, a leg wrapping, straps—anything. I'll tie this arm down. I don't move it, I'll be fine."

It worked. Boone helped him mount left-handed, and Scott was ready for action. Joe Totten galloped up on a horse he'd found somewhere, having made his own forward reconnaissance.

"Win," the stocky engineer said, "Vincent's moving fast, he's slipping us. Got maybe fifteen hundred together now and they're heading toward Queenston. Our second wave's coming up on the right but not near fast enough. Boyd's not with 'em."

"Where is he?"

"Crossing the river. Said he wants to be sure of orders."

"The son of a bitch—"

"Jesus, Win, we gotta move!"

"Let's hit 'em." Scott put the dapple gray to a gallop. A bolt of pain shot through his right arm and slowly faded. His troops were well ahead of him now, platoon and company officers keeping them in good order. The force he'd ordered across near Queenston to intercept the defeat had fouled the crossing—shades of Van Rensselaer!—and Vincent was slipping away to fight another day. Still, the Briton was moving south along the river, but his natural escape route was to the west. He'd have to turn to his right soon, and if Scott could swing southward—to his own left—and get around Vincent's right flank, he could turn the fleeing enemy back toward Boyd's troops in the second wave coming down from the north, pinch him between the two, force his surrender. Yes, it could work—

"Colonel Scott! Sir! Sir!"

He turned to see a captain in a fresh uniform who saluted and said, "Compliments of Major General Morgan Lewis, sir. He sent me across to tell you he wants you to hold up. Stop the pursuit. Consolidate your men and await further orders."

"For God's sake, Captain, that's just plain ridiculous. Get back over the river and tell the General I'm about to bag the entire British army."

"Sir—"

"Do as I tell you, God damn it!"

Before the other could answer, Scott had the dapple gray at a gallop. A dull ache in his shoulder was blossoming into something much more serious, but he held the arm still, cushioning himself as best he could against the horse's movement. He'd hold out long enough to bag Vincent, by God.

Now was the moment. Overwhelming numbers had forced the Briton to give up a little ground, but he was still loose and in good order and if left alone now would simply withdraw and be back to fight again and nothing would have been gained. You don't win battles by taking ground; you win by destroying the enemy army, killing its men or making them your prisoners.

And Scott was ready to do both. Roach's little battery caught up with him at a gallop, Boone riding the gun barrel in most unorthodox fashion. The big sergeant dropped off, clutching his crotch.

"Jesus, worse'n being rid out of town on a rail!"

Poppy Poppenheim passed him at a trot, a bloody bandage on his left forearm, and threw Scott a flashing grin. He looked . . . older, somehow, as if he'd grown up in a morning.

Scott heard firing ahead. His right—the second wave, the men Boyd should have been commanding—had engaged. Good. Vincent wouldn't stop, but he'd have to slow, hold off the Yanks, reduce his retreat to a crawl. That would give Scott time to throw his own men around on the left and charge straight in against the Briton's right, crush him between the two forces—

A colonel he didn't know galloped up on a lathered horse. The man's pant legs were wet—he'd just crossed the river. He had pointed little mustaches and his voice was high and girlish.

"Colonel Scott, General Lewis wants this army stopped and withdrawn to the river. You're to consolidate your position and await further orders when the situation has cleared."

"Colonel," Scott said, trying to keep his voice even despite his anger and the pain flaring in his shoulder, "General Lewis just doesn't understand the situation. We are closing with the enemy now. In another half hour we'll have Vincent and all his men as our captives."

"No, no, the General's orders were specific. He left no room for, ah"— the fellow's eyes glinted—"*entrepreneurship.*"

"Where's General Dearborn?" Scott said.

"He's still out on the lake with the navy." The fellow's eyes glinted again. "General Lewis is definitely in command."

"Then you go explain to the General—"

"Won't work, Scott," a new voice said.

Scott turned to see General Boyd sitting his horse. The veteran of so many battles in India with guns in his elephant's howdahs looked pleased with himself.

"Why the hell aren't you with your troops, General?"

"Well, now, Scott, I figured I'd better get instructions from the top man. Good thing I did, too. General Lewis, he was damned glad to see me. Sent me over five minutes after Colonel Jones here, figuring you might not pay him much mind. Look—Lewis knows the situation but he also knows a British army can turn and cut you up like crazy. We've won a hell of a victory already. Why put it to risk?"

"We've won nothing if we let Vincent escape." The pain was a rocket, flaring and brilliant, melding with the rage that battered at his control. The God damned miserable imbeciles!

Boyd shrugged. "Won enough to look good, and haven't lost our army. That's not so bad."

"Is that the way they did it in India, General?"

Boyd crossed a leg over the pommel of the saddle and clasped his ankle.

"Well, Win, the old Nizam was paying the bills and it wasn't smart to go agin him. Same here. It's the luck of the draw. Some days Dame Fortune smiles and some days she dips you in shit. Long as the whiskey's good, what the hell."

Scott didn't answer. Dame Fortune . . . today she was the hostage of fools. General Lewis wasn't a soldier, hadn't a shred of the instinct. He might be a hell of a judge, if anyone cared, but now he was in a perfect terror that something would go wrong and he'd be blamed. He pictured the man, plump, uneasy, belching away his dyspepsia behind his slender hand, his Revolutionary days far behind him, inured to the political equation of half-a-loaf that had no meaning on a win-or-lose battlefield . . .

Yet disobeying a direct order from a superior officer didn't so much as cross Scott's mind. He was a professional soldier and he knew the army lives and dies on discipline. If an officer can order a man to face the bullet that kills him, so he too must obey, and if that breaks, the army is finished.

"I'm a general officer," Boyd said, "and I'm giving you an order."

"Very well, sir," Scott said. And General Vincent would walk away unmolested, and what could have been the nation's first genuine victory was thrown away.

★ ★ ★ ★

The next day Dearborn sent Lewis in pursuit of Vincent and in a nervous frenzy recalled him the day following. By then Vincent was installed at the western end of Lake Ontario. Next General Winder set out with sixteen hundred men. He camped near Vincent's position and went to bed. Vincent struck him at midnight. Winder was captured—Scott could imagine the fussy Baltimore lawyer's mustache quivering as he recited prisoner-of-war rights—and his men crept back to the Niagara.

Lewis departed and second in command devolved to Boyd. Hungry for action not involving himself, Boyd sent one Colonel Boerstler whose five hundred men met three hundred Indians and thirty Englishmen. A cheeky British lieutenant told Boerstler he must surrender or the Indians would scalp his men, so Boerstler surrendered. Dearborn then abandoned everything on the British side of the Niagara except the ruined Fort George—and it was clear to Scott that it would go soon.

His collarbone healed. What didn't heal was the outrage of victory converted to defeat, of ground for which good men had fought and died returned to the enemy with whimpers.

Still, there was some cause for celebration. First, old Dearborn got his wish. The President sent him home to Boston and told him to stay there. He wasn't quite cashiered, but he plainly was no longer wanted around the army.

And Jake Brown, who had fought off a British attack on Sackett's Harbor with startling ferocity while Dearborn was throwing away the Niagara campaign, was plucked out of the New York militia and commissioned a regular army brigadier.

When Brown came to the Niagara he and Scott had dinner. He described his defense of Sackett's Harbor.

"Why," Scott said, "that's right out of Frederick the Great."

"The hell you say. I can't tell you I know piffle about Frederick the

Great, but it made sense. Key thing in a fight is, you want to get in there and *fight*. Surprising how often that takes the starch out of the other side."

"General," Scott said, "the technical side of war matches right up with the fighting side. I have an idea that between the two of us, we might make something of this war yet."

Brown grinned and put out his hand.

12

NASHVILLE
Late Summer, 1813

★ ★ ★ ★ The stage from the east rattled into Nashville, and Tom Benton swung down with a weary sigh. Two weeks on the road, bouncing and jouncing on deep ruts under a tower of dust in the baking summer sun, down the great valley of Virginia and into the mountains, laboring up to the Cumberland Gap and back down and across Tennessee, foul meals and crowded beds in the stage stops—good Lord, he was happy to be home!

Nashville had never looked better despite leaden heat that coated everything in white haze. Benton thought longingly of Stone's River on the road to General Jackson's farm—he'd strip and soak in its cool waters for an hour and arrive refreshed with all the details of winning the government's approval of the Natchez expenditures that had saved the grand old man from ruin.

He tossed his bag to Joe, the porter at the Nashville Inn where he lived, and ducked into Crab Early's shop for cigars.

"How's ol' Jesse?" Crab asked, opening a box of his best.

"M'little brother?" Benton said. "Fine, I suppose. I just got in."

"Then you ain't heard about Jesse's sore butt? Oh, God, it was the funniest thing! Whole town's been whooping over it."

It seemed that Jesse had had a duel with Billy Carroll, the most proper, punctilious, pompous young man in Jackson's army—everyone detested him except Jackson whom he courted assiduously. When Jesse fired—hit Carroll in the thumb, actually—he cowered away from the answering fire, turned sideways, bent over, and Carroll's bullet raked across both cheeks of his buttocks.

"So ol' Jesse's been taking his meals standing up." Crab finished with a braying laugh, then noticed Benton's expression. "Course, Tom, you understand, Jesse wasn't hurt bad. Been different if he'd been hurt. Everybody likes him, you know that. They're laughing 'cause they're—well—relieved, you know, that it wasn't serious . . ."

Benton went at a near trot the three blocks to Mrs. Sapson's boarding-house. He pulled off his coat and loosened his cravat, sweat-soaked all over.

"Hot enough for you, Tom?" Mrs. Sapson asked.

"Yes, ma'am, it'll do." He ran up the steps to Jesse's room. He found his brother in bed, lying on his side.

"Jesse, what in hell is going on?"

Jesse sat up, gasped in pain, raised himself slowly, tottered when he stood. He was like a pale copy of his older brother, the same cap of auburn curls, the same broad body, but Benton had always known that his brother had none of that underlying force that pushes a man to the head of the pack.

"It's that God damned Jackson's fault," Jesse said. The whine Benton had heard since boyhood was in his voice. "The old son of a bitch! 'Old Hickory,' my ass! He set it all up—figured to punish me 'cause he loves Billy so much."

"Wait a minute," Benton said. "What happened?"

"Well, you know what a shit Billy is? So he and Littleton Johnston quarreled and Littleton challenged him. And Billy backed off, said Littleton wasn't a gentleman. I delivered the challenge, so when he said that, I said, 'How about me?' "

"Shit!" Benton slammed his fist on the table. "Oh, Jesse, you are so dumb!"

"Yeah, I guess," Jesse said. His lips pulled down and he looked near tears. "But, Tom, they're *laughing* at me. Whole town is laughing . . ."

"How did Jackson get in it?"

"Well, he stood second for Billy. Delivered Billy's answer and his terms."

"He should of talked you out of it."

"He did, once. But then, well, the boys kept hoorawing me—they do hate Billy, you know—and it got going again. But see, Billy and Jackson set the rules. We had to stand back to back ten feet apart, then turn and fire. I never heard of such a thing. French rules, they said. So I bent over a little and I guess I was sideways when Billy fired, and the bullet plowed across my ass . . ."

Benton shook his head.

Jesse's whine deepened. He might have been ten years old.

"They're all laughing. Said I ducked—scared, you know—and got shot in the ass. But *they* wasn't up there facing the fire, they didn't risk nothing. And God, Tom, I do hurt—hurts to stand, to walk, I can't sit down, I can't sleep, and everyone thinks that's funny as all hell."

Any minute now he'd start crying. "Jackson done it," he said. "Billy sucks up to him like a calf on a tit, he thinks Billy's so precious, he thought up these crazy rules to give him the advantage . . ." Tears streamed. "I'm sorry, Tom, but—"

Jesse was dumb, but he was Benton's brother. He was family and Benton—as oldest, Pa long dead—had always looked after his family. And he'd made his own mistakes, too, and been called to account, and he'd promised himself that no one would call him or his family to account again.

"All right, Jesse," he said. "It's all right. They won't laugh while I'm around, you can be sure of that. I'd say it's pretty sorry recompense for going to Washington and saving that old man's ass to come home and find he's humiliated my family. And I'll tell that to any son of a bitch who asks, too!"

★ ★ ★ ★

"Hey, boys, here comes Old Hickory."

Jackson was on Sweet Lady Joan, his bay mare with the white blaze that foaled champions. He and Jack Coffee were bound for Winn's Tavern in Nashville. Phelps Austin would meet them there and they'd conclude the deal on the last eighty acres.

They were approaching Rich Stribling's store, where a branch of the Gallatin Pike met the Lebanon Pike. It was already hot, though early; Jackson peeled his coat and laid it over his saddle.

The boys in front of Stribling's set up a cheer—he recognized Dennis Pumphrey and Ewel Burganer, and a couple of others were familiar though none had been on the Natchez march. He lifted his hat and bowed in his saddle. He might have stopped at Stribling's for a cool drink but for the cheers, which affected him strangely.

"They love you," Coffee said in his rumbling voice.

They did, and it produced an odd confusion. He'd never been loved by the public, and the attention, the downright adulation, was pure joy. Governor Blount had given him a dinner at the Nashville Inn with a hundred guests and there'd been who knew how many toasts with variations on "Hickory," everyone stone drunk by the end. And the boys at Stribling's and every other crossroads were cheering.

He revealed in it. He wanted it never to stop. Yet that very feeling made him uneasy, vulnerable in a way he disliked. Something was sure to come along to unhorse it, for loving him was unnatural—respect him, fear him, admire him, yes, but love him? It threw him off balance, left him a little uncertain how to act, and he'd never been uncertain . . .

He rode along, ruminating. Coffee was a comfortable companion, rarely speaking. A good man to ride with. Yes, sir, the boys loving him, that was fine—but how long could it last with the administration leaving him frozen far from the scenes of action, unwanted, unremarked?

Months had passed since the return from Natchez without a word from Washington. No explanations, no apologies, nothing. That they'd paid the bills was a satisfaction but it reminded him that though Tom Benton was back, the scamp hadn't called.

What irony. Jackson didn't care for irony. He was a direct man, called a spade a spade, expected folks to lay their cards on the table like honorable men. Double irony, really. Washington sneered at the Tennessee general while displaying its own total ineptitude for war, one miserable defeat after another and now that old fool Dearborn had thrown away the Niagara campaign.

Yet the deeper issue was personal. Command was Andrew Jackson's metier. That's why the outpouring of love was uncomfortable. The military was his place, not politics. Orders, not persuasion. But in the democratic United States, pacifist to its core in the first years of the new century, the military had no meaning outside of war. For years he'd waited, treasuring his militia command and yet knowing that in peacetime it meant little.

But war was here, his time had come, and what blocked him? Politics. Being on the wrong side of the Burr question. Wrong side when Monroe challenged Madison in 1808. Politics as usual while the new nation strangled in military failure. He *knew* that given his chance he could forge an army into a fighting whole and save the South. What else mattered? But he couldn't do it as a mere state militiaman. He needed a regular army commission, brigadier or, better yet, major general. This fellow Brown was a regular brigadier now out of New York militia. That was good, he was a fighter, but what about the South's most potent figure?

Well, he knew the answer—but couldn't they see that New Orleans inevitably was the ultimate prize for the British and hence their certain target? And who else was to defend it? But they were blind in Washington, *blind*, God damn it!

"I don't see Phelps Austin's horse," Coffee said.

They'd reached Winn's; Jackson hadn't noticed. Inside, the barkeep said Phelps had sent a message: he was in bed with the grippe. Fever way up there.

Jackson asked for a julep.

"Ice is all gone for this year, General. Cool water from the spring house is the best we can offer."

Damn this heat! "It'll do. Set 'em up."

Winn served a stout julep, always had, and Jackson put one away and another, tried a little ham on a cracker with a pickle, decided it was too hot to eat, and settled for another julep.

Everyone was out on Winn's long veranda courting any passing breeze. He took a ladderback chair and sat with his boots on the railing gazing out at the white haze of the noonday sun. A tall fellow with a braying voice was sounding off about Creek Indians on the rampage down in Alabama country. Pete Olive, Kip Ball, Bernie Stughleman, and a few others listened, looking anxious.

Jackson finished his drink. What in fact was happening with the Creeks was a civil war within the tribe itself, and he said as much when asked.

"Well, Green Evans here, he says they're hitting whites, too," Kip Ball said. "Green, this is General Jackson."

He gave Evans a cool nod but kept his seat. "Fights among Indians always spill over against whites. But this Creek problem is just an extension of the larger war. Tecumseh set it off, and what's he but a British puppet?"

Jackson had the whole story. On Tecumseh's second visit he'd sung a witches' song of British victories and American humiliations and British arms that would flow to the Creeks in a golden stream from Pensacola if they joined his great confederacy to block farther white advance. Thirty-odd Creeks had gone north with him—where they'd taken part in the massacre on the River Raisin, and Tennesseans would remember that, too—and on the way home they'd murdered eight settler families. Creek elders in northern Alabama who understood the realities knew that could touch off war with the whites, so they punished the errant warriors—had them tracked down and killed.

"And that," Jackson said, "was tailor-made for Weatherford in the south to declare war on old-line Creeks in northern Alabama and attack whites as well." He hiked his chair around.

"Bigger'n I thought, then," Evans said. "I believe most folks down there just figure it's a local uprising. This Weatherford, they're all scared of him, I know that."

"With good reason," Jackson said. This was an extraordinary Indian, a worthy enemy whom Jackson had an idea he would meet on the field one of these days. William Weatherford—or Red Eagle, half-breed son of a Scottish trader who'd married into the tribe—was young, quick, smart, spoke French, Spanish, and English as well as he spoke the Creek language, and was possessed of a messianic power that set his warriors afire.

Evans said there'd been new trouble down on Burnt Corn Creek, just a good day's march north of Pensacola where settlers laid for Indians who'd been raiding their farms and had a tough little scrap. More of the same, really, but it was getting worse, and families were pouring into the fort the half-breed trader Mims built ten miles above where the Alabama and the Tombigbee meet.

"I was down to Mims's a year ago," Coffee said, "and the old fool, he calls it a fort but all he's got is a flimsy stockade. Indians could come over those walls like deer in brush country. I don't think he's closed his gates in years—I don't even know if he can close 'em. Has he made it any stronger?"

"Not a bit," Evans said.

"Look, General," Pete Olive said, "like you were saying, this is part of the big war. So how come Washington don't pay us no mind on these Indian matters? Don't they care? Can't they see it's a powder keg? I mean, even if they don't give a damn about them poor settlers getting their throats cut, can't they see the Creeks are giving the British an open invitation to land through Florida and hit New Orleans from the north?"

All of them were looking at him. Jackson bristled. He didn't like Olive's expression and he heard the hidden question, all right. Why did Washington ignore the Tennessee general? Weren't the settlers down on the Alabama paying the price for a general who couldn't mend his fences? The juleps boiled up and he had an urge to slap Pete into the ground.

Jack Coffee laid a restraining hand on his sleeve. "I reckon the gov'ment knows about it, Pete," Coffee said. "It'll take a hand when the time's right." His manner said the subject was closed.

"Well," Kip Ball said, "not much we can do about it now. Anyway, not to change the subject or nothing, but I expect you've heard what Tom Benton's saying, eh, General?"

Jackson felt rather than saw Coffee stiffen beside him. His senses suddenly alert, he set down his empty glass and put both hands on his knees.

"Tom hasn't been to see me. What's he saying?"

"It ain't nothing," Bernie Stughleman said. "Don't go making trouble, Kip."

Ball's little eyes glinted. "I'd want to know if I was the General."

"All right, God damn it!" Jackson said. "What's he saying?" Kip Ball was a miserable little tale-bearing pissant, but it's the tale-bearers who'll destroy a man's reputation, because folks will always listen, they say they won't but they will . . .

"He's all het up about the duel," Ball said. "Says you should have stopped it. Says you fixed the rules to favor Billy. Says he saved your ass in Washington and this is his reward."

Anger settled over him, welcome as a cloak on an icy night.

"If Tom wants to insult me," he said, "he should do it to my face. The fact is, I did my best to stop it, only stepped in when it was clear they plotted to kill Billy. As to the rules, Jesse's a good shot, probably why they chose him, and Billy's a novice. I tried to even it up."

He laughed. "So Jesse's whining, is he? And big brother's sticking up for him. My, my." He could feel glorious anger soaring. Anger solved so many things, settled things, painted them in black and white, removed doubts, burned with white flame.

"Did Tom say he was going to call me out?" he said.

"That wasn't clear," Ball said.

"Jesus," Stughleman said, "you watch out, Kip. I never heard him say nothing like that. Nothing!"

"Well, you know, he didn't exactly say it . . ."

At home that afternoon, the juleps had faded but his anger hadn't. Somehow it had to do with his new status, with Old Hickory. Tom was threatening that, challenging the love the community offered him. That love might make him uncomfortable, even uncertain, but it was *his*, he'd earned it, he didn't think he could bear to lose it, and by God, nobody was going to steal it!

"Andrew, Andrew, darling," Rachel said, "calm down. Please." She was wearing that shade of blue he liked, they were in the kitchen shed where he'd gone to find her and blurt out Tom's perfidy the moment he arrived.

"There's cool tea," she said. "Sit down, let's talk. Tom's just hurt about Jesse, that's all. He's talked to me often about family, it means so much to him. He's had some pain of his own in the past, too. Doesn't say what it is, but you can read it. Something happened, something that's made him sensitive."

"The jackanapes is talking of challenging me."

"He would never do that! Did he say that?"

"Not exactly, but Kip Ball—"

"Oh, Andrew, Kip Ball is just a nasty little gossip."

"That's true, but—"

"Darling, don't let this get out of hand. Please. Truth is, you should have stopped the duel. That's what you said afterward."

He nodded. "Yes, I wish I had. But now—I can't ignore this, Rachel. Can't have the question unspoken in people's minds. I'll write Tom and ask if he intends to challenge."

"Oh, Andrew, please don't stir it up. Let it lie."

"I'll be polite, but I have to know."

★　★　★　★

Tom Benton answered carefully. He thought it poor business for an older man to enter a quarrel between young men. He thought the rules should have been fair to both parties instead of savage, unequal, and base, as he put it. Base. Jackson wouldn't like that. As for a challenge, he had never threatened one nor did he intend one. At the same time, fear of the General's pistols was not to seal his lips; what he believed to be true he would say, and the General might make what he liked of that.

★　★　★　★

Impudent. Impudent! God damned outrageous, in fact. Who in hell did this young man think he was that he could talk so about Andrew Jackson, blacken the General's name in taverns—did he suppose he could so abuse his mentor and not be called to account?

Rachel was in tears when he left, but she didn't understand. Even after he'd mounted she stood by his horse, saying Tom was at heart a good boy, he'd been their friend, a good officer, loyal, a big-hearted lad who'd loved them. Standing by his brother, hurt because his brother was hurt, wasn't that to be admired?

Listen to Jesus, she said. What would Jesus say?—to seek Tom out, talk to him as a father, settle this growing evil between them. Tom had served them well in Washington, don't forget. But Jackson pointed out that

he'd merely done his duty, that others had helped—and anyway, did gratitude require Old Hickory to let a stripling as much as pull his nose in
public?

Old Hickory, he thought as he headed for Nashville, that was the point.
What of Old Hickory if his response to affront was to kiss and make
up? Jesus hadn't lived in Tennessee frontier society, where a gentleman's
willingness to defend his reputation was all that stood between him and
chaos.

The anger boiled in a cloud, familiar, comfortable as an old shoe interlaced
with the unsettling new aura now threatened, the instinct to fight as strong
as in a cornered wolf—

Rachel's face, white as paper, leapt to mind. "Andrew," she'd cried as
he was leaving, "there are things that can't be settled with pistols!"

He'd turned the horse away and she'd followed. "Look inside yourself,
stop yourself, you're destroying something important!" But he'd ridden away
before he had to hear more.

Benton had moved from the Nashville Inn, where Jackson stayed when
he was in town, to the City Hotel across the square. Rachel said he had
moved to avoid trouble, but as Jackson saw it, the scamp knew how to avoid
trouble—issue an apology.

Jack Coffee rode in with him. They registered at the inn and went for
their mail. The Post Office was near the City Hotel. When they came out,
they could cross the square to the inn and avoid the hotel, but how would
that look? Jackson, riding whip coiled in his hand, turned down the gravel
sidewalk to pass the hotel's long veranda. There stood Benton by the front
door, glaring at him.

"D'you see that fellow?" Coffee said.

"Oh, yes. I have my eye on him."

He shook out the whip and ran up the steps, shouting, "Now, you
damned rascal, I'm going to punish you. Defend yourself!"

★ ★ ★ ★

Benton had seen Jackson and Coffee coming, but not before they saw him,
and then it was too late to duck back into the hotel. He couldn't let Jackson
think he'd avoided a meeting. Anyway, the matter had become public—
well, he'd made it so, it was the only way he could salvage his family's
reputation—and now people were watching from the corners of their eyes,
avid and hot, it was the best show in town, the only show until it was
settled. Jackson's reputation was fearsome. If Benton seemed to quail now,
he would be ruined in Tennessee.

He turned his head slightly, said over his shoulder to Jesse, "They're
coming. Get ready."

Then Jackson came bounding up the steps, shouting at him, brandishing
his riding whip. Benton ducked back, half stumbled on the doorsill, touched

the double-shotted pistol under his coat to be sure it wasn't dislodged. Instantly Jackson shifted the whip to his left hand and snatched out his own pistol.

Inside Benton glimpsed Jesse hobbling and limping down the hall, his pistol already in his hand. Then Jesse ducked into the barroom to the left.

Jackson advanced, the pistol barrel level and menacing as Benton backed away. Rage distorted the General's face as if he'd lost all control of himself, more than that, as if he'd thrown it aside with joy—Benton had a sudden memory of his expression the day he whipped Eb Clute. He was nothing like the gallant soldier who saw his troops home from Natchez; his lips were flattened in a snarl, he looked absolutely . . . mad.

Over Jackson's shoulder he saw Coffee, following on. A damned dog, incapable of questioning his master. He backed slowly, not taking his eyes from Jackson. Where the hell had Jesse got to? Had he run? God damn it, where was he?

Still, it wasn't hopeless. Maybe he could draw his own pistol. Better, he could get in under the whip and close with Jackson. He didn't think the other would shoot if he didn't draw, and if he got under the whip one good punch ought to do it . . .

★ ★ ★ ★

Jackson stalked him step by step. Down the hall they went. Benton, the damned poltroon, kept retreating, his eyes shifting.

"Stand like a man and defend yourself!" Jackson roared.

Still, he could see in the other's eyes that he hadn't panicked. He was going to make a move, his eyes kept shifting, it would be certain death for him to try to draw, so he would try to get close and when he did Jackson would clout him with the pistol, knock him to his knees, then give him a whipping that would teach the miserable scamp once and for all what he could say about a gentleman and what he couldn't. Teach him manners that would save him a peck of trouble over the years—

He heard a click to his left, knew instantly it was a pistol being cocked, turned swiftly to see a door pop open, Jesse Benton's febrile face looming over a huge pistol—

An earth-shaking roar, a gout of flame, an immense blow strikes his shoulder, it's like a tree falling on him, there's a vast roaring that fills his ears and goes on and on, the gunshot reverberating, wrapping itself around him, shaking and rattling his body—

He was surprised to find himself flat on the floor. He had a moment's image of big Jack Coffee clearing him in a bound with pistol in hand, and then Jack was gone and he was lying there, his hold on reality suddenly slippery. He rolled onto his left side and felt a lightning shaft of pain, heard a scream and realized it had come from him. He saw a welling pool of liquid— his own blood, pumping and pumping and spreading on the polished floor.

Voices were around him, hands touching him, they lifted him onto a mattress, he couldn't see who, the blood poured out of his shoulder, the mattress was wet under him—

"Holy Jesus!" someone said. "It's soaked through, it's dripping on the floor. Get another mattress."

Rachel? Rachel?

Dear old Jack Coffee's voice, you can always count on Jack, shouting, "Get him to the inn. Hurry!"

Yes, he'd like that. The inn was comfortable. A second home. If only Rachel were there. He needed her just now. And then he would rest a little. Be quiet and rest and get well. With Rachel beside him. This wasn't really anything much; it wasn't the first time Andrew Jackson's hide had been penetrated.

The mattress lurched as they went through the door and he grunted with the pain of the movement and then they were out under the brilliant beautiful blue sky, the heat had gone somehow, he was cold and the sky looked like spring and he listened for birds and then the sky darkened until it was night, night without stars . . .

★ ★ ★ ★

Rachel sat by his bed watching his white face. *Two mattresses soaked through.* He lay still, scarcely breathing, swept by wound fevers. When the fever soared she and her sweet niece—little Mary Donelson who'd married Jack Coffee—covered him with cold sheets. When the fever passed and his teeth chattered, they warmed bricks in flannel for his bed.

The pistol had been double-shotted. The slug shattered his shoulder, the ball drove deep into muscle under the arm. The surgeons cut down to the slug and took out most of the bone fragments, but the ball was too deep and they had to leave it. After a few days fetid pus emerged and the doctors were encouraged.

Andrew muttered and mumbled as if dreaming, drifting in and out of consciousness; only once had he spoken clearly. When the surgeons told her they must amputate, his eyes opened and he fixed them with an iron stare.

"I'll keep my arm."

It was a command so absolute the surgeon answered by instinct, "Yes, sir!"

She was hugely cheered by this sign of life.

Days passed, the fever ebbed, the wound began to have the granulated look of healing tissue. He took broth and gruel and asked for beef cut very fine and then couldn't eat it, but did the next day. With help he could sit up, leaning against pillows, telling her in a thin voice that he was as good as new.

Daily she was on her knees in prayer to thank Jesus for the innate strength of her husband's constitution and his recovery, agonizingly slow but by its mere existence proof of her faith.

His color returned, he asked about the farm, he tolerated a few visitors. He ate a little more and grew strong enough to sit in a chair, wrapped in a comforter. They talked of her plans for a brick chapel she wanted to build on the farm and of the future they saw for the orphans and wards who filled their lives and lamented again that God had given them no children of their own. But he didn't mention the fight, nor did she.

One day they heard shouting in the street below and she ran to the window. A travel-stained rider stood by a lathered horse. She heard his voice only as an excited buzz, rising and falling. His right arm jerked up and down, sawing the air. The men around him shouted to others, waving them over, their voices urgent.

Then the door burst open and Jack Coffee dashed in. He was breathing hard and looked distraught in a way she'd never seen. She raised a hand as if to shield Andrew—

"Weatherford and his warriors overran Fort Mims," Jack cried. "Killed everyone there."

"Oh, my Lord," she said. "How many?"

"Five hundred, more or less, mostly women and children. This feller says about a dozen men escaped into the woods. Weatherford hit at noon when the bell rang for dinner and everyone was away from their weapons. He had maybe a thousand warriors massed, and they were inside before anyone could close the gates."

He looked at Andrew. "General, the whole town's going crazy. I have to tell you everybody's asking what you say."

"Yes . . . we must march immediately," Andrew said. Fire was in his eyes but his voice was barely audible. It tore her heart.

She stood up. "Jack," she said, "give us a few minutes alone. Then the General will have something to say."

As the door closed, Andrew groaned. "This means war—there's no other answer. And I'm . . . look at me. What irony! All my life I've waited for real need, a real chance to lead, a real demand for service. To save people, to punish enemies, that's the whole *idea* of the military—and here I am. Flat on my back. And I brought it on myself! It's my own stupid, miserable—"

He stopped short. "Can that be true? No, it's not. I had to do what I did. Didn't I?"

His voice trailed off to nothing. His mouth quivered and she had a sudden sense that he was frightened, as if he'd looked into something terrible. And he had—he'd looked into himself.

She wanted to fall to her knees and thank Jesus, but she must not let the moment escape. She made her voice soft and easy. "You must look at yourself. I think I know what you'll see—but you must see it."

"What?" he said. Was he slipping away? Denying? No—no more of that.

"What will I see, Rachel?"

She took a deep breath. "That in you there is a force, a will, a power that can make you great. And that that same force can destroy you—will destroy you—if you let it. That's what I think."

He smiled. "You're a pretty woman."

Her heart sank. He was making light of it, when he'd been so close. She shook her head.

"Pretty in mind as well as face," he said. "This force—"

There were new shouts outside. His eyes flicked toward the door.

"Let 'em wait," he said. "This may be important, this talk." His voice strengthened as the ideas gripped him.

"So. This force. I know you think I've been too strong, but it's what saved us all these years. We were under assault, don't forget, we were accused of every sin because we believed the report of Robards's divorce. And I wouldn't accept pillorying. It wasn't just my pistols, you know—it was this force you describe, I wouldn't let them traduce us, they wouldn't dare! That's what saved us, that force was the rock we clung to."

"Yes, when we were young. But we've grown so, we're beyond that. Don't you see? It's been years since—"

"Well," he said, "Dickinson wasn't so long ago."

"Yes, Dickinson, that poor, sad young man. He proves my point. You've paid a great price—we both have—for the security that defiance gave us."

He smiled. "I paid with Dickinson's bullet in my chest."

"But you paid too in what people thought of you with Dickinson dead and his children orphans. Now you'll pay more, for this. Maybe that quality saved us, but look at what it's cost us."

"Rachel, I'm no different from what I was. I've always been . . . well, determined."

"You've always been angry. Loving as you were, you were angry when I met you. You ran Robards off, that's the fact."

"And you were glad."

"Oh, I wouldn't change anything. I'd do it all again and I'd fly in their faces just the way we did—but that's not to say you weren't a pistol on full cock."

The door opened. Coffee's dark, anxious face appeared.

Andrew raised a hand. "I'm not ready, Jack. They'll have to wait." The door closed and he sighed and shut his eyes. Voice very small, he said, "That black-hearted British major . . ."

She knew the story of the Major. Andrew had been fourteen, his father long dead of overwork on their frontier homestead, when Tarleton's bloody rangers swept across the Carolina uplands to pillage Revolutionary Americans. A major who took quarters in their house told Andrew to clean his boots, and Andrew refused. The Major drew his saber and slashed him across his forehead and the scar was still there. Before he recovered his mother went off to nurse Americans held in British prison hulks in Charleston harbor, and there she died from what they called ship fever and left him alone in the world.

She'd heard the story often, but never this way. It was always full of youthful bravado, but now she heard the real child emerging, hurt, frightened, summoning his courage and his hate.

"I never told this to anyone. When he hit me I was so scared I peed my pants. Lay there bleeding, pee all over the floor, and he . . . he laughed at me. I never forgot that. And then Ma went off to nurse those poor devils, and God knows they needed it, but she left us all alone.

"It all told me there's only one way to lead your life. You have to run full tilt, throw yourself at it, and never, never let anyone push you. You have to *fight*, Rachel. That's what I've done and I reckon I always will."

"Oh, darling," she said. She knew what it had cost him to reveal, even to her, that ancient wound, the frightened boy soiling himself . . .

"But it *was* long ago," she said. "You've learned so much since then. That view, you know it's not enough, it's . . . well, too limited. You know there's more to life than that."

"Yes . . ."

"Then don't let it take charge of you!"

He didn't answer, and she said, "No one is born great. General Washington, he was a boy like any other. They say he made awful mistakes in the French and Indian War." She saw him nod. "He *grew* into greatness. And really, how else could one reach that exalted state?"

"What are you saying?"

"That power is in you, Andrew. I think you can be as great as you decide to be."

"But I must give up being who I am?"

"No, never—but I'm saying the very force that carries the seeds of greatness carries the seeds of destruction as well. You're right, I've only survived these years because you stood as a shield. But Andrew, that's fine when it's necessary but this thing with Tom—you know you had no real interests involved. You should have quieted the duel. Suppose Jesse had been killed? When Tom criticized you out of his family's humiliation, you should have had him to dinner and settled it with a word. You could have. You know that."

"Yes . . ."

"Well, I guess what I'm saying is that if you don't control this force, it will control you." She shrugged. "As for me, I doubt the families of great men are all that happy. I'd like to spend the rest of our lives on our farm, living as other people do. But you're . . . different. And if you let excess stifle what you can be in the world—oh, Andrew, I fear so for you! You'll turn dark and bitter . . ."

He didn't answer. The clamor outside seemed to grow. She knew Jack was pacing the hall. Time was running out.

She had to get it said. "I think you're at the most important crossroads of your life. This time that inner force brought you down—and now, just as the moment of greatness arises, when the people who look to you cry out, when the chance to lead will never be greater, you're flat on your back. The question is, which road will you take?"

"You're a wise woman," he said. "You always were. It wasn't just your pretty eyes that drew me, you know. And I've learned from you all my life." He winced from a sudden bolt of pain. "I think you're right. I've never seen it so, but I guess it's there to be seen."

She didn't answer; now it was up to him.

"Maybe I let that British major define my life. Funny, no? I do know that a wildness rises in me, and there's joy in letting it run. It's what I am, it's the essential me. That miserable man with his saber humbled me, but by Jehoshaphat, he was the last one to do it. That's been my strength— that inner capacity to explode in a magnitude to deal with anything—I can be killed, but I can't be beaten."

"All the force of gunpowder," she said.

"Yes."

"Do I understand that if you ignite gunpowder on a plate it will flash with little effect, but enclosed, in, say, a gun barrel, it's deadly?"

He smiled. "I do get your point."

"But it's an analogy worth pondering."

"Yes. Contained, directed, aimed—"

"Controlled."

"Yes, dearest girl, controlled." He was silent and she didn't speak. At last he said, "I've done everything I've set my hand to. I'll do this, too. You'll see." He nodded as if to himself, some inner confirmation.

"Now," he said, "let Jack in."

She listened to him give Jack instructions to call out the army. As soon as it could muster, they would march to settle this matter with the Creeks. The state would do it if the federal government wouldn't for this was intolerable.

"And, Jack," he added, "put exactly this at the end: 'The health of your general is restored. He will command in person.'"

She sighed. Had she saved him or was he advancing to an ultimate destruction? But she had done all she could.

13

★ ★ ★ ★ Dolley hurried from the visitors' gallery of the ornate House of Representatives chamber as soon as Henry Clay, the tall, elegant Speaker of the House, pushed through the vote that Jimmy so wanted. She went to the Capitol rotunda to treat herself to hard cakes she would dip in a stoneware mug of coffee. Deftly she threaded her way among vendors with their carts, tumblers and fiddlers and magicians seeking pennies, loafers in from the cold.

Actually, the rotunda between House and Senate was more a plan than a reality. At the moment it was a mere expanse boarded in against the weather where someday marble columns would stand if the Republic got around to raising them. But it made up in vigor what it lacked in looks— it was gloriously hurly-burly, a vivid place where congressmen and senators and pages and clerks hurried out for quick meals and stayed to do business, strike deals, make accommodations, honor and dishonor commitments, and thus grease the Republic's wheels.

She had just popped a bite of nicely saturated cake into her mouth when Henry Clay came hurrying toward her with boot heels clicking on the marble floor.

"Well, madam," he said with a vivid smile, his long, slender form bent at the waist, his silver snuffbox in hand, "I'll warrant you have no cause for complaint with us today."

Before she could answer, a swarthy vendor with pretzels on a stick aimed a kick at a yellow dog, and an urchin with sagging hose cried out in alarm. The man drew back a threatening hand.

"Now see here," Dolley said, "that will be enough of that! You leave that boy and his dog alone."

"Yes, mum." The pretzel vendor jerked off his cap.

Dolley turned back to Mr. Clay. "I thought you were brilliant," she said. "The Democrats were just wonderful."

The House had just passed the new embargo to stop all foreign trade. New England fought it, naturally, since the only foreign trade the United States had left came from New England—which was possible, obviously, only with the connivance of the British fleet that was supposedly maintaining the blockade. This treasonous trade infuriated Jimmy since it really went directly to the enemy, coastwise to Canada or to England itself. The embargo authorized the navy to hold vessels in port. New England would scream, but Jimmy said it would scream anyway. He wanted New Englanders to share the austerity of a nation under blockade.

"Yes," Mr. Clay said, "hard fought." She offered him a piece of her cake, which he broke off with long fingers and popped into his mouth. "Horse-trading and hair-pulling."

"I was proud of all of you," she said, though in fact it was Jimmy who had done it. Two embargo bills having failed in Congress earlier in the year, Jimmy had knocked heads this time, held feet to fires, called in debts, used all the leverage at his command. He'd always had the power; this time he used it, and she had an idea that the very use was a presidential elixir.

For it seemed to her that his mouth was firmer, his head straighter, his manner more forceful . . . when she said as much he'd frowned and said no, the situation simply demanded more forthright action. So she said no more, but she still liked it.

Mr. Clay grinned. "Of course, the President really did it."

"Well," she said, "there's credit enough to go around."

★ ★ ★ ★

Winfield Scott sat in a tiny chair at a tiny desk in the lobby of Davis's Hotel at Pennsylvania and Sixth. Congress was in session and the lobby swarmed with men in dark suits and white hose, in buff pantaloons and brass-buttoned coats, with women whose peacock feathers swooped behind them. They laughed, chattered, waved, called to each other. Men strolled to and from the taproom at the far end. The strains of Christmas carols from a street fiddler somewhere outside carried faintly over the chatter. Someone bumped the desk and murmured an apology; Scott crumpled the sheet and started over.

He was due at the President's House at three the next afternoon. The summons had caught him on the St. Lawrence River trying to digest the debacle Wilkinson had wrought—he wondered if the President blamed him for it. Maybe he simply wanted to talk strategy, but the peremptory letter that brought Scott back by day and night stage hadn't read like an invitation to chat.

Now—well, hell, writing Sally McQuirk was as uncomfortable as facing the President. He scratched a quick note. He'd just arrived, might not stay long, could he see her? He wadded it up. Too stiff. Five tries later he sanded and folded a slightly longer note, gave a messenger a coin, and sent it off. The answer came in an hour. She could give him a few minutes at five. A few minutes . . . Had his note betrayed his turmoil after all? Or was the turmoil hers?

When he pulled the bell cord she opened the door herself.

"Win!" She sounded breathless. "How good to see you." She caught his hands, but something in the set of her neck told him not to kiss her.

She led him into the parlor, where he bowed to her old auntie and followed her into a smaller parlor. They sat on a horsehair sofa, not far apart but not close, either. Dried flowers stood in vases and a cupid leered from a carved mantel. Auntie surveyed them over the book she pretended to read.

Sally seemed . . . different somehow, talkative, laughing, in no great hurry, interested in where he'd been and what he'd done and yet somehow brittle. His spirits flagged—he would have to broach the subject.

"I've been wondering, Sally, if we . . . if we . . ." There wasn't any good way to say it.

"If we're right for each other?" she said.

He sighed. "Yes. That is—"

"Oh, Win, I'm so glad you said it. I didn't know how."

In fact, *he* hadn't known how, and *she* had said it, but he let it go. She beamed at him, damn it all.

But then she took his hand. "Win, I do love you, and I think you love me—and if you don't, don't you dare say it!" She laughed.

"But it wouldn't have worked, and yet it was too strong for half measures." Her voice fell to a whisper. "I had to have all of you, mind and soul and body"—her eyebrows shot up—"or nothing. And I knew we'd end up destroying each other."

He nodded, comfortable at last. "Yes, dear Sally, I came out at the same place. But we'll be friends, won't we?"

She drew the back of his hand to her cheek. Her voice was very low. "Of course we'll be friends. But we won't—well, I couldn't stand it again. It was too wonderful. All my resolve would go."

So would his. "It's been precious, Sally. Precious."

"Yes. And it's our secret."

"Ours alone."

He walked away feeling exalted. Then he remembered the summons he faced the next afternoon.

★ ★ ★ ★

When young Scott walked into the office, Madison saw immediately that he was nervous. His uniform brushed to perfection, his hat tucked smartly under his left arm, he stood rigidly at attention. It hadn't occurred to Madison that an abrupt summons from the snows of Canada might unnerve a young man, but maybe it was as well that it so clearly had. He wanted answers.

"Sit down, Colonel." He nodded to the officer's bow.

Scott sat on the edge of the chair, that ridiculous hat still under his left arm.

"Put down your hat," Madison said. "We'll be here awhile, because I want the full story of what happened up on the St. Lawrence. What the devil went wrong?"

"Everything, sir." Scott looked a little more at ease. "One doesn't know where to begin."

"Begin with yourself. You were there?"

"Yes, sir."

"With your troops—the Second Artillery?"

"No, sir. I sent them on to Sackett's Harbor to defend our bases there, army and navy, against a possible counterattack. Sarenmajor Boone and I went on to the front."

"How long did that take?"

"Thirty hours in the saddle."

"Over how many days?"

"Thirty hours, sir, with stops to change horses."

"Straight through?"

"Yes, sir."

Ah, to be young again and consider a thirty-hour ride unremarkable. Or even possible. Madison couldn't have done it even in the flush of boyhood. He'd always been sickly . . .

"So you joined the invasion force?"

"Yes, sir. Overshot it, in fact. Struck the St. Lawrence twenty miles beyond General Wilkinson's position. I'd expected him to be farther along."

"I'd expected *everyone* to be farther along."

Scott didn't answer.

"So you backtracked," Madison said. "How was General Wilkinson?"

"In poor health, sir. The closer we got to action the worse his health. Diarrhea, dysentery, ague . . . I understand he'd been treating himself with opium, which may have been better for his bowels than his brains."

My. He saw he needn't have wondered if this young man would speak his mind. "Colonel," he said, "the first time I met you, Secretary Eustis described your court-martial for criticizing a general officer and your suspension for a year. That officer was General Wilkinson."

"Yes, sir."

"I looked up that case. It seems you said that serving under General Wilkinson was like being married to a prostitute. What did you mean?"

"That you couldn't trust him, sir."

"And that he was 'imbecility perfected.'"

"Yes, sir."

"And that if you had your wishes, you'd put a bayonet up his—well, in an undignified place."

"Yes, sir."

"My, my. Do you still hold those opinions?"

"Yes, sir."

"Were they eased or exacerbated by your recent experiences?"

"Exacerbated, sir."

"I see. Well, what was the battle plan?"

"As I understood it, sir, it was to bypass Kingston at the entrance of the St. Lawrence River. Commodore Chauncey's ships would hold British vessels there while the attack force moved downriver toward Montreal. There were two columns. General Wilkinson had seven thousand men in boats and on the banks, General Hampton was to bring four thousand more cross-country from Lake Champlain. The two columns would join on the St. Lawrence and advance together to take Montreal."

"Why not take Kingston—wasn't that the original plan?"

"General Brown told me Commodore Chauncey wasn't willing to risk his ships in an all-out attack." Scott smiled. "He does love those ships."

"But not using them defeats their purpose, doesn't it?"

"That's the military conundrum, sir. One works desperately hard to build a force, only to put it at risk."

Madison nodded. A distinction not all generals—or commodores—could make. He knew now that generals fell in two basic classes, those who liked to fight and those who didn't. Unfortunately, his didn't and the enemy's did.

"What was your role?"

"Took the point on the south bank, as General Brown did on the north bank. We were about ten miles ahead of the main army."

"Resistance?"

"I found a redcoat unit dug in. Flanked them and routed them. General Brown brushed aside similar opposition."

"So the advance was moving."

"Yes, sir. But Kingston was left uncovered after all—"

"Commodore Chauncey couldn't hold the British fleet?"

"His message said it looked too risky."

"He didn't try?"

"Apparently not, sir. So a fleet of British gunboats got in the river behind us to threaten our rear. They supported some eight hundred infantry under a Lieutenant Colonel Morrison. General Boyd commanded our rear guard, about two thousand. He landed his troops to beat off Morrison."

"And then?"

"I was ten miles in advance, but I understand Morrison took a good position in a clearing on a farm on the Canadian side owned by a Mr. Crysler. Three-pounders centered, line of skirmishers ahead, main line dug in with right flank on the river, left anchored in a swamp. Made him hard to flank. General Boyd came straight in and met very concentrated fire."

"Still, two thousand to eight hundred . . ." Really, that should be enough to do at least something.

"Yes, sir, but General Boyd didn't mass his force. He threw them against the British as they landed, unit by unit. At any given time, it was more like five ours to eight theirs. Our men were green, theirs highly trained, ours charging, theirs delivering sighted fire. Cut us up pretty badly."

"I thought General Boyd was experienced."

"In India, sir. With elephants and such."

Yes . . . at the start, any experience had seemed valuable. But Madison had learned a lot since then.

"Still," he said, "eight hundred men in your rear doesn't seem enough to stop seven thousand."

"Sir, General Wilkinson was quite ill. And just then General Hampton sent word that he wouldn't join the attack after all, said he was out of supplies and going into winter quarters. General Brown said that seemed to add considerable weight to General Wilkinson's doubts."

"Winter quarters. Getting cold, was it?"

"Bitterly cold, sir. Snow soon was certain."

"Why the devil wasn't the campaign started earlier?"

"No one seemed very urgent, to tell you the truth."

"But damn it all, Wilkinson still had his seven thousand, less Boyd's losses."

"Yes, sir. There were reports of substantial British forces ahead—grossly exaggerated reports, General Brown thought. He told me he voted to press on. General Wilkinson decided to withdraw."

"Wilkinson was ill, of course . . ."

"Actually, sir, his health improved dramatically as soon as he decided to turn back. We all noticed it."

Madison sighed. He could be more understanding of Wilkinson sick in the wilderness than a young man who'd just ridden thirty hours straight to join him, but the picture Scott drew left no doubt. Wilkinson had delayed as long—and quit as soon—as he could. He'd been useful long ago when Burr was exposed, and old Tom had decided to overlook his ties to the Spanish and to the smuggling fraternity of New Orleans, but now . . .

"Colonel," he said, "Mrs. Madison is having a small social in the family parlor; would you care to join it?"

"Very much, sir. Thank you, sir."

As he led the way, Madison said, "What do you think of General Brown?"

"A splendid officer, sir. A fighting officer."

"I have the impression he's not especially learned."

"But his instincts coincide with the dicta of the great theorists. I'd be honored to serve under him, sir."

"Good. General Wilkinson is leaving the army. So is General Hampton. And General Lewis and General Boyd. As of this moment, Brown is a major general, and you, sir, are a brigadier. You'll serve as second in command to General Brown."

A smile of utter delight flashed across the young man's face. Then he sobered.

"Thank you, sir. I believe you will not be disappointed." He hesitated. "Sir?"

"Yes?"

"Sir, I've argued often for better training, officers and men alike. Again and again, British troops outperform our men, not because they're smarter or braver than ours but because they're well trained. I know General Brown agrees. What I'd like, sir, is your authority to establish a training camp in the North and turn our men there into soldiers."

"By all means, General," Madison said, enjoying Scott's smile at this first use of his new title. "You do that. I'll see that the Secretary and General Brown approve."

★ ★ ★ ★

Following the little President along the long, solemn corridor of the mansion, Scott felt like dancing a jig.

Brigadier!

General's stars!

They walked into the family parlor, a small, graceful room with a tall window overlooking the south lawn, where the vegetable garden was strawed for winter. A Christmas tree decorated with a hundred candles, still unlit, stood in a corner. The President's plump wife turned toward them. She wore a vivid green turban; Sally said Mrs. Madison had made wearing turbans the current fashion rage, copied even in Paris.

Two slender young women stood by the window, their backs to the glass. Scott bowed to Mrs. Madison, saluted Ned Coles, met a couple of congressmen and a senator, a couple of lawyers, one from Boston named Thornton, the other a local man, Frank Key with Mrs. Key, and several others.

The taller of the two women at the window was Betsy Coles, Ned's sister, whose brief curtsy made it clear she was none too impressed. She had frizzy hair the color of carrots, quite unlike the smaller woman, whose rose-colored gown perfectly set off gleaming chestnut hair.

"And this," the President said, "is Miss Maria Mayo of Richmond. Betsy and Miss Mayo are spending the season with us."

Maria Mayo's brown eyes were deep and steady, the color of her hair, and as Scott bowed over her hand he had the feeling he could fall into them. They opened wide, they swept him in, enveloped him, left him a little dizzy.

"Miss Mayo," he said. "I'm honored."

She left her hand in his for a moment that felt endless, then withdrew it with a smile that seemed to say *she* wouldn't mind leaving it there forever, but what would the others say? Those wonderful eyes were wide-set and her coloring was russet and gold and quite perfect with eyes and hair and gown, low-cut under a cloud of lace . . .

"Colonel?" she said. Her voice had a lilt. "My. Such rank for one so young."

The President laughed. "He's a general now."

"Well!" Mrs. Madison's obvious pleasure lit her face with such a glow that in the warm flush of his own pleasure Scott saw for the first time why she was considered beautiful.

"Hear, hear!" she said. "Come, everyone, we'll drink a toast. General Scott!"

"Youngest general in the army," the President said. "I looked it up." He turned to his wife and left Scott with Miss Mayo and Miss Coles.

"Pay attention, everyone," Mrs. Madison said, clapping her hands, "Frank is going to give us his latest."

Francis Key apparently was a versifier of no mean skill, from the attention the group gave his rhymes. Scott, who had no ear for verse, waited patiently, politely attentive.

When Mr. Key and the applause were over, Betsy Coles turned to Scott.

"Now, General." She touched the back of her frizzy hair. "I suppose you are adept at campaigns?"

"I hope so, Miss Coles."

"Then you must plot a campaign immediately to restore Maria's tattered heart."

"Betsy!" Miss Mayo said.

"It was broken in Richmond," Miss Coles said.

"It was not!"

"Your face was as long as a basset hound's."

"*I* dismissed *him*, thank you."

"Ha!" Betsy said. "You see your objective, General."

"I do indeed, Miss Coles."

Betsy Coles danced away. Scott and Miss Mayo looked at each other. Both giggled at the same time.

"She's horrid," Maria said.

"Friends do that. It shows she loves you. And it broke the ice for us and I very much wanted it broken."

"Did you, sir? In truth, so did I. Isn't that awful? I guess I'm not so put out with Betsy. Come, pour me an eggnog and tell me if you know the Scotts of Dinwiddie Courthouse."

"Cousins, uncles, aunts, all." She took his arm as he led her to the crystal punch bowl. He felt immediately comfortable with her. He and Maria Mayo could be friends.

★ ★ ★ ★

Dolley sighed, very relaxed, and took a last cookie that she knew very well she should forgo. But she'd earned it, with her successful little gathering. She prized Frank Key for his poetry, and Jimmy said he sliced like a razor in the courtroom, that juries melted to his voice. You want something done, send Frank. Dolley hadn't always been so tolerant of verse's convoluted forms; that she had learned to appreciate poetry she took as a sign of maturity. Frank was charming, too, lithe and handsome with an elegant air—she wondered if his mousy little wife appreciated him. Of course, she'd given him six children with another coming, perhaps mousy was the best she could do.

And hadn't Maria brightened like sunshine over the young general? My! Dolley had wondered about the girl—she seemed sober and quiet, nothing like Betsy's bright flamboyance. Did she even like men? Some girls didn't, after all. Some girls liked girls, though of course one didn't mention such things, and some girls didn't like men but married anyway, you saw the unhappy couples all the time. Dolley noticed things.

But my goodness, the light in Maria's face when she met the young officer made Dolley's heart swell. And he had lit up, too. Of course, she'd seen him do the same thing over Sally McQuirk, but everyone tended to light up for Sally. Though she thought Sally held them off somehow—there was something hidden in Sally, something inaccessible. She had an idea that whatever had started between Sally and General Scott hadn't matured.

Another cookie? Well, one more. She saw Jennie peeping around the door and waved the child in, noticing the willowy way she walked, the sway of her hips. She was a pretty girl who soon would be a beauty.

"Take the dishes, dear," she said.

Joseph came in, and the look of joy that flashed across Jennie's face revealed for a moment the woman she would become. Dolley glanced at Joseph and saw him look away, his face a cold mask. Why, the child was in love with him!

And he ignored her? She was lovely already and rapidly filling out— obviously wild about him. Was he blind? Jennie would be ready for marriage soon, they could have a wedding right here in the mansion, the servants would have a party and she and Jimmy would drink a toast to the newlyweds—

Joseph walked out of the room with a tray and she watched the girl gaze after him. Then Jennie reached for her empty cup and saucer, and Dolley saw the tears standing in her eyes. Poor child—what *was* the matter with him?

★ ★ ★ ★

One piece of good news. One. Madison sat at his desk, digesting reports of a victory. He supposed he should savor good news, there was so little of it, yet he couldn't. So much was bad that it overwhelmed the good.

In the summer past, Commodore Oliver Hazard Perry's fleet on Lake Erie had defeated a British squadron in magnificent combat. Perry had sent General Harrison at Detroit a message that Madison suspected would last longer than the war: "We have met the enemy and they are ours." Would that Commodore Chauncey on Lake Ontario might so seize the initiative!

Harrison had set out along the north shore of Lake Erie, met a small force of British and Indians, and defeated them soundly. Lake Erie was ours, which reassured the West but hardly advanced the primary goal, the invasion of Canada.

But now it developed that one of the Indians killed in the fighting was Tecumseh himself. Apparently there was celebration all over the West, for with the death of the great chief came as well the death of his dream of an Indian buffer state supported by British arms and gold that would unite tribes from Hudson's Bay to the Gulf and put an end to settlers' westward movement. And the British losing the battle apparently had shattered Indian belief that men in red coats were invincible, with the predictable result that Indian allies were melting away.

All good news. Still, Tecumseh had been a genius, the greatest leader the Indian peoples ever produced, a man of towering vision who, born in a different age and circumstances, could have been a Caesar, a Napoleon.

Rare is the leader who can stir men to their hearts, yet has an intellectual vision of the future that spans continents and ages. Madison had the intellect, yes, but that blazing passion from within that brings followers to their feet with roars and launches them against the highest barricades—he would never have that.

He could help invent a country—he knew it was said he'd done as much as any man to create the U.S. Constitution, and he couldn't in honesty quarrel with the description. But how tepid an encomium compared to a Caesar of the forest able to mold incredibly diverse forces into a single whole. Of course they lit bonfires in Ohio and Kentucky and Tennessee, where fear of the Indian grew from hard experience. But Madison felt no jubilation. He understood that no king can celebrate the death of another king, for only a king can know a king.

★ ★ ★ ★

A hard, slanting rain drove out of the east, and the light was fading at four in the afternoon. Madison waited by a little-used side door on the ground floor, watching the rain and the bare limbs of a big oak shiver in the wind.

A carriage stopped and a long, lean figure swung down under an umbrella—Henry Clay, the Speaker and their best friend in Congress. It was Friday, the thirty-first of December; in the oval drawing room on the first floor Dolley was preparing the evening's celebration. It would be elaborate to a fault, though there was precious little to celebrate, that being, as Dolley said, the time to make merry. He held the door open as Clay bounded in, slinging water from his hat.

"Appreciate your seeing me on short notice, Mr. President." Clay settled into a deep leather chair in the library on the ground floor and wrapped both hands around a cup of steaming coffee Madison gave him from a pot on an alcohol flame.

"I've got a mini-revolt on the Hill. They're getting plenty of voter anger for passing the embargo, and it's got 'em worried. But worse than that, there's a new tone up there. Hatred, there's no other word for it. Federalist members won't speak to Democrats, as if the embargo tore something beyond repair. It's . . . well, it's disconcerting, open hatred right on the floor. As if they're New Englanders now, Federalists now, instead of Americans. Some of those Boston papers are flirting with sedition. What can become of a country so divided?"

Madison didn't answer. As a tongue searches out a sore tooth, Clay had raised the national nightmare, the tendency of a diverse nation to break into sections when stress is greatest.

"Another thing," Clay said. "On the Hill they're saying this administration looks as if it's coming undone. What the devil is going on, this business with Armstrong?"

The Secretary of War had yet to return to his duties. He was in New York City, where several newspapers carried extensive anonymous letters criticizing military failures and urging the appointment of a single commander. Everyone understood the letters were Armstrong's work, and who but himself did he have in mind for the lieutenant generalcy he proposed?

"Could he handle the top spot?" Clay asked.

"In the end, he lacks the courage to act. That's what happened to his fine plan on the northern frontier."

Clay nodded. "Suspected that. But you can't sack him."

"And won't," Madison said.

The Speaker was watching him carefully. "Good. There'd be an awful explosion." Armstrong was still popular in New York, and dismissing him would slap the state that had supplied more troops and seen more fighting than any other. And that had voted for DeWitt Clinton's siren song of an easy end to war. Anyway, as Madison pointed out, Armstrong had reorganized the army's staff and supply system with energy and skill.

"A thorn in your flesh," Clay said, "but I think you're stuck with him. Now, what about these Leipzig rumors? True?"

"Oh, yes," Madison said. "Reports from our agents all over Europe." German and Russian armies had smashed Napoleon's forces in three days of fighting around Leipzig. Already shattered in the terrible Moscow campaign, the French now were in another pell-mell retreat. Madison suspected the immense battle would emerge as a landmark in world history.

"A disaster for Napoleon," he said, "and that's a disaster for us."

"Think he's down? The man has nine lives, you know."

"Prussian forces are across the Rhine. And from Spain Wellington has fought his way through the Pyrenees. He's in Bayonne now. There's nothing to stop the advance on Paris—it's a question of who gets there first."

Clay gave Madison a canny look. "So the British will invade us next, right?"

"Our attaché in London hears they're ticketing fifty to seventy thousand men for transport to North America."

"Teach the pesky Yanks a lesson," Clay said. "God—remember when I said the Kentucky militia alone could take Canada?"

"Did you say that?" Madison smiled. Everyone had said something equally fatuous. And the President—the fatuous President—had believed it.

Fifty to seventy thousand . . . that made invasion certain. Madison stopped himself from lamenting the lost opportunities for taking Canada— the question now would be to make sure they didn't take us. Clay wanted details; he had to be straight with his members, no rosy views now and surprises later.

Madison saw two danger spots in the North and the big one in the South, where sooner or later they would make their try on New Orleans. So far, he had no one to meet a southern invasion.

"Well, Jackson's gone after the Creeks."

"Yes . . ." That bloody business at Fort Mims—five hundred settlers dead, apparently most of them women and children. The moment Madison heard the news, he knew it would rattle the nation, dampening the joy over the Lake Erie victory. Long before then Jackson had gone helling off with the Tennessee militia. With his arm in a sling, thanks to a shooting brawl of some sort that had reawakened Madison's distaste for the man. Imagine, someone of Jackson's age and position in a shooting.

"I hope he quiets the Creeks," Madison said, "but that's nothing like a serious invasion."

"You're underrating him, Mr. President," Clay said. "I know him well. He and I sure as hell don't always see eye to eye, but there's a power in him—and a powerful intellect."

"Jackson an intellectual?"

"No, but he has a great native intelligence that seems to work intuitively. I've never seen a man process information and come to a conclusion so rapidly, often by an intuitive leap."

Madison nodded; Clay's opinions were usually sound. And Jackson had wasted no time in pursuing the Creeks while the regular troops in the South lagged far behind.

"At least he likes to fight," he said. "Makes him a rarity among my generals."

Clay said members from New York were in a panic since the British crossed the Niagara and burned Buffalo. It was near criminal, he said, the way we whipped them last summer and then threw it away. Madison reminded him that the generals responsible had been cashiered and he'd put the Niagara frontier in the hands of Jake Brown and young Scott.

Lake Champlain was the other vulnerability. An invading force could run down the lake, cross to Lake George, jump over to the Hudson, and float right into New York City.

"Cutting off the whole of New England?"

"If we let 'em."

"And will we?"

"Of course not. They can't advance without holding the lake, and I have a young naval officer building a fleet there. Tom Macdonough, trained under Decatur, especially valiant in the Tripoli fighting and he knows shipbuilding."

"I know Macdonough, I think. Stocky, blocky fellow, eyes look like he's seen plenty of saltwater? Delaware man?"

"That's him." In fact, Madison knew that tremendous responsibility had been placed on the young naval officer, but Decatur vouched for him and in desperate days you took what you had. And he knew how to build ships as well as fight them, which here was a crucial skill.

"Now," Clay said, "what about closer to home? This loudmouthed Admiral Co'burn in the Chesapeake, burning towns along the coast and threatening to invade?"

"Pinpricks so far. He lacks the troops for a real invasion now, but of course, more are coming."

"You know, it's like when the lamp is burning low and all your chips are in the pot and you've got kings back to back and the other fellow has an ace showing—"

"I'll take your word for it." Madison didn't play poker.

"Well, Admiral Co'burn and his threats are the ace showing—has he one in the hole? Does he mean to attack or is he just talking? And is our Secretary of War watching that?"

"The Secretary tells me Washington has no military value."

"Horseshit! Washington's vulnerability is the hottest potato of all—if he sacks our capital, that's rubbing our nose in it. And since you're not a card-playing man, let me tell you from damned painful experience that when you see an ace showing the warning flags are flying."

Still, there was a new ray of hope. The British had rejected the Russian offer to mediate peace—but they had proposed direct negotiations between themselves and the United States. Madison was delighted, and he'd held this information to the end of the conversation in order to finish talking on a positive note. But when he told Clay the news, the Kentuckian threw up his arms and laughed.

"Now they'll invade us for sure!"

"You think they're playing with us? The offer not serious? Really, Harry, too much cynicism corrupts clear thinking."

"Of course they want to talk," Clay said, quite unruffled. "Why not? But first they'll up the ante. Grab all they can to bargain from strength. Building the pot, so to speak."

Madison laughed. A gambling man tended to get right to the gut of things. A new thought struck him. Albert Gallatin—exhausted as Secretary of the Treasury—had asked to join the negotiations when the Russian offer was still open. Madison couldn't refuse, though he was very fond of Gallatin and needed him desperately here. So the administration's financial expert was in Europe with young John Quincy Adams, old John's son, who'd become a brilliant diplomat. He and Adams would pursue the new negotiations—but why not put Clay with them? Let the British face a Kentucky poker player— they might learn something! He would broach it later, but he had decided.

But how will we respond to invasion, Clay wondered; he said members were deeply worried. Congressional reluctance to tax, to draft men into the military, even to authorize loans, all grew from the same thing: the feeling the people themselves were not behind this war.

"Harry," Madison said, "we fought the British once and set ourselves free. I don't think we're so different today."

"Damned if we don't act differently."

"Yes, but why? Because so far it's a political war. Second revolution to prove the first, yes, but the issues are those of diplomacy, our right to trade, our seamen's safety. This German, Clausewitz, he says war is politics by other means, but that idea works best with conscript armies.

"There's a lesson here that future presidents will do well to heed: free men don't fight well for political abstractions. But face them with real threats they can see and understand in their hearts and they're tigers—with all the imagination, the ingenuity, the initiative, the plain raw courage that a life of freedom demands.

"The British can invade us but they can't hold us. They couldn't before when we weren't a tenth of our strength today. We've had thirty-five years of freedom—will we give that up easily? No, sir, we'll fight. Wait and see."

Clay stood to go. "It'll be a rough year."

"Yes," Madison said, "a very rough year."

THREE

COMMAND OF DESTINY

★ ★ ★ ★

1814

14

★ ★ ★ ★ The brigade inspector, Billy Carroll, reined up before Jackson. "Sir, C Company's taking off. Say they're going home." He stood in his stirrups to point.

Jackson saw the tail of a column disappear into the woods.

"Those miserable bastards! We'll see about that."

He heaved himself onto his sorrel mare, gripping the saddle with his right hand. As always, the movement lit the pain in his frozen left arm, set it glowing and aching. He ignored it, willing its effect off his face.

"C'mon, Johnny," he said to Reid, "we'll head 'em off."

He set the bay to a swift trot through the woods, jumping downed logs, scrambling through draws, circling ahead.

"Mutineers, God damn their rotten souls!"

"It's not really mutiny, General," John Reid said in an earnest voice. "They just want to go home."

"But they shall not, sir! They can't run out on me. That's mutiny, and I'll see them in hell before—"

"Sir, they've fought well, you've got to give them that. And running out of food scared 'em. Winter's coming, they've got it in their heads they could starve."

"Nonsense. We have food now. It isn't an issue."

The arm, held stiffly against his side, throbbed damnably. It never let him forget. It gnawed and growled and wore him down, kept him on knife-edge. He refused laudanum, which dulled the mind, so he slept in snatches when he slept at all. Dysentery gripped him; his guts ached and his bowels boiled. These youngsters with their untouched faces, their complaints, their fear of short rations—what did they know of suffering?

Fragments of bone kept working out of his arm, pressing from the inside till he operated on himself with his clasp knife and pulled out sharp slivers and clamped his arm against bleeding, nauseated and trembling. He guessed the wound was better now, but who could say, what with the bullet still in there?

Your general's health is restored. He will lead in person . . . He'd done it, too, sick with pain—ridden into Alabama, paused on the Tennessee River to build a fort for the supplies he'd ordered in volume, then gone on to the Coosa River to build another, Fort Strother.

Despite pain and griping guts, soldiering was proving out for him, by God. He'd always believed he was destined to walk in great strides across his times—to be somebody who *mattered*. And sure enough—look at the fighting at an Indian town called Talladega. He'd aligned his troops with precision, the center purposely weak, cavalry on right and left bent forward in wings. The Indians attacked the center, it fell back, the wings swept in to close the trap—and he had them. Some escaped thanks to a lieutenant's error, but he was left with three hundred enemy dead and proof of his tactical capacities.

Lost forty-five killed, one hundred fifty-seven wounded. Burying forty-five good young men in the wilderness—drums rolling, bugles blaring, muskets thundering overhead in salute—sobered the boys, as did the screams of the wounded and the pile of arms and legs outside the surgeon's tent.

Every day he walked among the pallets of the sick. He drafted letters to those at home whose men were buried in the Alabama wilderness. War wasn't glorious, but it was necessary in an imperfect world and he knew that this war had just begun.

William Weatherford, as the charismatic half-breed Chief Red Eagle styled himself among whites, had started it with the massacre at Fort Mims. He was extraordinary—a master of rhetoric who could rouse his warriors to frenzy, an organizer who'd put six thousand troops in the field with discipline unheard of among Indians, a sophisticated manipulator who wore fine broadcloth when negotiating with Spaniards or Britons. They said he'd tried to stop the slaughter of women and children at Fort Mims, but what did trying matter? Jackson intended to see him stretched on a plank.

Maybe then the administration would focus on what mattered—the defense of the entire South. They must defeat the Creeks and eject the Spanish from Florida for the same reason: both were cat's-paws for a British invasion aimed at New Orleans.

Jackson was dead certain he was the man to smash the strike the British were sure to aim at the American underbelly. Big talk for a militia general? The point exactly: a militia command with its base in only a single state could only go so far. What he needed was a regular army commission. They'd elevated Jake Brown from the New York militia, hadn't they? Brown was a fighter, but could less be said of Jackson?

And who else did they have? Major General Pinckney, commanding in the South as Dearborn had in the North, was another old veteran, avuncular, kindly, dignified, rich—and not out here facing the enemy. Jackson grunted, dismissing Pinckney as the mare sailed over a rotting log. Time enough to worry about that—for now he had a war to fight and Indians to punish, and his damned shortsighted Tennesseans wanted to go home!

Of course his men had been hungry. What of it? They ran out of provisions, that's all, and only because contractors took their sweet time in filling his orders. What did those rotten greedy bastards care that fighting men starved in the wilderness? If he could lay hands on one of them he'd string him to the nearest tree and put some hurry in the rest of them.

With nothing coming down the trail from his supply dump fort, the food was about gone. There weren't deer for miles. He heard anxiety fluttering in his men's voices. He saw his muscular young sergeant, Pink Mims, fashion cakes from flour scrapings, acorn shavings, the last of the lard. Soon everything was gone; they drank acorn soup and waited.

Finally he set them on the road toward Tennessee, hoping to meet the supply column. That afternoon they did—beeves on the hoof and wagons full of flour, coffee, sugar, and fatback, a gift of angels. They gorged all night and in the morning he formed them up to march back to Fort Strother and the campaign ahead. He saw long faces—a few idiots who'd supposed they were starting for home had stirred them up.

And now a company had decided to decamp. Common sense said if he let one company go the whole army would follow, but more important, what did it say of Tennessee soldiers if they ran for home—and of their general if he couldn't control them?

No, by God, he wouldn't have it! He felt the old rage rising, warm and fine, like stepping into an old boot molded to his foot, clasping him like armor that made him invincible, omnipotent, conquering. The pain in his arm forgotten in the mists of rage, he sent the horse careening into a gully to lunge up the other side.

His handsome young aide from Virginia was still arguing for the men—they'd fought well, they'd been dismayed by hunger, they needed winter coats, they didn't understand the consequences—pleading for them. Major Reid was bright, able, uncomplaining, but was his loyalty a sometime thing?

"What's this?" Jackson said. "I thought I could count on you."

Reid gave him a stare as hard as his own. "If you doubt my loyalty, sir, I'll resign immediately and return to the ranks as a private. But I take it hard to be challenged for stating the men's case."

The arrogant puppy!

Just then they reached the road and he saw Jack Coffee and a company of cavalry. There came the errant company of deserters, swinging along as if on holiday—swiftly he arrayed Jack's troopers across the road and advanced to meet the miscreants.

They stopped when they saw him. He rode close and gave them a piece of his mind in a roar that lashed them, while Jack's troopers leveled their pieces, and when he was done he could see they felt lucky to be alive. Their captain looked shamed as an egg-sucking dog.

"Get on back, God damn you all—any more of this foolishness, I'll have you before a firing squad!"

And he followed them back, plotting their punishment.

But at camp the formation was drawn up facing in the wrong direction. They were ready to march home themselves!

He galloped forward. "What's the meaning of this?"

But the answer was obvious. The First Brigade—half his army, a thousand men—was pulling out. Deserting in the face of the enemy, a firing squad offense in any army in the world and most certainly in this army.

Rage flooded his mind. It soared and wrapped him in its wings and lifted him on high, made him a giant and a king. For a moment he saw Rachel's saddened eyes, heard her voice: *If you don't control this force, it will control you.* Control. Control. But God damn it, he wasn't out of control, he was *in* control, dominating, soaring, ready to crush everything that stood in his way.

Rachel was a woman, how could she know the ways of armies? Mutiny had to be crushed. Smashed. Throttled.

"You, God damn it," he shouted at a trooper, "give me that musket!"

White-faced, the lad handed him the piece. Holding it and the reins in his good hand, he galloped to the front of the errant brigade. A thousand faces stared at him, sullen, fierce, sour with hatred. Oh, they had a lot to learn!

He wheeled the sorrel mare before them, quieted her, and laid the musket across the pommel of his saddle, bearing dead on the ringleader bastards who'd put them up to treason.

"Hold it right there," he shouted. His voice was raspy from shouting at the company earlier, and that handful hadn't been a patch on this lot.

"Hold it. Nobody's going anywhere but back to Fort Strother and on with this campaign. Who do you bastards think you are? You're soldiers, by God—sworn to service for state and nation."

He glared at them. "Walk out on me? Run when the enemy's in sight? I'll see you dead first, every rotten one of you!"

Reid and Jack Coffee rode forward, positioned themselves beside him.

A rumble rose from the brigade. The men's faces were contorted. The sound of them, full of threat and menace, sent his rage soaring again.

"The first man who moves gets a bullet in the brain!"

He waited, finger curled around the trigger, the flintlock poised to flash down on the pan, ready to blow a heavyset sergeant in the front rank to kingdom come, and the moment stretched and stretched like a glassblower's strand drawing out and out—

And they broke. Their eyes fell, they shuffled their feet, some on the edges peeled off and then those in the middle turned, and those in front began backing away, and it was over. Turned their backs, walked shuffle-footed and shamed. He sat watching them go, and slowly his hand holding the musket relaxed.

He tossed the piece to someone and turned the mare toward his command tent. He felt exhausted, sick. Pain flamed through his arm like a fresh wound. His good hand began to tremble. Tremors coursed his whole body. He clamped hand to pommel, willing himself to hold steady in the saddle.

For now he saw it for what it was. He hadn't been in control at all.

Booted and spurred, anger had ridden him like the demon it was. The feeling he'd welcomed so, that soaring into omnipotence—it was just what he'd felt as he'd turned into the City Hotel on the Nashville square to chastise that miserable Tom Benton. Exactly. King of all he saw, swept on the wings of rage.

And flat on his back one minute later about to bleed to death.

He dismounted, leaned against a tree, and fought to hold down vomit. Toss his breakfast and they'd all be sure it was from facing them. But it wasn't. He needed desperately to vomit up what was in *him*. What lived inside him. What Rachel feared. What he'd promised her he would conquer.

"General?"

Young Reid was beside him.

"Are you all right, sir?"

"Dysentery cramps . . . I'll sit on that log a moment."

It wasn't dysentery, of course. It was fear. Not that he'd done wrong. He had had to stop them and he knew no other way than to pit his force against their weight. The fear was for how he had *felt*. He'd been luxuriating in the control he was so sure he'd mastered. On which he had promised Rachel . . .

So easy to make, promises.

★ ★ ★ ★

That afternoon they were back at Fort Strother. More supplies came—food, blankets, clothing, ammunition. But discontent flowered in minds set on going home. Young Reid pointed out they were mostly farmers with fields and cattle that needed tending, wives and children carrying the load alone.

Of course. They weren't professional soldiers, they were needed at home. And what of it? They'd volunteered, they'd gone to war in service of their country, and it was nowhere near over.

Then the First Brigade made a new move. Said their enlistments would expire in ten days. He found their reasoning faulty and told them to forget it, he'd never permit it. But they pressed. Ten days. Nine days. Eight, seven, six. Insisting. His arm throbbed. He walked stiff-legged and when the subject came up he got short of breath and all his officers looked worried. It raised a choking fury in him. Walk out on him? Fail in the greatest enterprise of their miserable molelike lives? Not, by God, while General Jackson was in command!

On the afternoon of the ninth day, Colonel Carroll came to him in a panic. "First Brigade plans to slip out in the night and head for home."

Jackson wasn't surprised. "Call 'em out on parade. Right now."

Bugle calls piped across the afternoon. First Brigade to the left, Second to the right, the two artillery pieces to the rear, cavalry on the far right. The men formed ranks, eyes shifting uneasily. Jackson sat his horse, staring at them.

"Major Reid," he said, "please ask General Johnston to move his Second Brigade two hundred paces to the rear. And ask Captain Smyth to report to me."

"Sir?" Captain Smyth said. He commanded the artillery. The Second Brigade was moving back. The First stood, the men craning their heads, puzzling over the shifts.

"Captain," Jackson said, "I want you to position both guns directly to the rear of the First Brigade. Load with grape and stand by, ready to light slow matches if I give the order."

"Yes, sir." Smyth hesitated. "Sir, you mean to aim—"

"At the First Brigade, exactly. See to it, Captain."

The two little guns swung into position. Gunners staked them down for firing. Loaded and rammed. First Brigade soldiers looked over their shoulders. A wave of uneasy murmurs went through the ranks.

"General Hall," Jackson said, "bring the First Brigade to attention, please."

The commands rang out and the men stiffened. Jackson rode slowly along their front, staring at them. He turned, came back, stopped his horse at their center. He sat very stiff and straight. Horse and rider were motionless, silent.

The artillerymen held slow matches still unlit.

Jackson began calmly enough, but his voice rose with anger until it was loud and blaring. They were fighting men, at least so they'd posed, they were Tennesseans pledged to protect their homes. They were volunteers; they'd signed on to avenge the horror of women and children slaughtered like shoats at Fort Mims; they'd pledged to protect the whole underside of the nation from a British invasion that would begin with the Creeks feeding intelligence to the enemy.

Had they forgotten cheering their nation into war? Forgotten Fort Mims, forgotten the River Raisin, forgotten that scoundrel Tecumseh, forgotten the ignominy forced on old Hull? The British burning Buffalo? The national insult?

Forgotten that their future and the future of their children and their children's children to the tenth generation depended on holding New Orleans? Would they bow to the mistress of the seas who would dictate their trade, the prices for their produce, their very hopes? Were they free men or serfs pulling their forelocks to the British manor house?

"Well, I'll tell you what you are. Deserters. Traitors. God damned miserable sniveling cowards, running for home when the enemy's in sight. Now, you think because you had a couple of tough skirmishes, you've won the war. Let me tell you something, you miserable bastards, the real fight is up ahead, it's coming, and if you run now the men who fight that fight will hold your names in infamy for generations untold.

"Ran from the enemy! Hid when the going was hard! Went home and tucked their heads under their women's skirts! You call yourselves men? Call yourselves Tennesseans? I call you scum. Cowardly scum. Traitorous scum. The kind of men who desert, who haven't the guts to stay the course."

His voice was a shriek now, and some of them had the stunned look men tended to get when Andrew Jackson exploded. But this time there was a radical, wonderful difference. He could shriek, rage, foam at the mouth, but he knew exactly what he was doing. He felt all the anger he hurled at them, believed everything he said, hadn't a moment's doubt he'd destroy them if necessary, and yet all this was contained, controlled. It was a revelation.

It *magnified* his power!

Wonderful!

A cry from the ranks: *"Horseshit!"*

Jackson stood in his stirrups. "Gunners, light your matches!"

It was an hour before sunset. A light breeze soughed against bare branches. When the matches were glowing, Jackson spoke. Now his voice was calm and deadly.

"Enough talk, we've come right to it. I won't let you leave. I'll cut you down like cornstalks if I have to but I won't let you go." There wasn't a sound. The wind had died. "Now, I want your pledge to stay. I demand an answer."

Dead silence.

He sat his horse in front of them. He could see the guns to the rear. Smoke from the matches drifted on the still air. He was squarely in the line of fire. He didn't move.

There was a clatter of hoofs. Young John Reid galloped up to sit motionless beside him.

A minute passed. Another.

"I'll use the matches before I let 'em burn down."

There was a sound like air gushing from a bladder. A captain stepped forward.

"Now, hold on, General, God damn, just hold on." He looked around. "Tom, Jack, Nat, get on up here!"

A half-dozen officers clustered around Jackson's horse.

"See here, General, I mean, this is crazy. We won't go—she-it, none of us want to go home so bad we'll take a load of grape up our backside. You tell those boys to put out them matches, we ain't going no place."

Jackson nodded, calm and austere. He sat his horse a long time watching them drift off to their tents. The pain in his arm ebbed away to a flicker. He nodded to young Reid.

"Come along, son. We need a cup of tea."

He knew he'd crossed a great divide and that all on the other side would be different.

Promises. Promises he could keep.

★ ★ ★ ★

"Do you mean to tell me he'd have shot down his own men?" Madison asked.

"Yes, sir," young Reid said.

"And he himself was in the line of fire?"

"Yes, sir. I was beside him. I noticed that."

"My God! Is the man mad?"

"No, sir. He's magnificent, sir. A magnificent commander."

Madison digested that. He'd had the most amazing letter from General Pinckney about Jackson—the man had broken Creek Indian power, probably forever, taken the surrender of that recalcitrant chief who'd been in Tecumseh's sway, and set the Spanish in Florida to quaking. And, though lethargic, Pinckney was no fool. He commanded regular army troops in the South, headquarters Charleston.

It was spring, dogwood a white glitter, new leaves an innocent green, the Blue Ridge startlingly blue. During a welcome month away from Washington, Madison had ridden out from Montpelier on a favorite mare to spend a few days in the mountain's shadow, stopping with friends.

At Carterwood, Jack and Penny Carter made him welcome. Dolley had come over in her new carriage, and he'd greeted a dozen guests when he spied young Reid, whose father he'd known for years. Johnny was home on leave from the Tennessee wars and Madison drew him aside to talk.

They sat in the gazebo at a white table, on chairs with red cushions. Early honeysuckle scented the air, monarchs were on the wing, prowling bumblebees buzzed, flowers the color of flame stood in pots on the steps. He thought of the spring mud miring Washington's streets, of the President's House with its grim responsibilities. Ah, Virginia in the spring!

He poured cups of Madeira punch from a silver pitcher, asked Reid to describe Jackson as a commander—and got this amazing story, Jackson's soldiers intent on deserting, the General stopping them twice by sheer force of will. It *was* magnificent, he supposed, what a Caesar would do, a Homer describe. Madison hadn't known things like that happened in real life.

The man was given to dramatic flashes, bursts of fire and flame—a dragon on the field. Appropriate, perhaps, for attacking savages . . . He left unspoken the corollary that dealing with British regulars might be a different affair.

Reid stiffened in his chair. "Mr. President, if you're suggesting that it amounted to a handful of savages with stone-age weapons, permit me to say you've been misinformed. The Creeks had massed some six thousand warriors, heavily armed with British muskets to say nothing of bows and arrows. I assure you, sir, they had no shortage of powder and lead."

The Indians were well generaled, too. Reid seemed to admire the war chief, Red Eagle, son of a Scottish trader and a Creek mother and carrying an English name as well, Weatherford. Handsome, charismatic, highly intelligent, he frequented the white world, traveled, spoke various languages—indeed, he sounded anything but a rude savage.

Gallant, too—after the terrible battle at Horseshoe Bend that destroyed the Creeks as a fighting force, he'd ridden into Jackson's camp to surrender. Came with a double-shotted musket in his hands and a doe across his horse's withers as a gift for Jackson—what a curious mix of cultures that implied!

A dozen pieces were bearing on him, but Jackson waved them down, shouting that anyone who would fire on a man so courageous as to ride right into an enemy camp didn't deserve to live himself! My. The General was a romantic, wasn't he?

At that, Reid grinned. "He has flair, all right."

This surrendering chief—though he appeared to have come more in triumph than in dismay and hardly sounded like Madison's idea of an Indian chief—had made a stunning speech in English. Said he'd fought Jackson as long and as hard as he could. Said if he had warriors and weapons he would fight to the end of time, but his warriors were dead and their weapons gone. Only the aged and the women and children remained and they were starving. So he surrendered himself to Jackson's vengeance but called on him to stop the war that the old might die in peace, the young carry on the race.

Whereupon Jackson sat down and poured him a glass of brandy! They drank, Jackson accepted the doe, and Weatherford went off to collect his scattered people. He and Jackson parted friends. Well, more or less friends. Interesting . . . The image of one potent leader recognizing another was very strong.

And how many of Madison's generals were leaders? Fat old Dearborn? That fool Wilkinson? Pinckney, comfortable in South Carolina? For that matter, how much of a leader was their Commander in Chief?

He thrust that thought away—he did his best and that was the best any leader could do.

"It's a remarkable story and I appreciate hearing it," he said. "But in the end, they *were* savages, however polished their leader."

The young man's eyebrows rose. "Mr. President, begging your pardon, you seem to be saying there wasn't much to it, after all. Now, sir, I haven't seen a lot of war, but I'll tell you I don't want to see hotter fighting than this."

Madison sighed. He himself hadn't seen *any* war. Too puny to fight in the Revolution, too elevated to fight in this one, who was he to question combat veterans?

"Tell me about it," he said.

"Well, the men who wanted to leave, the General finally had to let them go. Their time was up, legally, you see. And before long we were down to a bare hundred men deep in hostile country—I tell you, if they'd attacked then . . .

"Anyway, Jackson wrote Governor Blount a letter. I guess he burned the Governor some, for not ten days later here came eight hundred fresh men old Blount had rounded up. That gave us nine hundred and on the very next morning we marched for Horseshoe Bend, where the hostiles had an armed encampment.

"Camped on Emuckfaw Creek and they hit us at dawn and it was hot, yes, sir. Fought 'em off after an hour and the General sent Colonel Coffee to destroy their camp. But it was much too strong, and on the way back they hit Coffee again and the cavalry barely got in. Coffee was wounded.

"So the General pulled back. He simply saw that nine hundred wasn't enough for the knockout blow he wanted, so he'd wait till he had more. They hit us again as we crossed Enotachopco Creek—struck when the artillery was in the water. Our rear guard gave way, and if Constant Perkins hadn't gotten the six-pounder in action, I wouldn't be here remembering it."

Reid looked older than he had a moment ago.

"Did you consider Jackson's attack reckless?"

Reid shrugged, then smiled, boyish again. "Was it Julius Caesar who said fortune favors the bold?"

"My. Jackson's a classicist, too?"

"No, sir. Scholarship I can't claim for him. But he always seems to know what to do and hasn't a whit of trouble making up his mind."

Interesting. Just what Clay had said. "Still, boldness and rashness aren't the same."

"Actually, sir, he fights carefully. He plans well and likes to have twice the strength of the force he's meeting."

"I take it his troops grew, then, from the nine hundred?"

"To about five thousand, including the regulars, the Thirty-ninth Infantry. General Pinckney assigned them."

"Without denigrating the accomplishment, I suppose taking an Indian village hardly taxes a force of that size."

Again that cool expression that made Reid look older than his years. "This was quite a bit more than a village, sir. It was built on a peninsula— a big bend in the Tallapoosa River with a highly professional barricade of logs across its neck. Our guns—six-pounder and a three-pounder—worked on that for two hours with no more effect than knocking off a few splinters. We could hear them yelling, their shamans telling them that round shot bouncing off their wall proved our bullets couldn't touch them. So we charged—went over the wall."

"Where were you personally?"

"The Thirty-ninth led the charge and I was with 'em. Lem Montgomery was first over—killed atop the barricade. Sam Houston was right behind him, and I followed Sam. He took a bullet in the shoulder that near killed him."

"A Virginia man? I used to know a Major Sam Houston over in the Shenandoah Valley. Rockbridge County."

"His daddy, sir. Sam was real proud of his daddy. The family went to the Smoky Mountains after they lost the plantation and the Major died."

Madison listened carefully, letting the scene build in his mind. The Indians fell back from their barricade, dropped over a steep bluff, and fought on. Twice they killed the bearers of white flags Jackson sent to offer surrender. The fighting went on all afternoon, the Indians at last driven back to the river.

They had canoes?

No, Jackson had placed cavalry on the opposite bank and Coffee sent swimmers to take the canoes. Still the Indians refused to surrender, and in the end, none did. They plunged into the water under fire from both banks. Reid thought nine hundred warriors died that day; it ended Weatherford's power. Jackson had forty-seven killed, one hundred fifty-nine wounded.

"Then the General is not without tactical skills?"

For answer, Reid drew a notebook from his pocket and sketched a battle early in the campaign at an Indian town he called Talladega. Madison watched the pencil outline two solid blocks of troops with a small block out front representing a weak advance guard. Then Reid sketched the cavalry on two wings bent forward, the rear of each anchored to the right and left flanks of the two blocks.

He drew a short arrow moving the little advance guard out to meet the Indians, then a heavy black arrow in the opposite direction to indicate a massive Indian charge at the small contingent. It fell back hastily, the Indians pressed it, and the wings of the trap closed around their rear to surround them.

Madison stared transfixed at the rude drawing. These were the identical tactics Hannibal had used in his battle at Cannae. The same blocks of troops, the weak center, the wings ready to close. Madison had just studied the details—it was after the Carthaginian general brought his elephant train across the Alps two thousand years ago. Those closing wings trapped fifty thousand Roman troops for slaughter and broke Roman power. Hannibal in the Alabama woods.

"And it worked?"

"Perfectly, sir. Except one unit misunderstood orders and left a gap so some escaped."

"Do you know that was Hannibal's plan at Cannae?"

"Hannibal? No, sir, I didn't know."

"One of the turning-point battles of world history. Jackson didn't mention that?"

"No, sir. And frankly, I'd be surprised if he knew."

"Just lucked onto classic tactics?" Madison saw Reid frown and added, "No sarcasm intended. I'm asking your opinion."

"Well, sir, he's not a student. Very up-to-date, the office at his farm is full of newspapers from all over, but you don't see many books. I'd say if he used Hannibal's tactics, he shares some of Hannibal's abilities."

Madison smiled. Jackson as Hannibal? Johnny Reid was in thrall to his commander. Still, that intuitive grasp that Clay had noticed and Reid had described had played out again in an instinctive choice of classic tactics. He dismissed Reid with thanks and took a short pipe from his pocket. When it was filled and drawing well he sat alone in the gazebo, reflecting on General Pinckney's letter. Pinckney was an old Revolutionary veteran, plainly not the man to stop a British attempt on New Orleans. But was Jackson right to replace him? That, to Madison's amazement, was Pinckney's suggestion.

He had Brown and Scott on the Niagara. At Plattsburgh on Lake Champlain he was counting on Macdonough's ships. Soon he himself would have to name someone to defend Washington since his miserable Secretary of War wouldn't. Meanwhile, New Orleans. It was the cheese in the trap, sure to draw the rats sooner or later. Who was to hold it? Not Pinckney. Not Flournoy, who commanded the few troops there now.

But Jackson?

He smoked, letting the tobacco soothe him. What came through young Reid's account was the size of the man. Big in all ways. My God, what a scene, turning a cannon on men who wanted to desert. Facing a thousand men with a musket—they could have torn him apart, but they'd turned and gone back to their tents. Cowed by one blazing-eyed man facing them down, and he in excruciating pain from his own wound. And yet, his men loved him. That was evident. They were proud of him and he made them proud of themselves. And they would fight like devils for him. By now Madison knew that was a quality a man was born with—and that most of his generals had been born without it. Jake Brown had it, and so did Scott, but who else?

Horseshoe Bend was no Leipzig, nor Jackson a Hannibal, but on the evidence, he was tactically sophisticated and without real training seemed to understand military maneuver. A mind that could leap gaps to strong conclusions might just put to shame the brightest results of training, education, linear logic.

Decisions. The whole future of the country could hang on this. Lose New Orleans and it would be a very different nation—not at all the country Madison wanted, booming westward, ready to follow Tom Jefferson's dream, the trail Lewis and Clark struck, settlers advancing westward to the Pacific. Lose New Orleans and the United States would wither against the Atlantic seaboard, a plaything of the important states of the world.

He sighed and knocked out his pipe, weighing split images, Jackson challenging his men with a musket, ordering those gunners to light their matches . . . and brawling with Benton, one of his own officers . . .

Late that evening he drew Reid out of a whist game.

"Do you think Jackson learned anything from those encounters with his men?"

Reid considered, then said, "I'd say yes, sir. I couldn't put my finger on it at the time, but there was a difference between when he stopped the men with the musket and when he threatened cannon fire. The first time he was wild. Explosive. You didn't know what the devil was going to happen, and afterward, he was sick. Of course he *was* sick, with that arm and dysentery, but this wasn't the same. With the cannon business, he was just as angry, as implacable, but somehow he was solid where before he'd been—well—wild." Reid hesitated. "I'm sorry, sir. It's hard to put it into words."

"Thank you, John," Madison said. "You've helped."

When he went to their room Dolley was in bed, reading a French novel.

"You know what really matters about a general?" he said as he peeled off his white hose. "Whether he likes to fight. Most don't, I'm finding. And Jackson does."

"You're thinking of using him?"

"Pinckney says he should have the southern command."

"I liked him, I must say. He honors his wife."

"That's a qualification, I suppose, but—"

"It shows magnitude and—well—wholeness."

"You'd appoint him, then?"

She smiled. "How many fighters do we have?"

"Yes, that's the point. And yes, I'm going to give him the southern command. Major general, regular army, counterpointing Brown in the North. And the fate of New Orleans will hang on him—and that means the whole future course of the nation."

He was in his nightshirt. She closed the book and pinched the candle. "So come to bed, Jimmy. The future doesn't depend on Jackson, it depends on you. You're appointing him. Now, give me a kiss."

15

On the Niagara Frontier
Spring, 1814

★ ★ ★ ★ Brigadier General Winfield Scott paused in Albany on his way to the Niagara front to order supplies—tents, field kitchens, medicines, powder and shot, shoes, uniforms of regulation blue, cattle on the hoof, flour, fatback, barrels of apples, cords of sausages, enormous round cheeses, whiskey for the daily ration.

And vinegar by the cask. Vinegar was the soldier's balm—drinking it cleansed the system, pouring it on wounds flushed away poisons. No one knew why, but it worked and that was enough for Scott. Whatever was good for his boys he intended to have.

There was an exultation in command. He felt for his men as he supposed a man might for his children, knew he'd die before he'd fail them. Of course, he was on the line, too. He'd made training a cause, he'd promised results, and the President had said go to it. And by God, he and the boys would deliver!

And fast. He and Sergeant Major Boone covered the three hundred miles to Buffalo in less than six days, swapping mounts every three hours from the remuda they drove along.

Near the ruined village of Buffalo he found his campsite. Flint Hill had level ground for a drill field and a well-drained slope for tents. The owner, Isaac Fromton, was living with wife, seven children, horses, hogs, chickens, and milk cows in a new barn raised on the ashes of the old.

"Hell's fire, General, I don't want no rent." Fromton waved a hand at the ash pile where his house had stood. "You're gonna train up the boys and go punish them redcoat bastards, ain't you? They come in here in December with the snow four-foot deep and burn us out, house and barn both, and we hadn't never done nothing to nobody. Drove us out to live in a lean-to, m'little boy lost two fingers and three toes froze before I could get another barn up—I tell you, General, I'm an Old Testament man, I want to see the Lord work His vengeance on them British and I figure you boys are His instruments."

The four regiments that would form Scott's brigade marched in—the Ninth Infantry from Massachusetts, the Eleventh from Vermont, the Twenty-second from Pennsylvania, the Twenty-fifth from Connecticut. New England governors might refuse to turn out their militia, but patriotic men could join the regulars. They were damn fine men, tall and stalwart, and a glance told him their colonels were princes. He was delighted. Four companies of the Second Artillery arrived with six- and twelve-pounders. His old friend Nate Towson headed one company. All told, more than two thousand men, clay to be shaped into soldiers.

In four days the camp was set, tent sites leveled and tents up, field kitchens operating, privies positioned on the opposite side of camp. But when he turned around he found the privy crew digging near the kitchens. Why?

"Ground's no good where you picked, General," a sergeant said, displaying age-old sergeants' contempt for the inferior practical wisdom of officers. He stood with legs spread. "Too rocky. This here is nice and soft, we'll dig it in jig-time."

"Sergeant," Scott said, "you'll feel a lot better and live a lot longer if you don't eat and crap on the same spot."

Any caring officer would agree. A clean camp, privies far from food and water, and plenty of vinegar meant a low sick list. Scott was a bear on this. He went off to survey the creek that supplied their water.

Sure enough, he found a privy hanging over the stream. He told a work crew to rip it down and dig the owner a proper pit.

"If he objects, show him the business end of a musket."

On the fifth morning—a bright day in April with the ground still hard but the promise of spring in the air—he gathered his officers.

"Here's our situation," he said. "We have a campful of hunters and we're going to make them into soldiers." He pointed to a slender captain from the Twenty-fifth Connecticut. "Tell us the difference between hunters and soldiers."

"Hunter goes after deer, likely, or bear. We go after men."

"Exactly." He had their attention. He dropped his voice a little, made it conversational, made them strain to hear. "The difference lies in method. There was a time when warriors fought like hunters, mobs colliding with other mobs. But about four thousand years ago warriors in Mesopotamia— places called Ur and Lagash—grasped the meaning of formations. They lined men up, spears a bristling phalanx, and lo and behold, nothing could stand against them. Thunderstruck their enemies, too, until, of course, their enemies did likewise.

"The formation magnifies the soldier's power tenfold. The strongest men, as individuals, can't stand against organized power. But the corollary is that you can only achieve such power when each man accepts his role, learns his part, drills in it until he and the others become a single instrument, each individual essential to the whole. Soldiers, in short."

He let that sink in, pacing slowly back and forth.

"Now, gentlemen, the redcoats across the river, they're soldiers. Some of you have stood their charges, and for those who haven't had the pleasure, I can tell you it's a sight not to be forgotten." He raised his voice. "But what's the real difference between them and our men? Stronger hearts? Better brains? No! The difference is, they're soldiers. They're trained. And their power is magnified tenfold. Well, like the enemies of Ur and Lagash, we're here to do likewise."

His voice rose. "We're going to turn our boys into soldiers. Drill them till they drop. Till they learn to trust their units and then to love their units and then to fight by units—and then they'll be soldiers. When they march out of here they'll be as good as any troops in the world—and they'll prove it on the field."

He'd caught their imaginations, he could see it in their expressions.

"And it's bigger than just us. Make soldiers of your men and you'll be responding to the whole country. There's new movement out there, I feel it in my heart, and it says Americans are tired of being pushed. Tired of being beaten. The British think because they whipped Napoleon, we'll be easy! What do they suppose we'll be doing?

"Another thing. Look around you. Three out of four of us are New England men. By God, that makes me proud!" He punched the air with a forefinger. "The country's coming together. It's getting ready to fight. I say a new day's coming in America—and it's our job to usher it in."

Tom Jesup, the colonel of the Twenty-fifth Connecticut, stepped forward. A long, tall Welshman whose coal-black hair was shot with gray, he spoke with a distinct British accent and didn't seem to care that it would mark him if he were captured.

"General," he said, "that's jolly on the mark. I spent a few years in His Majesty's forces till I grew up and learned better and found me a new country, and it was drill, drill, drill, and by God, when the time came and your guts turned to water you just did it by the numbers. You didn't have to think, and it was damned comforting—you just did it."

He turned to the others with his arm raised. "Now, what I say, let's give the General a cheer! Hip, hip, HURRAH!"

God, Scott did love them.

★ ★ ★ ★

Major General Jake Brown marched in with two small brigades that joined Scott's camp. "Work their asses off, Win," he said before he went back to headquarters at Sackett's Harbor. "When they're ready, we're going turkey shooting."

The camp settled into a routine of ten-hour days. An hour of running and another of calisthentics and then they shouldered their muskets and drilled. Scott took one company after the next for two-hour stints, showing them—and, more important, showing their officers—how it was done.

Drill and drill and drill until a man lost track of time in a mad dance by the numbers, right flank, left flank, to-the-rear HARCH!, right oblique and left oblique and column turns, peel into platoons and then into squads and fan out and back to merge as smoothly as sand leaving an hourglass, left-right, left-right, left-right, LEFT! Obedience became automatic, instinctive, instantaneous as they turned and turned and turned again, developing a mind-set that would inspire similar obedience when the bullets were flying.

He led them into rough country, taught them to take cover, to approach dug-in troops, to follow their captain's hand signals, to vault a barrier and land ready to deal with whatever was there, to count on their buddies as they advanced under fire. He made them see they couldn't be singled out, separated, made victims, not if they stuck together.

Step by step—he could see it in their manner, hear it in their voices—they learned to trust their officers, their units, each other, themselves. And gradually they assumed what in the end becomes the soldier's greatest strength, what keeps him going forward under fire—the willingness to die rather than shame himself before his buddies.

Scott remembered the Glengarry Fencibles, desperately outnumbered against his landing force but falling back in perfect order despite heavy casualties. Compare that with the way his own line had broken on Queenston Heights and tumbled pell-mell down the hill at the very sight of British steel. Training, pride, confidence, love of unit, love of their fellows—there was the difference.

Then came that most fearsome assault, men coming at a run with bayonets glistening before them like killing teeth. With their weapons sheathed so that a thrust that scored might break ribs but wouldn't eviscerate, he set them at each other. And they learned—painfully—that flight was the worst defense, asking as it did for a blade in the back. Soon they were attacking each other with gusto, heads up, eyes on the other's weapon, parry, block, counterthrust.

Every man took his turn running ball in hand molds from bar lead, and then making paper cartridges, ball and a charge of powder in a quill of paper, the ends twisted neatly in place. He established a range against a sharp bluff and pushed them through, not just for marksmanship but for the smooth skill of loading the reliable old 1795 muskets under fire; break the paper quill with one hand, splash powder into the pan, pour the rest of the powder down the big barrel, and ram home the ball, the paper making the wadding.

He told the same story to each company before it fired. A century before, at the Battle of Belgrade, two battalions of Austrian troops had let the Turks come within thirty paces before opening fire. Despite the range, only thirty-two Turks fell. The rest charged and cut the Austrians to pieces.

"Bear that in mind, boys, when you're looking over your sights."

Supplies poured in—all but the blue uniforms. His men were dressed in homespun trousers and shirts, butternut overalls, and acorn-dyed hunting shirts with blousy sleeves and skirts to the knees. This was acceptable undress garb for soldiers, but the uniform was what tied a man to the army, made him part of the unit, made him belong. He fired off angry messages: get me my blue uniforms!

Contractor wagons arrived with beef salted in kegs. He was enraged—salt beef was for the march, when a man carried his rations on his back, not for training camp. He wanted fresh beef on the hoof. When the contractor tried to bluff, Scott shook him by his shirtfront as a terrier shakes a rat. Standing six inches over six feet tall did have its advantages—a week later the scoundrel showed up with a herd of decent animals.

He was everywhere and he loved it all. The ringing cadence calls on the drill field, the fierce popping on the range with black powder's blue smoke pinching the nostrils, the bright young faces, the growing precision as units marched and countermarched without a missed step, the joy when a man shot well and drew a bonus gill of whiskey, the serious look of men who'd laid trenches and built abatis and now were learning to attack them, the dress parades (even without proper uniforms), the flag snapping free at sunrise, the evening gun, the bugle calls, the rich smells from the kitchens, the men in line with mess kits in hand—it was all heaven.

He loved every one of them, and they—noting his obsessive attention to their training, their health, their food—reciprocated in full measure. He could see it in the smiles that greeted him, in the shy, respectful witticisms they offered when he stopped to talk.

At night, driven to exhaustion, he still felt the need to prowl his domain, checking sentries on the perimeters, wandering among the tents, inspecting kitchen pots for proper cleaning, visiting the remuda. He liked to finish atop the hill, looking across the starlit camp, the tents ghostly rows of dominoes, wood smoke drifting up from below, all his domain, his command—and then he would think, Maria should see me now.

Maria. The name set off late-night indulgences of memory, an after-hours treat. During his month in Washington he had seen her often—at the President's House, at dinners to which she arranged his invitation, on chaperoned afternoon drives in a rented carriage rattling across the Long Bridge that spanned the Potomac and up the hill to see the progress on the mansion called Arlington that Mrs. Washington's relatives were raising, all the while talking and talking about anything and everything but the stuff of war.

She would see and identify a bird before he even noticed it, then reel off plumage, habits, range. She knew as much about plants as about birds and in private was sharply critical of the mansion's gardeners. The shrubs were overpruned, the forsythia constrained—it should be allowed to grow free so that its yellow spears could greet the spring in glorious profusion. Such passion! It gave him a whole new sense of things.

She had a talent for cooking, though she couldn't invade the President's kitchens, and cooking was one of Scott's interests if not talents. Why should army food be bad? And wouldn't well-fed soldiers be healthier and fight better? With his traveling library of technical military works he carried cookbooks and consulted them often. Maria expounded on the nuances of flavor, the blending of sauces, the joys of garlic and onions, the use of bay leaves and basil and cumin the British brought from Egypt. They discussed the application of such seasoning to the army's big iron kettles of stew, and when he left she presented him with two pounds of bay leaves she had ordered from Philadelphia.

The beef stews at Flint Hill soon were better than any army food he'd ever tasted. And he believed Maria Mayo was in love with him and he thought he was falling in love with her.

This was nothing like his attraction to Sally McQuirk. Sally was dazzling with her bright hair piled atop her head, her sparkling eyes, her rich laughter, her fine body in gowns designed to show it off. Maria was quiet, dark-haired and dark-eyed, with a beauty that grew on you slowly because it emanated from within. She had a sweet nature, a serene inner strength, a presence that made being with her warm, comfortable, and highly enjoyable. The more he saw her the better he liked her, the more he looked forward to their next meeting.

Sally was anything but comfortable. To meet her was to want her, and their single encounter in bed could still shake him with memory and longing. Whenever he thought about it he would deliberately recall her confident sense of knowing more than anyone reasonably could, her quality of command, her steely determination. Sally wanted position, recognition, command—just, in fact, what he wanted for himself.

She had interrogated him so fiercely about General Wilkinson's debacle on the St. Lawrence that he'd accused her of using him for a newspaper article.

For once she had no answer.

"I think you've been writing all along," he said. "I think you wrote that election turn in New York, not your father."

Silence. They were on a sofa in her drawing room. At last she took his hands.

"Soldiers keep secrets?"

He nodded.

"I confess. I've been writing for a year, I love it, I'm good at it, and I'll never stop. But it's none of the world's business."

He felt that incredible pull, her hands warm in his, eyes glowing, lips parted; they hung there suspended for a dangerous moment, and then both pulled back as if simultaneously seeing the same precipice.

They settled at the ends of the sofa, breathing harder than usual.

"Will they invade?" she asked him.

"Yes. And when they do, we'll whip them."

"You're that confident?"

"I don't think a democracy fights well till it makes up its mind to fight and win. Then it can beat giants."

"And we've made up our minds?"

"Making them up, I'd say. Yes."

She nodded. "The President is different, somehow. Not so . . . apologetic."

"I always said he was strong."

"So you did. Where will they invade?"

"Down Lake Champlain from the north. Maybe the Niagara. And eventually they'll try for New Orleans in the South."

"You seem very confident of that."

"Believe me. I'm right."

"Oh, I believe you . . ."

For all her vitality—and all the excitement she generated—Sally was somehow tough and brittle, too. Once the bloom of youth was gone and the reins of the paper securely in her hands, she would be hard. Maria was just as strong, just as self-possessed, but he couldn't imagine her being hard. She focused confidently on what mattered to her, and home and garden mattered a great deal more than did the swirl of politics that filled the President's House. Since meeting him she'd taken an interest in the army and had a working idea of military issues, but she was more interested in whether a tent could be kept warm in winter (it couldn't) than in tactics and strategy.

Sally was a dynamo; Maria was soothing, calm, her company profoundly enjoyable. He had yet to kiss her. There had been a moment before he left when he might have, when he thought she almost expected it. But instead he'd taken both her hands in his and held them a long time, looking into her eyes, knowing that something wonderful was building between them.

★   ★   ★   ★

He drove the horses hard, lope twenty minutes, walk ten, swap mounts every three hours.

"Begging the General's pardon," Boone said when they paused at a creek to water the animals, drink upstream from them, and eat biscuit and beef without bothering to sit, "I fear we'll wear out these critters, this kind of pace."

"We'll get a new set coming back," Scott said. "Let's go."

He wondered if the President of the United States had seen a map of New York State. The order had had a casual ring: once Flint Hill was in shape, please ride over to Lake Champlain and submit a report on the adequacy of defenses there.

Ride over? God Almighty, it was three hundred miles plus of spring mud. He would be gone at least ten days; you'd think the President would understand the dangers of leaving his men . . . Then he thought of the little man's pale face and his steady eyes; he was carrying the whole war on frail shoulders. Why shouldn't he want a fresh professional opinion as to a crucial front? George Izard, Scott's old colonel from the Second Artillery, now a major general, commanded at Plattsburgh and doubtless was reporting as was the naval officer, a fellow named Tom Macdonough. But the President wanted another voice; well, why not?

As the sweating horses ate the miles, his mind went to his own problems. The uniforms still hadn't arrived. God damn it, he *must* have them. Essential to discipline and good order. His desertion rate was up, probably some connection there. He loved his boys, no question about that, but some of the bastards were crumbling under the pressure and heading for home.

You always had a few desertions but the upward trend infuriated him. He gave them a clean camp, the best food and training, a chance to share in national triumph—and they go home? He put out ranging patrols and set those captured to walking twelve-hour stretches with eighty pounds of rocks in packs and fed them bread and water. Flogging was outlawed but he had other weapons—sit a man on the parade ground with a stick under his knees, arms under the stick, wrists lashed before his shins, a tent peg tied in his mouth to keep him quiet, leave him there bucked and gagged for a few hours. They'd better not push him; desertion was serious business.

He came into Plattsburgh at a lope. It was a fair-sized village overlooking a handsome bay. He got directions to Izard's headquarters, and arrived to find a harried major who told him the General had just left for the docks— a British fleet was coming and he was crossing the lake ahead of it to Macdonough's yards. Down the hill Scott went at a hard gallop, slid to a stop on the docks where sailors on a heavy sloop were casting off, tossed the reins to a waiting soldier, and cleared four feet of water as he jumped aboard, Boone right behind him.

"Well, Win, that was some arrival," said Izard, who had taken on a dyspeptic look, as if high command didn't agree with him. "You always pressed hard." To Boone, he said, "Sergeant Major, good to see you again. Been taking care of the General?"

"Yes, sir. Thank you, sir. Like a reunion of the old Second, ain't it? As for taking care of the General, sir, he does a pretty good job of that himself."

Izard chuckled. "I don't doubt it."

The sloop's crew broke out sweeps and rowed them past a promontory called Cumberland Head that guarded the bay. A brisk wind from the north filled the sails, and the sloop heeled to dig into a heavy chop. Scott and Izard took shelter behind a midships cabin. After four days on horseback, the ship, the spray, the glittering waves, were exhilarating. Boone, immediately seasick, groped his way to the rail.

Scott explained his mission.

"Wants all the insight he can get, I expect," Izard said of the President. "I don't blame him."

Quickly he sketched the situation. The long, narrow lake, New York on the west bank, Vermont on the east, and the naval vessels struggling to control it were what mattered. Uncomfortable position, a soldier having to depend on the navy, but Scott knew his old commander's generosity of spirit.

Izard had about four thousand men. General Prevost, the British commander and governor general, would have about fifteen thousand if he invaded. Izard could delay him but not stop him. But Prevost couldn't supply such an army over local roads; to advance beyond Plattsburgh, he must have the lake.

That would give him a waterborne supply route that linked with Lake George and led on to the Hudson. From there, yes, he might take New York City and cut off New England, and given New England's state of mind—did Win know they were talking secession over there?—that could put us over a barrel.

"So, can this Macdonough fellow do the job?"

"If anyone can. You'll see. Tom Macdonough is tough and determined, and he knows ships. Wait'll you see his shipyard—he's turning 'em out right in the wilderness. But so are the British, at Isle Aux Noix at the head of the lake. It's a shipbuilder's race, really, but I'll let Tom lay out the tactics. Meanwhile the British are trying a preemptive strike. One of our spies at Isle Aux Noix rode all night to bring word. They've patched together a little fleet and hope to burn out Tom's yards."

"Can they?"

"Well, he just launched *Saratoga*, the biggest vessel on the lake, twenty-six guns, but she's not fitted out yet. Be a disaster to lose her, believe you me."

"Then we could lose it all this morning?" Scott said.

"We have a surprise for them." Izard smiled. "So—tell me about Flint Hill."

The sloop rounded a head. Her sails came down with a clatter, her anchor chain ran out, a small boat was lowered, and two sailors rowed them ashore. Izard set a hard pace up a heavily wooded, very steep hill until they vaulted over a parapet of camouflaged sandbags into a gun pit.

"Well, how do, General?" an army captain said. He waved his arm. "Bunch of damn sails out yonder I don't like the looks of."

Izard took his glass. "That's who we've been waiting for. Stoke that furnace for hot shot and stand by to open fire."

Five guns, twelve-pounders but the damnedest-looking pieces—and then he realized they were ship's guns, mounted on four-wheeled carriages. Macdonough's guns, Izard's artillerymen. The British vessels, two square-rigged brigs and two armed sloops rigged fore-and-aft, came confidently around the head.

"Commence firing," Izard said.

The slow matches dipped, the pieces bellowed with that roar an artilleryman loves. Shot went slashing through rigging, and at least one struck the forward vessel's hull. In the silence that followed they could hear the shrilling of bosun's pipes and the clatter of spars as the surprised ships came about hastily and beat toward safety.

Then howitzerlike columbiads on three of the vessels fired almost at once, the shells lofting high overhead and landing with shattering explosions. The Captain fell mortally wounded, and Izard leapt forward to take charge. Two gun sergeants were down, and Scott took command of both guns.

"Load and ram, load and ram," he bawled, "let's give 'em some God damned fire! You over there, stoke that furnace, I want hot shot in five minutes!"

The ships were running toward the security of open water. Scott's long twelves sent iron balls crashing through their rigging. They returned columbiad fire but it fell far short. Then the vessels' long thirty-two-pounders opened with a throaty roar. A massive ball, thirty-two pounds of solid iron, crashed into one of Scott's guns and knocked it askew with a shriek of metal. He heard someone screaming.

A gunner ran from the furnace with a glowing ball gripped in tongs and swung it into the barrel. They rammed it against damp wadding. Scott took a careful bearing, the gun fired, and the shot smashed into the largest brig's main cabin. The heavily tarred ship was a tinderbox, highly vulnerable to fire, and almost immediately wisps of smoke appeared and quickly grew. The vessels crowded on sail, now anxious to escape. Scott sent a few more hot balls after them, but they soon pulled out of range and he doubted they would be back.

"Good shooting, Win." Izard had a stocky man with pale face and oddly glowing cheeks in tow. He wore a naval uniform. "Commodore Thomas Macdonough, Brigadier General Winfield Scott. Tom came at a gallop when he heard the firing."

"Fine shot, fine shot." Macdonough wrung Scott's hand. "Arrogant bastards, think they can take us so easily."

Seven miles up Otter Creek, the naval officer had built the damnedest complex just below the waterfall. Scott was stunned. Macdonough had water power, ample timber, a vein of iron ore he was mining nearby, eight forges, air furnaces and a water-powered blast furnace, a rolling mill for working steel, a wire factory, gristmill, sawmill, fulling mill for making felt. His heavy guns came overland from Boston, but he'd manufactured a thousand iron cannonballs now stacked in neat rows.

Towering overhead was a shipbuilder's cradle with the ribs of a small ship rising like extended fingers of two hands. They boarded the *Saratoga* afloat in a small cove. Her masts were in place but she wasn't rigged. She rode high in the water without guns or stores, but he noticed how solid she felt.

"You did all this over the winter?" Scott asked.

Macdonough smiled. "Snow ranged up to eight feet, but war won't wait, you know." His square body would be stout someday, if he lasted, and Scott sensed his solidity; here was a man who would keep his head and get things done. Then Macdonough suddenly began to cough, turning away to bend double. There were tears in his eyes when he straightened, his face white but for glowing cheeks.

Scott glanced at Izard. When the paroxysm passed, he asked how Macdonough saw his chances.

"So far, so good. *Saratoga* is the biggest thing on the lake—eight twenty-four-pounders, twelve thirty-two-pounders, six forty-two-pounders."

"That's heavy firepower," said Scott, who was used to the Second Artillery's six-and twelve-pounders.

"Unfortunately, though, too many of those are carronades—short-range guns. The enemy outguns me at extended range. Means I have to get close to win, and he'll try to lie away and pound me with long guns. Still, weight of metal is the issue at sea." He smiled ruefully. "Or on the lake. I'm still not quite used to giving up saltwater. If we have more and bigger guns— and right now we do—we'll probably win."

"So once she's rigged, *Saratoga* will control the lake?"

"As things stand now. But that they would make so risky an attack means they know about her and are worried. They failed, but my guess is that next week they'll have something still bigger under construction. Then it'll be touch and go again."

"I have to give the President an estimate," Scott said.

Macdonough's face hardened. "You can tell him I don't intend to have those sons of bitches whip me."

Scott smiled and shook his hand. He knew fighting spirit when he saw it, knew it to be as important as firepower. His opinion was forming rapidly: Macdonough would defend the lake as well as anyone could and probably he would win.

Crossing the lake he said, "That's a nasty cough he has."

"Consumption—working in the snow all winter." Izard shrugged. "There's more than one way to die for your country."

★ ★ ★ ★

Black rain clouds sagged over Scott's troops standing at parade rest on the drill field at Flint Hill. In ten days the field would revert to Farmer Fromton's pasture, but now it had a military purpose. Five holes, six feet by three, made a neat row, dirt stacked alongside. Five poles were set in the ground before the holes and to each a man was tied, eyes blindfolded.

Scott had issued the plainest warnings: desertion in time of war is a capital offense. He had punished men with growing severity, leaving them bucked and gagged for hours plus unofficial punishment administered beyond the tents by hard-fisted sergeants, and still a few would drift away.

He granted leaves for provable hardship, but there were always some who couldn't stand the pace or feared the grim reality of approaching battle or were just lazy and worthless. The court-martial had been quick, the Sergeant of the ranging patrol testifying as to the capture of these five, their captains establishing that no leave had been granted.

Drums rolled and fifes shrilled. The musicians led a squad of twenty musketmen with weapons shouldered onto the field. They marched across the front of the troops, reversed, and halted at the center, stepping in place to the drumbeats, thirty feet from the blindfolded prisoners.

Scott sat a big bay gelding and read the Articles of War ordering death by firing squad for desertion in time of war, his voice loud and harsh. Dead silence in the ranks. When he was done the musketmen formed squads of four and took prone positions, weapons resting on their left hands.

He felt no regrets. Some of the men in the ranks before him would die when he led them into battle. He might die himself—he would be in front.

War was serious. Defense of your country was a noble calling. Let no man dishonor it. Those who fled the enemy deserved no mercy.

Each of the five was a repeat offender. Each had been punished before and warned. They were difficult men, all old enough to know better except for a youngster who probably wasn't of legal age. Sorry devils who didn't deserve the honor of serving, but that wasn't the point. The point was betrayal—of their fellows, their country, their oath. Now they would pay the penalty while their fellows watched.

He nodded to the Captain commanding the squad.

"Ready!" the Captain shouted, raising his saber.

The prone figures shifted, digging in their elbows.

"Aim!"

They lowered their eyes to their sights. One of the prisoners uttered a hoarse cry, the words indistinguishable.

The Captain's saber flashed down. "Fire!"

Twenty reports in unison struck the waiting troops like a physical blow.

Four of the targets jerked, blood immediately staining their shirtfronts, their bodies slumped against the bindings. The fifth—the youngster, whose firing squad Scott had instructed carefully to load powder but no ball— stood stiff and waiting. Then he jerked a hand free from the binding, tore off the blindfold, looked around, and fainted.

The musket roar rolled away and died. Powder smoke drifted off. The sky darkened, lightning flashed, rain spattered and became a downpour. There was no movement or sound save the thrumming rain. The men stared at the crumpled figures on the posts. War was serious business.

16

The White House
Summer, 1814

★ ★ ★ ★ Dolley hurried along the wide center hall toward Jimmy's office. Her Wednesday Drawing Room would start in an hour, and if she didn't remind him he would forget all about it. He hated large gatherings, where he was quite unable to be his real self.

Yet her drawing rooms were important, most of all for him. They had become the hub of the Washington social scene, where people could connect, transact, arrange, pass information, ask questions, get answers, issue challenges, make threats, relay surrenders, strike deals, learn how far they could go and the penalty if they did, and, incidentally, enjoy themselves. Jimmy needed to be there.

But at his office door she hesitated. He sat gazing out an open window, his shoulders slumped. She felt her heart lurch. So much had gone wrong in this awful war he'd never wanted. Battered by events, whipsawed by military failure and political attack—good heavens, would it ever end?

When he turned to face her, his features looked drawn. A letter lay open on his desk blotter. He tapped it.

"From Henry Clay. He's managed an advance look at what the enemy will demand when their delegation meets ours at Ghent. Ruinous terms—just ruinous. We can't even consider such a treaty."

When the British suggested holding direct talks Jimmy had said he had no real hopes, that sending Clay and Albert Gallatin and the others to Ghent, the city of negotiation in neutral Belgium, was a mere formality. But she knew one always hopes.

"What do they demand?"

"We cede control of the Great Lakes. They take northern Maine and northern Minnesota for access to the Mississippi River. And they want an Indian buffer state, no whites allowed. Obviously the intention is to kill our western movement."

"The old Tecumseh idea?"

"A vast area—Indiana, Illinois, Michigan, Wisconsin, a third of Ohio, half the Minnesota River country. A quarter-million square miles—in which, mind you, some twenty thousand Indians live with perhaps a hundred thousand white settlers."

"What would happen to the settlers?"

"Shift for themselves. Get out, theoretically."

"They'd never do it."

"Of course not—Dolley, this is a farce. If we were to accept such terms, it would be an armistice, not a peace treaty—in the end we'd go to war again." He slapped his hand on his desk so hard that his inkstand jumped. "Damn them! Dangle it in front of us like bait—"

"Well, dear, remember we said we expected nothing from it."

He managed a slight smile. "Maybe I was fooling myself. Maybe I did hope."

She kept her tone matter-of-fact. "They said they wanted to negotiate. Of course you hoped. I certainly did."

"Well, I suppose we're no worse off than we were." But his shoulders still sagged.

"The guests will be here in under an hour."

He started. "Oh, God, I'd forgotten. Give me a few minutes to think about this and I'll be along."

It was a dismissal, and she didn't argue. He turned back to stare out the window into the heavy green leaves that masked Pennsylvania Avenue. She watched a moment from the door, saw his fingers begin to tap on his desk, lightly and then with a quick drumming rhythm. When his shoulders slowly straightened, she nodded and went out; he would be all right.

★ ★ ★ ★

"Sally! There you are!"

Sally McQuirk turned to see Margaret Smith threading her way through the crowded drawing room with a tall, angular woman in tow. Maggie and Sally were newspapering comrades-in-arms. Until recently, Maggie's husband had owned the *National Intelligencer,* and Maggie's magazine articles and novels were justification in Sally's mind for her own ambitions. Maggie was a Bayard of Philadelphia, after all.

"Sally, dear, this is Betty Izard of Philadelphia and South Carolina. Betty's an old family friend—I'll leave her in your hands for a moment. Something I must see to." Maggie touched her friend's arm. "Sally knows everybody."

Izard? Sally's interest stirred. As Maggie dashed away, the two women looked at each other and laughed. Betty Izard was as tall as Sally, her dark hair coiled in a bun, her face full of hollows and sharp planes that made her look distinguished rather than pretty. Sally thought she was close to forty. Probably she could be stern, but her smile as she looked around was charming.

"What a gorgeous room," she said.

Sally paid more attention to people than to decor, but it *was* gorgeous. The red curtains were drawn back from the tall open windows, and people already were outside on the veranda overlooking the south lawn. She had seen Joseph drawing the Greek motif chairs into a uniform row along the walls when she arrived. Fresh flowers in crystal vases bloomed on every table, the girandoles and chandeliers balanced the harshness of outside light—

"Is that marble set in the walls?"

"Faux marble, I think, Mrs. Izard."

"Oh, dear, do call me Betty. And it's Sally, right? Yes, I see now, sort of a delicate blue shading—my, isn't that nice?"

They strolled around the room as Sally described the work that had gone into it—the genius of Ben Latrobe, but equally important, Dolley's instinctive taste coupled with her ability to make quick decisions.

"Some of her decisions upset poor Mr. Latrobe no end, but he told me once that in the end he'd always been persuaded. You've met Dolley?"

"Utterly charming. But the President . . . well, Maggie presented me, but I'm afraid he was offended."

Sally laughed. "That's just his way."

"He seemed so . . . cold."

"You have to know him well. Then he's a charmer."

"That's a relief. I thought—"

"Sally!" A deep masculine voice. "You pretty young thing!"

Stephen Decatur, resplendent in his brilliant sash from the Tripoli Wars, bowed over Betty's hand.

"Mrs. General Izard?"

She smiled. "I'm still not used to George as general."

"I hear splendid things about him," Decatur said. "His naval counterpart, Tom Macdonough, is an old friend. You might call him a protégé of mine."

"George seems to think the world of Commodore Macdonough. Tell me about him."

"Outstanding naval officer. He was with me when we burned *Philadelphia*, you know. Led the boarding party."

The story was familiar, but Sally enjoyed hearing it again.

U.S.S. *Philadelphia* had gone aground in Tripoli harbor during the fighting with that North African pirate principality and been taken by swarms of Tripolitans in small boats. In Tripoli's hands, she would have been a serious threat to the U.S. Navy in the Mediterranean. She was anchored under the guns of the fortress, quite unreachable. So the Americans captured a dhow, and with a volunteer crew Decatur sailed right into the harbor. The bay being full of dhows, they weren't noticed until they actually clamped onto the warship's cables.

Tom Macdonough took the lead. They swarmed aboard with pistols and cutlasses, cut down the prize crew, set fire to the great ship, cast off in their dhow, and raced from the harbor under thunderous fire, leaving *Philadelphia* a tower of flame.

"And old Tom, he's covered with blood—someone else's, it turns out—and he's got this light in his eyes, and he says, 'Ho, Steve, that does spice up an evening, doesn't it?'"

Decatur noticed the President beckoning. "Excuse me—I asked for a moment and I guess he's ready." He bowed. "His company is inferior in charm but superior, I'm afraid, as to command. With your permission, ladies."

"Captain?" Betty Izard said.

He paused. "Yes?"

"Then you think Commodore Macdonough will prevail? You understand my concern."

"I understand. Yes, if anyone can win there, Tom can. He's steady, strong, in control of himself and his men and—well, the point of my story was that he fights well. That's half the battle. Brains, skill, and experience supply the rest."

"Thank you, sir."

"Ladies." He bowed and left them. Sally saw him signal an officer she didn't know and lead him to the President.

"Frankly, I'm worried," Betty Izard said. She bit her lip and sighed. "George can take care of himself, but suppose he's wounded—who'll see to him then? I should be there, you know. I *want* to be there."

"Go to Plattsburgh, you mean?" Sally said.

"Why not? George is sure the British will advance with troops far outnumbering his four thousand. And suppose this naval officer can't stop their ships? Captain Decatur was kind and reassuring, but I've been told naval battles really turn on who has the most ships. George tells me to stay home and not worry, but how can I help it?"

"You were thinking of going, and he discouraged you?"

"I *was* going. Of course, he'd have a fit, but what could he do? My little sister was going with me, and then she fell in love and now she won't leave. I . . . I do hate the idea of going alone."

Sally hesitated. The thought had been hanging there for weeks, floating in her mind. Winfield Scott really had set it off with his conviction the lake would be crucial. She could hear his voice, see his serious expression, his blue-gray eyes, feel his hands on her—

No. She reined in the thought. She and Win were dangerous for each other, and that was that. She wanted to be where crucial things happened, wanted to write about them, and nothing was going to interfere. One couldn't have everything. And then, she believed in signs; things that happened indicated what was meant to be. Her meeting with Betty was no accident.

"I'll go with you," she said.

Betty Izard stared at her. "You *would*? But . . . but why? I mean, it would be very nice, but surely—"

"I have an interest there."

Betty didn't respond, but the oddly coarse smile that came and went in seconds made it clear that she supposed a man was involved. For a moment Sally wished there *were* a man there instead of a story, but the moment passed.

"My dear, if you can manage it," Betty said, "your going would be a great help."

"I can leave in two weeks."

"Done. Done! I'm so relieved!"

★ ★ ★ ★

Madison took champagne from Joseph's tray and held it without drinking, feeling, as usual, uncomfortable in the swirling gathering. He understood the value of these big affairs but they still were torture. Frank Key was telling some story that had everyone's amused attention, which blessedly left the President free to ponder those arrogant British terms.

Of course, he knew there'd been lots of loose talk in Commons about punishing the American cousins. This desire for revenge that British official-dom harbored against the United States struck Madison as ridiculous. They coerced our trade to their advantage, they stopped our ships at gunpoint on the high seas and stole our sailors, and then viewed our resistance to this treatment as a stab in the British back while the island nation was nobly engaged in challenging the Corsican tyrant. Until now, Madison had dismissed this chatter in Commons—it was the people's body, like our House, and so it played to the people. But could Parliament really believe such nonsense?

He sighed. Sometimes he felt a prisoner of himself. That Izard woman— his manner had dismayed her, he'd seen it in her face, but she was the wife of one of his most important commanders. He'd been trying to welcome her.

Now he saw her talking to Sally and smiled at both of them. Mrs. Izard flashed a quick answering smile, clearly relieved. My. He didn't know if he liked such power, that a smile could please a pretty woman, a frown dismay her. He looked around; Decatur had sent a note asking for a chat. Ah, there he was, bearing down on the women—trust Decatur to be gallant! He watched the officer telling some story, doubtless of derring-do, and when Decatur glanced his way, nodded to signal his readiness.

Soon the dashing captain approached with another officer. "Thank you, Mr. President. May I present Captain Joshua Barney?"

The officer bowed. "I'm honored, Mr. President." His voice was gravelly, the words forcefully ejected. His round face had a reddened, weathered look that bushy white eyebrows intensified. Madison saw he walked with a distinct limp that did not undermine his air of vigor, even of command. He belonged on a quarterdeck.

Decatur said that Barney had gone privateering out of Baltimore, twisting the lion's tail in the South Atlantic, and since had commanded a motley little naval flotilla, a dozen or so gunboats and small craft that a British frigate had bottled up in the Patuxent River and rendered useless.

"Two points I hoped to make to you, Mr. President," Barney said. "My vessels can't do nothing against a frigate's firepower, but I've got five hundred good men and eight or ten guns small enough to convert to land use. In six weeks I can have an artillery unit that'll make its weight felt."

"That's commendable, Captain," Madison said, "but—"

"Sir, that's where my second point comes in. All along the Chesapeake shore, the word is getting stronger that Admiral Co'burn really does plan to invade. Some say Washington, some Baltimore. Some both."

Decatur said that several naval officers had passed on reports the enemy was forming an invasion force on Bermuda.

"And we have eyesight confirmation, too," Barney said. "Swedish ship captain I know, really hates the British, he called at Bermuda and he tells me he saw a hell of a lot of troops. Nosed around and it wasn't any secret— they were ticketed for the Chesapeake. Tallies with what we're hearing, you see."

"Well, that's impressive, but—"

"Sir," Barney said, "my little ships are strictly coastwise, my sailors all local boys. They go home often and they hear all the talk. Now, you know the British sailors desert all the time, that's why the Royal Navy is so keen on impressment?"

Madison nodded.

"Well, these British tars, they talk. Looking for berths on our vessels, you see. Dozens of 'em tell me the same thing—major invasion. They're making up at Bermuda to hit us here, they're piling into Halifax, and they're forming up in Jamaica, maybe aiming at New Orleans. Given the uniformity of reports, I don't think we can dismiss 'em."

Madison sighed. This was new only in detail. He'd been convinced for months that Admiral Co'burn's threats were real. Smiting the enemy's capital made perfect sense for the British.

"Thank you, Captain Barney. I'll consider this."

Decatur spoke quickly. "Thank you, Mr. President."

But Barney didn't move. His legs were spread. He looked . . . belligerent.

"Sir," he said, "I've gotten my ass burned more'n once for speaking my mind, so I reckon one more time—"

"Now, Josh," Decatur said.

"No," Madison said, "let him speak. Go ahead, Captain."

"Well, sir, there ain't one God damned bit of defenses anywhere along the Chesapeake. I've ranged the whole coast, I've talked to everyone and I know. Not a thing! Now, sir, I can give you guns and men who know how to service 'em, but that's just the beginning. We got to have a real force. We got to have someone in command, someone who can pull everyone together, someone who can kick ass when he needs to, someone—"

"Josh!" Decatur said. "I think that's enough now."

But Madison liked what he was hearing. Wasn't it—in saltier language—exactly what he'd been telling his lackadaisical Secretary of War for months? He studied the red-faced sea captain. When he talked about making his weight felt, he sounded as if he knew precisely how to go about it.

"Maybe I'll give you that command, Captain Barney." Was he serious? He wasn't sure.

He saw he'd managed to shock Decatur. And Barney rocked back on his heels.

"Sir," the bluff captain said, "I'm honored you'd even have such a thought. But I'd be the wrong man. Shore battle needs an army man in command. I'll back him up with my guns, but he needs to be someone the militia will feel good about."

"Doubtless," Madison said. "But thank you for your impressions. Such a commander will be appointed soon."

As the officers withdrew he saw Monroe approaching and told him what they'd said. The Secretary of State looked down his long nose.

"Another failure of that miserable excuse for a Secretary of War," he said.

A voice said, "Speaking of that miserable excuse . . ." and they turned to see John Armstrong himself. Madison felt only a twinge of embarrassment—in fact, Monroe was right. Failure was becoming Armstrong's specialty.

"I've been hearing from the navy that Co'burn's threats against Washington are to be taken seriously," Madison said. "What have you done about our defenses?"

"Nothing whatsoever." The man gave him an ugly smile. His bluster was astounding. "Utterly unnecessary, since Washington is quite without strategic value. I've told you that repeatedly, Mr. President. Valueless, sir!"

"Well, now the navy reports—"

"Sir, talking to the navy about strategy is useless—they can't see beyond their own yardarms."

"Nevertheless, I think we should be prepared."

Armstrong heaved an exaggerated sigh. "If you say so."

Madison gazed at him. Armstrong meant maybe. Maybe, when he got around to it. If he got around to it.

"Mr. Secretary," the President said, "I will appoint an area commander myself. I'll expect you to work with him."

Armstrong paled and his eyes shrank to tiny points.

"As you wish, sir." He turned and walked rapidly from the room, passing close to Dolley without the courtesy of so much as a word or a nod.

"General Winder is back," Monroe said. "British released him on exchange. I saw him yesterday."

Winder . . . the man hadn't distinguished himself on the Niagara. A couple of days after that silly General Lewis stopped young Scott's advance, he sent Winder in pursuit of the retreating British with a thousand men, and Winder got himself captured. There'd been a nasty mix when the enemy struck at two in the morning. Much confusion—Winder got lost in the dark and stumbled into their lines. Still, things happened in war. It didn't say much for him but might not say much against him, either. He'd had some prior military experience, and maybe his adventures on the Niagara had taught him something.

"One thing about Winder," Monroe said. "He's cousin to Levin Winder." Levin was governor of Maryland. "You'll remember Levin hasn't been willing to call up his militia. Maybe with his cousin in command, we'll get more cooperation."

Maybe. That might make as much difference as tactical skills. And who else was there? He wouldn't pull a fighting general from the frontier. Too bad about Barney, but he knew better than to insist on a man who didn't feel up to a job.

"Ask General Winder to call on me, Jim," he said.

★ ★ ★ ★

Jack Tayloe was telling a long story about a horse that looked like a scrub but ran like the wind at the Washington track until one day he decided not to run anymore and that was that. Madison was a horse fancier and skilled at the track, but he listened with only half an ear.

A select handful of guests had gathered in Jack's dining room in his curious octagonal house, which he was about to turn over to the French minister, Louis Sérurier, for an embassy. Mr. Sérurier was here, as were Mr. Thornton, the Capitol architect; Jim Monroe; William Jones, Madison's Secretary of the Navy; Captain Tingey of the navy yard; William Rush, the bright new Attorney General from Philadelphia . . .

And young Daniel Webster, the arch-Federalist who was making a name for himself on the Hill, proving to Madison that high intellect didn't preclude execrable manners. Madison hadn't forgotten the visit to his sickroom. Still, Webster had asked for this meeting on neutral ground.

Like so many Washington dinners, it was a masculine party. Dolley was dining cozily with Mrs. Tayloe and Mrs. Thornton in a small side parlor. The President sat in the place of honor at the end of the table opposite Jack. He liked the Octagon—the graceful dining room was simple and classic with false doors in each of its oval ends to balance the real doors. A splendid silver plateau ran almost the length of the table, its bottom of crystal mirrors reflecting the light of three candelabra. As always, Madison ate sparingly, selecting from the plethora of dishes that servants presented only a slice of ham, venison, a potato, glacéed carrots, a glass of claret.

Was Jack purposely drawing out his story of the horse with a mind of its own to leave his guest to his own thoughts? In fact, the President was fond of these men and at ease in their company, but this was not a night for small talk. He was gloomily pondering Clay's letter in the light of Captain Barney's warning.

The harshness of the enemy's terms proved they still weren't taking us seriously, giving credence to the old rhetoric of a second revolution to prove the first. There had been plenty of London newspaper bluster—they'd been reprinting old Federalist speeches to prove the tired claim that the American government had served Napoleon. Rodomontade, like the drivel in Parliament. But specific terms to be laid on the table were different. And these were the terms of a victor taking a surrender. Demanding a quarter-million square miles, stopping America's westward thrust, limiting its growth—

Jack Tayloe stood and said they would take their port in the drawing room while the President and Mr. Webster talked. Madison scarcely noticed. The terms of a victor. It was outrageous. They weren't victors, they hadn't whipped us. And we weren't surrendering!

What would the American people say if they knew of these obscene demands? They couldn't know, secrecy being crucial to negotiations, but he didn't doubt that demanding surrender on the strength of threats would cause a popular explosion. Americans were getting tougher every day.

Enlistments were up, the last loan had found easier going, there was a different attitude in the air. What would the people say? Just what he was going to say in response to these arrogant terms: *Go to hell.*

For that matter, what would the British people say if they knew that they must ante up treasure and blood again for nothing more than to satisfy their ministers' pique against Americans?

He heard a crunching noise and looked up. He was alone in the room with young Webster, who was seated halfway down the table. Webster was cracking pecans in a silver nutcracker. Powerful-looking fellow with his bull neck, swarthy complexion, obvious self-confidence. He sipped his port and reached for another pecan. Plates laid along the table held nuts, candies, wafers, cakes, small pies. Perfectly at ease, the gentleman from New Hampshire awaited attention.

"Well, sir," Madison said, pouring port for himself and taking up his nutcracker, "what is your pleasure?"

"Mr. President, my recollection of my role in our last meeting is—well—less than pleasant, shall we say."

"But I understand you had considerable sport on the Hill as to the bitter medicine you delivered to my sickroom."

"An impertinence, I'm afraid."

"Ah. Then you wish to apologize?"

Webster laughed. "I hadn't thought of going that far. But I have concluded over time that I didn't cut so pretty a figure that day. If you construe that as apology, very well."

"I'll so construe it," Madison said. "Was there more?"

"I thought you should know the temper in New England."

"I know it's bad. Is that your message?"

"It's worse than bad. It's dangerous. You know that the British have extended the blockade to our coast?"

Madison nodded. "Apparently they've decided Massachusetts is part of the United States even if Governor Strong doesn't think so."

Webster didn't smile.

"You might suppose that would make New England realize we're all in this together," he said, and Madison was struck by the force in his splendid voice. No wonder he was dominating debate on the Hill. "But in fact, it's having the opposite effect. Questions on all sides—why must we suffer for a war we detest? Do we even belong in a country whose majority forces us to follow so ruinous a course?"

The heavy sectionalism—indeed, the real flavor of secession itself—alarmed Madison. Best to nip such trends in the bud.

"Such a statement smacks of treason, sir. It demeans your station as a member of the United States Congress."

"My status as a congressman is the least of my worries. What you should know is that in fact there is a real secession movement in New England.

Serious men, leaders, in Massachusetts and Connecticut—and some from Rhode Island—intend to call a convention to consider a motion to secede from the Union."

Madison felt as if he'd been slapped. It was much worse than he'd thought.

"I find that hard to believe, sir. I don't *want* to believe it. Are you actually saying that serious men contemplate so despicable a move? They would break the Union?"

"Exactly, sir. They've chosen Hartford as their site to consider just that. Make New England a new nation."

Madison put a hand on the table to steady himself.

"But that's treason." He stared at this complacent, thick-necked young man. "Where do you stand on it?"

"I'm of my people, Mr. President. In the end I'll support them. My own estimate is that no good can come of this, and I am not encouraging it."

"Do they hate us so much, then?" Webster didn't answer. "Would they so willingly shatter the nation with the greatest promise on earth because they dislike its short-term policy?"

"Perhaps it's not the greatest nation if it doesn't serve its people's needs. And it certainly isn't serving New England's needs and hasn't for years, not since the Democrats got in the saddle. Look, Mr. President, the nation isn't sacred. It's only thirty-five years old. And for the last fourteen years it's been in the hands of men whom many in my area believe to be evil."

"Evil, sir? Democratic-Republicans?"

"My personal view is that casting politics in terms of good or evil is inappropriate," Webster said, "but you should hear the talk from the pulpits in New England. And people listen. But my point is that a thirty-five-year-old government that has been sorely wounded for fourteen years is hardly sacrosanct."

"You are wrong, sir," Madison said.

"But—"

"Wrong. This government is as noble an experiment as exists on earth, a beacon of freedom in a world dominated by monarchy. I believe God's light shines on it, and on the document that guarantees its freedom. Neither New England nor anyone else may set it asunder."

"Fine talk. Very fine talk, sir." Webster's voice rose, his face reddened, his eyes were like darts. "But, sir, it's out of step with reality. The reality is that New England is sick to death of this war and this government and is considering separation. I'll regret that if it happens and so will others, but I will support it and so will they."

Madison drew a deep breath. He stared at the swarthy congressman.

"Mr. Webster," he said at last, "this is a movement that can destroy all who touch it. It sickens me that New England, the names of Bunker Hill and Concord still shining, should flirt with dissolution. But set that aside for now—two statistics tell a story. In 1810 the textile output for Rhode Island alone equaled that of any European nation before the French Revolution. Do you understand? Your manufacturing base is too valuable for us to let it go."

"Exactly the point, Mr. President. We are the industrial engine of the nation. We don't need you—you need us."

"But another statistic tells another story. Washington County, Pennsylvania, by itself is producing a half-million yards of cotton and woolen goods each year. You see: the rest of the country is catching up and soon will outstrip New England."

"With all respect, sir, I doubt it. We are the strength of America—those vast reaches to the south and west the Democrats are bent on including weaken the whole. We're strong. If we choose to stand alone, we'll do fine."

"Don't be ridiculous, Mr. Webster. Do you really believe that? Should we let you go, in five minutes you'd be the plaything of Great Britain. Even as you knelt in obeisance, they'd give you the knout. In the end they'd absorb you into Canada. But don't worry, sir, the United States will never let you go."

"Come now, sir," Webster said, "if our people decide to go, you'll have no say in it."

Madison smiled. He had regained his control.

"Of course we'll have a say. We won't permit such an insane move. There'd be civil war—which we would win and you would lose, at the cost of endless blood and treasure."

"Oh, come, come, Mr. President. If we choose to leave the Union we'll simply leave it. You won't fight us—you can't. My God, you can't even handle the British. Idle threats demean you, sir."

"Listen carefully." Madison extended a steady finger. "See that you convey what I say to your people at home. We will never allow you to break the Union. Never. We will win this present war, sir, and should your people be so insane as to try to break away, we will restore order with troops at whatever cost in blood it may take."

Webster didn't answer.

Madison stood up. He bowed, the coolest inclination of body, and walked from the room.

★ ★ ★ ★

The *Democratic-Republican* office was on Fourteenth Street a few doors off Pennsylvania. The low brick building had a narrow front on the street, a wider expanse at the rear where rows of type cases stood beside the big press. In front Susan Gooch sat on a stool at a counter laboring over ledgers and taking advertising orders. Sam Bartles, the day-to-day managing editor who was coming to understand and even to like Sally's true role—she was

decisive and could bring Micajah McQuirk to action faster than he could—
had a desk at one end of the room.

The two reporters shared a desk. Jack Early covered the Hill and the
crucial gossip murmured in the boardinghouses where congressmen and
senators lived during sessions. Angus Adams covered War, State, Treasury,
and the Executive in general. Micajah's office had a window through which
he could survey his domain, and Sally had partitioned off a little cubicle
where she read other cities' papers from Boston to Charleston. She marked
whatever she thought the *Democratic-Republican* should reprint, and though
she never insisted, she found that Sam Bartles was more likely than not to
take her suggestions.

She was reading the *New York Post* and trying to decide how she would
tell Papa she was going to Plattsburgh to cover the battle likely there when
she heard him cough. The cough deepened, and she was already on her feet
when he plaintively called her name.

"Yes, Pa, what is it? Are you—"

He waved an unfolded note. "The President." A new paroxysm seized
him. She thumped his back, then held him close. "I must go to him, Sally—
he says immediately. Most urgent."

He seemed disturbed by the summons, which surprised her. He stood
up, then leaned both hands on the desk as if exhausted.

"I want you to come," he said.

She scanned the note. "Papa, I'm not invited."

"But I need you." His voice rose. "This isn't social, it's business. He'll
welcome you. Please, Sally."

She felt new alarm. He was going down before her eyes, and no remedy
seemed to help.

"Don't fret, Papa. Of course I'll go." She would explain to the President
if necessary, but she wasn't going to send her father off alone, not the way
he looked at the moment.

As it happened, Mr. Madison smiled and said, "Sally's always welcome."
He chuckled, his manner quite buoyant. "And secrecy's the last thing I
want today."

They were in his office in the northeast corner. Ned Coles had brought
them up the long staircase, Papa breathing hard, Ned casting warm glances
on her. Mr. Monroe stood by a bookcase with a volume in his hand, radiating
displeasure.

The President handed Papa an unfolded letter—the terms, he said, the
British would offer at the forthcoming negotiations at Ghent. She glanced
at the Secretary of State's face and saw there an expression so hostile that
she averted her eyes. It seemed that Henry Clay had managed an advance
look at the British position. Her father's hand shook as he read the paper
while the President ticked off the British demands.

"Why," she said, "those are the terms of . . ." She broke off, remembering she was there as her father's nurse.

"Of a victor," Mr. Madison said. "Exactly."

"But they're not victors."

"And they'll never be," Mr. Madison said with surprising force. "They can attack our coastline but they can never, ever control us. They couldn't thirty-five years ago, and we're tenfold as strong today. Throw a hammer in a corn bin and what happens? The hammer bruises a few grains, certainly, but if you don't snatch it out in a hurry it'll soon be swallowed up. The British would do well to ponder that analogy."

Only two days ago she'd watched him with Captain Decatur, looking bowed by the cares of war. Now he looked . . . younger, lighter, as if he'd cast off a heavy burden.

"I've decided I want this text published," he said. "Write an article denouncing it in the strongest terms—I liked the forceful tone of that thing you did on the St. Lawrence debacle."

He was watching her face—which, she was sure, was scarlet.

"And see that you send copies to every paper in the country."

She stole a peek at Monroe. He looked as if he'd just bitten into a pickle.

"I don't know, Mr. President," Papa said. He'd been part of Monroe's delegation to France that had resulted in the Louisiana Purchase and had always considered himself a diplomat. "It's not right to publish this—not done, I'm sure of it. Ain't that so, Jim?"

"Oh, the Secretary of State doesn't agree with me," Madison said before Monroe could answer. "He's our chief diplomat, and publishing these terms is anything but diplomatic. But it's what I've decided to do."

"But, Mr. President . . ." Sally saw tears start in Papa's eyes. "It's not right."

"I didn't seek a debate," the President said. "I told you my decision."

"But why?" Papa said, his voice quavering. She wished she were close enough to seize his arm. "Why, sir?"

"Because, sir," the President said, "our people are getting ready to fight. These outrageous terms will infuriate them—you'll see their resolve stiffen. 'Who do they think they are?' they'll be saying.

"Now, the British have taken a false position. It's an expression of pride by power-mad ministers, when the actual issues between us could be settled overnight. They've already stopped coercing our trade. Let them stop stealing our sailors, and the quarrel vanishes. I believe that when the British people learn they're to sacrifice still more on the altar of pride, those ministers may get their comeuppance."

"But they'd be within their rights to break off negotiations," Papa said.

The President plucked the paper from his hand. "Very well, this will be in the *National Intelligencer* tomorrow. I thought of you first, but so be it. That will be all, Mr. McQuirk. Good day, sir."

"Pa!" she cried. "For God's sake! Of course we'll publish it. Don't you see—this is a great story!"

She caught Mr. Madison's shrewd glance and knew her cover was destroyed forever. Papa nodded and took the letter back.

"Thank you, Micajah," the President said. But he was looking at Sally.

17

NASHVILLE
Summer, 1814

★ ★ ★ ★ Rachel Jackson knew what was coming when she saw the men riding up the line of yellow poplars to the Jackson blockhouse compound. Until now the days had been heavenly. Andrew was here, he was well or at least not really unwell, and almost immediately upon his arrival she had perceived a subtle but marvelous difference in him.

She sighed and stepped out to meet them—Governor Blount; Jack Coffee and Billy Carroll, Jack as massive and solid as Billy was light; young Johnny Reid, of whom she was especially fond; and a man she didn't know. The stranger looked as if he'd traveled hard, though his shirt was clean and he was freshly shaved.

"Miss Rachel," Willie Blount said, bowing from the saddle.

She smiled. "Light down, gentlemen, the General's in the pasture with the foals. I'll send for him."

"Yes'm. Thank you."

"Aunt Rachel, this is Paris Yardley," Billy Carroll said when they dismounted. "He's just in from the south."

Of course. All their trouble came from the south. The man bowed awkwardly. There was something rough about him. A settler, she supposed.

"Hannah made a cake and it's just cooled. Chocolate, I think. With some coffee, gentlemen?"

"Yes, ma'am," Mr. Yardley said, "that'd be just fine. My missus makes chocolate cake when she can get the chocolate, but that ain't often, living so far out like we do." His voice trailed off and he looked uncertainly at the Governor.

"Mr. Yardley's come a long way with information for the General," Willie said. She liked Willie; he was loyal.

She smiled. "I'll give you a double piece."

"Yes, ma'am!"

The small domestic chores distracted her from the pain she knew was coming. The knife cut smoothly through the moist cake, cups rattled on saucers, cream from the springhouse formed little beads on the crystal pitcher. Bad news always came from the south—the Indians, the Spanish, the British . . .

He'd be going again. She'd known that all along, but until news actually came, she could push aside the thought and give herself up to sheer joy. She needed his presence, his iron self-assurance, the security he seemed to build around her. She just did. More so, perhaps, than other wives needed their husbands; but who could be sure of that and what did it matter? She was as she was. Meanwhile, having him home unharmed had been a gift for which she'd fallen to her knees morning and evening to give thanks to Jesus.

He'd been ill, of course, bent with dysentery, his innards ruined. Bone slivers from the wound in the Benton fight were still working out of his arm, and he was exhausted. She put him right to bed and dosed him with broth made from a whole chicken, tea with herbs and leaves in the Indian fashion, rice into which she sliced bits of chicken. For a week he'd let her cosset him, then pronounced himself well and gone out to see his foals and watch the yearlings work on the rope. She watched him touch young cotton plants thrusting from turned earth to test their firmness and break dirt clods in his fingers to assess retained moisture. He did love the farm.

As he grew stronger the difference she'd perceived in him became even more apparent. It was in what he said, in the texture of his voice, even in how he moved. Of course, he'd always been graceful. In her mind's eye she could still see him that day he rode in with the awful news that Robards threatened to take her by force, his body moving with the horse's gait as eloquently as a branch sways with the wind. But now there was a power, a precision, an inner authority in all he did and said. Nor was he just asserting authority, for he'd always done that; this was a controlled inner force that required no assertion, no raised voice, nothing to make it evident—it just was.

She had prayed to Jesus that he be given understanding, and her prayer had been answered.

When he told her, though she had a flash of dismay at the twin images of his facing rebellious troops with musket and cannon, his pleasure in his new self-control was so obvious that she'd offered thanks right there on the spot. He was standing by a window, looking out as if uncertain how she would respond, and she went to him and hugged him hard, her arms locked around his back.

The victory in the Alabama country had made him a hero. He was Old Hickory again, the damage caused by the fight with Tom Benton washed away, leaving him whole and strong in the public eye. She saw she'd have to get used to sharing him with the adoring crowd; he'd always been a public figure, but never with such acceptance.

And he handled himself smoothly and well, with an assurance she hadn't seen before. There were parades, receptions, public dinners. People praised his unaffected manner, his habit of sharing credit, gracefully calling attention to his men, citing this one and that for bravery. He was Tennessee's leading man, and he rose to the acclaim with new polish.

Then the commission came: major general, United States Army. Until now he'd been a state militia officer, significant at home but insignificant beyond, and as he had grown, she knew how much the failure of his rank to grow with him had vexed him. The British were sure to attack New Orleans, and who else would repel them? It was all simple, he said; why couldn't Washington see that he needed recognition for the duty lying ahead?

She was thrilled and horrified in equal measure, until his joy when he opened the letter from the Secretary of War overrode any dismay. Commander of southern forces of the United States, with orders to establish a headquarters at Nashville. The command made him a national figure. It was yet more evidence of that capacity for greatness she'd aways believed would be his if he mastered himself. He was soaring, and all at once she saw she must rise with him, in her own way, or be left behind. And she, in her own way, was as determined as he.

She made up her mind. This time she would bear his leaving well. No more paroxysms of lonely despair, no more hysterical screeds penned at midnight when she couldn't bear his absence. As he controlled himself, so would she control herself.

Silence, not especially comfortable, had settled over the group in her drawing room.

"I think I've found the plot for the memorial, Governor," she said to Willie. "A beautiful spot overlooking the Cumberland."

"The legislature will meet the price, you know."

"Half the price, Willie, please. I want the people of Tennessee in on this. It's *their* memorial."

She was absolutely determined. Those who died and those who came home wounded and suffering deserved a memorial. It would be carved from Smoky Mountain marble and would honor all who'd gone to war. She had another dream, too: a permanent fund to help men too crippled by war to work their farms. She'd put all the community leaders on notice: she would raise Cain until she got her way on this one.

Mr. Yardley demolished his cake, washing it down with noisy sips of coffee.

"This here is the best ever," he said. "Wish my missus could taste it. She's got some sweet tooth, and she's mighty partial to chocolate."

"Perhaps you'd like more, Mr. Yardley?"

"Well, ma'am, the Good Book says gluttony is a sin, my missus'd tell me to mind my manners, but . . ."

She liked a man who honored his wife. "I don't think one more slice would be a sin."

She saw Andrew coming at a fast walk, his face alight, his carriage radiating eagerness. In these past few weeks she'd been seeing only a part of him, of course. That part delighted in home and her company and life on the farm, but all it took to summon the fiery man of action was the call.

Mr. Yardley wrung Andrew's hand.

"General, I can't tell you how much folks down in my parts appreciate what you done. My brother, he's over to Mobile, he was about to go to Fort Mims when Weatherford struck it—and tell you the truth, I was thinking on it myself. We come that close to having our families murdered, and it made a sight of difference, you taking the poison out of that devil's fangs. That's how come when I saw what's going on, I knew you was the one to bring it to."

She listened—fascinated, appalled—as Andrew took a chair and leaned forward intensely, cradling his injured arm in his good hand. It seemed that Mr. Yardley lived near Pensacola, maybe within the Spanish line, maybe not, nobody really knew just where it was. He had friends there among the Spanish, who tolerated a few American settlers, and among the Scottish traders who did business there.

"Well, one day, in sails a British warship. Has her guns run out, she means business, and the Spanish fall all over themselves making her welcome. A captain name of Pigot, Cap'n Pigot, he comes ashore with about fifty marines and, I mean, they take over the place. And the Spanish let 'em! Wagging their tails like so many puppy dogs. Say they're neutral. Neutral, my—" He broke off with a glance in her direction.

"Well," he said, "like I say, they ain't neutral. They're hand in glove with the British. Been passing British arms to the Indians for years and now they're ready to help the invasion."

Andrew sat up straight. "Invasion?"

"Yessir, that's what I come to tell you about."

No different from what she'd expected. Andrew had been talking about it for years—foreseen every detail, forecast it step-by-step.

It seemed this Captain Pigot with his escort of Royal Marines and the Scottish traders as guides had gone around enlisting Indian allies. To gain acceptance he'd had to explain himself in some detail. The British intended to enlist a couple thousand Indians as guides and "light infantry," paying in goods and gold. Then they would march fifty miles overland to Mobile.

"But we hold Mobile now," Andrew said.

She knew General Wilkinson had taken it a year ago, after Andrew marched his men home from Natchez to keep them out of Wilkinson's hands.

"Yes, sir," Mr. Yardley said. "But my brother lives there, and he says there ain't a hundred troops on hand."

Andrew looked up. He was the commander now; these were his men, isolated in Mobile.

"They're in Fort Bowyer?"

"No, sir. In the town. Fort's thirty miles away, at the mouth of the bay, and it's a ruin. I been out there once. Fixed up, it could give invading ships a good tussle, but the way it is, wouldn't even be no point in manning it. No, sir, as things are now, if the British want to take Mobile, they won't have no trouble.

"But see, General, that's why I come hightailing. Mobile is just the start. They're telling the Indians they'll march from Mobile right across Mississippi Territory, cut the river north of New Orleans, then take the city at their leisure. Promising those savages soon as they have New Orleans, they'll go right up the Mississippi, tie into Canada, and give 'em the empire old Tecumseh told 'em about."

"Any idea of how soon?" Andrew asked.

"Well, the Scottish trader, he says Cap'n Pigot won't be the one to decide. He'll report and someone else decides. But Pigot told him they're already making up an army in Jamaica, ready to launch it, so it ain't gonna be too long. I figure Pigot got sent as sort of an advance patrol, so to speak."

Rachel shivered, sure it was true. Felix Grundy had written Andrew from the Senate: Washington talk said the British were making up in Bermuda to strike the Chesapeake, would do something in the North, and would try the South from Jamaica.

Andrew stood up. "Mr. Yardley, as major general commanding, I can say you've done signal duty for your country. I'll see that the President knows of your service. You'll return immediately? Good. Let our friends there know that I'll be going south in a day or two and I'll soon be in Mobile to reinforce that garrison. And you're to keep your ears open and report what you hear to me at Mobile."

In a day or two!

"I don't know, Andrew," Governor Blount said, "getting the army together again won't be easy. I sure can't do it in a day or two."

"General Pinckney has an army, regulars and volunteers, at the Hickory Ground now. I'm to relieve him, and as soon as I secure things there I'll move on to Mobile."

He glanced at her as he said this, and she saw that he'd known for some days he was going and had been waiting to break it to her. Cosseting her while she cared for him.

"But, Willie," he said, "better get ready. Jack, you and Billy get your men set. The British will aim at New Orleans, and then I'll want my Tennessee boys at my side."

"All right," Willie said. "Time comes, we'll be ready."

They were on their feet but she didn't stand up. She felt dizzy. Planning war. The fire in their eyes, the light in Andrew's face, the eagerness! She felt a bottomless dread and she knew that all her resolutions of bravery had been gasconade. She would smile and wave till he'd ridden down the long drive, and then the loneliness would come in waves, and in the dark of night and despair she would—

Mr. Yardley was making a clumsy bow and thanking her for her hospitality and she realized she'd forgotten his second slice. Well, that, at least, she could do something about.

She didn't look at Andrew. She told Mr. Yardley to wait, went to the dining room, cut a huge slab, folded it into a clean cotton napkin, and handed it to him.

"Eat it while you ride," she said.

"Yes, ma'am!"

When they were gone she put her arms around Andrew, laid her face on his chest, and held him. He sighed and drew her closer.

So soon . . .

18

THE WHITE HOUSE
Summer, 1814

★ ★ ★ ★ Captain Joshua Barney came into Madison's office ahead of Ned Coles like a squall breaking over the Chesapeake. The President was drawn to the fiery sailor, a burly man now in his middle fifties who'd gone to sea at thirteen and taken command of a merchant vessel at fifteen when the skipper died. In the infant U.S. Navy he'd made a fighting reputation during the Revolution, and afterward fought for the French Navy. Madison admired in about equal parts Barney's experience in the art of war and his healthy hatred of the Union Jack.

Barney came to rigid attention. "Sir! I figured I'd better get in here and report."

"At ease, Captain. Do sit down."

"Thank you, sir." He sat stiffly, still at semi-attention. Ned took a seat behind him. "Mr. President, things ain't going worth a fiddler's fart! That's my report, and I figured it's high time you hear about it."

Madison kept the dismay out of his face. "Tell me your own situation."

"Looks like I'll have to burn my vessels to keep 'em out of British hands. Royal Navy frigate's been nosing around the Patuxent, you know. But I got m'guns ashore and I'm turning five hundred sailors into a fighting artillery unit to give 'em a reception when they come."

"And you've reported this to General Winder?"

"Hell's fire, that's the problem. I can't even find him, and as far as I can tell, he ain't doing a blessed thing."

Madison had been afraid of this. He rarely saw Winder, who was active as a whirlwind and perhaps no more effective. The man spoke with vigor that sounded more nervous than forceful, and struck Madison as more the lawyer he had been than the officer he was. He was only about forty but seemed old for his age, with his little potbelly and miserly mustache. Madison remembered young Scott's reticence on the subject of Winder, who'd been involved in the fatal decision to stop the advance on the Niagara, just before he was captured. In Scott, reticence usually meant disapproval, and Madison had found the young officer one of the few men whose military judgments he could trust.

And his own instinct, too, told him Winder was no soldier. There was confusion and contradiction in the few discussions of plans they'd had, the man's voice hurried, his gaze roving around the room to fix finally on the President with hangdog supplication. Nor had his family connection with the Maryland governor, which had tipped the balance for his appointment, paid any dividends as yet. To all cousinly pleas for militia, Governor Winder had turned a deaf ear.

"I've been all over looking for the General," Barney said, "but everywhere I go, he's just gone somewhere else. He needs to take a lesson from Baltimore. Ol' Sam Smith is working day and night. I wish we could get *him* over here."

Madison saw Ned Coles start to speak and raised a restraining hand. Smith, just now leaving the Senate, was his harshest critic—nothing bites harder than the apostate's venom—and he raised a combative fury in Ned. Smith's brother Robert, Madison's first Secretary of State, had proved worthless as well as disloyal. Madison fired him in favor of Monroe, and the Smith boys had been pillorying him ever since. He remembered that Barney was a Baltimore native. But the Captain took the raised hand as rebuke and fell silent.

"Please continue," Madison said. Baltimore was important; measures being taken there reassured him. "What's Sam doing?"

"He has ten thousand militia on one-hour standby. A hundred thousand rounds for cannon, a million for muskets. He's dragooned a supply of heavy guns and he's rebuilding fortifications. Turning Fort McHenry into a powerhouse. They try to take Baltimore, they'll find it has a stinger. I figure that makes them even more likely to hit Washington, and like I say, Mr. President, damned little has been done here."

"Can you really be sure of that, Captain?"

"Well, the militia units along the coast, they sure ain't ready to get up and go. And nothing has been done to guard the key place the enemy will come."

"You can actually pinpoint a single place?"

"Yes, sir, it's pretty obvious." The Captain hesitated, plainly fearing he'd overstepped, then said, "May I take the liberty of sketching it out for you?"

"Please do."

As the sketch took shape on a bound notebook Barney extracted from an inner pocket, Madison realized that he had never considered the terrain from a military perspective. Washington was protected by deep water to the east, west, and south. The main branch of the Potomac lay to the west, what usually was called the Eastern Branch to the east. The two merged in a *Y* shape that nestled Washington in its crotch at the city's south side. Fort Warburton downstream on the Potomac—plus the river's shallowness—was enough to make an upriver attack unattractive for heavy vessels. So if they attacked Washington—and they were bringing an army, after all—they probably would come by land, cross-country from the Chesapeake.

"So there you are, sir," Barney said, sketching with a stub pencil, "they must cross the Eastern Branch to reach Washington, and the first place they can do so with any comfort is well to the north, at Bladensburg. See what I mean?"

Bladensburg was a hamlet in rural Maryland. But of course, the great battles of Europe generally turned on some anomaly of geography.

"What should we be doing, then, to get ready?"

"Fortify the Bladensburg crossing, for one. Have teams set to burn the bridge and make 'em ford—and guns to punish 'em when they do. Lines of defense keyed one to the next, so if one gives way the next one's ready. Outlying bastions, prepared so when they try to flank us we can turn as fast as they do."

He stopped and shook his head. "Things like that, I reckon. Hell, I don't know! Give me a frigate, I'll lay her barrel to barrel and blow the enemy out of the water, but land fighting ain't the same. But one thing I do know, land or sea, you gotta be ready. And we ain't ready!"

★ ★ ★ ★

"**M**y God, Mr. President, surely you know better than to ask a sailor for military advice."

It had taken Madison ten days to run Winder down, so furiously was he moving around the area, and he made no attempt to conceal his displeasure at being disturbed.

"Sailors know nothing about military matters. Really, sir! They're used to a self-contained unit, everything aboard before they leave port. Army's totally different—long before I call together my men, I've got to have lines of command, legal structures, positioning plans. Suppose I call up thousands of men, what do I do with them? Where do I put them? I must find horses, wagons, tents, medical supplies, food supplies. Doctors and chaplains. See that the senior officers meet my criteria. There's so much to do!"

Madison mentioned Barney's focus on Bladensburg.

"Well, yes, he may be right and he may be wrong, we'll have to wait and see, won't we? Other places are as logical."

"Really? Where?"

"I don't know! I haven't had time to study the ground. Yes, maybe Bladensburg, certainly that's a main point we'll be looking at. But it's easy enough to throw up parapets, set up lines of defense. Elementary. I'm surprised this sailor would waste your time with such talk."

Madison sighed. "Well, General, if you agree, perhaps we should be about it."

"All in due time, sir. But first I must line up my units. Check their commanders. Order supplies. Countless things, it's enough to drive a man mad."

"You need help, then?"

"No, no, I have it all in my head. Take me longer to explain it to someone else than to do it myself." He heaved a long sigh. "Rest assured, Mr. President, it all will be done. When the time comes we'll have a strong defense force dug in and ready, just as the good captain wants."

★ ★ ★ ★

Madison put on his hat and followed the curving gravel path to the little brick building housing the War Department.

"Damn it all, John," he told the Secretary, "I want you to give Winder some assistance. I'm afraid he's dithering."

"Oh, I suppose he is a ditherer," Armstrong said, "but it doesn't matter. They won't be coming here."

"You're so sure of that?"

"Military logic, Mr. President. With all respect, I think it fair to say I'm the expert in that field. Now, if they do attack in the Chesapeake, Baltimore will be their target. Standard military doctrine—strike at the enemy's heart. Baltimore is a powerful city. Home to the privateers that harry their shipping. Warships under construction, factories, foundries turning out cannons."

"I see some value in Washington, too."

"Value to us, yes. Political value. But no military value. Why, it's just a village. A pitiful collection of hovels studded here and there with a grand building, ankle-deep in dust one day, in mud the next. That's Washington, sir, a miserable village!"

"Well—"

"Believe me, sir, Baltimore will be the issue, if indeed there's an attack at all. That's why I'm putting all my resources there, feeding Senator Smith's splendid effort."

His ugly smile betrayed how much he relished supporting an enemy of the administration. Yet Madison found that his own rancor toward Smith was gone. Things had soared beyond mere political differences—if Smith could gird Baltimore for attack, Madison wished him Godspeed.

"Actually," Madison said, "I do understand Baltimore's importance. But listen to me carefully, John. I consider Washington a target whether you do or not, and I want Winder's efforts supported. He needs help and I want him to have it."

"Damn it, Mr. President, I can't say it enough, they're not coming here!"

"That's an order, John."

Armstrong's face froze. "Very well, sir. You will be obeyed."

When Madison went back to the mansion, the sun had given way to dark clouds. He sighed. Once again, he had infuriated his Secretary of War.

★ ★ ★ ★

"Well, Mr. President," Frank Key said, "it's about an even call. Winder and Barney—I have to say they're both right."

Madison wanted an impartial view of the military situation and Frank was the logical choice. Dolley valued him for his versifying, and perhaps for his slim, patrician good looks, but Madison knew him to be a trustworthy and able lawyer who had negotiated his way over many a tricky shoal. And not a bad poet, either, though poetry was hardly Madison's field. Dolley had a good many of Frank's verses by heart.

They were in the family sitting room. Curtains curled at the windows in a fresh breeze, and the sun outside glittered on leaves. Dolley filled cups with a cool punch made of fruit juices flavored with applejack and fortified with a decent little dollop of corn whiskey, while Joseph spread bite-sized squares of toast with spicy ham and mustard or curried chicken paste.

Madison noted Frank's sigh of pleasure when he took a plate from Joseph's hand. How did the man manage to keep that slim figure, considering the food he put away when he visited? Starved himself at home?

The lawyer was saying he'd spent a week touring the area from the Chesapeake to the upper Potomac. Yes, Bladensburg was the obvious entryway to Washington, and he'd walked the ground with Barney and seen immediately that his views on gun placements were sound. But he'd also found that militia across the whole area were hardly ready for the call and had precious little equipment of their own beyond their muskets. Few even had an adequate supply of ammunition. Every captain he met told him the gov'ment would supply all they needed soon as they mustered.

Since Winder had almost nothing ready, Frank understood why the man suffered from nervous stomach, belching continually. It had taken days to find him—he seemed always on the move—and he exploded when he realized Frank had been sent to question him.

"You know me, Mr. President, I can be pretty smooth, that's what negotiating is about, and I got him calmed down—but just barely. He's shaky. Overwhelmed, I think, but he won't hear of assistance. I offered to come back myself after I reported to you, to help him straighten it out, and he got mad all over again. Just about threw me out."

"That's a little alarming, isn't it?" Dolley said.

"If Admiral Co'burn lives up to his threats, yes, I'd say so," Frank said.

"Well, in the end, do you think Winder can get it done?" Madison let Joseph refill his plate. He was especially partial to the ham.

"As well as anyone, I suppose, in the absence of some towering military figure."

"I told the Secretary of War to get him some assistance."

"Really? Not much sign of that, I'm afraid."

"Maybe there hasn't been time," Madison said, but he knew better.

The door opened suddenly, and in came Monroe. He clutched a paper in his left hand.

"Good Lord!" he said. "There's no end to the tricks Admiral Co'burn will play. Listen to this. He's appealing to American slaves, says the British will guarantee freedom for any who come over to them. Free passage to Jamaica, a home, employment—"

He broke off just as Dolley raised a hand and Madison himself became aware that Joseph was in the room.

Joseph bowed to Dolley and said, "I'll get a plate for the Secretary."

★   ★   ★   ★

"Jennie!"

She was in the pantry scraping carrots for the evening meal, and though Joseph's voice was harsh as a rasp on wood and he could barely control his excitement, he noticed the slender pillar of her neck, the curl of dark hair, the way her thin shoulders moved with a motion that flowed down to her full hips. She turned suddenly and gave him a radiant smile. He rarely spoke to her, and now her expression carried a sense of something wonderfully new.

And it was, it was, thank the good Lord, it was!

"Jennie, listen to me." He slipped into the pantry and braced the door shut with his foot. "The British, they say we go with them, they make us free. Free! Do you understand?"

Her eyes were huge. She took a step back from him.

"What you talking about?"

"I just heard it. British proclamation—join up with them and they'll make us free!"

"You crazy? What kind of talk is that? They the enemy!"

"White folks' enemy, not my enemy. Nor yours."

"Why you come in here telling stuff like that? You get us in trouble! White folks don't want to hear no such talk."

"Jennie, we're going to go. You and me, we're—"

"Shut your mouth—you talking crazy. I been sweet on you for ages, you know that, and you never give me no reason to hope nothing, and now you're in here talking crazy—"

"Jennie, they'll take us to Jamaica, we'll marry, we'll—"

"Damn you, Joseph! I been never looking on another man but you— and don't you think they don't look at me, neither—but, no, no, I dream we'll marry, dreaming, dreaming, and now you come in talking like you done lost your mind—"

He released his breath in a long, shuddering sigh.

"I have to get back," he said. "Have to take a plate. But we'll talk—"

"No, we won't! You'll get us both in trouble. Get us whipped."

"Madisons don't flog, what's the matter with you?"

"Get us sold!"

"Damn it all, Madisons don't sell either, you know that."

"Oh, Joseph, I'm scared! You'll get us in trouble."

He stared at her. He'd held her off for two years, and now that he was ready he'd assumed she'd melt with joy but here she was pushing him away! When more than ever he wanted to hold her close, kiss her hard, make her his. He put his hands on her shoulders. She jerked away.

"No! Don't touch me. Joseph, you playing with fire. You get away from me. Leave me alone!"

"Jennie . . ."

She clamped her hands to her ears.

He took the plate, returned to the sitting room, and served the Secretary.

"Thank you," Mr. Monroe said.

"Thank you, Joseph," Miss Dolley said. She was smiling. She was a supremely kindly woman, and Mr. Madison was kindly, too. But Joseph was going to be free. He'd always known he would be someday. Now he knew when.

19

On the Niagara Frontier
Summer, 1814

★ ★ ★ ★ They were beautiful, that was the only word for it—three thousand men marching with all the snap and precision of hardened veterans, going through their paces for the last time at Flint Hill. Brigadier General Winfield Scott stole a look at General Brown—hell, yes, the General was impressed. He'd never seen anything like this. As if in confirmation, Brown turned and threw up his fist in a warrior's gesture.

It was a brilliant day, sun blazing, cool, winy air fresh and tangy. Glad-to-be-alive weather. Scott's throat was raw from shouting commands as he wheeled his big roan gelding about for each new maneuver. A big man needs a big horse, and the roan he called Rusty was just right, a soldier's horse that loved the drum and danced when he heard it.

The boys were equally invigorated, that snap in their steps, their backs like ramrods, dressing right to hold their lines on knife-edge, officers' sabers flashing in the sun. They were as proud as was their general, and were joined with him in a bond. He had made soldiers of them and they would be forever different; even at home with wives and children, even growing old by hearth fires, they would be different. They had been shambling recruits and now were men—how could they not be proud?

Oh, they were good. Drums rolled and fifes shrilled and he swung them

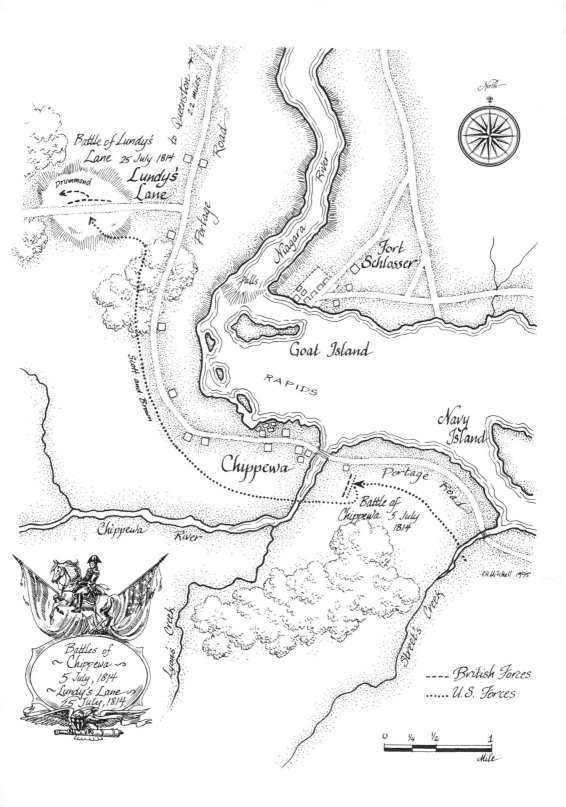

North

Battle of Lundy's
Lane *25 July 1814*

**Lundy's
Lane**

Drummond

Portage Road

to Queenston
22 miles

Niagara River

Falls

Fort
Schlosser

Goat Island

Scott and Brown

RAPIDS

Navy
Island

Chippewa

Portage Road

Battle of Chippewa *5 July
1814*

Chippewa   River

Lyons' Creek

Street's Creek

E.H.Mitchell 1995

Battles of
~ Chippewa ~
5 July, 1814
~ Lundy's Lane ~
25 July, 1814

- - - - *British Forces*
.... *U.S. Forces*

0   ¼   ½   1
Mile

here and there and back again, wheeling, reversing, by the right flank, by the left, advance by line, by column, by column of regiments. The thud of marching feet, lines adjusting and readjusting, dress right, soldiers! Clouds of little yellow butterflies jinked around their knees. A panicked rabbit bolted through the columns without causing a tremor.

He formed the men in fighting lines and threw them forward on the oblique—outside man on the point moving at a run, inside man at the base at a slow walk, so that the line steadily shifted to a forty-five-degree angle, and then reversed on a snapped command. Then rapid firing, highly accurate, and broken field advances, run, fall, dry-fire, reload, and up to run again. Bayonet drill, lunging and parrying and what to do when the redcoat parries you and comes in for the kill, all handled with skill, spirit, élan.

His own First Brigade was the leader, a single flowing organism in gray. Once the gray uniforms had been a sore point. The factories said there had been a run on regulation blue uniform material; gray jackets and unbleached linen trousers golden white in color would have to do. He was outraged then, but now gray had become First Brigade color, the uniform of men who could handle themselves; a color, finally, of pride well earned. He loved them for it as they prepared for war together.

★　★　★　★

Flint Hill broke up immediately. Tents collapsed, field kitchens were dismantled, excess supplies loaded for the run to the supply dump at nearby Fort Schlosser. There was a sadness in it; they were marching to war and Scott was eager, but this had been his domain and it was vanishing.

Toward dusk, Nate Towson and Ike Roach appeared at his command tent; the regimental commanders would be along soon. Ike, now a major, was serving again as aide, as he had when Scott commanded the Second Artillery, and good old Nate was still a battery captain. Four batteries from the Second were with Brown's army; Scott had made sure Nate and his three twelve-pounders were assigned to the First Brigade.

Old Nate . . . as solemn and steady as ever, as quietly confident. He would never be more than a captain, nor did he want more. He just wanted to go back to the family store in Pennsylvania. It seemed a girl from home had been writing, and—well, he thought he had a real chance . . .

"They're snappier," Nate said, puzzled by his men's response to the training. "Why, they've taken to saluting me."

"Good."

"Well . . . I guess."

Scott winked at Ike. "What'll we do with Nate, here, pretending he's a civilian at heart? Then, when the guns start up, he's a tiger. You go home, Nate, you'll miss those guns."

"Like hell."

"Sure you will," Ike said. His bright blue eyes flashed in his dark face, his voice had that South Carolina softness. "Those guns, you're going to help make history with 'em." He laughed. "Remember Queenston? Well, this is going to be teetotally different."

The army would march at two the next morning, cross the Niagara by small boat, and take a British redoubt that faced seaward and was open at the rear and hence couldn't be defended. Then they would march north along the Canadian bank of the Niagara toward a collision with the British army. And Scott would wipe away the stain of Queenston where his line had broken and his troops tumbled down the hill to huddle at its base like sheep awaiting roundup by the men in red coats.

Damned right it was going to be different.

★ ★ ★ ★

Tom Jesup walked in, chuckling. A tall, loose-limbed Welshman with an infectious laugh, he was independent of mind and operated best on his own; Scott would use his Twenty-fifth Connecticut as a hard-hitting ranger force.

"General," Jesup said, "you ought to see my boys honing their bayonets. They can jolly well shave with those blades. Say they'll slice the gizzard out of every redcoat they meet."

"My kind of soldiers," Scott said.

Jesup grinned. "Mine, too. I promised a gold eagle to the first man hands me a British gizzard. I know the Brits." He had done time, as he liked to put it, amongst the redcoats.

"Such bloodthirsty chatter, Tom," Henry Leavenworth said, appearing out of the dusk. He was a big man, solid, very steady, with an extravagant brown beard; Scott considered his Ninth Massachusetts the central rock around which to build a combat line. "Just shows how damned uncivilized Connecticut folk really are."

"Oh, my." Jesup rolled his eyes. "The Massachusetts gentleman wants soldiers to be likewise. My boys aren't gents, Henry. That's why they kick yours around when they go to town."

"Good evening, sir," Leavenworth said to Scott. "May I note for the record that only last week Tom was whining about how hard my boys had handled his in the Buffalo taverns?" He smiled, pleased with himself.

"Where are the other two?" Scott said. Hugh Brady had the Twenty-second Pennsylvania; he was a quiet, thoughtful man who rarely revealed himself. John McNeil, Eleventh Vermont, was a meticulous officer, able but fussily inclined to lose himself in detail.

"Brady's waiting on Mac, and getting madder by the minute," Leavenworth said. "Mac's gathering status reports from every platoon leader."

When the two arrived, McNeil offered a torrent of figures on his regiment. Scott raised a hand and he stopped in midsentence, looking offended and a little flustered. Brady leaned forward and punched his arm.

Mac sighed. "Well, I figgered the General'd want to know."

Scott said it was his confidence in McNeil's attention to detail that made him so willing to forgo its description. He saw Jesup wink at Leavenworth. But it was true. For all his fussiness, the Vermonter was a good officer; Brady could profit by emulating McNeil's daily reports.

Scott had just come from a meeting in which General Brown's three brigadiers got their marching orders. He explained the crossing they were to make and described the British redoubt with its open rear.

"Twelve-pounders set, slow matches glowing, they'll take notice," said Nate, looking much less the storekeeper.

"And then," Scott said, "in the words of General Brown, 'We go find the enemy and smack him good.'"

"Hip, hip, hurrah," Jesup said.

Leavenworth chuckled. "That's how to fight a war."

Scott saw McNeil frown and shake his head. He took everything seriously. But he was right: war was never so easy.

They were seated on camp chairs around a table on which Scott now unfolded a map.

"Let's trace out the plan."

Flint Hill was near the village of Buffalo, which lay at the starting end of the Niagara on Lake Erie. He tapped the chart with a finger. The Niagara wasn't a river at all but a massive channel through which water draining all the Great Lakes and their tributaries poured out of Lake Erie, plunged over the massive falls, and fed into Lake Ontario. Running a finger along its left bank—the Canadian side on which they would march northward—he came to four or five substantial creeks and then to the Chippewa River, a sizable stream feeding the Niagara just above the falls. North of the Chippewa lay Queenston. Continuing north—downstream, the water rushing toward Lake Ontario—he tapped two small squares. Fort George on the Canadian side, Fort Niagara on the American.

Fort Niagara was where Scott and Dearborn had planned the invasion that he had led the summer before, landing in small boats and fighting their way up that slope against the Glengarry Fencibles. And Fort George was the British fort they'd taken that morning, when debris hurled aloft by the exploding ammo dump smashed his collarbone. He rubbed his shoulder; it hurt when the weather changed. And it all had been for nothing. It wasn't even a British defeat: they'd had twelve hundred men to his five thousand and had executed a well-staged withdrawal, fighting as they went. And poor General Winder, sent in pursuit, had been outwitted and outmaneuvered, then captured.

Scott sat there tapping the map. It didn't say a hell of a lot for the future of Washington that General Winder now headed its defenses. But he pushed that thought away; he had his hands full here. Anyway, in the end, the British had regained Fort George, taken Fort Niagara from a skeleton force, and marched down to burn poor Buffalo to the ground. In cold fact, not once since the American regular army was formed had American regulars been able to stand against an equal number of British regulars on a level field. Not once.

Not yet.

"So we take those two forts, right?" Leavenworth frowned. "Will Nate's twelve-pounders do it?"

"Commodore Chauncey's naval artillery will—at least, that's the idea." He saw their doubt, the same doubt the other two brigadiers had shown when General Brown said Chauncey would meet them at the mouth of the Niagara. Scott would not forget the pompous sailor talking Secretary Armstrong out of his hopes for taking Kingston. Chauncey had never really cooperated with the army; would he, now?

"So!" Jesup rubbed his hands together. "We hit the lake, the navy arrives, we reduce those forts to kindling wood and mortar powder—what then?"

Then? "Then" was a long way off in Scott's estimation and could take care of itself when it came. But he tapped the map and offered Brown's basic plan. With naval firepower and ships to haul supplies, the army would swing west. His finger traced westward along Lake Ontario's south shore and stopped at Burlington Heights. They would take that fortified village. His hand moved up to find the north shore, then moved east to follow that shore to Kingston. Seize Kingston—and from there, the long thread of the St. Lawrence River stretched northeast, channeling lake water to the Atlantic. And Montreal stood on the banks of the St. Lawrence.

"Montreal?" Jesup's eyebrows went up. "Well, why not?"

Scott reminded them that Henry Clay and the others were at Ghent, in Belgium, trying to negotiate a peace treaty.

"I don't know that they'll have much luck, but if they do, I want a hunk of Canada in our hands instead of vice versa."

"Well . . ." Leavenworth smiled. "Does the General think the British will have anything to say about this?"

"Oh, yes," Scott said, "they'll talk to us about it, all right." The British forces on the Niagara were headed by a banty Irishman, Major General Phineas Riall, whose only error of judgment so far as Scott could see was the contempt in which he held American soldiers. Scott expected to change his view. Riall had some four thousand men, a thousand more than Brown, but they were scattered around the Niagara peninsula and it would take him a while to collect them.

Riall was a strong general by all accounts, but more formidable still was Lieutenant General Sir Gordon Drummond, who would be coming on with another thousand men from Kingston once he learned Brown was making his move.

"Let's go smack 'em, just the way the General says," Jesup said. "What's our order of march?"

Scott had given this plenty of thought. He wanted Jesup's Twenty-fifth Connecticut in the lead, supplying the skirmishers who must march far ahead on the point; Jesup would react in a hurry to emergencies. Then Leavenworth's Ninth Massachusetts, the solid core of the brigade, always ready to hunker down and fight. McNeil's Eleventh Vermont third and Brady's Twenty-second Pennsylvania last; the end of a column is always subject to attack, and he had less confidence in Mac to respond well. Fussy attention to detail didn't go with swift reactions; Brady might not be imaginative but he wouldn't hesitate a moment to swing into action.

"This General Riall," Leavenworth said. "Where do you think we'll meet him?"

Scott tapped the map. "Right behind the Chippewa River is my guess. In his place, that's where I'd be."

★ ★ ★ ★

It was the Fourth of July and the midmorning sun was a furnace overhead, cool winy air just a memory. Sweat ran down Scott's face. They were marching north on the Canadian bank of the Niagara, lifting clouds of dust, heavy timber to right and left, the falls thundering up ahead. Having crossed the day before and taken the little redoubt, General Brown was content to plunge ahead until he collided with the enemy. Scott couldn't quarrel with a fighter's stance, but it wasn't exactly subtle. Actually, he himself should be in command—he had trained the army, and he was a specialist in the science of war. But he had made brigadier before he was thirty—could he complain?

He was riding Rusty, his big roan, at the head of the column. Tom Jesup was with him and long files of Connecticut troops marched behind, Nate Towson's battery tucked in place behind the second company. Tom's advance squad, a full company this time, was on the point a quarter mile in advance.

Scott didn't think they would march undisturbed for long. Major General Phineas Riall of the British Army knew what he was doing. He would have pickets set, outposts of a squad or two ready to meet the enemy, feel him for his strength, and fall back, flashing news of his advance by rapid rider. Scouts must have alerted Riall to the crossing by now; doubtless he was gathering his scattered forces and marching to meet them.

A spattering of fire came from up ahead and he lifted Rusty into a gallop and went hurtling along an avenue of trees. Around a bend in the road he saw his men crouched and firing on a group of twenty or so British soldiers on a bridge spanning a creek that looked more morass than flowing stream. Half the Britons were firing while the others pried up the floorboards of the bridge.

Jesup caught up with him. "I can flank 'em, throw a company right and another left, root 'em right out."

"No—get Nate's guns up here, give 'em a taste of grape."

The first blast settled it. The redcoat soldiers melted away, dragging their wounded to work wagons, and disappeared around the next turn. Word would flash to Riall as fast as horses could run. Scott examined the captured bridge. In half an hour they could reset the planks and move on. He was proud of his boys. The men on the point had responded with high polish, and so had Nate's gun crews, while the Twenty-fifth Connecticut ran up and deployed left and right without a hitch.

★ ★ ★ ★

In the next sixteen miles there were three more contested crossings, which the boys handled with equal skill. It's rare that a man sees the results of his work so forcefully, but the difference between these troops and the recruits of the year before was unmistakable. Yet he didn't think training alone could take all the credit.

He saw a willingness in his men this year that was different from last year, an enthusiasm, a love of country openly expressed. Soldiers reflect the nation, and in the last months he had seen similar signs of change in the people at large. Townsfolk smiled when he appeared in uniform. Recruiting was up; he could still remember the agony of trying to get the Second Artillery together in 1812, but regiments now filled a little more readily. Scott didn't think much of the Secretary of War, but more and more the President was shaping military decisions, and he believed Mr. Madison to be steadily toughening. Certainly the President had weeded out army deadwood—incompetent generals had fallen on all sides.

The nation's financial picture, never bright, was at least a little less dim, so Sally McQuirk wrote. When Scott mentioned in a letter that three of the four regiments wearing First Brigade gray were from New England, she'd answered that Washington believed New England was growing isolated and now doubted that it could seduce New York.

She also said she was going to Plattsburgh on Lake Champlain "because I think there will be a great story there, though you must keep that secret." How startling! Women just didn't do such things, in Scott's estimation. Of course, Sally wasn't like other women—but then, maybe other women weren't really as he pictured them. It was a disquieting notion.

Sally was a power, all right, but on the whole he would take Maria. Not that he had declared himself or even decided anything, exactly, but oh, did his heart quicken when he saw his name in her sweet handwriting on an envelope. Her letters were warm and generous, reflecting exactly his estimate of her nature. She filled them with gentle commentary on the sort of Washington talk that he knew didn't much interest her and that she knew did interest him.

What she said reinforced his sense of a turn in the national attitude. She reported much admiration for Commodore Barney's energy—she'd heard

the President say he wished Barney were running Washington defenses—
but much dismay over General Winder's dithering. Until recently no one
had thought the danger of attack anything to bother one's head about, but
now folks talked of nothing else. Made them mad, too. Burn us out, will
they? The scoundrels! Personally, she thought Mr. Armstrong's insistence
that the capital would never be a target was downright silly. If we burned
London, she guessed, it would say something to the world. Scott chuckled.
Good for her!

So the sense of change was everywhere—which to his mind put even
greater pressure on the gray-clad First Brigade and the army Scott had
trained for General Brown at Flint Hill. What would the new attitude
mean—and how long would it last—if to meet us was to whip us?

The American soldier didn't have to win every battle, but he did have
to fight as an equal. Else who was he, this American, this new man conceived
in liberty and dedicated to republicanism in a world dominated by monarchs?
We believed the force of democracy would sweep away those monarchs and
change the world, but our democracy would die aborning if we couldn't
defend it. We said the second revolution was to prove the first, but what
were we proving? Was the new American the mere mongrel son of a mongrel
nation that had abandoned discipline, purpose, and integrity when it broke
from the mother country? Or was the difference just that the British soldier
was trained and the American, until now, was not?

The answer to that would tell whether democracy's bright promise was
real. Whether the American nation itself was significant. Whether it even
would survive—or whether it would die in the mud of broken dreams.
Questions for the warriors in gray . . .

★　★　★　★

The sun was a red ball low in the western sky but the heat was still fierce
when they found Major General Phineas Riall tucked behind the Chippewa
River as Scott had half expected. Street's Creek lay three quarters of a mile
short of the Chippewa. When no redcoats waited to contest the creek, Scott
galloped ahead and saw the enemy in force beyond the river with artillery,
the bridgehead well guarded. He pulled up short of musket range and
ignored a few pieces that popped at him.

He made a slow circle, checking the ground. The Niagara lay to the
right. Open fields extended a half mile to the left with heavy forest that
had not been cleared beyond. The hamlet of Chippewa hugged the shore
where the river entered the Niagara; the falls were a mile distant, and he
could hear their roar. The Chippewa was wide and slow at its entry point,
the bridge spanning it a good hundred fifty yards long. A twenty-four-
pound cannon was posted at the far end to sweep it like a broom.

Forcing the bridge would be murder, but it wasn't necessary. They would
simply cross upstream, then attack Riall on his flank while Nate's artillery

pounded him from across the river. The resulting crossfire would make his position untenable and he would withdraw to terrain that favored him. Scott made his camp short of the creek—two bodies of water thus stood between the two armies—and sent his engineers up the Chippewa to search out a ford or a place to build a bridge.

"Sarenmajor," he said, "think you can get a feel for their numbers?"

Boone grinned and swung onto a mule he'd taken to riding. "Yes, sir. Hang my head in shame if I can't."

General Brown had sent a note by courier: the other brigades, the Second and the Militia, were making camp. Scott rode back to report and was surprised to find the rest of the army had lagged by five miles. Brown agreed that the key to the Chippewa lay upstream and ordered the Militia Brigade to advance in the morning through the woods on the left to support the engineers.

Scott returned in deep dusk to find the First Brigade settled in along Street's Creek, a line of pickets across the bridge alert for enemy activity. Sarenmajor Boone awaited him with a lanky civilian in faded denims whose handlebar mustache looked oddly familiar.

"Sir," Boone said, "this here is Sergeant Belthasa Hoslie of the Eleventh Vermont."

"Sir!" Hoslie snapped to attention and saluted.

No wonder he seemed familiar. "Where's your uniform, Sergeant?"

"Sir," Boone said, "Hoslie, here, he grew up around Buffalo before he got mixed up with the Green Mountain boys. Talks like folks hereabouts, you see what I mean. So we borrowed some duds from a civilian—that's him over yonder." He pointed to a disconsolate-looking fellow in drawers whom two troopers were guarding. "So Hoslie swum the river, floated the clothes to keep 'em dry, you know, and paid them redcoats a visit."

"The hell he did!"

"Well, sir, you wanted their numbers. I'd as lief gone myself, but Kentucky lingo don't jibe with Niagara Canadian."

"So, Sergeant Hoslie, how did you handle it?"

"Went in with a notebook and a pencil and took orders for eggs and frying chickens. Made 'em pay a little down—I come out of it with a few shillings."

Hoslie had a good military eye. He calculated Riall's strength at about fifteen hundred regulars and five hundred Indians. Casual glances at their guns confirmed two twenty-four-pounders and a howitzer capable of lofting substantial shells.

Fifteen hundred regulars? Scott had his answer. Riall was too skilled to risk an attack on an American army twice his size. The First Brigade had thirteen hundred soldiers in gray, the Second Brigade nearly a thousand, and the Militia Brigade six hundred plus some friendly Indians.

Riall had no special need to fight now. He would pull back when they crossed above him, collect reinforcements, and sooner or later they would meet.

Scott slept easy in his mind.

★ ★ ★ ★

About four the next afternoon General Brown rode by, said he wanted a squint at the enemy, and took the bridge over Street's Creek. It had been a good day. Scott's engineers found a crossing suitable for a bridge that they could erect in a few hours. When Riall's Indians troubled them, they withdrew until the Militia Brigade with its own Indians could clear the way. Meanwhile, his men had eaten and were ready to drill on the field between the two streams. Give Brother Riall a show.

Scott led the brigade over the creek in its usual marching order. A bullfrog bellowed at them from a lily pad and a fish took a fly in the quiet water. Scott was just across the bridge when with a thunder of hooves General Brown came boiling out of a sunshot cloud of dust at a dead gallop, aides trailing behind him. Jesup's men jumped aside.

"You will have a battle, General Scott!" Brown yelled and then was gone.

What the hell?

It wasn't like Jake Brown to blow up over an enemy soldier or two. No doubt Riall had his picket line out to probe a little, but if there were three hundred Britons on the field, Scott would eat his hat. Then the breeze freshened and the dust cleared and he saw the whole damned British army spread across the field.

Coming on to fight!

He felt a sudden gut-clutching pressure. Without a moment's notice he was in it, without a second to plan he must *act*. And his men, yes, they'd learned their lessons, he had faith in them, but God damn it, he'd have liked to have had a moment's notice, a chance to get them ready. Prepare them.

Prepare *himself*!

He gazed across the field: a half mile from the Niagara on the right to the woods on the left, three-quarters from the Chippewa to the creek, and already Riall's advancing columns were halfway across. Marching in columns—the arrogant bastard hadn't even bothered to form a fighting line. It bespoke his contempt for Americans—

A galvanizing flash of rage tore through Scott's brain and came out as a plan.

★ ★ ★ ★

Jesup appeared beside him, his face smooth and hard.

"So we'll have us a fandango. Your dispositions, General?"

The enemy remained in columns. Good. A clamor arose in the woods off to the far left. The Militia Brigade had been pushing Riall's Indians there, but now two companies of redcoat regulars on the British right double-timed toward the woods with bayonets leveled, and the American militia fled. The British soldiers would follow the militia, and that would put them behind Scott's left.

Alarm bells rang in his mind.

"Tom, take the extreme left, get over there on the double and turn those bastards back. And, Tom—get clear in the woods, work around behind their main lines. We'll catch them in—"

A shocking, shattering, wind-tearing sound just overhead left him choking for breath. Three of Nate's men were down and several of Jesup's.

He whirled and saw those big British twenty-fours in place by the Chippewa Bridge, saw matches smoking in gunners' hands.

Christ, they had the range of the bridge over Street's Creek, but the bridge was the only way he could bring his own men across. Yet if he tried to withdraw, take his men back under cannon fire with the whole British army in chase, it would be a slaughter. They had to go forward—they had to!

But what agony that their baptism should be the very thing most dreaded by the most experienced troops, crossing a fixed point under totally unexpected locked-in cannon fire.

Everything could turn on this moment. Everything. He knew he would never ask more of his men than he was asking now. He tore saber from scabbard, he'd have to shout and roar, he must lift them, inspire them, drive them, give them the flat of the blade . . .

And then he focused on their faces.

They were steady. They were coming on at a fast trot, heads down, pieces unslung, faces set, wincing at the shattering noise when a shell burst, jumping over those who fell, but steady as stone. God, he did love them!

He shouted for Nate, and then the battery whipped past, Nate galloping by without a word, whirling into position, guns dropping from caissons, boxes flying open, load and ram, matches flaring, and the three twelves spoke almost at once.

"Dispositions, General?"

It was Leavenworth, reining in his horse and studying the field with a slight smile. The last of Jesup's troops were running hard across the field, the first of Leavenworth's following.

"I want you in the center, Henry. I want a fighting line three deep—but do not advance. I'll have Brady on your right, McNeil on your left. Repeat, do not advance!"

"No advance? Yes, sir, but won't that—I mean, that puts our backs to the creek, them coming on, there won't be any place for us to fall back—"

"You're not going to fall back." He grinned, suddenly full of a wild exhilaration. "Where better to fight than where you can't get out? Inspirational, don't you think?"

"Yes, sir." Leavenworth laughed. "You're right."

The Massachusetts men came across with that same steadiness, stepping around those who had fallen, running with their shoulders hunched and their heads down, fearing for their lives but steady, steady—

Soldiers.

The surgeon's wagon was across and surgeon's mates were pulling the dead and wounded out of the way, opening kits, pressing pads against wounds. A youngster at Scott's feet was white as paper and bawling out loud, clutching his belly, sure that a gut shot meant certain death and probably right. A sudden shattering thought: he'd have a lot of dead today.

But still the exhilaration bloomed like a flower in his mind. Everything had changed in an instant, he'd come out for a drill and would stay to fight an army of trained professionals bigger than his own. Oh, yes, General Brown would bring up the Second Brigade, but it was five miles away and it was slow, it would take an hour to prepare to move and an hour more to get here, and the battle was *now*.

A British drum was beating, and he heard fifes shrilling. Riall's columns came on, already two thirds of the way across the field, marching in exquisite drum-fixed order while Leavenworth's boys ran across their front. The enemy was still in column—no, they were shifting out now into a firing line, but Scott thought the movement was tardy. He saw General Riall wheeling a big golden-colored horse as he shouted orders.

At seventy yards—musket range—the redcoats opened fire. Several Massachusetts men fell. Then Leavenworth got them set and they turned with fixed bayonets and leveled muskets to return fire, aiming as they'd learned on the range. Cool, steady, and very fast, aim, fire, break the cartridge, pour the powder, ram, replace the rammer, aim, fire. A redcoat went down, falling so that his bayonet stabbed the ground and his musket remained impaled even as he rolled on his back. Another fell, then a half dozen, the ranks behind stepping over them. A sergeant extracted the musket as he passed and dropped it by the still figure.

Blue smoke from the guns burned Scott's eyes. His nostrils pinched. He saw Jesup disappearing into the woods on the far left. Heard the shriek of metal on metal and a man's shocking scream that went on and on—a British twenty-four-pound ball had struck one of Nate's twelves in the muzzle and dismounted it, flipping the long barrel up and dropping it across a gunner's back. Four men lifted it while another dragged the gunner free—

McNeil appeared, his thin face quivering but his voice steady. Scott sent him behind Leavenworth's regiment to bring his men up on what amounted to Scott's left flank. Jesup's men were out of sight in the woods on the far left. As Brady's Pennsylvanians appeared, a searing *boom!* ripped across the field. One of Nate's shells had exploded in a load of British ammunition. Scott focused his glass and saw that one of the big pieces was knocked askew and half the enemy gunners down. A wild cheer rang through American ranks. After a bit the other gun began to fire, the rate much slower.

He put Brady on the right, matching McNeil on the left, and galloped to the center, reining up before the Massachusetts troops. Twenty were down, maybe more.

"Hold your line, now!" he roared. "Remember, boys, shoot low, shoot low." Men under pressure invariably fired high. "Shoot low. Careful aim. Make it count, boys, make it count!"

He turned back to Brady on the right. By God, it would work! Riall's men were spreading out into fighting lines, but the British general had waited too long, his men were still bunched in the center. Now Scott would throw his wings forward on a long oblique firing line as he'd taught them. Fighting lines swinging forward right and left like gates on their hinges— their outer ends must overlap the enemy, enfilade his ranks, ultimately envelop him in deadly embrace.

Brady gazed at him wide-eyed, then began to laugh.

"Yes, God damn it, that'll work, damn right!"

The Pennsylvanian's arm flew up as he shouted orders and Scott paused a moment to watch the oblique movement begin, men on the outer end of the line running hard, those at the base pacing slowly, the line shifting to a forty-five-degree angle that would put it athwart the British lines . . .

"Sarenmajor?"

"Sir!" Boone, on his damned mule.

"Get around on the far left and find Jesup. You see the British layout— bring Jessup through the woods till he's *behind* their lines. Remember, behind. Tell him to come crashing out!"

Noise punched at him in waves. The musket fire was an almost steady roar, punctuated by the deep thunder of the British twenty-four, the lighter barks of Nate's twelves. Men were screaming as they fired, faces red, eyes bulging. A ball struck a corporal standing beside Scott with a meaty smack. The Corporal fell on his face without a sound. The man beside him turned to him with an expression of horrified grief, and in that instant a ball carried away his whole lower jaw and he fell on the Corporal's body with a piercing shriek.

Scott shook himself. He spurred Rusty to a gallop and reined up by McNeil on the left. The slender Vermonter listened alertly as Scott laid out his plan.

"D'you see? Work it right and we have 'em trapped between our wings. Pour in flanking fire the length of their lines, make 'em a God damned shooting gallery!"

A tic fluttered in McNeil's cheek. He looked from side to side and stuttered as he set the maneuver.

"C'mon, Mac," Scott said, his voice low, "steady now, steady. You keep the base fixed, I'll take the lead out."

McNeil flashed him a grateful glance, and then Scott was out on the end, where he saw a familiar face, long mustaches—Sergeant Hoslie, who grinned and flashed him a thumbs-up sign.

"Take the outer end, Sergeant!" he shouted. "Lead your men. I'll be right beside you." He sighted down the line, and when it sagged as the end swung forward, galloped to straighten it.

"Move it up here, boys, a little faster, step it up, dress right and dress left." They belled ahead then, and he pulled them back. "Easy, easy, dress your lines!"

A bullet clipped his right rein, left him holding only an end. Rusty faltered, turned his head. Scott leaned forward on the roan's neck, caught the cut rein, tied the end in place, and spurred on. The horse leapt forward, his whinny an absolute scream. What the hell?—gunfire never bothered Rusty, and the spurs had been just a touch. Then Scott saw a furrow plowed across the horse's broad rump, a line of blood starting. Rusty pranced, unhurt but clearly enraged, and Scott stood in his stirrups to survey the field.

Leavenworth's line was steady. Thirty or forty of his men were down, maybe more. A corporal with blood flowing from his mouth was on his knees but still firing. Leavenworth walked his mare along the front as he exhorted his men. Then his mare was hit; her knees buckled and Henry stepped off as if getting down from a carriage and walked his line, saber in hand.

They were beautiful. Beautiful! Fighting like a massive machine, all of a single mind.

The left wing was swinging around, Sergeant Hoslie controlling its outer end. Soon it would overlap the British line. Standing in his stirrups, he saw the same thing on the right, Brady's men matching McNeil's. Scott was only thirty feet from the nearest redcoat, a sandy-haired man gaping at the sight of an enemy suddenly materializing at his *side*.

"All right, boys! Fire! Fire! Fire!"

Muskets blazed all around him. The sandy-haired Englishman hadn't even raised his musket before a bullet struck his throat. His head snapped back and he fell.

That great swing had cost the line on the left three dozen or more, but now the boys were getting it all back, firing into the British flank. The best troops in the world can't take flanking fire. Cross fire from front and side and then both sides takes men down as a scythe takes grass, breaking the strongest of them. The British troops were looking around wildly—as horrified at this devastating turn of events as his own men had been at receiving cannon fire in the midst of a simple drill.

It was too late for them to recover. They were trapped and falling on all sides even as their bullets whipped around Scott and felled McNeil's troops left and right.

Now Jesup's Twenty-fifth Connecticut came bursting out of the woods with wild yells and threw a hurricane of lead into the British rear. General Riall's whole right began to melt.

Riall was a doughty little bastard, he didn't care that the lead was flying, and Scott saw him gallop that golden-colored horse into the center of things trying to rally his men with his saber flashing. Too late—his right was crumbling. He turned the horse, saw his left collapsing under parallel attack, Brady's Pennsylvanians pouring in their fire, Jesup's men coming up behind with bayonets—

And the British bugles sounded retreat. Scott swung his saber in wild loops.

"Come on. Come on! Now's the time to hit 'em, turn retreat into rout, break them for good!"

But McNeil's long flanking line was disorganized by success and momentarily out of control. Hoslie had snatched the ramrod out of his piece and was using it as a whip, lashing men into position, but precious seconds were going.

Across the field, Brady was having the same problem. Scott spurred Rusty toward Leavenworth's Massachusetts boys, who were standing openmouthed watching the British collapse.

"Forward!" he roared, and to a man the regiment lurched ahead, bayonets level, firing as they ran.

But Riall was a professional and so were his men, and he had them back in control again. Wheeling his golden horse here and there, he organized his retreat. As Leavenworth's line ran forward it met men backing steadily but facing them and firing relentlessly. Riall threw out wings to protect his retreat and soon was passing troops over the bridge at a run, their boots drumming on the plank floor.

So it ended. Scott felt sudden searing exhaustion. He wiped his face and scanned the field. Three hundred—no, four, maybe five hundred British soldiers were on the ground. Some were moving, most weren't.

His own men had suffered fewer but similar casualties. Bodies littered the ground. Surgeons and their mates ran from one to the next, checking hastily, leaving the dead and dying to try to save the living. He saw British surgeons still on the field, and realized doctors and mates from both armies were tending the wounded without reference to uniform. War's insanity: kill them ten minutes ago, try to save them now.

The field was silent save for the soft cries of the wounded, the silence as loud as the roar had been. Men stared, dazed, and sank exhausted to the ground. Others emptied canteens, went slowly to the creek to fill them, and began taking water to the wounded. Scott felt he'd been fighting for hours, but the sun was still bright and hot and his turnip watch said less than an hour had passed since Brown came galloping out of the dust and it all started.

The roan's bleeding had stopped. Scott rode among the men, nodding, smiling, shaking every hand thrust up at him. The feeling he'd had for them at the beginning now was magnified a hundredfold. They had faced the enemy together, some were wounded and some were dead but they'd come to fight and had succeeded brilliantly. Succeeded against a skilled professional army of fifteen hundred to their thirteen hundred, that had the advantage of taking the field first, that caught them by surprise—and under these worst of circumstances they rallied, fought like veterans, drove their superior enemy from the field, and won!

No American regulars had ever held their own on an open field against British regulars of equal numbers. Now that had changed forever. These men would live in American history, and by God—sudden tears formed in his eyes and didn't shame him—they deserved every honor their country could muster.

These wonderful men in gray.

20

ON THE NIAGARA FRONTIER
Summer, 1814

★ ★ ★ ★ Scott's engineers bridged the Chippewa upstream the next day, and Riall ran north with the battered remains of his army. Brown's three divisions followed as far as Queenston, which they occupied without incident. Scott and Boone tramped the now deserted hill where they'd fought that long-past day; there was no sign of the cannon the British had spiked before they abandoned it. Doubtless it was somewhere to the north now, spike drilled from the touchhole, loaded, and aimed toward them.

For Riall was still at large, and the Niagara campaign was not over.

They were waiting now for Commodore Chauncey's ships to appear off the mouth of the Niagara. With naval artillery—with the supplies that ships could carry, the speed with which troops could move by water—Brown considered his army invincible. Sweep west, take Burlington, continue around Lake Ontario's north shore, subdue the lakeside settlement of York, and rush on to Kingston where the St. Lawrence began—they'd give John Bull fits!

If the navy cooperated.

"Sir," Ike Roach said, "there's a British officer in our hospital tent who told me something you'll want to hear."

"All right. Is he wounded badly?"

"Leg smashed up. Surgeons took it off yesterday." He fluttered a hand. "I wouldn't want to bet."

Lieutenant Harrison Tittle of the Eighth Foot proved to be a long, slender young man with an angelic face, auburn hair, and a mustache that made him look even younger than he was. The missing leg was a conspicuous gap under the sheet, and his skin was waxy gray.

Scott drew up a stool. "Well, son, I see you caught the low end of the fortunes of war."

Tittle shrugged. "My family back in Sussex thought lawyering more appropriate than soldiering. Now they'll have their way." He sighed. "But, sir, as I told Major Roach, your men fought so well it surprised the bloody hell out of us. Surprised General Riall, too."

"Oh?"

"Yes, sir. I was with him. When your men came across the bridge and he saw those gray uniforms, he said, 'Why, that's just a pack of Buffalo militia—they'll scatter like quail.'"

Scott didn't say anything.

The youngster's voice seemed weaker. "I don't think I'm talking out of turn, I think General Riall would say it himself if he were here. When your men kept on coming across that bridge under direct cannon fire, the General couldn't believe it. He's standing there with his legs spread, his fists on his hips, and he says, 'Those are regulars, by God!' That's what I was asking Major Roach—your men *are* regulars, aren't they?"

"United States Regular Army, yes, sir."

"Good." Tittle sighed and closed his eyes. "That's what we thought. But why gray?"

"It's a fighting color," Scott said. He looked at the boy's waxy pallor and touched his shoulder. "There's a courtroom in Sussex waiting for you. Don't let go."

The faintest of whispers. "Yes, sir. Thank you, sir."

★ ★ ★ ★

"Those are regulars, by God!"

Riall had said everything in five words. It was a phrase, a motto, a benediction that would live in American military history—Scott himself would make sure of that. The American soldier had earned the right to pride at Chippewa: let no one forget.

A few days later papers arrived from Albany and New York City, and on the day following, from Boston and Philadelphia. They were full of celebration. Even the Boston editors recognized a signal American victory: for the first time American troops had stood head-to-head on level ground with equal numbers of British troops and defeated them. Editors in New York and Pennsylvania glowed and by the accounts, so did the people—victory bonfires, whiskey barrels broached at vast public meetings, orators outshouting each other.

Thus had his men in gray demonstrated that to meet us was not necessarily to whip us. They had fought as equals, anything but mongrel sons of a mongrel nation.

General Brown laughed when Scott repeated his conversation with Lieutenant Tittle.

"It do tell the story, don't it? Win, I'll say it again, your boys were magnificent. Truth is, when I crossed that bridge and went to fetch Ripley's brigade, I didn't know what the hell was going to happen."

Sixty good men in gray had died at Chippewa. There was no one in the brigade who hadn't lost a friend, and the fact that one hundred forty-eight Britons had died was no particular consolation. The chaplain held a long, impressive funeral ceremony. Some of the men wanted to speak, and Scott made time for everyone. Then the bodies, wrapped in canvas, were sent across the Niagara to be buried on U.S. soil.

There were two hundred thirty-five wounded; two thirds returned to duty in a few days; the others, most of them minus an arm or a leg, were going home to find what life held for them now. Scott was much among them, talking to all the wounded, showing how he valued them. He listened to reminiscences about the dead, and wrote wives and parents, including as many scraps of personal recollection as he could.

★ ★ ★ ★

Two weeks after the battle, General Brown summoned his brigade commanders. Scott arrived to find him pacing before his command tent, face white, lips a bloodless line, cigar clenched in his teeth. An open letter was in his hand.

"The Commodore," he snapped, "has found a new reason not to take part in the war." Sure enough, Commodore Chauncey was not coming. Said he could not risk his new ships against vessels the British had built this summer until he was ready to deliver the knockout blow.

That night Scott dined with the naval lieutenant who'd delivered the letter and learned that the Commodore's real problem was pride. He would fight—when he was ready—but he would not demean proud and beautiful ships by using them to haul soldiers and supplies for the army's glorification.

Chauncey's decision changed everything. They couldn't possibly circle the lake on foot carrying all the supplies they would need—food, ammunition, heavy weapons, and all the accoutrements of war. For that matter, even the Niagara peninsula wasn't secure without Chauncey's firepower. Two forts remained in British hands, and Riall was only thirteen miles inland from the Niagara. Word along the river was that more British were coming.

So things weren't settled at all, and what mattered now was to give the enemy another blow. Triumph though Chippewa was, it also was only a first step. The British had been badly stung; next time they would be wary, they'd take nothing for granted, and they would fight like hell. How would his boys do when the enemy was dug in, when battle went on and on, when their first charge and the next and the next were thrown back? If new skills and courage deserted them then, he knew the glories of Chippewa would be forgotten. It would slap the faces of all who'd celebrated, call the fresh turn in national spirit into question, give comfort to those willing to splinter the country.

Forget Canada. The answer wasn't yet in on the Niagara, and hard fighting lay ahead.

★ ★ ★ ★

Twice Scott proposed going out to find Riall and force the action.

"Dividing the army's dangerous," Brown said.

"So is waiting."

But Chauncey's refusal, Brown felt, impelled them to pull back. So they returned to camp on the ground they'd fought over at Chippewa.

The odds seemed to have turned, too. Each side had a good idea of where the opposition was and in what numbers. Civilians on both sides of the river kept watch, and those friendly to Americans passed information along. Riall had about twenty-two hundred men. Then Lieutenant General Sir Gordon Drummond arrived with another eight hundred. Three thousand plus. Brown had scarcely twenty-five hundred all told, while after Chippewa, Scott's brigade had trouble mustering a thousand. Like a move in chess, Drummond crossed to the American side, threatening Brown's supply lines. Brown sent Scott probing northward, confident that an attack would force Drummond's return.

At five on a hot afternoon under a brassy sun in a cloudless sky, they crossed the Chippewa, the bridge rattling under Nate's guns, a tower of dust rising as they took the river road north. Jesup's Connecticut regiment was in the lead. Next came Leavenworth's Massachusetts men, McNeil's Vermonters, and Brady's Pennsylvanians. Scott rode with Jesup, the big roan frisky, prancing and turning with obvious pleasure. A cloud of mist rose over the falls far off to the right, and he heard a vague rumble in the distance.

The river road—Portage Road, the locals called it—gradually swung west until it was a mile distant from the water. Now heavy woods stood between road and river. Within the hour, they sighted British officers.

A white-painted farmhouse an enterprising widow operated as a tavern stood to the right of the road. As they approached, five men in red coats boiled out the front door and untied horses. So General Riall was back—sooner than Scott had expected. The redcoat officers watched the Americans, then mounted and galloped away.

Scott reined up at the house. A barmaid stood smiling at Boone from the doorway, arms akimbo under bulging breasts, a dirty apron tied over her blue gown.

"Why, hello, Ducky. See them fellers? I told 'em you Yanks would bite 'em in the ass."

The Sergeant Major turned scarlet but didn't answer.

"How far off are they?" Scott said.

She frowned. "Seems Ducky don't know me today."

Boone sighed. "God damn it, Helen . . ."

She smiled. "Why, sweets, way you was acting, I thought you didn't remember we'd met." She rolled her eyes. "But I don't mind telling *you*, British army is right down the road. Maybe a thousand of 'em. Marched all night, so I understand, and their butts was dragging." She grinned. "Them officers fancied me, but I told 'em I was saving it for you."

★ ★ ★ ★

General Riall again. Scott rode on, knowing where he would find them. He had studied this ground, marking the terrain at Lundy's Lane for its defensive strength.

Then the river road cleared the woods and he saw them in the distance, placed just as he'd expected. He paused to restudy the terrain and scratch out a message to be carried to General Brown, urging him to advance the other two brigades on the double.

Lundy's Lane was a country road bearing off to the left, westward, from the river road. After some seventy yards it ascended a sharp hill—actually a ridge, long, narrow, roughly level on top. Scott, who had walked it foot by foot, estimated it to be three hundred yards in length, thirty to fifty in width. Its elevation was a good hundred feet and would be a tough climb under fire. On its eastern and southern flanks, visible from here as he sat his horse on the river road, it was sharp and difficult. Lundy's Lane ran the length of the ridge, dropped down its far end, and disappeared into heavy woods.

General Riall's troops were stretched along that road. His guns, the two twenty-fours and the howitzer, were in a churchyard at the center of his line, midway along the crest of the ridge.

Bugles shrilled in the British camp, and Scott saw antlike men begin to stir. He waved the brigade forward along the river road, the intersection with Lundy's up ahead. Troop dispositions were forming in his mind. To the right of the river road was a strip of cultivated fields. Beyond the fields were heavy woods.

He told Jesup to swing his rangers, the Twenty-fifth Connecticut, off to the right and across the fields. When they got well into the woods they were to work forward.

"Be ready to hammer them on their left flank—at the least, I want you to immobilize their left."

By the time Leavenworth came up, the Connecticut regiment was out of sight in the woods.

To the left of the river road were extensive cleared pastures now devoid of livestock. The open area was more or less a half-mile square this side of the ridge, the river road on the right, dense woods on the left. Scott formed his line in these pastures, Leavenworth anchoring the center, McNeil to the left, Brady to the right. Since his line lay east and west, just as the ridge before them ran east and west, they faced its side instead of its end.

He examined the British line through his glass. Nine hundred to a thousand—the barmaid wasn't far off. Those officers must have loose lips. He rode along his line, positioning his men.

"Sir!" Boone trotted up on his mule, pointing toward the hill. "Up yonder. Looks like they're fixing to cut and run."

Scott swung his glass and saw gunners moving limbers to guns, horses backing into wagon shafts, troops moving toward the river road. Pulling out. He lowered the glass and thought for a minute. Riall was scarcely outnumbered, yet avoiding the fight—Chippewa must have shaken him. Was there time to rush them in their disarray? They were a half mile off and moving rapidly, they'd be gone soon.

Damn!

He saw a commotion on the hill and clapped glass to eye.

"What the hell?" Ike Roach said. "They're turning around?"

They were. Long files reversed themselves, returning to position. The guns were swung around once again and placed to fire at the Americans. Horses were led out of sight. And then two, no, three, four—yes, four more guns appeared.

That was it! Reinforcements had arrived.

He ranged the glass here and there and found Riall, plump and short, looking hangdog even from here. With him was a tall officer in a fancy uniform who was shouting and waving his arms. Drummond! It had to be Lieutenant General Drummond. He had recrossed the river and was adding maybe another thousand men.

Scott studied the lines. Suddenly he was facing more than two thousand men, an army twice his size, with heavy artillery, even now digging in on a hill that wouldn't be easy to crack under opposition fire.

That was war for you. Everything changing in the blink of an eye. Expect the unexpected! Assume the worst will happen. Clausewitz. The men who'd fought the European wars knew every damned thing could go wrong and probably would.

Could he afford to engage so superior a force?

Or was the question whether he could afford not to?

They would attack him if he waited, two to his one, wearing his boys down by sheer numbers. But if he pulled out, his men would bunch up trying to get on the road, and the enemy would charge his rear. A disaster. And what of Jesup, alone off to the right? And suppose in retreat he collided with Brown coming up with the other brigades and threw everyone into panicky flight?

But that wasn't it, really. The last time he'd met these scoundrels he'd demolished them. This time he would run? Destroy his brigade's confidence in one stroke? They were proud of how they'd fought; if they ran, what was different from before? By God, he wouldn't do it!

If retreat was out, he must attack. Hit them now when they weren't set, when the new troops were trying to find places among the old, when the guns were not yet sighted in. Hit them now.

It was after seven. The lowering sun glowed on distant treetops. Swiftly he planned his attack, Brady on the right, McNeil on the left, Leavenworth the rock in the center. He saw a British regiment position itself on the enemy right to fire across the broad slope leading up to the guns. Frontal attack there would be deadly. Very well, they would angle to their own right, swing around the east flank of the hill, and drive a heavy wedge into the British left. Smash through their line.

If they could break the line, they would pivot both to the right and the left. His immediate right, under Brady, would turn to *its* right. Jesup, in the woods on the far right, would turn to his left. Then he and Brady would pinch the British left end between them.

He drafted orders to Jesup. Leavenworth in the center and McNeil on Scott's left end would turn leftward when they broke the British line, thus taking the British right in a flanking move. If things went well they could roll up the hill, rooting out infantry, taking the guns, and putting the enemy to flight. If things went well.

He made the plan sound simple and direct, but he knew better and so did his regimental commanders. That tic was back in McNeil's cheek, the stutter in his voice. Brady glanced at him, then draped a casual hand on his shoulder.

"I like it," Leavenworth said. "Fifty-fifty chance at best, but if it works, *bam!*" He punched fist into palm.

They formed in three lines. The drums rolled, the fifes shrilled "Yankee Doodle," and they started at a trot.

Scott was out ahead, Rusty dancing to the drum, throwing his head around so his bridle jingled. Three hundred yards to contact, effective musket range under one hundred yards. Bayonets fixed, pieces at the ready, running with faces set, lips drawn tight. Sweat streamed down their faces.

Scott tugged at his collar. His saber was slippery in his wet hand. Calf-high grass whipped at the soldiers' shoes. Insects boiled around them and rabbits burst out of hiding before them, driven by the thunder of running feet. A bird whistled blithely. Two hundred yards, hundred fifty, hundred twenty-five—

Wham!

The big twenty-four-pounders on the hill cracked with shocking noise, smoke billowing from their muzzles. Grapeshot slashed through Scott's ranks. Ten, maybe fifteen of his men were down, some moving, several not. He stood in his stirrups, saber high and pointing.

"Come on, boys, come on, let's go! On the double, on the double! Let's go get 'em!"

In the distance he heard Nate's cannon roaring, saw shells bursting in the British line. They were taking punishment, too. So far, Nate's fire hadn't reached the British guns.

The boys were coming on, running hard. Out ahead, he turned to study their faces, and when they were close he whirled Rusty and leapt ahead. Straining faces, lips drawn back in mad death grins, eyes fluttering, mouths open as they snorted for breath, running, running, a hundred yards, ninety, eighty. The guns above fired a second time, then a third. At seventy yards a blast of musketry erupted from above, a sheet of flame along the length of the British line. More of his men were down, perhaps seventy or a hundred. He wheeled the horse.

"Fire, boys! Fire! Kneel, aim, fire!" He jumped Rusty through a gap to give them a free field, and when all three lines had sent a blast of lead against the troops above, he lunged forward, saber flashing. "Let's go, boys, let's hit 'em. Charge! Charge! Charge!"

God, they were beautiful, running forward, not a man of them hesitating. He heard the deep roar of the British cannon, the lighter cracking of his own cannon in the distance, the blasts of musket fire from on the hill rising and falling, the wild yells of his boys. They tore paper cartridges with their teeth before ramming them down musket barrels, and flying powder made blackened masks on their sweaty faces. He heard a high wailing and saw a small man near him running with mouth wide open, veins throbbing in his temple, neck cords taut, scarcely aware of the scream ripping from his throat.

A bullet pinged off a buckle on Rusty's bridle. The big horse shook his head as if a bee were in his ear. He reared and spun an angry circle. Scott yelled and wheeled him back to the front.

The British advanced to meet them, cover abandoned, bayonets ready. Nate's shells ripped the redcoats like paper men.

Another blast of enemy grape tore through his own ranks. Men fell all around him, faces shot away, clutching their bellies, hysterical screams describing the knife-edge of pain. It broke his heart to see his ranks torn so, his mutilated men. But those still on their feet ran on, loading, pausing to fire—

Scott heard Ike Roach yell and turned to see his aide gasping white-faced. A bullet had shattered his left knee. He reached for his knee with both hands and toppled from the saddle.

"Sarenmajor!" Scott shouted. Boone appeared at his side.

"Get him in his saddle. Get him headed back. He can make it once he's mounted."

He wheeled to examine his line and saw it coming to a halt. Men can only take so much. They were slowing, looking around, tears streaking their powder-stained faces. Bodies littered the field. They were stalling, and stalling in range of British guns was deadly.

Leavenworth reined up beside him. "I think they've done what they can do, General."

A lieutenant appeared. "Sir, Major McNeil, he's down. Shot in the head."

Brady galloped up. "Can't hold my boys, sir. They can't stand no more. Sorry—"

"All right, gentlemen," Scott said. He kept his voice steady and even. "Take your men back. *With* the wounded—remember, we don't leave a single man!" And, to Leavenworth, "Henry, I'll count on you to hold the center if they rush us."

But the British were busy bringing in their own casualties under continuing fire from Nate's guns. Their cannon fired twice but misjudged the range, grapeshot thudding into the ground well behind the retreating Americans.

The First Brigade fetched up about where it had started and the boys fell to the ground, drank from canteens, wiped their faces, and lay still. Surgeons and mates ran from body to body, separating the dead and hurrying the worst of the wounded to a tent that became an operating room. Dull a man's pain with laudanum, give him a jolt of whiskey, and get the bone saw going. The surgeon's tent was placed at a distance; Scott didn't want his men listening to the screams.

The dead were laid in a long grim row; many in the operating tent would join them. Scott had about forty dead and three times that wounded—and who knew how many wounds that went beyond flesh and bone.

Men went to pay their last respects, walking that long row of bodies. Some stood long by a single friend, some knelt to pray, many patted an inert boot in farewell. Scott looked over the shoulders of a group clustered around one figure and saw the handlebar mustaches of Sergeant Belthasar Hoslie as fierce in death as in life.

He found John McNeil barely conscious. A ball had entered his open mouth and exited the rear of his jaw, shattering the joint and missing the carotid artery by a hair. Poor Mac: he might live on a liquid diet but he would live. Scott gave command of the regiment to a likely captain named Frank Ford.

"Thank you, sir." Ford was a handsome youngster with an earnest expression. "I promise I'll do my best."

Scott put a hand on the lad's shoulder. "That's all I ask."

He walked among his men while Boone took Rusty to water.

"You boys did fine. Proud of you, damned proud. You showed 'em what soldiers are made of. Rest awhile now, then we'll hit 'em again . . .

"You know, the soldier's life comes in ups and downs. Can't win on every charge, don't always make it the first time, but coming back and coming back, that's what wins. You'll see, boys . . .

"We're not done—and up there on the hill, they know it. They're worried. They figure we're coming again, and they're up there crapping their drawers . . ."

So he went, rebuilding his men. The golden burnish of dying sun had left the treetops now. The air cooled as the evening softened toward dark. It was after eight. There was no sign of Brown and the other two brigades.

Rusty looked rested when Boone brought him back. The horse whickered when he saw Scott. He deserved a carrot, old Rusty, and Scott found a stub in his pocket and fed it to him as he stroked the horse's muzzle.

★ ★ ★ ★

Dusk settled in, the sky bright only in the west, the distant woods dark. It was half past eight. The battered regiments, strength down by a quarter, formed again. The three lines took shape, wider-spaced this time. Scott rode along their front, looking into their faces. He saw set, firm expressions, well laced with dread but still unwavering.

When he signaled them forward, they stepped off in a rush. The overall quiet seemed heightened by the muffled thump of feet, the swish of grass brushed aside. He heard the same bird celebrating the evening—and then the shrill cry of a British bugle.

His plan hadn't changed. As before, they would bear to their own right to pass around the hill and crash into the British left. If he could break that line open and roll it up from the sides, he knew he could shatter them no matter their numbers.

The guns on the hill opened, that brutal slam slapping deep into their ears, and Nate's guns over by the river road barked in answer. Scott waved the boys on, running and firing, as flame sheeted along the British line and men fell all around him.

It was as before, dizzying, enflaming, the mind soaring and roaring with the sound of it, the horror, the exaltation, the sweet imperviousness to guns and death, the crescendo of noise blending into a mad roar, the General standing in his stirrups, saber high. C'mon, boys! They were closer this time, driving unstoppably, they had a chance now, break that line, plunge through. C'mon—

Rusty's head disappeared. Vanished, in a spray of blood. Scott had a split second of insane impression—the head just vanished—and then a ferocious blow struck his right side, lifted him, dropped him to hard ground like a sack of flour. Slowly he turned to look. His headless horse lay beside him, blood pumping from the stump of the neck. Old Rusty . . .

Silence, his ears ringing, and then the sound of firing came back with the impact of hands clapped together by his ear. He became conscious of vast pain in his right side. Cannonball, had to be. Twenty-four-pound solid shot, big as a hat and traveling fast as a lightning stroke, tore off poor Rusty's head . . . it must have glanced off, else it would have cut Scott in half.

Then a horrid thought. Maybe it had, more or less. The pain flared unbearably with every breath. Maybe his whole rib cage was shot away. Maybe if he touched it he would put his hand on his own beating heart, exposed to the world. The heart was on the right, wasn't it? He didn't think he could stand to put his hand on his own beating heart—

Stop it!

He clapped his left hand to his right side and foolish or not couldn't hold in a wild sigh of relief. He was whole. His uniform was torn but his ribs were all there. He examined his hand. No blood. The ball had creased him, bruised hell out of him, but he was all right.

Boone swung down from his mule. Blood still pumped from Rusty's severed neck. Had only seconds passed?

"I'm not hurt," he said. "Give me a hand—gotta see to things . . ." He cried out and fell when Boone lifted him.

The Sergeant Major knelt beside him. "You busted some ribs, General. Sir, the attack's breaking up—I reckon they stopped when they saw you go down. Pull-back's starting. Let's go."

Scott got to his feet with Boone's help, staggered, and then steadied, looking around. Dusk was fading into night. The men were moving back with their wounded, walking slowly under the protection of darkness, and their general walked with them.

His brigade was in tatters. He'd lost another forty or fifty, perhaps two hundred more wounded. Grunting with pain, he made his way to comfort his men. The brigade was cut in half. If he had five hundred effectives, he was lucky. They lay on the ground like rag dolls, faces covered with black powder streaked with tear tracks. Or sat with heads between their knees.

A ball had broken Brady's right thigh, and he was through. Handsome young Frank Ford was dead. Three lieutenants made it a point to tell him Captain Ford had done his best. Scott held his left hand to his ribs and reorganized the remnants of his men into a crippled battalion under Leavenworth.

"Brown will be along soon," he said. "We'll hold. British come after us, we've still got some sting."

"Let 'em come," Leavenworth said.

★ ★ ★ ★

It was after nine when Brown led the Second Brigade onto the field at a crisp trot. Scott explained his strategy; Brown agreed, placed the fresh troops between the enemy and the tattered First Brigade, and prepared a new attack.

The new men made the odds even. Two thousand on the hill, about the same down here. Let's see how things go now!

A rider galloped through the resting men. Scott recognized Tom Jesup's horse. A sergeant dismounted and saluted.

"Sir, Major Jesup's compliments, and he wants you to know another thousand redcoat bastards just arrived. Marched right by our position—we couldn't stop 'em but we could count 'em. Sir, he says to tell you we had that intersection, Lundy's and the other road, but they pushed us back. But we're hanging on their left like a tick on a dog and we don't aim to let up."

Another thousand against them. Three thousand on the hill, barely two thousand here. Still, it had been two-to-one before; now it was three-to-two. Better . . .

Scott struggled onto a fresh horse, his bruised ribs making him gasp with pain at the movement. The horse, a mare the color of liver, moved uneasily under his weight, nothing at all like old Rusty. He rode to Nate Towson's guns.

"Nate, for goodness' sake, can't you do something about those damned guns on the hill?"

Nate stood by the horse, his hand on Scott's stirrup. "Sir, we're playing hell with their troop line, you got to give us that, but their guns up on that hill, we're having trouble cranking ours up to where we can reach 'em."

"Well, keep trying." Nate looked so hangdog that Scott leaned over to pat his shoulder—and a bolt of pain all but threw him from the saddle.

The Second Brigade attacked and was hurled back.

A full moon rose behind the Americans as Brown prepared another charge, still trying to pass the guns to break the British left. Moonlight favored them; it was in the defenders' eyes. But though fresh troops attacked with fresh vigor, the result was the same—the guns on the hill thundered, musket fire slashed from the British line, and the boys stalled, stopped, turned back with more dead and wounded.

The British guns were the key. Scott hurried to Brown with a new plan. He'd seen the ground up close and understood it. The long face of the hill was still too protected to climb directly, but with a simulated attack there as diversion, a fresh regiment might be able to reach those guns through the heavy brush on the narrow eastern end of the hill.

Brown turned to Colonel James Miller's Twenty-fifth Infantry.

"Jim, I want you to go up and take those guns. General Scott here will show you the way."

Miller swallowed hard. "I'll—I'll try, sir."

★ ★ ★ ★

Boone didn't like it—wasn't any need for the General to expose himself this way. Scott was still young, that was the thing. Older a man got, the

more he realized bullets are real and can convert you to dead meat in a snap
of your fingers.

He wasn't overworried about himself. He'd heard bullets sing and was
still around, so what the hell.

But the General, now, that was different. Boone knew the way as well
as he did and anyway, a blind man could pick through the rhododendron
and find the guns. He'd said as much, and the General gave him a look
that told him that was enough of that—and now here they were, leading
Miller's detachment up the hill.

Heavy firing started around to their left, on the long face of the hill:
the diversionary attack. Above them he heard the British guns firing back.
Maybe all that would keep those gunners busy. Maybe they wouldn't even
notice the men coming up the hill to kill them. Boone had taken the lead,
the General and Colonel Miller right behind him. This was about like
walking a laurel slick back in Kentucky, not bad. He held a branch aside
for the General. You just had to keep an eye on that young man, help him
watch out for himself.

They had some First Brigade gunners with them, Captain Towson's
boys. Take those pieces and turn 'em point-blank on their former owners.

"There!" He spoke in a harsh whisper, and they stopped. They were
fifteen feet from a rail fence that marked the perimeter of the churchyard.
The guns stood in a semicircle. Colonel Miller took over. Obeying his hand
signals, his men rested their muskets on the fence and took careful aim.

"You done got us here, General," Boone said. "Nothing more you can
do here. Go on back." Then he surprised himself. He put his hand on Scott's
arm and said, "Please, sir."

Scott glanced at him. Boone saw he'd registered the note of entreaty but
wasn't offended.

"You're right." Gently he punched Boone's arm. "Good luck, Sarenmajor."

So the General was out of it, thank God. Boone laid his musket on the
rail and took careful aim. He chose a gunner at a distance, figuring the
others would pick the easiest targets, and when Colonel Miller signaled, a
crash of fire split the night like a thunderbolt and maybe half the gunners
went down like pole-axed steers in a slaughter yard and the others whirled
around staring as if they couldn't figure out what happened.

Boone vaulted lightly over the fence, saw the others coming after him,
went at a dead run toward the guns with his bayonet on the ready. He
picked out a gun captain, big fellow with sergeant's stripes, already the
bastard was reaching for a musket with fixed bayonet, and Boone lunged
for his chest. At the last instant the man ducked and the blade caught him
square in the throat, tore through and gleamed blood-shiny in the moonlight
and the big sergeant fell against Boone, head flopping like a rag doll, spine

severed, and with a grunt Boone threw him off, jerked his blade free, and turned to meet the next redcoat gunner.

But none remained. The handful that survived had bolted for the safety of their lines.

"Get set, boys," Colonel Miller said. "We've got to hold these guns. They'll be back, and soon."

Bet your ass on that, all right.

Captain Towson's boys horsed the guns around, loaded them with grape, and rammed them while the infantrymen took down the rail fence and stacked it in a barricade facing the way the British infantry would be coming.

Boone saw the redcoat soldiers jump up from the darkness only a hundred feet away, plain as daylight, with the big moon overhead. They ran forward, some stumbling, some shading their eyes with their left hands. Poor buggers were blinded in the moonlight, tough God damned luck for them.

He picked out a big one and fired and the bugger went down. Then the guns opened, grape slashing a couple of feet above Boone's head to cut a swath through the British that gladdened a man's heart. They came on, those redcoats, they had grit to spare, by God, but flesh and blood can only take so much. Boone was poised on the ground, ready to spring up and give 'em the bayonet when they broke, fell to the ground, crouched and panting, then scuttled away. He drew a bead on a back and didn't have the heart to pull the trigger.

Well, shit, without their cannon, these Brits weren't so tough! The regiment on the British right that had been protecting the front of the hill pulled back now, and at the same time General Brown's next attack on the British left succeeded and Boone heard yelling on both sides of his own advanced position, American voices, by God, and it came to him that they had pushed the damned British right off the hill. Just as the General said, the guns were the key. Right off the damned hill!

"Colonel's permission," Boone said, "I'll go take a little look-see."

"Granted. Get us a reading."

He vaulted the barricade and ran forward, tensing against possible fire. But none came. At the line the British had held, he found kits, canteens, cartridge boxes, muskets left behind. Fled! He ranged left, found no one, ranged back to the right, damned near bumped into Ripley's troops. Not a sign of the British, not a sign!

When he reported, Miller said, "They'll be back."

Well, Boone knew that. And we'd know what to do with them, too. So the gunners got the cannon ready and everyone blazed away. Those redcoats come up that long hill and the boys cut 'em down like turkeys at a turkey shoot. Like they'd been cutting us down a couple or three hours ago.

Fortunes of God damned war, now that's a fact! Boone wanted to yell, wanted to pound someone's back—and then he got an odd feeling.

Immediately he knew what it was. The General was in trouble or fixing to get in trouble. Needed old Boone. He felt it in his bones.

He grabbed a handful of cartridges from an English box, took a bone-handled knife he fancied off that sergeant he'd fixed—that poor bastard wouldn't have no more use for it—glanced around to be sure Colonel Miller wasn't watching, slid off to the side, went under the rail fence, and was on his way, slick as goose shit. The General needed him.

★ ★ ★ ★

They'd be back any minute now. Scott could hear the British in the distance—an odd rustling sound, clinking metal, voices, hoofs thudding. Getting ready for a third try, and it would fail, too. The Americans occupied the old British lines, the British driven a good half mile to the north.

Drove 'em, by God! Stormed strong positions and put Britain's best to flight.

The First Brigade, what was left, was back in it. He got them moving as soon as he came down from the hill, and they'd been in the van when the British broke. He wanted his boys in on that. They'd earned it. Let 'em go back to the wounded and the dead and say, at least we fixed their asses. Give 'em that.

No sign of Boone. He knew the Sarenmajor could take care of himself, but still, they'd been together a long time . . .

He heard them coming.

"Brace up, boys, brace up," he yelled.

His ribs like to split when he hollered, but otherwise he was all right. He was walking his lines, the boys well dug in, when the redcoats came roaring up from below.

He could see them in the moonlight. Fire flared from his own lines and many fell, but the others came on, firing as they ran, and he—

A great blow struck him. Spun him around. Threw him down. Had he stumbled?

He lay on his back, resting. The battle sounded distant. Must be almost over. But it went on and on . . .

His eyes closed. When he opened them, Boone was bending over him.

"I stumbled, Sarenmajor. Fell down. Damned foolish . . ." His voice sounded faint in his own ears.

"You're hit, General."

"Hit?" Yes, of course, the blow. That was it. Hit. Damn. He had things to do, he couldn't be—he turned, raised on an elbow . . .

★ ★ ★ ★

He swam up into consciousness. He'd been out again. Better not try to raise himself. That was a mistake. It must be bad, worse than the blow on the ribs. He touched his right shoulder with his left hand. Christ, felt like half the shoulder was shot away. It was wet, sticky, bleeding hard. Then Boone was back, pressing cloths into the wound. Instantly pain bloomed like a giant red flower.

"Easy, boys," Boone said. Two men laid a litter beside him. "Lift him gentle, now."

The Sarenmajor's voice was harsh, his face stern. He turned and the moonlight fell on his face and Scott saw that his eyes were full. Old Boone . . .

He screamed when they lifted him.

"Gently, God damn you!" Boone roared. "You jostle him, I'll break your fucking heads!"

Scott was sliding away, dizzy, slipping and sliding . . . but by God, they *did* it. No mongrel sons, no onetime soldiers and then run. They had stood to the test. Outnumbered, they'd met the British . . .

Those British professionals, now driven from their positions. Took their ground from them, his boys did, and held it. American soldiers proving themselves for all the world to see. For Americans to see.

The world was turning, Americans were coming to the fore, they would be a force to be reckoned with in years to come—and his little army had led the way. He was content.

Sliding away . . . He extended his hand and Boone took it and held it. He felt himself slipping toward great danger, but Boone wouldn't let him go. Boone would see to him. So thinking, he spun down and down into the black pool.

21

WASHINGTON
August, 1814

★ ★ ★ ★ James Madison sat drumming his fingers on his carved walnut desk. The windows on both sides of the corner overlooking Pennsylvania Avenue were thrown high against heat that was stifling. Even the leaves on the trees outside hung limp and exhausted. He had removed his coat, a breach of decorum he allowed himself only when he felt near collapse. The air steamed, it looked thick to the eye, birds were silent, the buzz of insects had faded to heavy stillness.

Still drumming, he reread the message. It had come by relay rider from Norfolk; guard sloops standing offshore had spied a British fleet arriving, twenty-two vessels of war, twenty troop ships. Troop ships in Chesapeake Bay meant invasion. But where? Baltimore was the logical target, just as the Secretary of War insisted. Third largest city in the nation, shipping center, shipyards thriving, home to privateers who harried British merchant vessels. Yet Madison's gut told him, *they're coming here.*

A day later he was sure of it. The blanket of steamy heat still lay across

Havre de Grace

MARYLAND

Baltimore
Godsfly Wood

Fort
McHenry
British
Bombardment.
13 Sept. 1814

North
Point

DELAWARE

Patapsco River

Choptank River

Nanticoke River

24 August
1814

Bladensburg

Washington
24-25 August
1814

Annapolis

Upper
Marlboro

Alexandria

Fort
Washington

Patuxent River

Benedict

Potomac River

Fredericksburg

British Lines

of Approach

British Advance

VIRGINIA

Rappahannock River

Mattaponi River

Pamunkey River

Chesapeake
Bay

North

0   5   10
Miles

CH Mitchell 1995

the Attack on
Washington
24-25 August, 1814
and
Baltimore
12-24 September, 1814

the region, and the message he received was damp with the rider's sweat. It said the British ships had entered the Patuxent, the river lying parallel to the Potomac thirty miles to the east. He unrolled his frayed Maryland map, now covered with minute pencil notations. The Patuxent was navigable to within forty miles of Washington, at least to the town of Benedict. Forty miles wasn't far.

But maybe it was farther than you'd think. He visualized the terrain—tobacco country but heavily wooded around the fields. Long, straight roads, tree branches laced overhead. And this overpowering heat. Hard on Americans, it would be worse on Britons just arrived by sea. It was difficult to believe they'd fetch horses clear from England, but Maryland farmers certainly would hide theirs. How many guns could they bring without horses? How much supply could they haul?

Suppose you burned the bridges over the creeks on those long forest roads. Suppose riflemen lay in wait for targets of opportunity. The redcoat column would halt and flood the woods with skirmishers and the riflemen would drift away. Half a day gone. The invaders would march on and an hour later meet new rifle fire. That forty miles might take a long time. Wouldn't tactics of the Revolution still work?

Delay the enemy, wear him down, abrade his confidence, increase his pain as his supply lines stretched ever tauter back to his ships at Benedict. Make him wonder if Washington was really worth it. After all, the Secretary of War was right when he said the capital was no military goal. It was a target of the mind and spirit, assuaging British desire to punish us, with hopes of breaking the American spirit. Would they fight to the last man for such ephemeral goals? Maybe not.

And if they did, how much better if we wore them down, slowed them while we lay a set-piece battle to stop them. Madison knew he was no military man, but he had read heavily in strategy and tactics by now and he understood that an army was analogous to a horse—great power if well handled but sensitive to terrain, not useful without equipment, always hungry and able to go only so far so fast. As a hornet can make a horse unmanageable, repeated stings can destabilize an army.

The British had miles to cover on the road to Washington, and we could make every one of those miles dangerous. Of course, the militia here were not as well trained as young Scott's brilliant soldiers on the Niagara, but surely they had learned the lesson all America learned from the triumph at Chippewa—men in red coats with bayonets aglitter were not necessarily invincible. They could be whipped and driven from the field. It was a lesson that America had needed and that was well understood, judging by the excitement in papers around the country. And now, the latest—Lundy's Lane, where Americans took possession of the enemy's field and his guns while he licked his wounds a half mile away.

What he would give for a Jake Brown or a Winfield Scott to meet the

enemy on the road from Benedict! But both had been wounded, Scott quite
seriously, though at last report he was still alive. But you never could tell
about serious wounds; a man could slip away any night on a tide of fever.
He bowed his head and prayed briefly but fervently for the tall young
general.

Chippewa and Lundy's Lane told him what he so desperately wanted to
hear: the country was turning. There on the Niagara we proved we could
stand against the world's best. But even before those victories invigorated
every hamlet, he had felt the change. Enlistments were up, the financial
strain eased at least momentarily, Congress less fearful, Federalists more
embattled—so let's march out and make the British approach to Washington
as painful as a scorpion in a boot!

But this was all theory, and six years in office, two of them in war, had
taught Madison the miles of difference stretching between theory and practice. He called in his Secretary of War, who continued to scoff at the very
idea of Washington as a target against the plum of Baltimore.

"You'll see, this is just a feint."

Madison didn't think so, but in any event he was reassured by Baltimore's
readiness, ten thousand men on alert, Fort McHenry strengthened to withstand attack from the sea. Baltimore might fall to concerted assault, but it
wouldn't fall easily. Whereas, Washington . . .

"I mean," Armstrong said, "there's no earthly reason for them to bother
with this miserable village."

Madison didn't respond. The man seemed to aim at provoking him. Of
course Washington was small. The government had been in residence a mere
fourteen years and few streets were paved as yet. Save for the monumental
Capitol and the White House, there were few fine buildings. But it was the
capital of the United States, and its spotty grandeur symbolized the American
dream. To denigrate it was to denigrate the nation.

The Secretary sat with his legs spread, stout and solid, his hair still too
long, his side whiskers too bushy, his nose too bulbous, the sly air that
Madison found so disturbing more evident than ever. The man had to know
he had made an enemy of himself, but his political weight in New York
saved him each time Madison decided to drop him. They dealt with each
other warily.

General Winder arrived, looking haggard and shrunken. His little potbelly had vanished and his mustache was ragged.

"I'm doing my best," he cried before Madison could ask.

Madison had known a lot less about soldiering when he appointed
Winder back in 1812 than he knew now. The man was a Baltimore lawyer
whose main strength then had been his political connections. Still, a country
that expands its army suddenly must rely on amateurs, and Winder did
work furiously hard, posting from place to place, reviewing troops and
checking defenses as he organized his new military district.

And his terse accounting at least sounded authoritative. Troops were pouring in, some with weapons, some without. He had quartermaster officers standing by at armories to equip the men, though, of course, each weapon and all ammunition must be counted out, signed, countersigned. Regulations.

"How many men can you count on?"

Winder hesitated, as if he were calculating. "Six thousand."

The number reassured Madison. Winder had his few regulars marching toward the Patuxent now, the militia to follow as the men arrived. He viewed them, he said, as a corps of observation under orders to watch the enemy.

"And harass them as well, I hope," Madison said. "Slow them, make their passage miserable. Make them wonder if it's worth it."

"*If* they come here," Armstrong said. "Which they won't."

The interruption gave Winder a moment to recover, but Madison had seen surprise and alarm flashing over his face. Had he had no such thoughts on his own?

"Well, you're exactly right, Mr. President," the General said. "Make 'em pay for every mile." He glanced at Armstrong. "If they come, that is." Sweat ran down his face and he loosened his cravat. "But it's risky. Our men are the only barrier, so we must be cautious." He swallowed. "And daring, too, of course. Stinging them. But carefully."

Madison asked about Bladensburg.

"Bladensburg, sir?"

The worn chart was on his desk and Madison unrolled it. Bladensburg was the key. Anyone approaching Washington from the east—from, specifically, the Patuxent—must cross the Eastern Branch of the Potomac. The Eastern Branch was deep and wide where Washington nestled against it, spanned by a bridge at the navy yard. The bridge could be defended easily with the navy yard's guns or it could be destroyed. So an attacker was likely to swing north until the Eastern Branch shrank to a narrow, shallow, easily forded stream, and that was at Bladensburg. From that otherwise unremarkable Maryland hamlet, an enemy could march south right into Washington.

"You are prepared there, I hope."

"Well, not in the immediate sense. But it's at the top of our plans, rest assured."

"Troops assigned?"

"Not just now, no, but I intend to put the Maryland brigade there. When it comes in. General Stansbury, very good man."

"Good. Now, what about Captain Barney?"

"The *navy*, sir?"

"Well, you know he's converted his guns to field pieces and has his sailors and marines ready to march." Barney had predicted an attack via the Patuxent. "I consider him a valuable resource, and I specifically want you to work with him. As with the Secretary of War." He turned to Armstrong. "You are assisting General Winder, are you not?"

He saw the two men glance at each other, their manner wary, just short of hostile.

Then Armstrong nodded. "Whenever I can be helpful, sir."

"I've been busy, Mr. President," Winder said. "Countless organizational details. After all, the fact that we have troops now, that's the result of all my spadework."

"Very well, gentlemen. Just make sure you do cooperate."

Madison saw them out; Ned was away, taking his sister and Maria Mayo home. He watched them walk down the gravel driveway. Pretty common clay, both of them, but they were all he had.

★ ★ ★ ★

Shouts outside drew his attention—a good deal of noise had arisen in the last hour. The street seemed to throb, men and women walking rapidly despite the heat, carriages on rubber tires threading their way among wagons. He watched for a moment, bemused, until it struck him that most of the traffic was headed west. Washington's people were leaving . . .

He found Dolley in the family parlor, drinking lemonade and fanning herself. The windows were open, limp curtains motionless. Joseph sliced a small cake, his black face moisture-beaded, his white shirt damp. Madison, surprised to find he was hungry, asked Joseph for a second slice of cake.

"The warriors were reassuring, I hope?" Dolley said.

"Rather the opposite, I'm afraid. You know Armstrong. And Winder— well, thank God for Captain Barney. There's something curiously unfinished about Winder. Or unfocused, perhaps."

"Out of his depth?" And then, her voice low, "You think they'll come here, don't you, Jimmy?"

Suddenly he knew that all his brave thoughts of challenging the enemy's passage were hollow. Yes, they were coming, and they'd be hard to stop.

"Well," he said, "they'll try, anyway."

"Today's Friday. When will they get here, if they do—Sunday? Monday?"

"They must land and march. I'd say more likely Tuesday or Wednesday if we don't stop them."

"And stopping them depends on what? Our determination?"

"I'd say on whether we can focus ourselves into a decisive striking force."

"On General Winder, then." She sighed. "I wish he were more . . . prepossessing." She looked out the window. The sky was so white with heat haze he couldn't see the Potomac. "Do you think he's up to it?"

"Yes." He heard the tentative note in his voice and saw she'd heard it, too. He sat up straight in his chair. "I don't see why not. If we harass them, delay them, make every mile costly, if we're ready at Bladensburg, it shouldn't be so hard."

Had his encouraging tone fooled her? He couldn't tell. Joseph collected the dishes and went out, leaving the lemonade pitcher sweating on the low table between them.

Dolley looked around the room as if committing it to memory—the crystal lamps, the polished chairs made in Philadelphia, the kneehole desk where she drew up menus for her banquets—and the anguish in her eyes shook his composure.

"This is our home," she said, her voice so low he sat forward to hear her. "Ours. If they come here it will be a . . . a *violation*. It would violate us, violate decency."

She hit the arm of the chair with her fist. "Damn them. Damn him! That vulgar, vulgar man!"

He knew she was referring to Admiral Co'burn and his rude tongue. "Blame Jemmy and his fat wench for your troubles—they're the fools who dared challenge the queen of the seas," the Admiral liked to tell Maryland citizens on his raids along the coast, while his men stole their goods and stripped their farms. And the King had knighted the man—Sir George, the plunderer. It debased knighthood, as such talk debased the honor of nations, the dignity of war.

"You know our friends are leaving?" she said. "Packing their bags and running?"

He nodded.

"Called their farm wagons in to haul away valuables, filled their carriages with linens and silver and servants. Fleeing before an enemy's even in sight. I tell you, Jimmy, it's disgusting!" Her fists were clenched. "I don't know if I'll ever speak to 'em again."

He shrugged. "Human nature, you know. They're scared."

"Well, I'm not. And you won't see me flying away. If they come here they'll find me standing in the doorway—they'll have to push me aside."

He set down his glass with a bang. "Madam, you will do no such thing!"

She stiffened at his tone, but the prospect of her presenting herself to an enemy appalled him. It would be just like her, too. If there was anything she was afraid of, he had yet to find out what it might be. He could well imagine her standing with arms akimbo to spit in the Admiral's face. The image made him shiver.

"Let's be absolutely clear about this. If the enemy draws near—long before he gets here, if he does—we must both be gone. To think otherwise is an indulgence in drama we can't afford. Do you understand?"

"But, Jimmy—"

"For me to be captured, taken aboard their ships in irons, exhibited like a monkey in a cage—God! It would be disastrous. It would wipe away all the glory Scott's men paid for with blood on the field of Chippewa and at Lundy's Lane. And the same is true for you."

In a small voice, she said, "Even a barbarian wouldn't handle a woman so."

"If you were captured, I'd have to petition on bended knee for your release. It's unthinkable." Then, a catch in his voice, "I couldn't stand it, you in their hands."

She came to him and put her hand on his cheek.

"Please, darling. It's all right. I won't be foolish."

He caught her wrist and turned her hand to kiss her palm.

Then watched her move wordlessly about the room, touching a curtain, plumping a cushion, straightening a picture. She came to rest with her hands on the carved back of her desk chair.

"I love it here," she said. Her voice was a whisper. "It's . . . it's *me*, somehow. My spirit breathed into it." The White House as it stood today was indeed her creation. "To see vandals come with torches—"

"That won't happen, dearest. We'll stop them. But in any event you'll be far away. Promise me."

She dropped into her desk chair. "We would go together, wouldn't we?"

"No. If it came to that, very likely I'd be with the army. You might be alone. You'll be sensible?"

"Yes, I will. But you . . ." He caught the tremor in her voice. "What do you mean, with the army?"

"That's where I belong."

"Jimmy, riding with troops isn't your place. You're sixty-three years old. Your power is in your mind—not your arm. You know it."

He shrugged. "It's my duty."

"But not in battle! You'd—why, you'd be in the way!'

She was right. Combat was for generals, not presidents. He knelt by her chair and drew her face down to kiss her.

She sighed. "Promise me," she said.

He held her face in both hands. "You won't lose me so easily."

★   ★   ★   ★

Joseph put the dishes on a table by Sophie's washtubs. Sophie's mind was addled but her smile was rich as Croesus, and he patted her shoulder. Through the open window he saw Jennie going to the springhouse beyond the vegetable garden and the stables. French John, who was looking over the cook's shoulder, tasted from a spoon and frowned. Joseph ducked out before John could call him.

Jennie was returning with a pitcher of cream when Joseph caught her wrist and drew her into the stables. She gave a little cry and nearly spilled the cream, which he took from her hand and set down on a bench.

She took a step closer. "You going to kiss me, Joseph?"

Damn! He very nearly did, she swaying toward him, sweet as a dusky rose . . .

"Listen," he said, his harsh whisper cutting the still air in the stable. He heard a horse stamp, a halter jingle. "The British are coming. Coming *here*!"

She shrank back against a stall.

"They ain't," she said. "Everybody says so. Army'll stop 'em—that what it's for."

"No, no—I was with the family. They think—"

"You mean Mr. James say they coming?"

"He says they ain't, but you could hear in his voice he don't believe it. Miss Dolley, she heard it, too, she got this look like she seen a ghost."

"*We'll* be ghosts, they hear us talking like this." She looked around; they were alone save for the coachman polishing Miss Dolley's Philadelphia carriage at the far end of the stable aisle well out of earshot.

Joseph took her hands. "Jennie, don't you see? When they come, we can go with them. To a new life. A free life."

"Joseph, you tell me something now. No fooling—I got to know for sure. You sweet on me, ain't you? Come on, tell me. You *is*."

"Ah, God!" It came out as a moan that told her everything.

She threw her arms around his neck. "Sweet baby, why ain't that enough? We can have each other. That's all I want."

"It's not all I want!" He reached for her hands and brought them together, cupped in his, between them. "My God, Jennie, don't you *want* to be free?"

She leaned back from him. "We wouldn't know what to do. We belong here."

He understood the fear. He'd felt it himself. It was the way of slavery, it fit you in a frame, and you hated the frame, but it had the comfort of familiarity, too.

"But that's what freedom means," he said. "You figure out what to do. What you want to do—not just do what a white man tells you."

Scorn swept her face, making her look old and wise. She pulled her hands from his and set them akimbo on her hips. "Joseph, you a black man. You'll *always* be doing what some white man tells you. They the bosses."

"I can choose my own boss if I'm free," he said. "I can work for this one and not for that one, I can work for myself—"

"You so smart and so dumb all in the same breath! We can't do nothing like that—white folks'd never let us. You imagine Miss Dolley saying 'Good-bye Joseph, good-bye Jennie, good luck to y'all going off with the enemy'?"

Sweet as a dusky rose. He could smell the rose's fragrance.

"Don't you want to be free?" he asked her again.

"I don't know!" She began to cry. "I s'pose—I ain't thought on it. You mean free like white folks? Do what you want, go where you want?"

"Like white folks. Why not? They ain't no better'n us. They leak out the same places we do, girl."

Again that look of ancient wisdom. "It'll never happen. We're *black*, Joseph." She folded her arms. "Don't talk this crazy talk. We get on all right, Madisons are good folk. Talking so could get us killed. Get us *sold*!"

"I'm going when the British come. I want you to go, too."

"No!" She started out the stable door.

"Jennie!"

She stopped. "What?"

"Take the cream."

She reached for the pitcher, her face averted. He watched her walk all the way to the house. She didn't look back.

★ ★ ★ ★

Joshua Barney's proper rank was commodore, commander of a fleet. But his little vessels were mostly splinters now, blown up to keep them from British hands. He was a land fighter at the moment—his sailors and marines ready to march, his ship's guns mounted on carriages and set to roll—and the rank of captain suited him just fine. He'd been so titled a long, long time.

The air was thick and steamy. He sat tilted far back in a protesting chair, his feet cocked on the rail of Salter's store, watching British troops marching off transports lying two by two against the single pier at Benedict, Maryland. It was Saturday and he watched nearly all day. In homespun and a slouch hat pulled low and sea boots wide enough to hide his glass when it was collapsed, he figured he looked about as much a country fellow as you could want. Sweat trickled from under his hat. There were a dozen men on Salter's porch, watching and not saying much. Time to time they passed a bucket of well water around. Said they'd seen some heat, but God Almighty, nothing like this. Said it could melt a man down to a puddle of piss.

Watching the British land on the soil of the United States of America like they were lords of the manor come to discipline the serfs! It didn't set well with a man who'd been master of his own ship—and captain of his own fate—since he took over a merchant vessel at fifteen when the skipper died at sea, and brought her home in fine shape with a profit that knocked the owners' eyes out.

That was before the Revolution, of course. Fought the British in that one, sailed for the French after—still fighting the Union Jack—and in this war his privateers out of Baltimore had slashed up enemy merchantmen pretty fair. That was the way he liked to see the British, through the smoke of his guns, and here he was watching them walk ashore like conquerors. The more he looked the deeper his anger stirred.

He counted forty-five hundred troops, give or take a few. Two guns swung ashore, light stuff, a three-pounder and a six-pounder. No sign of horses, so how were they going to drag the damned things, not to mention their supplies? There weren't more than a half-dozen horses within miles— soon as the farmers hereabouts heard those anchor chains rattling, they'd moved their stock out. Barney's own mount was hidden in deep woods.

The next day, Sunday, his horse again well hidden, he lounged at a crossroads with a half-dozen farmers watching the redcoat column stream down the road toward Nottingham. The line of armed soldiers was long but not at all awesome. In fact, he had to keep reminding himself the poor bastards were the enemy. They'd been at sea without exercise for weeks, and now they were humping along in a heat wave that staggered the natives.

A few officers were mounted, but whole squads of men were pulling guns and wagons like so many draft animals. They staggered and lurched, sweat soaking their red jackets. A towheaded youngster gone ghostly white dropped his musket and fell on his knees at Barney's feet. He swung out of his pack, and instinctively Barney reached for it.

"Jehoshaphat! You carrying lead in here?"

"Eighty rounds, three days' rations, and enough bloody shit to fell an ox," the boy said, and fainted.

Heavy pack plus musket, bayonet, and canteen—no wonder men fresh from sea life were falling out all along the line. Fifteen or so were down within his sight. Lord, what five hundred men with rifles couldn't do right here where thick woods pressed the road, slipping through beech and cow oak to knock over redcoats and drift away. These overloaded men towing their guns by hand wouldn't give much chase to hidden riflemen who knew the woods.

He sauntered off, turned into the forest when he was out of sight, found his horse, and rode like hell. It was near sunset on Sunday.

His sailors and marines waited amidst stacked cords of firewood at Henry Hunter's crossroads wood yard, where General Winder's army had camped. Tommy Tomlinson, his favorite lieutenant, had men and guns in good order. Tommy said the British were making camp at Nottingham, six or seven miles away, meaning they had covered twenty miles despite the heat. Bladensburg was only another twenty—they could be there tomorrow. Tommy thought two thousand Americans were at the wood yard, including the saltwater gunners, and no one seemed in charge. Hell's fire—the wood yard was farther from Bladensburg than Nottingham. They might find themselves in a race tomorrow.

No sign of Winder himself, about whom Barney had mixed feelings. He detested a man who dithered and piddled when it was time for action. He'd said as much to the little President, too, and then he'd had to back down when Madison offered him the command. But he'd been right to refuse—and he had to give Winder credit for pulling the militia together. Barney couldn't have managed it; he knew he'd have been instantly at odds with all those perquisite-conscious militiamen. Winder had them eating out of his hand, you had to give him that.

The General rode in an hour after dark. Barney was startled to see how much weight the man had lost in the last three weeks. He watched Winder striding around the camp with a tally board checking units; he seemed to be making a chart diagram of the camp. When he came to a militia company that styled itself the Rockford Rifles, he looked as though frustration was about to overcome him.

"But they're over *here*," he said, jabbing at the diagram.

The militia captain grinned. "So that's where them boogers went. Much obliged, Ginral."

When Barney tired of watching, he presented himself. The General looked at him with ringed eyes that lay atop pouches.

"Yes, yes, what is it?"

Barney outlined his plan crisply. The enemy would advance on the Upper Marlboro road tomorrow. It was forested as densely as the Nottingham road. Let's put riflemen—

"Attack the whole force, you mean? With five hundred? Are you out of your mind?"

"Harass them. Slow 'em down, make things difficult for them. I've watched them up close, General. Those men are suffering, they're pulling guns and wagons by hand and they're dropping like flies in this heat. Give me the men—let me put them athwart the road—"

"Divide my army? In the face of the enemy? Listen, Captain, you'd better stick to saltwater gunnery. Obvious that you have no concept of land warfare whatsoever. *Never* divide your force—least of all in the face of a superior army."

"I don't know that they're superior. They're sick."

"In numbers, they're superior. You just said so. My God! We're already divided—half my men are at Bladensburg and half are here and that doesn't even count the ones scattered around. Anyway, I regard this as a corps of observation."

"Observation? Does that preclude engaging?"

"For the moment, of course."

He sat down abruptly on a log and applied himself to his chart. Barney watched him pencil "Rockford Rifles" into a square, then draw a line to another square. He looked at it a moment. Then he drew arrowheads at each end of the line.

★ ★ ★ ★

By Monday the exodus was on. Government clerks loaded wagons with records while sailors at the navy yard prepared fires under warships well along in construction, to destroy them if it became necessary. Servants carried silver, rugs, family portraits, bags of linens and clothes to carriages and flogged teams off to the west, into Maryland and across the river to Virginia, to country homes or friends, anywhere far enough outside Washington to offer safety.

Yet the evacuation was fueled more by rage than by panic. Madison rode the streets with Rufe Dumster and saw fury stamped on every face, a good deal of it directed at him.

"You're the cause of this," a white-haired man standing on a corner shouted, "you pitiful excuse for a Commander in Chief!"

"What!" Madison, stung despite himself, wheeled the horse. "Because war was forced on us?"

"Oh, hell no, should have pulled their noses years ago. But what have we been doing for the last six months that our capital lies open to the vandals? What have *you* been doing—playing with yourself in your fancy mansion the government done bled the taxpayers to build?"

Madison fought a wild urge to quirt the old devil across his leering face and turned his horse away without answering. Yet as his heartbeat slowed and he fell into the horse's rhythm, he realized he hadn't answered because he didn't have an answer.

Posting up Pennsylvania toward Georgetown, he found himself hooted on his own streets. Catcalls from corners. Men shaking fists and bellowing threats.

"Don't try to run out on us!" howled a burly idiot in a sailor's striped jersey. "Hang you to a God damned lamppost, you go to running on us."

Madison spun the horse, lunged at the fool, and watched him stumble back against a building, face gone white.

"Never mind where I'm going," he shouted. "I'm going to the army. Question is, why are *you* standing here puling and mewling like a frightened baby? If you're such a fighter, get a musket and go meet the enemy, for God's sake!"

He whirled away, disgusted but also a little ashamed of himself. But only a little. Bastard!

Late Monday night he learned the invader had advanced a few miles from Nottingham to Upper Marlboro and there had stopped. Stopped at midday. But why? What were they waiting for?

Winder too had pulled back, still not engaging. The half of the army not at Bladensburg was at Old Fields, a bare five miles from Washington. Old Fields was on the road from Upper Marlboro to Bladensburg, at the intersection with the Washington road, which entered the city via the navy yard bridge.

On Tuesday morning he went there with a small party—Mr. Armstrong, Attorney General Richard Rush who had just come to Washington from Philadelphia, Mr. Jones the Secretary of the Navy, Mr. Monroe—just about

the whole executive branch escorted by half a dozen troopers carrying carbines.

Crossing the bridge, Madison gazed at the navy yard's heavy cannon.
Forcing the bridge would be fatal; hence the British must cross the Eastern
Branch at Bladensburg. But why had they stopped short? Or had they started
by now? Perhaps his own party would collide with the advancing enemy.
That prospect was a little frightening, but he was pleased to note that his
breathing remained even.

★ ★ ★ ★

At Old Fields Madison found Winder's army taking its ease. The soldiers
seemed to expect a speech, so he gave them a brief rouser that they cheered
somewhat halfheartedly, he thought.

Captain Barney, who rode in while he was speaking, presented a theory
to the group that Madison instinctively found appealing.

"How come the enemy hasn't budged out of Upper Marlboro in twenty-
four hours when it's a crossroads flyspeck without a whit of military interest?
Well, I ran into Will Beanes and it seems the two commanders took over
his house for a headquarters."

Madison knew Beanes well. He was Upper Marlboro's leading citizen,
physician, banker, one of those men to whom others turn naturally for advice.
Utterly reliable.

"Two commanders?" Madison asked.

"Yes, sir. Army's commanded by a General Ross. Admiral Co'burn's
along for the ride, but acting like he's a co-commander. Will Beanes has
an idea they're striking sparks off each other—said after hearing Co'burn
talk awhile, he downright liked Ross, by comparison, that is."

Madison listened carefully. The two officers apparently had radically
differing views of the campaign. Co'burn seemed to be waging a vendetta
against an upstart nation, while the General—who would be held responsible
if things went wrong—saw Washington as an emotional rather than a
military target.

"So why's he stopped?" Barney said. "He's a long way from his ships,
he has no real artillery and bare minimum supply, his men are wore out by
this heat—I believe he's having second thoughts and has stopped to see
what kind of opposition he's going to face.

"See what I mean, Mr. President? Maybe a good punch in the nose right
now will make him decide to go home."

Winder had been listening with barely concealed impatience. Now his
voice quivered with anger.

"Absurd! Likening the engaging of armies to a fistfight!"

Barney shrugged. "I've seen more than one feller who didn't much want
to fight decide to go home when his nose was busted."

"Suppose they broke through us—then there would be nothing between them and Washington. No—I can't risk it."

Madison glanced at Armstrong. "What do you think, John?"

His Secretary of War looked away, sniffed audibly, and said, "I wouldn't presume to direct a general in the field."

Instinct told Madison that Barney was right, but to override his general would be to take the command himself. That wasn't his role, nor did he possess the skills. He led his entourage back to Washington.

That afternoon the British advanced suddenly toward Old Fields, and Winder retreated in a wild dash that brought him clear to Washington. He camped at the navy yard, *in* the city.

★ ★ ★ ★

An hour before dawn on Wednesday, Madison called for his horse. Dolley was up. They lingered over coffee.

"Please, please, please be careful," she said. "Don't take chances."

"Well . . ."

"I mean it, Jimmy. Don't be a hero. You don't belong on battlefields, that's not your place—Jimmy, listen to me! You're a President, not a soldier."

"I know that, love. And you—no heroics here, either."

"Oh, I won't be foolish. Will I have some warning?"

"There'll be time to get out. But you must be ready."

"Can we stop them?" Her voice was barely a sigh.

"Of course. At Bladensburg—where we should have concentrated all along."

She smiled. "Good."

He saw that she didn't believe him.

"Are you frightened?" he said.

She looked surprised. "I'm *mad*. Through and through. At that rotten man. At the threats from our own people. In the clutch, they're proving themselves scoundrels."

He shook his head. "No, they're good citizens."

"Threatening us? Talking tar and feathers?"

"They're angry, that's the point. Not dismayed, not fearful—they want to fight. Dolley, we'll get through this and the country will be different. You'll see. Admiral Co'burn is outsmarting himself. He's triggering resistance the British haven't seen since the Revolution."

She smiled faintly. "You're an optimist."

"I'm a realist."

"Yes . . . yes, maybe you are. Maybe you're right." She put her arms around him and held him tight. Her breath was warm on his cheek. "God protect you," she whispered.

★ ★ ★ ★

Winder looked more like a corpse than a man. He'd slept for an hour—spent the night supervising the placement of explosives to blow down the navy yard bridge, a subaltern's job. Madison's heart sank.

"What about Bladensburg?"

"We don't know they're going there."

Wednesday morning and he still didn't know?

Winder hurried off. Madison looked at Armstrong, who shrugged but followed the General. A few minutes later he saw Armstrong alone on the bridge, Winder nowhere in sight.

Then a horseman galloped in. The British had pushed through Old Fields and were well on the way to Bladensburg.

Winder shouted orders—at last. The first units went streaming out of Washington on the road to Bladensburg that ran on this side—the west side—of the Eastern Branch.

Captain Barney presented himself. Winder had ordered him to keep his guns here to defend the bridge, just in case.

"That's madness, Mr. President," Barney said.

"So it is," Madison said. "There's too much madness afoot today. Of course, Captain—go and meet the enemy."

"Yes, sir!"

Madison turned to Armstrong. "Have you an opinion, John?"

Armstrong shrugged. "There'll be a battle, I suppose. And militia can't stand against regulars, so doubtless we'll lose."

He turned and walked to his horse. Madison mounted the big bay gelding and put him on the road to Bladensburg.

★ ★ ★ ★

It was a good thing the little President changed his orders, or Barney would've had to change them himself—he wasn't going to let himself be caught like a ship in a calm while the wind kicked up in the distance. Tommy Tomlinson put the boys in motion with their guns, and Barney loped ahead to place them.

What a tragedy of mismanagement! There would be no time to get carefully set—hell, they'd be lucky to beat the British to the battlefield. He passed the President's party, giving a quick salute. Whole cabinet but for Monroe, who had mounted and galloped to the front the moment word arrived. Fancied himself a military man, Monroe did.

Barney topped a crest and looked down on the battlefield. Good—no British as yet. He saw a long, steady slope that ran down to the river, which was quite narrow and spanned by a bridge. Beyond the river Bladensburg lay strung along the Baltimore pike. Partway down the slope and to the right an orchard provided some cover. The riverbank itself was lined with trees and scrub brush. He decided to place his guns on the crest where they could cover the whole field.

Stan Stansbury, the brigadier commanding these Baltimore militia, was arranging a reserve line at the crest. Barney had known him for years, an able man and popular with his troops. Stansbury had positioned his twelve hundred men wisely: a battery and five companies of skirmishers at the bridge, the rest up the hill in support, partly protected by the orchard.

Barney was marking sites for his guns when a thousand militiamen from Annapolis came across the bridge at a near run shouting they were barely ahead of the British. They formed a line on the crest where Barney's guns would go.

"What the hell!" Stansbury was placing the Annapolis troops when he pointed at the men he'd posted in the orchard. They were moving, a horseman directing them. Barney raised his glass.

Monroe! The Secretary of State was rearranging the battlefield. Stansbury didn't know about it?

"He didn't say a word to me. I didn't even know he was here. Well, maybe it's all right . . . But wait—look at that! He's pulled my reserve back five hundred yards. That means they can't support the first line. Damn it all, that was the whole idea. Leaves my skirmishers on their own. And look—second line loses the cover of the orchard. It leaves them bare."

He spurred his horse forward to shift them back, but then a long column of red came out of distant dust, and the lead files of the British line drew up just short of the bridge. It was too late to restore the line—Barney saw Stansbury gallop on to his first line, saber in hand. Now there were three lines, none placed to support another; each would fight alone, which negated all value of mass. Another failure.

Winder arrived with the Washington troops and placed them on the second and third lines. Barney's guns came and he sited them. When he looked up, he saw President Madison and the cabinet trotting serenely down the hill. They went right to the first line and started across the bridge! A scout galloped to warn them and they pulled back, looking startled even from where Barney stood, but they stayed with the first line. He had to admire Madison. A gutty little devil, obviously no soldier nor even an outdoorsman but not at all cowed by a British army.

A shrill of bugles, and without a moment to reconnoiter—let alone await the rest of their army—the first redcoat brigade started over the bridge. The cannon near the bridge opened, there was a ripple of musket fire that sounded like cloth tearing, and then his own big guns roared. British troops were falling on the bridge, but they were getting over, too, and fanning out right and left into the brush and trees.

The President was still in the first line, though bullets had to be cutting all around him. Even as it struck Barney that courage tested unnecessarily is foolhardiness, he saw Madison turn his horse and start up the hill at a quick trot, the cabinet with him. But even now, he wasn't fleeing. He rode turned in the saddle, watching like a student of war.

The British came boiling out of the riverbank cover and the little guns banged and the band of militiamen held their ground and drove them back to cover. But Barney saw officers waving sabers and exhorting, and the redcoats came up from the riverbank in another rush and this time they were too much and that first thin line of Maryland militia collapsed. It happened in a flash, one moment holding, the next in wild flight.

Now Monroe's disastrous misstep was evident—the second line couldn't help the first, and when the first crashed into the second the panic was infectious and the second began to crumble, too. The redcoats fanned right and left to flank the second line and shred it in crossfire, and it collapsed and fled.

The running Americans struck the third line, but Stansbury and Barney between them managed to rally that one. The big navy guns in the center bucked and roared, comforting music to infantrymen under pressure, and the line held. But barely. Barney stood atop one of his guns and saw immediately that both ends were fraying as the experienced British troops swung wide and came in on long slanting angles.

It was more than the militia boys could stand to see those implacable men in red come out of the blazing hot sunshot dust with bayonets shining to take their flanks in enfilade, get behind them, roll them up, and murder them. A week ago they'd been behind plows and store counters, and now they were being asked to die and it was more than they could bear. They broke and streamed from the field.

Barney's sailors-cum-infantry and his marines were regulars, and his gunners had smelled plenty of powder smoke. His musketmen ranged right and left to cover his flanks while he loaded with grape and fragmentation shells that sliced swaths through the enemy. But the redcoat soldiers came on and on, and at last he and his men were alone, the militia vanished, even Stansbury gone, and the guns roared on.

Half his men were down, empty caissons had stilled two of his guns, and the rest were low on ammunition. His gunners slowed down and spaced their shots—and just as he saw it was all over a giant force knocked him down.

His ears rang. He lay flat on his back with the sky brilliant overhead. He understood, he'd been hit before, no surprises here. No pain yet, but there would be soon. He felt his leg. Yes, in the thigh—shit, that could be bad, but what the hell, his ears were ringing, he heard music, a band playing "Yankee Doodle," and then he realized it was all in his own head but he liked it anyway.

Tommy Tomlinson knelt over him, lifted the leg—oh, *shit*, now, that hurt, all right—and then a tourniquet tightened and Barney knew at least he wouldn't bleed to death.

"Move the boys out, Tommy," he said. "We've done all we can and more. Pull 'em out."

"We'll rig a litter."

"Leave me. I'll kill your chances."

"No. We can haul you."

"God damn it, that's an order. Get the boys out—take care of 'em."

"Aye aye, sir."

Tommy saved the men still on their feet and some of the guns. Barney lay on the grass, shivering with cold in blazing sun. His heart ached. They'd failed. The militia had fled in every direction and the capital of his country lay open to the invader. The poor little President . . .

22

WASHINGTON
August 24, 1814

★ ★ ★ ★ The rumble of guns in the distance stopped at midafternoon.

Dolley Madison was in the mansion's center hall, surrounded by heavy linen bags that held the records of American executive government. Government in flight. In exile. And now the guns were silent and Jimmy was out there somewhere.

The silence seemed louder than gunshots, louder than cannon fire. It rang in her ears. Sodden heat accentuated this absence of sound. White haze pressed the city, leaves hung like rags, no air stirred, no birds sang. The ring of horseshoes on cobblestone and shouts from the street seemed loud and threatening.

The guns' deadly murmur had gone on for hours. The knowledge that men were being killed in distant earshot was horrifying—yet the sound was comforting, too, for it meant the contest was still on. Its cessation was ominous. The British wouldn't have quit so readily, and if they hadn't quit they must have prevailed.

But if so, if our army is broken, where is Jimmy now?

"We ain't got much time, Miz Madison," Rufe Dumster said. "Them guns stop, likely means we'll be having visitors soon."

"But there's all this . . ." She waved a hand at the pile of bags. "All the records—they're crucial."

"Coach is plumb full," Rufe said. "I left a little hole for you, but barely. You'll have to squeeze it as it is."

She caught a glimpse of herself in the vestibule mirror: hair straggling, face streaked, hands filthy, sleeves pushed up, half-moons of sweat under her arms. She used her fingers to comb a strand of hair from her eyes. They had worked for hours pulling records from oak file drawers, the whole staff stuffing them in the bags. All a jumble, of course, but at least they would be saved.

If, that is, she could find transportation. Obviously her coach wouldn't
be enough, and she had reserved the White House wagon to carry her
people to safety. They were family; she wouldn't dream of leaving them
to the Visigoths. She made sure they had food, cookpots, canvas for shelter,
for she had no idea when she would see them again. Though French John
would be with them, they would be adrift in a sea of angry refugees,
most of them white. She would not leave them afoot even to save the
national records.

"Rufe," she said, "you and Sime go find a wagon. Go to the navy yard,
the District of Columbia offices. Try Capitol Hill. Tell them we must have
one."

Rufe frowned. "I dunno, Miz Madison. Both of us? This situation brings
out the bad in folks, somehow. Leaving you alone—maybe that ain't a very
good idea."

She saw Sime nodding; he always took his cue from Rufe.

"I'll run the risk," she said. "You two go on."

People streamed westward along Pennsylvania Avenue, many with possessions tied in sheets and slung over their shoulders. As they passed, some of
them glared at the mansion with angry energy she could feel even from
here. A few shouted in raw voices, but none turned in; if any did, they
would have her to contend with.

From a side window she saw French John at the wagon, the servants
clustered around. They clutched their belongings in little sacks and peered
anxiously toward the east; with a start she realized they were watching for
the arrival of men in red coats. In anguish she turned toward her magnificent
oval drawing room. There was Joseph, dusting and straightening! His sheer
loyalty brought tears to her eyes.

"Maybe they won't come, Miss Dolley." His voice was gentle; he was
trying to comfort her, but she knew better. If he could, that dreadful man
would burn this lovely place out of plain hatred.

The thought was like a physical blow. She'd been with this house
from its beginning. Abigail Adams had lived here only a few months
before Tom Jefferson defeated Mr. Adams; Dolley had served as hostess
for Tom, a widower; then, after eight years the Madisons moved in. From
that moment on, it was hers. Duty and opportunity merged, and she set
about making the great house fit the faith in which Americans held their
country. And look—her fingers traced a faux marble facing—just look
at what she and Mr. Latrobe had done! On impulse she told Joseph to
take down her gorgeous red velvet curtains and pile them in the entrance
hall.

Could she save those curtains? Even the attempt was an expression of
grief that wrenched her heart. The mansion was beautiful, it was a national
symbol, but in the end what mattered was that it was her home. Any woman
would understand; any woman who had made the best of the simplest place,

hung curtains in the lowliest hovel, would feel the same. In a sudden shift, grief spun off into rage as necessary at the moment as it was un-Quakerish. That tall, jeering jackanapes of a barbarian—who had made war a matter of personalities, who would burn her home to express some mad desire to humiliate—may he rot in hell!

★ ★ ★ ★

She went up to the family quarters and found dear Sukey packing the bare necessities for travel. Sukey had two bags on the bed, one for Dolley's things, the other for Jimmy's.

The bags beside each other seemed to symbolize life with Jimmy over two decades. She saw that the rage she felt had less to do with the great house and its beauty than with Jimmy and with fear. She was sick with worry. He was sixty-three years old and not strong. Only a year ago he'd been terrifyingly ill—she remembered Sally McQuirk coming to cheer him when the city thought he would die. He had no business on a battlefield!

What was he trying to prove, that he must go and expose himself to danger? Yes, it disturbed him still that he'd been too sickly to fight in the Revolution, just as his small stature disturbed him. But that was the role God had made for him, and certainly God had given him a mind to make up for every physical shortcoming. But no. He was full of pride, he must take himself off to battle like a swordsman of old to prove his courage. Dear Lord, you couldn't be a President in war without courage that was tantamount to the worst demands of the battlefield!

What if his horse threw him? Or he fainted? Or was caught in a retreat, knocked over, trampled? What if he was wounded? Who would care for him? She had an agonizing image of his small figure lying in a roadway, raising a bloody hand in supplication, unseeing men stepping over him. She saw the hand sink, the face drop into the dirt, all motionless—

Tears streamed down her face and she rocked with grief. Sukey, who had been Dolley's maid for years, wrapped her arms around her mistress.

"Mr. James, he bound to be all right," she said. "He's smart, he won't let himself get caught in no soldier trap."

Dolley sighed and let herself be hugged. She could feel Sukey's calm washing over her. She hugged back, cheek pressed to cheek, and her courage returned.

"You're a dear, Sukey. A perfect dear. And you're right—he *is* smart. I guess it's up to us to do as well."

She went to the washstand, poured water from the pitcher, and got out of the sweat-stained gown. When she had washed she brushed her hair, touched her face with color, put on the lightest gown she had, and hurried downstairs. She felt clean and strong; that awful tension had gone out of her on the tide of anger and fear. She was in control again.

★　★　★　★

Rufe and Sime returned. No wagons were to be had. Navy yard wagons had departed with navy records, those on Capitol Hill were all in use, and the District offices were empty.

"I tried to commandeer a merchant's wagon," Rufe said, "and he drawed a pistol on me."

"Well, we'll see about that! Let's see if he'll point a pistol at me."

"Now, Miz Madison, I don't know—"

"Well, I do. Let's go."

Sime Puckett went off to see to his family. Rufe had already moved his, and she set out with him in the two-wheeled trap. Only a few men were on the streets, and the city had a furtive, dangerous look, as if unknown terrors might lurk around corners. The men she did see refused to meet her eye, giving her an uneasy sense that the very equations of life had changed in the face of the enemy threat. Rufe reached under the seat and drew out a heavy bat he propped between his legs.

Up on F Street they found a lantern-jawed fellow with a wagon. He'd shucked his shirt in the heat and stood holding the team as another man stacked boxes on the wagon bed. He stared at her as Rufe stopped the trap beside him. She smiled. His expression didn't change.

"Sir," she said, "I'm Mrs. Madison. We're moving the President's cabinet records from the executive mansion. I'm sorry, but we need your wagon—"

"Well, the hell you do!" The man slapped his hand against his thigh. "Just come up and tell me you want my wagon, just like that! Well, lady, you can—"

"Just one moment, sir! I am the wife of the President of the United States, and I demand the use of your wagon in his name!"

"Why, I wouldn't give that little shit the time of day—*he's* the one got us in this fix."

She fixed him with a look. "Now, you listen to me! I'm telling you your patriotic duty. I demand that wagon. I'll see you in irons after this is over if you don't give it to me right now!"

He stared at her a moment, then hawked up a wad of sputum from deep in his throat and spat it directly up at her. It struck the door of the trap with a thump.

She felt a flash of such rage that she couldn't breathe. Gripping her parasol like a club, she was half out of the trap before she stopped herself. She sat back, breathing heavily, just as Rufe stood with the bat drawn back to swing.

She caught his arm. There wasn't time to stop and beat some citizen to death for his wagon.

Rufe stared at the man. "I'll see you again, mister. I'll be looking for you."

The fellow took a step backward. Dolley prodded Rufe.

"Let's go—we'll find a decent citizen."

But they didn't. She found three more wagons that the owners refused to surrender. They were polite and regretful and yes, they loved their country and hated the British and they could hardly bear to think of White House records in the hands of invaders, but no, ma'am, they just couldn't give up their wagons . . .

At thirteenth and Pennsylvania she heard a wild clatter of hoofs. Rufe stopped the trap. A horseman galloped up, waving his hat.

"Clear out! Clear out! The British are coming!"

She stood in the trap. "Here, you! Stop! Stop!" The rider reined up. Foam flew from the horse's mouth.

"Our men are defeated?"

"Yes, ma'am. Whupped! Our boys broke and run."

"Have you seen Mr. Madison?"

"No, ma'am. I mean, he was there, but I didn't see nothing after. I come on ahead—them as ain't scattered, they're coming down the Bladensburg Pike. Likely he's with 'em. But you, lady, you better get on out of town." He tipped his hat and pelted away, shouting the news.

"We better go back," Rufe said.

"Yes," she said. She felt sick. Jimmy trapped in a boiling mass of defeated humanity, rolling down the Bladensburg road.

★ ★ ★ ★

Joseph cracked a shutter in a garret storeroom and peered down on the wagon. Jennie was sitting on her little bag, looking from window to window. He knew she was looking for him, her expression broke his heart—but that didn't matter. Her presence in the wagon confirmed her choice. He'd begged her one more time the night before, all the power of his soul in his voice, and she'd cried and clung to him and refused. Afraid.

So be it. The wagon would go soon and she would be on it and he would not and they would part forever. So be it.

He sighed. Would French John note his absence and search the house? He would crawl out on the roof if he had to, but he wasn't going. The British were coming—he'd known it when the guns stopped, and now the shouts in the streets confirmed it—and he intended to wait for them. He saw Miss Dolley alight from the trap. French John went to meet her and they entered the house together. Joseph tensed. Searching for him?

He'd made himself scarce when they finished emptying the file drawers in the cabinet room. And then Miss Dolley had found him in the oval room and he'd thought it was all over, she'd see the guilt in his face and order him bound and taken as a captive. But the moment passed. His hands trembled like leaves when she left the room.

Now he stood with his ear pressed against the storeroom door. Not a sound. He listened a long time, his body wet with the sweat of fear, but heard nothing. When he returned to the window, the wagon was gone. Jennie was gone. She was the only person he'd loved since Mam died. It had been a mistake to open his guarded heart, he'd known it even as he did it, but that smile, those warm eyes, the unfettered love that came from her in waves—ah, God! She was irresistible!

There would never be another. He would go through life empty and alone. But he would be free.

★ ★ ★ ★

To Dolley, the silence in the great halls matched the ominous quiet outside. Where was Joseph? She'd asked French John to leave him to drive the trap—hadn't she? Perhaps she'd forgotten in the confusion . . .

She went upstairs and extended her glass to gaze down Pennsylvania Avenue from an east bedroom. The street was empty but for occasional antlike figures that appeared and disappeared. Even the Capitol atop its hill looked deserted. Time itself had stopped to await the enemy. She gazed until her eye watered, the anguish over her house forgotten. All she cared about was to see that small figure on his bay gelding. Her heart called to him across the desolate mocking street—

What in the world was she thinking? She'd been so proud, so brave, so defiant—and here she was huddled in a window, crying over an empty street! Jimmy would be disappointed, he'd expect more of her, and by heaven she expected more of herself! She collapsed the glass and ran down the long steps.

Rufe was outside the north entrance, holding the bat with both hands. He turned when he heard her.

"We oughta move along, Miz Madison," he said. "Likely we'll see a whupped army coming through. I don't know—they might be pretty rough. I'd like to get you out ahead of that, ma'am."

"Soon," she said. "We'll wait just a little longer for Mr. Madison."

"I believe the President would want you to go, ma'am."

"Soon, Rufe."

Her gorgeous red curtains lay neatly folded on the bags of cabinet records, but what did it matter now? Nothing could be saved. Those records could never be reconstructed. A gaping hole would forever mar the history of the United States and of the Madison administration. Surely the inability to maintain a continuity of records described disgrace more clearly than lost battles or burning buildings. Years after buildings were rebuilt, that hole would tell its awful story—and all for the lack of a wagon, for scoundrels who refused to help, for a President's Lady who couldn't inspire a single soul to patriotic sacrifice. If she must cry, *there* was a subject for tears!

Then she heard hoofs and iron tires on the driveway gravel, and there like a vision from heaven came an empty wagon and beside it a tall man in a white suit on a gorgeous dapple gray. Why, it was Charles Carroll, who once had owned most of the land on which Washington was built and so considered the city more or less his, a conceit he was more than wealthy enough to indulge.

She could have kissed him!

"Madam, you must be gone," Carroll said in his august, commanding manner. She saw a pistol tucked in his waistband. "It's very dangerous now, and you must not be captured. I came to fetch you—"

"With a wagon, you wonderful man!"

He blinked, then smiled almost shyly. "Figured you'd need it. But, Miz Madison, we must go. I'll escort you."

"When we've loaded."

While Rufe and the driver stacked the bags on the wagon bed, Dolley darted upstairs with her glass. She stared down the empty street. Nothing. Mr. Carroll followed her.

"Mrs. Madison, truly, there's no time to lose."

"Yes, of course." He led her down the stairs. But what if Jimmy came? What if he were wounded?

"Take the records and go," she said. "I'll stay. If the enemy comes, Rufe and I will slip away—"

"My God, woman! In a carriage that stands out like a sore thumb, that attracts attention wherever it goes, you'll just slip away? Madam, show some discretion! I'll keep you safe, but you must get in your carriage right now and go!"

"All right, Colonel Carroll, all right." But then a new thought struck her—what about Gilbert Stuart's great full-length portrait of General Washington?

It was irreplaceable, taken as it was from life. But even more important, if that British ruffian found himself under the eyes of the man most responsible for the American separation from Britain, wouldn't he work unspeakable indignities on it? By heaven, she would not give him that satisfaction!

"We must take the portrait," she said.

Carroll looked from the huge picture in its heavy gilt frame to her.

"Why, madam, there's no room for it. There's no way even to get it down." He grabbed the frame, which didn't move. "It's screwed to the wall!"

"Rufe," she said, "get an ax. And a ladder."

"Madam, this is madness."

"Now, you listen to me, sir! There is nothing whatsoever mad about saving a great portrait of a great man, and that's exactly what we're going to do."

That silenced him for the moment. She felt momentarily ashamed—he had rescued them, after all—but then Rufe chopped the frame apart and brought down the painting on its stretcher. She knelt with a kitchen knife to pull out the tacks, then rolled it loosely in one of the curtains. Rufe produced a length of twine and made it secure.

They would have to tie it to the coach, there wasn't room inside, and they'd be lucky if it survived. But it was the best she could do—

"Halloo . . ."

A stranger was at the door, a youngish man with a white linen coat slung over his shoulder, a fine cambric shirt rolled up at the sleeves, a black cravat loosened.

"Miz Madison," he said in a sweet voice, "Jacob Barker of New York City, at your service. I bring letters from Martin Van Buren and Mr. Astor . . ." He dug in an inner pocket of the coat. "I came to offer any help."

It was ludicrous. "Really, sir," she said, "there's hardly time—" But then she had an idea. "Let me see those letters."

She studied them while Colonel Carroll stamped like an impatient horse. She knew both signatures—they were genuine.

"Yes, sir," she said, "you can render your country an immense service if you will."

"Anything, madam."

She lifted the curtain with the rolled painting. "This is General Washington's portrait."

"Yes, ma'am." She saw he understood its importance.

"Guard it with your life and promise me you'll deliver it."

She gave him detailed directions to Mr. Carroll's farm in Maryland.

"Go now," she said. "God be with you."

"And with us, madam," Carroll said. "Now may we go?"

"Not without a last look, Colonel. Mr. Madison may be but a block away as we leave."

He didn't answer. She ran up, leveled the glass, and focused on a crowd at the far end of the avenue. They carried muskets, some wore bloody bandages, they were coming at a trot—and there was no sign of Jimmy. He was somewhere in that mob if still alive, but there was no more she could do here.

She walked down the stairs for the last time. Mr. Barker and the wagon were gone, Rufe was waiting on the box, Colonel Carroll held the coach door open. He gave her his hand and she stepped in and drew his hand to her lips.

"Thank you," she said.

He bowed, then swung onto the big dapple gray and led the carriage out into the street.

She looked back once at the house standing noble and serene among its shelter of trees, and then she looked ahead.

★ ★ ★ ★

Joseph waited in the storeroom under the eaves. He had built a cave, shifting boxes artfully to leave a space into which he could crawl, drawing a last box behind him. Only French John might notice that boxes had been moved, and John was gone. He heard Miss Dolley's footsteps below and slipped out in time to see the coach leave, Rufe on the box, Miss Dolley looking back from the half-open coach door.

The great house was silent as death, the quiet emphasized by the murmur of men passing on the street outside. He went from room to room making sure he was alone. It was exhilarating if a little frightening, the familiar made strange. And sad. He hadn't been unhappy here; he might have enjoyed serving if he'd been free. Free to come and go, draw a salary for his labor, have a home, raise a family.

Free like Rufe and Sime. Yet Rufe and Sime were ignorant men. Joseph knew his own mental capacities far exceeded theirs—he read what Mr. James read, and from overheard conversations knew his own thinking was consistent with that of Mr. James. But Rufe and Sime were free; they did as they pleased, stood eye to eye with any man in the world. Because they were white. Inferior but white. The thought hardened him; sentimentality was a conceit he couldn't afford.

Enough moping! Freedom was at hand—click your heels, man! But how could he, when the cost of freedom had proved to be throwing away his woman? His woman . . . it was a phrase he had refused even to think, lest it bind him to slavery forever. But it was she who had failed, love crushed by fear. She who had refused life, who loved but maybe just didn't love enough.

And she who had left a wound in his heart that he knew time would not heal. The image of her wan face gazing up at the windows from the wagon would be with him when he was an old man. And the look of the empty yard a little later, all his hopes gone.

Evening was coming on. The haze was darkening, shaping into storm clouds. The beaten army streamed past the gates, still running from an enemy that might or might not follow. Most men carried muskets, and in the waning light he saw bloody bandages on arms and legs and heads. Their boots shuffled and they cried with pain and rage. It was a frightening noise, full of despair, and Joseph felt something wild and dislocating in the air as if for these men the world had exploded and would never be the same. It was more mob than crowd, and he understood that passing through it could be deadly for a small black man with no rights.

Suddenly he was sick with fear. Nausea clutched his throat. His whole body shook. How would he fare in a vast world filled with white ruffians?

What did he even know of the world he was so determined to enter, the world of those men crying in their defeat?

Nothing. He'd lived in the shelter of a great house and an ordered universe, his days absorbed in domestic details while he dreamed his dreams of freedom. But what of the unknown, of the world's mean side, of the stunning capacity of random chance to reverse every facet of a man's life in an instant? These things he knew only from books.

He calmed himself, breathing deeply and flexing his shoulders until he regained control. This fear wasn't new. He'd always known he would be afraid when the moment came. Nor was it any different from Jennie's, except that he refused to submit to it. So he must plunge, take the risk, win if he could, die if he couldn't.

Still, he hadn't counted on having to pass through a mob of beaten American soldiers to reach the British. He decided to wait until midnight. If they didn't come to the mansion by then he would go find them, at whatever risk. He sat at Miss Dolley's desk as the last light faded and drafted a pass for himself, just in case. It said he was Colonel Carroll's boy, was going for the Colonel's horse, and was not to be disturbed.

★ ★ ★ ★

Horsemen turned in at the gate. Joseph ran lightly up the stairs to peer from an upper window. In the last light he made out Mr. James, sliding off his bay gelding. The difference from the last time he'd seen the President was startling. Mr. James—always so confident, so assured, such a model of behavior—looked . . . lost. As if he'd seen ghosts. His shoulders sagged. He raised his face as he passed into the house and for a moment Joseph thought he was crying, but he was sure that couldn't be.

He heard steps on the stairs and darted to his hiding place, pulling the box behind him. Arms wrapped around his knees, he sweated in utter darkness, straining to hear. Nothing. After a while he crept to the door, listened, then went to a window. The horses were gone.

Nothing to do now but wait. For the British or for midnight. He climbed a ladder to a trapdoor that opened to the roof and sat with his back against a chimney, watching the night. It was very dark. Clouds sagging low had supplanted the haze. Sooner or later blazing heat and boiling moisture always produced a storm; it would break before dawn. He sat quietly. Puffs of wind swirled against him and died. The metal roof was hot to the touch. He waited.

Lightning flashed in the far distance, thunder nearly a half a minute in following. But the flash was enough to show him the length of Pennsylvania Avenue clogged from side to side with fleeing soldiers, hundreds upon hundreds of them. That ominous sound they made as they streamed around the mansion continued, that murmur radiating rage and pain. He shivered. But at midnight he would step into it no matter what.

A faint glow appeared in the east, like the first hint of dawn. Had he slept, had hours passed?

Then he understood. The Capitol was on fire. Soon the clouds in that quarter were clearly evident and then they took on a reddish tint. The red deepened and brightened until the clouds looked illuminated, and then a thin spout of flame lanced into the air from the roof of the House side and a shower of sparks flew down. The spout fell back, soared up again, and then he saw the whole roof was aflame.

He could see the upper windows; they glowed from within as if all the chandeliers were ablaze with candles. He sighed. The British were here. All the Madisons' fears and all Joseph's dreams had come true.

He leaned against the chimney watching smoke boil into the red of the clouds above. Flame pierced the roof on the Senate side and spread until the entire roof was a sheet of fire. The light playing against the clouds blazed brighter and brighter; now the whole city was illuminated as if by reddish dawnlight.

The mob coursing Pennsylvania Avenue was thinning out. The men still there walked faster. They twisted their heads to watch the flames behind them, and even from the roof Joseph could sense the panic in their movements. They began to run, still watching, and many of them fell. At last there were only a few, then none. The long avenue was empty. If Joseph had to go to the British, at least his way wouldn't lie through a mob.

Off to the right an explosion threw a new column of flame to the heavens. The navy yard. Joseph knew Captain Tingey had orders to burn the yard if the enemy approached lest the Royal Navy ensign fly over the ships under construction there. The British had arrived, no doubt about that—but would they come here, to the mansion? He watched the empty avenue. The hot glow over the Capitol began to fade as the one over the navy yard grew.

It was near midnight. The Capitol had been burning for hours. If they were coming, you'd think they would be here by now. He stood up, ready to go brave whatever dangers lay between him and his dream. Then he saw new movement on the avenue. Backlit by the flames and the glowing sky, a column of men swung along Pennsylvania Avenue in disciplined cadence. A single horseman was with them, astride a white horse. The Admiral, coming in person . . .

He saw them turn in at the President's gate. Fearful now that the moment had arrived, he hesitated at the top of the stairs. Harsh commands halted the troops, and then with a splintering crash the front door flew open. A tall, skinny man in blue with a huge cocked hat laced in gold stood with his foot raised after kicking it in. Joseph stood transfixed, hidden in shadow at the top of the stairs.

"Jemmy!" the Englishman bawled. "Are you home, you little devil, you? Here's Admiral Co'burn come to call, just as I promised. Don't tell me you didn't wait up for me!"

A cluster of young officers followed him, laughing at his sallies.

"Jemmy, you little fart, what kind of welcome is this? I thought you'd be waiting with open arms. Come out of the closet, you little mite, and bring your fat wench to do the honors. Don't you see—we've come calling!"

He did an odd little jig of triumph, boots shuffling, and Joseph's reflexive thought was that he would scratch the polished floor. Then the man's expression changed.

"If anybody's up there, come down now or you'll roast! This place is going up in flames!"

Now or never. Joseph skipped down the stairs.

"Well, well, well. Lookee here—a bloody little wog." His amusement seemed to have returned. "I'd rather have seen the lady waggling her charms at me, but you'll have to do. Any more up there? Fat Dolley hiding in a closet?"

"No, Your Honor," Joseph said, hating the tremor in his voice. He saw the Englishman had heard it.

"Scared shitless, eh? And I suppose Jemmy ran off to hide? Took Missus Fat Arse with him, eh? Well, come on, speak up, speak up!"

"Yes, Your Honor."

"What a pity. So much for American hospitality. But surely they left dinner for us. So get some candles lit and scare up a meal, you God damned little scoundrel, and be quick about it!"

Joseph lit a taper from the banked fire in the kitchen and ran from room to room lighting candles and crystal sperm-oil lamps as he had done so many times before. He cut slabs from a huge joint, sliced fresh loaves, splashed oil and vinegar on washed greens, found mustard and horseradish, put out bowls of stewed fruit, and set the silver that Miss Dolley had left because there wasn't room in the wagon.

As he worked he could hear them moving from room to room, laughing at the Admiral's jests, now and then a crash sounding as if lamps were knocked over or chairs kicked out of the way. Then the Admiral leaned through the kitchen door.

"This picture frame broken up—what did it hold?"

"Portrait of George Washington, sir."

"Haw! Bloody George Washington, eh? Now listen, you little turd— you wouldn't fool me, would you? Sure it wasn't a portrait of fat Dolley in the nude?"

"No, sir."

"I'd have come a ways to see that. George Washington, now, I'd have cut him a mustache with my saber. Well, come, come—where's the dinner?"

"Coming, sir."

Joseph laid it on the long table in the state dining room and poured Mr. James's best wine in crystal goblets. They drained the glasses in great swallows and poured more, carelessly spilling wine on the damask tablecloth as they tore at the meat and bread.

"To Jemmy!" the Admiral roared, raising his glass.

"To Jemmy!" the young officers shouted, emptying glasses and pouring again.

"To Dolley—I'm told her titties would make Michelangelo weep!"

"To Dolley's titties!"

"Boy," the Admiral said, "where does the lady sit at dinner?"

"At the far end, sir."

"Lieutenant Jenson!"

"Sir!"

"On your feet, lad. How dare you profane the cushion that has had intimate communion with the sweetest arse in all North America? Bring it to me—it shall be my prize of conquest, filling my cabin with ambrosial fragrance to comfort lonely days at sea!"

A young officer raised his glass. "To the sweetest cushion in Christendom!"

"Hear! Hear!"

Joseph stood in the doorway and thought of all the dinners he'd served here, the wine he'd poured, the conversation he'd heard, the bright remarks, the decorous jests, graceful music drifting from the next room, usually the work of that prolific young Mozart whose sound Joseph had come to love.

This casual desecration was excruciating, somehow. But it wasn't *his* place they violated. He was a mere slave. That graceful talk had never been addressed to him, Mozart wasn't played for him. What did he care?

But he did. He felt pain in his heart and knew he was seeing an assault on decency. Miss Dolley and Mr. James had invariably thanked him for his service, slave though he was. He knew what the world could be, should be, and this—it made him sick. For it gave him again in a different, more intimate way the dislocating message that the mob outside had given him— the world into which he intended to plunge was very different from the one he'd known and vastly more dangerous.

The Admiral drained his glass and tossed it over his shoulder. It shattered on bare floor. He stood up and thrust his chair back.

"All right, gentlemen, let's get on with it."

The officers hurried outside and Joseph followed. Soldiers in red coats lounged on the grass. A number held long heavy poles. Sacking had been wrapped on the ends and soaked in pitch. A fire burned on the crushed gravel driveway.

"Ready, sir?" a subaltern said.

"Go right ahead," Co'burn said. The pillow was under his left arm. "I want to see it blaze."

The soldiers dipped their torches into the fire and withdrew them ablaze.

They made the night bright. Joseph held his breath as the soldiers poised themselves, one beneath each window.

On a shouted command, each rammed his torch pole through a window. Glass shards fell in tinkling rain. Then they thrust the poles deep into the building. One fell back; a trooper cursed and with a quick run hurled it like a javelin.

Wisps of smoke appeared and then a dull orange glow. The glow brightened, shards of flame appeared, and the soldiers cheered. Joseph stared. It hardly seemed possible that what had been talked of so long was happening, that so splendid a building could so casually be destroyed, that hatred's flames could so easily consume grace and magnificence . . . yes, it was a different world.

Dancing fire leapt up the curtains in lightning puffs, blossomed through the broken windows, crept up the walls, ignited the ceilings. The British watched in silence. There was a crash inside. The upper floor was giving way. A shower of sparks appeared in the higher windows, and then that fatal glow.

"Let's go," the Admiral said. A subaltern snapped commands and the troops formed a line.

Now . . . Joseph fell to his knees before Co'burn. "Oh, sir, Your Honor, Your Excellency, it was said slaves could go with you—"

Co'burn laughed. "Lookee here, the bloody little wog wants to be free. Hell, yes. Come along. Fall in at the end and mind you keep up. You'll still be a nigger, but by God you'll be a free nigger!"

Free! Oh, darling Jennie, why didn't you seize your courage? Why didn't you come!

He took his place at the end of the column, the soldiers there glancing at him curiously, and when they went swinging down the drive he clung so close that he stepped on a man's heels.

A sandy-haired sergeant with a mass of freckles grinned.

"Don't worry, little fellow, we won't leave you. Ship you off to the bloody islands a free man. Count on it."

Heavy bushes stood by the gate. As the column passed, a small dark figure darted out and crashed into Joseph.

Jennie!

"I got off the wagon," she whispered. "I couldn't stand to leave you. We going to be all right, ain't we, Joseph?"

He put his arm around her, holding her close, marching in step with the men ahead, his heart soaring.

"Ain't we, Joseph? Ain't we? You gonna take care of me, now, ain't you?"

"Take care of you all my life, girl. Not ever let you out of my sight. We gonna be free together."

As the column swung around the Treasury, Joseph turned for a last look at the mansion. The upper windows were full of brilliant flame. There was a muted crash as part of the roof fell and a shower of sparks shot up, dancing and boiling in the heat. He glanced at the Admiral, who had turned his horse to sit gazing with a look of satisfaction.

Within minutes the gorgeous mansion with all that had been done to perfection within it would be gone. Yes, the world was cruel and dangerous. He held Jennie hard against him and walked into the unknown.

23

WASHINGTON
August, 1814

★ ★ ★ ★ Across the Potomac and well upriver, Madison stood on a high bluff with water glinting dully far below and gazed back at Washington. He held the bay's reins loosely as the animal cropped grass. The men with him stood in a little group to one side, leaving him alone. That was his preference as he watched his city burn.

The flames from the Capitol and the navy yard died down as those in the White House mounted. When the mansion roof fell, geysers of sparks boiled into orange clouds, and the odor of charred wood and paint and fabric rode the breeze.

He stood there a long time. Gradually the fire in what had been his home for seven years, where his papers, his clothes, his memories were stored, died down to a hot glow. Dolley had put her soul into that building. It was a drafty barn when old Tom had it, and she had made it a showplace the American people could love as they would never love the Capitol. That was why the British saw only a target in its beauty. Now Dolley was abroad somewhere in the Virginia night.

Wind gusts, newly cool, newly strong, stirred the grass at his feet. Lightning, long and jagged, struck across the river with an intensity that made the air sizzle, and then thunder crashed to knock a man's breath from his chest. The clouds opened as if by a blade and rainwater gushed in torrents. Madison stood motionless as his companions scrambled for cover under nearby trees. Water streamed from his hat brim, soaked through his coat, and ran in rivulets down his chest. The last firelight from the city vanished as rain doused the embers. He stared into the black night.

The disgrace of it! A proud nation's capital abandoned to the enemy, left open for the vandals to burn as a lord of the manor might burn a squatter's shack. What vast contempt was expressed in destroying those fine buildings that were without a particle of military value. It was so unnecessary, so out of the pattern of war as prosecuted by civilized nations. Perhaps the time would come when burning cities would be the norm—war seemed ever to grow more cruel and abusive—but it wasn't the norm now. When two Canadian hamlets were burned, Americans had court-martialed the officers responsible.

Yet he knew the disaster was his own fault. All his fault. He was the leader, inadequate as he might be. He'd sought the job, the people had given it to him, and he had failed. He'd known that Winder was weak, that Armstrong sulked in his tent like an adolescent. He'd been warned that it wasn't going well. Should he have taken command himself? No—not the President's role nor his strength. Forced Barney to take command? No—Barney's self-estimate was wise. But he should have taken hold, made Winder calm himself, flogged Armstrong out into the field whether he liked it or not, summoned officers from every side until he found one capable of command. Or he could have gone much further—dragooned state militia into national service, punished recalcitrant congressmen who trifled with the national economy, kicked open the bankers' vaults, used the President's strong voice to rouse public fury against governors who sat on their hands—

But that would be to destroy democracy in order to save it. It would violate the most basic democratic themes that he himself had helped design, beliefs that went to his core, body and soul. Yet perhaps that was the real measure of failure. General Washington had held the nation together by sheer force of character and conviction when it was much newer and in much greater crisis, and he'd done so without sacrificing democracy. And Madison could stare across the reaches of the future and imagine other times when other Presidents would face great crises, and rise to the occasion without damaging democracy. That, he thought, not just the burned city, not just the staggering effort in the war, but the inability to rise to ultimate challenge, that was the failure . . .

He shook his head. Water sluiced off his hat brim. Enough of that! Self-recrimination was another form of self-indulgence. Of course it was his fault; he was the President. But what now?

The moment he looked ahead, the picture brightened. For parse it all down and what did you have? Since burning these great buildings had no military value to the British, it must have emotional value. It made them feel good. It was spiteful, disdainful, contemptuous. They wanted to punish us. And why?

Wasn't it really for taking our independence these three decades past? For having the effrontery to demand that we be treated as a member in full of the family of nations? What they really wanted was for the American to bend his knee and pull his forelock as the lord of the manor passed. And how would the American respond to that?

Standing in the dark, the rain that even now was quenching the last embers of his destroyed home dripping steadily from his hat, he thought the British had outsmarted themselves. A new determination was in the air, at Chippewa and Lundy's Lane and, he thought, everywhere—and instinct told him this contemptuous abuse would quicken it tenfold. Their capital in flames would pull Americans together as nothing else had done.

He turned, nodded to the men huddled under the trees, and swung onto his horse. They mounted and followed as he rode into the dark night.

★ ★ ★ ★

All the next day men came down the dusty Virginia roads. They carried rifles on their shoulders and blanket rolls slung under their arms, water bottle and little skillet, powder horn and buckskin bullet bag. They walked in long streams in no particular order. When Madison crossed into Maryland on the second day he found even larger crowds, all armed and packing their gear, hats pulled low against the sun, faces dark and angry, their march steady—toward Washington.

They had come to fight.

The outrage in the capital had stirred them at last. Perhaps the war until now had been more an abstraction than a call to arms, but the Capitol and White House in flames was concrete and they put rifles across their shoulders and poured off their farms in spontaneous droves, come down to fight.

"Them bastards still in Washington? I reckon we'll see about that. Just don't believe they can do that to us, not and get away with it."

Madison was riding to join the army at Montgomery Courthouse. He had found Dolley the day before at Wiley's Tavern, shaken but calm. When he told her he would go to the army, she touched his cheek and held him close but didn't answer.

It was late morning and he was near the village of Rockville when an officer of the District of Columbia militia galloped up.

"Captain Tartle, Mr. President! Compliments of General Smith. He's got a dozen runners out looking for you. Sir, the British have gone. Their nerve broke and they ran!"

"They're retreating, you mean?" Madison knew Brigadier General Walter Smith well. He headed District militia and had no command initiative but was a competent observer.

"Tell me about it, Captain."

For Captain Tartle, everything had joined with the seamless simplicity of a fable. Militiamen who had fled to their homes after the battle emerged in small groups on the next day. The flow of men streaming into Washington joined them and sizable bodies grew. On the afternoon of the second day a violent storm broke that made the downpour of the night before mere prelude. Madison himself had been forced to stop and take shelter. The storm spawned tornadic winds that threw down trees, lifted roofs, collapsed walls. More violent than usual, this was still within the normal range of Washington weather, but Tartle said it seemed to dismay the British, who'd actually had men killed by falling buildings and flying debris.

"So they ran," Tartle said. He laughed. "See, they were camped on the Capitol grounds, and they built these big fires like they were scared of the boogerman. I reckon they figured that big storm was God's retribution for the evil they'd done. That's sure how I saw it."

Madison doubted that God was so simplistic or that the British thought so, but he liked the idea nonetheless.

"Anyway, they had these big fires, but after a while we saw there was damned little activity around them, so our scouts snuck up and found their pickets gone. Went on into their camp and they'd cleaned out. Folks living along the Bladensburg road said they'd passed that way, going the same way they came.

"Mr. President, the men are flocking into the city and General Smith is forming 'em into companies as they get there. Way I see it, the British figured they were getting in deep water. They knew the boys were coming in mad as hornets, them burning us out, and they knew they were going to have a real fight." He grinned and spat.

"Not like the Bladensburg Races. Have you heard? That's what the boys are calling that afternoon. Well, believe you me, they've had enough of running to last 'em a lifetime. British could figure that out, too—they'd tipped a hornet's nest, and by God, they scattered like quail flushed in a field."

Madison smiled. Probably Admiral Co'burn and General Ross had simply made a tactical withdrawal when their mission was accomplished. But they were sixty miles from their ships in hostile territory, and he knew that like Captain Tartle, most Americans would interpret their stealthy withdrawal as flight. Slipped off in the dark of the night, by God. Ran like rabbits when they figured retribution was at hand. Exactly the attitude he wanted.

★ ★ ★ ★

"Sir! Sir! Mr. President, sir!"

It was Tartle again. Orange hair stuck up in tufts and his face was freckled. He looked agitated.

"Sir, General Smith sent us. Major McKenny, he's looking for you, too, he'll be along any second—sir, in the militia camps, there's hell to pay, begging your pardon for my language, sir—"

Another disaster, then. Madison and Ned had been sitting their horses staring at the ruins of the Capitol, the walls stark and scorched, the graceful dome collapsed into ashes that now lifted and swirled in the slight breeze.

"Yes, Captain," Madison said. He saw the man was younger than he had supposed.

"The Secretary of War come to the militia camp and the boys like to blew up. Mr. Carroll—you know Mr. Carroll?"

Madison nodded. There hadn't yet been time to seek Charles Carroll out to thank him for the help he'd given Dolley.

"Well, Mr. Armstrong stuck out his hand, to shake, don't you see, and Mr. Carroll wouldn't take his hand, and he told Mr. Armstrong right to his face that he was a God damned low-life scoundrel, he ought to be ashamed of himself, he wasn't no more military man than a dog scratching his ass on the grass." Tartle stopped, suddenly abashed, and then turned bright red. Lamely, he added, "Well, I'm only telling you what he said, I ain't talking that way my ownself."

"I understand, Captain. Is that your report?"

"Oh, no, sir—General Smith told Mr. Armstrong, he said every officer in this army would tear off his epaulets if the Secretary of War was to have anything to do with them. But, sir, the General said to tell you this ain't no mutiny—we'll all serve happily under any other cabinet officer."

"Captain Tartle, please tell General Smith that the contingency of Mr. Armstrong attempting to command troops will not arise again."

Full of sudden resolve, he lifted his big bay gelding into a lope, Ned following, hurrying toward Armstrong's quarters on F Street where the Secretary, wounded by the encounter, probably would retreat. And sure enough, Armstrong turned the far corner and they met on horseback at the boardinghouse door.

The Secretary looked pale and drawn, only his bulbous nose a blotchy red, his gray side whiskers fluttering in agitation.

"Sir," he cried, "the troops are in mutiny." His voice was low and breathless. "I have been insulted in the gravest manner. For myself I don't care, I hold myself above petty squabbles, but to insult me as a cabinet officer insults the entire administration—"

Madison could barely contain himself. How he did detest this pompous man! "There is huge dissatisfaction with both of us," he said, "with you and with me, but most of all with you. The destruction of Washington is laid at your door."

"Yes, how utterly outrageous—inspired by intrigue, sir, and founded on falsehoods!"

"I rather think it's with good cause."

"Cause! Why, sir, I have not failed in a single task enjoined upon me. Not one!" Sly as a mouse over cheese, his little eyes peered from his fleshy face, bluffing to the end.

Madison should have done this long ago. Repugnance for the man's insubordination, the contempt he'd shown, the actual desire for the administration to fail that his own chances of succeeding Madison in office might be enhanced, had slowly grown into utter outrage. Over and over, Armstrong had said the British wouldn't come and defense was unnecessary. He'd sat on his hands and sulked and taken malicious pleasure in the administration's humiliations. And then in the desperate moments before the battle, he had had the cool effrontery to predict failure, the very failure that grew from his own inattention to duty. In that shocked instant, without even coming to clear decision, Madison had known that the man was finished. And now the mountebank's air of injured innocence lifted him to fury.

"Your role, sir, was not to follow but to lead!"

The bay pricked up his ears, catching the tension between the men, and began to dance. The nondescript livery animal Armstrong was riding responded equally, turning this way and that, hoofs clattering on cobblestones. Madison rode the bay easily, erect in the saddle, shifting his weight and enjoying the beast's quick, alarmed movements as counterpoint to his own tension. But Armstrong, much the poorer horseman, obviously was discomfited. He reined the fractious horse angrily, glancing apprehensively at the ground. Mean as it might be, Madison felt an undeniable joy in watching the hapless Secretary, usually so arrogant, flummoxed by a livery animal. He reined the bay at the other horse, making the hapless beast jump away as his rider clutched his saddle.

"Mr. Armstrong," he cried, "never once did you propose or suggest a single precaution, a single arangement to secure the safety of the capital city of the United States and its government. Everything done in that respect—everything!—was done by myself. You, sir, are a disgrace!"

"Mr. President—"

"Be silent, sir! Above all I wanted harmony in my cabinet. I wanted the country to be spared the dismay of seeing disorder in the national government. That and that alone has kept you in office despite countless acts of insubordination and shameful indignities worked by you upon your government."

Armstrong looked ready to weep. "I have tried—" His voice broke off in a groan.

"I want you out of my sight, sir, out of this city, out of this government!" Madison cried. "Begone, sir!"

To the core of his being, this crashing denunciation so richly deserved and delivered in the hearing of a half-dozen bystanders felt wonderful. Armstrong left at dawn the next day. In Baltimore he drafted his resignation and newspapers that hated the administration took his part. But Armstrong and his partisans had been reduced to the force of popguns.

Dolley laughed when he told her. "Something to cheer about, at last!"

Monroe willingly took over the War Department while remaining as Secretary of State. Monroe was hardly perfect, of course, but then, who was? By now, Madison had the full story of his disastrous shift of the lines at Bladensburg but he ignored it. He needed Monroe. They were friends— they had had their differences, yes, but they were mature men and they had

put them aside. He trusted Monroe, and the man was vastly experienced—
he'd been governor of Virginia, had served in Washington's administration,
had been Jefferson's ambassador to France where he'd collaborated with
Robert Livingston in negotiating the Louisiana Purchase. He understood
the issues.

Yes, he did fancy himself a military man when he had no military talent,
and he was painfully ambitious, seeking military glory to assure his succession
to an office that Madison couldn't wait to vacate. But his loyalty was
unlimited, his efforts to help unceasing, his advice uniformly good, his
self-control strong, his most self-serving actions never vicious, his excesses
growing most often from excess zeal—in the face of such virtues, Madison
could forgive the urgency of his ambition. And he would see to it that
Monroe played general no more.

★ ★ ★ ★

Dolley insisted on going to the mansion.

"Just us, Jimmy. I don't want anyone else around. We'll take the dray—
you drive."

They were at the Octagon, Colonel Tayloe's fine house which Louis
Sérurier, the French ambassador, had offered to vacate in their favor. Madison
had arranged for the Senate to meet in the Post Office, the House in the
Patent Office, and his government was coming together. The cabinet would
meet that afternoon. Dolley's Philadelphia carriage was in the Octagon's
barn, but this was not the moment for display. They rode in the Ambassador's
utility cart, appropriate for the day.

At the mansion's gate he clipped the horse to a gate picket and handed
Dolley down. They walked together up the gravel driveway and stopped,
neither speaking. She folded her arms and stared, her face set. The sandstone
walls alone still stood, looking gaunt and forlorn. Window frames were
burnt out, the outer walls flame-streaked above. He could see sky through
the naked window holes. The roof was gone and the flooring, here and there
a charred corner joist remaining. Masonry interior walls still stood, but the
shape of rooms had vanished.

The woodwork, the paneling and wainscoting, the furniture, the portraits
of prominent Americans, the Madisons' clothes, his books, his papers, his
big desk with its comfortable, familiar chair and its inkstand with freshly
cut quills in a bowl and the little knife he used to sharpen them, all the
familiar accoutrements of living and of the work that gave him such pleasure,
everything was gone, vanished in smoke and flame, reduced to ash.

And so were her years of labor, the focused concentration she and Mr.
Latrobe had given countless details, the faux marble facings, the delicate
shadings of blue and gray worked into creamy painted walls, the Greek
motif chairs with eagle and shield, each with its crimson cushion to match
the curtains that in the end she'd had to leave, the kneehole desk where she

planned her Wednesday Drawing Rooms, the magnificent oval room in which they were held, all of it gone.

She didn't speak. He stole a glance; her eyes were dry. They were past rage by now.

"We'll rebuild it, you know," he said. "They'll try to move the capital, back to Philadelphia or New York, but they won't get away with it. We'll rebuild right here." He waved an inclusive hand at the blackened walls. "You'll see—it'll be like new."

"We'll all be like new," she said. "The whole country, don't you think?"

"I do, actually."

"We'll be a great nation. We weren't before, with all our divisions, our uncertainties—I mean, we've been wondering about ourselves."

"Wondering if we wanted to be a nation, a single nation, even a free nation—that's what you mean?"

"Yes, trying to figure things out. And I think we'll come out of this knowing our way. I think all will be different."

"The second revolution to prove the first?"

"It's the hard knocks that turn youngsters into mature men and women," she said. And she smiled.

★　★　★　★

On a sunny afternoon a horseman galloped through the streets of Washington.

"Great news! Great news! Baltimore done whipped the British! Broke their attack, drove 'em off, sent 'em back to their ships with their tails tucked! Great news! Great news!"

Madison was in the Octagon gazebo having tea with Dolley and Ned Coles after a long day at his desk scanning reports from around the country. In the three weeks since Washington was attacked, the growing threat to Baltimore had lain like a weight against his mind. How empty would be the sense of American renewal if the enemy took over the nation's third largest city, its mid-Atlantic commercial center.

The droves of men pouring into Washington had hurried on to Baltimore, where Sam Smith welcomed them. The retiring senator cum general refused any communication with Madison, so fierce was his hatred, but the President made sure every armed man available was with him. Baltimore had more time to get ready, but its danger was greater, too, facing as it did both an enemy army and an enemy fleet that could sail into its harbor.

And now, glorious news shouted by a rider galloping past on a lathered horse. Madison ran to the iron fence and gripped its pickets, hearing still the horseman's distant cry.

His heart full of thanksgiving, he turned to Dolley who had followed him to the fence and threw his arms around her.

Washington was almost normal again, residents returned to the bustle of daily life. Work crews were clearing the rubble at the President's House and the Capitol. Congress had met in its impromptu quarters, the cabinet was sitting regularly if not comfortably, and government was functioning. French John had returned with the servants; Joseph was missing somehow, but doubtless would appear eventually at Montpelier.

The details of Baltimore soon were in Madison's hand. Royal Navy ships had bombarded Fort McHenry, which was placed to guard the harbor. Until they reduced the fort they couldn't pass, and in the test, their guns didn't dent the stone bulwarks. So the Royal Navy pulled back and left the attack to the army.

The troops had landed at a distance to march toward the city. In the first skirmish a sharpshooter braced a long rifle against a tree and blew General Ross off his horse. The General bled to death in fifteen minutes. The army, perhaps unsettled, marched on to find vast rows of fortifications it would have to storm one by one, deep trenches with firing platforms, each trench linked to the one behind so that defenders could fall back line by line while making attackers pay a fearsome price. American cannon were placed in angled redoubts, ready to rake the field in cross fire.

The redcoat soldiers made one savage lunge—doubtless to see if the militia would fly as they'd seen the militia do at Bladensburg—and these militiamen rocked them back with heavy losses. Military prudence reared its head and the British hesitated. Madison saw instantly that Fort McHenry was the key to it all, for stopping the navy meant the British army faced heavy artillery fire with none of its own. British bugles sounded and the redcoats turned and marched away to the wild cheers of the Americans.

Now he couldn't wait to hear from Frank Key. He had sent Frank to try to negotiate the release of poor old Doctor Beanes of Upper Marlboro, whom Admiral Co'burn had made a prisoner on an apparent whim. Frank must have been there, must have seen the whole thing.

But meanwhile, celebrate good old Sam Smith! Thank goodness he was leaving the Senate, for he heaped calumny on Madison at every opportunity, and couldn't be a fiercer, meaner, more troublesome, or more damaging enemy, but bother that—he had saved Baltimore! While Winder dithered and Armstrong sulked, Smith had sent Ross home in a pickle barrel and rubbed Co'burn's nose in failure. The humiliation of the capital in flames still stood, but Sam Smith had stamped paid on some of the debt—and Madison had an idea more repayment was in the offing.

★ ★ ★ ★

He felt a boundless confidence that was quite different from anything he'd felt before. Scott's success on the Niagara, Washington recovered if not restored, Baltimore saved—all these told him the very texture of the war was changing. There was a cheerfulness on the street that he hadn't seen in years, and talk of moving the capital back to Philadelphia or New York died even as it was born.

The weather cooperated. A fresh, dry breeze from the north swept the city, leaving a crystal sky that seemed to reflect the new attitude as well as making it clear why folks came to love this confluence of river and valley and wild weather shifts on which General Washington had sited the capital.

Still, he knew the war was entering its most serious phase. Harsh new threats loomed. In the North ten thousand veteran British troops newly arrived from Spain were massing on the Canadian border under Sir George Prevost, governor general of Canada, a mere twenty miles from Plattsburgh, New York, on Lake Champlain.

The *Democratic-Republican* ran a strong story from Plattsburgh over Mr. McQuirk's signature. That told Madison why Sally had hurried north and Dolley said what a pity—better that a romantic interest should have drawn her. Madison was glad she'd gone; he found more clarity in the article than in either army or navy reports. What was painfully clear was that everything depended on Commodore Macdonough's fleet stopping a British fleet of about the same size.

And in the South, the danger was at least as great—with a new development that could shake the country to its foundations. As usual, Major General Jackson, now of the regular army commanding all southern forces, knew just what he wanted to do. He wanted to kick over the diplomatic applecart. The man apparently possessed not an ounce of self-doubt, a quality that Madison was ruefully aware was central to his own nature.

"Jim," he said to Monroe, "write Jackson and tell him no. We can't do it. Yes, the offense is great, quite outrageous, and yes, it certainly calls for remonstrances which we'll certainly make, but we are a responsible nation and there are channels, et cetera, et cetera. You know the sort of thing— lay it on pretty heavily."

"Very well, sir," Monroe said. That had been his recommendation, and he always glowed when his advice was taken.

"But, Jim," Madison said, "you're a busy man. Washington's in turmoil and you're running both State and the War Department. You have lots to do. So take your time. Hold up your reply for two or three months. Or more."

Monroe stared. "Are you saying . . . ?"

"General Jackson is interestingly volatile, you know. And decisive. Yes, give him some rope."

★ ★ ★ ★

"It was an unbelievable sight," Frank Key said, "our hearts in our mouths all night long, waiting for the dawn . . . sublime, magnificent, if I may say so, almost holy—"

Madison cleared his throat. These poets did wax on. He was in the Octagon drawing room with Dolley and Monroe and Ned Coles, gathered to hear Frank's description of the attack on Baltimore. But Madison wanted to know what happened.

"They released Doctor Beanes, did they?" he asked. Might as well get him started at the start.

Frank said he found the British willing enough to free the old man but by the time he found Beanes on a supply ship being used to hold prisoners the attack was ready to start and they were told they couldn't go until it was over. So they stood by the rail and watched; Beanes finally went to sleep, but Frank watched the night through.

"They were several miles from Fort McHenry—I was quite surprised. I asked an obliging young officer why so far, and he said the Americans had sunk twenty-odd vessels in the channel. When he pointed them out, I could see the masts sticking out of the water. Apparently that made it impossible or at least dangerous for their ships to get much closer."

He said the death of General Ross appeared to shake the British officers badly.

"Very poor sportsmanship, shooting at officers, they were saying, bad American habit, not cricket at all. All things considered, I decided to keep my mouth shut."

At any rate, efforts to force a passage stopped after this news arrived. Madison took it that the navy doubted the army's commitment without its fighting general.

"So you could see Fort McHenry in the distance," Frank said, "with its powerful stone bulwarks, and there was this huge flag flying, the old one with fifteen stars, rolling and snapping on the breeze, defiant and gorgeous. Warmed my heart to see it. And then I saw a flash from the walls and in a minute I heard a thump, and realized the fort was opening fire on the ships. Made me so proud, even if I was standing on one of the targets.

"It was getting dark by then, and soon I saw the American fire couldn't reach this far. But the crescendo of noise when the ships opened was beyond all experience—I thought it like a descent into hell. And my heart sank, because I saw immediately that nothing could stand against it. Cannon firing on every side, flashes of light, the smoke swirling, those great rockets that soared through the sky as if ridden by Satan's imps—oh, Lord, it was awful!"

"But what a sight it must have been," Dolley said.

"It was, madam, it was. The rocket's red glare, the bombs bursting in air—forgive me, I'm quoting myself. One of the prisoner lads in the hold—they couldn't see—kept calling up to me, asking was the flag still there? Well, it was. The gallant fort was holding. Its own guns were silent, but by the flickering light I could see the flag still gleaming. But then about one in the morning the ships' firing stopped. I was sure it meant the fort had fallen and my heart sank, but in dawn's light, there was the flag. What a joyous vision."

Dolley waggled a finger at him. "What did you mean, quoting yourself? You wrote about it, didn't you?"

"Couldn't help myself, madam. Scribbled some lines on the back of an envelope and fleshed it out the next day. Well received, too—the Baltimore *American* printed it and it's been set to music—to an old drinking song, 'Anacreon in Heaven.'"

"Anacreon?" Ned Coles said.

"Greek lyric poet, half a millennium B.C.—celebrated wine and love and must have been a rousing fellow. Probably he livened heaven when he arrived."

"Well," Dolley said, "you must give it to us."

Madison saw Frank's uneasy glance. "I wouldn't want to weary the President," the poet said.

"Oh, Jimmy loves your work," Dolley said.

"Go ahead, Frank," Madison said. He didn't like being singled out as insensitive to the arts. "A verse, perhaps." Maybe Frank would take the hint and not drone on forever.

Frank's voice altered alarmingly when he recited his poetry, deepened, became portentous. Still, it was effective.

"I call it 'Defense of Fort McHenry,'" he said.

> *"O! say can you see, by the dawn's early light*
> *What so proudly we hail'd at the twilight's last gleaming,*
> *Whose broad stripes and bright stars through the perilous*
>   *fight,*
> *O'er the ramparts we watch'd, were so gallantly streaming?*
>   *And the rockets' red glare, the bombs bursting in air,*
>   *Gave proof through the night that our flag was still*
>   *there—*
>   *O! say, does that star-spangled banner yet wave*
>   *O'er the land of the free, and the home of the brave?"*

Tears filled Madison's eyes. Amazed by his own visceral response, he stood to join the applause.

24

★ ★ ★ ★ The schooner ran down Mobile Bay under the August sun. Andrew Jackson stood in the bow, hat pulled low to his eyes against the glare, alert as a gundog on point. Any week now, any day, the British army making up in Jamaica and the fleet gathering there would strike across the Gulf of Mexico for that plum of plums, New Orleans. The city was the key to everything. It was the choke point on the Mississippi, and the river was the jugular of the American West, on which turned the dream of a continental nation. But General Jackson was on his way, and by God, they'd have the city over his dead body.

And it was here, in this strange sunshot land, all water and sand and shells and crusted salt, wind off the Gulf roaring in his ears, shark heads strung along wharves for decoration, crushed shell used for gravel on walks, that the defense of the West would begin.

He heard yells behind him and turned to see Johnny Reid and Jack Gordon and the others landing a big snapper. The ship's cook took the fish, promising a meal in an hour, and the men joined the General in the bow.

The shallow-draft schooner was an old fisherman, Spanish built, wood that had never known paint weathered to a satiny gray, muddy canvas every color but white. The sun burned through his hat and he stepped into the shadow of the sails as she went in broad reaches over ruffled water that bled from lime to blue to lime. Off the port beam an explosion tore the surface: mullet fleeing from barracuda. A brown pelican crossed the bow, folded its wings, and plunged a full fifty feet into the sea to emerge with fish in its beak and water draining in long plumes. Enraged gulls screamed as it continued its stately course.

Mobile Bay with its fly-specked village and handful of dories offered a natural attack route, for New Orleans was not necessarily a simple nut to crack. A good fort at the mouth of the Mississippi blocked attack directly from the sea, and dense cypress swamps all around made land approach difficult. But the enemy could sail into Mobile Bay and march overland to the Mississippi, and then he could float down with ease to take the city from the north.

But that wasn't the only danger. Pensacola would do as well. And there Spain's perfidy was staring him in the face.

"Now, General," Jack Gordon said, "this don't look no different than Pensacola Bay—'cept there's British warships riding at anchor there." Jack was a good man; he'd stood with the General when it counted at Fort Strother, and now headed the scouting company. A compact fellow, face

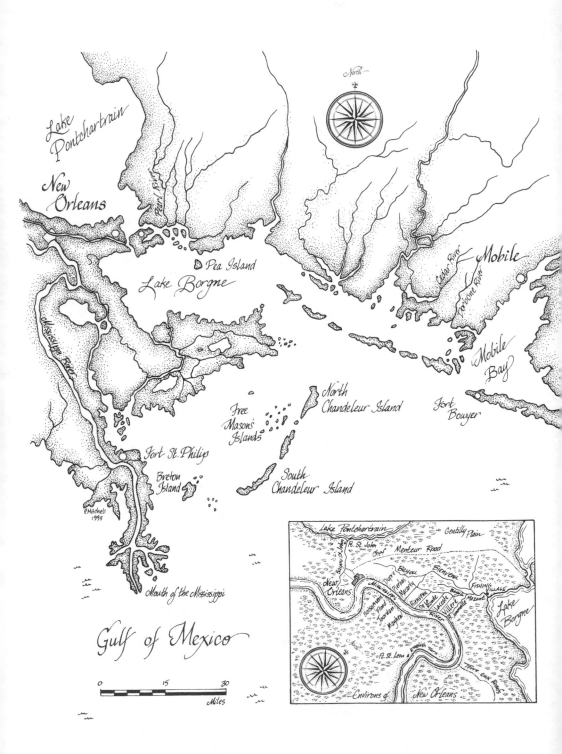

Lake
Pontchartrain

New
Orleans

Pearl River

Pea Island

Lake Borgne

Mississippi River

North

Cedar River

Mobile

Fowl River

Mobile
Bay

Free
Mason's
Islands

North
Chandeleur Island

Fort
Bowyer

Fort St. Philip

Breton
Island

South
Chandeleur Island

PMitchell
1995

Mouth of the Mississippi

Gulf of Mexico

0   15   30
Miles

Lake Pontchartrain   Gentilly Plain

Ft. St. John
Chef   Menteur Road

Bayou St. John

Bienvenu

New
Orleans

Dumb Bayou

Portius McArty

FISHING
VILLAGE

Mississippi

Bienvenu

Ox Bend

Villere

Jugeac
Mazant

Bienvenu

Lacoste

Jordan

Macarty

Bienvenu

Mayhew

English Turn

Ft. St. Leon

Lake
Borgne

Terre aux Boeufs

Environs of   New Orleans

lined by sun and wind, carroty hair gone thin, he usually talked around a cigar clamped in stained teeth.

And he well understood Spain's knife-in-the-back. He'd ridden over to Pensacola on a quiet scout dressed as a local settler, ridden right in and taken his look-see. He'd been waiting when Jackson reached Mobile with the troops.

"Four warships, big as you please, and a hundred marines under a loudmouthed Irish major. Says he's just the vanguard, says they'll take Mobile from Pensacola, land that army of theirs, and march over to Baton Rouge like taking a summer stroll."

Well, either bay could handle a fleet, no doubt about that. And it didn't amaze Jackson that the British would so violate Spanish neutrality. Spain had been feeding British arms to the Creeks all along. What we ought to do was violate its neutrality our ownselves, march in there, and throw the bastards out—British and Spanish both, for that matter. And that was just what Jackson had proposed in a letter to the War Department. And gotten no answer. Well, he could only wait so long—if the administration felt he'd tossed it a hot potato, they'd better start juggling.

The village of Mobile faded from view with its hundred odd houses of mud and sticks and its surly folks who'd been American citizens for barely a year. After some thirty miles, a ribbon of white dead ahead emerged as a low barrier island across the mouth of the bay.

Jack gestured off the starboard bow. "See yonder to the right, General? The opening to the sea ain't barely a mile wide, but even that'll fool you, too. Four to six feet, most of it, a ship of any size'll go aground in a minute. There's just one deep channel the tide keeps plowed out, and it runs right around the tip of the island. And Fort Bowyer, it sits on the end like a fly taking a rest on your pecker, and any ship comes along would be looking up its gun muzzles. A few repairs, and it'll give the Royal Navy plenty to think about, all right."

Johnny Reid leaned on the rail, staring wide-eyed at the low island now off the beam as they ran toward its end. He'd removed his hat and the wind was making his light brown hair fly so that he looked even more boyish than usual. "What remarkable terrain," he said. "Not a bit like the Atlantic coast. All this sun and sand and shallow bays and this finger of an island defying the surf—as if land gives way to sea with great reluctance . . ."

Gordon took the cigar from his mouth and spat over the side.

"Shit, Johnny, it's just a damned sandbar flung up by the wave action. Like you see forming and dissolving in the Mississippi all the time, only this one's permanent. You ought to be a poet, thinking them fancy thoughts."

Reid bristled; he saw himself as a hardened soldier, and in Jackson's view, he'd proved his claim beyond question the day he sat his horse without a tremor when slow matches were glowing over cannon set to blow them both to kingdom come. But he was a thinker, too, and he'd read the classics and had the kind of polish the great houses of Virginia gave one—that kind of life seemed to buff a man right up to a glow—and all told, the result tickled earthy fellows like Jack Gordon.

This ribbon of sand they ran along was one of a chain of barrier islands that sheltered most of the Gulf coast. To the west the chain ran a hundred sea miles through the Mississippi Sound, past Pascagoula and Pass Christian and on to Lake Borgne and Lake Pontchartrain, a pair of brackish sea lakes, half lake and half bay, that lay within a dozen marshy miles of the city.

To the east the island chain ran fifty miles to the pass that opened into Pensacola Bay. It had been a great naval center in the days when Spain's empire yielded streams of gold. Pensacola's fine anchorage and ample wharves under the guns of Fort Barrancas stood not only for past glories but also for present potential.

As the schooner neared the end of the island, Jackson saw a massive structure of upright logs. Crumbling into sand-scoured decay, it had a lonely, desolate look.

The anchor chain rattled out and the sails went slack. A jolly boat swung over the side and Jackson went down a rope ladder. The boat lurched as Gordon boarded and Jackson steadied him. The scout was a horseman, clumsy in boats. Reid, who'd grown up around small craft, dropped neatly into the bow with a superior grin for Gordon.

"Up your ass, young'un," the scout said, but he smiled.

The two majors, Howell Tatum and Bill Lawrence, came on a second boat. Tatum was the army's chief engineer, a soft-spoken man whose round spectacles gave him an owlish look. Jackson had found his opinions sound, if never daring and always diffidently delivered. Lawrence commanded artillerymen. Gunnery was an American strength, proved in the Revolution, and Jackson was counting on his guns in this second revolution.

Tatum and Lawrence approached the fort frowning, and no wonder. It looked like hell—stood a couple hundred feet in each direction, the seaward side a semicircle with guns, the rear a diamond-shaped bastion against overland attack. Its log walls sagged and rippled. Here and there some of the pickets had fallen, to lie atop one another like straws.

Gates were carelessly ajar. The sun was low now, the shadows long, and the only sound was the wind and the gulls. The walls consisted of a double row of upright logs with sand filling the space between. Inside the fort he found more pickets down, the sand spilled out. Cannon of green-coated bronze and rusty iron pointed helter-skelter at ground and sky from sagging gun platforms. The platforms quivered when he climbed them.

Still, it stood on a rare patch of clay hardpan, so the pilings could be dug out and reset. The guns could be cleaned, their carriages rebuilt, their platforms squared.

He walked around the tip of the island. The sun lay on the horizon in a red glow across the channel that enemy ships would have to use. Wet sand was firm underfoot and littered with countless shells, round and pointed and conical, some with bloodred lips, some rosy, some of pedestrian gray shading into blue. Terns ran chattering before him and tiny gray crabs popped into view with each spill of surf and dug back into the sand. He looked up. From here the fort was menacing, its faults scarcely evident in the warm orange light. Repaired, it could challenge any ship in the world.

Gordon had a fire going and Johnny was in the surf dragging a net full of fish ashore with a couple of crewmen from the schooner. Only Tatum and Lawrence, just leaving the fort, looked discouraged.

"You have your work cut out for you, gentlemen," Jackson said. "I want this fort ready to fight in two weeks."

"Two weeks!" Tatum's pale eyes blinked rapidly behind his glasses. "Sorry, sir—that's impossible."

"Royal Navy vessels are in our waters. I expect they'll try us before long, and I intend to be ready for them."

"But two weeks?" Tatum cried. "*Damn*, General!"

Jackson turned to Lawrence. "How many men to fight this place with all guns ready?"

"Hundred sixty, I'd say."

"You'll have 'em. Refurbish the guns while you rebuild the walls. Fix it, then fight it, the latter to inspire the former."

"General," Tatum said, "I must say—"

Jackson raised a hand. "Any fool can tell me what can't be done, Major. I want you to figure out how to do it."

"Easy enough to say, but—"

"Major Tatum!" Both men came to attention. "This fort will be ready in two weeks, and if you and Major Lawrence can't do it, by God, I'll see to it myself."

Lawrence nodded. "We'll get it done, General."

Jackson glanced at Tatum, whose expression was unreadable. "Better start improvising, Major."

"Yes, sir. I was just thinking that myself."

"We'll be fine, gentlemen. I'm counting on it."

★ ★ ★ ★

The fish, poached in wet seaweed, was delicious, the flaky meat easy on his tortured stomach. He was dangerously thin and was convinced the diarrhea he'd had since the Creek campaign had ruined his digestion permanently. Gordon produced a bottle of Tennessee corn, the very thought of which hurt Jackson's stomach. The bottle made a couple of rounds.

He saw the scout studying him in a speculative way, his face reddening, and knew he was getting up his nerve to say something.

"Now, I may be talking out of turn, but you know what I think we ought to do? Go over to Pensacola and take the damned place and be done with it. Hoist the stars and stripes, God damn it, and tell the world it's ours and that's that."

Jackson made no answer. It was precisely what he himself had urged on Washington.

"Hell, Jack," Reid said, "we can't do that."

"Don't see why not," Gordon said, glowering. Then he sighed. "That Irish bastard got under my skin, tell the truth."

Jackson grinned. "Tell 'em about Major Nicolls," he said.

"Well, now, this sumbitch, he's got about the loudest mouth in North America. I told him I might join him since the U.S. government never did nothing for me, and he fell all over himself promising this and that. Said if I got some more settlers, he'd make me a commander. Said he was recruiting Indians for light cavalry and settlers for guides, and when they had Mobile and New Orleans, believe you me, he'd make it all worth my while."

He grinned, good humor restored. "And when I told him I heard General Jackson was coming and that might slow him down, he laughed. Big braying laugh, you could hear him all over town. Said they'd slap the Americans aside like dust from their hands."

There was a burst of laughter at that. "Still," Reid said, "Spain is a sovereign country." He understood diplomatic realities as Gordon never would. "And the British are there by invitation. If we went in, it would be by force."

"Sovereign?" Gordon said. "They knuckled right under to Nicolls. Why, the British flag flies over Fort Barrancas side by side with the Spanish. Hell, Johnny, them dons are lucky their visitors even let 'em stay. I tell you, we'd better grab it before the whole British army gets there."

He took another nip. "Spain's so poor it can't hardly feed its people, you know. Hungry Spaniards aren't going to die for the cause, believe you me."

"Sure," Reid said. "We'd win in Pensacola, but we'd lose all over the rest of the world."

"Horseshit, Johnny," Gordon said. "Right's on our side, damn it all."

He raised a finger and rattled off all of Tennessee's arguments for seizing Florida. It was a haven for Indians who attacked settlers. It welcomed America's enemies. It was a natural invasion route. The West could never grow to its full potential with Florida in enemy hands. All in all, the hostile nation crouched on its southern flank was an arrow aimed at the West's heart.

"Anyway," Gordon cried, whiskey and anger reddening his face, "it's so God damned *arrogant*—why, it ain't even theirs. It's ours. Part of the Louisiana Purchase, Florida and Texas, too. Sure, Spain was the original settler, but it swapped the territory off to France long ago. And we bought it fair and square and God damn it, it's ours!"

"That's true enough," Reid said, "but the French didn't get around to occupying Florida or Texas, and the Spanish never actually gave either one up—you know they still run Texas out of Mexico City, Jack. So the world doesn't know who owns what, but it knows Spain occupies that territory."

"Well, they occupied West Florida, too, but that didn't stop us from taking it. Mobile wasn't always ours, you know."

Jackson wouldn't join this fireside chatter, but this was just the point he'd made to the administration. Florida had once reached clear to the Mississippi River. East Florida and West Florida, all Spanish. In 1810 American settlers at Baton Rouge seized the western end and named it Orleans Territory. Madison welcomed it into the Union. When Louisiana became a state in 1812, Orleans Territory formed the toe of its boot shape. In 1813 American troops under that idiot Wilkinson took the rest of West Florida as far as Mobile but stopped short of Pensacola, which was considered East Florida.

He sighed. Both Johnny and Jack were right, that was the truth of it. The Spanish empire was dying—revolution already had started in Mexico, Cartagena had declared itself free, and other places were boiling.

He didn't have a moment's doubt that someday Florida would be ours, but someone still would have to make that happen. The Spanish were always hostile, saying the Louisiana Purchase cheated them when the truth was they were scared of the growing strength of the young United States. American adventurers trying to seize chunks of their territory to form independent kingdoms in Texas and Central America didn't help, either. These attacks were the same as a pirate like Jean Lafitte attacking ships— but given the allure of a mortally weakened Spanish empire, they were hard to stop.

Yet Johnny was right, too. He hadn't named the sources for his certainty that a diplomatic explosion would follow a move on Florida, but Jackson knew his father was close to Monroe and saw Madison and Jefferson frequently. They were all figures in Johnny's world.

It was the conundrum that Jackson had turned over in his mind again and again. Of course the rule of law must hold among nations or banditry and war would follow. And then, suppose war with Spain followed—could we afford that, however weak Spain might be, when we already had our hands full? And would we stand before the world as an outlaw nation that took what it wanted at gunpoint? A British incursion in Florida as part of its war with America actually would justify our seizing the place, but that raised yet another point: could Jackson do it without authority, as an individual?

"You know something, Johnny?" Jack said. "You think big, see things in a big frame and all, but I think real. Maybe you're right, but in the end, it don't matter. Pensacola is a danger we can't tolerate much longer. In the end, mark my words, we'll have Florida, whatever it takes."

The fire was burning down. Jackson stood up, and soon the schooner was running wing-and-wing up the bay on a path of brilliant moonlight. He rocked with the vessel's motion, the conversation still vivid in his mind. A name everyone was too polite to mention in his presence had hovered over it like a buzzard over dead meat. Aaron Burr. How attractive the man had seemed back in 1806 when he came to Tennessee—smooth and gracious, a former Vice President of the United States, an official voice of Washington inviting Jackson into his vague plan. Whatever it was. The way Jackson heard it, they would take over Florida and Texas, doing just what Tennessee wanted.

Why shouldn't he pitch in? Seizing Florida was long overdue—it appeared that Washington had awakened to reality at last, and he figured better late than never. So let's go!

He liked Burr and that the man had killed Alexander Hamilton in a duel wasn't at all disturbing—dueling was part of the gentleman's code. Burr was charming, too, it was no wonder that women warmed to him. There was a story around that Burr had introduced Dolley Madison to her husband. If it was true, he'd bet a bale of cotton that Burr had made a run at the lady himself before bringing little Jimmy into the picture.

So he was flattered to be taken into what seemed a national enterprise. Willingly he lined up the Nashville gentry, put out a call for volunteers, ordered boats to run them downriver—

And then one of Burr's people said something about when they took over New Orleans. New Orleans? Wait a God damned minute! We already had New Orleans. Just what the hell was going on?

No sooner had Jackson posted a letter to President Jefferson letting him know that maybe Burr had something of his own in mind, such as separating the Southwest into an empire with himself as emperor, than it all blew up. Burr was arrested and the plot was pinched off. Whatever the plot was . . . Jackson finally decided even Burr himself had no fixed idea. He hadn't realized the extent to which Burr had cooked his own goose in Washington in 1800 when he used a quirk of the law to challenge Jefferson for the presidency when the voters clearly had intended him for the second slot. All the poor bastard had in mind in the West was to shimmy back up on top somehow—and he didn't scruple to use a patriotic Tennessean to his own ends.

Jackson's timely letter to Jefferson cleared him of criminal complicity, if not of Jefferson's hatred. But more important, he'd learned an indelible lesson: international adventures must have the color of law. Nations can declare war, invade, seize territory, and suffer the consequences, but individuals who try the same thing are pirates.

So he waited for the authorization he needed to make the Gulf coast secure. There was only silence from Washington.

★ ★ ★ ★

The Spanish lieutenant was gorgeous as a cockatoo, and his manner radiated insolence. He brought a message from—clicking his heels and looking down his nose—"His Excellency, Don Mateo Gonzales Manrique, governor general of all the Floridas." To a polite note pointing out that harboring a combatant in an ongoing war raised doubts as to the neutrality of Spain and its colony, Señor Gonzales Manrique saw fit to respond with a blast of rodomontade denouncing the United States.

Jackson felt a slash of pain in his gut like a sword thrust. Next time he spoke to the Governor General it might be from the mouth of his cannon. He controlled his expression with an effort.

"You are dismissed," he said. "You will await my reply."

"Am I a prisoner?" Lieutenant Cockatoo was haughty.

"You are a messenger, sir. Messengers await the convenience of superiors. You will be informed when convenience permits."

He was in his room in Mobile's only inn, a clapboard structure on the square just off the waterfront. There was a deal table with chairs, a bunk nailed into a corner, and mouse droppings on the floor. Pain tore at his gut. In a yellowed mirror he glimpsed his face, white and sweating. Carefully he draped himself across the back of a straight chair, the hard wood holding him doubled as a tent pole holds a tent, and let his whole weight bear down on the pain. Tears stood in his eyes. Dear God, how he needed his Rachel now!

The Creek campaign surely had given the coup de grace to his system, capping years of abuse. Drinking whiskey, living on acorns and squirrels in starving time, those boiling rages—now he felt rage in his gut before it stirred in his mind.

Ah, Rachel . . . It wasn't just the food she gave him—he'd been living on gruel for weeks now, milk when he could get it, the fish the other night—what mattered was her soothing presence. He was never fully content unless she was near.

He'd just sent her a message saying her plans to join him must wait: the enemy was too close. Lying across the chair, pain bleeding into the hard wood, he wondered again, why do I ever leave her? But he knew the answer. He had always burned with possibility, and more than ever, he burned with it now.

He'd been born to command, he knew that in his heart, born to defend his country from its enemies. He remembered that major's flashing saber, the shocking pain, the iron resolve taking hold even as he lay shamed in a puddle of urine: he would not submit. His destiny was set that day, inchoate at first, now clearly formed: he must save the opening West and thus save the burgeoning country that he had first defended when he stood up to the enemy. *Clean my boots, boy!* He'd paid a penalty, but by God, he hadn't cleaned the bastard's boots.

He was calmer now, the pain easing. He straightened up slowly with a deep sigh. The impertinence of the Spaniard's reply had touched off that wild part of him again. It burned in him, as intoxicating as hard corn whiskey, he could feel it sweeping him in like a giant whirlpool—and like a whirlpool, it would take him down if he let it.

That was Rachel's great gift. He understood rage now, recognized its onset and the mad temptation it offered, and recognizing, he could refuse it. Ever since that explosive moment, poised in the saddle with a musket over the pommel staring down a thousand angry men and sick afterward, he'd held himself in firm control. Never again would he surrender to himself. That flinty fierceness that had carried him through life he now applied to mastering himself—and doing so, found his power magnified a hundredfold until he felt he was as hard as a Toledo blade and honed to a razor edge.

★　★　★　★

Still no answer from Washington. He saw that none would come. But the government wanted Florida, no question. Nor was there any lack of nerve— Madison had proved himself a gutty little devil. Did they want him to act on his own so they could repudiate him if necessary? Make him the cat's-paw?

The next day the courier sloop brought an urgent message from Major Lawrence. The fort was ready—and four British sails stood offshore in battle formation while a force of marines and Indians prepared a land attack from the rear. He needed reinforcements.

Jackson had come to Mobile with the Fourth Infantry, nucleus of his regulars, hard-handed men who'd been in the army long enough to under-stand soldiering. Lawrence had one hundred sixty with him now, and Jackson put another eighty on the schooner and told its skipper to crowd on all sail. He held three hundred twenty on full alert in Mobile in case the British broke through.

Now he must wait. Tension mantled the village. Men stood at corners talking in low, compressed bursts of Spanish with very little laughter; women lounged in low windows, calling to each other in urgent voices. Jackson saw Lieutenant Cockatoo on the inn's patio, where Mobilians plied him with drinks and talked as earnestly as petitioners.

He took a quick turn around the square with its wooden bandstand in the center where every Sunday the people came out to hear brassy music— unmarried women marching in one direction, single men in the other in that bright Spanish ritual. There were always people here in the shade of the oaks, people who rarely met his eye. They were Spanish, after all; they hadn't asked to be absorbed into the United States the year before, and no doubt they would like to be Spanish again. He had come to rescue them but felt more occupier than rescuer.

The rumble of guns in the distance began about four in the afternoon. The sound froze people where they stood. They were silent, staring in the direction of the sound as if straining to see over the horizon. Jackson stood on the wharves in anguish, wanting desperately to be in the battle. But Lawrence was a skilled regular and would fight well. The General must wait here, ready to deal with the battle's aftermath if it went wrong. That was the penalty of command . . .

Minute by minute the firing increased in intensity until the distant rumble became a roar, thunderous and breathtaking. At sunset it stopped. He took that as a bad sign since he doubted the British would quit that easily. Gordon led a patrol down the bay shore to sound the alarm if enemy sail approached.

As night fell, the glow of a massive fire rose on the south horizon. He thought of those pine pickets in the fort, seeping pitch. Surely the glow would fade—but it didn't. At eleven a thunderous explosion ran up the bay and rattled the town. It was huge: even at this distance it thumped in his chest. It had to be a magazine detonating, and that meant . . .

Lanterns appeared and suddenly the streets were full. Women clustered in the square in groups; men milled about, calling to each other in high, jocular voices. Lieutenant Cockatoo was surrounded, Mobilians shaking his hand and buying him drinks.

Jackson pored over his maps, studying the bay shore, marking ridges and rises that could be defended, timber that would conceal movement. Getting ready.

★ ★ ★ ★

At dawn the schooner returned, the Captain mumbling, his eyes shifting. They'd met adverse winds and were still three miles from the fort when the firing started, so he waited in a handy cove. The glow told him the fort was burning and that told him Lawrence would blow the magazine soon. The explosion came as confirmation, and he hurried back.

"So you didn't actually see it?"

"No, sir, but I figured . . ."

It took all of Jackson's strength not to start his whole army down the bay by ship and by shore. Lieutenant Cockatoo at his patio table raised a glass to the General in mocking salute. Jackson looked through him. If the fort was gone, by God, he would take it back. Land on the island, advance by stages, storm it in the dark—he would not allow such a loss to stand!

He held himself in tight control, fighting the vast temptation to plunge, remembering Rachel's face . . .

Control.

At noon Gordon rode in with Howell Tatum, whom he'd plucked from a courier sloop. The engineer's dusty eyeglasses lay askew on his nose. He smiled, exhausted but cheerful.

"Do you have a report for me, Major?" Jackson's voice was level and calm.

"Yes, sir. We shot the hell out of them. Sank their flagship, crippled another one, two of 'em fled. Their Indians and marines tried to come on our rear but we laid charges of grape among 'em that scotched that plan in a hurry."

"Drove them off, then?" Voice cool, not a hint he'd considered any other possibility.

"Whipped 'em, sir." His eyes were snapping. "Beat the bejabers out of them."

"By God, Major, that's grand!" He felt a wild elation, wanted to throw up his arms, stand, prance, yell. He controlled himself. "Every man there shall be commended. Every man."

Tatum sketched in the battle. The channel was narrow, and two ships had come in: H.M.S. *Hermes,* twenty-two guns, in the lead, followed by H.M.S. *Carron,* twenty guns. Two others stood offshore, waiting their chance. Within bare pistol shot, *Hermes* dropped her hook to hold in the channel and fired a broadside. The American gunners answered—slowly at first as they got the feel of guns they were firing for the first time, and then at ever greater speed until the roar was continuous, a mighty thunder that shook a man's heart.

A ball clipped *Hermes'* cable and she drifted out of control to ground stern to the fort, and for twenty deadly minutes the American gunners raked her fore and aft. Her rigging fell, her guns wouldn't bear, her crew was slaughtered. The Commodore loaded his survivors into longboats, fired the dying ship, and rowed away. The Americans let the longboats go. *Carron* picked them up, then limped off, badly damaged, and what was left of the British fleet took a bearing for Pensacola.

"By nightfall, *Hermes* was a tower of flame," Tatum said. "You could read by it. She burned to the waterline, and about eleven her magazine went—an unbelievable noise."

"That it was," Jackson said. "We heard it here."

Mobile's gaiety had vanished. Women disappeared behind closed shutters, and men stood disconsolately on corners. Jackson shrugged. He couldn't blame them if they wanted to be Spanish, but it was proof more positive than he'd had before that he was surrounded by enemies. And that was important to where he stood and what came next.

Four days later Gordon's company rode in from a long scout with the rest of the equation. Yes, the tattered British ships had gone straight to Pensacola and were there now. The marines and Indians had returned to Pensacola on foot.

In the end, the decision made itself. It scarcely was a decision—what he must do was so evident that no other course was possible. He must have Pensacola. He had deprived the British of their hopes for Mobile, but Pensacola would serve as well for the attack on New Orleans. Their willingness to strike Mobile from Spanish territory meant they wouldn't shrink at making it their base for the march on New Orleans. The people of Mobile would make sure that all he did was relayed to Pensacola, and little that happened there would reach his ears.

It was clear and simple: he could not leave a festering sore open in his rear as he rescued New Orleans, so never mind Spanish sensibility or the world outlook on piracy or the long-term future of Andrew Jackson. If he was the cat's-paw, so be it.

His destiny was set. To save New Orleans was to save the West and thus the nation. What else could matter?

Rachel's lovely face, softened with the gentling touch of age and the deepening of wisdom, filled his mind. He had led her on a wild ride from the beginning, from the moment he settled the issue of her marriage to Robards. But she had never complained and never lost faith in him, for all his excesses. And as he'd paid with pain, so had she with perhaps worse pain.

Now he would plunge again, and if he were branded a pirate and disgraced, she would share his exile. Yet he believed she would be content, for he knew he had given her her due: calmly, steadily, breathing easily, he had examined himself. His action, however the world took it, would be choice, not reaction.

25

PLATTSBURGH, NEW YORK
September, 1814

★ ★ ★ ★ Sally McQuirk was standing on the shore of Plattsburgh Bay with the Saranac River pouring into Lake Champlain at her feet when the fleet came in. She gripped a wooden rail, thrilled despite herself as the big square-rigger, preceded by a stout brig, followed by a schooner and a slender sloop, swept around the massive headland that formed the bay and let go anchors with a rattling clatter.

U.S.S. *Saratoga*, the square-rigger, towered over the mercantile vessels scattered across the bay. She saw men running aloft to dress ship, strings of pennants fluttering brightly in errant winds. A boat started ashore. Presently the ships swung in unison as the wind shifted. The breeze usually was steady on the open lake but it broke into fitful gusts as it flowed over Cumberland Head. Ships struggled for wind on Plattsburgh Bay.

She lost track of time, half-intoxicated by sheer physical joy in the crystal sunshine, the bay a glittering brilliant blue, whitecaps flashing out beyond in the lake proper, air as clean and vivid and bright as a draught of spirits. It made her want to run and dance, throw up her arms, and drink the winy air and laugh and shout . . . even with a British army massed on the Canadian border only seven leagues distant ready to pour down upon them

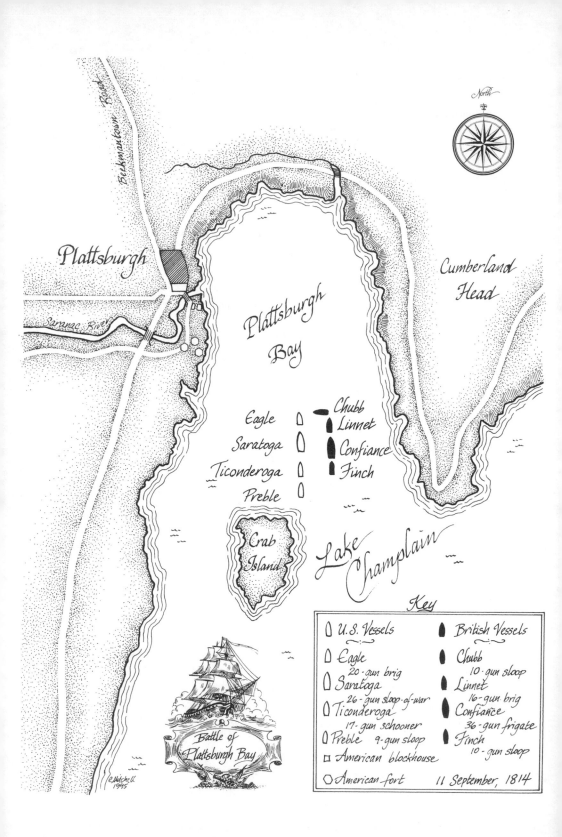

North

Belkmantown Road

Plattsburgh

Saranac River

Plattsburgh
Bay

Cumberland
Head

Eagle · ◗
Saratoga · ◗
Ticonderoga · ◗
Preble · ◗

Chubb
Linnet
Confiance
Finch

Crab
Island

Lake Champlain

Battle of
Plattsburgh Bay

e.Mitchell
1995

Key

◗ U.S. Vessels   ◖ British Vessels

◗ Eagle
  20-gun brig
◗ Saratoga
  26-gun sloop-of-war
◗ Ticonderoga
  17-gun schooner
◗ Preble   9-gun sloop
□ American blockhouse
⬠ American fort

◖ Chubb
  10-gun sloop
◖ Linnet
  16-gun brig
◖ Confiance
  36-gun frigate
◖ Finch
  10-gun sloop

11 September, 1814

in unthinkable numbers . . . even with a leaden lump of fear that seemed to have taken permanent residence deep in her belly.

Fear and beauty—what an ironic mix! She still marveled at the differences she found here in the far north—Canada a healthy day's walk of twenty miles, Montreal a mere hundred, Quebec just beyond. The Richelieu River poured out of the northern end of this long slender finger of a lake and struck the St. Lawrence above Montreal. If she dropped a leaf here it might well flow on to that great artery river, on past Quebec City and into the Gulf of St. Lawrence and on to the North Atlantic where sailors said icebergs stood like white mountains in the sea.

Yet it was fragile beauty; as a butterfly spends its moment of glory and passes, these golden days must die on a tide of cold from the north. Already there was a thread of chill, she needed her shawl in the morning, at night there was a shivering whisper that said snow as clearly as words.

Winter was coming and war was coming and in her mind they became one. Literally, of course, time was short for Sir George Prevost's massive army, too. If it was to invade, it must act ahead of the coming weather. But the connection that stuck in her mind was metaphoric—the implacable harshness of northern winter and of war merged into a lump of dread.

★　★　★　★

There was a wooden bench carved with scrolls on the promenade overlooking the bay, and she sat gratefully. Presently she saw Ham approaching, walking determinedly on his cane, his limp more pronounced today. Stubborn man— it was a point of masculine pride to walk on that wounded leg. He was a naval officer and obviously a good one, and she supposed that and his response to pain went hand in hand.

He bowed. "Sally." His voice was low and melodious. She felt a little tingle of pleasure. Then he said, as casually as if he were discussing the weather, "General Prevost launched his invasion. He's in New York State now, advancing slowly."

She stared at him. It was one thing that Sir George Prevost threatened, that war and winter would come; it was entirely different that the British actually were doing it, actually were on their way. Twenty miles; he could be here by morning!

Ham gestured grandly as if he'd produced the fleet entirely for her pleasure and began explaining the finer points of *Saratoga*'s rigging, but she tugged at his arm.

"How many men?"

"Prevost? Oh, twelve thousand, about."

"Moving slowly, you say?"

"Poking along. He has to wait for the Royal Navy, and we hear they're not ready. We have a while."

And General Izard and the army—most of it, anyway—were gone. She was shaking and she couldn't stop herself. That idiot, John Armstrong. Oh, that idiot!

General Izard had been in command with six thousand troops. Secretary of War Armstrong had ordered him to take four thousand of them and march over to the Great Lakes—three hundred miles from *here*, where the enemy threatened. Izard protested but Armstrong had left no time for a six-week round trip for comment, and on the appointed day, Izard and the army marched. A bare fifteen hundred ready troops remained in Plattsburgh.

"Hey, hey, hey," Ham said. He smiled, looking happy. She saw his uniform was freshly sponged and brushed. Even with the pallor of his wound, he seemed to burn with healthy vigor. She found him hugely reassuring.

"It doesn't matter," he said. "This is the navy's show. Izard couldn't have done much against Prevost anyway, not with six thousand to twice that many of the best men Lord Wellington ever trained against old Boney. In fact, the army's irrelevant." He had a loud barking laugh which she'd found came easily. "Drives the soldiers crazy to hear it, but it's true. Prevost can march clear to New York City, but if he leaves Lake Champlain behind him in our hands, we'll gut his supply lines, land an army behind him, and cut him to pieces. I promise you, if we hold the lake, General Prevost turns around and goes home. And we will hold the lake—Commodore Macdonough will see to that."

She raised a hand to stop him; she knew all that. But now it was different with an army actually advancing on her, not on some academic, strategic, general goal, but on *her*! She felt a little sick, and it struck her that her absence of fear in the Baltimore riots had been a measure of ignorance. Then something Win Scott told her once popped into her mind—that courage wasn't the absence of fear but the control of fear.

She touched Ham's arm. "We'll be all right," she said. "I have total confidence in the United States Navy." She didn't, in fact; she knew the battle to come would be touch and go. The British were building a huge ship at the northern end of the lake, a frigate, mind you—frigates were *big* ships—called *Confiance*. When the ship was ready, she would sail down to engage the American fleet, which the British commander already was boasting *Confiance* could handle by herself. And Ham had told her the old bare knuckle ring adage was analogous—a good big man will beat a good little man. A good big ship . . .

But this wasn't the time for such talk. "Total confidence," she said. He nodded—again she had that comforting feeling that he understood her so well—and began explaining *Saratoga*'s virtues. Soon she was lost in a welter of unfamiliar terms. She smiled and fixed an expression of interest . . .

★ ★ ★ ★

First Lieutenant Horace Hamblin, U.S. Navy, on convalescent leave from duty as U.S.S. *Saratoga*'s executive officer, had come as an answer to a prayer.

A melodramatic answer, but that was all right, for war was melodrama by definition. And she was about to be inundated in war.

He appeared around the time Izard announced his departure and said Mrs. Izard and Miss McQuirk would leave in three days for safety in Albany. Leave? She didn't intend to leave.

She and Betty Izard had come to this crystal paradise by an easy run, Philadelphia and then New York and up the Hudson in one of Mr. Fulton's steamboats to Albany, over the little land bridge to Lake George and on to Lake Champlain and a pleasant voyage north in a passenger sloop. It was clear how easily Sir George Prevost could float down to New York City and split off New England like picking an apple. Geographically, at least.

General Izard was billeted in the Northern Star, a substantial tavern with rooms that passed for a hotel in the village of Plattsburgh, and he arranged a room there for Sally. Lieutenant Hamblin, recovering from a wound and apparently a person of some means, took quarters there a few days later. They met at the last reception General Izard gave.

Ham was slender, about her height, and at first he looked young and rather inconsequential. She noticed the cane, and when he moved she saw a spasm of pain on his face and perspiration stood on his lip. But he wasn't inconsequential; as they talked she saw confidence and authority in his expression. Something about his voice warmed and drew her. His cheeks were blue with closely shaved beard, and black hair curled off the back of a muscular hand and into his sleeve. When he talked to her, the cane was hooked casually over his arm but the muscles in his jaw were tight knots. She suggested they sit but he shook his head, his face suddenly hard. She liked him and felt at ease.

Sally had come a long way for this story and given up a lot, and she didn't intend to leave now. The latest reports said the British definitely were aiming at Washington—poor sick Papa left at the mercy of enemy troops, to say nothing of their invaluable printing presses at risk, let alone what a great story an attack on Washington would have made if she had stayed home. She was desperately afraid the shock might kill her father, but she put the thought aside. She was here and war was coming here, too, and that was that. She wouldn't leave, but since arriving she had made the discovery that some compromise was necessary: she must be with a man to justify her own presence.

She came to this realization reluctantly, disturbed by its air of calculation and especially pained by the cost to her treasured independence. But she couldn't remain alone in a tavern with a hostile army approaching. Some things just weren't done. That it was unthinkable would increase the danger of defying convention because it would suggest a woman who was careless of herself, or one who sought adventure.

Mrs. Donnelly, the motherly wife of the landlord, already had inquired as to a lone girl's plans. Sally couldn't remember her own mother and she warmed instantly to the older woman. She explained herself frankly, suddenly confident, and found she had tapped a vein of independence that the landlord's wife probably kept well hidden much of the time.

"Dearie," Mrs. Donnelly said, brushing a strand of gray hair from her eye and smiling, "you stay and do what you need to do, and if it comes to that you'll be my daughter and by Jiminy, won't nobody harm you while I'm around."

And they'd hugged and for a moment it was like having her own mother and tears came in her eyes. Mrs. Donnelly patted her shoulder, murmuring. But still, to move about, she needed a man.

War forces rapid decisions on everyone, not just on generals. On the day after Izard's announcement, she made her move. She and Ham both dined at the first shift of the Northern Star's long table. She placed her shawl on the chair beside her. When he came in she said she was chilled and spread it over her shoulders. He took the empty chair.

"And you, sir," she said, "when it starts, you'll be there on the quarter-deck—is that the right term?"

He grinned. "That's the right term, but I won't be there. The British attacked our base in May, and though we drove them off, one of their shots troubled me a little. I'm beached, much to my regret, though I suppose I'd just be in the way. No, I'll be ashore on lookout bluff watching my ship fight without me."

She nodded. "Tell me, that attack in May, did shore batteries turn them back?"

"Why yes, the guns on the hill fired hot shot—"

"Perhaps a friend of mine was involved—General Scott, Winfield Scott?"

"Win Scott? Was he ever! Win is a friend of yours? What a first-rate fellow. He took over a gun when some of our boys were put down, and poured the shot into them. They fled like dogs, too. But I heard he was hit bad at Lundy's Lane."

"He's in hospital in New York City. Says he's ready for duty, but his handwriting doesn't look it."

"Well, give him my best. He and Tom Macdonough got on famously— two of a kind, you know, quick to action."

She took a deep breath. "Lieutenant Hamblin, my father owns a newspaper in Washington. The *Democratic-Republican.*"

He gave her a canny look. "And so you're here . . ."

She felt herself coloring. "Others write for our paper, of course, but I fancy my observations by letter are of some value. Since I find myself here, you see."

"Oh, of course . . . since you're already here . . ."

"Yes . . . so tell me, do you think the danger would be great—to me, I mean—with an enemy army coming?"

He shrugged. "I expect the navy to win and Prevost will turn back, but how soon, how far he'll penetrate, who can hazard that? But, Miss McQuirk—if you should choose to stay, it would be my great honor to watch over your safety."

"You're very kind, Lieutenant Hamblin." She gave him her most vivid smile. "Perhaps I'll call on you."

★ ★ ★ ★

Of course Ham Hamblin fell in love with her. It amused her to perceive that she'd have been hurt if he hadn't. What wasn't so amusing was her own reciprocation.

He was charming, able, forceful, steady, often kindly, and rarely harsh, and while he wasn't unduly handsome, his smile was good and his wit made the hours fly. She found herself awaiting him each day with eagerness that she understood too well. They laughed together; they saw things alike; he was a Virginian and the rural oddities of northern New York struck them identically; they had mutual acquaintances and parallel experiences; they fitted together, seemed to belong together—but wait! She admonished herself fiercely—this wasn't real, it was the just the pressure of war that made things so intense and romantic.

She needed him as protector, not as lover, and to slide down the slippery slope of the latter would be to jeopardize the former. Yet she wanted to kiss him. It was vexing. He rented a carriage and together they scouted the country roads down which the British army would come. Once when he helped her down her skirt caught on her boot and she fell into his arms. With sure instinct, those arms tightened around her and she raised her mouth longing for his kiss, and then he released her, backed off, face gone crimson, and apologized.

It made her value him more highly. His pledge to protect her precluded approaching her as a man. That this was as it must be—given her confidence in her capacity to drive their newspaper to the heights against all competition—was on the one hand infuriating and on the other so ingrained in the social fabric by which she lived that she readily set it aside. Dolley Madison was as bright, forceful, and independent a woman as anyone she knew, and Miss Dolley didn't seem disturbed by the way things were. Still, one of these days . . . there were whispers even now that women should be allowed to vote. Maybe someday newspapers—her paper—would fall in behind that radical idea. But now twelve thousand enemy troops were close and this was no time for complications. But oh, the unruly heart!

★ ★ ★ ★

Sally was in the kitchen of the Northern Star peeling potatoes with Mrs. Donnelly. The forward units of General Prevost's legions now occupied Plattsburgh north of the Saranac. They were bivouacked, waiting for the

Royal Navy to arrive and make the lake secure for their supply lines. It was all quite methodical and unhurried, and seemed the more deadly for that.

The fifteen hundred American troops Izard had left here plus some Vermont militia were dug in on a ridge below the river for what could only be a delaying action when Prevost decided to cross. Fortifications had been raised on the ridge—three strong redoubts and two blockhouses, all connected with interrelated field works. Patrols ranged the south bank of the river, watching for the next British move.

Ham had rowed out to report to the Commodore, which is why Sally was in the kitchen with Mrs. Donnelly. There was tension in the streets that made even a simple walk alone inadvisable. Late in the afternoon Ham returned, looking pleased. She smiled—oh, she *did* like him—like, mind you.

"Compliments of Commodore Macdonough. Will you do him the honor of gracing his table aboard *Saratoga* one hour from now?"

"My!" Mrs. Donnelly said. She clapped her hands together.

Saratoga rode trimly at anchor; when the barge carrying them came alongside, the ship's bulk loomed overhead. Menacing square gunports, now closed, were at eye level. A gangway was lowered, a bo'sun piped a shrill welcome, and she came on deck to find the Commodore awaiting her. He was a solid man of thirty or so, just short of burly, squint lines around very steady blue eyes, a long Caledonian face. She almost expected him to speak with a Scottish burr, but of course he was from Maryland.

She met the ship's officers, and then with obvious pride the Commodore walked her along the deck talking easily of masts and spars and sheets and halyards. But what she noticed were the guns. Of brass and iron, they were mounted on timber carriages with iron wheels so they could roll back against restraint ropes with the recoil of each firing. Some were long and slender with tapering lines that swelled smoothly at the end of the muzzle, and then narrowed in a pretty curve. But most were short, squat pieces without grace that looked simply brutal.

In the captain's quarters stern ports were open to the dying day and oil lanterns on gimbals threw smoky light. The Commodore seated her to his right for shellfish bisque followed with a leg of lamb. He poured a good wine and talked of books and music and affairs of the capital. But when she could she shifted the talk to the guns. She thought the long, slender pieces might be for signaling, at which the men smiled and Macdonough said they were the real power of the ship. Long twenty-four-pounders, they could reach a mile or more with great accuracy.

"You understand, Miss McQuirk, naval gunnery is a science all its own—you're firing from a moving platform, the target is moving, likely there's a fresh wind cutting in another direction, and you must lift a twenty-four-pound ball a mile through the air and drop it into his cabin. No small matter, I assure you."

"But those ugly little—well, not ugly, but I mean—"

He smiled tolerantly. "Carronades, short-range weapons, good to three hundred yards, but not much more. Nothing like the long guns—they're really more like shotguns in that they fire point-blank. We have eighteen of them, some huge, and I assure you, they can wreak havoc at close range."

At close range. She thought about that as Macdonough rattled on. He refilled her glass and she sipped and studied him, glancing now and then at Ham, meeting his warm eyes. She saw that Macdonough was in his element and she was sure that even discounting some hero worship, he was just as strong as Ham said he was. She remembered Steve Decatur talking about this man in Miss Dolley's oval drawing room. The memory gave her a shiver of dread; the British were aiming at Washington, and would the room even be there when she returned?

Captain Decatur's tale was still stirring though she heard it years after the event—how the Tripolitans had captured the frigate *Philadelphia* and to deny them her use the Americans had sailed a captured dhow into the harbor, boarded, killed or scattered the prize crew overboard, set her on fire, and sailed away. Macdonough had led the boarding party, cutlass in hand, and come back covered with someone else's blood. To sit in this quiet cabin sipping good wine with this affable yet very proper man, the thought reminded her of the horrors within the capacity of the human creature, men and women alike.

He told her of the industrial complex he'd raised at Otter Creek across the lake to create his fleet. He touched the rough sternpost that ran through the cabin to the deck.

"This was a tree on March second of this year. We laid the keel March seventh and she was in the water on April eleventh. Now, that's fast!"

A shipyard in the wilderness . . . power from the falls on the creek, timber nearby, puddled iron from a smelter he'd built on bog iron beds, blast furnaces and air furnaces, eight forges to shape iron, rolling mill to work steel, wire factory, grist mill, sawmill, fulling mill. Heavy items—guns, balls, anchors, hawsers—came by wagon from Troy, New York, hub-deep in mud.

It fascinated her. They must first be industrialists, then fighters. But perhaps the two callings weren't so different . . .

Yet the British were building, too, putting all their hopes on that monster ship, the mighty *Confiance*, a frigate, Lord ha' mercy—the very word had an awesome sound.

On deck, Ham wrapped a peacoat about her, and she was grateful for there was real chill in the air as he helped her into the barge in bright moonlight. She turned to him, the coat's high collar shielding her whisper from the oarsmen.

"Ham, how much bigger is a frigate, really?"

He shrugged. "Near twice *Saratoga*, I suppose."

"And its long guns can engage from a distance?" She knew something about ships; most everyone did, for until the war most travel was by coasting vessel. "They'll be coming on a north wind—won't they lie upwind and fight long-range? Our eight long guns to their, what, twenty?"

"Thirty-one, actually. Plus six short-range carronades."

"Good Lord!" Impulsively she put her hand on his. He covered it with his left hand but she withdrew it.

"Look, Sally," he said, "he'll deal with that. This is an American lake and we'll hang on to it."

"He has a plan, you mean?"

He gave her a quizzical look and didn't answer. She said no more, huddling in her peacoat and fighting the urge to lean into him. So there were plans, maybe the disparity ashore wouldn't be repeated afloat. Maybe it would be all right. Maybe.

★ ★ ★ ★

She stood with Ham on a promontory overlooking Plattsburgh Bay an hour before dawn. A sliver of moon lay on the horizon and she could see Cumberland Head lying across the bay like a sleeping bear. But the bay between shore and headland was an inky pool, nothing visible. The headland was an extension of the lake's western shore that thrust south and then turned back on itself, the turn-back enclosing the bay. On the charts it looked like a giant hook held upside down. An island and its surrounding shoals partly plugged the bay's opening.

She shivered, drawing her borrowed peacoat closer to her throat, stood on one foot and then the other, swallowed, started to choke, coughed, her mouth was too dry, what if, what if—

"It'll be all right," he said. His voice was warm and reassuring. "First light and they'll be here."

She nodded and put her arm through his and thought better of it and removed it. Well, all right, admit it, she was scared—that oversize frigate that could outgun their fleet, the vast army ready to smite them, everything coming to a head, the entire North in the balance, maybe the war, maybe the nation itself, all to be decided this morning and she right in its middle!

At least she would see it. Or would she? Maybe the vessels would fight so far out that only distant gunfire would echo on shore. Ham had told her not to worry, but when she asked how he could be so sure he got a look that she had decided not to press. But she wondered. Maybe she'd see nothing, the whole venture a waste, she'd accomplish nothing and still be caught—

Then she realized she was supposing the British would win. But that was ridiculous! She had faith in the navy, in Macdonough and Ham and the others she'd met. Never examine the future in the hour before dawn.

So she calmed herself and burrowed deeper into the peacoat and waited. As if sensing her mood shift he turned to her and smiled.

Light broke in the east and suddenly it was day and from the hilltop everything in the bay was open to the eye. And to her great surprise, she saw Commodore Macdonough's four ships anchored in a long and obviously calculated straight line. They were facing north into the bay, one to two hundred yards apart, and the mercantile vessels that usually dotted the bay were gone.

On this chain of warships now placidly at anchor but soon to sail out to meet the enemy the American future might well depend, and she listened carefully as Ham cited each ship's features.

At the head of the line was the brig, *Eagle*, sizable at five hundred tons, square-rigged on the forward mast, fore-and-aft on the after mast. Ham was as proud of her as if he'd built her himself. She was their newest, scarcely two weeks old, and she carried twenty guns. But for all the brig's magnitude, Sally thought she looked small beside *Saratoga*, the next in line. The flagship wasn't much longer, but she looked deeper and heavier, her masts were taller, the guns she carried threw bigger balls; she was, at seven hundred plus tons, of a different magnitude.

At dinner that night aboard *Saratoga* Sally had asked how one weighed a ship, since sailors were always talking tonnage. That had earned her superior smiles that amused even as they irritated her—men love to feel superior in matters of mechanics—and the explanation that hull size was measured by the weight of water it displaced. Power grew from hull size—beam, depth, weight—more than mere length. Tonnage told number and size of the guns it could carry, the weight those guns could throw.

Directly aft of *Saratoga* lay *Ticonderoga*, a three-hundred-fifty-ton schooner with fore-and-aft rigging that was a solid ship but obviously was armed with lighter pieces. Abaft the schooner, too close to the island shoals, Ham said, for a ship to pass safely to her stern, was the smallest vessel in the fleet, *Preble*, a mere sloop that Ham rated at eighty tons. He said she carried seven long nines, potent guns but nothing like the twenty-fours and the forty-twos on the larger ships.

The line of ships was somewhat closer to the distant headland than to the immediate shore. Ham said there was shoal water on this side, and of course, the island with its six-pound gun made the near side approach difficult. Yet Macdonough had left a relatively narrow channel between his position and the headland. He'd have to up-anchor and make sail soon, and it looked crowded to her and she said as much.

Ham shook his head. "He won't move. He's set to fight as he is—he'll make them come to him."

"Fight at anchor?" She thought the whole idea was to range this way and that, darting in to strike a blow and dancing away again. "Isn't he a sitting target at anchor?"

Ham shrugged. "Common enough in tight places. See, he's purposely laid close to the headland which leaves them blessed little room. I think they'll wind up on the hook, too."

"But can he make them come to him?"

He glanced at her with that same hard look. "They're attacking. They want our lake. They have to come to us."

"Wait a minute!" The significance was dawning on her. "If we make them fight up close, the advantage of their having long guns cancels out! Isn't that right? Our short-range guns are as good as their long-range if we can keep them close."

He laughed, very pleased. "That's the whole idea."

She felt huge relief—at least they wouldn't be so outgunned. That Ham had held the Commodore's plans secret reassured her. She focused the handsome old brass one-piece telescope on a tripod that Mrs. Donnelly had loaned her, relic of the days when Mr. Donnelly was on the lake and his wife watched for him from the headland.

The power of the glass startled her. She trained it on *Saratoga* and plainly saw the Commodore, moving about the deck followed by a slender figure she thought must be the young midshipman, fourteen or fifteen, who'd been at the table the night of the dinner—his name was Bellamy and the ship's company called him Salty.

A boat was lowered on each side, and she saw a small but stout-looking anchor weighing down the stern of each. Oarsmen drew off at forty-five-degree angles as men near the stern on both sides played out heavy hempen cable that sank from sight. When the boats were well spread out on a line about even with the bow, the anchors were tipped into the water.

"What are they doing, Ham?"

"Wait and see." Another secret. Good: they had plans.

The sun came cracking over the Green Mountains in Vermont, dazzling rays of orange and scarlet, and ignited a golden glow on the Adirondacks behind them. And almost as if the sun was their herald, four ships rounded Cumberland Head with sails taut, white water splashing at their bows, wakes streaming behind. They were running abreast in a broad line. With the sun striking them from behind, their sails glowed like otherworldly lights and she was struck with awe—and then she understood that what gripped in her gut was the immensity of that big ship.

For *Confiance* was of a whole different order, not in length but in her height, her weight, the breadth of her beam, the vast reaches of canvas crowded onto her yards, and the rows of men already aloft to shift sail to every nuance of wind, long guns run out port and starboard—my Lord, this was a ship! She made *Saratoga* look like a coastal lugger. At twelve hundred tons she was near twice *Saratoga*'s size, her deep hull supporting huge masts and clouds of canvas and thirty-seven heavy guns to *Saratoga*'s twenty-six.

As *Saratoga* towered over the American fleet, so *Confiance* towered over *Saratoga*.

Sally felt stunned. Was it over before it started, America's fine hopes and brave talk to be scattered like chaff? For a moment she felt dizzy but she saw that Ham, gazing through his own glass, appeared unperturbed.

The other British ships were more modest. The largest was a brig Ham said was called *Linnet*, at three hundred fifty tons substantially smaller than the five-hundred-ton American brig, *Eagle*. There were two sloops, *Chubb* and *Finch*, each about a hundred ten tons with a dozen smaller guns, so Ham said.

The four swept around the headland like hawks in search of prey, swung to the north, charged furiously into the bay—and their sails went soft and the bones at their bows died and they looked as uncertain as lost travelers. They were in the weak and contrary winds of Plattsburgh Bay that regularly tested sailors who must maneuver under fluttering canvas. It wouldn't be so easy as the British Captain Downie surely had hoped.

Signal flags flew and the British line broke up. A sloop, *Chubb*, she thought, tacked to windward and moved ahead, first in what soon became a single line of ships parallel to the line of American ships. *Linnet*, the brig, came next, square sails on her forward mast drawing, then *Confiance*, finally *Finch*.

She swung the glass back to focus on *Saratoga*. There was Tom Macdonough on his quarterdeck, Salty Bellamy beside him hopping from foot to foot in youthful impatience. Macdonough held a long glass to his eye. He looked steady as stone.

The British column came on slowly, clawing for wind. *Chubb* in the lead passed the American *Preble* and then *Ticonderoga* and finally *Saratoga*, all in utter silence. But as *Confiance* approached Sally saw Macdonough shouting as a gun crew horsed a long twenty-four toward the frigate—and then it fired with a startling boom that rolled across the bay. Smoke bloomed from the muzzle and faded. Hurrah! First shot! The ball hit true—she saw it smash through the big ship's railing and crash against a deck house. Stretcher bearers moved toward an inert figure. But *Confiance* didn't answer.

Then the British brig *Linnet* fired a broadside. It sounded light—twelve-pounders, Ham said. The balls crashed across *Saratoga*'s deck. Sally swung the glass with her heart in her mouth and saw the men looking up into the rigging and cheering! And there, all at once filling her glass, she saw a rooster, a gamecock, obviously crowing lustily.

"Hurrah for the fighting cock!" Ham cried. "They smashed his cage and he's telling them off!" He glanced at Sally. "Boys see a fleet like this, it gets them in the gut, you know?"

She did, too well.

"So they need an omen, a lift. Rooster'll do just fine."

Then *Confiance* swung hard aport.

"Good Lord!" Ham cried. "He wants to cross *Saratoga*'s stern and rake her fore and aft. Pray he can't do it."

She held her breath. Broadsides poured down the length of the American's deck could end it before it started. But the frigate's sails went slack and she lost way and started to fall off, and then slowly turned back into line.

"He'll anchor," Ham breathed. "Has to."

The frigate came up to the American ship at about three hundred yards. She remembered that was the range of Macdonough's short-range pieces, and it struck her that he was in control, he was forcing them to fight on his terms and to his advantage.

Immediately *Saratoga* opened on the frigate, rolling gunfire that pounded into the big ship's hull and deck houses and threw showers of deadly splinters. Sally had picked out the British captain in her glass by now, a tall, impressive figure in a fine uniform, his hat awash in gold, standing motionless on his quarterdeck ignoring the American balls. His ship made no answer. Indeed, there was a certain arrogant pride of execution in the very way *Confiance* loosed her anchors and prepared her guns. Taking her time made her the more ominous.

And then she fired. Eighteen guns to her broadside and one on a swivel— nineteen heavy guns erupted at once with a roar that shook the ground where Sally stood. The massive charge slammed into *Saratoga* with such force as to heel her violently, men sprawling across her deck. Sally swung to the American ship—my Lord, it was a disaster! Guns knocked askew, spars falling, the deck a scrambled tangle of lines, halyards, and sheets, men clawing up to return to the guns—

"Skipper's down," Ham said.

She saw Macdonough sitting on deck, his hat gone and one side of his face dark and bloody. He was holding his head. She didn't see his midshipman shadow. He held out a hand and someone lifted him but his legs folded and he sat back down.

"Oh, God," Ham said, "I think Salty's head hit him."

Salty's head? She shifted the glass and saw a human head in the scupper. She gasped as bile rose in her throat.

"Don't look, Sally," Ham said.

"But—but what?"

"Shot took off Salty's head and it hit the skipper's face, I think . . . poor kid."

She saw the headless torso twenty feet away and then he pulled her away from the glass and sat her down. Her stomach was roiling. She felt like a voyeur, watching men die in the distance. Salty was just a child, all his life before him. She remembered his boyish enthusiasm, his eager answers, and tears formed on her cheeks. For the first time she understood the power and the horror of ships in close combat.

She had assumed *Saratoga* was finished, but then the American ship's starboard guns thundered and heavy shot slashed into the Briton. She looked again; Salty's body had been moved, his head was gone. Macdonough was up and moving from gun to gun. Several guns had been thrown over but others fired on and on. Gun flashes sparked in boiling clouds of smoke. The Briton was taking a beating, too. Guns knocked apart and raw wood scars were everywhere. The two ships pounded each other like raging bulls crashing horn to horn.

Then she saw one of *Confiance*'s guns lifted into the air. It fell back, skated across the deck, and knocked down a group of men. One didn't get up. The others bent over him. She saw the gold stitching in his uniform, the gold-laced hat nearby. The British captain was down. She waited for him to rise but he was inert, and then she saw them drag him out of the way and cover his face with canvas. Captain Downie was dead.

The fire was a rolling, rumbling bellow now, too general to distinguish individual shots, all eight ships slashing at each other. Clouds of gunsmoke rose so that at times smoke shot with brilliant gun flashes was all she could see. Then the vagrant wind would swirl bits of it aside to reveal scraps of the fight in deadly vignettes. She clung to the scope on its sturdy tripod, fascinated, horrified, the anguish she'd felt on seeing the child's head torn off and canvas drawn over the British captain's face refocused into a breathless anxiety as a battle that seemed beyond human endurance went on unslacked. Brushing away unnoticed tears, she felt overwhelmed by a sudden recognition of the magnificent grandeur of the human creature, so murderous and yet so splendidly willing to sacrifice for ideas, for faith and country and freedom. And consequent to this understanding of the meaning of great events came a deep humility as she stood safely on a hill in the distance watching men die, watching history come to its vast decisions.

The smoke lifted at the north end of the line just as the brig *Eagle* slammed a broadside squarely into the British sloop *Chubb* and wrecked her. Mainstay parted, mast left a jagged stub, tangles of rigging and wreckage covering her deck, scarcely a moving soul evident aboard, she drifted out of control. Someone hauled down her flag and now Sally saw a handful of survivors moving about her deck like men stunned by catastrophe. The destroyed ship drifted between the anchored vessels and the firing stopped on both sides as she passed, as carriages pause for the plodding horses of a funeral procession. Like a ghost ship through the fog of smoke, *Chubb* floated on, passing between *Saratoga* and *Ticonderoga* as she drifted sadly toward the shore.

At the lower end of the line *Ticonderoga* and the sloop *Preble* were under wild attack by the British sloop *Finch* and a dozen galleylike gunboats with oars that scattered jewels to flash in the sunlight. The American ships fought them off, but *Preble* was near destroyed. Guns silenced, hull holed, masts and rigging gone, she cut her cable and drifted off like a wounded veteran on crutches. Three American ships were left to three British, but then the big schooner sent the second British sloop, *Finch*, floating helplessly away. Two British ships remained, but they were the big ones, massive *Confiance* and *Linnet*, the brig.

Linnet's broadside, eight long twelves still mostly intact, fired again and again. A ball cut the anchor cable of the lead American ship, *Eagle*, which drifted slowly to leeward of *Saratoga*, turning as she floated. Masts shattered, rigging a tangle, there was no hope of raising sail and regaining power. But when she came midway between *Saratoga* and *Ticonderoga* a bit to leeward, her skipper let go his stern anchor and she held place and opened fire again. It wasn't over by a long shot.

Yet the two brigs and the schooner, after all, were small vessels with light guns. The real quarrel was a pounding grudge fight ship to ship, gun to gun, between the giants, *Saratoga* with her starboard flank aflame with gunfire that became visible as the smoke eddied and flowed, and the much larger—a whole different order of ship—British frigate, her port batteries laying hammer blows as fast as men could swab, load, ram, advance the guns, and slam match to touchhole. Sheets of flame flared along her port side.

The two ships were taking fearsome punishment. *Confiance* fired high and *Saratoga*'s rigging came crashing down, spars flying, masts shattered. Sally ran the glass along the deck looking for Macdonough, but he had disappeared. She watched a work party heaving aside fallen spars with an urgency that held her attention, and then she saw a prone figure on the deck. Macdonough—that solid blocky form must be he. He was motionless and she thought he was dead, but then he raised a hand and someone pulled him to his feet and *Saratoga* opened again.

Her shots were slamming point-blank into the Briton's hull, and Ham said the frigate was taking water. Indeed, Sally saw men sawing on pump handles and a bright stream squirting over the side and the ship looked lower in the water. But her guns were still firing, and *Saratoga*'s were slowing and a cold dread settled in Sally. One by one the American's guns were being silenced, knocked about, shattered, thrown aside. She was still firing, but all at once Sally thought the sound had taken on a hollow, aimless ring, as if the ship's heart was gone.

Confiance was winning. Paying a terrible price in damage and loss of life and pain of awful wounds, but winning. The adage was holding, good big ship against good little ship. She thought it would be over in minutes.

"Now, Cap'n," Ham whispered, his eye fixed to his glass. "Now, now, *now!*"

She stared at him. "Whatever—"

"Watch! Watch, Sally. Now's the time, he'll do it, I know he will— yes! He's starting—look!"

She saw Macdonough shouting, his arms waving. A bo'sun put pipe to lips and she could imagine the shrilling sound. Men ran to a heavy anchor dangling off the stern and it dropped.

"Stream anchor away," Ham murmured.

Men stumbled along the deck, carrying forward the heavy line from that anchor. She saw another party on the starboard quarter just above the stern heave on a line that—yes, there!—rose from the water like an apparition. And all at once she understood. That line was attached to one of the anchors carried out by boat so much earlier.

"Kedge anchor's holding," Ham said.

The men pulled and pulled and *Saratoga*'s stern swung up to the right. Another party hauled hard on the line attached to the stream anchor that now had become a bow anchor. She saw axes flashing as men cut the ship free from the original bow anchor. Then a group maneuvered the line holding the port kedge anchor until it passed under the vessel. When it came clear, they hauled in vigorously. The result was a neat reversal, a completely unexpected turnabout that could not possibly have been managed under power with rigging torn and masts mere stubs.

And now a full broadside that hadn't been fired, that had been sheltered from enemy fire and was scarcely damaged, was ready to erupt on the British frigate like the scythe of God.

The men on *Confiance* saw their danger and tried desperately to turn their ship. But they had only springs, the light extra lines usually attached to anchor cables. And springs gave only limited turning range—even Sally knew that.

Confiance turned halfway and there she stalled and would turn no more. Her stern was toward *Saratoga*'s fresh broadside. None of her guns would bear.

And *Saratoga* fired.

Her full broadside went shrieking down the length of *Confiance*. She reloaded and fired again and again and again and she scourged *Confiance* as a holystone scourges a deck. It was sublime, it was horrible, it made Sally want to cringe and cry for mercy and shout for joy. Emotions in wild conflict ripped through her as she saw the bodies piled on *Confiance*'s deck, the guns torn and broken and tossed about like straws, saw the deckhouses disintegrate under the iron battering. Officers shouted on the quarterdeck but the men they called were crouched in fear, protecting themselves as they could from fire that surpassed human bearing, and then the shouting officers were carried away, vanished in the maelstrom.

And the Union Jack came fluttering down.

What was left of the proud, towering frigate surrendered.

A boat crossed from *Saratoga* to take possession. *Confiance* was low in the water and appeared to be sinking. A twitch on the kedge anchor swung *Saratoga*'s guns onto *Linnet* and after a single devastating broadside, the brig's flag came rattling down.

Sally was crying and laughing and shouting, it was over, it was over! Tom Macdonough had done it with his courage and foresight and his brilliant kedge anchors that snatched victory from defeat's ravening jaws. And we won and the lake was ours and the North was saved and General Prevost with all his legions would have to turn back to Canada. The British had staked everything on that great ship and the wonderful doughty Macdonough and *Saratoga* had met them and destroyed them.

And the blood had run in rivers, how many widows and orphans had this morning made, how much pain and agony, how many maimed men and blighted lives? And what of the child Salty who would never be a lieutenant? Sublime, magnificent . . . and heartbreaking. Her legs felt weak and she had an overwhelming need for human connection, for surcease of pain and horror, for reassertion of the root of humanity that is love.

Ham's face was tear-stained, too, and she turned to him with a deep sigh and fell against his chest and his arms closed hard around her. There would be kisses later—now she wanted just to feel his heart beating against hers.

26

NEW ORLEANS
December, 1814

★ ★ ★ ★ When Andrew Jackson reached New Orleans on the first day of December, he knew a British invasion fleet was as little as ten days away. By now, sixty warships carrying upward of fifteen thousand troops must have weighed anchor in Kingston harbor, Jamaica. Ten days was cutting it dangerously close, but by sealing Mobile and taking Pensacola he had forced their hand. They would come straight in to the city, and there lay his best chance of whipping them.

If, that is, he could get ready in time. Grasp the terrain, figure out their exact approach, line up the navy's support, collect troops and weapons, establish sources of supply . . . His barge bumped a dock on the south shore of Lake Pontchartrain and he led his horse ashore. It was just after dawn.

Ten days to prepare to shatter a force two to three times the size of his own and made up of veterans of the finest army in the world, the army that had just beaten Napoleon Bonaparte.

He was about to mount when he saw good old Ed Livingston hurrying down the bank to meet him. Ed stumbled on a rock, looked as if he would fall, recovered, grinned, and rushed on. Clumsy as ever. He pumped Jackson's hand vigorously in both of his own. Ed was an old friend and now a leader in the New Orleans community; he would pave Jackson's way.

"It's all set, Andrew. A fine headquarters building, three-story brick on Royal Street, I cleared the mercantilists out last week. Folks are waiting for you on pins and needles."

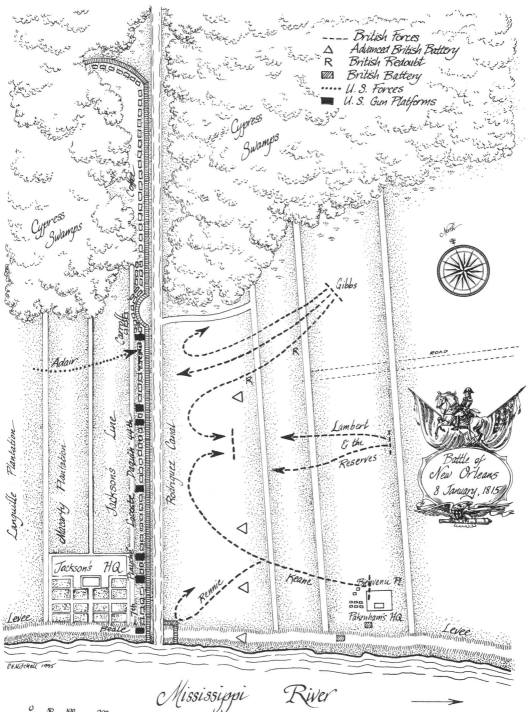

Battle of
New Orleans
8 January, 1815

British Forces
Advanced British Battery
R   British Redoubt
British Battery
U. S. Forces
U. S. Gun Platforms

North

Cypress
Swamps

Cypress
Swamps

Cypress
Swamps

Gibbs

R

R

Lambert
& the
Reserves

Adair

Keane

Rennie

Bienvenu Pt.

Pakenham's HQ

Jackson's HQ

Languille Plantation

McCarty Plantation

Jackson's Line

Carroll

Coffee

Rodriguez Canal

Laronde Dupuis 44th

7th

ROAD

Levee

Levee

Beale

Mississippi   River

C.H.Mitchell 1995

0   50   100   200
yards

"Ready to fight, are they?"

An odd speculative look flashed over Ed's face.

"Well," he said, "you'll want to take them in hand."

Tall, as awkward physically as he was smooth mentally, Ed had a wonderful way of getting what he wanted without making enemies. They'd been in Congress together in the days when Congress still sat in Philadelphia; Ed was a New Yorker then, a city man skilled in the legislative arts that Jackson was learning would never be his strength. It was an unhappy time, and old Ed had seen him through many a rough patch while matching his fervor for the then-new Democratic-Republican party.

Johnny Reid and Jack Gordon led their horses ashore, followed by the engineer, Howell Tatum. Pink Mims maneuvered the bivouac cart ashore; he made the General's life on the trail almost comfortable from that cart.

"Let's go," Jackson said.

He shivered and drew his worn blue uniform coat closer to his throat. It was cold for South Louisiana; there'd been ice on the washbasin that morning and frost silvered the debris of the cane harvest in plantation fields they passed. His mare stepped along at a brisk pace.

Ed reported quickly. The New Orleans militia planned a review. Commodore Patterson, commanding U.S. Navy vessels on the river, was standing by to coordinate with the General. A wizard mapmaker, Major Latour, was waiting at headquarters to discuss terrain. Ed said Mrs. Livingston was giving a ladies' dinner that evening for the wives of the city's leaders and hoped the General would join them.

"And finally, a meeting with those selfsame leaders. They'll be coming to headquarters." Ed hesitated. "You'll want them on your side, of course."

Jackson turned in his saddle. "What do you mean? Where else would they be?"

Again that hesitation. "Well, the Creoles are more or less at war with the Americans. I serve as a buffer between them—or go-between, as the case may be."

"At war with the Americans? Hell's fire, Ed, they *are* Americans."

"Yes, of course. Or technically, at least. But you know the Creoles."

An elderly man with a pointed beard and a slouch hat reined a trap to one side of the road and called to Ed in French.

"A client," Ed said. "You'll forgive me a moment, General? He's not just a client, he's a client who pays."

Jackson rode on, considering. He knew the city reasonably well; business had fetched him here over the years, starting with that wild run to Natchez with Rachel so many years ago, and yes, the Creoles were touchy as hell. In some places the term Creole included black and mixed-blood people; here it meant Louisiana-born descendants of mostly French and a few Spanish settlers. France had settled on the river bend a hundred years back, then lost it all even before the American Revolution, when the British won the

French and Indian War. Out went France, and Britain turned New Orleans over to Spain. But Spanish rule could not touch the city's inherent Frenchness.

The city went crazy with joy when Napoleon regained Louisiana. Jackson, who had visited the city not long after, would never forget the force of their celebration. French again! Long live Napoleon! They didn't dream that even as they hoisted glasses, the Emperor was peddling them to the United States, offering everything from New Orleans to Oregon in a bargain sale. As chance would have it, Napoleon and Talleyrand made the deal for the Louisiana Purchase with none other than Ed's older brother, Robert Livingston. Diplomacy seemed to come naturally to both brothers.

So as of 1803 these passionate Frenchmen became Americans, like it or not, and some didn't. Once he'd nearly come to pistols with one who'd said as much, more forcefully than had seemed necessary—though, of course, that was in the old days. And since then they felt that after getting them with no say-so of their own, the United States had ignored them. The nation had a lot on its mind just then, what with Jefferson consolidating the new democratic turn of government while trying to stand clear of war in Europe, but that didn't matter to the Creoles.

Which was just too damned bad. They were Americans, they were about to be attacked, and he wanted action.

"Well," he said, "all that matters is, are they loyal?"

"Loyal they are, certainly. But not always cooperative, I'm afraid. And they detest Governor Claiborne."

"Nothing new about that," Jackson said. "They always hated him." And with good reason, far as he was concerned; William Claiborne had been a mistake when appointed territorial governor in 1803 and he'd been at war with the people ever since, beginning with his refusal even to bother to learn French. As for why Louisiana had elected him its first governor when it became a state in 1812, Jackson figured mutual hatred had become as comfortable as a pair of old shoes.

"Well," he said, "they can forget Claiborne. Now they're dealing with me."

Ed chuckled. "They're only too aware of that. Your reputation goes before you—they won't want to ruffle your feathers. But in turn, you need to see there's lots about our ways that disturb them. Take the matter of Jean Lafitte—you know he volunteered his forces for the defense of New Orleans?"

"Of course I know. I'm the one who refused him. Told Claiborne to clap that damned pirate in prison if he could."

"Lafitte is popular in New Orleans—a hell of a lot more so than Claiborne."

 Jackson stared at his old friend. "He's a pirate, Ed. Barataria Bay has been a pirate's nest for years. What are you telling me—that New Orleans folk look to hellish banditti for their defense?"

"You know the British tried to enlist him in their attack, and he refused them?"

Jackson shrugged. Ed represented the Lafitte brothers on various criminal charges, but even he couldn't claim that Lafitte's offer to fight on the American side in return for amnesty for his crimes was patriotic. The U.S. Navy under Commodore Patterson had raided Barataria Bay and chased the pirates into the swamps. Lafitte could see the end coming and was trying to dodge the hangman's noose.

"He's not the only one here with an interesting past, you know," Ed said. "Folks don't ask. This is a live-and-let-live town, believe me. Lafitte says he's a privateer, sails under letters of marque from a breakaway Spanish colony in South America—Cartagena, I think. Preys on Spanish shipping. Folks here don't see much wrong with that, and what the hell, Andrew, our privateers are sailing out of Baltimore, aren't they?"

"A substantial difference there, Ed. Substantial."

"All right, all right, so they don't equate. But people here accept Lafitte as legitimate, and they saw the navy's raid as plain old harassment. Way they look at it, Barataria Bay is part of commerce. You'd be surprised at how much local trade comes through there."

"Smuggled, doubtless."

Ed laughed. "Of course. U.S. revenue laws don't impress New Orleanians. This is an easy-minded place."

Jackson turned in his saddle. "Look, Ed, I'd sup with the devil if it was going to aid my defense. But how could I trust a thief in my camp? He'd betray me for a handful of gold."

Ed shrugged. "Still," he said, "one thing—if you meet with Jean Lafitte, you'll find him an interesting man."

★ ★ ★ ★

"Andrew," Ed said, "tell me true—did you have authorization when you seized Pensacola and ran the British out?"

Jackson grinned. "What do you think?"

"I think you went on your own. I think you asked Washington and they—what? Said no?"

"Didn't answer."

"Good. That's what I'd have done in their shoes. They figured you knew what to do. But it leaves you the cat's-paw, doesn't it?"

Jackson shrugged. "If I hadn't attacked it would have canceled the victory at Mobile and left my rear open. Could have been fatal. I expect Washington can figure that out."

"And throw you to the wolves if a diplomatic explosion follows."

Jackson smiled. "Yes, I expect that's the plan." He ignored a hollow in the pit of his stomach at the thought.

"Well, you always were a tough old bastard, even when you were young. I guess dealing with Florida was basic to defending New Orleans, and that's what matters to me. How tough was it? We had conflicting reports here."

"The Spanish put up a little resistance, mostly for their pride, I guess. I wanted to kill as few of them as possible and it took a half hour to clear them out, and that was long enough for the British to blow up the old fort."

"Barrancas?"

"Dominated Pensacola harbor, did before they blew it up. Then they ran like hell for their ships. You should have heard Jack Gordon crowing. The British major, he'd shown himself a big talker, and now he showed that's all he was. So it all worked out—Pensacola is useless with the fort gone and they'll have to come here direct—and after that I didn't waste much time getting on over here."

★ ★ ★ ★

He sent Ed galloping ahead to alert the city to his coming, and rode on, pondering the balances he faced: fifteen thousand enemy troops on the way, against the five or six thousand he could muster. Jack Coffee's fifteen hundred dragoons were holding upriver at Baton Rouge. The twenty-five hundred Creek War veterans Billy Carroll had enlisted in Nashville were coming down on flatboats and couldn't be very far from arrival. Two solid regiments of regular infantry were on hand, the Forty-fourth, a Louisiana outfit, and the good old Seventh, enlisted in Tennessee, crossing Lake Pontchartrain right behind him. Two hundred Mississippi dragoons said to be born to horse and rifle were due in a day or two under a colonel named Tom Hinds. And he could count on some fifteen hundred Louisiana volunteers, including a strong battalion in New Orleans, most of whose members had soldiered with Napoleon.

About a hundred regular army artillerymen serving under a veteran colonel named Bill McRae were with the Seventh. They had a couple of little six-pounders, but he also was counting on a good supply of naval cannon with powder and shot long stored here in case of attack. Guns designed for a ship's deck wouldn't be the easiest to handle in the field, but they'd be welcome.

Broad plantation fields began to give way to neat little farms; he was nearing the city. The British advantage wasn't just in numbers: these were highly disciplined troops, carefully trained, men who'd proved their skill with the bayonet. In European fighting, after all, it was assumed that steel would settle things after the initial exchange of fire.

But he had some advantages, too. He was here first and could study the ground and get ready. He probably had more and heavier cannon than they could wrestle ashore, and he had the rifle and a frontierman's experience in the deep woods that told him how effective men in leather shirts could make it. It was good to three hundred yards, even four hundred in the hands of masters, and he had some masters in his ranks. Modern armies stuck with the musket, effective range only a hundred yards but able to load and fire twice as rapidly as the rifle. But with the field carefully set, the accuracy and range of his rifles might just catch the British short.

He felt a burst of that urgency he knew so well and had to resist putting spurs to the mare. Take control at the start, by God, know the ground, see them coming, force them into sheets of aimed rifle fire while his cannon hosed the field with grapeshot.

An old man passed, spoke, then spurred away like a rabbit when Jackson answered in English. The old fart probably didn't have a word of what now was his national language, so why shouldn't he and his fellow Creoles find it a little difficult to fetch up center stage in an epic they hardly could comprehend? It made him see the gulf between them, for that same epic defined his very nature—that pale-eyed major's saber introducing him to the Revolution, the struggle to pass the Constitution, the battle under Jefferson and Madison to recast the nation into a democracy serving mankind instead of an oligarchy limited in hopes, aims, and territory . . .

And everything came to a head here, on this key to the continental future. Of course the enemy wanted New Orleans and just as certainly we would die to keep it. He'd always known that destiny would bring him here, just as he'd understood how necessary this second revolution was to the nation's soul. He'd taken Madison for a weak sister, but the little President and his lady had proved him wrong on that, thank the Lord. Nothing seemed to shake the little President as he stood like a stone amid political opposition, failing finances, public fear, a tremorous Congress, sagging enlistments, untried generals, green militia, cruel defeats on the battlefield.

Years ago Jackson had owned a four-miler he called Steamboy, who always took two miles to get set. That horse won races all over Tennessee, men betting him down when he lagged at first; he had a way of shaking his head when he was ready to go, and then he gave you heart palpitations. We'll come on like Steamboy, he told Rachel, and sure enough, by 1814 the country was shaking its head and getting set—Winfield Scott's regulars throwing back Britain's best at Lundy's Lane, Madison slapping aside that contemptuous peace offer, enlistments on the rise.

When Tennessee heard they'd burned Washington, the boys who'd fought the Creek War swarmed into the recruiting office Billy Carroll opened on the Nashville Square, the same troops coming downriver now. Break our spirit? Burning the Capitol *made* our spirit. He saw it everywhere. The British fleeing Washington after setting their barbarous blaze. His own guns stopping the Royal Navy at Mobile Bay. General Prevost and his big army hightailing it back to Canada after that tough-minded sailor up on Lake

Champlain blew their fleet apart. Old Sam Smith, always a fighter, hurling them back from Baltimore. And Pensacola, bells ringing all over Tennessee.

Hell, yes—they couldn't hold us down!

Even the war's dark side, bankruptcy and disunion, had peaked. The treasury was empty, financiers refused all loans, Congress still wet its drawers at the thought of taxes. And now, the indelible stain of treason up in New England—a convention was meeting in Hartford to consider secession. Talking treason. By *God*, if he could lay hands on them, he'd hang them from every tree in Hartford!

They were fools, too, abandoning ship just as the tide turned. Still, nothing else would matter if the British took New Orleans. There was the great test. And he was ready—never had man and destiny merged more perfectly.

★ ★ ★ ★

He liked Major Latour immediately—Arsene Lacarrière Latour, military engineer, late of the French army, a smallish man of indeterminate age with dark face and eyes and a pointed mustache, who spoke with a mapmaker's precision and the dignity of one whose dueling pistols were well oiled. Latour carried a roll of his own maps, drawn from surveys he had made himself. He clicked his heels and said he wished to acquaint the General with the oddest terrain he was ever likely to see.

It was ever-forming land, nature caught in the act—Latour permitted himself a small smile—as the continental artery poured topsoil into the delta. Land formed first at the river's edge, accounting for the mile-wide riverfront on which New Orleans stood. But go down eighteen inches, and voilà—water!

"Water at eighteen inches?" Howell Tatum took off his little round glasses and put them back on. "Good God! How do you dig trenches? How do you build defensive lines?"

Latour bowed. "With engineering ingenuity, my dear major."

Major Tatum threw up both hands and laughed. "By God, General, we'll need all of that we can get!"

They were in the brick headquarters at 106 Royal Street, in a huge, airy room on the second floor with an iron balcony. That mile-wide strip, plantation land above and below the city, was clearly marked on the map Latour anchored with four little brass weights he took from a case. Beyond the strip were vast crosshatched areas of less formed land—swamps studded with cypress trees or covered with sawgrass. But it was not impenetrable; bayous teeming with alligators wound through it, marked more by openings among trees hung with Spanish moss than by actual banks.

"Smugglers move readily enough on these routes," Latour said. "My friend Jean Lafitte is a master of swamp travel."

His friend? Interesting . . .

"So, Major," he said, "where will the attack fall?"

"Here." Latour pointed on his chart. "The sea lakes."

So Jackson had thought all along. That fort guarding the mouth of the Mississippi precluded attack via the river, if it was as strong as reported. He was going to see for himself.

So it would come to those sea lakes, first Lake Borgne and then Lake Pontchartrain, extensions of the Mississippi Sound that ran within its barrier islands all the way from Florida.

"Brackish water," Latour said, his English excellent if accented. "Half lake and half bay, so to speak, and both shallow." He tapped the chart. "You see the point, of course. A deepwater fleet must anchor well out in the Sound—they'll have to move everything into the lakes by small boats. Men, guns, supplies. A considerable chore."

In his mind's eye Jackson could see longboats or small luggers with square sails in a vast spread across the water. Fixing them early and divining their landing place would be crucial; he intended to have troops ready to meet them. Navy gunboats were standing watch on Lake Borgne.

"Now," Latour said, "note how slender are the channels connecting Borgne to Pontchartrain. Will they force them? Possible but difficult—the fort on the main channel is small but strong—so I think they'll take this peninsula."

Called the Plain of Gentilly, this bulge of land between the two lakes had a broad, flat, open strip down its center with cypress swamp on each side. Jackson figured that's where he would strike if he were attacking. He must ride out immediately to begin plotting its defense.

"That's the front door," he said. "Is there a back door?"

Latour pointed to a mile-wide band of plantation land along the river below the city. Five miles of swamp lay between that strip and Lake Borgne, and various bayous meandered through it to empty into the lake. An enemy following a bayou through the swamp could pop out on the river *below* the city in a position to deal a devastating surprise blow. And that would knock Jackson's planning into a cocked hat. But ten to fifteen thousand men, heavy guns, supplies, all coming up narrow waterways in small boats?

"Possible, I suppose," Latour said, "but hard to imagine."

★ ★ ★ ★

He invited the city leaders to walk with him to the Place d'Armes, where the Battalion d'Orleans waited to pass in review. Ed introduced them, the Mayor, several legislative leaders, a number of leading merchants, and the militia general whose troops he was to meet—Jacques Villeré, a tall, slender man in his middle fifties whose patrician manner seemed just short of arrogant. With a couple of questions, he discovered that General Villeré knew next to nothing of military matters.

And the group seemed remarkably glum, given that he had come to save their city. He didn't expect roses underfoot, but still . . . he laid out his concerns as they walked, hoping to elicit sparks of enthusiasm, but none appeared.

He wanted the militia mobilized statewide and ordered here, the city armory emptied of weapons—"I'll need all I can find," he said—and the warehouses thrown open. He would need meat, flour, cornmeal, blankets, coats, powder, shot, and would give vouchers on the government in payment.

Black freemen, most of them refugees from revolution in Haiti, had begged for the chance to help defend their new country, and he had ordered them formed into two battalions that needed outfitting.

The sun came out and made the wet street sparkle. Women looked down at them from marvelously intricate wrought-iron balconies, and he saw more French flags than American. A handsome woman with black hair blew him a kiss and he swept off his hat and bowed, but he saw no gratitude in these men. They frowned and shook their heads.

"Am I missing something?" he said. "New Orleans welcomes our defense of all it holds dear, does it not?"

Bernard Marigny de Mandeville spoke for the lot of them. He was a man of middle years, ruddy-faced and vigorous-looking, his manner commanding. He was an absolute power in the legislature, apparently regarded as the voice of the Creoles.

"Of course," he said. "But arming blacks? Emptying the armory? And these vouchers—who knows when they'll be paid?"

"You understand that a British fleet is ten days away? With fifteen thousand professional soldiers?"

"Yes, but—"

"I expect cooperation, and by God, I'm going to have it!"

He saw the look that flashed across Marigny's face. Was it fear? Of course, he understood the implications of arming black men, even free black men. Slaveholders lived in terror of slave revolt, slaves being slaves only by force and oppression. The weapons were in the armory in case of slave revolt, which was why emptying it alarmed these burghers. It was no different back on Jackson's farm. He wouldn't arm slaves, but neither would he deny freemen the chance to fight.

The magnificent central square glowed in the sunshine, the levee on one side before a forest of ship masts, the fine St. Louis Cathedral on the other, flower beds in the center banked against winter. A band heavy on brasses and drums played with a remarkable lilt. A crowd had gathered, and peddlers with drinks and sweets on trays were doing a lively business.

Six hundred troops in vivid uniforms were assembled in four companies. They were society soldiers, only the best people admitted, but he knew that men who considered themselves an elite often fought well on sheer pride. They surely drilled well. He was particularly impressed by one of the officers,

Henri St. Gême of the Dismounted Dragoons. Compact and muscular, ruddy-faced with startling blue eyes, St. Gême radiated decisive assurance.

"Henri's activities may interest you," General Villeré said with a sly air. "He's an important banker, but he also has a privateering vessel sailing out of Barataria Bay. With Lafitte."

"Quite so, sir," St. Gême said, well pleased with himself.

"And you pay duty on all you bring up the river?"

St. Gême spread his hands. "But of course!"

Jackson grinned. Another smuggling scoundrel—and this one the General intended to use.

★ ★ ★ ★

Next, the front door and the back door. He and Latour rode in blessed silence through the city, Latour being one of those confident men who didn't speak until he had something to say. The others followed, Johnny Reid looking about eagerly as Jack Gordon, an old New Orleans hand, pointed things out.

Unfortunately, the front door might as well be a welcome mat for the British. There were dozens of places along the shore of Lake Borgne where a small-boat flotilla could land. Too many to cover; he must set a roving watch, with troops in reserve and ready to move. And then Gentilly Plain itself, the peninsula between the lakes, provided a natural attack lane. It was broad and level, most of it cleared for cane fields, with occasional clumps of trees. Fence rows, hedge lines, ditches, canals, a few buildings that he must level—these were the only barriers to a rapid enemy advance down the center of the peninsula.

Just looking at it intensified the ache in his gut. The cold, so unlike South Louisiana, made the pain worse, and he was developing a rattling cough.

"Let's see the back door," he said.

Taking the road south along the levee on that mile-wide strip of dry land skirting the river, they passed a series of plantations. Each was relatively long and narrow, fronting on the river at one end and on the swamp at the other. Amid cane fields littered with harvest debris he saw orchards, gardens, stout fences with heavy gates, handsome houses with broad verandas and flower beds, barns and slave hovels nearby. Each plantation had its own canal to drain ground water and river overflow to the swamps. Several appeared to feed directly into bayous that wound away into cypress-studded water.

The last big planter, several miles downriver, proved to be General Villeré of the militia. He presented his son, Gabriel, a handsome young major with a winning smile and no more apparent substance than his father. Over fine coffee as welcome for its heat as its flavor, Jackson asked Villeré's view of an attack through the back door.

Young Gabriel laughed and answered before his father could speak. "Through the swamps? Impossible."

"But you have a canal that feeds a bayou. Doesn't the stream extend eventually to Lake Borgne?"

"Granted, a pirogue makes it easily," General Villeré said. He looked at his son and chuckled. "But boats for men by the thousands and heavy guns? No, I hardly think so."

"Hardly," Gabriel said.

"I think we'll block those streams," Jackson said.

"Block them?" Gabriel said. "How?"

"Drop cypress trees into each for a few miles, I suppose." He glanced at Latour. "They'd be weeks chopping through."

The engineer beamed but Jackson saw Villeré and his son exchange amused glances.

"I'll make that an order," he said, "each plantation on a stream responsible for blocking it."

"Well, if we must," General Villeré said. The smiles were gone. "Gabriel will see to ours."

★ ★ ★ ★

It had been a long day, in Johnny Reid's estimation, when he and the General dismounted in front of Ed Livingston's house. It was a handsome house in the Creole manner—the General had told him that Ed, after a bankruptcy in New York, had opened a law office here, married a Creole widow known for her beauty, and grown rich while serving as a buffer between American newcomers and the old-line Creole society.

Reid was delighted with New Orleans after so long in near wilderness, in which, privately, he included Nashville, and he hoped the widow Ed had married would measure up to her city. Narrow streets, houses flush to the sidewalks and wall to wall with those alongside, graceful belled bars on windows, those lovely balconies of wrought iron, a throbbing central market, shops catering to every taste—and crowds everywhere, polyglot babble punctuated with laughter, snatches of song, music wherever he turned, gentlemen and ladies and soldiers and sailors and peddlers and vendors and whores and swamp rats mingling on its busy riverfront. Twenty-five thousand people lived here, only three thousand of them from other states.

They passed from a patio open to the sky with flower beds and iron chairs and entered a long parlor. A plaster statue of St. Andrew with a crown of brilliants stood alone on a narrow table. A woman left a group to sweep lightly across the polished tile floor. She was slender and lissome with dark hair and eyes and a way of moving that made him think she would be as comfortable in a sidesaddle as in her drawing room.

The General made an old-fashioned bow from the waist as Livingston presented them to Madame Louise Livingston. Reid bowed in awkward emulation, sure he looked clumsy, and she, as if sensing his discomfort, smiled suddenly. It was a dazzling look—warm, commiserating, generous, forgiving—and it captivated him. She was beautiful, scarcely older than he, twenty years her husband's junior, a magnificent woman not at all his idea of a widow.

"Come, sirs," she said, her voice melodious and low, her English rendered with piquant accent, "and meet my guests."

Yet as they approached the group of a dozen women, Reid sensed that she was nervous and it struck him that the ladies of New Orleans might view Jackson uneasily, given the immediacy of war and his reputation for violence. The General was modestly dressed, his high boots innocent of blacking, the brass buttons on his worn uniform coat gone greenish.

But he seemed fully at ease as he strolled into a drawing room full of strange women and bowed to each of them, repeating the name with attention to French pronunciation. He made a graceful little speech: these were difficult and threatening times, but they could rest assured that he intended to crush the invader, that their lives might go on undisturbed amid the pleasures of their lovely city. Graceful indeed—where was the man of mad temper? In fact, though, it now struck Reid that the General's old explosive quality seemed to have been replaced by a steely force.

After the dinner, he watched the women cluster around Mrs. Livingston.

"Is this the rude backwoodsman you described?" one said in high, clear French. "Why, madam, he is a prince!"

Mrs. Livingston accepted their laughing compliments graciously, making it seem a tribute that was her due, and when she caught Reid's eye over the women's heads she smiled with conspiratorial warmth, as if to say, *see what you and I have achieved with our fine general*, and on the spot he fell in love.

★ ★ ★ ★

U.S.S. *Carolina* and U.S.S. *Louisiana* lay bow to stern, snubbed against a wharf along the levee. Brown water sucked at their hulls, whirlpools forming and disappearing. Their firepower could be decisive if the British reached the river. Gulls screamed overhead and Jackson watched a half-dozen brown pelicans at rest on the water float by with the detached expressions of stagecoach riders. In the distance a huge uprooted tree passed, slowly spinning. The river looked a mile wide.

Commodore Daniel Patterson proved to be a thick, muscular man who described his ships with real passion. *Carolina* was eighty-seven feet, a Charleston-built schooner carrying fifteen guns, three long nines, and a dozen short-range carronades of twelve pounds each. *Louisiana* was a hundred-foot sloop carrying twenty guns, four of them massive twenty-fours.

He led them into a shack on the wharf. A coffeepot on gimbals emitted a rich aroma to mingle with heavy tobacco smoke. Patterson took up a pipe but didn't light it. Charts were open on a table, and he used the pipe as a pointer—yes, the attack would come through the sea lakes.

"I have five of my gunboats on watch there," he said, dropping dried beans on the chart to indicate position, "under Lieutenant Jones, here." He nodded to a slender young man with a shock of light brown hair tied in a queue.

"Got a lot resting on you, son," Jackson said.

"Yes, sir."

"I think they'll land on Gentilly Plain, too—means they'll come right by your location. Now, what I must have is continuous reporting on their progress. Understand? Everything depends on our having time to get ready for them. So don't take any chances. Once they start, fall back—you've got plenty of small boats aboard these craft? You can send frequent messages as their intentions become clear?"

"Yes, sir. Plenty of boats."

He liked the boy's looks; those dark eyes had a spark that suggested a man of action. Of course, he had nothing to say in the choice of Jones; Patterson's was an independent command. But he felt he could rely on the young sailor, and in the end, every general is hostage to the men carrying out his orders.

He shook Jones's hand. "You'll be fine. Just make sure you don't get caught in an engagement. I'm sure Commodore Patterson agrees: your role is to watch, not fight."

"Correct," Patterson said.

"I'd as lief fight," Jones said.

Jackson smiled. "But see that you don't."

"Aye aye, sir."

Jackson turned to Patterson. "Now, if I have to fall back to near the river, your ships' guns can pour in the grape?"

"One ship, at least. *Louisiana* isn't manned. *Carolina* brought her own crew of regulars when she slipped the blockade to come in from Charleston, but the other ship outfitted here."

Jackson stared at him. "Are you saying only one of your ships is operable?" The river was full of ships idled by the blockade; there should be plenty of sailors.

Patterson shrugged. "The problem stems from our raid on Lafitte. All New Orleans seems to have a romance with that damned pirate—I suspect a good many of 'em are getting rich off him." He described his raid on Barataria Bay. "That put a hell of a crimp in smuggling. Seems the New Orleans economy turns on smuggled goods, and the people here were mad as all get-out. Plenty of sailors on the beach, but I guess half have family connections at Barataria and the others figure to get a knife in the ribs if they sign on."

Of course there was no forcing them—old Dominic Hall, a hanging judge with a hair-trigger temper, would grant writs of habeas corpus in an instant if Patterson tried.

"Well," Jackson said, "we'll get a crew, come what may. Now, this Lafitte—tell me, is he privateer or pirate?"

Patterson shrugged. "Letter of marque from Cartagena? Pretty thin. They've been pirates for years. Nothing wrong with privateering as such, you know, preying on enemy merchant vessels with proper authority. My old skipper Joshua Barney did well out of Baltimore until the British shut him down. Heard from him, by the way—wounded at Bladensburg. Says the enemy could have been stopped before he ever reached Washington." He hesitated. "Tell you one thing about privateers *or* pirates—every ship they take has weapons and powder, and they seize it all. Hell's fire, we took twenty guns with powder and shot, and that's not a patch on what he's holding."

"Really?"

"Oh, Lord, yes. He has dozens of caches back in the bayous, powder kegs all waterproofed and stored against need. You'd never find them without a key. He's got a thousand men, you know—they've all been squirreling away ammunition."

A thousand men? With heavy guns and ample supplies of powder and shot?

He stored the thought; meanwhile, he wanted both of Patterson's ships operating, and Judge Hall could go to hell.

★ ★ ★ ★

Rachel Jackson was taking the sunshine in front of the blockhouse compound when a slender figure in black on a dark horse rounded the bend at a lope. Her heart turned over, and for a disorienting moment she was swept back to the day when Andrew galloped up the lane to Ma's blockhouse full of the peril posed by Robards's threat to return and claim her. Then she saw it was young Mr. McIntyre, Dr. Hume's new assistant, come to pay a pastoral call.

Yet so powerful was that momentary vision that she had to sit down, hand pressed to her chest. She was still shaken with disappointment over Andrew's last message: once again, she could not join him. He'd wanted her in Mobile, then had said the risk was too great but she should order a keelboat for the journey to join him in New Orleans.

So Tom Larson had made a beautiful craft in his boatyard; Harriet Larson even hung pretty blue curtains at the cabin windows. And then the last letter—danger mounting, he could not risk her presence in New Orleans. Nothing had disappointed her more save the realization that the Lord would deny her the children she and Andrew wanted so desperately.

So she would wait here at the home they called the Hermitage. The name seemed a forlorn expression of hope rarely answered, with Andrew so often gone. She waved as the young man dismounted and led his horse around to the barn to be watered and fed. It wasn't just that joining Andrew would have ended the agony of those long, bitter nights spent pacing in the dark, old Hannah coming to her with cups of hot milk, and then a breaking dam, wild laments scrawled pell-mell—*I have borne it untill now it has thrown me into feavours. I am very unwell—the mercy and goodness of Heaven to me you are Spard perils—my prayers is unceasing how Long o Lord will I remain so unhappy. No rest no Ease I cannot sleepe I never wanted to see you so mutch in my life*—letters that shamed her for the pain they gave him.

No, it wasn't just that. He was sick. There was no disguising it from her. Between the lines she read his pain, the ashen face, the spasms that shook him so he could scarcely stand. How long could indomitable will triumph over body?

And now he was in the gravest danger. He always said New Orleans was the key, so the enemy's huge army would never be more determined. And he would be in front, ignoring peril—oh, God, what if she lost him? She couldn't bear it, she would go mad or die. Of course she was too dependent, but it was what life had done to her with its gift of joy and burden of pain. God's will.

If she could just go to him, be with him—oh, if she were there she would protect him, cosset him, see to his diet, make him rest. But what could she do from so far?

What could she *do*?

Mr. McIntyre appeared, bowed, suggested they pray together. Later they would have coffee with pound cake fresh that morning, but now they talked to the Lord together and a calm came over her. It always did when she talked to the Lord.

What could she do? She was an able woman, active, she had ideas, she ran the farm well in Andrew's absence—think!

The monument to those who had served in the Creek War was complete; the Governor led the dedication, Dr. Hume preached on service and duty, and the crowd came for miles. But now she wanted something immediate, something that would help.

"Why don't you go to New Orleans, Mr. McIntyre?" she said. It was inspiration from the Lord.

She saw she'd startled him, but she rushed along.

"Don't you see? Andrew and all his men will be in danger—surely they'll never be more in need of spiritual comfort. Oh, what a difference you could make—you speak so clearly for Jesus, you know. Your faith is so strong."

"Do you think so?" He smiled. "I do try."

"Dear Mr. McIntyre, you try and you surely do succeed. You're an inspiration. But there are five thousand men there or more—my goodness, why not send you and several ministers. Of different faiths, perhaps."

She saw him frown at that but rushed along. This wasn't the time to debate her view that all faiths spoke equally to the Lord, except maybe the Pope's minions, they talked only to the Pope, as she understood it. New Orleans was French and Catholic, the more reason to send Presbyterians and Baptists.

"Think of the good work you could do. Several ministers—well, why not send doctors, too? There's always work for doctors in war, there'll be countless poor devils wounded, I'm afraid, and they'll need care for the body as well as the spirit. The two go hand in hand, don't you think?"

"They do, Mrs. Jackson. You're wise to see that. I've noticed it over and over. And this is a wonderful idea—folks always think on Jesus when they're not well."

"Or in danger."

"Exactly—oh, it's a wonderful idea." He stopped and his face fell. "But the cost . . . the medicines and things . . ."

"And horses, packhorses and saddle horses."

"Horses?"

"Yes, of course—you must go the fastest way possible, right down the Natchez Trace, with extra horses so you don't wear out your mounts and face delay. Not wasting a moment—oh, the spiritual joy that you can spread! And of course, we must collect ample medicines, bandages and balms and tinctures and extracts, balsam and belladona and simples and opium."

"But the cost . . ."

"I'll raise the funds, don't you worry—let men of property pay to ease the suffering of younger men who fight for them. I'll see to that, never you fear."

Mr. McIntyre's eyes were snapping. She saw he leapt at the idea there is more to life than leading old ladies in prayer. Then he looked dismayed.

"Dr. Hume might not let me go."

She smiled. "I think Dr. Hume will listen to me."

"Bless you, Mrs. Jackson. Bless you."

★ ★ ★ ★

The music was one of those new waltzes that were the rage of Europe, but played with a New Orleans beat, a lilt that made Johnny Reid think of the crowded market on the levee with its shouts and laughter and curses and guitar music, the old men over their chessboards with an audience to cheer adroit moves, the stalls with piles of fruit and nuts and shellfish and alligator hides, black women in scarlet and yellow gowns with baskets on their heads. Reid loved to waltz, a pretty woman in your arms, round and round till you were giddy with the motion . . .

He was in the Livingstons' drawing room, furniture pulled back, a brace of violins playing, feeling easy with General Jackson away on his inspection trip to the south, admiring the décolletage of his partner, a young woman named Michelle Frontenac, his admiration the more pleasurable because she so plainly enjoyed it. Slyly, teasing him with those lush parted lips, she asked if the navy had found its crewmen. He shook his head.

She laughed. "Of course not—after the cruel way it attacked poor Captain Lafitte, who would join?"

But Lafitte was a pirate.

"No, no—a privateer. A pirate is very déclassé. Vulgar, surely. But Captain Lafitte is a gentleman. Handsome, too." She shrugged. "He's often in our home, he's charming, witty, full of the latest news from Paris—an ideal dinner guest."

Reid was astounded. Pirates at such a woman's table?

"Anyway," she said, "he hasn't been charged with piracy."

"He's under indictment for smuggling."

"Yes—an accusation surely in the poorest taste."

"But smuggling is a crime."

"Oh, I hope not. My grandfather was a famous smuggler. Honored for it. A criminal? How misguided, Johnny."

"You astonish me."

"Under the French, the Spanish, now the Americans, there has always been smuggling. It's a game, you see. Sometimes we get careless and are caught. Sometimes they become clever and catch us." She gave a fetching little shrug. "But we're all friends."

"You slip through what you can, and pay when you're caught?"

"There! *Now* you understand. You see? That's why Captain Patterson's raid was so . . . well, it broke the rules."

She laughed and pressed his hand when the music ended and whispered that with a little forethought she could evade her father's eye, should Johnny send her a note. There was punch well laced with brandy, and he was pouring her a cup when a bearded Frenchman bowed and whirled her away.

Madame Louise Livingston appeared beside him.

"Well, monsieur, did Michelle persuade you that the Creoles are not ogres after all?"

"Ah, madame," he said, "I have found them charming."

"Would that your fine general agreed."

"He hopes to persuade you that he's not an ogre."

Her quick smile was intoxicating. The music began, they were alone at the punch bowl, she raised her arms in invitation, and he swept her onto the floor. They danced without talking, she with a feathery lightness that made him realize he'd been carrying Michelle. Madame Louise was delightful, able to fascinate him without the least suggestiveness and leave him sick with envy of her husband.

"Ah, well," she said, "anyone who was born and reared in Haiti and driven out by the slave revolt knows real ogres."

He saw the sudden pain in her eyes and was silent for a long moment.

"The slaves, you mean?" he said finally.

"Not really. They just wanted what the revolution in Paris promised—freedom. It's what the slaves here doubtless want and will have someday, I hope not so bloodily for us. No, I was thinking of man's everlasting capacity for cruelty. They killed my two oldest brothers and threw their bodies on the veranda."

She turned her face aside, and they went the full circle of the room before she looked up at him with a crooked smile.

"We ran out—I was already a widow then—and saw that the bodies had no heads. Jacques and Pierre. We recognized their clothes. Then—from the dark, you see—they threw my brothers' severed heads. They bounced on the veranda and rolled to our feet. My mother was out of her mind for weeks, my father died within the year. And eventually I came to New Orleans and became an American."

He was stunned—and yet, he thought now that he had sensed from the beginning that she carried pain in her heart.

"Would that you had . . . had happier reasons for coming," he said.

She nodded. "Thank you, dear sir. But the past . . . is past. I'm an American now, and I'm happy to be here."

★ ★ ★ ★

Jack Gordon was ready to report when Jackson returned from his trip downriver, where he'd found the fort guarding the river entrance from the sea more than adequate. The British wouldn't be coming that way. It would be the sea lakes, all right. And it would be soon. Already a week had passed since his arrival.

He was in his headquarters, gloves and crop still on the table, the mug of hot coffee Pink had given him in both hands. Johnny nodded in confirmation as Jack described the situation.

The new militia units were getting no volunteers. The warehouses were locked and their owners not around. No vouchers had been accepted. The armory was still locked—said they would open it, but hadn't. And Patterson had found no sailors.

"Ain't just the leaders, neither," Jack said. "None of 'em know what they want. You go in the taverns, they're snapping and snarling about the Americans, talking about hiding their goods from the army, maybe they'll join the new militia units and maybe they won't. What they need is a kick up their backside."

He removed his cigar and spat into a gaboon.

"And then some of them really sound like British agents, talking about how the redcoats would turn the place right over to the Spanish. The average Frenchman, see, he figures Spanish is closer to French than American. I got enough French to keep up, and I'll tell you, General, I had to bite my tongue right smart not to knock some of those big mouths down. Not that they're such bad folks, but they sure do want taking in hand."

★ ★ ★ ★

Dressed in black, Louise D'Avezac Livingston sat in the tiny study off her drawing room, blinds drawn, the door cracked just so, and watched the men file into the room. She was deeply worried; those who have seen war want never to see it again, and she had seen a lifetime's worth in Haiti. That she had lost a husband and three gorgeous babies to fever was simply part of life; war was what she couldn't forget. She regretted telling Johnny Reid of that awful night. She rarely spoke of the horror she'd known, for people who hadn't known it could comprehend it only with their minds, not their souls. Young Reid was handsome, of course, with that lock of brown hair falling across his forehead and the power—still latent but already forceful—so evident in his face. And then he was a little in love with her, and of course that was touching; her awareness of it had loosened her tongue.

Now war was seeking her out again. She still had nightmares peopled with soldiers in Haiti. They were black and barefoot and armed with cane knives, and these would be white in red coats with bayonets, but they were the same. These soldiers would be coming in awful numbers, professional troops who'd beaten a military genius—and facing them were citizen troops from Tennessee and Louisiana, led by an untried general. She had drawn Jackson's dossier from Edward, and though the man was impressive, his dossier was not.

And these foolish French squabbled among themselves, petty men spoiling over trifles in the face of disaster. General Jackson had returned from downriver to find the city pulling in all directions and had asked Edward to assemble these men that he might—what? Appeal to them? He didn't strike her as a man who appealed.

She watched Rosemarie passing the tray of demitasses, her round rump quivering as she maneuvered. Everyone who mattered was here. General Villeré and his son, Gabriel; something light in the son, and in the father for refusing to see it. Bernard Marigny, who might speak for the Creoles but didn't speak for her. Governor Claiborne, looking as innocent as the day he was born.

Major Plauché of the Battalion d'Orleans, with that tedious St Gême who always tried to flirt. The nasty old judge, Dominic Hall, looking as if he absolutely hungered to hang someone. Major LaCoste, who had the black battalion, sitting with Jean Daquin, who had formed a second battalion. Little Major Latour with his bristling mustaches and unshakable dignity. General de Flaugeac of the senate, a key commander under Napoleon, the epitome of the old soldier. The white-haired merchant Tom Beale, once a citizen soldier in America, now a dealer in dry goods, who intended to raise a rifle company. Mayor Girod, a shuttlecock in the war between Claiborne and the legislature.

They were puffed up, a bit hostile, their vanity showing, such importance in the very way they stood. What peacocks! They made women's small ministrations to self, ruffles and feathers and paints and powders, seem modest indeed . . .

General Jackson stood with his back to the fireplace, window light full in his face, and waved Rosemarie aside. Something in his face made her think he was in pain.

"Gentlemen," he said. He spoke slowly, his voice shrill, and a little shiver ran through her. "I don't have the French language, but that isn't to say I don't appreciate the glories of French culture. In recent memory France came near conquering the world, and the valor and fury of the French fighting man is not in question."

Very good, she saw slow smiles forming.

"But you are Franco-Americans now. *Americans*—and I want your help in the test that lies ahead. I want it given willingly," but—his voice rose suddenly, startling her—"I will compel it if necessary."

She felt a slight tingling in her skin, listening to him. She studied the men's faces; they didn't like such talk.

"Now, gentlemen," he said, "hear me well. I expect full cooperation and I'm not getting it. I want warehouses open and goods flowing. I want every weapon in the armory, every able-bodied man enlisted—and believe me, I intend to have a crew for Commodore Patterson's second ship."

No answer. They sat like toads.

She saw he'd expected the reaction. He raised a baleful finger.

"Understand, if I don't get it, I'll declare martial law and compliance will be at bayonet point."

Judge Hall stood abruptly, his normally pallid face flushed.

"You would trample the Constitution, sir!"

The others watched apprehensively. No one trifled with Judge Hall. But the tall general was unmoved.

"I believe the Second Amendment grants a clear exception to the writ of habeas corpus in time of invasion."

The Judge hesitated, then said, "Perhaps the President could declare it under these circumstances. You, sir, cannot."

Jackson smiled a bleak smile and didn't answer. Judge Hall sat down, looking oddly discomfited. The General walked to a window and turned with his back to the light. Blazing light behind the dark figure made him look . . . awesome.

"Does anyone really not yet understand the situation?" he said. "Gentlemen, the British are coming and we're going to fight them so long as one man lives—fight when they land, fight here if we must, fight street by street, house by house . . ."

Her eyes blurred. Images of Cap Haïtien after the rebels had fought house-to-house mixed with memories of what was left of their own great manor house. He would burn what he couldn't hold, he would leave nothing to the victors—couldn't these fools understand? Then she realized that they understood too well and were sick with fear.

He paused, letting them think. "So . . . British agents are at work in New Orleans, saying if Britain should win, it would pass control to the Spanish. But I tell you in plain language, that is a God damned lie. The British vision of the future depends on joining Louisiana to Canada—they would never get out willingly, and you would live forever under London's command."

London? Dismay settled on French faces. The General paced, and their eyes followed him. His voice slipped to a lower register, and she heard a cajoling thread in its force.

"But there is a deeper reality here, too. Britain could never hold New Orleans. We would fight for it forever, and in time they would weary and go home. But we would never weary—for losing New Orleans would mean the death of the American dream, the westering dream, the dream of a continental nation. And we won't let that dream die. We won't give up the West."

Silence, pacing, pacing, watching them with that eye like an eagle's, imperious, demanding, brutal, seeing visions and depths denied others. Her fists were clenched, her breath short.

"We are a hardy people, gentlemen. Had you walked across the Cumberland Gap as I have done and seen the people coming with packs on their backs and rifles in hand, long-limbed Scotch-Irish men and women with resistance in their blood, highland Celts who've always known they must fight to live—oh, if you had seen the westering dream in action you would never doubt its strength. They are violent and resolute and no one on God's earth can turn them back. Should the British take New Orleans, it would never last, for these people will fight forever to live as they see fit, and their sons and grandsons will fight on."

She was stunned. She had never heard the American strength so expressed; suddenly she saw that in coming here she had joined what she hadn't even understood, and she felt a surge of joy.

"And you," Jackson said, "what of you? What matters to us is an open Mississippi, not this city as such. Think about it. If we spent ten years whipping the redcoats, what would be left here? Ashes and rubble. And when we drove them out, we would build a new port and the New Orleans of today would be cane fields for our grandchildren. All that you are and all that you have would be a fading memory."

His voice sank lower and vibrated with intensity.

"Now, gentlemen, I intend to win and I expect to do it with your help—but I advise you to make your people understand that the day I fail will mark your descent into hell."

No one moved. She released her breath in a long sigh. The force of him! The men looked at each other, red-faced and shaken. It was Tom Beale, the merchant, who spoke for them.

"Well, General, we're with you. Not a man here wants the British to win. Or thinks they will. And me and my men will be beside you when the time comes. But you said it plain, so I will, too. You mought better be thinking about Jean Lafitte. All his men and guns, it don't make sense not to use him."

Jackson stood like a statue. Then he smiled a faint smile and said he would give that point due consideration. And in a flash of insight, even as the men nodded in foolish triumph, she saw that he had given them nothing—he already had decided.

Louise Livingston sighed. She had dealt with powerful men, she knew the breed well, and this one—ah, this was one to make others pale. She watched the men file out, and when they were gone Edward came to her and she slipped inside his arm with a sigh. She felt his arm tighten around her and she turned to press her body hard against his.

27

New Orleans
December, 1814

★ ★ ★ ★ Sixty Royal Navy vessels—half warships and half troopships— decks stacked high with nests of small boats, dropped anchor in the deep water of Mississippi Sound just beyond the entrance to Lake Borgne. The small boats went over the side and lay against the vessels like clusters of insect eggs. It was the fifteenth of December.

A gig came flashing across the lake, then a party of scouts raced from lakeshore to headquarters with Lieutenant Jones's terse message: his gunboats were standing by to withdraw as the enemy advanced, and he would send regular advices.

Jackson lifted both arms over his head, stretching, smiling, feeling good. The pain in his gut was scarcely noticeable. He was forcing the issue—he had made them come by sea, had figured they would choose the sea lakes, and he was as ready on Gentilly Plain as mortal soldier could be. The gunboats would keep him posted step by step as they advanced, and when they landed he'd be waiting for them. The situation was tenuous and fluid, that's the nature of war, but he was in a solid position to press his advantages.

He dashed off orders, quill scratching, ink drops flying. Jack Coffee's dragoons were to come from Baton Rouge by forced march; Jack had posted relays every ten miles along the river road so the message would reach him in under twenty hours. And Carroll with his twenty-five hundred Tennessee volunteers couldn't be far now—Jackson sent a hard-riding search party to cut the river's turns and find him with orders to abandon his flatboats and advance overland at a driving pace.

Both regiments of regulars were to collect in the city, save for those assigned to outlying forts. Louisiana militia was to move a couple of miles out on the Gentilly Plain. A second battalion of free blacks formed only last week would join them. The original black battalion would hold just north of the city with the regulars and the uniformed companies, poised to move in any direction from which a threat came.

Tom Hinds arrived with his two hundred Mississippi dragoons. They lined up on Royal Street in three ranks, handling their horses with easy skill, and Jackson reviewed them from the balcony. Fine big stalwart devils in gorgeous uniforms of blue with snowy white crossbelts, carbines in saddle scabbards, silvery sabers at their sides, bedrolls fixed to their saddles. Hinds was a big man with a booming voice, a shock of tawny hair, and odd tawny eyes to match.

"Now, sir," he roared, "we're cavalry, and God damn, we come to fight! Put us up front—we'll grind their ass, we'll pick off their pickets, we'll keep 'em so God damned upset they'll feel like their drawers are on backward. Just don't leave us lying around—we want to whup 'em and go home!"

Jackson laughed. "One thing I can promise—there'll be fighting enough for everyone."

"Hear that, boys?" Hinds shouted. "General says we're going to burn their butts!" A cheer echoed down Royal Street. Some of the men shook their carbines in the air.

Hinds and Jack Gordon were old friends. Jackson rode out to Gentilly Plain with them as they established a system of patrols that would keep him as closely in touch with Jones's reports as horseflesh could manage.

He was content, for short of knowing exactly where to look for the enemy to land, he'd done everything he could—old French fortifications repaired, check lines and fallback lines set, rises and hedge rows that provided cover identified, angles of fire calculated, places for guns figured. Of course he hadn't committed men or guns, not yet. He was flexible, ready to shift as enemy plans became evident.

At dawn on the seventeenth of December, watchers on Gentilly Plain reported a crackle of distant gunfire. What the devil—Jones had explicit orders not to fight, but what else could it be? Jackson rode out to find Jack Gordon and Hinds staring across Lake Borgne. It was cruelly cold, the air heavy, wet, and so still the cold penetrated to the bone. Clouds that looked within reach of his hand leaked light rain. He clutched his coat to his throat and stifled a paroxysm of coughing.

Another gig hurried across the lake and a saturnine bosun older than Jackson stepped out with a crumpled message in hand. Jackson unfolded it with dread. It was addressed to Commodore Patterson. A single drop of blood obscured a word and there were water marks that might have been salt spray or might have been tears.

Sir
Casualties at more than half my men, all my ships disabled, I am striking my colors and surrendering my command.

Jones

Disaster. In a single blow the enemy had struck him blind. It didn't matter how or why—he stood there trying to absorb the impact while Jack quizzed the bosun. It seemed the enemy had mounted three-pounders in some forty longboats and attacked just as this oily calm froze the gunboats in place. Jones broke out his sweeps but his heavy vessels were no match for the light longboats, which closed rapidly and opened fire. Jones had two hundred men, the British twelve hundred. Those little boats came head-on into brutal fire, closed, boarded, and overwhelmed him.

Jackson sighed. A graphic picture of his enemy was forming. They were resourceful—no one had expected a small-boat attack. And they were tough and they didn't let enemy fire slow them and they kept on coming. Such were the men who would be charging his lines with bayonets.

And who now with a single blow had shattered his plans. For how could he maximize his own advantages and minimize theirs and thus overcome their numbers if he couldn't see them coming? Everything had depended on his having time to lay his lines, position his guns, guard against flank attacks. He would send out small boats on scout, but those same longboats would surely drive them away. He told Gordon and Hinds to post day and night roving patrols and keep men with glasses in trees all along the shoreline. Give him the earliest possible warning—with that he would have to make do.

He returned to the city at a gallop. Ed Livingston met him in the street.

"My God, I just heard. The town's in an uproar—panic in the streets, people running around shouting. Sat on their hands for months, now they're chickens with their heads cut off."

"Are they ready to fight?"

"Ready to dither, damn them. They're all over the place. Some want to shoulder a musket and fight; some want to run to the enemy and capitulate; some couldn't believe it would ever happen and now they're having trouble holding their bowels—and the British sympathizers or agents or whatever they are, they're telling everyone it's all for Spain's benefit."

He ran up the stairs to his office and Ed followed.

"Look, General, there's something else. Governor Claiborne took the news to the legislature to ask for action—appropriations, authorizations, gearing up for war, you see—"

"And?"

"They blew up. Yelling, cursing, quarreling—right on the edge of panic. It scared Claiborne, I think—he urged them to adjourn for two weeks and tend to war matters."

"Claiborne's first good idea."

"But they denounced him, more or less chased him out. They're over there now fuming and fulminating and—well—dithering. No other word for it."

"I need your help, Ed," Jackson said. He scrawled out an order. "Get this to a printer. Have a thousand copies made and see it's posted everywhere—market, taverns, every square, the churches, the armory, city offices. Deliver it personally to the Governor, the Mayor, the legislature. And Judge Hall—put a copy in that little prune's hand."

Ed scanned the sheet. "My God—this is strong medicine."

The order declared martial law.

"It's just too late for confusion and vacillation," Jackson said. "I won't have it. And no more talk of capitulation. Make it clear, Ed—I'll treat any attempt to talk to the enemy as treason in wartime, and that means firing squads."

The capacity to end confusion at bayonet point if necessary felt so good— so delicious, in fact, that a flash of caution gave him pause. Power is sweeter than wine and much too easy to love. In a stroke he had suspended the writ of habeas corpus, giving himself the right to arrest without explanation. Everyone entering and leaving the city must report and account for themselves. Nine o'clock curfew; those abroad after nine without a pass to be taken as spies. No boats on the river without naval permission. The armory to be opened immediately, the arms therein to be held under guard until they were needed. Every able-bodied man to report for duty, in one of the new militia units or for the labor battalions needed to perfect his lines in a hurry once the enemy's intentions became clear.

"Saddle up," he said to Johnny Reid, "and get this over to Patterson. Tell him I suggest he start his marines scouring the waterfront for seamen. I want that ship of his ready to fight."

"Yes, sir!"

★ ★ ★ ★

The next day he stood on the levee and watched U.S.S. *Louisiana* cast off, sails clattering into place in a stiff breeze from the north. She swung well out into the muddy river, came about smartly, and came straight at him. When it seemed her bowsprit must graze the moored vessels, she whirled and her sails took the wind on the opposite quarter with cracks like gunfire. She ran upriver making a bone, spun about, came down before the wind with sails spread. When she was squarely abeam she fired a thunderous broadside, her guns making the sterile sound of powder exploded without a load. Jackson swung his hat overhead.

By the Eternal, that was a sight to see! But the lift was momentary. The ship was on the river, and his problem was on the brackish waters washing Gentilly Plain. Never had he felt more blind, more discomfited. He could only wait.

★ ★ ★ ★

Major Latour's cousins were merchants—Descloseaux Bobé, a fishmonger, and Andreas d'Arges, a hide dealer—both of them balding, too heavy, over fifty, and down at the heels. Jackson shook their hands warmly.

"You can do a real service, gentlemen. I want you to take a launch and carry a letter from me to the British commandant inquiring as to the condition and safety of Lieutenant Jones, if he's alive, and the crews of the five gunboats."

"Reckon they'll tell us?" Bobé looked cannily doubtful, but maybe it was just the way one eye turned outward.

"Oh, no," Jackson said. "They won't answer and they'll detain you till this is over, but I judge they won't harm you."

"Well, shit, General, what's the use?"

"They'll interrogate you. They'll want to know about our troops here. You are to tell them General Jackson has fifteen thousand men and more coming every day."

"Well," Bobé said, "what good'll that do?"

D'Arges poked his cousin in the ribs and winked at Jackson.

"C'mon, Des—General wants to fool 'em."

★ ★ ★ ★

He paced on the wrought-iron balcony, trying to pierce the mind of that British commander in the distance, wherever he was. Did the man know he operated in the comfort of invisibility? Did he care? Would it make him careless?

Cob Farr, his chin fiery red from squeezed pimples, poked his head in the door.

"Say, there." Cob was the guard; he hesitated, remembering military etiquette, and put his yellow shoes together. "Sir, a fellow here, he wants to see you. Won't give his name, but you can tell he's a gentleman."

The visitor was scarcely thirty, tall, slender, handsome, light brown hair well trimmed and brushed, wearing a fine woolen suit with a gold watch chain, impeccable linen, boots well blacked, hands clean and rather delicate.

He bowed in the doorway and said in accented but easy English, "Jean Lafitte, sir, at your service."

The gall of him, walking into his enemy's lair like a prince of the realm!

But it was more than that—there was princely courage in his bearing, in the cast of his eye. Jackson remembered William Weatherford, the Creek chief, half Creek and half Scot, riding in with that buck across his saddle, facing a dozen leveled muskets, shoot and be damned! They were enemies, he and Weatherford, but he'd come to admire the man.

"Sit down, Captain Lafitte. I understand you want to join the defense of New Orleans—for a price."

"The price of forgiveness of sins, if in fact there were any sins. It seems not unreasonable."

Jackson tented his hands and studied Lafitte. The man's low, well modulated voice had a timbre that hinted at strength, at familiarity with power, even at the whiplash of command. Jackson knew he was fluent in Spanish, Italian, English, and, of course, French, and that the ladies of New Orleans couldn't get enough of him. He scarcely looked the pirate, but Jackson was too old to imagine that evil is evident to the eye.

"Actually, Captain," Jackson said, "it's not your price that disturbs me but the problem of trusting you in my camp. Pray show me why I should."

"I came to Louisiana ten years ago," Lafitte said, "when I was twenty-two. This is my chosen home. What would I be if I didn't burn to defend it? And yes, if I prove myself, if my men serve well, who is to say that past crimes, if any there were, should not be forgiven? What is the point of redemption but that one changes? The point of punishment but that it deters crime, and what is punishment but service?"

"Punishment as service?"

"Payment for crime, is it not? To be shot or flogged is to pay all at once. Brand my cheek, hold me in jail, that's surely service. Why not have me serve usefully?"

Jackson didn't answer.

"For example," Lafitte said, "I know these swamps as well as any man."

"As a smuggler."

Lafitte shrugged. "As a sportsman, say. A naturalist. But I could have delivered that asinine Englishman to within a mile of your camp." His lip curled. "What a fool, offering to bribe me. I am French, sir, to my very core, which is reason enough to hate the British. And I have my own reason for hating Spain, whose ships I've troubled a bit, always as a privateer."

"A bit?"

"More than a bit. I make no apology for attacking Spain. My grandfather died in the Inquisition and my father fled to Haiti. I grew up there on tales of Spanish cruelty. When my brother Alexander became a privateer, Pierre and I—we are the youngest—we could hear our grandfather cheering from his grave. Joining Alexander was our duty to family and heritage. And we've made the Spanish pay. And pay, and pay."

He laughed out loud and with a vivid smile slowly snapped his fingers.

"Now, sir," he said, "you can defend New Orleans without me, but why should you? I can give you a thousand men, fighting men who've heard the cannon roar. I can take you into the swamps to powder caches that are an artillery officer's dream—we were prepared to hold out for years, if it came to that. I have guns in those caches, too, grease-coated twelves and twenty-fours awaiting the defense of my country."

"Why do you suppose this patriotism has a hollow ring?"

Lafitte chuckled and spread his hands. "Because, sir, you are a man of the world. I am French by heritage, American by persuasion—am I to bow to Britain? But wisdom leads you to suspect more."

He slowly shut his right eye, and to Jackson's surprise, this gave weight to his words.

"I loved our life in Barataria. We were wild and free and the world was ours. Who could resist it? I admit that. But now the world is shifting. The United States is growing strong. When I came here, Louisiana was sleepy and backward. But look what my new country has done—challenged the mistress of the seas, the conqueror of Napoleon. I think it will win. I want it to win with my help. And winning becomes a devil of a lot more likely with that help.

"And what then? Why, I sense a new order coming. The lazy old days of smuggling are gone, never to return, because the United States will never again let Louisiana languish. Florida will prosper as a state in time, and I'll wager Texas won't be far behind. Commerce will flourish on the river. And if there are smugglers, they will be miserable wretches living in shadow without pride. I could not live without pride."

Again he smiled broadly and spread his hands in that Gallic gesture.

"Patriotism, sir, laced with self-interest. Surely you agree—self-interest is the most honest motive?"

Jackson laughed. By God, he liked the man! More and more, Lafitte made him think of Weatherford. They wouldn't be friends and might remain enemies, but here was a man he could respect even if he had to kill him. And yes, of all motives, self-interest was the most reliable. To use him was risky, but he had men and guns, and Jackson judged the risk was tolerable.

"Very well," he said. "I'll accept your offer and arrange amnesty for you and your men. I'll want you to leave in an hour with Captain Spotts of my artillery to go to your caches. I want all your guns and powder—all, mind you."

"They're yours, sir."

"We'll muster your men and divide them into companies—well-separated companies. I'll take frequent communication among those companies as a sign of treachery. Impress that upon them. And you, sir, when you return from your caches, I'll want you near me at all times. If I suspect treachery on your part, there'll be no trial and no delay. I'll put a pistol to your ear and blow your brains out. Do you understand?"

Lafitte's right eye closed. "Sir, you would have prospered at my old trade."

Jackson stared at him, unsmiling. "Don't try me, sir."

★ ★ ★ ★

Big Jack Coffee marched in from Baton Rouge with his fifteen hundred dragoons. They went into bivouac on Avart's plantation four miles up the river, and Jackson hurried out to see him. God Almighty, his Tennessee boys did look good! Rangy devils in homespun with eyes used to looking over a rifle's sights, they were firing tobacco juice all over the place. They crowded around so hard he had to climb on a wagon to see them and they gave him a cheer to make the air ring. They'd made a hundred and twenty miles in two days and seemed well satisfied they'd impressed a man not easily impressed.

"Well, shit," Sergeant Passman said with a laugh, "we didn't want to miss the fandango, now, did we?"

Coffee was his strong right arm. And right behind him came the other strong arm: Billy Carroll reached Avart's four hours later with his twenty-five hundred. Compact of body, neat of mind and manner, marked by a reserve that made him seem cold, he was quite the opposite of warmhearted Jack Coffee. A relative newcomer to Tennessee, he'd arrived with capital, gone into business, and was making himself wealthy. You couldn't love Billy—no one he knew did, certainly—but you had to respect him.

In the end, that's why Jackson had taken his part in the silly duel with Jesse Benton that had such awful consequences—they were ganging up on Billy because they didn't like him, and it was damned unfair. And he'd served well; how could Jackson refuse when asked to speak for him? It cost him, though, and not just the wound. Tom Benton was one of the best men he'd ever had and now, of course, there was no communication between them. He'd heard Benton was talking of leaving Tennessee. Missouri was opening up now; maybe he'd go there. It would be better. If they met on the street, Jackson might cane him again, whatever the consequences. Let him go to Missouri . . .

Billy, now, was his usual efficient, effective humorless self. En route by flatboat, he had intercepted a portion of the shipment of arms and ammunition coming from Pittsburgh. Where the rest of the shipment might be God only knew. Billy's gunsmiths put the muskets in working order to augment those he'd scraped up in Tennessee, though the bulk of his men carried their own rifles, which they knew as well as they knew their wives. Billy also had made up fifty thousand cartridges, ball and three buckshot pellets in a paper twist. And he'd built a foredeck on each flatboat and drilled his men all the way down, brushing up these old Creek War veterans' military skills. They were damned good soldiers when Jackson sent them home last time, but Billy had added polish.

"Plus," Billy said, "they know the woods, they know how to shoot, and they know how to take care of themselves. Put them in the line and by God, they'll do you proud."

Jackson led both his generals out on Gentilly Plain, pointing out the few defense elements—ditches, canals, fence rows, rises, here and there an orchard. They met roving scouts every few minutes. At a beach where a handful of men huddled around a fire and one watched from high in a cypress, they dismounted to stare across water that revealed nothing.

Jack Coffee grunted. "God damn, General, you know I don't often question nothing, but 'pears to me we're leaving it in their hands. Setting here waiting for 'em to hit us."

"That's about it."

"That ain't usually your way, nor mine. Any situation you can name, it's better to have control. Especially in a fight . . ."

Jackson stared at Coffee. For a moment he wanted to slap his old friend— the impertinence! He clamped his jaw shut, realizing his spurt of anger grew from hearing his most ardent desires voiced as if they were new. But there was no man he trusted more than Jack Coffee, even if he did have to explain things now and then.

"What would you do, Jack?" His voice was soft, but Coffee looked a little uncomfortable.

"Well," the big man said, "get ready, I guess. Pick a likely spot, throw up some barriers, get a few guns set up—get set to meet 'em, you know."

"Suppose we moved out a ways and they put in behind us?" Jackson was holding his troops at the one-mile point outside the city, ready to move onto Gentilly Plain in response to a landing.

"Well . . ." Coffee shrugged, face coloring.

"It's like business," Billy Carroll said. "I'm going to bring the first steamboat up the Cumberland one of these days."

"So?" Jackson said. Sometimes Billy was hard to follow.

"Time's not right for it, don't you see? Investment unclear, return unclear. I don't know enough, not yet. Same as this here—if I understand it correctly, we don't even know they'll attack this way or not."

"Where the hell else?" Coffee growled.

Billy shrugged, looking aggrieved.

"Point is, we don't know. That's the point."

Coffee's fists were doubled. He turned suddenly and walked up the beach, looking much like an angry bear. Jackson pondered the question. Where else might the enemy come? Force the narrow straits leading into Lake Pontchartrain? A secondary role for the gunboats had been to protect that route, and now the gunboats were gone. Circle both lakes and attack from the north? It would be a hard march, but he'd better ask Hinds to send out a strong patrol just to be sure.

He shook his head, refusing anger that he knew could sweep him away. That was the cost of the gunboat loss—he could only wait. It was the nineteenth of December and he thought they would hit the next day. Then we'd see.

"Shall we ride, gentlemen?" His voice was harsh as a nail scraped on slate.

★ ★ ★ ★

Jack Gordon brought in an old fisherman who lived on the north shore of Lake Borgne. Pierre Altariva was a stocky man, burned deep brown by the sun, most of his teeth gone but a gleam of intelligence in his eyes.

With Jack translating, he reported the British massing on Pea Island offshore from his home, countless small boats with eight or ten oars, each delivering thirty to forty men or riding low in the water with a single heavy gun.

That described the enemy's forward staging, but unfortunately, it told Jackson little more. Pea Island was near the passage to Lake Pontchartrain; would they force that route after all? But then, Gentilly Plain with its multiple landing places was not so far beyond. In fact, from the island they could land anywhere, and that meant he still was blind.

The fisherman gazed at Jackson's map, then tapped the cross-hatching marking the cypress swamps that lay between the south shore of Lake Borgne and the river below the city.

"*Oui, oui*, Pierre," Jack said. "General, he says there are *beaucoup* bayous back in there—he can put you in a pirogue and take you to the river in three hours."

Beaucoup bayous . . . anyone could see the back door. But it was closed. Jack Gordon had waded a half mile into three separate bayous to check, and in each he found trees dropped with their leafy branches inextricably tangled. He said gators would have trouble getting through. And Gabriel Villeré reported every route locked tight as a reluctant oyster shell.

★ ★ ★ ★

At dawn on the twentieth of December the patrols on the shores of Lake Borgne and the men in the trees were on full alert, staring into the fog, waiting for boats spouting fire to emerge from the gloom. Nothing. Terns skittered along the beach. Gulls took exception to their presence and said so. But the water was still as glass.

Where in the devil were they?

Jackson sighed. He had a scarf wrapped around his throat. He signaled Johnny and they started in. The situation was baffling and more painful every day.

Johnny said Sam Spotts had crossed the river during the night with the first arms from Lafitte's caches and could hardly contain his excitement. Jackson headed for the Place d'Armes, where the artillerymen had set up workstations.

Captain Spotts was a loud and likable young man, tall, ungainly, prematurely bald, with a brilliant feel for guns and the precise calculations that made the difference between a loud noise and a weapon as deadly as man possessed. He had trained in the old Second Artillery under Winfield Scott, the same who'd made such a name at Lundy's Lane, and would be more than welcome in the front line—assuming they had time to form a real line when the enemy emerged from Pea Island gloom.

When Jackson rode into the square, Spotts was still bubbling over his trip into the swamp. "Yes, sir! More guns than we can haul, and powder— my God! Shoot all day and shoot all night and not even wonder about supply, there's so much."

He rubbed his palm across his bare scalp from front to back, smoothing hair that wasn't there. "Now, sir, this Lafitte, he's a prize. He was a different man once we got in the swamp—shed that fancy suit, handled a pirogue like you guide a horse, knew every turn on a bayou that looked like all the rest of the water to me. And how those cutthroats do jump to his commands. They love him, I guess, but he gets a look in his eye that scares them, too, and, sir, I don't think they scare easy."

The guns lay on sawhorses, from little six-pounders to massive twenty-fours. They were of all ages and came from across the world, so each was different. Spotts was cutting new sights based on careful individual calculations, notches of precise depth in the base ring and the swelling of the muzzle of each.

"Damn, General," Colonel McRae said, "ain't that boy a wizard? Did the carts, too. Wherever you want a gun, you can count on us getting it there pronto."

Moving such guns overland would be hard work. McRae led Jackson to a row of carts with high frames and huge wheels originally designed to move massive sugar hogsheads on plantations. Now slings dangling from each were positioned to hoist and move the heaviest guns wherever they were needed.

Howell Tatum was at work on the next artillery problem. If fired on dirt—and where else did guns fire in the field?—those carriages with little wheels designed for a ship's deck would flip over backward. Major Tatum had devised a platform of interlocked timbers that provided a floor on which the gun could roll back smoothly against restraint ropes as it fired.

Jackson rested a foot on Tatum's bench and looked over his shoulder. Wouldn't recoil soon shake the platforms apart? Not at all, the engineer said, and sketched rapidly, showing how recoil forces transmitting through the locked timbers would jam them tighter and strengthen the platform.

He was ready. Now he had ample guns and nearly unlimited supplies of powder and shot, while his enemy would have to carry every gun, every ball, every pound of powder on his back. He had sling carts ready to move the guns in a hurry, firing platforms for which the timbers were being pre-cut now, crack gunners to lay the pieces, riflemen who could stop a deer at four hundred yards, regulars whose muskets were loaded with ball and buckshot and tipped with bayonets ground to a fine edge—he was as ready as ready could be.

All he lacked was an enemy . . .

★   ★   ★   ★

With Michelle Frontenac and a half dozen of the women she had recruited into her Corps of Mercy, as she styled it, Louise Livingston hurried toward the Place d'Armes, boot heels clicking on stone sidewalks.

There was to be a dress parade, every outfit marching and turning and whirling and presenting arms and saluting—why, those Mississippi dragoons just arrived were said to rival Napoleon's guards in equestrian pomp. And General Jackson would give an oration to stir men's hearts. Edward had written much of it and would read it, so she had heard it at length. "Soldiers . . . I expected much of you . . . and you surpass all my hopes . . . the nation shall applaud your valor as your general praises your ardor . . ." Heady stuff, all right, and Edward had the voice for it. That voice of his . . . when it was pitched low in the language of love, my, my, it was enough to stir her.

The sun had broken the fog and was climbing a perfect sky, water clinging to sidewalks and buildings and trees like glistening jewels. She heard music ahead and another military band approached from the left. The streets were full of marching men and martial music—"Yankee Doodle" and "La Marseillaise" and "Le Chant du Départ"—music you could step right along to, that made you want to fight, that promised glory as the reward for valor.

"Johnny will be riding next to the General in the parade," Michelle whispered, clutching her arm.

The girl's eyes sparkled and she was ravishing at the moment, though often enough she seemed coarse. If she hadn't taken young Reid to bed by now, Louise missed her guess—and she found that the thought irked her. He worshiped Louise from afar, and she didn't mind that at all. But could she be . . . jealous of this sensuous creature with her parted lips and hot eyes? She laughed out loud because in fact the thought was accurate, and Michelle laughed with her.

"Isn't it grand?" the younger woman cried. "All the marching and the music and the spirit the men show? Why, the women I know do nothing but stand at their windows to cheer the passing parade. And look how proud the men are!"

That they were. Peacocks marching with that self-satisfied swing of the body, each convinced he was the center of attention, the focus of all admiring eyes. Still, what a change! And all the tall general's doing. She suspected he was ill and was sure he was often in pain, but he burned with energy, was everywhere at once, thought of everything, noticed every detail, let nothing go unchecked.

Before he came they had been loose, vacillating, confused, fighting each other. Now they were focused, intent, anxious to face the enemy. More militia units were forming, every able-bodied man summoned. Men exempted for age were forming Corps of Veterans to guard the city's streets.

That plain talk he'd given the leaders, the impact of martial law—he'd made everyone see that this was real, that now was the time. And the people responded with hot enthusiasm, denouncing an enemy who supposed he could cow a proud French culture—*mon Dieu*, hadn't the French been fighting the English since the beginning of time? Balls and dinners were staged in the afternoons now, and by half-past eight the streets were abustle with people hurrying home before the nine o'clock curfew. Discipline, ardor, demands for service, had had exactly the effect the General had intended.

She realized she was marching in step to a drum and fife, full of warlike zeal. Her Corps of Mercy was making bandages and lint—for men who surely would be wounded and in pain—and would be ready to help the doctors as needed. Meanwhile they would see to the needs of wives and children left alone when their men marched to war. It was heartwarming, the opposite of war's harsh side.

She already had incorporated young Mr. McIntyre and his corps of chaplains and doctors who had arrived the day before. Apparently his mission had been devised by Mrs. Jackson, about whom Louise was intensely curious. She had heard all the stories about Rachel, the mad rush to Natchez fleeing a furious husband, the raging affair with young Jackson—how *potent* he must have been then, given his fire today—the adulterous marriage. Blazing passion, Parisian in scope! Now the lady was said to be not just matronly of figure but fat, with religion absorbing her passion. But Louise knew that embers must survive in such a vital woman's heart. She couldn't wait to meet her.

Soon her Corps of Mercy would be at battalion strength. She laughed again: General Louise. And Michelle laughed with her and in unconscious step with the drums, they all turned into the Place d'Armes.

She was well pleased with herself.

★ ★ ★ ★

December twentieth, twenty-first, twenty-second. The enemy didn't appear. Not on Gentilly Plain, not circling the lake, not forcing the passage to Pontchartrain. He sent scout boats toward Pea Island, and Royal Navy longboats mounting small cannon drove them away. Were they waiting at

Pea Island for more troops before launching their attack? More supplies? More boats?

Each dawn he and Johnny were on the shore of Lake Borgne, waiting as the light unfolded, straining their eyes for that moment when the surface was visible; every morning they saw birds, not boats. And he rode back coughing in the cold, the old blue coat with its faded marks of rank clutched to his throat, willing himself to remain calm in the face of an ever-strengthening premonition that something was dreadfully wrong.

Control, Rachel said. She meant of rage and of self, but it applied to this moment just as fully. It struck him as he rode that the man who had walked into the City Hotel to cane Tom Benton might not have survived this pressure. Indeed, since then there had been many places where that man might not have survived, might have plunged, rushed in, lost his head, might have yielded to the wild temptation he now felt to do something, do anything.

He thought of young McIntyre and his frustration eased. The preacher had come down the Natchez Trace at real speed, in less than two weeks, swapping horses as he went. A couple of the doctors had played out and would follow on, but the rest of the party came through with packhorses of supplies intact. He had delivered a letter from Rachel describing quite wittily the pressure she'd put on Dr. Hume to release his assistant from pastoral duties.

But he'd brought a second letter, too, this one another incoherent cry in the night's agony of loneliness. Old Hume seemed to have no comfort to offer against these terrible hours of darkness. Jackson thought that something had broken in her under the pressure of Tennessee's response to their bigamous marriage, leaving her vulnerable if not defenseless without his physical presence.

Some of his own inner power had grown in response to that pressure, too. She had grown, too—she was able, intelligent, persuasive, kind beyond imagination—and yet there was that pain that struck to her heart and never quite healed. Of course, having written in the dark of night, she didn't have to send the letter, but she did; she was saying, he feared, that she *couldn't* bear it alone. He knew the strain she felt, he'd seen how short of breath she was, how often she pressed her hand to her heart—dear Lord, what would he do if he lost her?

★ ★ ★ ★

At one in the afternoon on the twenty-third of December, footsteps drummed on the stairs and Johnny Reid propelled young Gabriel Villeré into the room by his arm.

"The British!" Villeré cried. "They're here—out of the swamp—they're on my plantation!"

He was crying. Jackson grabbed him by the shirt.

"Get a grip on yourself, man. South of here?"

"Yes! There's naught to stop them—"

Through that locked and barred back door? Here was disaster to sweep all before it.

"How many men?" he said. "How many guns?"

"I don't know. Oh, God, I don't know. I have disgraced myself, dishonored my father's name—"

He had Villeré's shirt in both hands and he started to shake him, wanted to destroy him—and, as quickly, thrust him away so that the young man skittered across the room into a wall. Everything was clear in a flash—the contemptible creature had been sure no enemy would come by the bayous, so that he'd left his own open to avoid the expense of reopening it later.

"General—" Villeré's mouth quivered.

Jackson jerked his thumb at Reid. *Out with him!*

And then he was calm, cold, collected. British troops, no telling how many, five miles away and nothing to stop them as they came in at a run to exploit their priceless surprise. Jackson's troops were all on the north edge of town looking toward Gentilly and the empty lake. It would take an hour to orient them, turn them, bring them through the city, and in an hour a swift column of British shock troops would be here.

Jack Gordon thrust his head in the door, eyes frantic.

Jackson held his voice low. "Easy does it, Jack. Take a patrol and get on out there. How many? How fast are they coming? Move right along— I need this information now."

He turned to Johnny. Send separate runners to every commander. Every unit ready to march in fifteen minutes, each man with weapon, powder, and shot. Come through the city and head south; their general would join them en route.

"Yes, sir! That includes the militia on the plain?"

Jackson hesitated. He wanted everyone! But no . . . this could be a feint to draw him south, then land in force on the deserted plain. Probably that was exactly the plan.

"No, but put them on the highest alert."

Major Latour walked in. "I see you have the news," he said, calmly removing his gloves.

"Hold it, Johnny," Jackson said. "Major?"

"I was south of here when plantation hands told me the British were at Villeré's. So I rode over—cautiously, I must say—and counted them."

Thank God! "How many, sir?"

"About nineteen hundred. An early contingent."

"How rapidly do they advance?"

"Why, they're not advancing," Latour said. "I watched them quite a while and they're clearly making camp."

"Camping?"

"Bivouac fires, picket lines set, headquarters tent erected, couple of sentries posting before the tent. Typical British. Making themselves right at home."

He couldn't believe it. But then he turned the equation and it made some sense. The British commander was badly extended, reinforcements couldn't come rapidly, he was in an isolated spot pinched between swamp and river with no place to retreat, and Jackson had been ardently spreading the word for British agents to hear that he had fifteen thousand men and more coming every day. Having made a daring step, having found the only chink in the American armor, the Briton was having a fit of caution.

And offering a reprieve to General Jackson and his men.

He raised his arms overhead and stretched and smiled, the picture of comfort and confidence.

"Well, gentlemen," he said, "let's plan. We will attack an hour after nightfall . . ."

28

New Orleans
December, 1814

★ ★ ★ ★ Jackson stared at Latour's map spread on the table before him. His hand moved along vivid black lines, sensing through his fingers the mile-wide strip of plantation land between the deep, coursing river and the impassable swamp where the British were . . . making camp.

What a precious sliver of time!

"Do they have such maps?"

"Hardly possible," Latour said. Jack Coffee stood by the window, rapping a crop against his knee; Johnny Reid waited with open notebook. "No others have been done with theodolite and chain, and there are no copies of this."

He'd been blind after the loss of the gunboats, but now the enemy might be more blind than he. He tapped a cross-hatched line running from river to swamp. It was two miles short of the Villeré plantation.

"What's this?"

"You have a quick eye, General." Latour had the cat-over-cream look of a man whose professional judgment has been vindicated. "That, sir, is the key military point in my view—but other maps take no notice of it. The Rodriguez Canal, a sometime millrace, now just a drainage ditch."

"A ditch, eh? What's it like?"

"Grassed over now, five feet deep, ten wide, muddy bottom."

At just that point, the swamp suddenly jutted into that strip of dry plantation land, reaching toward the river by a good half mile. So there— and only there—the mile-wide strip was reduced to a half mile. What if that ditch became a moat before a fortification?

But that was for later; now there was business at hand. Tom Hinds, on patrol with his Mississippi dragoons, had confirmed Latour's report. They were camping. No preparations to move.

"Then let's go hit them, gentlemen."

★ ★ ★ ★

When he reined up at the Rodriguez Canal he heard rice birds chirping. A hare burst from the grass. He loosened his coat. The day had turned soft and warm under a glowing afternoon sun; his quarry was two miles distant and all was quiet. This was wet plantation country, level cane fields still covered with harvest litter, occasional plantation houses with their outbuildings, orchards, hedges and stately rows of trees, stout fences and drainage ditches.

The canal was perfect—just deep and wide enough so that a man crossing it must jump down, slog through mud, and then crawl up the far bank. From a fortified firing line thirty yards away, every man scrambling through it would be a target. He gave Jack Coffee terse orders—eight hundred of his Tennessee dragoons to join the advance, sixteen hundred to start building a fallback line here.

He sent new orders to Billy Carroll north of the city: double patrols on Gentilly Plain against an attack there, should this one prove to be a feint. Tatum arrived with wagons full of tools, and the boys went to work. The sun eased toward the tree line and damp rolled in from the river. The sound of shovels made a cheerful clinking.

Both regular regiments marched in, Tennessee's Seventh and Louisiana's Forty-fourth Infantry. The sun slipped from sight and the air cooled; it would be dark in an hour. Coffee's boys were nerving themselves for action.

"Told you, General," Sergeant Passman said, the troops looking pleased, "we didn't figure on missing no fight."

Sam Spotts arrived on a sway-backed mare with the two little six-pounders and a company of United States Marines to guard them. The day faded toward purple night. Major Plauché's battalion of uniformed militia came at a run; St. Gême's saber flashed and his men presented arms smartly.

Tom Hinds trotted in from the south, riding a rough buckskin with the easy fluency of a born horseman, his dragoons in a long column behind him. His hat was off and his shock of tawny hair flew in the breeze.

"How do, General?" he roared. "We got right up agin them, believe you me. Drove in their pickets and got close enough for a good look. Two thousand and more coming, but they ain't planning no battle anytime soon. They're taking the sun."

"A regular holiday, eh?"

"Yes, sir. Skinny-dipping in the river, laying out in the sun. Poor fellers, they was chilled in them little boats getting here. Now they're making themselves right to home, got supper in the pot. We going to hit them?"

"Damned right."

"Good. You know, when we drove in their pickets, they formed up and of course we backed off. And they laughed like hell. Figured we was scared, you see. I understand they was at Bladensburg, where the militia run off, ain't that right?"

"So I hear."

"Well, I'll tell you, I didn't like them laughing like that. Let's go show 'em we're cut from different cloth."

The last of the light was gone. An orange moon lay on the treetops as they marched to meet the enemy.

★ ★ ★ ★

British campfires were pinpoints in the dark fields around the Villeré house when the attack formed behind a screen of mature oaks on the next plantation. It was half after six; soft mist rose from the river, and the moon's sharp edges went fuzzy.

U.S.S. *Carolina* appeared in the dark and put Patterson ashore in a small boat. Would the Commodore be so good as to lay alongside the British camp and open fire at half after seven? The army would strike at eight, when the enemy was well diverted. Soon the ship slid gently down the current.

Jackson would anchor the attack line himself from the far right with the cannon and the marines on the levee road. He walked his line and came to the Louisiana regulars, the Forty-fourth Infantry, who were cracking jokes in French and looked as ready as troops can be. Then the pride of New Orleans, the uniformed companies, St. Gême exhorting his men, saber whirring.

Jackson nodded appreciatively and walked on to the black freemen from Haiti who trembled with enthusiasm; they set up such a cheer, arms waving, feet dancing, that he had to quiet them lest they stir the British. He went on to his good old Tennessee regulars. Their steady colonel, George Ross, was rolling a cigar in his fingers; when the action started he'd light it and puff away, knowing that the sight of the old man calmly smoking while bullets flew was highly soothing to his boys.

He found Jack Coffee's troopers, dismounted now, preparing to circle still farther to the left to strike the British flank. Hitting them from three sides should rattle them. He left the boys' morale to Jack and went back to the guns.

The air rolling in from the river, now heavy and damp, grew steadily colder. The moon faded in the mist and disappeared. At seven-thirty a red bloom flared, and thunder punched their chests as *Carolina* laid a broadside into the British campfires at point-blank range. He heard thin cries in the distance, fright mixed with fury, commands bawled, bugles piping, muskets popping.

The chill mist curled around them. At eight the line stepped off. The marines were ahead in a point, bayonets ready, the guns trundling along behind with a gunner holding each horse's head, the cannon wheels crunching on the sandy road.

He swung his horse to the left. The Louisiana regulars forged ahead as the uniformed companies tangled in a deep ditch and fell behind. There was a scattering of fire from the front, marines on the point driving in the British pickets. Gunshots, louder now, seemed all around them. He heard sharp cries in French as the militiamen fired blindly. Angry shouts from ahead: the Forty-fourth had veered in front of the militia.

"Hold your fire!" He galloped ahead to restrain the Forty-fourth and restore his line. There was scattered fire off to the left, the Haitians and the Tennessee regulars engaging. He counted on Colonel Ross to guide the eager but inexperienced Haitians, and when he heard the six-pounders boom on the road he turned and galloped back. The guns were properly swung and blazing, but the marines were on their bellies, firing on British pickets who had rallied after falling back fifty yards.

He could hear his troops to the left pushing through broken British lines, but directly ahead a tall colonel with a voice like a horn had stopped their retreat. Jackson saw him windmilling his arm to bring on more troops. He was getting his men ready to charge, and Jackson could see their courage growing.

Gutty bastard—the kind of man who could rally his troops to great feats, who could hold like a stone.

Jackson swung down from his horse. The six-pounders snarled, hurling swaths of grape right over the heads of that colonel and his men. Powder smoke bit his nostrils, and in murky light brightened by gun flashes he saw his men running forward like shadows in a dream, the Forty-fourth and the Creoles charging with level bayonets.

Then from the left, new firing as Coffee's dragoons engaged, a distant tattoo over the deep bellow of *Carolina*'s guns and the hammering fire all around him. The bugles that piped madly in the British camp sounded thin and frightened.

The fire from just ahead slackened. The troops there were wavering, crouched, looking around for reinforcements that didn't come; Jackson could feel the onset of their fear even from where he stood, and then that colonel with the big voice had them again. Saber flashing as lead howled around his head, the officer was on his feet, whipping his men up, knocking their fear aside. What a fighting man he was! Jackson felt a thrill of admiration even as he shouted orders to kill the bastard.

And then, by God, leading a charmed life, the big colonel brought them charging right into the American guns!

Rocketing along the road into a metal storm, coming and coming at a dead run as if lead couldn't touch them—and Jackson saw his own marines hesitate. Their firing went slack, they stared at murderous bayonets they already could feel ripping their guts, and then they scrambled back. Broken and running! The gunners stared white-faced as the marines passed through them and left them open to the enemy, and then they dropped rammers and tumbled backward—

The guns were exposed!

Yet even in his horror, even as he leapt to hold his men, he felt a burst of admiration—these bastards in their red coats were *good*, they were dangerous, never, never underestimate them—and then he was among his men, his own saber flailing.

"Save the guns!" he roared.

Sam Spotts was pulling muskets from a caisson, but it was too late to turn his artillerymen. Jackson spun marines around and whipped them forward with his saber. Out of the rolling mist and smoke and noise popped St. Gême, saber in hand, flailing at the men and cursing in high-pitched French. Jackson slammed his blade flat across a big marine sergeant's chest.

"God damn you, hold your men! Hold your men!"

The Sergeant shook his head like a bear fighting bees and recovered himself. He grabbed marines with both hands and flung them forward and then another pair and another, cursing them by name with a fury that left them gasping.

A skinny, sandy-haired man, his mouth working, cried, "I'm gonna puke!" and then he was laughing and the Sergeant spun him around and kicked his ass and he ran forward.

But the redcoats were still coming and the guns were still exposed. Jackson leapt between them, saber in his right hand, pistol in his left. And Johnny Reid appeared beside him, swinging an old navy cutlass, his mouth wide open as he howled a mad cry of rage and courage and desperation.

"Come on! Come on!" Jackson bellowed.

He heard a volley behind him, the boys together again, and glanced back to see the marines coming on at last, bayonets thrust before them. He spun back to the front and plunged forward with his saber straight out— and saw the British colonel take a bullet in the throat.

The saber flew from the officer's hand, his bull voice was cut mid-word, he started a long fall with blood pouring down his chest and struck the ground like a meal sack, dead or dying, and his men hesitated. They stared at him, then at the charging Americans, then back at the fallen figure.

Jackson was no more than ten feet from them when they broke. They were backing up, still facing forward, and then the whole body turned and ran. A sergeant with tears coursing down his cheeks lifted the fallen colonel and carried him back.

Jackson stopped his men before they could plunge into the entire British army. Powder smoke stung his eyes. They were all shouting in wild triumph, and then St. Gême whooped and danced a little jig and swung an open hand to deliver a clap on the shoulder that almost knocked the General down.

"Mother of God!" he cried, "that's *fighting!*"

Fog and drifting powder smoke thickened, and the ship's cannon booms dulled to a sodden rumbling.

Jack Gordon groped his way toward Jackson with his cigar clamped in his teeth to say the lines were breaking up.

"It's getting so you can't tell ours from theirs."

All right. They'd done well, they'd knocked the enemy off balance. The British would pause and think it over now.

And he would hit them again in the morning.

★ ★ ★ ★

Back at the next plantation, the chill air was still heavy with powder smoke. He hurried to check his casualties. His troops stood in little clusters, swapping experiences, exulting in being alive; he knew those new to combat were changed forever.

Both doctors were busy in the Seventh Infantry hospital tent. Jackson crouched by every wounded man, told them all they'd fought well and he was proud of them. Johnny Reid gathered reports. That cutlass hung from his belt; where had he laid hands on it? Johnny said they had a dozen dead and another dozen who wouldn't last till dawn. Of a hundred wounded, half were in danger—eyes shot out, head wounds gaping, belly wounds that were touch and go, shattered limbs that called for the bone saws.

A Tennessee lad—from Franklin, Jackson thought, though he couldn't call the boy's name—was hit in both knees and gasping with pain, laudanum to a dangerous level scarcely helping. He knelt by the youngster, not sure if his cries to God were prayers or curses.

Jack Gordon appeared. "They're bringing up reinforcements like crazy. Fresh troops, General." He rolled his cigar around. "Been coming along the bayou all night, at least two thousand more. We're looking at four thousand now and I reckon it'll be six by dawn."

"You can count in this fog?"

Jack sighed and rubbed his cheeks. "Cap'n Lafitte—that fellow's a wizard in the swamp, you know, like he has an instinct for where the water's deep enough to float a pirogue. See, they lighted the way with pitch torches and we slipped up pretty close, and believe me, they're in one hell of a hurry. You can hear it in the officers' voices, way they keep their men cracking. Looks like we lit a fire under their tails."

Jackson began to pace. That urgency—had they planned all along to make this their major attack, or had he forced their hand? The latter, he'd wager—first step toward taking charge, staying ahead in the fight, holding the initiative.

Yet, Lord have mercy, how he wanted to smash them at dawn. Catch them over their cookfires and bowl right through, knock their damned heads off! He'd lived his life ready to go right up to the edge and beyond if necessary. Never measure cost—that's the first step toward losing!

His breath was short. He felt that visceral rage rising, appearing as an old friend, welcome, comfortable—and, suddenly, frightening. He stared into the mist toward his enemy—and he heard Rachel's whisper, *control.*

He had no more than three thousand men here. They had six. Was surprise enough to defeat such odds? He thought of that colonel with the big voice—these men were professionals, never to be underestimated. He must hoard his advantages.

It was like rassling the devil, but he would pull back to the Rodriguez Canal and make them come to him. He sighed. Rachel's voice piercing the fog of war; he would have to tell her of the power of her words as he grappled with desire.

★ ★ ★ ★

Coffee's boys had raised enough parapet behind the Rodriguez Canal to shelter prone riflemen. Jackson went on full alert: would the six thousand come boiling out of the mist at dawn in all-out attack? That's what he would have done in their place.

But the sky lightened and slowly warmed to the color of roses, rice birds twittered, rabbits sat up eating seeds. Tom Hinds said *Carolina* and now *Louisiana* were dosing the British camp with grape and solid shot, keeping them huddled in ditches behind the levee. If they looked to attack, it didn't show.

Jackson laid out his plans. He wanted a massive parapet raised from river to swamp, wanted it a good twelve feet high and twenty thick at the base with the gun platforms built right behind it. They would have to haul dirt from miles around, but the result would be a formidable barrier, and each day the British delayed would add to its strength.

The day passed, the night, the next day, and the enemy didn't move. Probably waiting for heavy guns to drive off the ships that now would scourge any advance. Balls heated glowing red in an artillery field furnace were death to wooden ships caulked with pitch. He sent urgent warnings to Patterson.

He was intent on holding the initiative. The dragoons controlled the two miles of land lying between the armies—foot soldiers can't stand against mounted attack. Tom's men drove in enemy patrols so regularly they gave up, and without patrols they were blind.

At night St. Gême rattled them with mock attacks, volunteers coming out of the dark yelling and firing. Enemy pickets fell back, bugles called the army out to fight, and the boys melted away. The little Creole came in whooping: we're pushing them, not vice versa.

Tennessee marksmen went out at night, too, and pushed them in a different way. These were men who could nail a squirrel through the head, which mattered on the far frontier because there's little enough meat on a squirrel anyway, and a ball through the body often left none. Now they were picking off sentries from the dark, keeping enemy troops nervous, keeping control, keeping the initiative. Jackson was a gut fighter; he wanted war at every level.

He watched the barricade rise foot by foot thirty yards behind the moatlike canal. Work gangs on neighboring plantations scraped up dry topsoil, loaded it in wagons and in woven mule panniers that usually held sugar, and hauled it to the line. He slapped a draft on New Orleans citizenry: every able-bodied man must join a militia unit or show up for work on the line.

They worked in shifts around the clock. Tatum studded logs with pegs like giant cribbage boards and laid them across to stabilize the growing wall. He stepped the inside with firing platforms faced with cypress planking. Pitch torches were kept low at night, out of the enemy's sight. Men wrapped soft cloths around hands that first blistered, then bled.

The first gun platform went up, massive timbers resting on a base of springy cotton bales Tatum hoped would absorb recoil shock. The little engineer sunk bales two and three deep in the mud and laid the first timber. Jackson planned a half-dozen platforms, each to hold several guns high enough to sweep the ground directly ahead—where, sooner or later, the enemy would appear in attack formation.

Squeezed between river and swamp, the British must come this way or retreat through the swamp, which he figured their pride wouldn't permit. They had only a handful of boats, so if they tried to cross the river it would be no more than a light thrust. He summoned militia from downriver to shore up defenses on the opposite bank, then sent Latour to position them effectively.

The enemy could move when they drove the ships back, but he thought the barricade would surprise them. Naval cutters patrolled the river, and Jackson posted guards along the bank to block British sympathizers who might carry information to the enemy. Keep them blind and in his hand.

★   ★   ★   ★

Christmas Eve faded into Christmas Day and the day after Christmas and the barricade went up foot by foot and the enemy didn't move and the work never stopped. Jackson summoned St. Louis Cathedral priests to say midnight mass on the parapet while Mr. McIntyre, bless Rachel's loving heart, gave Protestant services.

Jackson liked Mr. McIntyre. He found the young man's fervent faith richly touching; his own belief, such as it was, would never transform him as Mr. McIntyre's so obviously did. The minister roamed among the wounded and the well, seeking those troubled by fear and spreading the balm of conviction. Preachers are never more welcome than in war. Rachel had chosen wisely; the lad had a rangy, springy look reminiscent of himself at that age. Had she noticed it?

The canal was on Augustin Macarté's plantation, and his big house became the headquarters. It was in an orange grove about a hundred yards behind the new line and was completely circled by a veranda scattered with wooden lounge chairs and tables. Comfortable place, the more so after Pink Mims moved in and made it theirs. Out in the barn the doctors opened a hospital for the wounded.

Jackson often saw Louise Livingston when he visited the injured men. She was good for them. A beautiful woman's smile, a soft hand holding yours—strong medicine when you were racked with pain and scared of dying. He thought her remarkable, as courageous as Rachel herself. He'd seen Madame Livingston listening the day he dressed down the Creole leaders, heard her murmured "Bravo," when she touched his arm afterward.

Ed Livingston was his link with the civilians of New Orleans, whom Ed described as patriotic enough but quaking with fear. On the one hand, Christmas parties were held to roll bandages and knit blankets for men sleeping in the open with ice crusting their canteens. On the other, householders darted to their windows at every strange sound, fearing the army had collapsed and the conquerors were at the door.

A party of Creole legislators appeared unannounced. They paced the length of the line, shaking their heads, their expressions dubious. Jackson didn't take time to dismount.

"Gentlemen," he said.

Bernard Marigny tried to maintain his dignity, his big gray mustache quivering.

"Sir, we have come to ask your intentions for our great city should you be defeated."

Jackson felt a wild urge to quirt damned poltroons who dared come on his line and speak of defeat. Should he be defeated he would burn the city, leave the enemy its ashes, and fight on. But why turn their anxiety to panic?

"I don't intend to be defeated. Good evening, gentlemen." He trotted away, glad to be free of their stink of fear. Men of property were often fearful; he hoped to God he would never bow to an enemy to save his farm. Better he should live on acorns!

A small figure on a huge dapple gray reined up beside him and saluted. He saw it was General Garrique de Flaugiac, a wealthy member of the senate, seventy years old or more, slender and very erect, with a white mustache and a stern eye.

"Your fellow legislators were just here," Jackson said with no greeting.

"A pox on them and their fears, sir!" De Flaugiac waved a hand, dismissing caitiffs. "I, sir, have come to fight. I commanded a division of the

Emperor's artillery, so I know something of guns. Let me lay a piece when the moment arrives. If your artillery officers approve, I'll serve the gun, if not, I'll put my rifle on the line."

Jackson smiled and shook his hand.

"Welcome, sir—in any capacity."

★ ★ ★ ★

Jeff Farnsworth was tall and skinny with arms that dangled loosely at his sides. But Jack Gordon could see he was strong, the way he held the heavy rifle as lightly as a toy.

Jack was on night patrol with a sharpshooter. He didn't know what the hell he was doing here, really, and already regretted accepting the invitation, which had contained enough challenge to make refusing difficult. But he didn't like being maneuvered, and that added to his unrest.

Well, damn it, neither did he like killing a man out of the dark, enemy or not. Jeff walked with a loose, easy stride, making scarcely a sound, the long piece balanced in his hand. He had a thin face with an overbite and an underslung jaw that made him resemble a rat. Once the thought had fixed, Jack couldn't shake it from his mind. Or maybe it was the way Jeff slowed and fell into a crouch, or the gleam in his eyes when he gestured with a hand and flattened himself.

"We go on our bellies from here," he said.

They slid forward through cane trash until they came to a fence line. Jeff laid the piece over the lower rail.

"This'll do," he said.

A cloud drifted off a quarter moon and faint light lay over the scene. Jack could make out the British outpost beyond a small clump of bushes. He shivered, not entirely from the cold. Jeff laid his cheek against the stock and stared down the sights.

"C'mon, baby, step this way." His voice was a whisper floating in the dark. "Just a little more, that's the boy, little more. C'mon, sweetheart, papa's waiting—shit!" He glanced at Jack. "Stepped back in. But he'll be out. See, he thinks I'm over yonder." He jerked a thumb to his left. "Where I was last night, so he's watching out there—yes! There you are, baby. Right in papa's sights. C'mon, c'mon—"

He looked at Jack, eyes oddly bright, tongue caressing his lips. He drew up trigger slack.

"He's dead meat, the little sweetie. Watch now."

Jack could see the man, too, standing in the dark, rubbing his hands, cold, probably hungry, far from home. Well, you take your chances when you go soldiering, but still . . .

"Another inch, baby, another—there!"

The report rang and the sentry fell.

"I'll go get his piece," Jeff said. "Then we'll want to move right smart. They'll be out directly."

"You take his piece? Why?"

"Why, because it's worth money, that's why. What else?"

"You can sell it?"

"Already have. I got orders for four. This one goes to a captain from Decatur. One hundred dollars flat, yes, sir."

When Jeff returned with the British musket, they walked back to the line and parted without a word.

★ ★ ★ ★

At noon on Christmas Day, cannon fired in the British camp. Hinds rode in, looking puzzled. He dismounted wearily and rubbed his fleshy face.

"Hear them guns, General? They was all lined up like for firing a salute. Reckon some high sachem could've showed up?"

Could the General sent out from London to capture New Orleans have delayed till now? Jackson told Johnny Reid to question the British deserters.

There was a core of toughness in Johnny. He might be young, somewhat naive, perhaps a bit overeducated, kindly by nature, and usually polite, but he was quick to fight and no one trifled with him. Jack Gordon's jokes never crossed a certain line. And Johnny was an effective questioner.

Every night a few more deserters crept in, begging guards not to shoot. The desertion rate of British sailors—which had led to British impressment, which led America to declare war—applied as well to their army. Soldiers weary of floggings and a diet of hardtack and salt pork yearned for America's freedom and opportunity, and they expected to sing for their supper.

Yes indeed, they said, Lieutenant General Sir Edward Pakenham had just arrived, and the rumor among the troops was that he'd given the junior general bloody hell for landing the army here when he'd intended to attack through Gentilly.

Jackson knew from his Jamaica correspondents that London had assigned Sir Edward to head the New Orleans campaign after a Yankee sniper on the road to Baltimore picked off the General originally ticketed, the same fellow who'd seen fit to burn Washington, may his soul rot. From a distance, at least, he knew Sir Edward quite well. Pakenham had gone to college in Scotland with one Redmond Barry, who had emigrated to Sumner County, Tennessee, where he and Jackson became fast friends. Pakenham had married the great Lord Wellington's favorite sister and gone on to military glory against Napoleon, which Barry followed with rapt interest, tracing his exploits on maps of Spain. A look at his campaigns in Barry's drawing room made it obvious to Jackson that the man had fully earned his lieutenant generalcy.

Was soldier gossip accurate in saying that Sir Edward was furious to find his army where it was? Probably—every army lives on rumors and usually there's a core of truth in them. If so, the British general had started off balance; Jackson intended to keep him that way, but he didn't imagine it would be easy. Sir Edward was determined and dangerous, and Jackson already had tasted British professionalism at close quarters.

★ ★ ★ ★

Johnny brought his report late on the night of the twenty-sixth of December. Cold had returned on a tide of wet air; he felt an icy rime on a gun platform. He thanked Johnny and swung into his saddle—only to experience a sudden sensation of pitching backward, as if his body wouldn't work. He hadn't really slept in three nights, though he'd rolled in a blanket to nap on a wagon bed, and he wondered if he was approaching some limit. He swayed in the saddle and steadied himself, saw Johnny's look of alarm, and reined the horse away. No one must see his exhaustion.

He rode slowly, the workers on the line ghostly figures in flickering torchlight. He had done all he could. He was sure Sir Edward would attack here, whatever he did about Gentilly. If they broke the American line, their bayonet skills would be hard to handle, but the line daily grew more formidable. And until they breached it, his rifles outranged their muskets and his guns were set to scourge the ground just beyond the canal.

The temperature was falling. Cold seeped through him until the ache always in his gut spread over his whole body. He turned toward the Macarté house. God, he wished Rachel were there. She would give him that gentle creamy soup he liked and he would pull off his boots and lie down and she would cover him with a blanket and sit with him, his hand in hers, and he would drift away . . .

His spirit seemed to leap all the miles between them. She probably was up, probably in her private agony—and here he'd been thinking only of the comfort she would bring him. He shook his head. Did she know she filled his thoughts? Would that comfort her? He could see her pacing their bedroom in her robe, her graying hair loose nearly to her waist, old Hannah bringing her warm milk, clucking helplessly. So fiercely courageous in all outer matters, Rachel still looked to him for that bedrock strength that had seen them through their perils. What would become of her if he died?

The thought startled him. He didn't intend to die. But it had been close the other night when he charged the enemy, not sure if his own marines would follow. Chance had taken the British officer and spared him, but a stray ball could have finished him in a moment.

If he was killed when the British struck, she would be in desperate need. What could he give her that would mean the most to her if he couldn't give her himself? A letter—something she could hold in her hand as bulwark against despair. Telling her that he was thinking of her in the moment of danger. That he loved her, that he always had and always would, and—

He snapped his fingers. Yes, the one thing that would matter above all else, that he shared her belief in the Father and the Son, that if the Father should take him, he would be waiting for her on the other side, waiting to welcome her home.

★ ★ ★ ★

Soon after dawn on the twenty-seventh of December, Jackson heard a distant hammering that was different from the ships' cannon—lighter, sharper. He ran up the stairs in the Macarté house to focus a long telescope, a wonderful instrument volunteered by an old Creole who shyly admitted he was an amateur astronomer, and through its crystal lenses saw a pair of British long nines mounted on the levee and between them a hot shot furnace.

He swung the telescope to *Carolina*. She was at anchor! And close, much too close. Jackson relied on that ship—what in the devil was Patterson thinking? He saw a sailor on the forepeak swinging an ax at the anchor cable.

British gunners using tongs swung balls glowing red into the muzzles. He saw the steam gush when the balls hit the wet wadding that separated them from the powder, heard the hard crack of firing, saw the ball smash through *Carolina*'s cabin to fall into the river beyond and make a little tower of steam.

"Get that ship out of there," he whispered.

There was no wind. Pulling boats were launched, but they went upstream, against the current.

"Downstream, *down*stream . . ."

At greater range in the distance, he saw *Louisiana*'s crew land cordelles on the far bank and begin dragging her out of range. But it was too late for *Carolina*. Solid shot crashed through her freeboard and into her hull. Smoke wisped from a companionway and in minutes was billowing. So the shot had lodged somewhere beyond reach, down against the hull where her caulking pitch was ready to burst into irreversible flame.

Soon men were dropping over the side, and then she exploded with a heartbreaking roar. Pieces rained into the river. Her bottom blown out, she settled into the water like a dropped stone and disappeared, leaving only a ball of steam.

His floating firepower, so crucial in holding the initiative, had just been halved.

★ ★ ★ ★

Jack Gordon was a mile south of the line at midmorning when a Mississippi dragoon sergeant he knew hailed him. The Sergeant was with a redcoat officer who had a white flag on a long staff.

"Them sailor boys losing our ship wasn't so smart, huh, Jack?" He jerked a thumb at the officer. "This here booger's got a message for the General. You want to take him in?"

Gordon knew that Jackson wouldn't dream of letting a Briton see his line and go back to tell about it. "Hold him right here," he said. "I'll see if the old man will come out."

The Lieutenant was a pale young fellow with wispy hair of no particular color and a way of swallowing his words. The General was on a big gray, Jack following, and did the air ever freeze when the Lieutenant protested the American habit of shooting sentries. Jackson let him talk, a haughty little speech that made Jack feel like kicking him in the ass. He said the practice was barbarous and uncouth. But what the hell was war itself? He said the great armies of Europe wouldn't think of doing such things. Was that so?

"Quite outrageous, sir. Those are General Pakenham's words, and he charged me to express them directly."

"Do tell." The General peered at the officer. God, he was a tough old boot. "Where are you from, Lieutenant?"

"Surrey, sir."

"Ah, Surrey. 'Tis beautiful, I'm told."

"Indeed, sir. Very much so."

"Are there Americans in Surrey?"

"A few. Only a few."

"And are they shooting at your people? Killing them? Do they seek to grind your people under their heels?"

"Well . . ."

"Answer me, sir!"

"No, sir."

"But you're here trying to crush our people, control them, or kill them. Does that give you your answer, sir?"

"But, sir, begging your pardon, I must take a proper response to General—"

"Give General Pakenham my compliments. Tell him that in due time I shall handle all his men in like fashion."

★ ★ ★ ★

Josh Mason was dying. Louise Livingston sat beside him in the makeshift hospital in Macarté's barn, his hand gripping hers. He was nineteen, from Franklin, Tennessee, he'd been hit in both knees in the night battle and had been in agony ever since. Until four the next afternoon he'd alternated between screams and exhausted whimpers, and then they took off both legs above the knees, and after that he just cried silently, tears welling from open eyes and running down the sides of his face.

Now fever was taking him, his skin so hot it smoked. He was barely conscious. Sometimes he called her Ma and sometimes Judy, and once he shouted that the cows were in the crazy weed and then fell back with a fresh stream of tears. He lasted longer than she'd believed possible and then he died, a look of blessed peace gentling his face.

"Take his young soul into your care, dear heavenly Father," she whispered, crossing herself. She needed air, sunshine, relief from pain and fear. She walked outside. The air was brisk and brilliant, the sky cloudless; a sassy mocker perched on a fence, and she heard a bobolink bubbling.

Mr. McIntyre paused in his rounds. "Did Josh pass on?"

She nodded. "Surely a blessing."

"Death rarely is."

She sighed, brushed away tears, and started to walk along the barricade. It was a full twelve feet near the river, tapering lower near the swamp. She supposed they considered that end less dangerous; perhaps the swamp precluded attack. Three gun platforms were up and others had been started.

It was the morning of the twenty-eighth; this had been farmland only five days ago. If the people of New Orleans could see the vigor here, their puling fears might ease. Won't Jackson be defeated, they asked—he's only an amateur general. Won't he burn us out as he flees? Their anxiety had spawned an insane idea: they would go to the British themselves and offer to surrender the city. When Bernard Marigny mentioned the scheme she'd been ready to slap him until it was clear he was opposed.

Better these Creoles hope General Jackson could hold, for she didn't imagine white conquerors would be much different from black ones. It was all over New Orleans that the British password was "beauty and booty," and while a captured British officer she'd met said it wasn't true, it sounded real to her. If Jackson lost he might as well burn the city—they'd have nothing left anyway. Edward tried to calm them, patiently smoothing the way between rough-handed Americans and volatile French, all of them infuriating.

The line was a beehive. Someone said the General had brought in fifteen hundred of Carroll's Tennesseans from Gentilly, leaving a thousand on watch there. She heard cheering and shouts in French and turned to see a column of men in red shirts arriving at a trot, dragging handcarts that no doubt held ammunition. The leader was smallish, about fifty, stocky and strong, a shock of gray hair to his shoulders, a wicked cast to his dark eyes. He whipped off his soft cloth cap.

"Mademoiselle!" he bawled. Mademoiselle. She liked that. "You are too beautiful to be a soldier!" She liked that, too.

Smiling, she raised hand to forehead in mock salute.

"*Magnifique! La belle soldat!*"

"Hi-yo, Dominique!" someone shouted, and then she realized this was the mysterious Dominique You, and the men behind him Baratarian pirates. He was said to be Jean Lafitte's oldest brother, the one who had introduced him to the sea rover's life.

Quite to her surprise, General Jackson greeted the pirates warmly, shouting some gaiety as they swarmed onto one of the gun platforms. Dominique turned to the gun and she saw his smile vanish and his face harden as men leapt to obey him, and she realized that here was the real man—and that he was dangerous.

A bugle sounded, brassy piping near at hand. Others up and down the line answered. There was a quickening in the air, a sudden sense of urgency. Men ran here and there, and their shouts had a new force. Then she heard more distant bugles, and with them the skirl of bagpipes—

They were under attack!

She stood frozen as men all around her snatched up weapons and bounded onto the barricade. No one seemed to notice her. She shrugged and walked to the barricade. She climbed two steps but the next was high and her gown constricted movement. She stood there feeling conspicious, knowing it wasn't ladylike but determined to see for herself, and then two gallant Creoles from the Forty-fourth reached down to put hands under her elbows and swing her up. She looked across the fields and her heart almost stopped.

In the distance she saw a long, thin column of men in red advancing in perfect rhythm to the sound of drums and bagpipes. The line swayed slightly with the supple, implacable assurance of an approaching snake. Sunlight glittered from polished bayonets on rifles held on shoulders row on row.

It was like a Napoleonic painting, like a Parisian opera march—and then her mouth went dry and her legs went weak. These men with their weapons and discipline and vast numbers were coming to kill her. She glanced at the men beside her and saw in their faces the same fear and horror that shook her, and at once she was relieved. They too had never seen death on the march, and no ounce of levity was left them.

A vast convulsive roar slammed against her from behind, filled her ears and smote her back and threw her against the parapet. Smoke and flaming debris was all around her. One of the soldiers brushed a coal from her shoulder. The cannon must have fired almost directly overhead.

Before she could see the result, someone shouted, and off to her left she saw a second enemy column, marching up the field near the swamp, extending the attack to both sides. Then all the heavy guns on the line went off, and the air was buffeted with violent sound. Smoke and spent wadding boiled around her. More distant guns sounded, and *Louisiana* slipped into view, smoke blossoming from her side, and she saw at once why Edward had termed Patterson's loss of *Carolina* a disaster.

She stared at the dreadful scene. The distant barks of British cannon seemed faint compared to the sound waves buffeting her. Then, almost beside her, dirt atop the parapet exploded into the air when an enemy shell struck. Someone screamed, and falling dirt pelted her. She should duck, run, hide—but she stood frozen, gazing at the mad panorama. The British column to her right broke up all at once, men scattering to find cover, spreading into a long line parallel with the parapet. But now they were crouching in muddy ditches to escape the cannon fire. The grape that slashed around them sent dirt and grass and bodies flying willy-nilly.

The proud British column was shattered. Men jerked like stricken insects as they dug for cover. Many didn't move. One struck her as oddly shaped until she realized with a start of horror that she was seeing a body without a head.

But off to her left, the British right had not stopped. She saw immediately that the long column there was beyond the range of the ship's guns. A slender file of Americans in butternut went out to meet it; she saw smoke puffing from British muskets. Many Americans fell and the rest hurried back, British soldiers leaping after them. That low parapet at the swamp end of the line looked frightfully vulnerable to her.

She heard shouts in French and saw Captain Lafitte running leftward, men leaping down to follow him, and even amid the turmoil she could see the difference in him. He looked anything but the charming dinner guest, and for the first time she understood that everything rumored about him probably was true.

An aide she didn't know stopped General Jackson's horse. He was immediately below her, the horse stamping impatiently.

"Sir," the aide said, "we have a report that the legislature intends to give up the city. Capitulate to the enemy!"

"I don't believe it," Jackson said. "Who said so?"

"A Colonel Declouet—he speaks with great authority."

Declouet! She was stunned. The man was an ass, forever seizing on some rumor and dashing about like a headless hen—

"I don't believe a word of it," Jackson said, his voice so strident it hurt the ear. "But tell Governor Claiborne to investigate, and if there's truth in it, he's to blow them up!" And he galloped away.

She stared after him, wondering what she should do.

"Louise! What in God's name—why are you here?" She turned to see Edward on the parapet.

"Never mind that." She stopped his lips with her fingers and told him what she had just heard. "You must go see to it before something terrible happens."

He begged her to take cover, then ran to his horse. Before she could move she saw a horde of American troops in butternut and blue converging on the left, leaving her end of the line denuded. Her legs went to water again—was a new attack focusing on her? But the British left still crouched in ditches, and cannon fire from overhead slashed them again as she watched.

Still, their right came on with frightening strength against our left. She looked at that awful low parapet, and now no one need tell her it was dangerous—of course it could be climbed—and then a horseman came galloping across the field to the British contingent and immediately the attacking column halted. It paused as if deliberating, and then the men turned and started back. They were withdrawing!

Cheering on the American line rose to a thunder and she found herself cheering, too, fist in the air, tears on her cheeks.

Little St. Gême—she stood half a head taller—bounded onto the barricade beside her.

"*Mon Dieu*! What a fighting man is our general!" For once he didn't seem interested in flirting. He was gazing across the field. "Stopped them cold—caught them off guard. They didn't dream we were here."

"How could they not?"

"They were pinned, off balance, their scouts driven in. We kept them on edge—I, if I may say so, played some slight part in that. And the ships, ah, the ships! So the British General Pakenham brings up his guns, you see—inexcusable that Patterson lost that ship, but note that bringing the guns commits General Pakenham—he can hardly haul them back through the swamps, now can he?"

"So they expected to march right to the city?"

"They thought Americans would run—but this American general will never run. You should have seen him the other night, charging the enemy like a boy. What courage! Believe me, madam, he proved himself forever with his troops."

"You actually saw him?"

A modest smile. "I was beside him."

She liked St. Gême better than she ever had.

"And now," he said, "he has stopped them cold. It's a matter of military initiative, of controlling the battlefield, of handling the enemy. Oh, my, that British commander so proud of his victory over the Emperor must be reeling with humiliation, being handled without gloves by a general from Tennessee."

"But off toward the swamp," she said, "they stopped of their own volition."

"No such thing, madam. They stopped because General Jackson crushed their attack. The British general knew if his men got inside our lines, he couldn't support them. Calling them back saved them." He glanced over his shoulder, saw the General approaching, seized her hand, swept it to his lips, and murmured in liquid French, "What a magnificent woman! What courage! But poor me—I should be with my troops." And he was gone.

"Madame Livingston!" General Jackson sat a big bay, frowning up at her. "What are you doing here?"

She was cowed only a moment by his fierce expression and harsh voice. She wasn't one of his soldiers.

"I'm watching the battle," she said, "and I'll thank you not to speak in such a tone, sir."

At which, to her surprise, he smiled.

"Mr. McIntyre," he called to the minister, "would you be so good as to escort Madame Livingston to somewhere more . . . appropriate."

He bowed to her from the saddle with another little smile.

Mr. McIntyre bounded onto the barricade.

"Well!" he said. "I see you've been enjoying yourself—you're absolutely glowing. And wasn't it a sight? I wish Mrs. Jackson could have seen it."

"You surprise me. Mrs. Jackson?"

"No one is less warlike. But there is no shortage of nerve in that lady, I'm entirely sure."

Rachel Jackson must be quite a woman. Louise could hardly wait to welcome her to New Orleans.

★ ★ ★ ★

He rode toward the swamp end of his line. There'd been an anxious moment when their right came on; he needed more weight at that end. What if they'd splashed into the swamp and flanked him? Jack Coffee jumped off the parapet to meet him.

"They were in a position to give us a good tussle there," Coffee said. "I expect we'd better beef up this end?"

"I think they can flank us through the swamp, Jack."

Coffee pushed his hat back to scratch his forehead. "I been calculating on that—maybe we can go a ways out in the water."

Johnny Reid bustled up with Lafitte in tow. "Now, General," the pirate said, "if I were fighting on the other side, I'd come around the end of your line and climb up your backside."

"Through the swamp?"

"Of course. They have three-pounders—I'd bring a couple around and start blasting balls up your line."

"I'll bet," Coffee said. He didn't like Lafitte and didn't trouble to hide it. "Drag cannon underwater, for Christ's sake?"

"You could use more imagination." Lafitte held a cold eye on Coffee. "Build a litter for each gun, ten men to carry it, bring a few around, and stick 'em up your ass to see if they couldn't blow your mind free."

"You're pretty God damned smart, mister," Coffee growled.

Lafitte's face hardened. "Call on me when you please."

"That's enough of that!" Jackson put a crack in his voice that brought both men up short. "The enemy's out there, not here. Now, what do we do about that line?"

"My apologies, sir." Lafitte was the gentleman again. He closed one brown eye and fixed Jackson with the other. "Point is, most people don't understand swamps. They take water for water, like river or lake. That it's full of snakes and gators worries them. But actually it's shallow, often only inches, rarely more than chest deep, and the snakes and gators are more scared of us than we are of them. We need to push the barricade right out there."

"How far?" Jackson said. "A hundred yards?"

"Five hundred yards, no less."

"Good God!" Coffee said. "That scarcely seems possible."

"And when you're five hundred yards out, curl it back on itself another hundred yards." He shrugged. "Surprising what you can do in a swamp. Push the dirt out foot by foot, barrow by barrow, plank the sides as you go, set rafts on the inside so men can sleep at night and fight by day. Four or five feet of height is enough—see, it's easy to wade the swamp, but it's not fast. You can't see your footing, water impedes movement—no, you're slow, and if you're coming up on a proper line it's like shooting fish in a barrel—you're the fish. Trust an old swamp rat, General—a proper line, they'll never crack it."

"Makes sense," Jackson said, and Coffee nodded.

★ ★ ★ ★

Johnny Reid felt it had been days since he'd rested, and the wild excitement of the enemy thrust along the swamp had drawn his last reserves. All he wanted to do was sleep. Until he received Michelle Frontenac's note in florid French.

"Come to me, my darling, tonight, at my sister's house. I can't bear the thought of you in danger—" There followed a delicious row of dots he thought pregnant with meaning, and, "We will be alone," the last word underlined heavily.

His exhaustion vanished and he headed for New Orleans. Patrols stopped him twice but he scarcely noticed, consumed as he was by thoughts of Michelle. So beautiful, so fine—and yet, something about her led him to shamefully carnal thoughts. She was so warm, so sweet that sometimes he wondered if she wanted to be overpowered . . . but that was silly.

It was near midnight when he dismounted at her sister's house. Michelle herself opened the door, took his hand, and led him into a parlor where a fire blazed and a crystal decanter of port was on a tray. The room was warm, and she insisted he take off his coat as she poured him wine and refilled her own glass. She wore a velvet gown, the front laced with a silken cord that held her fine breasts in suspension. Somehow he came to understand that her sister had retired with her husband and the servants were down and they wouldn't be disturbed. She gave him cake and poured more wine in each glass. A flush moved up from the knotted cord to her cheeks. Her eyes sparkled.

"I've been so worried since I heard of the battle," she said. "Were you in great danger?"

He answered truthfully enough that behind the barricade he'd felt reasonably safe.

"Oh, you're so modest!"

The wine went straight to his head—but for the cake, he hadn't eaten since breakfast. Her amber eyes were huge and moist, she brushed aside a strand of hair the color of honey, her lips parted, she leaned toward him—

"Well," he said, "of course we did have casualties, poor devils."

"Oh, I *knew* you were in danger. And when I heard of those wounded and . . . and"—she broke off, in her tenderness quite unable to say the terrible word—"well, I was sick with worry, I thought what if—what if . . ."

Oh, God, she was gorgeous!

"What?" he whispered.

She caught both his hands and held them tight. "Promise you won't think me a goose? Well, I thought, what if I lost my chance to say how much I care, how you fill my life? And now this awful war—I just had to say . . ."

He was breathless. "Say what, dear Michelle?"

"That I love you."

"Oh, my beautiful dear girl!" Visions of marriage—and of the night that would follow—flashed through his mind. "I love you. I want—"

Her hand stopped his lips. "Hush, my darling Johnny. Let me look at you. Let me memorize your face."

Suddenly her luminous eyes filled with tears. He was dizzy with wine and love. For just an instant something cold in his mind compared her to Louise—Louise was truly fine, but she wasn't his and never would be—and he thrust the thought away. Michelle was beautiful, melting before his eyes, here, *now*—

"Oh, darling," she murmured, "I so fear for you." Her hand toyed with the knotted cord that her breasts held taut, the knot fell, the dress opened. She stared at him, her lips parted. Suddenly she half stood and slipped a leg beneath her, and in the process a flash of bare knee appeared. She made no attempt to cover it and sudden intuition told him that she wore nothing under the gown, and the very thought seemed to strangle him.

She put her hands on his neck, he could feel her breath warm on his face.

"Kiss me, kiss me." And she drew his mouth to hers.

★ ★ ★ ★

On the first day in January in the new year 1815 the fog lifted about ten, and British cannon mounted overnight opened fire. Jackson was in the Macarté house when several balls struck it in rapid succession. Dishes flew onto the floor, plaster dust cascaded down.

He dashed toward his line. Brilliant sunshine flooded the field. Standing on his parapet with soldiers pell-mell around him, he saw five brazen enemy batteries in plain sight eight hundred yards distant. The redcoat infantry was posted three hundred yards ahead of the artillery.

His own guns were answering with painful slowness; he turned angrily until he saw they were firing single shots to feel out the range. He had thirteen pieces in action now, on five platforms. Dull booms echoed from across the river, where Patterson had landed three guns from *Louisiana* before moving her to safety.

He stood on the parapet, scarcely breathing, until his fire picked up speed as gunners saw their balls crashing consistently into the British batteries. What a sight it was then, the cannon thundering, smoke burning his nostrils, flaming wadding filling the air, his breath locked in his throat, men beside him transfixed and oblivious to the enemy fire. He turned to watch his own cannon, noting the way Dominique You handled the big twenty-four with swift and easy rhythm that spoke of long experience. What gunners these Baratarians were!

He ran his glass over the redcoat infantry. Pakenham's plan was obvious: open fissures in Jackson's parapet and pour his bayonets through. Would the line hold? Jackson had steeled his men against such an attack, but he knew that troops penetrating several openings would turn the day to blood.

The balls smacked into the wall like gladiator blows—*thwack-thwack-thwack*. Gradually the sound became wet and sucking. The barricade scarcely trembled. That beautiful mud was eating the enemy balls!

The British infantry, ignominious in muddy ditches, waited for openings that didn't come. They managed but a single stab, probing along their right toward the weakness they had uncovered last time. But now the barricade reached five hundred yards into the swamp, and he watched it throw them back.

After forty minutes the first of the enemy guns fell silent. Then one by one the rest shut down, the long barrels tumbled askew, those of their gunners who survived fleeing for their lives. Jackson cheered and waved his hat; the reasons for American artillery's fame had never been clearer than on this bright first day of January on the Rodriguez Line.

Lafitte and Gordon had described the weight of the British guns that nearly swamped the rowboats bringing them up the bayou. So, Jackson had wondered, how much powder and how many balls could they carry as well? He had the answer now: not enough. The British batteries went up overnight and apparently they too were plagued by the shortage of dry dirt for bulwarks, which would explain their using wooden sugar casks in place of sandbags. But his guns shattered the casks immediately, and he realized some of the barrels had been filled with sugar instead of dirt when he saw what he'd taken for sand sticking to gunners' feet in big clumps as they slipped and slid around their cannon. The sugar looked like brown sand but acted like sugar. He even saw a barrel shatter and splash molasses across a gun!

It was over, enemy forces pulling back, their third clash another failure. What now? Jackson stared across the field, trying to penetrate the mind of his opponent. Was the lean and handsome—and certainly angry—General Pakenham getting that frantic feeling that comes when you find nothing is working? When you're a long way from home and it's all on your shoulders and you've gone too far to turn back?

Maybe. But that would make a skilled and professional officer even more dangerous. The preliminaries were over now, the easy tries finished and failed.

Now the fighting would be real.

29

New Orleans
January 8, 1815

★ ★ ★ ★ Midnight was long past. He stood on the parapet, listening. Fog lay against the ground, dense and heavy and bone-cold. It seeped into his clothes, lay wet on his face. He shivered—

There! That soft, distant clinking. A murmur—muffled, distorted, but real. He'd heard it before and understood its meaning very well. Out in the open field between the two armies, the British were setting up their guns again. And that meant they would attack at first light, and this time they would come in a tide to crash against his wall with all the bone and muscle and grit of the most professional army in the world.

No more hesitation, no more waiting. The guns being placed in battery out there were to suppress his fire, not to batter his walls. He was quite sure they had given up taking the easy way. Now they intended to do it the old-fashioned way, the hard way, the British way. They would rely on their great strength—soldiers schooled in iron discipline and utterly confident in their skill with the bayonet in numbers two to three times greater than his. They would cross that field at a run, plunge through the canal, and swarm up his walls if he let them. He drew his coat closer to his throat. *If* he let them.

A week had passed since they tried to open his walls with cannon fire. They hadn't moved in that time, and he thought he knew why. Sure enough, Jack Gordon and Captain Lafitte had reported yesterday that a fresh brigade had come through the swamp, another two thousand men.

"Stalwart bastards who look ready to charge the gates of hell," Jack said, and he wasn't easy to impress.

Jackson used the week to build more gun platforms. He had eight now, most with two or three pieces. He had solidified his wall, completed that curl-back in the swamp, and rested his men. He estimated he was facing about ten thousand; he had thirty-five hundred on his line, the rest on Gentilly Plain where a sneak attack was still possible, or across the river. The British clearly planned a foray on the other side; troops there wanted reinforcement, but he knew the real attack would be here.

His guns would be loaded with grapeshot or loose musket balls, and his hand weapons would carry ball and three buckshot. Did Sir Edward Pakenham have any idea of the power of the American long rifle, source of story and song and legend in Kentucky and Tennessee, accurate at three hundred yards and even four hundred in skilled hands? Sir Edward was used to muskets, faster in firing but a waste of powder beyond a hundred yards. The rifle might surprise him yet.

Tom Hinds rode out of the fog, Jack Gordon behind him. "Can't get close to 'em tonight, General," Hinds said. "They got pickets out in skirmish force."

Gordon sighed and nodded, a cigar clamped in his teeth.

Jeff Farnsworth sat on a bucket nearby, his long rifle cradled in his arms. "Ought to go see what I can do," he said. He sat with his head thrust forward the way his daddy always did. His daddy looked like a rat, too—Jackson thought it ran in the family.

"And get a bayonet in your damn gizzard," Jack Gordon said.

Jackson turned to Hinds. "They'll come at dawn. Have all your men inside."

He stepped off the wall to walk his line. The fog enveloped him in its dense cold and he shivered, an involuntary shudder instantly controlled. All along the line little fires glowed. Men crouched around them with their hands extended. They talked in murmurs softened by the weight of the air and their laughter was a little off-key. Mule carts came and went, delivering powder kegs and casks of balls and heavy roundshot and shells. Ammunition was stacked at each gun, and each infantry unit had its own dump. The mules were weary; they shivered in the cold and stood with their heads down while men unloaded the carts.

The Macarté barn was dark now. The wounded had been moved out the day before, and Louise Livingston had gone with them. He'd let her know in blunt language that he didn't want to see her on his line again during a battle. He'd stung her—meant to, in fact. She'd gone red and then white, and he'd been a little startled by the force in her stare, but she'd heard what he said and he didn't expect to see her here again.

Nat Berkins had stretched an awning from the side of the barn to shelter his stew pots. In easier times, Nat ran a famous barbecue house out near Granny White's place in Nashville. He'd rounded up a half-dozen iron vats normally used for soap, scoured them out, cut up the makings, and now that warm smell floated up and down the line. Jackson wanted the boys to meet the enemy on full bellies. Columns of steam rising from the pots mingled with the fog. Beyond this impromptu kitchen the tent where gunsmiths were repairing broken firelocks glowed with lantern light.

"Eat up, General, God damn it," Nat said. He was a heavy man, a patron of his own cooking, and the apron girdling his bulk was splashed with stew. He ladled a white crockery bowl full. "You look like you ain't had a square meal since Christmas."

Jackson grinned and spooned up a bite—by God, it was good! Beef, pork, fish, fresh oysters, sort of a Tennessee bouillabaisse with rice, tomatoes, okra, peppers . . . The familiar twist in his gut didn't come, and suddenly he was ravenous. He ate rapidly, felt a surge of well-being and, with it, confidence.

Silas Burger cut a great plate-rattling fart, his moon face glowing, and Rufe Peeler, who'd turned into a right good soldier since Jackson had had him flogged on the Natchez road, ran around holding his nose, and Pink Mims said they were uncivilized bastards.

Good. They were in the right frame of mind.

And so was he. As he started up his line toward that troublesome redoubt on the right, he was calm, steady, filled with implacable force that was utterly different from the wild personal rages of the past. His heartbeat was slow, his breathing even—Rachel would be proud of him. He was in control. He had a notion that had she not made him cross that great bridge within himself, he would never have reached this crossroads of national destiny. He could see her now, pacing through another night made darker by her knowledge of the battle that loomed on this field so far from her. He had sent the letter; if the worst happened, at least she would have that.

He walked up his line, past the little fires, the huddled figures, exchanging an easy word here and there, throwing a quick answer to a nervous question, his ranging eye checking and rechecking men and guns and ammunition supply as he reflected anew on the form he thought the British attack would take.

Sir Edward would have his troops ready when dawn broke and the fog lifted. He would drive hard up his own far right, along the edge of the swamp, to crash into the American left. That seemed almost certain: only there would the bulk of his army be out of the range of Commodore Patterson's heavy guns mounted on the opposite bank of the river.

Jackson laid out his line accordingly. On his left were his Tennesseans. Jack Coffee's dismounted troopers manned the impact point at the swamp line. From there they stretched leftward along the parapet they had extended into the water with its impregnable curl-back. Billy Carroll's infantrymen met them at the impact point and stretched rightward toward the center.

Both brigades were full of old hands who'd been with him on the march from Natchez and through the Creek War. Most were there the day he turned the cannon on them, and they were stronger for it. If anyone could withstand the concentrated blow coming, these men could.

He expected less pressure on the middle of his line, so he put his least experienced troops there—the Louisiana militia, volatile little St. Gême and the other New Orleans companies, and the black freemen from Haiti with their machetes.

But the right, where the parapet butted flush up against the river, long his strong point, had become his weak point. He never should have let Howell Tatum build that miserable redoubt. It was the first time in memory he'd gone against his own best judgment, but the little engineer had insisted he could finish it. And he'd been wrong.

Jutting forward, the unfinished redoubt filled the space along the river between parapet and canal, but with much lower walls. The advantage of a redoubt ahead of the line was that guns mounted there could sweep the face of the wall as the enemy tried to scale it. But if an all-out attack did reach its low walls, the enemy certainly would get inside. From there, penetrating the parapet proper would be simple—and then their bayonets would be inside his main wall.

Patterson's guns across the river would make such an attack costly, but blinding fog might hang over the river after it lifted here. And even under the heaviest fire, determined troops are hard to stop. He could still see that tall British colonel leading his men till a bullet tore out his throat. There were more like him, and one of them would come helling up the levee with his men hard behind him, trying through sheer momentum to ram his way into that redoubt and then into the parapet proper.

Still, the line overlooking the redoubt was strong. He looked at the water where the fog seemed heavier, the current sucking at the shore. A floating tree, perhaps carried from the Ohio, wedged itself momentarily, and as he watched it turned ponderously and pulled free.

From the parapet wall he walked a narrow, cleated plank down into the redoubt. A pair of six-pounders were set to sweep the outer face of the parapet if the enemy got that far. Tom Beale was in the redoubt. He was comfortable with Tom, a New Orleans merchant with a rough tongue and a choleric temperament, long white hair bound in a queue, his nose as red as an apple and shaped similarly. Beale's Rifles were marksmen; they would hold the redoubt with the marines on the parapet above them.

"They'll come fast," he told Beale. "If they get in, spike the guns and get out in a hurry, up and over the parapet."

"We'll stop 'em." Beale bit off his words. Manners of a bulldog—or of a fighter. Then he added, "But I'll tell you, General, I don't like to hear no jumping back talk."

"I should kick your ass for that remark, Tom." Jackson kept his voice low. "You just be God damned sure you don't fail me."

The red in Beale's face deepened. "Guess I spoke out of turn. All right—we'll be waiting for them."

Jackson turned to the marines, grouped along the parapet overlooking the redoubt. Their muskets could deliver ferocious rapid fire if the enemy came near. He'd fought beside these men; man for man, they were the best he had, right for this danger spot. That big sergeant who'd been at his side when the guns were threatened in the first fight grinned around a huge wad of tobacco and threw a quick salute.

"May be up to you," Jackson said. "That redoubt's weak—"

"That's the damn truth, General," a lance corporal said.

"Beale may have his hands full. If they get in there, you boys don't leave a one of them alive. Understand?"

"Mow them down like hay," the Sergeant said. "Take my stripes if we don't."

Two brass long twelves on the first gun platform behind the marines were ready to lay sprays of grape into the attack. He set out what he expected to Enoch Humphrey, a hard-handed old regular artilleryman who fired his pieces with his cigar—said it perfected the cigar's flavor. Next to the marines went his best regiment of regulars, the Seventh Infantry—they would hold if the marines were overrun. Then came the society soldiers, St. Gême miffed to find himself where less action was likely, and beyond them the smiling Haitians.

Dominique You was tending a small pot on a tiny fire under the Baratarian's gun platform. Rich aroma lay on wet air.

"*Café,* General?" Dominique said and filled a cup.

Again he had that odd sensation of never having tasted anything better. It went down like honey . . .

"My," he said. "Smuggled?"

Dominique smiled and didn't answer. He jerked a thumb toward the gun platform above when Jackson asked for Lafitte.

The pirate was alone, back resting against a gun, staring into the dark. He was easy with his people, but he possessed the reserve of the natural commander, a separation from others that Jackson knew in himself. His face looked cut from steel, and as strong. Heavy triangular piles of black balls were beside the two big twenty-fours. Lafitte stood as Jackson explained the coming attack; these guns must destroy the batteries the British were setting up in the dark right now.

He hesitated, then said, "The guns you've supplied, the ammunition, have made a crucial difference—and will again today. I'll see that's not forgotten."

Lafitte bowed. "Thank you, sir."

The smell of Dominique's coffee lay on the air, but his fire was a pale flicker in fog that swirled and boiled around them. The platform seemed suspended in a separate world.

"You chose the right side," Jackson said. "We'll win, today, tomorrow, next year. We will not be put out of the West. In the next twenty years you'll see amazing growth—for a man with your instinct for command, opportunity will be unlimited. See that you use it well."

"You're a bit of a pirate yourself, you know," Lafitte said.

"No. I'm honest."

Lafitte shrugged. "Everything is relative."

"If you believe that, I may yet see you over my guns."

"I don't think so. If I cross the line again, it will be far, far from here. And you'll have bigger fish to fry."

Jackson nodded. "Good shooting, Captain," he said.

★ ★ ★ ★

He walked leftward along his line, back to the primary focus of the battle, the full-scale assault he expected along the swamp line. The gun platforms there were crucial. He had a massive naval thirty-two-pounder on one, commanded by a Patterson lieutenant, Charley Crawley. General Flaugiac was handling a brass twelve on another platform. On another, looking squarely down what Jackson was sure was the British route, Sam Spotts had two long eighteens. Jackson wanted all these guns charged with grape or loose musket balls; he wanted a hailstorm of lead slashing the attackers.

"Fill her to the muzzle," he told Crawley.

The naval Lieutenant patted the big thirty-two as he might a favorite horse. "Too much weight in front of the powder can split her, sir." He knew guns; he radiated authority.

"Let's take the chance," Jackson said.

"Aye aye, sir."

Flaugiac, erect as always, scarcely looked his seventy years. He had proved himself a master of artillery; light guns had been Napoleon's great forte, and Jackson guessed some of that fame had been Flaugiac's doing. He needed no instruction.

"Load with grape, please. You'll have ample targets."

"We'll make ourselves felt, this lady and I," Flaugiac said, voice low and raspy. Something in the way his hand cupped the brass gun's knob made Jackson think of a hand on a woman's rump under the sheets.

The fog seemed deeper and colder. Major Latour, who appeared as Jackson walked the line, tested the little breeze stirring the fog and said it all would clear soon after first light.

The General found Jack Coffee and Billy Carroll together on the parapet at the swamp line. Jack was massive, ponderous, ever good-hearted; Billy cool, compact, neat, unsmiling, an unmistakable crackle of authority in his manner. They didn't like each other, but then, not many people liked Billy and he seemed to find it enough that they respected him.

He reviewed the attack he expected, a tide of up to ten thousand rolling along the swamp line, maybe with bundled fascines to throw in the ditch for a bridge, maybe with ladders to scale the wall. They would be shooting, but only at musket range and then not a lot—their aim would be to get their bayonets inside, and they would waste very little time.

"Put your best rifles here. What do you consider the rifle's range?"

Billy, at heart a merchant, didn't answer, but Jack said, "I've taken down deer at three hundred yards myself."

"I'm told standard British practice is to advance to seventy-five yards, fire a volley, and charge. Between three hundred yards and seventy-five yards, that's your killing zone."

Kentucky militia had arrived at the last minute, two thousand men who brought only seven hundred rifles! Sending men to war unarmed? Jackson was amazed. He ordered five hundred to empty the armory and cross the river to support the troops there and posted the seven hundred riflemen fifty yards behind his line, facing the juncture point between Coffee and Carroll where the British tide would cross if it got that far.

The Kentucky brigadier, John Adair, a chesty man who held himself as if ready for a gut-bumping contest, wanted his men on the main line.

"Kentucky's honor demands it," he said.

Jackson, who felt like kicking his backside, explained the backstop role they were to play.

"Put your men in ranks to fire in rotation—if you let them blow their wad in a single volley against the first redcoats they see and then have nothing left, I'll see you hung from a God damned tree. Do you understand?"

Adair backed off. He looked down. "I've got some real marksmen, though. They could do some good on your line."

"Pick your hundred best, we'll make room for them."

"Thank you, sir."

The mist was thinning, darkness softening in the east. He moved along the parapet step with an easy word for every man, letting them know they mattered. They stamped their feet and drew their collars close, rifles looped in their arms, Silas Burger with that unshakable innocence in his expression, Nat Berkin with rifle in hand still wearing the cook's apron in which he felt most at home, Farnsworth with hungry eyes and his piece leveled and ready on the parapet's sandbag cap, Rufe Peeler with face as solemn as a preacher talking on judgment day, Pink Mims with the rifle his daddy used at the Battle of King's Mountain, holding it in one hand with strength that made it look light as a toy . . .

The tension etched in the rigid lines of their necks matched that solidifying in his own chest, and somehow this increased his calm, smoothed his voice, focused his inner control. He stared over the parapet. The faint noises in the distance had ceased. Their guns were ready, and so were they.

Suddenly the night was gray instead of black, and a light breeze broke the fog into patches. Everything seemed suspended in a mad instant of waiting, and then a rocket rose from near the swamp and broke in a bluish-silver shower that glowed in the mist, and in a moment an answering rocket rose from beside the river.

"Their signal to attack, I expect," Jackson said.

★ ★ ★ ★

And the fog lifted, all at once, a theater curtain rising on players assembled, the puff of wind that set it boiling up and away, and there under a leaden sky the British army was arrayed in all its amazing magnitude. He was ready for it, he'd imagined it a thousand times, and yet the sight of it was like a kick in the stomach.

He had never seen such a body of troops spread across a field, and for a moment he had the sense of a man on a beach before a tidal wave, towering wall of water that must destroy all it strikes—and then he blinked and the thought vanished and he was filled with exaltation, a giant who could smite his enemy with a single stroke. A throbbing sense of fitness and command swept him. As a glass multiplies the sun's strength, so control he'd never fully known before had focused him.

A murmur swept his lines, then muffled cries, ejaculations, whispers, whimpers, a horrified moan.

He snatched off his hat.

"All right, boys! We're going to take these sons of bitches down like we're chopping cotton!"

A ragged cheer ran down the line as they got their feet set; he felt perfectly wonderful, strong as Samson, rich as Croesus, sure as Abraham.

The fog lifted and swirled, revealing and hiding moment by moment. It lay as a heavy bank over the river and even as his glance swept the field he saw he'd be denied Patterson's guns until it cleared. Even the British guns were still out of sight. He looked back to the left as bugles sounded and the distant column lurched into motion. It still was five hundred yards or more away but it was moving rapidly over the silver-frosted cane stubble, men in red, white crossbelts making a great X across their chests. A target X.

He saw immediately that the attack was laid out almost exactly as he had expected—the bulk of their troops was here, on his left side, coming along the edge of the swamp in a massive column sixty men wide and God knew how many deep. He checked the right and saw a smaller column advancing near the river, ducking behind the levee, but coming more slowly than he'd expected.

Then, like a sword slash across the silence that had enveloped his lines, General Flaugiac's brass twelve erupted, thunder that jerked their heads, smoke a black-blue bloom, and in the distance he saw a half-dozen enemy soldiers down, others filling their places as smoothly as water flows so that the wide line came on unbroken.

As if Napoleon's old artillery general had announced the battle's start, everything burst into sound and action at once. The British guns opened behind the fog, muzzle flashes brilliant flickers in the gloom. His own cannon fired to each side of him, Sam Spotts's long brass eighteens almost overhead, the big twenty-fours on the right aiming at the British flashes, Dominique You capering in a wild dance as he plunged match to touchhole and the big gun gouted flame and snapped backward.

From the corner of his eye he caught a dark streak in the sky that arced from the fog as British balls crashed down on his line. A couple of them slashed the top of his parapet nearby, and the boys ducked down with yells, crouching to peer at the riveting sight ahead. No more leaning on the parapet top like spectators; even Farnsworth had snatched his rifle off its rest, and Silas Burger's round face was pale as paper. One of the six-pounders had been knocked askew on a platform that held two, but the other was firing with a rifle's speed.

He glanced down the line where the big thirty-two-pounder crouched like a monster just in time to see it go off with a roar that went all the way down into his chest and rattled his heart against his ribs. Fifteen feet of flame streaked from its mouth like an awful tongue, and a smoke blossom became a giant ring floating across the canal. He peered through the smoke for Charley Crawley on the platform. Had that massive load split the piece? Crawley ran his hands over the gun, then turned and waved triumphantly. Still whole!

Jackson wheeled to see the great charge flying across the field. The mass of balls was too fast for the eye and yet somehow was visible as an impression, a hint of something awesome—and then it plowed a furrow in the British column, throwing bodies aside and opening a gaping lane, and an image of an ax biting into a log flashed through his mind.

But the lane closed, the gap disappeared, the men in red came on and on, and in the distance he heard their music playing. They were near four hundred yards out when the Kentucky brigadier, General Adair, appeared on his line.

"Ensign Ballard, here, he's a right good shot. He can take them down at that range."

"From four hundred yards?" Ballard wasn't very big, and his piece looked taller than he, a good .70 caliber or more. He laid it on the parapet and stared down his sights.

"See that feller on horseback?" Adair said. Only a few British officers were mounted—most of the local stock had been driven off the moment they arrived. "You can do him, can't you?"

"Might could if the son of a bitch would hold still."

The officer turned, peering over his shoulder; Ballard sighed and his piece cracked and the man flew out of his saddle. Ballard screamed in triumph, a roar went down the line, and Jackson, disbelieving, extended his glass—sure enough, the officer was lying motionless, his men staring at him, then glancing forward, and even from here he read apprehension in their expressions.

He checked the right again. Yes, that column, bigger than he'd expected, moving fairly slowly. He was deciding he'd mistaken their plan when his eye caught a flash of color along the levee and he saw the slender column he'd been expecting moving up at a dead run. Enoch Humphrey's twelves on the first platform roared. Jackson heard a crackle of rifle fire, leapt into the saddle, and galloped to the right, Johnny hot behind him.

When he reached the end of his line, that light column was only fifty yards out and coming at a run, not firing, bayonets fixed, blades gleaming in odd pearly light. Running for that vulnerable redoubt. Another big colonel was in the lead, he might have been the brother of the one killed the other night—tall bastard with a big voice, saber in his right hand and pistol in his left, the kind of man who can move disciplined troops to superhuman efforts, who can carry your lines in a mad rush on sheer grit and run through a curtain of lead to do it.

"The officer," Jackson shouted. "Get him—he's the key!"

Beale's men were firing rapidly from the little redoubt and the marines were pumping lead from the parapet, and still the British column came on and on, thirty yards, twenty, ten, the big bastard leading a charmed life as he windmilled his saber. He reached the canal, leapt into it, splashed across, and scrambled up the low walls of the redoubt and he was inside!

A half dozen were with him and more coming. Beale's men rushed toward the slender plank that would carry them back inside the parapet to safety. The marines' fire fell off—they couldn't shoot for fear of hitting their own—but Beale kept his head. He was at the plank, yelling, his face purple, his white queue swinging as he hustled his men up to scamper across, their feet clawing the cleats. A big British trooper lunged ahead of the officer, and Beale swung his short-barreled carbine and fired from his hip. The ball—it must have been .75 caliber—caught the redcoat square in his belly and slammed him back against the officer, who was thrown off-pace.

In an instant Beale scrambled up the plank and the marines on top snatched it up as the officer below reached for it, missed, fell against the parapet proper, and came scrambling up its face, a half dozen of his men with him. As he cleared the parapet, looming huge against the sky, a rifle ball from a foot away tore out his left eye and spun him in the air, saber and pistol flying from his hands, and two more balls hit him before he fell.

Three of his men followed him over the wall. Two were killed instantly and the third threw down his piece and fell to his knees with a look of entreaty that saved his life. Beale's riflemen and the marines crowded the wall to fire into the redoubt. The British troops, thirty to fifty men, milled there, half killed in less than a minute, the others fleeing the way they had come.

Jackson heard a shriek and whirled to see the British officer sit up, hand clamped to his eye, and then pitch backward, body flopping in agony. He plainly was dying. Jackson felt a twinge of pity and dismissed it in a flash—the bastard came here to kill us and got what he got.

The big marine sergeant let out a howl and seized Jackson in a mighty bear hug.

"What did I goddam tell you! We did it! I guess I'll keep my stripes after all."

"Keep them?" Jackson shouted. A moment of wild exuberance swept him, he had to restrain himself from leaping and capering. "You'll get another! A stripe for every man here!"

"Hear that, boys?" the Sergeant bellowed. "Every one of you buck-assed privates are privates first, now!"

Jackson's attention jerked back to the attack on his left. The red tide had advanced considerably, it was within two hundred fifty yards, good rifle range, and still moving with authority. He snapped out his glass and saw immediately that his riflemen had been busy. The British skirmishers in front were mostly down now, and the advancing men were stumbling over bodies in red lying amid the cane stubble. He snatched the mare's reins and galloped down the line.

At the attack point where his Tennessee units met, ranked firing had already broken down. The boys were loading and firing at will, fast as they could ram balls down the muzzle and jostle open a firing position on the wall. There was loud talk, laughter, wild excitement edged with hysteria in their voices; Jeff Farnsworth crowed like a rooster every time he thought his target fell. On the platform above them Sam Spotts had the two big eighteens firing one and one, hurling sheets of lead balls to mesh in cross fire with the charges from the massive thirty-two.

"What the hell is that?" Jack Coffee rumbled, pointing.

Jackson saw men coming through the British troops with huge bundles. He focused the glass. Yes, it was sugar cane tied in bunches four feet in diameter, and he realized he was seeing fascines prepared to throw into the canal as a bridge for troops to cross to attack his parapet. Cane was heavy—no wonder they staggered as they walked.

Behind them came more troops carrying crude ladders, obviously to be thrown against his wall when they reached it. At once he realized how effective his use of Hind's dragoons had been from the beginning. The British had never gotten close to his wall or the canal—obviously they thought both were more formidable than he knew them to be. Fascines and ladders!

But why are they coming from the rear? Surely they should be in front, special troops ready to run through fire and plant the bridges and ladders that unlock enemy doors. There was a sense of . . . confusion. He braced his glass on the parapet and studied faces and even from this distance he could feel a fury in them. They were late, something had gone wrong, but he didn't make much of it; things always go wrong in war, and the attack was still rolling like a wave toward his lines.

Over the cannon roar he heard the Battalion d'Orleans band burst into "Yankee Doodle," and a cheer went up all along the line. The band played with ornate Latin flourishes, nothing like the shrill fifes of his boyhood, but it still gave a fine fighting spirit that he could feel in his blood and see in the way the boys squared their shoulders and leveled their pieces.

Then a thunderous "Marseillaise" began and all along the line French voices took up the soaring hymn to revolution, and his Tennessee boys grasped its meaning without knowing its words and shouted its moving tune as they loaded, gazed down their sights, fired, loaded, leveled their pieces . . .

"Aim right above the X, boys, right above the X," Jackson said, pacing up and down the firing step. "Right above the X."

The men carrying the fascines and ladders stalled. Many were hit but others just stopped, some walking away from their burdens, some firing their muskets. A mounted officer with gold lacing on his hat, surely a general, galloped to the front on a handsome bay and veered the troops to their left, toward the center, clearly trying to escape the fire Sam Spotts's eighteens were delivering one and one.

The music, the sharp crackle of the rifles, the shouts and laughter of the men, the deep-throated roar of the cannon, the smoke burning eyes and nostrils, smoke gushing blue-black, blinding, destroying aim—

"God damn that God damn gun!" Farnsworth squealed. "Spoils my God damn aim!"

And to Jackson's own amazement, he felt the same shrill surge of rage within himself. He couldn't see his enemy, didn't know what they were doing—

"Johnny," he said, "get up there and tell Sam to space his shots. Let the smoke clear after each round."

Even as Johnny leapt off the parapet, the smoke did clear and Jackson saw the enemy at two hundred yards, and by God, those vaunted British soldiers were beginning to stall!

They slowed, some stopped, some fired though they weren't yet in effective musket range, some stumbled over bodies and once on their knees stayed there. Some in the front ranks turned back, which threw those behind into confusion. They were milling, barely advancing, and then the General in his gold lace hat galloped in front of them.

"Take that son of a bitch down," Coffee shouted, but the horse was dancing, the rider lunging this way and that, saber flashing, obviously shouting, and then he had them up and moving again. They dropped their packs on order and moved on with new life, hurrying lightly over ground littered with bodies.

The grape and loose musket balls that Sam's eighteen and Flaugiac's twelve and the big thirty-two were hurling swept away British soldiers in swaths, wholesale maiming, but he saw that at this range rifle fire was even more effective, men staring down the long barrels, bearing on the white X . . .

They stalled again at a hundred fifty yards, and this time there was nothing lace-hat could do. Through his glass, Jackson could see the officer's face, red as his uniform, as he shouted, slashing at them with his saber, running his horse at them. But they ducked away, crawled away from him like dogs dodging the lash—and then he wheeled his horse and galloped across the field to another officer mounted on a big dapple gray whom he addressed with a curious look of supplication in the set of his shoulders.

That slow column Jackson had noticed earlier on the British left along the river now veered across the field to the right. The officer on the dapple gray snatched off his hat and spurred to an instant gallop. Jackson held the glass steady—by God, that must be Pakenham himself. The man's hat was off, and Jackson could see he was young, handsome, a superb horseman as he galloped across the field, the lace-hatted officer following.

The stalled troops made stationary targets and many more had fallen, but the man on the dapple gray wheeled in front of them. He was shouting, exhorting, commanding, and Jackson could see their reluctance in the very way they stood, and then, by God, they got up and started to come on. Must be Sir Edward—

Then lace-hat's body jerked and snapped and flew off the bay. Sir Edward's head jerked around. Lace-hat lay like a dropped meal sack and didn't move.

"I got him, I got that son of a bitch," Farnsworth howled. His lips were pulled back and his eyes glittered.

"Go to hell, Farnsworth," someone yelled. "We all got him."

With a start he realized the British guns were silent now; Dominique and the others had done their work and now were firing grape across the field. The fog on the river was gone, too, and he heard the dull rumble of Patterson's guns in the distance, slashing the field with cross fire. The boys were standing straight now, sightseers, laughing, pointing, cracking wild jokes as they fired. Cannon smoke floated along the line and when it cleared he saw the enemy was nearing the hundred-yard markers Hinds had set. Their muskets would bear at that range, and they were firing and reloading as they came.

There was a yell beside him and he whirled to see Connie Perkins knocked off the parapet, hand clapped to his head. Then Connie sat up and pulled off his hat. The right side of his head was bloody but he held up the torn felt he'd been wearing.

"My best hat," he bawled. "My lucky hat. Bastards shot a hole in it." He touched his head. "Pinked me, no more."

They were laughing, and then someone said "Jesus," in an entirely different voice, and Jackson turned to see Silas Burger sitting with his hands pressed to a growing stain on his chest, his round moon face crumpled and gray.

"Aw . . ." Silas whispered. "Shit." His eyes shut and he toppled sideways. They carried him off the parapet and put a coat over his face.

After that the boys exposed themselves less, peeping over the wall, aiming, firing, and getting down. They were different now, laughter and jokes gone, their manner grim and deadly. It went on and on, rifle fire and musket fire rippling along the line in staccato bursts, the thunder of the guns overhead, the blinding smoke that enveloped them and then skittered away on the wind, the noise that beat deep in his chest like heavy drums—the British were within a hundred yards now and slowing again, more of them down, those coming from behind stumbling over bodies, falling, slow to rise . . .

Sir Edward rode among them, swinging the flat of his saber as they ducked away, and then in a flash he was down, flat on the ground, the dapple gray wandering a few steps before it fell. He got up, left arm hanging uselessly, hat gone, and someone brought him a small black pony and he went one-armed into the saddle, almost fell, righted himself, and galloped again among his men.

And Crawley's overloaded thirty-two-pounder roared and the hail of balls crossed the field like swarming hornets and slashed into the British general. Horse and rider went down together as if the hand of God had slapped them into eternity. Jackson focused the glass; if ever he'd seen a dead man he saw one now, no tremor of movement, the body lying at odd angles.

The advance stalled. Stopped cold, the men gazing at their general, no further thought of movement. They crouched, or crawled toward the swamp to escape the relentless fire, or sheltered themselves behind men already wounded or dead, or flattened and scratched out shallow trenches with their bayonets.

And then he heard the bagpipes and across the field marching on a diagonal straight into the fire came the Scotsmen—Ninety-third Highlanders—the only enemy regiment Jackson could identify specifically—stalwart big bastards marching heads up, kilts swirling around their knees, their pipes sounding shrill Celtic pride, the kind of men you had to kill to stop.

The boys gazed at them in awe and their firing fell off and stopped. Jackson read consternation on their faces—they saw the same inevitability of conquest in these iron men that their general saw. He walked calmly along his line.

"All right, boys, take them down, take them down, aim careful, square in the chest, they're men just like we are, they sleep at night and shit in the morning, take them down, boys, take them down. Fire, fire, fire!"

Rifle fire exploded up and down the line, cannon boomed, grapeshot slashed across the field, and the Scotsmen marched through as if noticing such distractions was beneath them. But then they started to fall. They stumbled and fell and their pieces flew from their hands, and the men still on their feet stepped around them and came on.

More and more of them went down, and still they marched in decent formation, still the bagpipes skirled. Their colonel fell and their sergeants fell and their formation went ragged but they didn't stop. Jackson watched, holding his breath. They were beyond belief, beyond human endurance, it looked as if they would march until only one was left, and he would charge the wall—

But at last they staggered to a stop, two hundred still standing out of the eight hundred who had started, their officers gone, their sergeants down, and they milled for a moment and then stood and opened fire from a bare seventy yards, loaded and fired again, loaded and fired, and now they started a slow withdrawal, firing as they went.

"Let 'em go," Jackson whispered to himself. "For God's sake, let 'em go." He was about to shout the order when he realized his line had gone silent, firing had stopped, the cannon momentarily stilled, and the Scotsmen pulled back with a single bagpiper still skirling.

And then, on his far left along the swamp came a last desperate effort, an officer who shouted to his men to follow and came running forward. Perhaps a hundred men followed him and they ran through crashing fire, through curtains of lead, came to sixty yards, fifty with some down, forty with more down but still coming. Fifty men plunged into the canal only thirty yards from the line, and twenty came out, that officer in the lead. He was a major, Jackson could see his pips clearly now, and with flushed staring face, not looking back, he hallooed his men and ran full tilt for the parapet. Ten of the twenty reached the wall.

They chopped steps in the parapet and came charging up, the Major in the lead. At the top of the parapet he stood poised against the sky, and for the first time looked back.

"Why don't the troops come on?" he bawled, heartbreak in his voice. "The day is ours!"

A half-dozen rifles crashed and he fell lifeless into the arms of a Kentucky major. Tenderly they carried his body off the parapet and covered it with a Kentucky flag.

Two soldiers followed him and surrendered before they could be killed. The others at the base of the parapet threw away their muskets and stood with hands raised in supplication.

It was over. Over! The British had done their best, they'd died trying, they lay out there dead and broken and covered with gore, and New Orleans was saved. It was over.

He bowed his head and prayed.

★ ★ ★ ★

Louise Livingston waited at Monsieur Languille's plantation, next to Macarté's. M. Languille had sent his womenfolk to the city and doubtless she should be there, too, but she had to know the outcome. She knew the great test was at hand and she was on edge. Captured British officers she'd met and their unshakable confidence that professionalism would overcome a backwoods general had rattled her nerve more than she would admit. The firing at a distance went on and on, rumble and thump of heavy guns, rifle fire like paper tearing, and then, gradually, it slackened. Did the great wall lie open to the enemy at last?

A lone rider came down the road, a rough-looking American wearing a blanket coat.

"We're whupping them," he yelled, "whupping them good!" And he galloped on.

She called for her horse, took a lift into the saddle, hooked a knee over the horn, and trotted toward Macarté's, a waterproof across her shoulders. Misty rain struck her face. Why was she drawn so, she who had seen too much of war? She lifted the horse into a lope as the firing ahead began to fade. Because she was part of it—Edward's role in smoothing Jackson's way with the Creoles, hers in organizing women for knitting and making bandages, her recognition of Jackson as a gentleman and of the honor he paid his wife, but most of all the duty she had assumed to the wounded. Josh Mason died holding her hand. That tied her to this war, and this could be its climax; she had to know.

The last firing died away as she came to the line and with a quick glance saw that the enemy hadn't crossed. She felt a momentary surge of sheer partisan joy, the strength she'd perceived in that granite general fully justified. But the men weren't cheering. They stood motionless and silent on the parapet. She didn't see the General. No one seemed to notice her, and she dropped from the sidesaddle and struggled up to an unoccupied place on the line. As she did the clouds parted and for a moment brilliant sunlight bathed the field.

She gazed out and saw . . . nothing. Everything still, frozen, motionless. The field oddly red—

Red? Then, bile rising in her throat, she saw that the red carpeting flung across the field was made of the bodies of men in red, hundreds and hundreds and hundreds of bodies, bodies in heaps, bodies swept in windrows like the detritus of floods, bodies—

"Mother of God!"

She crossed herself. Her knees wobbled, she braced herself against the sandbags, tears blurred her vision—

She dashed them away. The smell of gunpowder was still acrid and heavy, and her eyes stung. Then she saw most of the dead were at a distance. Only a few were near the canal, only a handful on this side of it. Eight or ten British soldiers were alive near the wall, kneeling with their arms held high in supplication.

Beyond the canal there were more scattered bodies, and beyond them that sea of red. She tried to grasp the meaning of so many dead, so many young lives snatched away, so many mothers and wives and children waiting for them on the other side of the sea.

She glanced at the men on the line near her. They hadn't noticed her. They stood transfixed, staring at the horrid scene, looking stunned and full of human pain. How strange is war, turning humans into beasts to tear at each other's throats, and in the next instant teaching them of humanity with an intensity unknown in ordinary life.

She looked back across the field and now she saw movement. Slowly, painfully, men were rising from among the bodies, some with obvious wounds, some who must have fallen in terror and lain unable to move, praying for relief. They stood facing the American parapet with their hands held high and slowly came forward as prisoners.

Wounded men were stirring on the ground, too, twisting in agony. One of them raised his arm and dropped it, raised and dropped, metronome on a bloody field, its owner probably not even conscious. An officer in kilts walked in a circle with a stump of sword in his hand, the blade shot off. He stumbled against a body, fell, rose, fell again and rose, and resumed his stumbling circle, and she saw his eyes were gone.

Mewing noises came from the wounded, men crying for help and for water. She already knew that bullet wounds, especially belly wounds, produce ferocious thirst.

"Poor bastards," a Tennessee voice near her said. She saw a tall fellow with a water bottle in his hand. "C'mon, boys, let's go give 'em a hand." And a half-dozen men followed him with water bottles, sliding down the outside of the parapet and running to kneel by the wounded. Men went out from the French battalion, too—she saw little St. Gême leading a party armed with water bottles and knew she would not sneer at him again.

More figures were making their way onto the field now. Mr. McIntyre and several of the doctors he'd brought from Tennessee were moving from body to body, and farther out, British doctors were moving forward, until the medical men of both sides were mingled in a sort of communion.

She found she was weeping, tears streaming unnoticed down her cheeks. There would be work for her. Hundreds and hundreds of wounded. Many would die, but many could be nursed back to a semblance of health. She would struggle to save them as she had supported killing them. Yes, they were enemies who had come to oppress her, but that didn't matter now. All humans suffered alike.

She shook herself. Better get ready. She turned and stepped off the wall.

★ ★ ★ ★

Word of the victory reached Nashville in late January. Riders galloped to the Hermitage with the news. Church bells rang, people came for miles to celebrate, a victory bonfire blazed on the square, families raised hymns of thanksgiving for their men, preachers talked and speeches were made and folks danced by the bonfire's light—Tennessee's warriors had triumphed over the British with astonishing results, some two thousand British casualties against a handful of American dead and wounded, praise God.

New Orleans was saved, the Mississippi River secure, the West free to thunder into the explosion of growth that surely was its destiny. Tennessee's future was assured and the name of Andrew Jackson emblazoned forever on Tennessee's heart and on the hearts of its people.

At the Hermitage, Rachel Jackson was on her knees, offering fervent thanks and praising God for His wondrous generosity. Oh!—how benevolent His gaze on Andrew and on her, holding Andrew in His hand safe from all dangers. And how benevolent to the young United States about which Andrew cared with such passion, though she herself would be happy enough to live the rest of her life in quiet here on the farm with her husband beside her.

She prayed raptly—thank you, thank you, thank you. But mere prayer was not enough to honor God for His boundless generosity, His rescue of His faithful servant from her despair. Laboriously she levered herself to her feet against a chair, breathing hard; too much weight, but it wasn't that, somehow her body didn't work well anymore, her heart thundering in her chest as it so often did, nothing like the dancing girl she once had been. The thought swept her back to those wonderful wild days when Andrew rescued her from her mad husband and they sealed their love in glorious meeting . . .

She decided to ask Dr. Hume to come here and preach a special sermon of thanksgiving. Everyone would come, especially all the women and children whose men were at war, come for a giant preaching here at the Hermitage— and they would roast as many beeves as they needed and have cider and candied yams and candied apples and cakes and all manner of things that ladies for miles around would cook, and they would thank the dear Lord properly that Andrew and his men would be coming home.

How she yearned to see him! He would summon her soon in the pretty keelboat with the blue curtains that still lay snubbed to the river pier. She would embark with utter joy, she and Mary Coffee. And in time she would bring him home to life in Tennessee on their tranquil farm. But even as this wishful thought registered, doubt stabbed her. She had the feeling from the way people talked that Andrew had gained a level of recognition in his country that meant his life—and therefore hers—would never be the same.

She sighed, then straightened; she would take with joy what the Lord vouchsafed to give. Now to summon Dr. Hume.

★ ★ ★ ★

General Jackson stood on his parapet watching Tom Hinds and a small patrol come in at a brisk trot over the field on which British bodies had made a carpet. The check gate was open now, no need to close it, and he was alone on the wall, though the bulk of his troops were still in the immediate area. He was taking no chances.

"That's the last of them gone," Hinds said. "Got in them little boats of theirs and went back up the bayou, same as they came. Kept their pickets out to the end, too. You know, you were right, they had plenty of stinger left."

They had been withdrawing to their ships for nearly two weeks, showing no signs of interest in further attack. He had small craft watching on Lake Borgne, but their boats headed straight for the deepwater ships as they emerged one by one from the bayou.

He had no intention of attacking their retreat. Of course it was standard military doctrine to counterattack and drive a defeated enemy—indeed, he'd had to restrain Tom Hinds, who'd wanted to gallop across the bloody field with his tawny hair flying and smite them then and there. Their casualties were awesome, but he calculated they had at least six thousand men whole and ready to fight if attacked—they still had double his numbers.

Johnny Reid, showing the advantages of a classical education, had pointed to the grim lessons of Crécy and Agincourt, where he said the retreating British had whirled when attacked and converted defeat into victory. Jackson would not give them a like opportunity here.

He had gained immense respect for his enemy. Watching them march across that field into the jaws of hell, his old hatreds had eased a little. Here were brave men not to be taken lightly. He would never like the British nor forget that pale-eyed major, and warmth to his enemies would never be his way, but he had to admit that these redcoats had fought till human flesh could take no more. Prisoners had told him since that in all their battles on the Continent they had never encountered such fire, nor had death dealt to them so relentlessly. Jackson knew that some of his own men had wept to see the carnage they had done.

British casualties, as best he could determine them, were two hundred ninety-one dead, twelve hundred sixty-two wounded, and four hundred eighty-four captured. General Pakenham was dead. General Gibbs was dead. General Keane was on a Royal Navy hospital ship with a bullet through his throat; Jackson had sent him his sword, found on the battlefield, with a note. Only General Lambert survived to oversee the retreat. Lambert had left some five hundred of his more seriously wounded men behind, on the American agreement to care for them.

Jackson had lost seven men killed and six wounded on his line proper.

Only the west bank marred the totality of the victory. A light British force had crossed in the night and driven General Morgan and his men, and for a few minutes it had been tricky indeed. Everything went wrong. Patterson placed guns ahead of Morgan's position, so the militia general advanced to a less favorable line to try to defend them. The British struck, the militia collapsed, and the enemy was on the way to capturing all the guns on the west bank. The guns there in enemy hands would have been difficult but not fatal—in Patterson's hands, after all, they had not subdued the British. The eastern bank was what mattered, and when the British attack there was crushed, they were forced to withdraw from the far bank and that was that.

He sighed. So it was over, for now at least. The British might be back, he had no thought of relaxing his guard, but for the moment he could rest. He stepped down from the parapet and walked slowly to the Macarté house.

He had proposed to the Abbé Guillaume Dubourg, apostolic administrator of the diocese of Louisiana and the Floridas, a great Te Deum in St. Louis Cathedral, and he understood the people were combining it with a salute to the General who had saved them. It was to be wonderfully grand, troops parading in the square to military airs, a triumphant arch already raised, girls in diaphanous gowns representing each state, two children on a pedestal holding a laurel crown to be placed on his head to salvos of artillery, ballads and odes to be performed, and then into the august church to prostrate themselves in gratitude before, as Jackson had phrased it in his note to the Abbé, "the *ruler of all Events.*"

He would dress in his one fine uniform. Pink Mims would see that his only decent pair of boots were well blacked, and in manner he would do his best to merit the title that Louise Livingston had told him with obvious pleasure was on everyone's lips: the Hero of New Orleans.

He smiled. Better the hero than the dog. Yet triumph seemed lonely. He thought of the farm in Tennessee, serene and secure, Rachel on vigil there. It would be weeks before he could leave New Orleans, but the immediate danger was past and he no longer need be alone. He sharpened a quill and wrote swiftly.

Come to me as quickly as you can. Come in your keelboat, bring young Mary Coffee to see you safely through. Oh, Rachel, waste no unnecessary time. I need you more than ever.

Come to me.

30

★ ★ ★ ★James Madison sat at his desk in the cubbyhole office that was all the Octagon House afforded him. He was very straight, his back barely touching the cushion behind him, a soldier facing combat. The flash of victories now long past—Chippewa and Lundy's Lane, Baltimore and Plattsburgh—were fading sparks this dark and painful winter, the ice edging the Potomac a fit metaphor for the state of the Union he must soon describe in a bootless exercise before the Congress.

Dolley walked in, teapot and cup on a small tray.

"Your mouth is turned down," she said. She poked his shoulder and smiled. "Where is the dashing cavalier I married?"

"'Cavalier' . . ." He had to laugh. "All my dashing is to stay ahead of our creditors." He tapped the papers on his desk. "Seventeen million shortfall this year. Fifty-five million needed next year, against fifteen million revenue—why, it takes fifteen million just to service the debt! As for the piddling taxes the Congress authorized . . ."

"At least they authorized the three-million loan."

"Of which sum . . ." He dug in his papers. "The banks say they'll take six hundred thousand."

"Only six hundred?" He saw her hand go to her mouth, but she recovered immediately. "Drink some tea," she said. "It's just more of the same."

That was true enough, as the State of the Union message in March would say. He would put it on paper, then let the clerk read Congress the sorry tale of its own peccadilloes. He started to say as much—but no, there was ample blame to go around.

The nation was effectively bankrupt yet the Congress feared to tax; trade with the enemy was greater than ever, and what specie there was flowed in a golden stream toward Canada; the army needed men but Congress wouldn't draft them; the Federalists were a steadily growing minority in implacable opposition and secessionists dreamed of ripping New England from the union—while the talks dear old Albert Gallatin and Henry Clay and the brilliant younger Adams were holding with the enemy at Ghent dragged on as Britain sought revenge though the causes of the war were long settled. And over it all like a Damoclean sword hung the threat of that massive redcoat army approaching New Orleans.

"At least those idiots in Hartford pulled back from secession," Dolley said. "For now, anyway."

"Peeped into the fiery chasm and drew back. I think New England will come to its senses."

"You like to believe the best, but people in politics often act their worst. Like this vile Refederator, whoever he is."

That anonymous writer of hostile articles in northern papers *assumed* that the British army approaching New Orleans had crushed the backwoods general by now. British control of the Mississippi, Refederator wrote, meant the western states would cut their ties to the old Union since their economic life depended on the river. Then the states on the coastal shelf east of the Appalachians could return to sanity. The old federation was dead anyway, killed by Madison's excesses, so the old thirteen could refederate into their original neat little seaboard form and live happily ever after.

"Refederator," she said, "is an ass."

He had to smile. "You're right, and there's no running backward. Whoever he is, he speaks for the British, all right. Another letter from Ghent— my, is poor old Albert sick of Belgium and yearning for Hannah!—says London plans to hold New Orleans as a sugar colony and thereby control everything west of the Appalachians. Be *the* power in North America."

He shook his head. "But let them hope. This Refederator preaches to an audience of fools. We've moved beyond his listeners' narrow desires and there's no way back. The West is real, it's ours, we'll never give it up. Abandon Tennessee and Kentucky and Ohio? And the lands opening now in Illinois? Never! If we should lose New Orleans, we'll recover it. If that takes years, we'll spend years—"

He broke off. She was miming applause—hands patting each other, mischief filling her face.

He laughed. "Oh, all right, I was making a speech. But it's true."

"Every word of it, darling, and Refederator should stick his head in his chamber pot. My, Jimmy, such a sterling speech calls for celebration."

She always associated celebration with food and was really quite deliciously round. The way she filled that special nightgown flashed through his mind and he felt a stirring . . .

She jumped up. "Coffee—you've let your tea get cold—and plum cake for us both, then early to bed. What do you say?"

★ ★ ★ ★

The delegation of local folk walked into Octagon House looking hangdog. Dolley knew only a few—Jack Bostick, a lawyer, Ambrose Peckaloe, a surveyor who boasted he'd helped on the original Washington City plat, a couple of city officials she recognized. They had come to admonish the President, and she saw it would be a harsh meeting. She let French John lead them into the drawing room and offer them morning coffee and sweet breads. When they were settled she sat quietly in the back of the room. She knew she inhibited them; they talked in murmurs.

When Jimmy strode in she could see through his vigor to the exhaustion beneath. Seven years as President, three of carrying all the responsibility for war . . . she knew as others couldn't the effort and the iron that lay behind his calm, controlled manner. He stood like a rock to the worst news, never seemed afflicted by the panic or fury or doubts or hesitations of lesser men. But she saw him at night. Long past midnight she would get him to bed and an hour later awaken to find him sitting by the window, staring into the snowy dark, and she would stir the fire and wrap a blanket around him, and often it would be near dawn before he returned and she could sigh and move close to him.

"Gentlemen," he said, seating himself in a wing chair.

Ambrose Peckaloe had designated himself spokesman. He just naturally seized the floor wherever he was. He wore fawn trousers tucked into high boots and a coat the color of violets with huge brass buttons.

"Mr. President," he said, "I speak for a multitude that cries out to you—"

"Just say what's on your mind, Ambrose," Jimmy said.

"Well, all right. We figure things are going to hell in a handcart." He glanced at Dolley. "Begging the lady's pardon."

He rattled off the problems—finances, recruitment, divisions, secession talk, the West in danger, and who knew what might happen in New Orleans—

"Yes, yes," Jimmy said. "Your point?"

"Point is, a whole hell of a lot of us feel only draconian measures can save us. So why not declare martial law? Then, see, you can make things work like they ought to—dissolve the Congress and the courts, impose a draft to fill the army, force banks to disgorge their holdings, bring all these miserable, squabbling contentious folks by God to heel!"

That sounded simple; it just meant discarding the Constitution of the United States that Jimmy had helped write. She awaited his explosion, but he smiled and spoke gently.

"Now, Ambrose," he said, "that's shortsighted. Let me tell you the reality. I believe this nation is working out God's will to bring democracy to a world locked and hobbled by monarchism and autocracy. It's the hope of mankind."

"Well, sure," Peckaloe said, "that's the truth."

"Now," Jimmy said, "the day will come when any other government form will seem an aberration. And, sir, all that bright promise rests on the document that you would throw aside for the ease of the moment."

"Wait, now," Peckaloe's voice went whiny. "To save the country and the document, I meant."

"Destroy the Constitution in order to save it?" Jimmy said. "That, my friends, is . . ."

Dolley held her breath.

"An oxymoron."

Oh, splendid.

"Gentlemen, we'll never abandon the Constitution—our liberty is the basis of our strength."

★ ★ ★ ★

The noise reached Madison first as a faint twittering and then, louder, as voices. Shouts with a glad ring. He and Ned peered down New York Avenue from the Octagon and saw the flames of a massive bonfire leaping toward the sky just this side of the ruined mansion. Figures with torches were dancing around it. Something new, something to celebrate . . .

Ned went to investigate. Dolley came out and they stared down the street. Ned was back in ten minutes.

"Marvelous news from New Orleans—they're saying Jackson destroyed the enemy. It's an unbelievable victory!"

His heart lurched. He so wanted to believe. But rumors run like wildfire and often far outpace the truth. He was quiet as Dolley pressed Ned for details. He must not yield to hope—

A horseman swung around the corner. "This here where President Madison stays?"

"I'm President Madison."

"Then I got a message for you, sir. From New Orleans."

He took the packet inside. His hands shook. Ned opened it and handed it to him.

From General Jackson. Incredible . . . amazing . . . his eyes filled with tears and he couldn't see and he stood there with the paper rattling in his hands—

Oh, thank God, thank God!

★ ★ ★ ★

The New Orleans victory was changing everything—the people Dolley saw in the streets seemed bright and vigorous, given to smiles and laughter. At night houses blazed with light and parties ran late. Add New Orleans to Baltimore and Plattsburgh and the victories on the Niagara, and she could accept the ashes at 1600 Pennsylvania Avenue. There were signs the banks might loosen their grip on money, enlistments rose, and a fierce new mood swept Congress.

So she broke out the Philadelphia carriage she had ridden into the country as the enemy burned her home. Its splendor was fitting now. The burning was past; the future glowed, the West was saved, the nation would boom, its right arm grow strong. But there was more in the air today. The cold had eased, sky softening in a foretaste of spring. She was going to hear Congress debate in its new quarters in the Patent Office, and people were running, laughing, shouting—

"Rufe," she said, "pull up."

Rufe glanced back at her. He'd gone prowling with a cudgel when they returned to Washington, and had told her that the gross beast who'd spat on her carriage would know a whole lot better next time. Which, she thought, was good and as it should be.

"What happened?" she cried to a man on the sidewalk.

He snatched off his hat. "It's peace! Peace treaty come, so they say. Whupping 'em at New Orleans won us the war!"

"Let's go back, Rufe," she said. "Quickly."

Jimmy was outside at the gate. "I've heard the rumors," he said. "They're saying a British sloop of war landed an envoy in New York, and riders are dashing south to give advance word in Richmond and Charleston to buy tobacco and cotton before the prices boom with peace."

"My Lord," she said, "that sounds real enough."

He smiled. "That commerce would hear first? Yes, I found that reassuring."

And she thought, yes, maybe this is how life shifts and the old dies and the new begins and wars end and peace comes and the future explodes in sunrise—with a rumor running on the wind.

An hour later the Secretary of State, dour Mr. Monroe, his long, grave face broken into smiling planes, put the treaty in Jimmy's hands.

"Congratulations, Mr. President," he said, his eyes moist.

The British had abandoned all their punitive demands, which were unreal since the only issues of the war had been settled. There had been just two, really—British coercion of our commerce and their impressment of our seamen. They had dropped the first at the start, which was why the Federalists had been so outraged and so suspicious of motives when the administration pressed on. And she had to admit, one fraction of the Democrats had believed we soon would conquer Canada. Those foolish days!

Britain still insisted it had the right to impress seamen, never admitting it took any but its own deserters, but with war in Europe finished and the Royal Navy shrinking they had stopped doing it, which was what mattered. So Jimmy told our negotiators to strike impressment as an issue.

In other words, we'd said, let's return to our standing before the war. But oh, no, they wanted to punish us, rub our noses in our mess as one London paper inelegantly put it, and Jimmy prepared to fight on. And now, suddenly, they dropped their punitive demands. They accepted our proposal: restore the status quo and get on with life.

Had the victory at New Orleans changed things so radically? But no—the treaty had been signed *before* the battle. Something else had turned them . . .

Jimmy poured the best Madeira into cut-crystal glasses—there never would be a happier toast—and raised his.

"To *status quo ante bellum*!" he cried; she thought he sounded as young as he must have the day he finished Princeton.

They raised their glasses and drank, Jimmy, Jim Monroe, and the pale ethereal Mrs. Monroe, whom he'd summoned hastily; Hannah Gallatin, for whom Dolley had sent the carriage the moment she heard, for if anyone deserved to be here it was Hannah; Ned as always, and, of course, young George Dallas, who'd brought the signed copy of the treaty from Ghent and who already had given Hannah a letter from her husband. And most precious of all, he'd given Dolley a wonderful letter from Payne, her darling son who'd gone to Belgium with Albert.

"Mr. President," Dallas said, "I hesitate to intrude, but Mr. Gallatin instructed me to speak to you the moment the treaty was in your hands. He impressed me most strongly, sir."

"Very well," Jimmy said. They were in the Octagon drawing room and he waved an inclusive hand. "Let's sit down and hear what Albert had to say."

Young Dallas sat on the edge of his chair. He was scarcely more than a boy, handsome and eager, the son of Alexander Dallas who finally had agreed to become Secretary of the Treasury and was even now, she hoped, making some sense of the nation's finances. Alexander had steadfastly refused to join the administration until that miserable John Armstrong departed . . .

"Sir, as you see, the treaty was finally signed on Christmas Eve, late in the day. Mr. Clay ordered a great dinner and led a round of toasts that I assure you neglected no one. No one. And in the morning, I—"

"You had a big head," Jimmy said.

"Yes, sir, I'm afraid that's true. But it didn't keep me from—"

"I'm sure it didn't. Now look, son, sit back in your chair, cross your legs, relax. There's no rush. I'm very interested in what you have to say. So proceed."

"Yes, sir. Thank you, sir." He sat back, crossed his legs rather tentatively. Then he smiled and she thought how fresh and young and sunny he looked.

"I left Ghent at five on Christmas morning. Stage on the Calais road, an hour getting over the frontier from Belgium into France, ferry sloop from Calais to Dover, and there the sloop of war. Mr. Gallatin roused me a half hour early and we walked up and down in the cold with our breaths making clouds of steam and the bells of Christmas ringing and I listened very carefully and folded all he said into memory . . ."

Good old Albert! She raised her refilled glass to Hannah and smiled. She could see their dearest friend's dark, slender face, always calm and controlled, that razor-edged mind of his slicing to the heart of every conundrum. Trust him to think ahead to the consequences of the treaty and to prepare them.

"Mr. Gallatin said the treaty was sure to excite various claims for credit— he was very definite, he didn't want American Federalists to get away with saying it was their friendly attitude toward the British that brought those recalcitrant devils around at last. Because it wasn't. It was Federalist clamor that encouraged them to keep on as long as they did. Every time a Boston paper reached London there was new confidence that Americans were too divided to continue."

Yes, she'd thought from the beginning that if the British had talked less to Federalists, with whom they felt such easy rapport, everyone would have been better off.

"Mr. Gallatin says two things—two things only—turned the English tide. One was the gathering strength of our army. The other was your actions." She saw Jimmy's eyebrows go up at that, but he didn't interrupt.

"The way our men fought at Chippewa and Lundy's Lane, the battles under General Scott and General Brown—the British saw a professionalism there that opened their eyes, I know that myself. And Mr. Gallatin believes that told them this was becoming a real war and punishing us might be costly. And then Baltimore—they were puffed up over attacking Washington, and then they couldn't dent Baltimore—"

And that star-spangled banner waved on, Frank Key's wonderful phrase having entered the language by now.

"And then Plattsburgh, Plattsburgh was crucial. There was a rumor in London which of course we heard; it seems Whitehall asked the Duke of Wellington to take over the American command. Well, Wellington is their soldier of soldiers after he beat Napoleon, and he told them that without Plattsburgh their chances were about zero. Told them that in light of their performance they didn't have a right to a square foot of our territory. Wellington himself!"

Dallas dug a small notebook from an inner pocket. "But Mr. Gallatin really wanted me to stress what you did. He believed the British expected us to fold—with all our problems, they didn't see how we could go on. He says it was your steadiness that convinced them."

Dear Jimmy, steady as stone.

"And then, Mr. President, when you released those outrageous terms the British first offered . . . Oh, were their envoys furious! It's just not done, they kept saying, sniffing the way they do, looking down their long noses, barbarous, contrary to diplomatic decorum, outrageous—but all the time you could see what was really burning them. Mr. Gallatin thought it stiffened our people, but it really stiffened the British public.

"I mean, the British people found they were being taxed and their men being sent to die because their ministers were mad at us—and that made British common folk mad and they kicked the props out from under the war. And Mr. Gallatin wanted to be sure you understood how important that was."

My, the boy was a credit to his parents and she would say so when she saw the Treasury Secretary that evening. And as usual, Albert had put his finger on the key issues. The causes of the war had vanished. Only British pique kept it going—once the people found they were paying for pique and the British military found the fighting had become real, it was all over.

"Thank you, Mr. Dallas," Jimmy said. She had rarely seen her husband look more satisfied. "You've reported well."

★ ★ ★ ★

Nervous? No, no—French John was nervous, appropriately, but Dolley was merely alert as she swept through the Octagon public rooms with John at her heels checking odds and ends in the moments before guests began flowing into her newly resumed Wednesday Drawing Room. It was late afternoon, the light outside beginning to fail, candles in girandoles and many-faceted crystal chandeliers giving the rooms a warm glow. Waiters were in line, white shirts clean and pressed, the wine was uncorked and ready, ham and roast well sliced, fresh baked bread on boards with slicing knives, cheese in variety, silver polished, glasses gleaming, punch cups neatly stacked. She tasted the punch—just the right mix of tart and sugar to gentle the whiskey—and saw that what rural congressmen often wanted, corn liquor, was in good supply.

Handsome though it was, the house really was too small, even using all three rooms, the circular entrance room, the drawing room, and the fine oval dining room with its false doors matching its entrance doors for classical symmetry, the long table pushed to one side. The thought made her heart ache for the glorious room she and Mr. Latrobe had created. Even now the barbarous brutality of fire set to abuse beauty and to humiliate gave her nightmares. She dreamed of torches rammed through windows in showers of glass, flame leaping up lovely burnished walls, polished chairs and tables igniting, crystal chandeliers collapsing—and awakened to the awful reality that the dream wasn't a dream.

But then, she was lucky to have a place to sleep, let alone a place to entertain. And she was grateful to Mr. Sérurier for shifting his French Embassy out to give them the finest home in Washington. When he arrived she would remark on the beauty and the comfort of the house. But it was still too small.

The preparations made her remember little Joseph and his polished manners. When he didn't reach the plantation she reluctantly concluded he'd gone north and taken Jennie with him. Then one day French John said he'd learned that Joseph was on the household staff of the British high commissioner in Jamaica and Jennie was expecting their first child. Apparently there'd been a letter. So they had fled with the British. Well.

"He especially wanted his respects paid to you, Mrs. Madison. He said you were good to him."

She had nodded. What was there to say? If she were glad he'd gone on to freedom, why not free all the slaves? Go down Papa's road to disaster, then die and leave it to Mama to deal with the consequences. But she wished them both well.

The guests were arriving. Mr. and Mrs. Monroe entered with Hannah Gallatin on a nephew's arm. Stephen Decatur came arm in arm with Captain Barney, who had recovered from his wound and was his pugnaciously hearty self. John C. Calhoun of South Carolina—tall, handsome, courtly, and yet essentially awkward, fire deep in his eyes—led a congressional delegation that went straight to the food table. Frank Key came with his dowdy wife; she wondered if she could tame this crowd to hear Frank's latest poem and decided not to try. She turned into the drawing room and saw Jimmy taking his accustomed place by the fire.

The Chevalier de Onís, Spain's fat little ambassador, walked in looking cross. He had come in a fury after General Jackson seized Pensacola, threatening war. There had been plenty of diplomatic dithering when that news broke, but Jimmy had stared it all down, reminding everyone that the belligerent had occupied the ostensible neutral and America had acted in self-defense. And he'd gotten away with it. Barely.

As for Onís, Jimmy had ignored his bleating. After all, Jackson had done just as Jimmy wanted—he'd shown the nerve to plunge in without orders that Jimmy was reluctant to give. With a dismissive wave of his hand, Jimmy had told Onís that those who could not control their territory— Indians attacking from it, British using it at will—deserved to lose it, so he should count himself lucky Jackson hadn't thrown them all into the sea.

William Thornton, the Boston lawyer and banker, bowed and delivered greetings from Mr. Astor, the merchant banker he had brought to their rescue last year. Thornton also had delivered the disastrous response of Boston bankers to the three-million loan, but that was a problem now moot, thank the Lord. Felix Grundy joined them with an effusion of gaudy rhetoric. The canny Tennessee senator remarked on Thornton's last visit to Nashville, and both bubbled over General Jackson's triumph. They said Mrs. Jackson would go to New Orleans soon.

"I think the General depends on her much more than he'll admit," Grundy said.

"Second that," Thornton said. "He's totally devoted."

"Whenever either of you speaks to Mrs. Jackson," Dolley said, "tell her that when she comes north—and she will, you know, General Jackson has quite a future unfolding before him—tell her please to call on me. I want to meet her."

She saw Ambassador Sérurier in the round entrance hall. She touched his arm. "This lovely, lovely house," she said. "It makes entertaining a joy." He smiled and bowed.

The Treasury Secretary, Alexander Dallas, and Ben Crowninshield, the new Navy Secretary, a Massachusetts Democrat, were deep in conversation. She saw George Dallas with his father. He looked a little left out, so she waved, and he bowed deeply, clearly pleased to be recognized.

Sally McQuirk kissed her cheek and presented a handsome naval officer— well, not that handsome but interesting-looking and strong—a Lieutenant Hamblin. Dolley saw at a glance that he was wildly in love with Sally. She was a connoisseur of such connections, and of this one there was no doubt. But how Sally felt—well, Sally was as mysterious as ever. Or maybe just divided. Sally loved that newspaper and, my goodness, the account it carried of the naval fight at Plattsburgh—well, it made Dolley *see* the battle in a way she hadn't supposed possible. Jimmy said it had been reprinted from Boston to Charlotte to Lexington. Sally was the source, that was obvious, but Dolley thought she was the writer, too.

She masked a moment's uneasiness. That handsome young general, Winfield Scott, sufficiently recovered from his wound to travel but far from well, had promised he'd come today. She'd always thought something had gone on between him and Sally. But now Sally's lieutenant was here, and Ned had brought his sister Betsy up from Richmond, and with her had come Maria Mayo. Dolley was sure Scott's presence accounted for Maria's, for the girl was sick with love, and her trip to New York had been more than daring. Outraged her father, but then, who consults a father in matters of love?

French John was replenishing the punch bowl; Dolley glanced from waiter to waiter with practiced eye, making sure trays were full and moving. There were new voices at the front, more guests arriving, and she moved to greet them, cocking her ear to the clamor as she went. The loud steady hum suggested guests well fed and well wined. Dolley Madison was a supremely skilled hostess, she knew how to assemble a party, how to shape it, guide it, control it when necessary, and the smooth loud sounds she now heard told her this one was going well. Very well.

★ ★ ★ ★

"My God! It's just outrageous. Everyone is saying we won the war, you hear it everywhere, we whipped them at New Orleans and they quit and went home and sued for peace. You know that's ridiculous. Why, the treaty was negotiated two weeks before the battle. I mean, we didn't lose, but neither can you really say we won. And now they're saying it was *Jackson* who won the war!"

Madison smiled. That was the nub of Mr. Monroe's complaint—the situation elevated Jackson. Madison stood with his back to the fireplace where he could survey Dolley's crowd; he and Monroe talked in low voices and their manner barred anyone interrupting them. He knew he'd better deal with Monroe's fears now, lest they get out of hand. Monroe was obsessed with the office Madison couldn't wait to vacate in just a little more than a year. Now, having vanquished one rival, John Armstrong, he was confronted with a new one. Yet his nervous hunger for the office irritated Madison, too. It was unseemly to lust so openly. More important, Jackson was a man of great, instinctive power; if Monroe was foolish enough to contest directly, he would be eaten alive. And Madison didn't intend to have the end of his term and the glory of a successful peace marred by some new squabble.

"Oh, literally speaking, New Orleans doesn't relate to the treaty, but in a larger sense, the people are right." He shrugged. "They usually are, you know, in the large scale. We won by not losing, and New Orleans was crucial."

Of course Monroe understood the victory's import. The U.S. Senate had ratified the treaty the day it arrived, but Parliament had yet to act. Gallatin said British ratification would await news from the Gulf. Had Britain won at New Orleans, possession of the mouth of the Mississippi would have given her a lock on the West—and then, he was quite confident, the English could only have been ejected by force, and the treaty, unratified in London, would have died.

"I don't deny the victory," Monroe said, "but they're glorifying Jackson—that damned song they're singing."

Madison chuckled. "Yes, it has old 'Yankee Doodle' giving John Bull fits, doesn't it?" He beat time with his hand.

> *Yankee Doodle, keep it up,*
> *Yankee Doodle dandy,*
> *Andrew Jackson went to war*
> *And fed John Bull lead candy.*

He smiled. "Quite the rage in music halls, I believe."

Monroe's face went stiff. "Well, Mr. President, it may amuse you, but it elevates him falsely, it seems to me. Of course the battle was won, but does he deserve such credit? The British commander must have been mad, throwing his men to their deaths against an impenetrable barrier. Apparently it was a turkey shoot, which is hardly a triumph over the turkey."

"Jim," Madison said, "drop that idea. It demeans you more than it does him, and he certainly doesn't deserve it. In fact, the whole campaign was sort of an intuitive mastery of generalship, though Jackson really hasn't had much military experience. Young Johnny Reid arrived with his report and I talked to him for hours. Fascinating—such a talk would profit you, too. He makes it clear that Jackson took command of the situation, held the initiative, and forced the conclusion."

He glanced about. The noise was louder, the crowd denser. He saw Reid deep in conversation with Betsy Coles; the two looked intoxicated with each other . . . ah, youth. Several men waited to speak to him, but he wanted to settle this with Monroe. Jim must see Jackson as an asset, not as a rival.

He laid out Reid's points. The loss of the gunboats had been devastating because it left Jackson unable to track the enemy. But when enemy troops did emerge from the swamp, his quick attack threw them on the defensive. Thereafter he made sure his scouts and night patrols held them there while he built the line against which ultimately they destroyed themselves.

The presence of the powerful parapet forced the British to call up heavy artillery to blast through it—and this committed them so heavily that it was no longer possible to pull back and strike from a more favorable direction. Yet once committed, their supplies shrank rapidly and they lacked the ammunition needed to make their guns truly effective. When Jackson's artillery outdueled theirs, Packenham's only choices were ruinous retreat or head-on attack.

Reid said prisoners afterward talked about it at length. None had doubted they would win—the bayonet was their primary weapon and they'd charged into more difficult barriers in the Napoleonic battles. What they hadn't counted on was American artillery and the Kentucky long rifle. Officers and men alike told Reid that they'd never encountered fire so murderous.

But it was Jackson taking control of the situation as soon as they came into view and holding control that kept them constantly off balance and eventually forced them into their disastrous attack.

"Well," Monroe said, "that's interesting, and it was a great victory, of course. But this . . . well, this deification . . ."

"That's too strong a word," Madison said. "But Jackson is just beginning—I think his future is absolutely unlimited. It's not that he's brilliant, or even profoundly intelligent in the conventional sense. But I think he has a great instinctive capacity—he's one of those rare men whose thinking can't be exactly traced but who can leapfrog others to profound conclusions."

He saw doubt, anger, perhaps fright in Monroe's expression. He took the Secretary's lapel in his hand and held him close, giving the coat little tugs to emphasize his whispered words.

"Jim, Jim—Jackson isn't your rival. He's your successor's rival. In fact, likely he'll *be* your successor. But you, my friend, you will be the next president. No one can block you now, certainly not Jackson. He's not ready. But mark my words, he'll be a fiery streak across the heavens in the twenties, the thirties—that will be *his* time. And now is *your* time. So make Jackson your ally, your friend. Keep him on your side. You'll need him—for you, not against you."

Monroe shrugged. "You read me too well, I'm afraid. But you know, I really do want the office—want it a lot."

"And why not? You've earned it, and you'll have a golden time. The country will explode in new growth, new activity, new attitudes. We'll see changes in your eight years like nothing we've seen since the Revolution. And the new thrust will be westward—the opening of the West as we scarcely can imagine it now, men and women, wagons and flatboats, flowing westward. Why, they're pouring into Ohio and Tennessee and Missouri now, but it's a trickle compared to the coming flood. It's no accident that the man of the future is a westerner. A western President will follow you—the national balance is tipping."

He saw he'd mollified Monroe by this endorsement of his hopes and thought he might as well get the point anchored now.

"The Federalist Party will fade away and the West will be our growth engine—in time, western agriculture will feed the world—but the East will remain the country's bedrock, financial base, manufacturing base. Our infant industries need protection now, but with American shipping, American inventiveness, ample raw materials—why, there's no limit.

"We're coming of age, Jim. Putting adolescence behind us, moving into the full bloom of adulthood. That will be the glory of *your* period."

★ ★ ★ ★

Madison caught the Boston lawyer's eye and beckoned. Thornton was wearing pantaloons and looked very dashing; Dolley wanted her husband to modernize his dress, but small clothes with white hose and buckled shoes had been good enough for Madison's father, and he saw no reason to bend to the whims of fashion.

"I have a mission for you, Mr. Thornton," he said. "It would mean a sea voyage . . ."

Thornton bowed. "An honor to serve, Mr. President."

"Good. See me tomorrow and we'll discuss the details."

★ ★ ★ ★

Winfield Scott stood with a shoulder wedged surreptitiously against a false doorjamb. The pain was readily manageable now, the terrible fevers of the wound long past. Still, it was better to move no more than necessary, and he welcomed the door's support, his glass held casually in his good hand.

He was a different man today from the eager youth he felt he had been before the wound. Sinking helplessly toward death had burned his mind with a firm understanding of his own mortality. He'd always been tough, he knew that, but now he felt a calm intensity that seemed rocklike.

But then, too, the way the boys had fought on the Chippewa and at Lundy's Lane had solidified him. What magnificent men they were! The whole country had rallied in honor of those men in gray—and now he'd heard talk in army circles that cadets in the little academy at West Point henceforth would wear gray uniforms as a memorial. And by God, that would be fitting!

He believed he was alive because he'd made the surgeon wash his hands. Of course he couldn't prove it—and the surgeon had taken it for delirium, amazed and then furious when Scott, barely conscious, murmured, "That's an order, Captain."

And Sergeant Major Boone had leaned close to the medical officer and added, "An order from the *General*, Sir."

Thank God for the Sergeant Major. Old Boone had simply separated himself from the army and seen to his commander. He left the paperwork to Scott and if Scott died he would be a deserter, but that didn't seem to bother him. Anyway, he didn't let Scott die. Operation followed operation— hands washed each time—and he was moved in stages across New York and finally into a big hospital room with forty other men, and there, slowly but surely, he began to recover.

And so it was that while lying abed reading Machiavelli's *The Art of War*, he heard Boone's loud voice.

"Cover up, gentlemen; lady's coming in."

He drew a sheet to his chest. Boone looked at him critically.

"Better spruce up, General. You need a shave. And a clean shirt."

Scott protested, but Boone had a way about him, so he sat on the edge of the bed and shaved himself and let Boone slip on a clean shirt before he sank back to the bed exhausted. He heard a low murmur but didn't open his eyes. Nothing really mattered.

"Sit up, General," Boone said. "You got a visitor."

He opened his eyes. And stared. Maria Mayo stood gazing down at him, something frightened in her eyes, and then she slowly smiled.

"Hello, Win."

She wore a yellow scarf. She looked like a flower in summer grass. He thought if he touched her she would disappear.

And she touched him. She took his hand.

"Hello, Win," she said.

She bent down and kissed him, her lips warm and smooth and gentle on his. The room erupted with shouts and cheers, forty men whistled and whooped, and Maria turned and smiled and threw up both arms in acknowledgment.

Scott caught her hand. "I love you," he whispered.

Now he stood in the President's house watching Maria across the room. She was talking to Betsy Coles and Johnny Reid. He and Johnny were to dine soon, and Johnny would walk him step by step through the military nuances of New Orleans, but at the moment it looked as if in Betsy Coles Johnny had found a different sort of match.

He glanced around the graceful room and saw the President talking to Mr. Monroe. The little man caught his eye and nodded; Scott bowed, ignoring a jolt of pain. If ever a man deserved salutes for staying the course, it was James Madison. And the President had been generous to him, too. In the lively competition for position in the army at war's end, Scott had emerged as one of six permanent brigadiers.

Brigadier general: permanent rank. He was twenty-nine, and this was just the start. There would be two major generals, Jake Brown in the North and Andrew Jackson in the South. But Jackson wasn't a professional soldier, and his star already was soaring. Jackson would leave the army before long and Brown would command the whole, and when that happened Scott intended to be his deputy—and, in time, his successor.

Meanwhile, Madison was sending him to Europe for a year. He was to walk the great battlefields and talk to the generals who'd fought there and the theorists who'd studied the flow of battle. Already a professional with substantial combat experience, he would make himself the most intellectually polished soldier in America. He was profoundly grateful. A year in Europe for a honeymoon? Maria's father hadn't yet recovered from her trip to New York, but when Scott returned they would marry, with or without Papa. There was a core of iron in Maria.

And then Sally McQuirk walked in. She was with a familiar-looking naval lieutenant whom she presented to Mrs. Madison and whom Scott saw at a glance to be thoroughly smitten. Presently the officer went to pay his respects to Captain Decatur and Sally began working her way across the room to him.

He glanced at Maria with a moment's apprehension and then decided his concern demeaned her as much as it did him.

"Sally!" he said with a warm smile.

★　★　★　★

The sight of him standing there so tall and handsome did give her a turn, Sally had to admit it. She took his hand, glancing as she did so at Ham's sturdy back. He was deep in conversation with Captain Decatur.

"So," she said, "the wounded warrior home from the wars. You had us worried there for a while. But now you look fine. Whole, are you?"

"Not quite whole, but getting there."

She saw he felt an awkwardness analogous to hers, but soon they were talking like the old friends they were. He told her sketchily about the battles on the Niagara and his wounds. They talked about Plattsburgh— he remembered Ham the moment he made the connection—and he told her he'd read a most handsome account of the fighting that had carried her father's line.

"I thought it beautifully written," he said. "It brought sea fighting to life, even seen from a distance. I'll never again wonder if a fight on water is any easier than one on land."

"I'll tell my father," she said. Why did she bother?

He touched her arm, giving her that warm smile she knew so well.

"A very fine writer," he said.

The size of him, the round, open face, the heavy masculine timbre in his voice, his relaxed generosity, the sensitivity to share her secret—she felt a surge of the old emotion. She had loved him and let him go—because, and there was the truth of it, she hadn't loved him enough.

And with a start she realized that as she had felt for Winfield Scott so did she now feel for Ham Hamblin—that much and no more. The thought made her sad. Was she condemned always to love a little but never enough?

But she'd made her choice. Maria Mayo would marry Win and be a soldier's wife, and that was what she wanted. Sally had different dreams, she had a gift that sharpened each time she used it, and she was going to make her name or at least her work blaze across the nation.

Her father was dying and soon the paper would be hers. He rarely left his bed, but he was full of visions and she talked to him for hours on end. She'd heard old people looked back, but he looked only ahead. Mark my words, he said in his dry, papery, and yet curiously vital voice, ten years from now we'll be very different. Coming of age—first revolution for freedom, second revolution to use our freedom. He said Monroe would be just an adequate President, but that didn't matter because the East would be restabilizing and the West growing like weeds.

The opening of the West: oh, what a story!

This fellow Jackson might be the key to it all, her father said. "He'll be coming north soon, and you should get to know him. The next twenty years will bend around him—our paper can present him to the nation."

She loved the idea but he hadn't stopped with that.

"The country's fine, but what about you? Oh, Sally, you need a man."

"Now, Pa, don't start."

"But you do, child. How else will you have your own daughter to give you the joy you've given me? You filled my life, Sally, I want yours filled, too."

She saw tears in his eyes. "Hush, Pa. It'll be all right."

But would it? We choose our roads. Now she was talking to Winfield Scott whom she hadn't loved enough. And glancing across the room she saw Ham Hamblin approaching, Ham whom she didn't love enough—not yet, anyway.

"Ham admires you greatly, Win," she said.

"I remember him well. Fine fellow—is it serious, Sally?"

Again that bleak chasm opening at her feet.

"As serious as I get," she said, trying to smile.

He squeezed her hand. "Try harder," he said, and turned to greet Ham.

★ ★ ★ ★

Dolley was talking to Ambassador Sérurier when Daniel Webster presented himself.

"Well," she said. "I didn't expect to see you."

"I thought it appropriate to pay my respects, madam. I hope to do the same with the President. The war is over."

"With no help from you."

But immediately she regretted the words. The war *was* over, it was past time for recrimination. Then she saw skulking in a corner—afraid to present themselves, no doubt—two members of the Hartford Convention come to offer that perfidious meeting's resolutions, which stopped short of secession but kept the threat open in a flurry of bombastic reproach. If they dared offer Jimmy their written denunciations, she knew he would look through them. She pointed them out to Webster.

"Have you come to carry their cause?"

He chuckled. "They can give it all the carriage it needs, which isn't much. Frankly, madam, I opposed the convention. But I am a New Englander, they are my people, and I stand with them."

Ambassador Sérurier sniffed. In accented but flawless English, he said, "Doubtless, doubtless, but surely your diet these days is humble pie."

"Not really, Mr. Ambassador." She saw Webster was talking to her. "You must remember that New England was hit harder by this war than anywhere else. Its shipping is in ruins, its manufactures are worse. It disapproved most bitterly and believed England right in its contest with your dictator."

Sérurier's lips tightened.

"Now, sir," Webster said, and this time she understood the potency of that rolling voice, "I see you don't care for that reference. But it's true, and I make no apologies for the beliefs of those I represent. And I might say"—he broke off and glanced at Dolley—"with all respect to my presence under your roof, madam, and your toleration thereof—I might say to you, sir, that I think you have very little standing to comment on any aspect of New England and its people."

"To the contrary, sir!" Sérurier said. "I have *world* standing, sir. Your region posed itself not just against your own government but against every right-thinking nation. And the world stood to applaud the American victory."

"Victory? Surely a draw, sir."

"A victory—a great victory! To stand alone against the world's mightiest sea power, to fight it to a standstill, to drive it from your shores, to bring it to the treaty table more than happy to get out alive—that, sir, is victory!"

"As the French might interpret it."

"As the *world* interprets it. Chippewa, Lundy's Lane, Baltimore, Plattsburgh, New Orleans—names that ring in the world's ears, that stand for the young lions, for a nation come of age. Do you know, sir, when news of New Orleans struck Paris, theater audiences stood to cry, 'Vivent les américains!'"

"Ah, well," Webster said, "Parisian theatrics."

"No such thing, sir. Do you know what thrilled the French? That it was all done without violence to your magnificent Constitution. We of all people understand the perils facing democracy—we've lived with that pain. And your President avoided those perils. Of all his accomplishments, perhaps that is his greatest. You, sir, you should be proud."

Now Webster's dignity and control were unmistakable. He would go far.

"Mr. Ambassador," he said, "I think I need no instruction on honoring my country—or my President. I am of my country, my people are Americans. And they will march into the future arm in arm with those from Virginia and Tennessee and Louisiana. I think that is all I need say to you."

He turned to Dolley. "And now, madam, perhaps I should take my leave. The evening seems cool."

"No, no." She smiled to Mr. Sérurier and took Webster's arm. "Come, now, we'll find you a glass of wine and a bite, and then you must speak to the President."

★　★　★　★

It was late and the house was quiet, guests gone, servants retired. Madison stood by a bedroom window watching snowflakes drifting fat and white against the light of an oil lamp down on the corner. He'd spent many a night by bedroom windows, pounding weather outside matching his mood. Now the snow seemed a benediction—peace lay over his land, a blessing from God.

He heard her put the chamber pot back into the cabinet in the dressing room, and then she was framed in the doorway. She was in that special nightgown and he thought her inexpressibly beautiful, the single flickering candle casting dark hollows in her face. She poured two glasses of sherry, left the stopper out of the decanter, and sat beside him on the sofa, one knee drawn up. He put his hand on her smooth thigh, and she sighed.

"Do you remember the day you proposed?" she said.

"I was terrified. Never been so frightened since."

"Do you remember I told you you would be President?"

"Did you? I remember how you looked."

"I told you you'd be a good one."

"I wanted to kiss your breasts. It was all I could do to restrain myself."

"But you remember what I said, too. I know you do."

"Yes, my love, but I didn't believe it would happen. Nor that it was my strength."

She refilled their glasses.

"Life's funny," he said. "Old Aaron Burr—such a scoundrel he was, but what a favor he did us. I'll always have a soft spot for him. Suppose he hadn't introduced us?"

"Why," she said, "you'd have found some other way."

"I don't know."

"I do. It wasn't Aaron's idea, it was yours. Aaron had a totally different idea."

He looked at her, smiling. "He wanted to seduce you?"

"Of course. He wanted to seduce everyone. It was only after I offered to slap his face that he said you asked to meet me. And I thought, the great little Madison wants to meet me . . ."

"'Great little Madison . . .'" He chuckled. "And what did you think of that?"

"That it was the most exciting thing I'd ever heard. But then, of course, I feared you wouldn't get yourself together to propose." She poured a third sherry, stoppered the bottle, and added, "And that was frightening. I wanted you."

His hand was on her thigh again and she leaned toward him.

"Thank you, Aaron Burr," he murmured.

"Bosh," she said. "You'd have knocked on my door. You'd have broken it down if necessary. And now I know my fears were quite unfounded— you'd have asked, all right. You're strong, Jimmy. I told you that the day you proposed and I was right and I've been right ever since. Look at the way you held this country together—you went to war against opposition and stood like a rock against the naysayers, against military disasters, against financial collapses, against all the odds while the casualties mounted. You're strong, darling—don't you dare tell me you wouldn't have found a way. And by the time you asked, you know, you had burrowed straight into my heart. And you've been there ever since."

He smiled and took the empty glass from her hand and pinched out the candle. She turned on the sofa and lay across his lap and his hands moved over her rich round goodness and his lips found hers.

★ ★ ★ ★

Rachel Jackson was bound for New Orleans. She and Mary Donelson Coffee, her pretty niece who'd married John Coffee, cast off from Nashville in the double-ended forty-foot keelboat with the blue curtains that Tom Larson had built for her. With Mr. Larson in command and a small crew to man the sweeps, they floated the Cumberland to the Ohio, the sweeps swinging the craft from one side of the river to the other in search of the swiftest runs of current.

Where the broad Ohio merged with the massive Mississippi, at Cairo on the southern tip of Illinois a hundred fifty miles below St. Louis, they paused to reprovision. She was at a reception when she saw a tall man with auburn curls watching her. Why . . . it was . . . surely it was Thomas Hart Benton!

"Well, Aunt Rachel . . . will you speak to me?"

Impulsively she stretched on tiptoe to kiss his cheek.

"It's so good to see you," he said, "and never did a man deserve triumph more than General Jackson."

"You should have been there."

"Oh, Aunt Rachel, would that . . ." He hesitated, then plunged on, "Would that none of it had happened!"

"Tell me about you," she said. The great lesson—the value—that had grown from that terrible wound was Andrew's secret, and hers.

Immediately he brightened. "St. Louis is booming! You wouldn't believe how rapidly the West is opening."

"You're doing well, then?"

"Yes, ma'am. Law practice growing and we'll be a state one of these days and I've got my eye on a U.S. Senate seat. Wouldn't that be something!"

★ ★ ★ ★

Down the great river they went. There was much traffic, most of it broadhorns, the big oblong flatboats that rode the current down and were broken up for lumber at their destination, bringing countless families with their livestock and farm implements out to the new lands now opening and hauling the bountiful farm produce of the West down to the sea. Now and then they encountered keelboats being poled or dragged upstream, and once they met a steamboat thrashing its way north.

Day after day she watched the bank slide by, everything familiar and everything strange. She was forty-nine now, too heavy, her breath short, her heart often feeling like a seed rattling around in a gourd, and memories slid through her mind with the same ease as the passing bank. She'd been only thirteen when John Donelson took his family down the Cumberland to settle in the great bend long before it was called Nashville. That was in 1779, and it was 1788 before Andrew arrived with flaming hair and manner, and by then that devil Robards had captivated her, a fascination lasting to the day they were wed and little longer.

And that other long float in flight from Robards, down the river on Colonel Robertson's flatboat, the way Andrew looked with his rifle when he came in from prowling the dark around the campfire, the way he would fold into his blankets beside her and every night she would fight the same desire to slide under his blanket, his eyes glittering in firelight with the same passion, and he would bring her hand to his lips and they would pass the night hand in hand—that and no more, not once, and so Colonel Robertson had testified and the community had accepted.

Twenty-five years had passed, the fraudulent divorce rumor, the illegal marriage, the terrible adultery charge, the thunder of the community, the sheer, desperate pain—well, forget it! The war was over and she was going to Andrew and he would fill her heart.

As she wound day by day down the Mississippi the very magnitude of its waters made her aware of the immense continent it drained, everything from the Appalachians to the great Stony Mountains in the far west. It seemed a metaphor for all the vast possibilities of the American shift unfolding before her eyes, coastal nation with lightly settled edges becoming a continental nation overnight. She couldn't help seeing—no one could—that this was a nation poised on the brink of greatness.

The differences were evident at each turn. Colonel Robertson's flatboat had gone for miles without seeing a settlement. It passed the occasional Indian village, the occasional lone settler's cabin, now and then a hamlet glowing as a touch of civilization in wilderness.

But now the Indian villages were fewer and farther between, and a settlers' hamlet came in sight at every turn with fresh cornfields between. Each had a wharf and a road with a dozen buildings along the bank, and some had a second street running off into the woods and some had several.

The farther west they went the more giddy the optimism she encountered. They were all newcomers, from the Carolinas and Virginia and New England with their odd accents, come out by broadhorn or wagon and positive that with the war over their little hamlet was destined to be the city of the future. They'd make a state out of the territory any day now, they told her, and this here little town would be on the map in a big way—and the land each man had carved out would make him rich, as newcomers flocked in and boosted values.

General Jackson's lady is here! Delegations of matrons in out-of-fashion finery with the fold marks showing it had been pulled from trunks invited her to tea, and there would be a dinner with successive toasts to General Jackson and his lady and New Orleans and the victory, all very decorous in respect for her with scarcely a man drunk enough to fall down. Little girls in long dresses and button shoes carrying baskets full of garlands recited poems extolling General Jackson's prowess.

It was joyous—they were so kindly and decent and genuine in their enthusiasm for her and for Andrew—and yet there was a sinking in her heart, too. For now she could see and feel what was only hinted in Nashville—Andrew was being swept to the heights on this flood tide of growth and expectation. Would he be swept away from her?

She knew what she wanted. She wanted to live out her days on the farm with Andrew beside her, live quietly in the ways of God and church. She wanted Andrew with her, safe, well, eating good food, restoring his health. And every day that future became less likely.

The vast tidal surge lifting them would suit Andrew perfectly with his yearning to do, to lead, to triumph—but what of her? At Natchez, where the whole town turned out and proposed a three-day celebration with a mock reenactment of the battle if she'd stay, a new dread overtook her. Could she keep up? Would Andrew be a star blazing across the world's sky and she a fat little woman on a farm?

Oh, he always would love her. That love was her pole star and she never doubted. But would he . . . pity her? Be ashamed? She was devoted to God's ways instead of men's, her heart would put her down one day, she wasn't a bit fashionable, and she was going to a city where Andrew was a savior and fashion was supreme. New Orleans's urbanity had always disturbed her. The city was full of the pride that Scripture warned against. But every report said Andrew was a commanding presence there; as his lady, she knew she must measure up.

She lifted her chin, suddenly furious with herself. She'd come this far to be intimidated by fashion doyennes? No, indeed! She was who she was, and Andrew was a hero today because after the fight with Tom she had forced him to look into himself that he might master what he found there. They had come a long, long way together and they would be together now and she would be herself and the people would have to take her as she was and that would be that. Yes, that would be that!

But she was still uneasy as the crescent city came into view, much larger than she had remembered it, and she saw the crowds along the wharfs and heard the music, saw the flags, heard the saluting guns thundering . . .

★ ★ ★ ★

Word of the keelboat's approach reached Jackson when it was still ten miles upsream. Everything was ready for Rachel's arrival, and long before the boat appeared he ran up the levee through a gathering crowd to scan the river. Jack Coffee and Ed Livingston and the lawyer from Boston, William Thornton, waited below as he paced the top of the levee and the people intent on seeing Rachel arrive stood apart so as not to intrude. The General's lady was coming; in a city of romance and love, as Major Latour had observed, touching his mustache, this was a sacred moment.

Still, the Hero of New Orleans, as he'd just learned the American public was calling him, was unsettled. He glanced down at Thornton; the lawyer had arrived the day before, sent with the President's glowing commendations on a swift twenty-gun corvette that came slipping up the river under full sail.

Apparently Thornton had conquered Washington as fully as he had Nashville, where he'd cut a wide swath as agent for John Jacob Astor. And it told Jackson a good deal about the West's future that though Thornton was here for the President, he also carried a trading commission from Mr. Astor, who believed things would bust wide open out beyond the Appalachians with the great river and its terminal city now made safe.

But the banker's report of public acclaim sweeping the East was as disturbing as it was gratifying. Thornton said people were hungry for a hero—there hadn't been a man in seven-league boots since General Washington. And folks seemed to feel that the Tennessee general who'd whipped the British and won the war—Thornton said it was an article of faith by now that we won the war at New Orleans—fit the bill perfectly.

Which was all right. Jackson and his boys were heroes for what they'd done on the Rodriguez Line, and he'd known since he was in knee britches that somehow he carried the capacity for great leadership in his mind and heart, and the chance to demonstrate it had come. Damn right he was a hero, and so were all his boys.

But then Thornton said talk back East had taken a new tack. Said he heard it everywhere he went: Jackson for President.

President!

And Jack Coffee went to crowing.

"See, General, damn me if I didn't tell you that my ownself!"

"Yes, and I told you I wouldn't hear a word of it." He'd turned to Thornton. "That's dangerous chatter, sir. I'm an officer, the President is my Commander in Chief—"

"But you can't stop what's in the people's hearts," Thornton had said.

"Just what I told you!" Jack cried.

"Jack, that's enough of that!"

Jack chuckled. "All right, General, but I think what I think."

Now, pacing the levee, he found it the more disturbing. The people were honoring him, folks clear across the country. Hero . . . Well, he *liked* it, by God, he was human and it made him glow with pleasure. But if he tried to capitalize on it for political gain, what would they think of him when they saw their gift cheapened . . .

Still, the idea glowed in his mind like a hot coal. President! It wouldn't be beyond him, either; he had the capacity, all right. And it might happen, too, for now the West would rise and he intended to rise with it. But then he would appear as a product of his region, not as a mountebank who tried to capitalize on the people's gift.

Everything would boom in the West now, he was sure of it, trade would course the river, cotton and grain flowing in streams of white and gold to a world hungry for both. New Orleans would be its entrepôt and the day would come when these Frenchmen would shout for joy that they had become Americans.

More and more land was opening, more towns, more settlers, more traffic on the rivers. Cincinnati and Louisville and Nashville were becoming small manufacturing centers. Statehood was possible when the citizens of a territory passed the sixty thousand mark, and he'd heard that ambitious men in Missouri were talking statehood already. But the way other territories were growing, Indiana and Mississippi and Illinois and Alabama might slip in ahead of the Missourians.

For the American die was cast—we would be a continental nation. The promise of Jefferson's great Louisiana Purchase and the daring trek that Meriwether Lewis and William Clark led to the Pacific would be played out in time by streams of wagons, men, women, and children on the move, herds of lowing cattle, rivers full of broadhorns and keelboats and the new steamboats now making their appearance. Trails would become roads and villages towns and towns cities. Oh, it wouldn't be easy, there'd be suffering aplenty and many a westering man and woman and child would end in a shallow grave, but the day would come when the nation would stretch from sea to sea and its trade would flow toward China. The West . . . ready to rise, ready to be led, ready for full membership in a nation exploding with youthful vigor.

He stared up the river, anxious for the keelboat to appear, a little breathless from the force of his thinking. Her face was vivid in his mind, quiet, patient, gentle; she was central to all that he was and all the routes he might travel in the future. She had opened him to that future, sitting beside his bed when his shoulder was shattered out of a fool's quarrel and the evil wind of Fort Mims blew outside, when she made him see himself, reckon with himself, *deal* with himself.

He understood now that without her he would have destroyed himself—with her he had found triumph. He stared up the river and at last the boat came into view, moving with the current, and he waited, his gaze fixed. Presently he could make her out; she was standing on the bow and she was wearing that blue gown. The boat turned toward the wharf and he ran down the levee to leap the narrowing gap and sweep her into his arms. Bathed in her smile, secure in her warmth, it came to him that, as did nothing else in the world, she made him whole.

From the levee where a thousand men and women watched came a mighty cheer that buffeted the soft river air. He felt her shrink at this noise and his arm tightened around her as he turned her to face the crowd. That cheer was for them both—and if he had earned it, she had earned it more.

A Note on Methods and Sources

1812 is a novel, a work of the imagination. Yet it is in general accurate both to the history of the events it chronicles and to the character and personality of the various individuals. To sum up in a phrase, this is the imagined inside story of a known outside story.

So I believe that with a few exceptions, most listed below, the novel is a close account of what happened and why, and of the individuals involved. I base the words I put in their mouths on the records they and their contemporaries left and on my own estimate of how reasonable men and women might reasonably respond. In areas where there can be no record, I have followed what seems logical and reasonable; in giving Winfield Scott a love affair, for example, I take the position that he was a handsome, robust young soldier, and it is hard to believe that he knew no women before meeting the woman whom he did in fact marry, Maria Mayo. I base Aaron Burr's attempt to seduce Dolley before he introduced Madison on his reputation for extensive sexual activity as reflected in his own diary.

History strives for reality, for what is provable, documentable. Historical fiction should strive for the story that underlies reality and thus become an imagined reality. To present that reality I have used a few imaginary characters who in their interaction with historical figures allow me to amplify those figures' viewpoints. Thus the greatest departure from reality in this novel is the fact that Sally McQuirk is a fictional character. But all that she says and does, including her view of the battle of Plattsburgh, is completely consistent with the facts of the time. Sarenmajor Boone, Scott's sidekick, is fictional, but the battles of Queenston, Chippewa, and Lundy's Lane with him at Scott's side are as accurate as I can make them.

William Thornton, the banker, is fictional, but all that he represents is accurate. Eb Clute, Jackson's antagonist, is fictional, but the encounter is true to Jackson's explosive nature. Joseph, the slave who gives us the British in the White House, is fictional but accurately represents the Madisons' views on slavery and the vulgar manner of Admiral Co'burn (Cockburn but pronounced Co'burn).

Some of the oddest things are historically accurate. Jackson did marry Rachel before she was divorced from Robards. Scott did acquire his military education while sitting out a court-martial sentence of a year's exile from the army for insulting the notorious General Wilkinson, and did demand a promotion. Thomas Hart Benton with whom Jackson brawled went on to become the great senator from Missouri, and the fight is entirely accurate. Jackson's change in demeanor after the fight is based on his conduct. Daniel

Webster did invade Madison's sickroom with his denunciations and Madison did kick the papers onto the floor. Secretary of State Monroe's ambition was, in fact, overweening, and Secretary of War Armstrong did plot against his own administration.

Close readers of history will see a few discrepancies. The greatest is in placing Jackson in Washington at the start of the war. His attitude toward war and toward Madison, made clear by mail to the President, is portrayed accurately, but he did not leave Tennessee that year. Scott and Joe Totten were friends but not from New Orleans. Occasionally I place characters a few days before or after their actual arrival. Chauncey and Dearborn did defeat Armstrong's plan, but by mail, not in person. Madison published the British terms later than I describe.

Language in the early nineteenth century bore a certain formality, but I'm sure thoughts were as fluent, angers as quick, analysis as surefooted as they are today, and that all were rendered from one individual to another just as fluidly. My aim is to create for modern readers the intimacy of decisions and pressures then affecting these individuals, and so, while avoiding modernisms, I have chosen language that sounds more formal than modern usage but that is probably somewhat less formal than what was actually used then.

Party names can be confusing to modern ears. At the start there were no political parties. The nation was governed by an elite. As the democratic spirit rose, reaction to the elite took form as the first Republican Party under Jefferson, Madison, and others, and the opposition took the name Federalist. As the latter died, the former gradually took the name Democratic Party and has retained it to this day. The modern Republican Party was formed in the 1850s, John Charles Frémont its first presidential candidate.

Obviously this novel depends on extensive research, and I owe great debts to the Butler Library at Columbia University, the Library of Congress, where my friend Bruce Martin has so often helped, the New York Public Library, the library of the Century Association, and the library at Greenwich, Connecticut, one of the finest and busiest community libraries in the United States.

For further reading, Donald R. Hickey's *The War of 1812* is the best modern history. Harry L. Coles's *The War of 1812* is more compact. John R. Elting's *Amateurs to Arms!* is a military history, as is John K. Mahon's earlier *The War of 1812*. For biographies, Ralph Ketcham's fine *James Madison* is the one-volume biography of choice, not supplanting Irving Brant's earlier six-volume treatment. I relied on Robert Remini's great three-volume biography of Jackson, but dipped frequently into Marquis James and James Parton. For Winfield Scott, who deserves a more modern biography, I relied on Charles Winslow Elliott's *Winfield Scott*.

Henry Adams's magnificent *History of the United States During the Administrations of Thomas Jefferson and James Madison* is brilliant but must be read with some caution. Adams was the grandson of John Quincy Adams, and he had little use for his grandfather's predecessors, Jefferson and Madison, and none whatsoever for the man who defeated his grandfather after a single term, Andrew Jackson. His animus toward Jackson finally becomes ludicrous.

D.N.

the United States of America
British
Oregon Country
Unorganized Territory
Spanish Possessions
Pacific Ocean
Spanish Texas
North